THE WRITINGS OF

William Gilmore Simms

CENTENNIAL EDITION

VOLUME III

THE WRITINGS OF

William Gilmore Simms

CENTENNIAL EDITION

VOLUME III

As Good as a Comedy:
or THE TENNESSEEAN'S STORY.

and

Paddy McGann;
or THE DEMON OF THE STUMP.

Introductions and Explanatory Notes by Robert Bush
Texts Established by James B. Meriwether

UNIVERSITY OF SOUTH CAROLINA PRESS
COLUMBIA

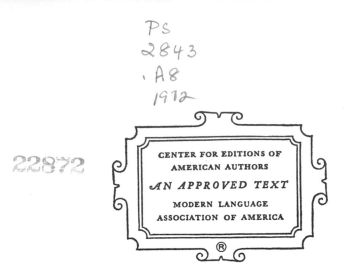

Copyright © 1972
by the University of South Carolina Press
Published in Columbia, S. C.
by the University of South Carolina Press, 1972
First Edition
International Standard Book Number: 0-87249-181-1
Library of Congress Catalog Card Number: 74-120585
Suggested Library of Congress classification furnished by
McKissick Memorial Library of the University of South Carolina:
PS2840.A1 1969

Manufactured in the United States of America

*The publisher gratefully acknowledges the assist-
ance of the Friends of the University of South
Carolina Press in meeting the manufacturing costs
of this book.*

ACKNOWLEDGMENTS

I should like to thank the following scholars for their helpful suggestions in the preparation of the explanatory notes: Edward C. McAleer of Hunter College, Hannah E. Bergman and Meriwether Stuart of Herbert H. Lehman College, and Padraic Colum. Special thanks are also expressed to the staffs of the libraries of the University of South Carolina and Herbert H. Lehman College of the City University of New York. Of the latter, Zosia Seitz Diamond was particularly helpful in the search for the sources of quotations. I am also grateful to Herbert H. Lehman College for grants in aid for this project and to the Newberry Library, Chicago, where, some years ago as a resident fellow, I first read *Paddy McGann.*

R.B.

CONTENTS

vii

INTRODUCTION TO
AS GOOD AS A COMEDY: OR,
THE TENNESSEEAN'S STORY.

William Gilmore Simms introduces his novel *As Good as a Comedy: or, The Tennesseean's Story* (1852) with a long "Proem" that suggests an allegory of the precarious journey of the American union. Representatives of various seaboard states are traveling together on a rough road through a stormy night. They have come from the Georgia town of Madison, a symbolic name for the American Constitution; they are bound for Montgomery, the capital of Alabama. Their driver is drunk and reckless. The state representatives frequently encroach on each other's space. Like the American states that communicated and wrangled with each other without ever knowing each other, they can not "see each other's faces," but they can "hear each other's words, and feel each other's hips and elbows" (p. 5). The Virginian bemoans the fact that Tyler was the last of the Virginian presidents, but he is consoled by the South Carolinian, who believes there will be no future need for a president since the Union is about to dissolve.

The common feature of both Proem and narrative proper is Simms's perennial interest in the social and political differences among the states and between North and South. The Proem depicts the states allegorically; the narrative proper recounts an authentic tale of the life of one of these states, Georgia. The narrative is also concerned with the character of rural life outside the pale of restricted urban society. Thus it depicts the South generally and also includes characteristics found in Northern rural life. The Proem also provides an effective frame for the narrative. The Tennessean tells us that he heard his story from a man he met during the fighting in the Seminole War. In the final chapter of the book we learn who this man is and why he was a fugitive in Florida.

ix

It is possible that Simms at one time intended to write a series of tales for which this Proem, or a version of it, would serve as a prologue, after the fashion of the *Decameron* or the *Canterbury Tales*. Several narratives, we learn, have already been told before the Tennessean begins his: the Mississippian's account of the "Yazoo rogues," the Georgian's story about catching alligators, the South Carolinian's experiences with abolitionists in New Haven, the North Carolinian's ballad of Blackbeard the Pirate, and the Massachusetts man's story of a cruel seduction. These may be vestigial remains of a series which Simms had planned to carry out as he did in *Southward Ho!* (1854), a series of tales told by travellers brought together on a vessel sailing from New York to Charleston. When Simms unsuccessfully urged Henry Carey Baird to publish a new edition of *As Good as a Comedy* in 1854, he did so with the suggestion that the Proem be omitted,[1] and his dissatisfaction with it may be an indication that he had concluded the Proem did not serve so effectively as prologue to the one tale as it might have introduced several.

After Simms had spent many years building his reputation as an author of historical romance and idealistic biography, the 1852 narrative *As Good as a Comedy* marks a distinct change of genre. Neither this work nor *The Golden Christmas*, published in the same year, is a romance. In his essay on "The Writings of James Fenimore Cooper" (1842), he had disparaged what he called "a very inferior school of writings, known as the social life novel."[2] Both of the 1852 fictions bear a relation to this class; but they both are attempts to improve the genre by an admixture of humor. Simms's experimentation may be explained by his hope to earn more from fiction of lighter tone and shorter length. He may also have wished to prove to himself that he could succeed in a very different genre from that for which he was well known. And if he did not rank realistic humor with serious romance, he was most conscious of it as a secondary tradition in English literature, and he was aware of its vitality in the humor of the South.

[1] Simms to Henry Carey Baird, April 14, 1854, *The Letters of William Gilmore Simms*, ed. Mary C. Simms Oliphant, A. T. Odell, and T. C. Duncan Eaves, 5 vols. (Columbia, S. C., 1952-1956), III, 293.

[2] *Views and Reviews in American Literature, History and Fiction*, First Series (New York, 1845), p. 210.

The first indication we have that Simms was planning to write a short comic novel is found in a remark in a letter to his friend James Lawson in 1845. He wants him to ask a publisher "how he would like a story with the title 'A Dead Shot, or as Good as a Comedy'—a thing of 150 pages to be written . . . ."[3] The second of these proposed titles was to become the title of the novel, which would not be published for seven years. The passage of time may be explained by the fact that Simms chose to go slowly in the writing of comedy, and it may be that some time passed before a publisher was found.

The firm of A. Hart of Philadelphia published the novel in their series known as "The Library of Humorous American Works." Between 1846 and 1849 Carey and Hart had published eighteen volumes in the first series, including such important works as William Tappan Thompson, *Major Jones's Courtship* and Johnson Jones Hooper, *Some Adventures of Captain Simon Suggs*. *As Good as a Comedy* appeared in the second series, published by the successor company. In writing to Abraham Hart before the publication of his book Simms showed some diffidence in insisting on anonymity: "Be particular in maintaining the secret of the anonymous book, as it enters a field which I had but partially before attempted."[4]

Simms had, of course, successfully used humor in his novels before, particularly in their subplots. His romance *Border Beagles* (1840) had been delightfully lightened by the character of Harry Horsey, the stage-struck yokel who mistakes a gang of outlaws for a troupe of strolling players. The new works, however, were not romances at all, but social comedies, *As Good as a Comedy* with a background of middle Georgia, then a relatively recent settlement, *The Golden Christmas* with a background of Charleston, where tradition had long since found a permanent home. In both novels the author functions as a genial observer who wishes to record his observations of regional life within the range of his own memory and his own countryside. Here Simms has no need to idealize his characters or to heighten the excitement of his plots as he did in his romances. Especially in *As Good as a Comedy* there is the note of something new. The novel is an amalgam of several ingredients that reflect

[3] *Letters*, II, 84.
[4] *Letters*, III, 105.

two old traditions in English literature and a new one in American literature.

From his critical writing on humor and from his fiction itself we can reconstruct this theory of a new genre. In "The Humorous in American and British Literature" (1845)[5] he dwells on those phases of humor that he most admires. They are three: the comic tradition of the English theater stemming from the Elizabethans, the eighteenth-century masters of comic fiction (especially Fielding and Smollett), and the native Southern humor of the United States that stems from the oral tradition, exemplified in print by Augustus Baldwin Longstreet's *Georgia Scenes* (1835). These three elements are the major sources of the Simms novel of humor; they are to be seen most distinctly in *As Good as a Comedy*.

Both the title and the narrative of *As Good as a Comedy* either allude to drama or imitate it. Simms begins his work with a dedication to Harry Placide, the comic actor. The "Advertisement" that precedes the novel is spoken coyly by the author as "L'Allegro"; it is a brief "speech" that has the effect of a prologue to an old comedy. In the Proem the Tennessean promises the story he is about to tell will be *"as good as a comedy!"* and the New Yorker proposes to make of the tale a play to be enacted by Harry Placide. The main plot has something of the neat simplicity of an eighteenth-century comedy, involving the courtship of a young girl by three gallants and her eccentric decision to marry the one who wins a horse race in competition for her.

The style of *As Good as a Comedy*, too, seems to owe something to Simms's theory of humor, particularly that of the stage. "It is the great characteristic of poetry in general, and the drama in especial," he writes, "that language should be suggestive rather than full. Something must be left to the imagination of the audience. The clue must be put into their own hands, and they left to follow it; and it is because of the actual part which they thus are made to take in the progress of events, that the drama forms an intellectual exercise much more exciting than any other which mortal genius has yet been able to conceive. The spectators are, themselves, to a certain

[5] *Views and Reviews in American Literature, History and Fiction,* Second Series (New York, 1845), pp. 142-84.

extent, participators in the scene."[6] Brevity had never been a virtue
of the Simms romances; the style left little to the imagination of
the reader. But the narrative of *As Good as a Comedy* never becomes
bogged down in excessively descriptive passages, and its dialogue
frequently resembles the terse, racy speech of the kind of drama
Simms had in mind when he wrote his essay.

Among the eighteenth-century novelists, Simms singles out Fielding and Smollett as most worthy of praise. He points out that their
humor "grew naturally out of the situation,—was unstrained,—the
result of the regular progress of events, and not of cunning con-
trivances, merely set in operation to provoke the cachinnation of
the reader." To them fun "was the spontaneous effusion of a faculty
in themselves, and in the character and the event upon which they
were engaged,—and the action of circumstances upon character, gave
form and effect to the situation. Nothing was derived from mere
quaintness of expression, peculiarity of phrase, or oddly-sorted
phraseology."[7] A similar theory is suggested in the Proem to *As
Good as a Comedy*. When the Tennessean is asked if the story made
those who heard it laugh, his answer is equivocal: "Laugh! I guess
some did and some didn't . . . . 'Twas something a'most too strange
for laughing; the more, too, as we know'd it to be nothing but the
truth, and it happened here, too, in one of these western counties of
Georgia" (p. 15). To Simms, the comic writer begins as the observer
of truth, not as the creator of humor.

Simms admired *The Merry Wives of Windsor* of Shakespeare
because it was "a story from humble life avowedly, yet with just such
an admixture of the high with the humble, the several constituencies
of society in such combination,—as we find ordinarily in society, and
by which that curious moral amalgam is kept from becoming utterly
monotonous and wretched."[8] He believed that in humorous writing,
low life should not be presented exclusively, for this would give
a false impression of the general character of society. The higher
classes should be placed in juxtaposition with the lower, in order
that the one "idealize" the other. In *As Good as a Comedy* the
focus of the plot is upon the middle class of small planters in rural

[6] *Ibid.*, p. 157.
[7] *Ibid.*, p. 175.
[8] *Ibid.*, p. 153.

Georgia, but characters and scenes from lower life also play their part in the novel. The racetrack scenes, coming early in the book, bring all the people of the district together. All classes participate in the pleasures of the race-course, whether they own horses or not.

Several characters in the novel cannot be placed precisely in the respectable upper and middle classes or in those below them. The heroine's stepmother is a vulgar woman who has achieved some degree of social standing through her marriage to a planter. Jones Barry, the heroine's richest suitor, is also her coarsest; despite his wealth, he has more in common with the drunken, brawling lower classes who watch the races than with planters who race their horses against his. Simms emphasizes strongly the crudeness and cruelty of the sport of gander-pulling, and then shows Barry delighting in it.

Simms's masterful circus scenes similarly depict a broadly popular activity in which all classes take pleasure, and again afford the opportunity of revealing the vulgarity of Barry in his drunken involvement with the "Sultana." Altogether, Simms devotes eight early chapters of his novel to this panorama of rural enjoyments, before the action of the main plot of high life begins in earnest. These chapters, the most vivid and most comic portion of the novel, convey a realistic picture of the life and the language of the plain people of the area that serves as more than a background for the actions of the genteel upper-class characters of the main plot. If these characters "idealize" the low-life characters of the work, they, in turn, give an earthy strength and truth to the gentry-oriented main plot.

This kind of writing is rarely found in the novels of the antebellum South. Neither John Pendleton Kennedy, nor William Alexander Caruthers, nor John Esten Cooke attempted to show the plain people of a rural district enjoying the pleasures of a Saturday afternoon in town. Such subject matter was gradually working its way into the literature of the time primarily through newspaper sketches which were widely circulated by such journals as William T. Porter's New York *Spirit of the Times* and, ultimately, in book form, most readily in the paperbacks of the "Library of Humorous American Works." During the decade after the publication of Longstreet's *Georgia Scenes* a number of works appeared which established a new genre in American, and particularly in Southern, writing, and which unquestionably influenced Simms's humorous fiction. Probably Longstreet's sketches "The Turf" and "The Gander Pulling" in

Georgia Scenes were the primary inspiration for Simms's depiction of the varied activities of "Hillabee Race-Course," but Longstreet's had been followed by many other treatments of such subject matter, along the same lines, which Simms may well have known. Other models were probably supplied by William Tappan Thompson's vivid picture of Muster Day in *Major Jones's Courtship* (1843) and Johnson Jones Hooper's circus scenes in *Some Adventures of Captain Simon Suggs* (1845). Though Simms's best contributions to this literary genre, the tall tales "Bald-Head Bill Baldy" and "How Sharp Snaffles Got His Capital and Wife," were not written until much later, he showed his awareness of the tradition, and made it serve his ends as a novelist, in *As Good as a Comedy*.

In thus combining the materials and tradition of Southern humor with those of English comic drama and fiction, Simms failed to create a thoroughly unified novel. His early chapters (II-X), with their realistic depiction of society in early nineteenth-century rural Georgia, contribute little to the progress of the major plot. Despite the presence of Jones Barry in both, the sub-plot and main plot of the novel have little connection, and the early chapters comprise too large a portion of the work as a whole, depriving it of balance, so far as the working out of the action of the main plot is concerned. Had he reduced the scope of his race-course realism and made it simply the background for his plot of the courtship of Geraldine Foster, Simms would have produced a more unified work. But he would thereby have lost or diminished its best features. Simms succeeds fully as a writer of humor in the early scenes of the work, with their vignettes that follow the subjects of contemporary genre-painting—the spilled barrel of whiskey, the wrestling match, the excitement of the circus.

The originality of the main plot of *As Good as a Comedy* is largely dependent upon the character of the heroine, Geraldine Foster. We have seen the other characters before—Mrs. Foster, Geraldine's vulgar and socially ambitious stepmother; young Hammond, the gentlemanly hero; and his mother, the upholder of the traditional rules of genteel behavior. Geraldine is new, and characteristically national rather than regional, as a type. She is a young woman who behaves according to her own impulses despite the dictates of convention. Simms recognized this essential independence of behavior as the dominant characteristic of native American backwoods character. Such freedom might be expected in a young woman of a pioneer family, but the fact that Geraldine belongs to the upper class of the landed gentry, in a settled society, is what makes Simms's observation important. In the Proem, when Simms interprets the symbolic importance of Geraldine Foster, his thought comes surprisingly close to Emerson's. The transcendentalist had urged individualism on a new country, too dependent upon the conventions of the past. Simms as novelist-observer was pointing out that self-reliance and freedom from convention were qualities often disguised as eccentricity in the society of the hinterland:

"The story illustrates curiously the variety and freedom of character which we find everywhere in our forest country, where no long-established usages subdue the fresh and eager impulses of originality, and where, as if in very mockery of the conventionalities of city life, the strangest eccentricities of mood and feeling display themselves in a connection with the most unimpeachable virtue—eccentricities of conduct such as would shock the demurer damsel of the city, to whom the proprieties themselves are virtues—yet without impairing those substantial virtues of the country girl, whose principles are wholly independent of externals. Let the reader only keep in mind the perfect freedom of will, and the absence of prescriptive or fashionable discipline in our border countries, and there will be nothing strange or extravagant in what is here related of the heroine" (p. 16).

This interpretation could describe the milieu for Henry James's Daisy Miller except for the fact that provincial Schenectady is the later novelist's equivalent for "our forest country." In her innocence and in her freedom from convention Geraldine Foster anticipates Daisy Miller because both Simms and James observed the same trait of American character at two widely separated locales. Simms's Geraldine Foster is one of the earliest appearances in American fiction of the innocent girl who shocks conventional society.

James, of course, brought his innocent to a pathetic end, illustrating society's destructive cruelty. There is a threatening suggestion of this in Simms's proud Mrs. Hammond, the conventional mother of the successful suitor. But Simms sees little reason to anticipate tragedy for Geraldine because he never moves his story beyond the confines of her native "forest country." Savannah is mentioned as the center of sophistication, where Geraldine's eccentric behavior would have been as unacceptable as Daisy Miller's was in Geneva or in Rome. From Simms's point of view Geraldine's freedom of character is admirable until she carries it to a ludicrous extreme. When, at the behest of her scheming stepmother, she agrees to marry the suitor who wins a horse race in her honor, she is indulging in an extravagance that nearly destroys her happiness.

As Good as a Comedy was well received by the critics. *Godey's Lady's Book* compared the anonymous author to Dickens at his best. The *Southern Literary Gazette* reprinted a scene from the novel and called its humor "absolutely irresistible." A review in the *Literary World* spoke of the fulfillment of the promise of the novel's title and added: "The publishers have given us many amusing books in their humorous library, but the last is worth all the others. Far from a broad caricature, it is on the contrary the most faithful and amusing description of the bright side of Georgia Life that we have yet seen .... [It is] one of the most truly amusing and thoroughly American books that we have met with."[9] But the novel never achieved popularity. Simms made at least three attempts to interest publishers in reprinting it, on one occasion suggesting that the title be changed.[10] He acquired possession of the plates and attempted to reissue it at Columbia in the fatal year of 1865. The coming of General Sherman's army destroyed that possibility in the destruction of the city itself.[11]

As Good as a Comedy is a novel that combines the calm eighteenth-century comic spirit with the earthy reality of the humor of the early nineteenth-century South. It is the fiction of a romanticist who, in this phase of his work, was chiefly concerned with the regional. If Simms was looking back to the tradition of Old Comedy, he was also anticipating the vogue of realism yet to come. He would not attempt such a book again. With the approach of war his mood became somber. He did not attempt humor again for more than a decade, when he wrote *Paddy McGann*, a dark comedy, less concerned with genteel planters than with backwoods folk, and with the character and mood of the people of the embattled South.

[9] For an account of the reception of *As Good as a Comedy* see *Letters*, III, 105, note 79.
[10] See Simms to Baird, April 14, 1854, *Letters*, III, 293. Simms suggested as the new title "Tom Nettles, or a Race for a Wife" or "The Fair Geraldine, a Story of the Backwoods."
[11] See Simms to Evert Duyckinck, Sept. 9, 1865, *Letters*, IV, 518.

INTRODUCTION TO
PADDY McGANN; OR,
THE DEMON OF THE STUMP.

The short novel *Paddy McGann; or, The Demon of the Stump* [1] (1863) appeared under the name of W. Gilmore Simms in sixteen installments in the Richmond weekly *The Southern Illustrated News*. It was the first Simms novel to appear since the publication of *The Cassique of Kiawah* (1859), the work that completed the long series of romances on which the South Carolina author had built a sound reputation. The falling off of his production after 1859 was certainly due to the coming of war and its attendant dampening of the impulse to create. During the month before the beginning of the serialization of *Paddy McGann*, Simms wrote to a friend, "I have done little or nothing in literature for two years . . . . I am now trying to do something—working up an old story for the Illustrated News, but the work is uphill entirely. I need leisure, repose & my wonted conveniences for composition. I need not say to you, also, how much a man of my excitable temperament may be kept from his tasks by the condition of the Country. It will need a year of peace to bring me back to that calm of mood which Literature demands.—" [2] The reference is to *Paddy McGann*, but it is not possible to say whether the "old story" was a novel that Simms had begun some time before or whether it was a new novel based on a story that he had had in his mind for some time. Much of the local material of the "old story" centering around his own mid-South Carolina plantation area had been in his mind for a long time; the episode in New York reflects his own experiences there about fifteen years before. It is the element of the South

---

[1] For the first extended criticism of the novel see Robert Bush, "*Paddy McGann*, William Gilmore Simms's Devil Story," *Bulletin of the New York Public Library*, LXIX (March, 1965), 197-204.

[2] Simms to John Reuben Thompson, Jan. 10, 1863, *Letters*, IV, 421.

and her ordeal of invasion that is current and that colors the tone of the novel and deepens its meaning in all its episodes.

It is likely that Simms's affection for the Edisto River and its countryside began in 1836 after he had married for the second time and settled at "Woodlands," his father-in-law's plantation home near the village of Midway, South Carolina. In 1839, a few years after that event, he published in *The New-York Mirror* a personal essay in the form of a letter describing the beauty of the plantation setting and the swift-flowing Edisto, a major artery for the transportation of cypress and long-leaf pine and an inexhaustible source of trout, rock, perch, bream, and cat.[3] It was several years after this that Simms must have begun to see the river country as a source of legend which the fiction writer might exploit in much the same way that Washington Irving had made use of the Hudson River country. The earliest Simms story about his river is "The Boatman's Revenge, A Tale of Edisto," which appeared in *Graham's Magazine* in 1845.[4] This tale was to be retitled "Sergeant Barnacle," as one of the collection of *The Wigwam and the Cabin* (1845). The story concerns the revenge taken by a raftsman against a rival in a love affair. The setting is pre-revolutionary. Little stress is placed on the activity of the raftsman, but it is evident that Simms saw rafting as a romantic career for a rustic hero. Sergeant Barnacle, like Paddy McGann, is a man of high principle and a devout patriot. Both men are disappointed by the tragic loss of their loves, and it is for this reason that they have remained bachelors. A curious character at the conclusion of "Sergeant Barnacle" is the comic Judge Burke at Orangeburg who exonerates the hero. He is an Irishman with the brogue and some of the wit of Paddy McGann. Sergeant Barnacle is a good man, but he is much too sober and evangelical to be an endearing one. Simms seems to have fused the qualities of the upright raftsman, Sergeant Barnacle, with the Irish qualities of Judge Burke to create the vigorously humorous Paddy McGann.

Another story appeared that probably contributed to the development of Paddy. In 1852 Simms published a series of sketches based on the legends of the Charleston area and its hinterland: "Home Sketches, or Life Along the Highways and Byways of the South."

---

[3] Simms to *The New-York Mirror*, XVI (June 22, 1839), 412-13.
[4] *Graham's Magazine*, XXVII (March, 1845), 109-20.

One of these sketches[5] is a story the author says he has heard—
"Ephraim Bartlett, the Edisto Raftsman." In this tale there is a
greater stress on the routine of the boatmen as they pilot their rafts
from Lexington District down to Charleston. Two new elements
are added that suggest the Paddy McGann character—whiskey and
the supernatural. Ephraim is sober on his voyages down river, but
once his commission is completed, he and his Negro assistant set out
for upcountry on foot, armed with a jug of whiskey. Ephraim drinks
his fill and observes a ghostly hunting party ride through the deserted house where the two have settled for the night. Whether
it was a spectre hunt or whether he saw it because he was drunk
is a question left unanswered. The development of the raftsman
theme has taken a livelier and a more comic turn. Ephraim is made
a picturesque figure as we see him with a red bandanna tied around
his head, jumping into the cool Edisto to sober up when his rafts
demand attention; but like Sergeant Barnacle he lacks a spark that
would make him memorable. In his series of variations on the
raftsman theme, Simms found that spark in the Irish wit and character he had tried out somewhat incongruously in Judge Burke, who
ended a solemn story with a touch of humor.

There were other reasons for the use of an Irish immigrant's son
as the hero of the 1863 novel. Simms was attempting to record the
authentic life of his own countryside, where, during the 1840's and
1850's, the Irishman was frequently seen, an interesting working
man because he was white and free and because he spoke an amusing
dialect. The 1850's and 1860's were decades when amusing stories
about Irishmen appeared in abundance in newspapers and in oral
tradition as well. But if the Irishman was usually the butt of the
jokes of the time because of his innocence or ignorance, Simms raised
him in Paddy to the higher dignity that he had conceived in the
character of Sergeant Barnacle. Paddy McGann is fully respected
by his creator for his honor, intelligence, and manliness. That he
is ignorant of books and given to an inordinate love of whiskey
makes him delightfully human and subject to imaginative visions
that open the door to the folklore of diablerie.

Paddy McGann is not a coarse work, but its subject matter would
be more attractive to masculine than feminine readers in the 1860's.

---

[5] *The Literary World* (New York), (February 7, 1852), pp. 107-10.

The heavy drinking of the raftsmen, their pleasures in bawdy houses along the river, the attempted seduction of Paddy in New York— these subjects would have been distasteful to most mid-Victorian ladies. Paddy tells his adventures to a group of gentleman planters and intellectuals. In his experiences there are no colorless, fragile ladies of the sort frequently found in the Simms romances. Paddy's mother is credible as a decent country woman who is foolish enough to try to urge her son into a marriage for which he has little enthusiasm. His wife and mother-in-law are predatory and ostentatious; the women of the New York salons are pretentious and overemotional. However it may deal with the supernatural, this novel is not a romance. It is a curious amalgam unlike most of Simms's previous fiction. Broadly speaking, it has much of the narrative spirit of the realistic oral tradition of Southern humor. Paddy McGann tells his story in a mixture of Irish brogue and Carolina backwoods talk. His story is intended to amuse his readers. It sparkles with comic adventure and racy satire. But the full import of the novel and the underlying tone is one of high seriousness. It is this combination of elements that tempts the reader to compare it to *Adventures of Huckleberry Finn*. Both novels stem from a similar tradition and both partake more or less of the picaresque, an element that links them with the European tradition.

Simms's Devil derives from the comic Old Nick of folklore. The idea that drunkenness brought about visions of the supernatural had been popularized by Burns in "Tam O'Shanter"; here and in *Paddy McGann* there is the wry ambiguity as to whether the visions have an existence of their own or whether they are only in the drinker's mind. Closer as a possible influence on Simms is "Mike Brown," a story told in John P. Kennedy's *Swallow Barn* (1832; revised edition, 1851). Mike Brown is a rustic hero, who meets the Devil only after heavy potations. Other elements that suggest *Paddy McGann* are the Devil's derisive "ho, ho, ho!" and his fight with the doughty hero. Mike Brown's Devil appears in human form, but Paddy McGann's never does. When Paddy cheerfully fights the demon it is in the form of an animated stump. Paddy's Devil is also a great owl, an immense buck deer, or a pair of red eyes. Another difference between Paddy and earlier Devil stories is the lack of resemblance to the Faust legend. There is no pact for the purchase of the hero's soul as in "Mike Brown" and in Washington Irving's "The Devil and Tom Walker." In *Paddy McGann* the Devil plays several roles according to the plot of the individual episode. In the earliest adventures he is Paddy's moral nemesis and a dramatic projection of his conscience.

At least in the first part of the novel Paddy's Devil seems to have a purposeful mission. He hinders the backwoodsman from shooting the creatures of the woods and from catching fish from the river. Although Paddy is frustrated and angered by the jinx cast on his usual skill as a huntsman and fisherman, he himself realizes that the Devil's aim is the protection of wildlife. The Devil rarely speaks to Paddy to explain the reasons for his harassment; when he does it is in the role of protector of the birds:

" 'I raised 'em, you dirty fellow, jest as an old woman raises chickens, by good usage and good feeding. And for you to come and murder 'em. Murder, I calls it,' says he, 'to take 'em in a line upon the ground! To give 'em not the shadow of a chaince! You a sportsman! you a hunter! Sorra's the day when you got a gun into your clumsy fists. But I'll punish you for your murdering acts, you dirty villain. I'll see that you get no more meat! You a hunter. Hoo! Hoo! Hoo!' " (pp. 315-16).

This is indeed as curious a Devil as is to be met with in literature—a kind of avenging angel acting as protector of the gentle partridges against the depredations of the cruel huntsman. Paddy is not by nature cruel, although up to this point he has had no qualms about making his rather lazy living by exploiting the wildlife of the forest. Simms conceives of him as the type of European settler in his relation to the frontier. The period during which natural life was understandably exploited for the sake of the living of the settlers is now past. The stage of settled diligence for the frontiersman is now at hand. He must give up the easy life of the professional hunter and fisherman and assume the duties of the useful villager who follows the trade of local carpenter or pilot on the Edisto. The narrator explains that "His demon, if he had a demon, was a blessing to him! Before he was troubled, as he tells you, he had a score of other demons at his heels; the worst of all, such as accompany the idle life of hunter and fisherman in our country; not one of whom did I ever meet who was not worthless in all other respects. The moment

Paddy ceased to lead a desultory life he prospered" (p. 446). In this transitional phase of Paddy's career, Simms is taking a realistic look at the American backwoodsman, who had been idealized for too long a period during the previous half century by authors like James Fenimore Cooper.

Paddy's demon is best interpreted psychologically as a projection of his own conscience. He tells his planter friends that whenever he committed one of the Seven Deadly Sins he could expect a visitation of the Devil, not at the time of temptation but after the committing of the act, in the form of a punishment for wrongdoing.

There is a shift in the burden of the story when Paddy describes his experiences on the raft. Commissioned to pilot seventy lumber rafts down the Edisto to Charleston, he at one point falls asleep in a drunken stupor and is carried out to sea on his caboose raft. The demon actually causes the catastrophe after Paddy has indulged in a riotous party at one of the brothels along the river. The demon would then seem to represent the punishment for indulgence in gluttony. Other members of his crew indulge in lechery as well, but apparently not Paddy. Why then is he singled out for punishment by the demon and why does he find himself in the most dangerous situation in his life, adrift on the ocean with little expectation of rescue? One answer is that Simms is writing a picaresque adventure and must engage his hero in danger that will eventually get him to New York, where very different adventures will befall him. Another is that the raft adventure is no longer concerned with the exploitation of nature; nature itself seems to be Paddy's enemy as a shark-infested sea surrounds him. The drama of his struggle is the testing of man's endurance in the face of adversity. Confronted with despair, the hero refuses to surrender his belief in the providence of God.

Simms was a man of staunch faith in the Deity. At the time of his writing of *Paddy McGann* "Woodlands" had been burned for the first time. His soldier son was home from the army, ill with typhoid. If the Confederate success at Fredericksburg elated him, there is no doubt that the war seemed a horror that he had not counted on and a catastrophe, the end of which was hardly in sight. In his many comments in letters discussing the desired secession for at least ten years before the war, he never seems to have had the foresight to predict a terrible ordeal for his country in the achievement of independence. In his letters of 1862 there is the new note of ordeal sustained by the strong belief that God may test the South's endurance but will not let her sink. Even at the beginning of *Paddy McGann* the note has been sounded, suggesting that in 1862 Simms has already contemplated the possibility of disaster. In the character of the planter Wharncliffe he says, "It cannot be that God will deliver us into the hands of these atrocious heathens. As between us and the Deity, there is no doubt a sad reckoning to make; but as between us and these accursed Yankees, no reproach lies at our doors, unless that single one of having too long slept within the coil of the serpent. I have faith in God, my friend.—He may punish us, and we must suffer, for this is the meed of our desert; but he will not let us sink" (p. 221).

Except for Paddy's eventual enlistment in the Confederate army no direct connections are made between his story and the war. Why then does Simms introduce the theme of the ordeal of war at the beginning of the novel, if he does not intend to present the entire fiction as a comment on Southern character in times of trouble and in relation to her mortal enemy? Paddy McGann at his best is an emblem of the essential character of the Southern masses, representing values that Simms wished to see preserved. In the episode in which the hero is helpless on his raft on an indifferent ocean, his ordeal seems to be equated to the wartime ordeal of the Confederacy itself. There is a curious parallel between the planter's references to God quoted above and the elaborate vision Paddy experiences at his most desperate moment on the raft. Three stars appear during the night that Paddy refers to as the "staff of God." He says, "I will hold on to this staff of God. It is a sign to me, He will not let me sink" (p. 351). In this episode the Devil is disguised as a stump in the woodpile on the raft. When Paddy struggles with the stump it is his own struggle with the temptation to despair when his fortunes are at their lowest point. The episode has the didactic function of encouraging the people of the South to hold on in their own struggle, to trust in God's providence. As Paddy is rescued by a passing merchantman and the danger to his life evaporates, so also the South will survive through endurance and faith.

In the third part of the narrative, Simms began to draw on his own experiences in earlier years. It is probably more than a coincidence that the captain of the merchantman who rescues Paddy is a Scotsman named Wilson, a foreigner who can take a less than idealistic view of Northerners. Captain Wilson is a man of the world who can not only introduce Paddy to the social life of New York, but he can also warn him of the evils that will befall the greenhorn. The parallel to be recognized in the early life of Simms is that he too, the son of an Irish immigrant, was introduced to New York society by a Scotsman, James Lawson, who remained his friend through life. Of course Simms and Lawson were gentlemanly intellectuals in the New York of the forties, but the now mature Simms could look back on himself as a greenhorn and write something that approaches a parody of his own experiences.

Paddy's enforced visit to New York gave Simms an opportunity to air his recollections of the literary celebrities of the city during the later years of the life of Poe. The people whom he caricatures are of the same group that Poe himself evaluated in his series of *Literati*. Simms avails himself of the chance to castigate at least two of his old enemies—Lewis Gaylord Clark and George Pope Morris. The absurdly sentimental ladies of the salons are here satirized in Anne Statia, who may be a caricature of Anne Sophia Stephens, queen of mid-century scribblers and later the author of the sensationally successful first dime novel—*Malaeska, or The Indian Wife of the White Hunter* (1860). This New York episode, when Paddy McGann is made much of because of his exciting ordeal at sea and his romantic background as frontiersman close to the heart of nature, recalls the historical lionization of Davy Crockett over a generation earlier. The picturesque figure of Montgomery Damon, the woodsman who is lionized by the city in William Alexander Caruthers' novel *The Kentuckian in New-York* (1834), was perhaps also in Simms's mind as he conceived the episode. In the Era of Good Feeling Dr. Caruthers wrote his novel to contrast the character of the people of the two sections in order to bring about tolerant understanding between North and South; Simms, in the midst of war, used the material primarily as propaganda to show the innocence and virtue of Paddy as a Southerner as opposed to the chicanery and pretentiousness of those who had become the enemy. The details of his satire lack subtlety, but the picture of Miss Pynch's early Victorian salon (based on the celebrated salon of Miss Anna Lynch) is historically amusing.

The concluding episode is the story of Paddy's unfortunate marriage to Susan Pogson after his return to South Carolina. The marriage is engineered by well-meaning meddlers, Paddy's own mother and her friends. Paddy has grave misgivings about the Pogson family, even though he is made to see Susan as superior to other members of her family. The now settled, diligent Paddy despises the ill-kept Pogson farm, the laziness of the elder Pogson and the showiness of the mother and daughters. Once married, he gradually realizes the folly of taking other people's advice against his own better judgment. The entire Pogson family exploit Paddy, selfishly usurping his property and even evicting his own mother from her accustomed quarters in his house. The Pogsons as a family are successfully drawn by Simms as an entirely believable group of poor whites for whom the reader can generate no sympathy whatever. They have all the worst qualities of the poor white families without any indications that they would be better people if the economic system favored them to a greater extent. When Paddy finally discovers that his property has been stolen by his wife's father and brother, he gives way to violence, banishing the brother from his house and striking his own father-in-law. For some time he has been estranged from his surly wife, and in desperation the disappointed man goes off to join the Confederate army, thus bringing his story up to a time contemporary with the narrative with which the novel began.

All of the story of Paddy in the first three episodes has a general bearing on the destiny of the South in war and peace: part one, the shift from exploitation of the wilderness to village diligence and responsibility, part two, the primitive Southern hero enduring his ordeal with the help of God; part three, the rural Southern hero's innocence in contrast with Northern urban chicanery and avarice. On the surface, part four is a good picture of an unfortunate marriage among the poorer classes of the backwoods, contrasting the now prosperous and diligent Paddy with the irresponsible family into which he has foolishly married. If Paddy's early adventures are to be interpreted on a general level as an objectification of the

Southern experience, then it is highly likely the final episode also bears such symbolic meaning. If so, the unfortunate marriage is an allegory of the American Union itself, which Simms had long proclaimed a grievous mistake on the part of the South. Once married, the innocent Paddy is fully exploited by his wife and her entire family. This would seem to carry out Simms's views on the relation between the sections.

In the earlier episode when Paddy was on Captain Wilson's ship heading for New York, the idea that the North exploited the South was expressed by the captain himself. Paddy quotes him as calling America "a nation of rogues and swindlers. Their only idee of vartue is *smartness*, and they uses their smartness only to take a fellow in!" When Paddy resents the slur on the national character, declaring himself an American, Captain Wilson laughs at him: " 'Oh, pooh!' he says. . . . 'You're a Southern—you're one of the *geese;* the *fox* is in your feathers! The Amerikin charackter . . . is made by the North. The people of Europe knows nothing about *you*, 'cept that *you* keeps the niggers and the Yankees keeps *you*. Why, man, . . . they'll cheat the very eyes out of *your* head . . . .' " Paddy sees the point and admits that "that's what our people in Carolina thinks . . ." (pp. 373-74). In the marriage episode Paddy's patience endures until he finds his stores stolen by his wife's father and brother. He is driven to violence against them himself; the marriage has long since been an unhappy one, but now the rupture is complete. On the historical level the South is now at war. The symbolic story melds with historical actuality as Paddy enlists in the Confederate army to escape from his intolerable predicament. Other elements tend to reënforce this interpretation. Paddy's excellent, well-meaning mother seems to represent the spirit of the Southern founding fathers, who strongly favored the foolish marriage; but Paddy's mother came to rue her part in the plan before her own death. By Civil War time, of course, the founding fathers and their enthusiasm for union had long been dead.

The tone of *Paddy McGann* is curiously complex, but quite successfully varied to suit the author's purpose. The frame of the narrative is rhapsodic in its presentation of the life of the Old South and both belligerent and apprehensive whenever a threat to that life appears. Paddy's own story, within the frame, is told seriously, but buoyed up by the liveliness of his character and wit and his insatiable love of spirits. Caught up in the adventures of this attractive personality, the reader, before he is aware of it, has been led to the contemplation of an ideal. Paddy has much that is the essence of the primitive South to Simms. He has the virtues of great heroes—honesty and courage and the sense of duty to old people and children, to his mother and his country; he has the weaknesses of heroes—self-indulgence, pride, and anger. He spans a goodly cross-section of Southern life from solitary frontier huntsman to raft pilot in the lumber industry to innocent ambassador to the North, and finally to Confederate soldier. He belongs to the folk, but he is a natural aristocrat who can hold his own with the planters and the learned men who assemble to listen to the tales of his adventures. The planter Wharncliffe and his friends have high respect for Paddy. As a symbol of the spirit of Southern energy and character, he bears comparison with Captain Porgy, whom Simms had introduced in his early romances of the Revolution and developed fully in *Woodcraft*. The Porgy symbol is that of the Old South landed gentleman who is broad enough in his scope to be a part of the life of the folk. Paddy McGann, who belongs to the folk, is broad enough to embrace the gentry.

As a serialized novel in an obscure weekly, *Paddy McGann* passed unnoticed by contemporary critics. Because it dealt with themes too sectional to interest Northern publishers who might have brought it out as a book, it was ignored in the later nineteenth century when other Simms novels were reprinted. William P. Trent mentions it only briefly in the first biography of Simms (1892). Our own era, however, should find value in it as a document in our civilization: it dramatizes the spirit and character of the Old South during her short life as an independent state. It is one of the sprightliest works in early American fiction to depict the clash of regional characters— the Southern backwoodsman against the New Yorker and the Yankee, the man of native wit and little learning against the men of commercial skill and the ladies of Byronic sentiment. If we see its origins in Irving, Longstreet, Caruthers, and Kennedy, we also see it as an early example of the dialect novel, which would come into its own in Mark Twain's time, some twenty years later.

As a regional novel *Paddy McGann* depicts the life and character of the Edisto River country with unquestioned truth. Without false sentiment it celebrates a picturesque vocation on a picturesque river. Many of the characters are traceable as people who once lived—men of note like General Jamison, Dr. Bruns, and Paul Hamilton Hayne. Of course such people have often appeared in novels. The more remarkable fact is that many obscure names are a part of the work's reality—Isaac Bamberg, the Reverend Lucius Bellinger, Britton Elzy, and John Brunson. So authentic do most of these names appear to be that one is inclined to believe that Paddy McGann was himself a real figure, who drank heavily and was harassed by the Devil, who rafted on the Edisto and was washed out to sea, who visited New York and returned home to marry the wrong girl, who made his escape into the Confederate army, and perhaps at last found his way into one of the unkempt graveyards that mark the crossroads in what was called Barnwell District.

AS GOOD AS A COMEDY:

OR, THE

TENNESSEEAN'S STORY.

"I have some purpose in it;—and, but beat off these two rooks, Jack Daw and his fellow, with any discontentment hither, and I'll honor thee forever."

BEN JONSON.

TO HARRY PLACIDE.

My dear Harry:—

You have been, in your day and mine, as good as a thousand comedies to me. Why should I not endeavor to requite you, after a very poor fashion of my own? Yet will you not know, any more than the Custom-House, when some repenting sinner of an importer makes anonymous restoration of defrauded dues, whose conscience it is from which this poor acknowledgment is drawn. It is, you may be sure, a very sincere one, coupled with the single misgiving that my little "Comedy" will scarcely prove half so agreeable to you, as yours has ever been to me. Nevertheless, you excellent wretch, be you grateful with the philosophy of Sancho, and look not the gift-horse too narrowly in the mouth.

L'ALLEGRO.

New York.

ADVERTISEMENT.

In good faith, I very sincerely hope that the title which this little volume bears upon its face will take nobody in. Now that it is written out, I am not sure that there is anything comic in its pages. I am certain that I have made no effort to make them so; and if merriment should be the result, I shall certainly congratulate myself upon the possession of an involuntary endowment, which takes its owner quite as much by surprise as anybody else. But no; even if there be comedy in the narrative that follows, it will be none of mine—I were a Pagan to lay claim to it. These, in fact, are but jottings down from the lips of another; and I don't know that I was greatly beguiled, when I heard them, into that happy humor which makes one cry out in defiance, "Sessa! let the world pass!" Were I to confess honestly, I should rather admit myself of that graver order of monkhood which never tells its beads on the face of a tankard. I don't see a jest readily at any time, and, knowing my infirmity, I very frequently suffer it to escape me by keeping too closely on the watch for it. It so happens, accordingly, that, being very amiable and anxious to please, I blunder after the fashion of Dr. Johnson's butcher, who was procured to help bolster up Goldsmith's first comedy, and do all my laughing in the wrong place, and after the mirth has fairly subsided from the muscles of my neighbors. This makes me modest of judgment in all matters that affect the humorous, and hardly a proper person, therefore, to recount that which is so. But, indeed, I propose nothing of the kind. The title chosen for this volume is in some degree in compliance with necessity: it can scarcely be said to have been a matter of choice.

3

This will be explained by our Introduction, to which I shall hasten with due speed, promising to make it as short as possible, since I have no hope to make it funny.

L'ALLEGRO.

New York.

PROEM.

We were nine of us, packed snugly enough in a close stage, and on the high road from Madison, in Georgia, to Montgomery, in Alabama. The night was dark, and the rain falling. The roads were bad, and the driver as drunk as the least reasonable desperate could desire under the circumstances. Everybody has an idea, more or less vivid, of a dark and rainy night; most persons can form a notion of the drunken driver of a stagecoach—a swearing, foul-mouthed fellow, pestilent, full of conceit and insolence, fully conscious of his power over his nags and passengers, and with just reason enough left to desire to use his power so as to keep all parties apprehensive—his horses of the whip, and his passengers of an upset. But if you know nothing of a Georgia road in bad weather, at the time I speak of, you can form but an imperfect idea of the nervous irritability of the nine within our vehicle that night, as, trundling through bog and through brier, over stump and stone, up hill and down dale—as desperate a chase, seemingly, as that of the Wild Horseman of Bürger—we momently cursed our fates, that had given us over to such a keeping and such a progress. We could not see each other's faces, but we could hear each other's words, and feel each other's hips and elbows.

"Hech! There we go!"

"You're into me, *stranger*, with a monstrous sharp side of your own."

"Beg pardon, but—" [Jolt, toss, and tumble.]

"We're gone now, I reckon!"

A general scramble followed the rolling of the baggage in the rear, and sudden silence of the human voice, while each strove to maintain his equilibrium, seizing upon the nearest solid object.

"She rights!" said one.

"Eh! does she? I'm glad of it," was the reply of another, "since I hope this gentleman will now suffer my head to get back fairly upon its shoulders."

There was a release of the victim and an apology. Indeed, there were several apologies necessary. We were momently making free with the arms and sides and shoulders of our neighbors, under the impulse of a sudden dread of the upset, which it is wonderful how we continued to escape. We compared notes. Our apprehensions were general. The driver was appealed to; we howled to him through the pipes of a Down Easter, entreating him to drive more gently.

"Gently, be hanged!" was the horrid answer, followed up by a tremendous smack of the whip. Away went the horses at a wilder rate than ever, and we were left, without hope or consolation, to all sorts of imaginable and unimaginable terrors. We had no help for it, and no escape. We could only brood over our terrors, and mutter our rage. There were curses, not only loud, but deep. It was in vain that our individual philosophies strove to silence our discontents; these were kept alive by the suggestions of less amiable companions. Our very efforts to conceal our fears sufficiently betrayed them to all who were cool enough to make the discovery. But self-esteem was reassured by the general sympathy of most of our comrades. There were various emotions among us—the modified exponents of the one in common—modified according to age, temper, and education. Our various modes of showing them made us altogether a proper group for dramatic contrasts. We could have played our parts, no doubt very decently, upon any *stage* but that. We could have strutted manfully, and shown good legs, but scarcely upon boards which creaked and cracked as with convulsions of their own, as we hurried headlong up the heights, or rushed whizzing through the mire. And we should have had variety enough for character. Our nine passengers might have represented as many States. Never was there a more grateful diversity. There was a schoolmaster from Massachusetts. Whither, indeed, does not Massachusetts send her schoolmasters, teaching the same eternal notion of the saintly mission of the Puritans, and the perfect virtues of their descendants? The genius of that State was certainly born a pedagogue, with birch in one hand and horn-book in the other! There was a machinist from Maine, a queer, quaint, shrewd, knowing, self-taught Yankee, who had lost half his fingers in experimenting with his own machines, and who was brim-full of a new discovery which is to secure us that "philosopher's stone" of the nineteenth century—perpetual motion! The principle of our machinist seemed to lie in the amiable good-nature with which certain balls, precipitating themselves upon certain levers, would thus continue a series of ground and lofty tumblings which should keep the great globe itself in motion without other motive agencies. Our New Yorker was an editor, bound first for New Orleans, and then for Ashland, where he proposed to visit the god of his political idolatry. We had a Pennsylvanian, who seemed to feel as if all the shame of State repudiation lay on his own particular shoulders; and a Mississippian, who appeared to deplore nothing so much as that he could not claim more than the merit of a single vote in the glorious business of defying the foreign creditor of the Union Bank. The encounter between these two parties—the humbled and desponding tone of the one, contrasted with the exulting and triumphant convictions of successful right in the other—furnished a picture of opposites that was perfectly delightful. The leading idea which troubled our Virginian was, that Tyler was to be the last of the Presidents which his State would furnish to the Union; while the South Carolinian, with whom he seemed intimate, consoled him with the assurance that his regrets were idle, as the Union would not much longer need a President. He indulged in the favorite idea that a dissolution was at hand. "The Union," said he, "answered the purposes of the time. It has survived its uses." Our Georgian, on the contrary, was for the extension of the confederacy by the incorporation of as many new States south of us as we could persuade into the fold. He was even then upon his way to Texas, provided with his rifle only, in order to be in the way to help in the matter of annexation. Then we had a North Carolinian, a lank-sided fellow from Tar River, who slept nearly all the way, spite of toss and tumble, talked only (and constantly) in his sleep, and then chiefly upon the trouble of looking after his own affairs. Our *ninth* man was a broth of a boy in the shape of a huge Tennesseean, who filled up much more than his proper share of seat, and, trespassing upon mine with hip, thigh, and shoulder, compelled me (will he, nill he) to reduce myself to dimensions far more modest than I have usually been disposed to insist upon as reasonable. But, there was no chiding or complaining. He was so good-natured, so conscious of his involuntary trespasses; at least, so dubious about them.

"I crowd you, *stranger;* I'm afeard I crowd you;" and he laid his huge paw upon my shoulder with the air of one who solicits all possible indulgence. If I had been utterly squeezed out of proper shape, I could scarcely have forborne the assurance, which I instantly made him, that he didn't crowd me in the least.

"Well," said he, "I'm glad to hear you say so; I was a little dubious that I was spreading over you; and if so, I didn't know what to do then; for here, if you can feel, you'll see my fat lies rather heavy upon the thighs of this perpetual motion person, and my knee is a little too much of a dig for the haunches of the man in front. In fact, he's cutting into me—he's mighty sharp!"

The man in front, who was the Yankee schoolmaster, said something in under tones to the effect that men of such monstrous oversize should always take two places in a public conveyance, or travel in their own. I caught the words, but the Tennesseean did not.

"I'm jest as God made me," he proceeded, as if apologetically; "and if 'twould be any satisfaction to you, stranger," addressing me, "I'm willing to say that I would not be quite so broad if I had my own way, and the thing was to be done over agin. But as that's not to be hoped for, I don't complain at all, ef you don't."

How could I complain after the last suggestion—complain of a man who felt his own misfortune with such a proper conscience! The schoolmaster had something to say. His tone was exceedingly indignant, but too much subdued for the ears of the Tennesseean. My amiable recognition of his bulk seemed to have won his affections, if, indeed, his great size and my unavoidable neighborhood did not sufficiently account for them. His great fat haunches nestled most lovingly against me, threatening to overlap me entirely, while his huge arm encircled my neck with an embrace which would have honored that of the Irish Giant. It was fortunate that we had no such sulky scoundrels within the stage as he who lorded it from the box. If we swore at *him*, we kept terms with one another. If the storm roared without, we were pacific enough within; and it was wonderful, with such a variety, and with so much to distress and disquiet! Vexed and wearied with the aspect of affairs without, we succeeded in maintaining good conditions within; our curses were expended upon the driver; for one another, we had nothing but civility; good *nature*, if not good *humor*, keeping us in that sobriety of temper in respect to one another, when an innocent freedom passes without offence, and we tolerate a familiar in the barbarian whom, at another season, we should probably scarce recognize as an acquaintance. But mere good-nature has no chance, in the long run, against the protracted fatigue and weariness of such a ride as ours; and, as if by tacit consent, all parties seemed to feel the necessity of an effort to dissipate our dolors. The Maine man, it is true, discoursed of machines, and the Massachusetts man of Webster; the one was full of saws, the other of maxims; but the very square and compass character of their mutual minds was a worse monotony and fatigue than the wallowing of our wheels in mire. A lively account, which the Mississippian now gave us, of the pursuit and hanging of the Yazoo rogues—that terrible tragedy, which still needs an historian—soon led us upon another and more agreeable track, upon which the Georgian entered with a narrative of his own experience in catching alligators, in winter, with barbed stakes. To him succeeded the South Carolinian, with an account of a famous set-to which he had enjoyed the season before with certain abolitionists at New Haven, and which he concluded with an eloquent showing of the necessity for a Southern confederacy by next July. A stout controversy followed between him and the representative from Massachusetts, in which the grievances and quarrel between the two States were particularly discussed; the Carolinian concluding by proposing gravely to his opponent that the territory of North Carolina should be hired by the belligerent States for the purpose of settling their squabbles in the only becoming and manly way, by a resort to the *ultima ratio*. This dispute thus determined—for this strange proposition seemed to confound the man of Webster—we all had something to say in turn, each mounting his favorite hobby. It was an easy transition, from this, into anecdote and story, and even our North Carolinian roused himself up with a grunt, to yell out a wild ditty of the "old North State," which he heard from his great-grand-mother, and which he thought the finest thing in the shape of mixed song and story which had ever been delivered to mortal senses since the days of the prophets. It was one of the many rude ballads of a domestic character, which we have unwisely failed to preserve, which rehearsed the doings and death of Blackbeard the Pirate, "as he sailed" in and out of the harbors of Ocracoke and Pamlico. The strain was a woful and must have been a tedious one, but for the interposition of some special providence, the secret of which remains hidden from us to this day. It was observed that the voice of the singer, pitched upon the highest possible key at the beginning, gradually fell off towards the close of the second quatrain, sunk into a feeble drawl and quaver ere he had reached the third, and stopped short very suddenly in the middle of the fourth. We scarcely dared, any of us, to conjecture the cause of an interruption which displeased nobody. If this "sweet singer" from Tar River fell again to his slumbers, it is certain that not a whisper to this effect ever passed his lips. He gave us no premonitions of sleep, and no sequel to his ballad. We were all satisfied that he should have his own way in the matter, and never asked him for the rest of the ditty. He will probably wake up yet to finish it, but in what company or what coach hereafter, and after what season of repose, it is hardly prudent to guess, and not incumbent on us as a duty.

His quiet distressed none of us. There were others anxious to take his place, and we soon got to be a merry company indeed. Gradually, in the increasing interest of the several narratives, we forgot, temporarily, the bad roads and the drunken driver, recalled to the painful recollection only by an occasional crash and curse from without, to which we shut our ears almost as fervently as did Ulysses, when gliding among the dogs of Scylla. Our singers were, in truth, no great *shakes*, and our story-tellers scarcely better; but we grew indulgent just as we grew needy, and our tastes accommodated themselves to our necessities. It was only after all parties seemed to have exhausted their budget, their efforts subsiding into short and

feeble snatches—when there was only, at long intervals, a sort of
crackling from dry thorns under the pot of wit—it was only then
that our mammoth Tennesseean, who had hitherto maintained a very
modest silence, as if totally unambitious of the honors of the
raconteur, now suddenly aroused himself with a shake not very
unlike that of a Newfoundland dog fresh from the water.

"Stranger," says he to me, "ef so be you will only *skrooge* yourself
up so as to let me have this arm of mine parfectly free for a swing,
as I find it necessary, I'll let out a little upon you in relation to
sartain sarcumstances that come pretty much to my own knowledge,
a year or two ago, in Florida."

To *skrooge* myself up, in the expressive idiom of my neighbor,
into a yet narrower compass than I had been compelled to keep
before, was a thing wholly out of the question. But a change of
position might be effected, to the relief of both parties, and this was
all that he really wanted. I contrived, after a desperate effort, to
satisfy him, and, in some degree, myself.

"I can't, somehow, talk easy, ef my arms ain't loose," he continued,
apologetically. "My tongue and arm must somehow work together,
or I ain't half the man I ought to be. It's like being suffered to
spout out, when you're rushing upon the inimy; and when you can
halloo as you rush, you feel wolfish all over. I've had the feeling.
Now, it's so in talking. Ef you can use the arms when you talk, your
words come free, and jest of the right nature. It's like what people
mean when they say 'the word and the blow!' They do help each
other mightily. Now, I'll try, as we're mightily close set for room
in this wagon, to jest make as little a swing of the arms as possible;
for you see, I might, *on*intending anything of the sort, give a person,
standing or sitting on *eny* side of me, a smart notion of a knock;
that is, in the heat and hurry of the argyment. I've done such a thing
more than once, without meaning it; only I'll try to be within
bounds this time, and I beg you'll take no offence. I'm sure, gentlemen, if my motion don't trouble you, though it's a rether oneasy one,
I shan't mind it at all myself."

Here was an excellent fellow! In his eloquence, he might swing
his great mutton fist across my mazzard, and the thing, if not
positively disagreeable to me, would be of no sort of disturbance to

him! It was difficult to conceive in what school he had acquired his philosophy. It was certainly as cool as that of St. Omer's, but rather lacking in its refinements. At all events common sense required that, as I could not entirely escape his action, I should keep as sharp an eye upon it as possible. It might have been the safest course to reject the story in regard to its accompaniments, but that would have seemed unamiable, and I might have incurred the reproach of being timorous. Besides, there was some curiosity to hear what sort of a story would issue from such a source, and we were all too much in need of excitement to offer any discouragements to a new hand proposing to work for our benefit; so, after modestly suggesting the propriety of using as little action as possible, we began to look with considerable anxiety to the reopening of those huge jaws, from which, to say truth, whatever might be the good things occasionally going in, but few of us had any anticipations of good things coming out. But he was slow to begin. He had his preliminary comments upon what had gone before. His previous silence seems to have been due to his habit of bolting all his food at once, and digesting it at leisure. We were now to hear his critical judgment on previous narratives:—

"I've been mighty well pleased," quoth the Tennesseean, "with some of them sarcumstances you've been telling among you, fellows, and I've made considerable judgment on some of them that don't seem to me made to carry water. But I won't be particular jest now, except to say that I don't see that the narrow man thar, with his hips cutting into the saft parts of my knee at every turn down hill (the New England schoolmaster), I don't see, I say, that he made so good an one of it as he might have done. Though that, agin, may be the misfortune of the sarcumstance, and not his fault in telling it. The sense is, ef so be the thing happened as he tells it, then the whole town and country ought to be licked to flinders for suffering the poor gal to be so imposed on. By the powers! I'd fight to the stump, *eny* day and *eny* how, but I'd make the men see that the poor weak woman was not to be the only sufferer!"

It would be a tedious task, wanting our Tennesseean's air, tone, and manner, to follow up this trail, and show upon what grounds our backwoodsman took offence at the *pro*prieties in our Yankee's story. It was one of those cruel narratives of seduction, so frequent in large commercial cities, where the victim is the only sufferer, and the criminal the only one to find safety, if not sympathy. The narrator had given it as a fact within his own experience, as occurring in his native city; and the offensive defect in his narration, which the skill of the Tennesseean was able only to detect and not to define, consisted in his emotionless and cold-blooded way of unfolding his details of horror, without showing that he felt any of the indignation which his tale provoked in every other bosom.

"Such things can't happen in Tennessee, I tell you, stranger; and ef they did, nobody would be the wiser of it. You'd hear of the poor gal's death, the first thing, and she'd die, *pre*haps, of no disorder. But she'd rather die right away, a thousand deaths, sooner than have her shame in the mouth of any of her kindred; and ef so be it happen to leak out, there would be somebody—some brother, or friend, or cousin, or, may-be, her own father, or may-be a *on*known stranger like myself—to burn priming for her sake, so that the black-hearted villain shouldn't have it all to himself. But I ain't a going to catechize your story. I rather reckon it can't be true, jest as you tell it, stranger. I can't think so badly of the fellow, Compton, though I reckon he's bad enough, and I can't think so meanly of your people, that could let him get off without a scratch upon his hide. I reckon it's a made up thing, jest to make people sorry, so I won't believe a word of it. But the one I have to tell is in sober airnest. It happened, every bit of it, on good authority. Indeed, I'm a knowing to a part on it myself, as you'll see when we get on; though the better part of it I got from the mouth of another. It's a history I picked up in Florida, when I went down to fight the Simenoles. You know that when the rig'lars got on so badly with the Injins, splurging here and there with their big columns, and never doing anything, old Hickory swore, by all splinters, that we boys from Tennessee should do the business. So we turned out a small chance of volinteers, and I was one among 'em. Down we went, calkelating to ride like a small harricane through and through the red skins; but twan't so easy a matter, after all, and I don't think we Tennesseeans did any better than other people. It wa'n't our fault, to be sure, for we'd ha' fit fast enough, and whipped 'em too, ef the sneaking varmints would ha' come up to the scratch; but they fought shy, and all the glory I got in the campaign for my share, would lie on the little end of a cambric needle. But I learned some strange things in the campaign, and I ain't a bit sorry that I went. One sarcumstance, it seems to me, was a leetle more strange than anything I've hearn in this wagon, and if I could only tell it to you, as I heard some parts of it tell'd to me, I reckon you'd all say 'twas *as good as a Comedy!*"

"*As good as a Comedy!*" was the hopeful exclamation all round.

"Let's have it, by all means," was the eager chorus of arousing spirits.

"Ay, Tennessee, out with it, in short order," was the abrupt cry of the Georgian.

"Oblige us," was the condescending entreaty of South Carolina.

"Go ahead, old horse," yelled the Mississippian, wheeling about from the middle seat of the stage, and bringing his hard hand flatly down, and with great emphasis, upon the spacious territory of thigh that Tennessee claimed for its own, while trespassing greatly upon that of its neighbors; and the entreaty was promptly followed up by the machinist from Maine, the ex-editor from New York, and even the lymphatic pilgrim from Tar River, who, starting from his seventh heaven of sleep and dream, cried aloud, in half-waking ecstasy—"A comedy, O! yes, gi's a comedy. I'm mortal fond of comedy."

"Let it but prove what you promise," said the New Yorker, "and I'll send it to Harry Placide."

"Harry Placide?" exclaimed Tennessee, inquiringly.

"The great American actor of comedy!" was the explanatory answer from New York. "I'll write out your story, should it prove a good one, and will send it to Harry. He'll make a comedy of it, if the stuff's in it."

We spare all that New York said on the occasion, in honor of comedy and Harry Placide, and in respect to native materials for the comic muse; particularly as the Mississippian wound him up, in the most prolonged part of his dissertation, with—

"Oh! shut up, stranger, anyhow, and don't bother your head about the actor until we get the play."

Not an unreasonable suggestion. Our Tennesseean seemed to fear that he had promised too much. He prudently qualified the title of his narrative; apparently discovering, for the first time, that "comedy" meant something different from story.

"Comedy," said he; "comedy! Well, gentlemen, I tell you that when I first heard the affair, everybody said 'twas as 'good as a comedy,' and I thought so too. 'Twas over a camp-fire that we first heard it, and it mout be that we were all of us jest in the humor to find a comedy in anything. The story mayn't be like a comedy, the way I tell it, for you see I don't profess to be good in sech histories; but I reckon ef you could ha' seen and heard the chap that first tell'd us, by them old camp-fires, on the Withlacoochee, you'd say, as we said all of us, 'twas as 'good as a comedy.' "

"Did it make you laugh?" demanded New England, abruptly.

"Laugh! I guess some did and some didn't," was the satisfactory but simple reply. "What I saw of the affair myself was no laughing matter; but we'll keep that back for the last. 'Twas something a'most too strange for laughing; the more, too, as we know'd it to be nothing but the truth, and it happened here, too, in one of these western counties of Georgia."

Here the Georgian put in, confidently—

"I reckon I know all about it. I've heard it myself."

"Well! you'd better tell it, then," quoth Tennessee, very coolly.

"Oh, no!" modestly responded Georgia.

"But, oh! yes! Ef you know it, you've a sort of right to it, sence it's in your own country; and I rather reckon you can make a better mouthful of it than I. I'm but a poor stick at such things, and am quite as ready to hear you, stranger, as to talk myself."

"Pshaw!" exclaimed the Georgian. "Go ahead, man. I'm a mighty conceited fellow, I know, but that's no reason you should hold me up to make me say so."

"Gi's your hand, my lad; you're a good we'pon, I see; though, may-be, a little too quick on trigger."

A gripe of the extended fists followed in the dark, and the Tennesseean proceeded.

"The sarcumstance that I am going to tell you tuck place in one of the western counties of Georgia, not many years ago, and there's many a person living who can jest now lay their fingers on the very parties. I've seen some of them myself. You must take the thing for its truth more than for its pleasantry; for, about the one I can answer, and about the other I'm as good as nobody to have an opinion. I'm not the man to make folks laugh, unless it's at me, and then I'm jest as apt to make them cry, too; so you see I'm as good as comedy and tragedy both, to some. But, as I confess, a joke don't gain much in goodness when it leaves my mouth; and ef so be—"

We silenced these preliminaries *viva voce;* and, thus arrested, our Tennesseean left off his faces and began. In a plain and direct manner, he related the occurrences which will be found in the following chapters. He was no humorist, though he suffered us all to see in what the humorous susceptibilities of his story lay. It was the oddity of the circumstances, rather than their humor, that held out the attraction for me; and I could readily perceive how, without confounding comedy with the merely humorous and ludicrous, the materials thus thrown together might, by a dexterous hand, be converted to the purposes of the stage. The story illustrates curiously the variety and freedom of character which we find everywhere in our forest country, where no long-established usages subdue the fresh and eager impulses of originality, and where, as if in very mockery of the conventionalities of city life, the strangest eccentricities of mood and feeling display themselves in a connection with the most unimpeachable virtue—eccentricities of conduct such as would shock the demurer damsel of the city, to whom the proprieties themselves are virtues—yet without impairing those substantial virtues of the country girl, whose principles are wholly independent of externals. Let the reader only keep in mind the perfect freedom of will, and the absence of prescriptive or fashionable discipline in our border countries, and there will be nothing strange or extravagant in what is here related of the heroine.

In putting these details together, I have adopted a fashion of my own, though without hoping, any more than our Tennesseean, to bring out the humorous points of the narrative. These must be left to the fancy of the reader. "As good as a comedy" need not imply a story absolutely comic; and I do not promise one. Still, I am disposed to think and to hope that the title thus sportively adopted will not be found wholly inappropriate to the volume.

New York.

AS GOOD AS A COMEDY:

OR,

THE TENNESSEEAN'S STORY.

CHAPTER I.

A GEORGIA BREAKFAST.

LET us start fairly, and not on an empty stomach. Reader, we begin with a Georgia breakfast. We are at one of those plain, unpretending, but substantial farm-houses, which, in the interior of Georgia, and other Southern States, distinguished more especially the older inhabitants; those who, from time immemorial, have appeared pretty much as we find them now. These all date back beyond the Revolution; the usual epoch, in our country, at which an ancient family may be permitted to begin. The region is one of those lovely spots among the barrens of middle Georgia, in which, surveyed from the proper point of view, there is nothing barren. You are not to suppose the settlement an old one, by any means, for it is not more than twenty or twenty-five years since all the contiguous territory within a space of sixty miles was rescued from the savages. But our *family* is an old one; inheriting all the pride, the tastes, and the feelings which belonged to the old Southern "Continentaler." This will be apparent as we proceed; as it is apparent, in fact, to the eye which contrasts the exterior of its dwelling with that of the neighboring settlements among which it harbors. The spot, though undistinguished by surprising scenery, is a very lovely one, and not unfrequent in the middle country of the Atlantic Southern States. It presents a pleasing prospect under a single glance of the eye, of smooth lawn, and gentle acclivity, and lofty forest growth. A streamlet, or *branch,* as it is here called, winds along, murmuring as it goes, at the foot of a gentle eminence which is crowned with a luxuriant wealth of pine and cedar. Looking up from this spot while your steed drinks, you behold, perched on another gentle swell of ground, as snug and handsome an edifice as our forest country usually affords; none of your overgrown ambitious establishments, but a trim tidy dwelling, consisting of a single story of wood upon a brick basement, and surrounded on three sides by a most glorious piazza. The lawn slopes away, for several hundred yards, an even and very gradual descent even to the road; a broad tract, well sprinkled with noble trees, oaks, oranges, and cedars, with here and there a clump of towering pines, under which steeds are grazing, in whose slender and symmetrical forms, clean legs, and glossy skins, you may discern instant signs of those superior foreign breeds which the Southern planter so much affects. The house, neatly painted white, with green blinds and shutters, is kept in admirable trim; and, from the agreeable arrangement of trees and shrubbery, it would seem that the place had been laid out and was tenanted by those who brought good taste and a becoming sense of the beautiful to the task. There was no great exercise of art, it is true. That is not pretended. But nature was not suffered to have her own way entirely, was not suffered to overrun the face of the land with her luxuriance; nor was man so savage as to strip her utterly of all her graceful decorations—a crime which we are too frequently called upon to deplore and to denounce, when we contemplate the habitations even of the wealthy among our people, particularly in the South, despoiled, by barbarity, of all their shade-trees, and denuded of all the grace and softness which these necessarily confer upon the landscape. Here, the glance seemed to rest satisfied with what it beheld, and to want for nothing. There might be bigger houses, and loftier structures, of more ambitious design and more commanding proportion; but this was certainly very neat, and very much in its place. Its white outlines caught your eye, glinting through openings of the forest, approaching by the road on either hand, for some distance before you drew nigh, and with such an air of peace and sweetness, that you were insensibly prepared to regard its inmates as very good and well-bred people. Nor are we wrong in these conjectures. But of this hereafter. At this moment, you may see a very splendid iron-gray charger, saddled, and fastened in the shade, some twenty steps from the dwelling. Lift your eye to the piazza, and you behold the owner. A finer-looking fellow lives not in the country. Tall, well made, and muscular, he treads the piazza like a prince. The freedom of carriage which belongs to the gentlemen in our forest country is inimitable, is not to be acquired by art, and is due to the fact that they suffer from no laborious occupation, undergo no drudgery, and are subject to no confinement, which, in childhood, contract the shoulders into a stoop, depress the spirits, enfeeble the energies, and wofully impair the freedom and elegance of the deportment. Constant exercise on foot and horseback, the fox hunt and the chase; these, with other sylvan sports, do wonders for the *physique,* the grace and the bearing of the country gentleman of the South. The person before us is one of the noblest specimens of his class. A frank and handsome countenance, with a skin clear and inclining to the florid; a bright, martial blue eye; a full chin; thick, massive locks of dark brown hair, and lips that express a rare sweetness, and only do not smile, sufficiently distinguish his peculiarities of face. His dress is simple, after an ordinary fashion of the country, but is surprisingly neat and becoming. A loose blouse, rather more after the Choctaw than the Parisian pattern, does not lessen the symmetry of his shape. His trousers are not so loose as to conceal the fine muscular developments of his lower limbs; nor does his loose *negligée* neckcloth, simply folded about the neck, prevent the display of a column which admirably sustains the intellectual and massive head which crowns it, and which we now behold uncovered. Booted and spurred, he appears ready for a journey, walks the piazza with something of impatience in his manner, and frequently stops to shade his eyes from the glare, as he strains them in exploring the distant highway. You see that he is young, scarcely twenty-two; eager in his impulses, restive under restraint, and better able to endure and struggle with the conflict than to wait for its slow approaches. Suddenly he starts. He turns to a call from within, and a matron lady appears at the entrance of the dwelling, and joins him in the piazza. He turns to her with respect and fondness. She is his mother; a stately dame, with features like his own; a manner at once easy and dignified; an eye grave, but benevolent; and a voice whose slow, subdued accents possess a rare sweetness not unmingled with command.

"We need wait for Miles no longer, my son," was the remark of the old lady. "He surely never meant to come to breakfast. He knows our hours perfectly; and knows, moreover, that we old people, who rise with the fowls, do not relish any unnecessary delay in the morning meal."

"Well, mother, have it in, though I certainly understood John that he would be here to breakfast."

"Most probably he did not understand himself."

"He is, indeed, a stupid fellow. But, there he is. Ho! John"—calling to the servant whom he sees crossing the lawn in the direction of his house—"ho, John! what did Miles tell you?"

"He tell me he will come, sa."

"Ay, but when?"

"He say dis morning, when breakfast come."

"Ay, indeed! but whose breakfast; his or mine? Did he say he would come to breakfast with me, or after he had eaten his own?"

"He no say."

"Why *did* I send that fellow!" muttered the youth to himself as he passed into the breakfast-room. Let us follow him. How nice are all the arrangements! betraying the methodical and tidy hand of one brought up in the old school. The cloth white as snow, and neatly spread; the silver shining as brightly as if just from the burnish of the smith; and the *tout ensemble* denoting the vigilant care of a good mistress, who *sees,* as well as orders, that her servants do their duty. A single colored girl stands in waiting, dressed in blue homespun, with a clean white apron. The aged lady herself wears an apron, that seems to indicate her own readiness to share in the labors of the household. And now for the breakfast. A Georgia, indeed a Southern breakfast, differs in sundry respects from ours at the North, chiefly, however, in the matter of breadstuffs. In this respect our habits are more simple, particularly in the cities. In the South, there is a variety; and these are valuable chiefly in proportion to their warmth. *Hominy* itself is a breadstuff; a dish that our mush but poorly represents. It is seldom eatable out of a Southern household. Then there are waffles, and rice cakes and fritters, and other things of like description, making a variety at once persuasive to the palate and not hurtful to health. These were all in lavish array at the table of the widow Hammond, for such is the name of the excellent lady to whose breakfast board we are self-invited. The breadstuffs had their corresponding variety of meats. A dish of broiled partridges, a steak of venison, and a vase of boiled eggs, furnish an ample choice for a Spring breakfast, and take from us all motive to look farther. Coffee for her son, and tea for herself, constituted the beverage of the breakfast; and we are not unconscious that the platter of white fresh butter, that occupies a place in the centre of the table, is suggestive of a pitcher of foaming buttermilk that stands at the extremity. Why look further into the catalogue?

For a while the parties ate in silence, or rather they did not eat; one of them, at least, seemed to need an appetizer. Randall Hammond took several things on his plate at the suggestion of his mother, but he merely tasted of them. The partridge was sorely gashed at the first stroke, but the morsel taken from its breast lay upon the fork unswallowed. The youth seemed more disposed to exercise his ingenuity in balancing his spoon upon the edge of his cup; a feat which, having succeeded in, he abandoned for the more difficult experiment of standing the egg upon its point, as if to solve the problem which Columbus submitted to the Spanish doctors. The mother watched with some anxiety these movements of her son.

"You do not eat, Randall."

"No," he said, "I have somehow no appetite;" and he pushed away his plate as he replied.

"You have eaten nothing; shall I send you another cup of coffee?"

"Do so, mother; I am thirsty, though I cannot eat."

The cup was replenished. The mistress dispatches the servant-girl on a mission to the kitchen, and then, after a preliminary hem or two, she addressed her son in accents of considerable gravity, though so coupled with fondness as to declare the tender interest which she had in her subject.

"My son, you well know the regret which I feel at your going to this horserace."

"But I *must* go, mother."

"Yes, I understand that. You must go, as you have promised to do so, and I suppose it's quite unreasonable on my part to desire that you should not comply with what is customary among your associates. I can believe, also, that horseracing is a very different thing, nowadays, from what it was twenty years ago in Georgia."

"O yes, indeed; a very different thing!"

"I hope so; I believe so! If I did not, Randall, nothing should persuade me to give my consent to your exposing yourself to its dreadful influences."

"You need fear nothing on my account, mother."

"Ah! my son;—that is being quite too bold; persons who are thus strong in their own belief are always in danger. But, I trust, you have heard me too frequently on this subject; I trust you feel how deeply I should suffer, did I suppose that you could run a horse, or risk a dollar, in such a practice; to be misled by the persuasions of others, or your own natural tendencies."

"But, why do you think I have any such tendencies, mother?"

"Why have you spent so large an amount on these foreign horses?"

"For the sake of stock, mother. I have an eye to the merits and the beauties of the horse. I know his fine points. I love to look upon them. I know no spectacle more beautiful than a group of these beautiful creatures, wheeling and dashing over the lawn; and as a captain of cavalry, I must be well mounted myself. Beyond this desire, I do not see that I have any natural tendencies that should occasion your fears."

"These tendencies come from this very passion for horseflesh."

"But with me, mother, it is no passion."

"Alas! my son, I know better; all passions begin very modestly. That you have the tendency is enough for me, and, at the risk of giving you pain, I must repeat what I have said before, that you inherit this passion from your most unhappy father."

"No more of that, mother, I entreat you."

"Nay, Randall, but there must be more of it. It is needful for your safety that I should remind you that your father lost his life and fortune both by this insane and dangerous passion. What remains to us of former wealth was happily secured by my father's providence. We had else been destitute. You resemble your father greatly in most respects. You have his sanguine temperament; his hopeful confidence in himself; his eager will; his lavish expenditure, and his passion for horses."

"But, dear mother——"

"Restrained only, as I trust, my son, by the constant lessons of your mother."

"And by the love I bear her."

"I believe it, Randall; it is God's blessing that I do believe it; otherwise, this would be to me a moment of the dreariest hopelessness of heart. Promise me, dear son, that you will neither run a horse, nor bet upon a horserace."

"Promise, mother!"

"Nay, I ask no promise; I will only pray, Randall, that you will never for a moment forget how much the small remnant of your mother's life depends upon the heed you give to these lessons of her fears and sorrows. Let me not mourn the fate of an only son, as I must always mourn that of a husband."

The youth passed his arms about her, and kissed her tenderly. They had both risen from the table, and they now approached the piazza together.

"There is another subject, Randall, about which I wished to speak with you, but my heart is quite too full just now. I must keep it for another time. It relates to this young lady, Miss Foster."

The youth colored deeply. The flush did not escape the penetrating eyes of the mother. She did not seem to observe it, however, but continued with rare quietness of manner to remark:

"They tell me that you are pleased with her."

"Who tells you?"

"No matter. Enough, that I hear also that she is a maiden of singular levities, of bold, masculine habits."

"O mother! who could have told you this? What a scandalous story!"

"What! has she not some singular habits?"

"Some slight eccentricities, perhaps; something in thought and manner more free and confident than is common to the uneducated girls of the country, and which they accordingly censure—but—"

"Well, another time for this, my son. There comes Henderson."

The youth was not unwilling to waive the subject. His eyes were eagerly fixed upon the highway, where a horseman now came in sight.

"Ay, there he is at last, riding like the high-sheriff, as who but he! Should he want breakfast, now, mother?"

"He can have it in a moment; but, unless I am greatly mistaken, he has considered his wants of that sort some time ago."

A few moments sufficed to determine the doubt. The new-comer cantered rapidly down the road, and was soon within the inclosure.

"Well, Randall, are you ready?" he cried, as he alighted from his horse. The bridle was thrown to a servant, and Henderson ascended to the piazza, where he shook hands with mother and son.

"Ready," said Hammond, "and have been this hour. What has kept you? Why did you not come to breakfast?"

"For the best of reasons. I overslept myself."

"Then you have breakfasted, Henderson?" asked the old lady.

"O yes, ma'am. I wouldn't keep you waiting; though I sent word by John that I would take coffee with you."

"And a pretty tale he made of it. We waited for you."

"I'm sorry—" he began to apologize, but the old lady silenced him gracefully, and then took her departure, leaving the young men together.

"So, you overslept yourself, Miles?" was the remark of Hammond. "Something singular for you. Where was you last night?"

The inquirer darted a swift but half-smiling glance of suspicion directly to the eye of the other. The answer was somewhat hesitatingly delivered.

"Where was I? Oh! at Mrs. Foster's."

"Ah!" was the significant exclamation of Hammond, and a pause ensued between the parties. The tone with which the exclamation was uttered was subdued, the word seemed to escape the lips of the speaker involuntarily, and a keen eye might have detected a slight contraction of the muscles of his brow. But this passed away in a single moment, and putting his arm within that of his guest, with a glance behind him to the breakfast-room, Randall Hammond led his companion down the steps, and they walked away in silence to some distance in the park.

CHAPTER II.

THE new-comer, whom we are already taught to know as Miles Henderson, was tall of size and graceful of person. In these respects, he resembled his companion; though it needed no second glance of the spectator to discover the superiority, in all that regards bearing and general manner, in the person and carriage of the latter. Henderson was a fine, sprightly, and rather sensible fellow, but scarcely so courtly, so well-bred, and well-looking as Randall Hammond. Still, there were those by whom the former was preferred. He was more frank and less commanding, as a character; more accessible, and accordingly more agreeable to the many, than the man of superior will and general endowments. It does not need, however, that we should strike the balance, just at this time, between them. Such a proceeding will serve hereafter. Enough for us, that the two are most excellent friends; true, whole-souled, and confiding; with neither doubt nor distrust of any kind between them; ready to share their resources, and to peril life, if need be, in behalf of each other. And such had been their terms of relationship from boyhood. They had few other associates to divide their sympathies or provoke jealousies between them. Both of them were the only sons of widowed mothers; and both of them were equally docile in respect to the wishes of their parents. They were not absolutely faultless, but very good fellows, as the world goes; the one being supposed to have a very decided will of his own; the other of having a tendency to good-fellowship of every kind, without losing his equilibrium, in the license which good-fellowship among young men is supposed to engender. We may state, at the beginning, that, on the occasion of their present meeting, there was something more of shyness and reserve in their mutual bearing, cordial and frank as it really appeared, than had ever distinguished it before. The secret of this, of which each was duly conscious, will be shown as we proceed. They had got to some distance from the dwelling, when, somewhat abruptly, Randall resumed the conversation with an inquiry.

"So you dined at Mrs. Foster's yesterday, Miles?"

"No. I got there in the afternoon. I went down to the village to see Ferguson about that land business, and took the good lady in my way home."

"By going four miles out of the way," said the other, drily.

"You're right, Randall," answered the other frankly, while a slight flush tinged the cheek of the speaker. "You're right; but I reckon it's only what you'd have done yourself."

To this nothing was answered. A moment's pause ensued, when Hammond resumed.

"Was that foolish fellow, Barry, there?"

"No! not then; but I gathered that he had been, during the morning, from something that passed between Geraldine and her mother—"

"Ah! What?"

"Why, as far as I could guess, Geraldine had been rather sharp upon him, in some of her answers; and her mother was quite displeased in consequence. She gave Geraldine a lecture as long as one of Brother Peterkin's, particularly when his dinner has been a good and comforting one; and Geraldine—"

"Minded it quite as little as my roan horse does the snaffle. But how often, Miles, you name her in the space of a sentence!"

"Name her! How often! Who?" The response was stammeringly made.

"Who, but Geraldine Foster? In a single half sentence, I think, you contrived to bring in her name at least half a dozen times."

"Nay, Randall, you're joking. But *once*, 'pon my honor!"

"Pawn nothing, or you lose. The offence is not hanging, unless agreeably. The name is one to be repeated. It is a sweet and musical one."

This was said good-humoredly, a slight smile lightening pleasantly the otherwise grave face of the speaker. His companion discovered a something significant in the look and speech, was himself slightly confused, and concealed it in silence. Hammond quietly turned full upon him, and, laying his hand with affectionate emphasis upon his shoulder, thus addressed him:—

"Look you, Miles, old fellow, there is one small knot between us which remains to be untied."

"Knot between us, Randall?"

"Yes; and the sooner we take it between our fingers, the more certain are we to escape the necessity of putting our teeth to it. We are here by ourselves, and a few moments more—"

"But, have we time, Randall?"

"Time! Yes; we neither of us care much for the race; we shall lose but little."

"But little, in truth. The horses I hear of are only common ones. There is Vose's gray, pretty good at a quarter; and Biggar's young filly out of 'May Queen;' and the old horse 'Bob,' of Joe Balch, which you know was never of much account; and Barry, I understand, means to run his 'Fair Geraldine,' of which he brags so much; and—"

"Enough of your catalogue," said the other, with a smile: "I perhaps know quite as much as yourself with regard to the horses likely to be upon the ground; for Tom Nettles was with me yesterday, and he has all the news. The race, he agrees, will be no great shakes, so that, if we lose some of it, we lose nothing—"

"Yes, but Randall, Geraldine will be there early, and without any male attendance. In fact, I promised her to be on the ground at the beginning, in order to let her know all about the horses. She is full of it, and is prepared to bet a world of gloves, and purses, and handkerchiefs. She expects you there early also. She told me, indeed, that you had promised her—"

"Ah! she remembered it, did she?—well!" after a moment's pause; "we shall still be there in season; what I have to say won't take many minutes. The chief difficulty was to get up the resolution to say it at all, Miles."

"The resolution, Randall? Why, what can it be?"

"Can't you guess?" replied the other, fixing his eyes keenly upon those of his companion. The orbs of the latter sunk beneath the scrutiny.

"I see that you know. Let us sit here, Miles."

They were now beneath a magnificent cluster of oaks, covering five or more acres of ground, and looking forth, from a noble eminence, on lawn and field, and plain, and high road, that stretched away below. Sylvan seats, manufactured rudely, but not without a native ingenuity, out of wands of hickory and elm, into Gothic and fantastic forms, were conveniently distributed for the lounge, while great streamers of drooping gray moss festooned the outstretching arms of the several trees with a drapery not less appropriate than natural. Hammond pointed his companion to one of these seats, while he took another close beside him. An inconvenient pause followed of a few moments, which was finally broken by the strong will of the former, which was of that fearless and frank character that could soon shake itself free of all feelings of social awkwardness when resolved on the performance of a duty. His hand again rested kindly on the shoulders of Henderson, as, looking him affectionately in the face, he thus proceeded to unfold the matter which troubled him.

"Miles, old fellow, it won't do, after so many years of close and brotherly communion; years when we were all in all to each other, and seemed to live for nobody beside; I say, it won't do for us now to suffer any mistrust or misunderstanding to grow up between us."

"Surely not, Randall!—I wouldn't for the world!—But what mistrust—what misunderstanding?"

"Hear me, Miles; mistrusts and misunderstandings grow very naturally and very silently between friends from the slightest beginnings. There's no seeing them at first, unless the heart is watchful of itself, and even then they are apt to be let alone to grow apace, as all ill weeds do, unless the heart is properly jealous of itself. Now, it may be that my heart is equally mistaken in its suspicions of itself and of yours—"

"Of mine, Randall?"

"Yes! I have reason to believe that there has been a slight falling off between us ever since Geraldine Foster returned to the neighborhood."

"Randall!" said the other, reproachfully.

"It is even so, Miles; but it must not be so any longer. For this reason, I have determined to speak out plainly before the weed grows too strong for the ploughshare. We were friends from boy-hood until now, and your friendship has been, and I trust will continue to be, quite as precious to me as any love of woman. We must continue to be friends, Miles, even though we should both of us love Geraldine Foster."

The other clasped his hands together, as if with a sudden anguish.

"Ah, Randall!—I did fear it; I did!"

"It is unfortunate, Miles, that such is the case, but it is no longer to be feared, and it need not be fatal to our friendship. I can love Geraldine with all the passion of a Georgian's heart; but, Miles, I can love you too, and I will love you to the last. To be sure of this, we have only to understand each other. There must be no doubts, no mistrusts, no suspicions between us. You love her; you will seek her; you will try to win her love if you can; and for this I shall afford you every proper opportunity, not hesitating to avail myself of the chances that seem to encourage me. Thus far, we have both sought her without interference of each other. We will continue to do so. It is the instinct of a true friendship which has compelled this forbearance. I frankly admit to you that, as yet, she has given me no proofs that she cares one straw for me more than for another. If you can say that you have been more fortunate, speak it out, Miles, like a man, and I pursue her no longer; I leave the field entirely to yourself."

"You are a noble fellow, Randall, and deserve the girl; which I don't. I could no more have mustered the heart to talk of it to you, as you have just done to me, than I could have found wings to fly; yet I felt that that was the only way. I do love her, as you say; but I must own that, like yourself, I have had no encouragement. But no more does she seem to show favor to others. She has several suitors, you know?"

"Yes! but none, I think, that either of us has need to fear. You, at least, are the only person whose chances disquiet me. She has the sense to perceive your worth—to respect you—"

"I don't know that," was the somewhat sullen answer, with a discontented shake of the head; "she treats me mighty scurvily, at times. You know her way!"

"Yes; but I know it is her way, which shows itself to all others as it shows itself to you, though each person naturally thinks himself the worst treated of all. She is a tyrant, knows her power, and is but too fond of abusing it; but she is a noble creature, nevertheless, with all her faults."

"A beautiful creature, Randall!"

"I don't speak so much of her beauty, Miles, though, as you say, she is very beautiful; but she is a *genuine* creature. She is wrong frequently, and says and does wilful and mischievous things; but I do not think she has any cunning, which I look upon as fatal to all the beauty that woman could possess. She speaks, and thinks, and feels, very much as if a feeling and honest heart was in her bosom, which had not yet been tortured out of shape and nature by the tricks of society and the teachings of other women. It is this for which I love her chiefly, and which reconciles me to so much of her eccentricities and wilfulness. I suppose she treats you only as she treats me and all others. The truth is, she not only feels her power, and is rash because of her own impetuous spirit, but she has learned to distrust the professions and attentions of gentlemen. She has met with flatteries and flatterers at Savannah and Charleston, and has learned perhaps to despise them, not because she did not like attention and homage, but that she required them to be interesting as well as suppliant. It is the insipidity of beaux, rather than their devotion, that her bold mind, which resents the commonplace, has learned to distrust and to contemn. Fortunately, you and I are no *beaux*, Miles; but she has yet to discover what we are. That she will find out, if time be allowed her, I make no question. I confide in her sincerity of mind; in what seems the very wilfulness of her heart; in its warmth, its impulse, and the shrewd good sense, which is quite as apparent to me in her conduct as her eccentricities."

"Ah! Randall, you need to fear nothing," was the somewhat desponding answer of the other; "I'm thinking she already sees you with kinder eyes than anybody else."

"Scarcely, Miles; for I am not taking the course to win her affections suddenly. I confess to some policy in this respect. She would rate me with the rest, if I sought her like the rest. I must approach her as a man, and not as a schoolboy."

"You were always a man, Randall, even when a schoolboy."

"I'm not sure, Miles, that you pay me any compliment in this opinion. My consolation is that it is not just. Your mannish schoolboys are usually destroyed by their precocity. Still, if I can persuade Geraldine that I am a man now—"

"You will—you will!" said the other, with a sigh.

"Nay, nay, Miles; I must have none of this despondency. You must pursue your chase with as much hope and ardor as decision. As I have said already, I am not taking the usual course for success, and there is one evil influence particularly at work against me."

"What is that?"

"Her stepmother's dislike to me, which flows naturally from the slights which she complains of at the hands of my mother. My mother, who comes from an old stock, and a very proud one, dislikes the obtrusive and bad manners of Mrs. Foster. It is not that she is of humble origin, but that she is pert and presuming, and has made several efforts, without success, to find her way to my mother's intimacy. Besides, Mrs. Foster evidently inclines to this little fellow, Barry, who treats her with a degree of deference which amounts to sycophancy, and who, besides, has the prospect of much greater wealth than either of us could possibly hope to acquire. The step-mother must have succeeded before this, had it not been for the native good sense and the strong will of Geraldine. Yet she may at last—"

"Who, Geraldine? Never! She despises Barry."

"Very likely; indeed, I know she must; but that don't materially impair his chances, should circumstances favor him. Many a passionate woman, taken in the lucky moment, has married the object of her loathing. This is woman's weakness. But we needn't linger in this discussion. I have made a clean breast of it. You have done the same. What next? Why, that we should pursue our objects, Miles, as we have always pursued them, with candor, with mutual sincerity and love. Fair play between us will always keep us friends, let who will get the lady."

The cordial gripe of their hands which followed was as an oath between them. Much more was said, which it does not concern us to repeat. A few moments found them mounted, both on blooded steeds of the best breeds in the country, and on their way to the country race-course, not yet famous in the sporting calendar, which was honored with the name of Hillabee, after an ancient tribe of Indians, all of whom are extinct.

CHAPTER III.

In the more thinly settled regions of the South and West, a thousand sports are resorted to, to compensate the want of society, and to supply equivalent pleasures for those of a great city. On public days, the villages, or hamlets rather, are always crowded with people. The County Court brings together hundreds who rejoice that they have no business within its precincts; while on days of sheriff and public sales, other hundreds appear within sight of the auctioneer's hammer, who have neither means nor wish to buy. Muster-day calls forth its hosts in addition to those who come for training; and Charity, availing herself of the popular need, opens her frequent fairs for philanthropic purposes, relying on the universal desire for society to persuade into useless expenditure those whom it would not be easy to tempt to a benevolence for its own sake. Saturday, in these regions, is almost as much a holiday with the full-grown farmer as it is with the schoolboy, and usually takes him to the nearest place of gathering, which is usually a grocery, under the pretence of laying in the supplies for the week; but really with the no less human motive of procuring those social excitements which do not always result in the elevation of his humanity. Here, he rewards the patient labor of five days at the plough with potations which exhaust much more certainly than any labor. He calls for his quart of whiskey, which he shares with comrades, who find similar supplies, and, towards evening, he may be seen wending homewards, balancing himself with no little difficulty upon his steed, with a jug well filled, hanging in one end of a sack across his saddle, the other end being stored with such supplies as will soothe the apprehended anger of his spouse. It is not unfrequently the case that, overtasking his capacity, he imbibes too many potations for his equestrianship, and man, jug, and saddle find their way into ditch or thicket, while the unincumbered horse gradually crops his way home. This, fortunately, is but an occasional history now. There was a time when it was much more frequent, and associated with other practices—the brutal scuffle, the vindictive fight, the blasphemous language, which left our hopeful humanity but little of which it could really boast. Happily, this period is one of which the memory grows daily more and more imperfect. The sports of the people of the South and West, even along the border settlements, are of a more grateful character. The horserace is that which more nearly resembles those of the past, since it necessarily brings into most decided activity the animal tendencies of the people. It is here that the great masses prove their affinity with the ancient Saxon family of Bull! The picnic and the fishing-party will suffice for girls and boys in the season of romance, which is one simply of mutual confidence and hope; but the *turf* for all parties, at all seasons. It is here that all meet as upon a common ground, and amidst a thousand inequalities of wealth and life, show and condition; no one thinks so much or so meanly of himself as to be absent. Few think of themselves at all, at such a period. The horserace commends itself to the great body of the forest population more than any other amusement. It is an image, in some degree, of war. It appeals particularly to a people scarcely one of whom fails to keep, and not one of whom is unequal to the most excellent management, of a horse. Commend us, accordingly, to the Southern turf. Here, the sport is not an affectation. It is enjoyed with a zest. Here life and nature speak out in all their varieties of character. The dullest peasant looks animation as the sleek coursers wind beneath his sight. His eye becomes bright and knowing. He looks at head, heels, and neck, with the eye of a connoisseur. He feels the breast and shoulders knowingly. He adopts his favorite, and then shouts his preference in defiance to all comers. He is ready with or for a banter. He is prepared to stake his earnings of a year upon his judgment. His greasy pocketbook lies ready in his grasp. His bales of cotton are folded up in tens, and twenties, and hundreds, waiting deliverance or companions in bondage. He is no longer a person of drooping and grave aspect, drowsily going forward as if without hope or purpose. He is now all life, eager for opposition, and confident of success. Nor is it the inferior taste and understanding only to which the announcement holds forth temptation. Education here is not construed to assume the total subjection of the animal nature, and the elevation of the moral at the expense and sacrifice of the passions. The excitement which arises from the contemplation of the bold, the fleet, the strong and energetic, is supposed to be clearly consistent, within certain limits, with the laws of refinement and civilization; and the young damsel, who will prattle sentiment with you by the hour, quoting freely and understandingly from the pages of Moore and Wordsworth, yet bounds at the tap of the drum which warns the courser to depart, and glows at the progress of the contending *bloods;* her soul as much excited at what she sees as the young dragoon for the first time jingling his spurs in the heady tempest of the fight.

But a glimpse at the race-course of Hillabee itself will afford us a much better idea of the scene, as it ordinarily appears, than we could possibly convey by any process of generalization. The ground is chosen in a pine barren, which, being entirely level, and free from ridge or inequality for a space of several miles, renders it suitably firm and hard for the required purpose. The trees are cleared away, leaving a spacious amphitheatre something more than a mile in circumference. Within this space the course is laid out in a circle, and designated by ditches running parallel, with a track of eighty feet between them. The original forests surround the whole; a deep green girdle of massive pines, at whose feet have sprung up, taking the place of those which have been eradicated from the outer edges of the course, a narrow belt of scrubby oaks. Among these, you see numerous carts and wagons. These contain supplies of food and liquor. Here are ginger-cakes and cider, of domestic manufacture. Here are cold baked meats in abundance, ham and "chicken fixings," mutton and pork, spread upon long tables of rough plank, and waiting for customers. On one hand, you see rising the smokes of a *barbacue;* a steer is about to be roasted entire above a huge pit, over which, by means of a stake, he hangs suspended. Steeds are fastened in every thicket, and groups of saddles lie beneath every tree. Their owners are already scattered about the turf, while hundreds of negroes are ready, within and without the circle, pushing forward wherever there is promise of novelty, and anxious to emulate their betters in perilling every sixpence in their possession on the legs of their several favorites. There is a yet greater attraction for these in the huge white tent, spread at one extremity of the area; over which hang, in greasy and tattooed folds, the great stripes and stars of the nation. The attraction here is a novelty. It is a company of circus-riders. Their steeds, gayly caparisoned, have already gone in clamorous procession over the course to the sound of music; a thousand negroes have followed at their heels. Their exercises begin at the closing of the races, which cannot possibly take place before the afternoon. The interval to these is one of the most trying anxiety; to be soothed in part only by the events of the race. For this, the preparations are actively in progress. A glance at the opposite extremity of the ring, where the judges have a rude but elevated structure, not unlike a Chinese pagoda, shows us a handsome sprinkling of other visitors, on horse and foot. Many of these have a deeper interest in the progress of the day than arises from simple curiosity. There are the sportsmen, the jockeys, the owners of horses, their admirers, riders, and those who, in some way, look to the future with some selfish consideration. They dart about in large survey, or crowd in groups around some favorite steed or speaker. There, you may see a dozen around the drum, whose office it is to give the signal which sets horse and man in motion; and not far distant, you may behold the amateur fifer that perambulates merrily by himself, discoursing through his instrument, somewhat imperfectly, of Robin Adair and Roslyn Castle. Others, again, are more busily and officially employed. They are weighing steed and rider, measuring the track, taking down bets and entries, and, altogether, looking and behaving as if the next movement of the great globe itself depended upon the wise disposition which that moment should make of their affairs.

Looking beyond this circle, the prospect is equally encouraging. The eye naturally falls first upon the imposing *cortège* of the higher classes. Here you perceive, in coach, carriage, barouche, and buggy, that the upper ten thousand are tacitly permitted by the multitude to form a little community to themselves. The vehicles crowd together, as if in sympathy, the carriage-poles interlacing; the horses withdrawn and fastened in the shade of neighboring thickets. Here, seated in their carriages, appear the ladies, as various in their ages as in their separate style of beauty. They form close compact knots, or circles, according to the degrees of intimacy between them, and jealously force out all intruders; leaving such avenues only as will permit the approach on horseback of their several attendants and gallants. Showily and richly dressed, and surrounded by these dashing gentry of the other sex, all well mounted and eager to show their horsemanship, they give to the scene a gayety and brilliance which wonderfully add to its life and animation. Their gallants whirl around them with anxious attentions; now fly off to ascertain the course of events, and now dash back, at full speed, to report progress. They describe and designate the horses to the delighted fair ones, direct them in their choice of favorites, and lose to them glove and ribbon with the happiest gallantries. You may note the emblems and badges upon each fair bosom; these are white and pink, and red and green; they designate the colors of the selectest horses; and *beauty*, in this way, does not feel mortified at being made tributary to the *beast*.

The more numerous multitude, if less attractive in their exhibitions, are much more various and not less imposing. A glance to the right confines the eye to a crowd in the midst of which a wagon appears, surmounted by a red streamer which waves twenty feet high from the peak of a pine sapling. The shaft is rigidly held in its perpendicular by the embrace of a group of barrels, from one of which the more abstemious may obtain a draught of domestic cider or switchel; while from another, the stronger head imbibes his modicum of whiskey or apple brandy; a poor Western apology for Irish *poteen*, which, after the first season, our Patrick learns to swallow with something of the relish with which he smacked his lips upon the brown jug in his native island. Other wagons and flags appear, each in the margin of the thickets, sheltered by its shade, yet not hidden from the eyes of the thirsty and hungry citizen. They divide themselves, according to their experience, between the several wagons; and it's—

"Ha, Uncle Billy, and what have you got for a dry throat to-day?" Or—

"Thar you ar', Daddy Nathan, as bright as a bead of brandy, always bringing something for a tharsty sinner!" And Uncle Billy responds with a smile:

"Yes, Joel, my son, and it's I that's never too old for the sarvice;" —or, Daddy Nathan shouts back, with the voice of a "blood-o'nouns,"

"And what would you hev', you great jugbelly with a double muzzle? Ain't I here for the saving of such miserable sinners as you, that never think you're half full till you're fairly running over and can't run no more. Ride up, and see if you can find the way to your own swallow. Here's the stuff that'll make you open your mouth, though your eyes never seed it; as a hungry pike jumps up for the bait, jest because his nose tells him it's sartainly out somewhar' in the pond."

Then comes the rugged wit in answer, fashioned after the same model; a mild, good-humored banter; ending with a summons to the boys, to "come up to the rack," and try the peach or apple brandy, the whiskey or the cider, each according to his taste, of the uncle or the daddy.

"Whose treat?" demand two or three in the same breath.

"Who's but Joel Norris's?" or Pete Withers's, or Ben Climes's, or some other well-known boy of the masses, whom they have learned to reverence for that equal freedom of hand which enables them, with just the same readiness, to bestow buffet or beverage, according to the mood of the moment, or the character of the provocation given. And thus the groups form; and the meeting leads to the drinking; the drinking to the betting; and they part, or group themselves together, busy, from the moment in which they appear upon the field; much more earnest in the pursuit of fun than in the prosecution of their daily tasks.

He must be of difficult taste, indeed, whom such a theatre will fail to satisfy. Yonder, upon the grass, sit a cluster of rustic damsels. They are only spreading their baskets of cakes, *gunjas,* as they call them, and boiling huge vessels of coffee. Beyond them, at a little distance, appear others of the sisterhood, busy in preparing their tables with plate, knife, and fork. Towards noon you will see them smoking with hot dishes, and well surrounded by hungry gamesters.

Cards and dice already begin to interest other parties, that crouch away in remoter places along the skirts of the wood; and the more personal matters of "poker" and "old sledge" render many an ardent spirit momentarily indifferent to the approaching horserace, upon which he has no sixpence left to stake. You will see him start to his feet as the shouts of the crowd without, and the rush of the horses, announce the approach of the contending steeds; but a glance suffices; and, satisfied that he neither wins nor loses by the event, he sinks down upon the turf or log, and renews the game of "brag" with fresh *nonchalance* and audacity.

Look, now, at the ring forming within the wood, where an eager circle encourage two rivals to a stand-up wrestle. They are stripped to the buff; the broad breast, and full, rigid muscle, promising a noble struggle. They approach with equal deliberation and good-humor, and the hug is fairly taken. They pause, and each lifts the other from his feet; and now they bend to it and wave to and fro, like tall saplings shaken adversely by capricious winds; now yield, now recover; a stern, close issue, very doubtful to the bystanders, who, soon forgetting their individuality, unconsciously follow the wrestlers in all their contortions, and, before they know where they are, glide into the ring and into the embrace of well-matched opponents, with whom they tug and tumble about without a single word of preliminary. In the shade of yonder avenue, you see a couple attended by their admiring followers, coats and shoes cast off, hands clasped, and about to dart forward in a footrace of a hundred yards. Beyond them, still farther in the wood, you are called upon to witness a trial of skill between the crack rifles of two adjoining counties, of whom their respective friends have been boasting for several seasons. They have now, for the first time, been brought together. A race-turf, like that of Hillabee, will assemble the best fellows of several counties upon extraordinary occasions. They have planted a dollar at eighty yards. Could a shilling be seen at that distance, the smaller coin had been preferred.

And thus the field is laid off and divided. Thus the parties group themselves throughout the day, except when the race is of peculiar interest, when all small matters are necessarily merged in the one result. But many wander about nearly listless, who depend for their pleasures rather upon the sports of others, than because of any direct participation with them. These sway to and fro at every summons that promises novelty or excitement. Now, there are sounds of strife and clamor, that declare a fight; and they hurry with open-mouthed delight to the scene of action. Now, a barrel of whiskey rolls from the wagon, and the owner, attended by the yells of a delighted circle, prances and rolls over it to his own confusion. Now a table of plank yields beneath the elbows of the guests, and the bacon and the pans go over with the company into the sand; and now an ill-trained horse bolts from the track, and scatters the clustering group of terrified spectators, compelling them to a use of their heels not less eccentric than his own. So much for the general aspect of the race-course at Hillabee on the memorable day in question. But it is high time that we should be more particular, and concentrate our regards upon those personages in whom our reader is expected to take the deepest interest.

CHAPTER IV.

FLATS AND SHARPS.

A RACE-COURSE has its music; at all events, we are now among the flats and sharps. Here you see, on a small scale, some of those characters who, on a more extended field, and with better training, might become famous financiers, or equally famous diplomatists. Here you may encounter some inglorious Rothschild, and witness instances of petty dexterity in policy which might honor Metternich. Look you now, for example, at the person who approaches us. His shabby exterior and lounging manner would hardly fix your attention, unless you were first assured that there was a meaning under it; mark him closely, and you will discover a certain significance in his eye and bearing which shows that he has his object. He is not the stolid indifferent that he seems to the casual observer. His eye, shrouding his glances as he may under the heavy penthouse of his bushy brows, is that of the hawk, as, wheeling aloft, he casts sidelong glances upon the covey of partridge that crouch along the bramble thicket. His quiet, cool, and easy carriage; the half smile that plays about his mouth, while his face presents a dull, unmeaning gravity; his manner, at once listless and observant; his evident acquaintance with everything and everybody; and the fact that, while he seems to seek nobody, he is seldom himself without a follower; all declare a character and talent of his own. But, what sort of talent? The scene in which he appears so entirely at home, and the costume which he wears, present us with a clue to his secret. He is one of the heroes of the turf. This, though on a somewhat humble scale, is the scene of his victories. He knows every race-course and horse of heels in Georgia; knows every jockey, and his dimensions; and, a well-known *sharp* himself, his constant study is to extend his acquaintance among the *flats*, who are too numerous in every country to be so easily canvassed. His province is, particularly, horseflesh. He knows clean heels, at a glance. He reads the speed of an animal in his eye, and its bottom in its quarters; and knows the art, as well as any man, of so disguising a horse as to deceive the eyes of other judges. This is exclusively his world. His library is the stables; his place of worship is the race-course; his prayer-book, the little dirty envelop of loosely folded sheets, rudely stitched together, in which he notes his bets, and records his obligations. His costume speaks, however, for nothing of his method, though it sufficiently declares his character. His trousers are loose; hang about his hips, without suspenders, something like a sailor's; and are occasionally jerked up for the purpose of a brief interview with the short and open vest that hangs somewhat distantly above; the legs are thrust into his boot-tops, which are themselves wofully in need of covering, torn at the sides, and crushed down upon the ankles. His hunting-shirt has seen like service; the fringe is dilapidated, the cape half torn away. His cap, which rests jauntily on one side of his head, has its own fractures; the peak of it flapping, with a constant threat of departure, over his left eye. The vest flies wide, in consequence of the entire absence of its buttons. His breast is partly bare, from a like condition of his shirt-bosom; and the greasy black kerchief, which is wrapped about his neck like a rope, with the ends almost hanging to his middle, has suffered the shirt-collar, on one side, to escape entirely from its folds. You would suppose him the poorest devil on the ground. But that is his policy. He is a *chevalier d'industrie.* He lives by his wits; but these are so much capital; they command capital. Note him, where he goes, and you see that he is still followed by another, whose externals are quite unlike his own. This is a tall, good-looking stranger, from another county; well dressed,—rather too much so,—and with quite a fashionable manner. He finds the capital, while his pilot finds the wit. Still, they do not seem to work together. The stranger does not too closely follow on the heels of his associate. He suffers him to keep ahead, and somewhat distant, but never loses him from sight. He is simply convenient when the fish is to be taken, and suffers the other to proceed after his own designs without interruption or communication. Let us follow, for a space, our first acquaintance. How quietly and successfully he makes his way among the crowd; without any effort at doing the agreeable, he is yet everywhere received as a favorite. He has a good-humored speech for all, and knows just the subject which appeals most directly to the fancies or the feelings of each. He is, in fact, a nobleman, from whom more pretentious persons of this order might well receive a few lessons.

"Well, Burg," he says to one, whose ear he first tickles with the end of the whip which he carries, and who turns only at the voice of the speaker, "so 'Betsey Wheeler' died of the staggers?"

"Ah! Ned; yes. She did, poor thing, she did!"

"Good heels had 'Betsey' for a quarter stretch. That was a most beautiful run she made with Latham's 'Buzzard.'"

"Worn't it, Ned?" responded the man addressed, with a delighted expression of countenance, as he clasped the hand of the new-comer. "Ah! she was a critter. My darter hain't got over the loss of the mar' yet."

"She *was* a mare!" was the emphatic reply of Ned. "She hasn't left many with cleaner heels behind her, Burg."

The latter was greatly flattered.

"Ah, Ned," said he, "you're the man to know when a horse *is* a horse!"

"You've got her filly?"

"Sold her to Captain Barry."

"Ah! You shouldn't have done so. Is he here to-day—Barry?"

"Yes, I reckon."

"Has he the filly yet?"

"Yes, that he has; and will run her, too; for he counts her about as good flesh for a brush as any four-year old in the county."

"If she's like her dam, Burg, she can't help it!"

"As like as two peas from the same hull; only, I'm thinking, she has a little more bone than 'Betsey.'"

"So much the better. That's where 'Betsey' failed."

No more was said between the parties. Our acquaintance passed on: the next moment his follower came up with him, sufficiently close to catch the whispered sentence—

"I put a spoke in there that'll help to make the wheel. Barry's a fool! and Burg will tell him everything I've said."

The other falls back, and our jockey pursues his way, until, stopping short, he applies his whip, with a gentle cut, to the shins of a person; who, leaning against a sapling, betrays but little interest in what passes. He turns gently round at the equivocal salutation, and, as he encounters the features of the assailant, his words and looks of defiance give place to those of banter and good-humor.

"Halloo, there, monkey! ain't you afeard of that tail of your'n getting in the wolf-trap?"

"No, Jake; for I know you hain't got the teeth to raise the skin of that varmint."

"Hain't I, then? Just you try it, then, with another sort of look in your face, and see if I ain't a peeler."

"Will you peel?"

"Won't I, then?"

"Jake, my boy, I've come here to-day to strip the skin off you altogether."

"You! Tain't in your skin to do it, Ned."

"Yes, or there's no snakes. I'm here with the best nag at a heat that ever was seed in Hillabee."

"Oh, shut up! Where's the cow?"

"She's out in the bushes; I'll show her, when the time comes. They call her 'Graystreak;' and she does go it like lightning. Now, didn't I hear, from some old buzzard that never found out the value in a horse until he come to be carrion, that Lazy Jake Owens had something of a nag, with three legs, or more?"

"Didn't you hear? Yes, that you did, Ned Ramsey; and there the critter stands; 'Crazy Kate,' they call her; but she does her running sensible. There's no crazy in that. She's the mare to strike your 'Graystreak' all in a heap, and take the shine out of her, or any animal you ever crossed."

"What!" said the other, following the direction, and with the most contemptuous curl of the lip, and wave of the uplifted whip. "What! you don't mean that poor old bay, yonder, that looks as if she hadn't shed hair, or tasted corn, since the beginning of the Seminole war? Why, Jake, the poor beast looks more like lying down on her last legs, and begging a judgment upon her master. You've starved her, Jake, I reckon; and she only keeps on her legs by the help of her halter. Just you let down the critter's head now, and all natur' couldn't keep her up till you'd half curried her."

"Say no more, Ned, till the run's over. We always know'd you was a nice person to say hasty things of other men's cattle. If 'Crazy Kate' can't stand, it's because she prefers to run. But we'll go and look at this 'Graystreak' of your'n; and I'll tell you, when I set eyes on her, what we'll be doing. I didn't know you had such a horse. When did you get her, and whar's she from?"

"She comes from Mississippi. I traded for her with a man named Myers, that brought her out. But she's to pay for herself, yit; and that's one reason why I'm greedy for Hillabee. So get ready to shell out handsome."

"Yes, empty the chist, Jake! Go your death on the bay mar', old fellow. I don't reckon she'll find her match on this ground to-day." So cried one of his neighbors.

"I reckon you think yourself a judge of horseflesh, Owens?" quietly said Ned Ramsey.

"I reckon, then, I do. I ought, by this time!" was the answer.

"Well! if a man's judgment's worth anything, it's worth what he's got in his pocket."

"Guess it is; and I'm willing to come down a trifle on Jake's bay mar', though I never seed your critter."

"That's coming out, like a man. But you shall see her."

"On sight, on seen, same to me. I'll go all I've got on the bay, whether or no!"

"That's right! into him, Charley Owens. He's a suck," cried one of the bystanders.

"He'll dive, if you shoot," said another.

"A suck! Yes! that's it," responded Ned Ramsey, very coolly. "Ready for any bait, boys, with a swallow that never refuses. I'll dive too, that's cla'r; but you may let drive first, and I'll carry off your load if I can. Load for buck, if you please. The larger the shot, the better. Here's 'Graystreak' agin 'Crazy Kate,' or agin the field. Who cares? The nag's got to be paid for. Here's steam agin wind! I'm wanting money mightily. Who'll sweat for the sake of charity? Here he stands; the Georgy railroad agin, besides a line of stages. Whar's the passengers?"

"Into him, Charley Owens!"

"Deep as I can go," said Charley, pulling out a greasy pocketbook, and laying bare its contents; no great matter; in bills and silver, some nine dollars thirty-seven cents, chiefly Georgia and Carolina currency. It was instantly covered from one of the pockets of Ned Ramsey, who cries out for more customers.

"But whar's the gray mar' all this time?" demanded Lazy Jake.

"It's a bite!"

"A bite! It's your bite, then," answered Ramsey, at this outcry. "You've jaw enough, I reckon, for any sort of bite. As for the critter, look out, boys, there she comes. Yonder's the gray; a foal of the hurricane, sir'd by a streak of lightning."

"Hurrah for Ned Ramsey; he can go it!"

"Graystreak" was now brought up by a groom.

"Thar she stands, ready to fly. Thar's legs for you, and a head and neck to make a pretty gal jealous. There's no want of heels whar the sire was the lightning. No want of wind, with the hurricane for a dam! Ain't she a beauty, Jake?"

"A decent-looking thing enough, but not a crease to 'Crazy Kate.'"

"You say it? Well, chalk up your figure!"

"Cover that V."

"Thar it is, and I'm willing to face its brother."

"It's a go!" cried a huge-handed fellow, who called Jake "uncle," unfolding a greasy bank-note of the same denomination.

"What the dickens!" cried another, interposing; "can't I have a grab at some of them pretty picters? I believe in Uncle Jake, too. I've seen 'Crazy Kate's' heels before, at a three-mile stretch, and I'll back her agin a five myself."

"Will you!—you're a bold fellow," answered Ramsey, as he began to fish up the contents of his pockets. It seemed low-water mark with him, and his bank-notes began to give place to a curious assortment of commodities, which he brought up very deliberately, and without any blushing, from the capacious depths of two enormous breeches-pockets. There were knife and gimlet and fishhook; whistle, button, and tobacco; gun-screw, bottle-stopper, and pack-thread, and a dozen or more of pea-nuts. It was only here and there that the pieces of money turned up; a quarter eagle, a few Mexicans, and a couple of dollars, in small silver, making their appearance somewhat reluctantly, and contrasting oddly enough with the other possessions of our jockey. These were soon brought together, and, the sum ascertained, it was quickly covered by friends of Jake Owens, who had a faith in his creature. Owens was quite a knowing one in the estimation of his friends, and so indeed was Ramsey; but "Crazy Kate" had shown herself a *"buster,"* and her very *loggish* appearance led the crowd to expect a great deal from an animal whose own looks promised so little, while her sagacious owner seemed to expect from her so much. Her skin really looked unhealthy; she carried her head low, almost between her legs; and her eye drooped sadly, as if with a consciousness of the disappointment which she was about to give her friends. But all this was regarded as deception by the backers of Uncle Jake. It was known what arts the cunning sportsman employed to disarm the doubts of the gullible: and the matted mane of "Crazy Kate;" the coarse, disordered hair; sorted, rough hide, and sullen carriage, were only regarded as results of a shrewd training and preparation, by which the more completely to take in the "flats." Very different was the appearance of "Graystreak." She did look like a thing of speed and mettle. She was clean-limbed and light of form, with a smooth, well-rubbed skin, and such a toss of the head, and such a bright glitter of the eye, that every one saw, at a glance, that her own conceit of her abilities was not a whit less than the conviction of her master in her favor. But this really made against her, in the opinions of the betting portion of the multitude, most of whom had, at one season or other of their lives, been taken in by just such a dowdy-looking beast as that of Lazy Jake Owens. Ramsey relied upon this result, or the appearance of "Graystreak" had been less in her favor.

"I reckon," said Ramsey, looking around him, "that I've hooked all the bait in these diggings."

"If you had anything that a chap might kiver," cried a greasy citizen, thrusting himself forward, and holding out a couple of shinplasters, of single dollar denominations.

"And who says I hain't?" answered Ramsey, as, with his forefinger and thumb, he drew from his vest pocket a small supply of similar I O U's.

"Well, kiver *them!*"

"A short horse is soon curried."

"Are you man enough, Ned Ramsey, to curry a long one?" cried one from the crowd, who now pressed forward and appeared amid the ring. His presence caused a sensation. It was well calculated to do so. He was small of person; a lively, dapper-looking person, seemingly of gentle birth and of occupations which implied no labor;— a smooth, pale cheek, and a bright, restless black eye. His hair was long, and fell from under a green cloth cap, from which hung a gay green tassel; and several great rings might be seen upon his fingers. But the rest of his equipment was what fixed every eye. It consisted of a close-fitting jacket, with a short tail like that of a light dragoon, and small-clothes, all of scarlet, after the fashion of an English jockey, and his white-topped boots completed the equipment. The habit had been copied from an English print; and a good leg, and rather good figure, though *petit*, had justified, in the eye of vanity, the strange departure from all the customs of the country.

"It's Captain Jones Barry," says one of the spectators, in an under tone, to another who had made some inquiry: "He's rich enough to make any sort of fool of himself, and nobody see the harm of it." At the same moment, it could be seen that Ned Ramsey exchanged significant looks with the well-dressed stranger, who had been his shadow through the morning, as if disposed to say, "This is our man."

"I say, Ned Ramsey," cried Barry, "are you man enough to curry a large horse? I've seen your nag; she's a pretty creature, that's true; but I know something of Jake Owens's 'Crazy Kate,' and I don't care if I could put a customer on her heels, against your'n."

"You don't, eh! well, Squire Barry, you're a huckleberry above my persimmon, but I reckon something can be done. I believe in 'Graystreak,' and will go my death on her. 'Twon't take much to bury me, that's true; but what thar is—"

"There! can you roll out against that?" asked Barry, as he laid a fifty dollar note upon his palm.

" 'Twill go hard to drain me dry, but I ain't to be bluffed, neither; and though it takes from what I put away to pay for the nag, here's at you!" and the required amount was brought forth; but this time it came from a side pocket, in the coat of Ramsey, who, it was observed, seemed to find some difficulty in detaching it from its place of security. Lazy Jake Owens was not insensible to this demonstration. It seemed to open to him new views of the case, and he now proceeded to re-examine the strange animal upon which so good a judge as Ned Ramsey had so much to peril. But the new-comer, whom we shall know hereafter as Squire Barry, was not similarly impressed with the proceeding.

"Too much," said he, "for 'Crazy Kate,' Ned Ramsey! I have a nag of my own, as nice a little bit of filly as is on the ground to-day. I reckon you never saw or heard of her. Her name was 'Betsey Wheeler,' a crack mare of this county, and her sire was a New Orleans horse, whose name I now forget."

"I know the mar' you speak of," answered Ramsey, looking up, but without appearing to discover the man Burg, who stood behind Barry, and to whom he had spoken of this same mare an hour before in terms of exceeding admiration. "The mar', 'Betsey Wheeler,' *was* famous at a hunt. I can't say for the filly; I don't know that I ever seed her. But you can tell me what about her, Squire?"

"She's mine, and I believe in her; I believe in her against your 'Graystreak,' there: that I do!"

"Well, Squire, you have a right to believe in your nag; she's your own, and you know her. 'Graystreak's' mine, though not quite paid for yit, and I've a notion that I've a right to believe in her; she's got the heels to believe in. But what's the use of believing when every *pictur* (bank-note) that you have has got its fellow already? If you was to go your belief *very strong*, I couldn't say a word agin it!"

"What say you to another fifty?"

"It's tough, but let's see your filly; if she's much like her dam," hesitating.

"What! scared, old fellow?"

"No! not exactly skeared, but a little dubous! I know'd the dam; *she* was a clean-heeled critter."

Looking up, he pretended to discover Burg, the former owner of the filly, for the first time. "Ah!" said he, "Burg, you're a keener." Barry looked gratified. He exulted in the notion that he had bluffed the bully; and Ramsey walked forward, with a side-long air, switching his whip as he went with the manner of a man half discomfited. He was pinned suddenly by Lazy Jake Owens, who had just returned from a reinspection of "Graystreak."

"Ned," said the latter in a whisper, calling him aside, "I see your game! We've got but three V's on this brush; if you'll let me, I'll take the fence and say quite?"

"What, hedge?" said Ramsey; "no you won't!"

"It's as you please; but, if this bet's to hold, you don't do Jones Barry."

"You'll not put your spoon into my dish, Jake?"

"I won't be dished myself if I can help it."

"Well! I'll let you off, if you'll let your nag run. Keep your tongue, and you may keep your V's."

"It's a bargain—mum's the word!"

"Do you know this filly, Jake?" said Ramsey, half aloud, as he saw Barry approaching.

"A nice critter to the eye, but I never seed her run. Her dam was a beauty for a mile stretch or so."

"There she stands!" cried Barry; "I'll back her against the field for any man's hundred."

"I'll take you!" quickly responded the stranger, who was Ramsey's shadow.

"Who's he?" inquired Ramsey, in a whisper of Barry himself.

"I don't know him at all," answered Barry. "But I reckon he'll show his money."

"I'm ready to cover, sir," was the remark of the stranger, showing his money just as if he had heard the whispered reply of Barry to Ramsey. The bet was taken down, and the bill covered in the hands of a third person. Ramsey did not linger to behold these proceedings, but occupied himself in a close examination of Barry's filly. The eye of the latter, with an exultation which it could not conceal, beheld the grave expression in that of the jockey. He saw the head of the latter shaken ominously.

"Isn't she a beauty, Ramsey? I call her the 'Fair Geraldine,' after the most beautiful lady in the world."

"You're right, to pay the filly such a compliment. She's the most sweetest little critter! Will you sell her, squire?"

"Sell her; no! not for any man's thousand dollars."

"You'll not get *that*, I reckon. But she's got the heels; that's cla'r! she'll run!"

"Will she? well! Can she *do* 'Graystreak?'"

"N—o! I don't exactly think she can."

"You don't? well! Can 'Graystreak' *do* her?"

"Y-e-s! I reckon."

"You reckon? well! If such is your reckoning, I suppose you're ready to match your mind with your money. What'll you go, on the match?"

"Well, squire, you see I'm quite clear up. Bating what I've put aside to pay for 'Graystreak,' I don't suppose I've got more than a single Mexican or two. I might raise three, or, *pre*haps, five upon a pinch; but I shouldn't like to go more."

"Be it five, then," said Barry, eagerly; and the seemingly reluctant pieces were fished up to the light out of the assorted contents of the deep pockets of the jockey.

"Now," said Barry, tauntingly; "what's the value of a horse, if you're afraid to risk on her? You say you've got money to pay for 'Graystreak?' How much did you give for her?"

"Oh! that's telling, squire."

"Well, I don't care to know; but how much have you made up towards paying?"

"Well, a matter of seventy-five or eighty dollars left."

"Which might be a hundred. But whatever it is, Ned Ramsey, I'm clear that if you valued the heels of your horse at all; if, indeed, you were not frightened, you'd see it all covered before you'd be bantered off the course."

"Squire, you're a little too hard upon a fellow," was the somewhat deprecating reply.

"Oh! it's the turn against you, then, Ramsey," was the retort of Barry. "You had the laugh and banter against everybody before. Well! you can taste the feeling for yourself. Now, if you're a man, I banter you to empty your pockets on the match; every fip down; and I cover it, fip for fip, and eagle for eagle. I'm your man, Ramsey, though you never met with him before."

It was with the air of the bully, desperate with defeat and savage with his apprehensions, that Ramsey dashed his hands into his bosom, drawing forth, as he replied, a pocketbook which had hitherto been unshown—

"I'm not to be bantered by any man, though I lose every picayune I have in the world. I'm a poor man, but, make or break, thar goes. No man shall bluff me off the track, though the horse runs off her legs. Thar, squire, you've pushed me to the edge of the water, and now I'll go my death on the drink. Thar! Count! Ef my figuring ain't out of the way, thar's one hundred and five dollars in that heap!"

"That's the notch," said a bystander, as the bills were counted.

"Covered!" cried Barry, with a look of exultation. He had obtained a seeming victory over the cock of the walk. The more sagacious "Lazy Jake Owens," however, muttered to himself, with the desponding air of one who was compelled to acknowledge the genius of the superior:

"A mighty clever chap, that Ned Ramsey, by the hokey! His mar' is paid for this day, if he never paid for her before."

Barry, cock-sure of the result, now slapped his pocketbook with the flat of his hand, as he lifted it over his head, and cried to the circle around him:

"There is more money to be had on this match, gentlemen. Here are a couple of bran new C's (hundreds) ready for company. Who covers them against the 'Fair Geraldine?'"

The stranger, the distant shadow of Ramsey, again modestly approached with two similar bank-notes already in his hands. The bets were closed.

"I must find out who that stranger is," muttered Ramsey, in the hearing of Lazy Jake Owens and Barry. The latter did not seem to hear or to attend to him; but, as he walked away, Lazy Jake whispered to Ramsey:

"If so be you ain't pretty well knowing to each other a'ready, Ned."

The latter simply drew down the corner of his eye, in a way that Lazy Jake understood, and the parties dispersed in search of other associates and objects. The scene we have witnessed was but a sample of that which was in progress, on a smaller scale, perhaps, all over the field. It needs no farther description.

CHAPTER V.

WE left our two sworn friends on the road, rushing forward, at a pleasant canter, for the race-course. They were within a mile of it, when they were joined by one who came forth suddenly from a private avenue through the woods, which conducted to his homestead. The parties at once recognized each other as old acquaintances. The stranger was a good-looking person of thirty; not exactly one whom we should call a gentleman, but a frank, hearty, dashing, good companion, such as one likes to encounter at muster-ground or hunting-club. He was simply dressed in the habits of the country; not those of the plain farmer, nor those of the professional man. A loose, open hunting-shirt of blue homespun, with a white fringe, was not considered a habit too picturesque for the region, and it sat becomingly upon the large frame, and corresponded with the easy and not ungraceful carriage of the wearer. Tom Nettles was a character, but not an obstrusive one; a man, and not a caricature. He loved fun, but it came to him naturally; was something of a practical joker, but his merriment seldom left a wound behind it; his eyes were always brightening, as if anticipating a good thing, and they did not lose this expression even on serious occasions. Tom Nettles was much more likely to go into a fight with a grin on his visage than with any more appropriate countenance. But let him speak for himself.

"Good morning, Miles; good morning, Hammond; you're on the road something late, are you not?"

His salutation was answered in similar manner, and Hammond replied to his inquiry:

"Something late? No! We are soon enough, I fancy."

"Quite soon enough for the race," said the other; "but Jones Barry rode by my house two hours ago, and stopped long enough to tell

me that he was to be on the ground early to see Miss Geraldine
Foster. He said you had both made the same promise, and he was
bent to have the start of you. He seems to think it a rule in love
matters, as in a barber-shop, first come first served, and the first
comer always the best customer." Randall Hammond smiled, but
said nothing; while Miles Henderson, taking out his watch, looked
a little anxious as he remarked:

"We *are* later than I thought for."

"Soon enough, Miles," said Hammond, assuringly. Nettles continued:—

"But you should see the figure Barry has made of himself. He's
dressed, from head to foot, in scarlet, and pretends that it's the
right dress for a man that means to run his own horse. He says it's the
dress of one of the English noblemen—I forget his name—who has
grown famous on the turf. He owns, you know, that clever little filly
of 'Betsey Wheeler,' that belonged to Burg Fisher. The dam was a
good thing, and the filly promises to be something more, if Barry
don't spoil her with his notions; and he's full of them. He means to
run the filly to-day, and has christened her the 'Fair Geraldine,'
after a young lady you know, both of you, I reckon. But, though he
may get the lady, if he's not wide awake he'll be chiselled in the race;
for Ned Ramsey is out, with his eye set for game, and he's too old
a hand at the game not to *do* a young, foolish fellow like Jones Barry,
with mighty little trouble."

The friends allowed their companion to talk. He was a person
to use the privilege. They interposed a "no" or "yes," at intervals,
and this perfectly satisfied him. Hammond, meanwhile, was good-
humored in his replies, and quite at his ease. It was not so with
Henderson. He referred to his watch repeatedly, and more than once
made a movement for going forwards at a pace more rapid than that
into which they had fallen after Nettles had joined them. But his
companions, on the contrary, seemed both equally determined not
to second the movement. They hung back, and Hammond pointedly
said—

"Don't hurry, Miles. This good little fellow, Barry, attaches so
much importance to his being first in the field, that it would be cruel
to disturb his prospects."

Nettles smiled. He understood the speaker, and knew equally well his character and that of his companion.

"If being in a hurry," said he, "would win a lady, then Barry's the boy for conquest. But there's the mistake. It's my notion that it's the last comer that's most likely to do the safe business, and not the first. A young girl likes to look about her. She soon gets used to one face and the talk of one man, and likes a change that's something new. I wouldn't be too late; I wouldn't stay off till the very last hour; and I'd always be near enough to be seen and heard of now and then; nay, I'd like to be caught sometimes looking in the direction of the lady; but then I'd make it a rule never to be too soon or too frequent. It's most important of all things that a man shouldn't be too cheap. Better the girl should say, 'I wonder why he don't come,' than 'I wonder why he does.' "

Our philosopher of the piny woods might have gone on for a much longer stretch, had he not been interrupted by an event that gave a new direction to the party. They had reached a bend in the road which gave them glimpses of another which made a junction with it, and not fifty yards off they discovered the carriage of Mrs. Foster coming directly towards them. They at once joined it and made their respects, Miles Henderson taking the lead, and Hammond and Nettles more slowly following at his heels.

The party of Mrs. Foster consisted of that lady herself, her stepdaughter, Miss Geraldine Foster, and her niece, Sophia Blane, a girl of twelve. Mrs. Foster was an ill-bred, pretentious woman, who had succeeded the mother of Geraldine in the affections of her father, at a time when his feeble health and the impaired condition of his intellect rendered him too anxious for a nurse to be too scrupulous about a companion. He had raised her from an humble condition to one which she was ill calculated to fill; and, with the ambition to be somebody, she determined to carry her point by audacity rather than by art. She was a bold, forward beauty in her youth; was a bolder woman now, still pleasing in her face, but no longer a beauty; a woman given to petty scandals, and satisfied with petty triumphs; envious of the superior, malicious where opposed, and insolent when submitted to. What was defective or censurable in the manners of her step-daughter was clearly referable to the evil influence of this woman, and the doubtful training of the distant boarding-school to which she had been confided at a very early period of her life. That she was not wholly spoiled by these unfavorable influences, was due wholly to the native excellence of her mind and heart. She was a passionate, self-willed damsel; not easily rendered submissive in conflict; capricious in her tastes, yet tenacious of her objects; delighting in the exercise of power, without any definite idea of its uses or value; and by no means insensible to those personal charms which, indeed, were beyond all question, even of the hostile and the jealous. But, in opposition to these evil characteristics, she was magnanimous and generous; her heart was peculiarly susceptible to treatment and impressions of kindness. If her tastes were capricious, they at least were always directed to objects which were delicate and noble; if she was passionate, it was when roused by sense of wrong or supposed injustice; if she was slow to submit in conflict, she was never long satisfied with a victory, which a calmer judgment taught her was undeservedly won, and she knew how to restore the laurels which she had usurped, with a grace and a sweetness that amply compensated the injustice. Her mind was vigorous and active, and this led to her frequent errors; for it was a mind untrained, and steadfast and tenacious of a cause which, it was yet to discover, was not that of truth and justice. She was a creature, indeed, of many contradictions; a wild, high-souled, spiritual, but capricious creature; the very ardor of whose temperament led her into tumultuous sports of fancy, such as only shock beyond forgiveness the staid and formal being to whom there is but one God, whose name is Fashion; but one law, the record of which is found only in what my neighbor thinks.

Randall Hammond was by no means insensible to her faults; but he ascribed them to the proper cause. He felt that she was a character; but a character which could be shaped, by able hands, into that of a noble woman and a faithful wife. He looked upon her with eyes of such admiration as the Arabian casts upon the splendid colt of the desert, whom he knows, once subdued by his art, he can manage with a whisper or a silken cord. But he strove—as earnestly as the Arab who conceals his purposes, and scarcely suffers the animal whom he would fetter to see the direct purpose in his eye—to keep his secret soul hidden from the object of his admiration. He was not unwilling that she should see that she had awakened in his bosom an interest, a curiosity, at least, which brought him not unfrequently to her presence, but he strove, with all the success of a man who has a will sufficiently strong to subdue and restrain his passions, to guard his eyes and his tongue so that the depth of his emotions could not easily, or at all, be fathomed. It is sufficient here to say that Geraldine Foster was not insensible to his superiority. She had very soon learned to distinguish and to discriminate between her several suitors; but the bearing of Hammond, though studiously respectful, in some degree piqued her pride. If a suitor, he was not a servant. If he spoke to her earnestly, it was the woman, and not the angel he addressed. This reserve seemed to betray a caution which no maiden likes to detect in the approaches of her lover, and seemed to imply a deficiency of that necessary ardency and warmth which was, in truth, the very last want which could be charged upon this gentleman. Mrs. Foster first insinuated this doubt into the bosom of her step-daughter, and the feeling of the consciously underbred woman made her studious in keeping up the suspicion. She was not satisfied with the superior rank of Hammond's family; was mortified at the coldness and distance of his mother, whom she well knew to have been intimate with the first wife of Mr. Foster; and, though the peculiarly respectful deportment of Hammond himself left her entirely without occasion for complaint, the very rigor of his carriage, the studious civility of his deportment, by restraining her freedom with his own, was a check upon that vulgar nature which is never satisfied till it can subdue the superior nature to its own standards. Mrs. Foster could say nothing against Randall Hammond; but she could not conceal her preference for all other suitors. Miles Henderson was decidedly a favorite; but there was a charm in the idea that Barry's fortune could positively "buy the Hammonds out and out," that inclined the scale of her judgment greatly in behalf of the latter. But we are at the course, the horses are taken from the carriage, the three young men are in attendance, and Barry is approaching.

"Dear me, Captain Barry," exclaimed Mrs. Foster, "how splendidly you are dressed!"

"Is that your uniform in the militia, Captain Barry?" was the demand of Geraldine.

"They'd set him up for a scarecrow, if it was," said Nettles; "and he'd have to treat as long as the liquor lasted, before they'd let him down."

"O hush, Nettles; you're always with your joke at everything and everybody. I wonder what there is in my clothes for you to laugh at?"

"Not much, I grant you, while you're in 'em," was the reply. "But answer Miss Foster. She wants to know what uniform it is you've got on."

"Oh! it's no uniform, Miss Geraldine. This is the exact suit worn by the Earl of Totham, at the last Doncaster races."

"You don't say that the Earl of Totham sent you his old clothes?" responded Nettles.

"No! no!" said Mrs. Foster. "I understand. Captain Barry has adopted a dress like that which the Earl of Totham wore at the Doncaster races. Well! I don't see what there is to laugh at in a costume borrowed from the best nobility of Europe."

"But who is the Earl of Totham?" demanded Hammond. "I know of no such title in the English peerage."

"No? But it may be in the Scotch, or Irish," said Mrs. Foster, anxiously.

"No. It belongs to neither. But it makes no great matter. We are in a free country, Captain Barry, and can wear what garments we please, in spite of the English peerage."

"Ay, and in spite of our neighbors, too, Captain Barry," said Geraldine.

"Yes, indeed!" exclaimed Mrs. Foster, exultingly. "There's many of those who decry the fine equipments of superior fortune, who would give half their lives to enjoy them. Now I think, however strange it appears to our eyes, that this costume of the Earl of—what's his name?"

"*Tote*-Ham! I think," said Nettles, with a smirk; punning, with a vulgar accent, upon the first syllable. *Tote*, among the uneducated classes of the South, means "to carry."

"*Tote*ham!" continued Mrs. Foster, innocently. "Well, I repeat, this beautiful costume of the Earl of Toteham appears particularly adapted to the use of gentlemen who are fond of field sports."

The eye of Barry brightened. He looked his gratitude.

"I agree with you, Mrs. Foster," answered Nettles; "the red would not suffer from an occasional roll among the soft crimson mire of our own clay hills; and as our sporting gentlemen drink deep usually before they leave the turf, the prospect is that they become deeply acquainted with the color of the hills before they reach home."

"O, Mr. Nettles!" exclaimed the maternal lady.

"Nor is the advantage wholly in the color," continued Nettles, with great gravity. "The cut of the coat is particularly calculated to show off the fine person of the wearer. The absence of all skirt is favorable to the horseman; though I confess myself at a loss to guess what use to make of that little pigeon-tail dependence in the rear. I can scarcely suppose it meant to be ornamental."

All eyes followed the direction thus given them, and one of Barry's own hands involutarily clutched the little puckered peak which stuck out in the most comical fashion above his hips. Barry began to suspect that he was laughed at, and Mrs. Foster interposed, to change the subject.

"You mean to run your horse and ride him yourself, Captain Barry?"

"That I do, Mrs. Foster; I have pretty nigh five hundred on his heels, and I'll trust to no rider but myself."

"Well, that's right; that's what I call manly," said Mrs. Foster.

"You have certainly a very beautiful creature, Captain Barry," was the remark of Geraldine, turning from a somewhat subdued conversation with Henderson, to which Hammond was an almost silent partner. "You gentlemen," continued the fair girl, "are to teach me how I am to bet. That is, you are to give me your opinions, which I shall follow as I choose. See, I have a world of ribbons here, and am prepared to wear all colors. Who has the best horses, and how many are there to run?"

"You hear of one, certainly, Miss Foster," said Nettles.

"Yes! and certainly Captain Barry rides a very beautiful creature."

"She has the legs of an angel," said Barry.

"Better if she had its wings, I should think," was the immediate remark of Geraldine.

"Very good, very excellent, Miss Geraldine; certainly, for a race, the wings of an angel might be of more service than its legs. But she will scarcely need them. Her legs will answer."

"Should she lose, Barry, you'll have to change her name. Do you know the name of this beautiful creature?"—To Miss Foster. She answered quietly—

"O, yes! I have heard how greatly I am honored; and, in truth, I shall feel quite unhappy if she does not win. I must certainly, at all hazards, bet upon my namesake."

"You may do it boldly!" said Barry, with confidence; "I'll insure your losses."

"Who'll insure you, Barry? Your chances will depend upon what takes the field!" quoth Nettles.

"Do you know the mare of Lazy Jake Owens, that they call 'Crazy Kate?'"

"I do! your filly can trip her heels."

"I know that! my 'Glaucus' shall do that. He's here, and will be ridden by little Sam Perkins. Well! here's, besides, Vose's 'Grayshaft.'"

"Pretty good at a quarter, but—"

"And Biggar's filly, 'Estella.'"

"Her dam, 'May Queen;' sire, 'Barcombe;' a good thing, but wanting bottom."

"Joe Balch's 'Nabob,' Zeph. Stokes's 'Keener,' and 'Flourish,' a gambol-looking nag from Augusta, or thereabouts."

"I know them all except the last. The 'Fair Geraldine' ought to give them all the wind."

"She'll do it!"

"But these are not all the horses out, surely?"

"No! there's another animal, that Ned Ramsey claims. I never saw her before, and don't think a great deal of her now; they call her 'Graystreak;' she comes from Mississippi. I bluffed Ramsey so tightly that I almost scared him off the hill; but I brought him to the scratch, and I have covered for him to the tune of a hundred and more on the match between 'Graystreak' and 'Geraldine;' besides something like half the amount on Lazy Jake's mare against 'Graystreak.'"

"And where's this 'Graystreak?'"

The animal was only at a little distance. The proprietor, the renowned Ned Ramsey, was busy, at the moment, in preparing her for the course. The eyes of the party were directed to the beautiful creature in admiration. She shipped to the sun finely, as if clad in velvet. Her clean limbs, wiry and slender; the spirit in her eye, and the airy life in all her action, at once fixed the regards of so good a judge as Nettles. Nor was Randall Hammond indifferent to the beauty of her form, and the promise in her limbs.

"This fool and his money have parted!" said Nettles, in a whisper to Hammond. "*Your* horse is the only one that can take the legs from this filly, and it would give *him* trouble!"

The answer of Hammond was unheard, as they reapproached the carriage where the ladies sat.

"Well, gentlemen!" said Geraldine, impatiently; "I am eager to be busy. Come, let me have your judgment. What horse shall I adopt as my favorite?"

"Are you not fairly committed to your namesake?" asked Hammond, with a quiet manner; his eye, however, looking deeply into hers. She answered the gaze by dropping hers; replying quickly, as she did so:—

"No, indeed! the compliment to me must not be made to lose my money or discredit my judgment. For sure, Captain Barry himself has no such design to injure me. But I do fancy the beauty of his horse, and if you think her fleet, Mr. Hammond—"

She paused:—

"The 'Fair Geraldine' is doubtless a very fleet, as she is a very beautiful creature!"

"But," said Nettles, finding that Hammond hesitated, "that strange mare you see yonder undressing, is sure to beat her."

"Sure to beat her!" exclaimed Barry, who drew nigh in season to hear the last words. "What'll you go on the word?"

"Horse, house, lands, ox, ass, and everything that is mine!"

"Nay, nay! to the point; look to your pocketbook!"

"Well, if you will have it, we'll say a hundred on the match; 'Graystreak' against any horse in the field, unless Hammond runs his 'Ferraunt,' and then 'Ferraunt' against the field!"

"'Ferraunt!'" said Barry; "what, the large iron gray he rides. Why, he came on him!" looking to Hammond inquiringly. The latter had yielded his horse to his groom, and was now sitting on the box of the carriage, the driver being withdrawn to look after his horses. "Ferraunt" was already groomed, and resting in the shade at a little distance under the charge of the servant. The finger of Nettles pointed where he stood. The eye of Geraldine at once followed the direction of his finger, and while Barry and Nettles arranged their stakes, and withdrew to look at "Ferraunt," a short dialogue, not without its interest, took place between herself and Hammond.

"Is your horse so very fleet, Mr. Hammond, as Mr. Nettles says he is?"

"He has the reputation of being a very fast horse, Miss Foster; indeed, he is probably the fastest on the ground."

"Well; you mean to run him, of course?"

"Why of course?"

"Oh, why not? To own a race-horse, indeed, seems to imply racing. What is the use of him otherwise?"

"One may love to look at a beautiful animal without seeking always to test his speed; at all events, without seeking to game with it."

"To game! Is not that a harsh expression, Mr. Hammond?"

"Perhaps it is, since gentlemen have not often the motive of gain when they engage in this amusement. It is as a noble and beautiful exercise of a beautiful animal that they practise this recreation, and not for its profits."

"Well; and *you* could have no eye to the gains, Mr. Hammond?"

"No. But how small is the proportion of gentlemen, governed by such principles, to those who usually collect at a scene and on an occasion like this! What a greedy appetite for gain does it provoke among thousands who have no other object, and find no pleasure in the exquisite picture of the scene—in the glorious conflict of rival blood and temperament—in the wild grace of the motion of the steeds—in all that elevates it momentarily into something of the dignity of a field of battle; who think only of the wretched results which are to fill or empty their pockets. And of these, very few can afford to win or lose. If they win, they acquire certain appetites from success, which usually end in their ruin; and if they lose—though more fortunate in doing so, as they are probably made disgusted with the pursuit—they yet rob their families of absolute necessaries, in this miserable search after a diseased luxury for themselves."

"I confess I am no philosopher, Mr. Hammond. I don't see things in the same light with yourself, and can scarcely believe in such dreadful consequences from a spectacle that is really so fine and beautiful."

"Oh," said Mrs. Foster, interposing, sneeringly; "oh, Mr. Hammond, you get all those queer notions from your mother."

"You will permit me to respect the woman of my opinions, Mrs. Foster?" with a respectful but measured bow.

"Oh, surely. She's an excellent woman, and I respect her very much; but her notions on this subject are very peculiar, I think; though, in her case, natural enough."

This was said with a degree of significance which did not suffer Hammond to misunderstand the speaker. His face was instantly and deeply suffused with crimson, as he felt the allusion to the fate of his father. His head was, for the moment, averted from the speaker. In that moment, the malicious woman whispered to her step-daughter, "At him again. I know where the shoe pinches."

A slight expression of scorn might have been seen to curl the lips of Geraldine. A pause ensued, which was at length broken by Hammond, who drew her attention to a showy procession of the pied horses, the calico steeds of the circus company. Some comment followed on the performances of the *troupe*, when the young lady, in the most insinuating manner, resumed, with Hammond, the subject of his own horse.

"But, Mr. Hammond, though you inveigh against racing as a practice, you can have no objection to running your horse, upon occasions, once in a way, as much for the satisfaction of your friends as with any other object. Now, I am quite pleased with your dark-looking steed. What do you call him?"

" 'Ferraunt.' "

"Ah! his name indicates his color. He seems to me a military horse."

"I got him chiefly as a charger."

"Oh, yes; I forgot; you are a colonel of militia. But, for a charger, you need an animal at once high-spirited and gentle."

"He is both. That, indeed, Miss Foster, is the character of all high-blooded animals. The rule holds good among men. The most gentle are generally the most high-spirited—at once the most patient and the most enthusiastic. The race-horse, next to the mule, makes the best plough-horse."

"But that is surely a contradiction; the mule being the most dogged, stubborn, slow—"

"He need not be slow. He is only slow when broken and trained by a drowsy negro. But, though it seems a contradiction, as you say, to employ animals so utterly unlike for the same purposes, and to find them nearly equally good, it is one that we may, and perhaps must reconcile, on the principle that finds a sympathy in extremes."

"Mr. Hammond, it seems to me that all this is perversely intended to divert me from my object." A playful smile and arch manner accompanied this remark of the young lady. "But I am as perversely resolved that you shall not escape. Now, then, let me hear from you. Do you not intend that 'Ferraunt' shall run to-day?"

"I really do not, Miss Foster. I came out with no such purpose."

"I'm ready for you, colonel," was the remark of Jones Barry, who had just that moment reappeared with Nettles. "I'm not afraid of your 'Ferraunt,' though Nettles tells me he's good against all this crowd. I'm willing to try him. I don't believe in your foreign horses, when they come to this country; the climate don't seem to suit 'em. They're always sure to be beat by the natives; and, after the first talk on their arrival, you never hear anything said in their favor, and you never see anything they do. Now, your 'Ferraunt' comes of good stock, but he's awkward—"

"Awkward!" said Nettles; "ah! Barry, if you could only dance as well."

"Well, I'm willing to see him dance; and, if Col. Hammond chooses, I'll go a cool hundred on the 'Fair Geraldine' against him. There's a banter for you."

"I won't run my horse, Mr. Barry."

"What, bluffed off so soon?" said Barry, coarsely.

"Call it what you will, Mr. Barry; I don't run horses."

"But, Mr. Hammond, if you are content to underlie his challenge, you surely will not be so uncourteous as to refuse mine. The 'Fair Geraldine' against 'Ferraunt,' for a pair of gloves. I must maintain the reputation of my namesake."

"The 'Fair Geraldine' must excuse me, if my courtesy will not suffer me to accept her challenge."

"What! you pretend that your horse must beat?"

"I know it, Miss Foster."

"And what if I say that I don't believe a word of it? that I equally know that the 'Fair Geraldine' is the fastest horse? and I defy you to the trial? There, sir, my glove against yours."

This was all sweetly, if not saucily said. The eyes of Hammond were fixed gratefully upon the speaker; but he shook his head.

"You must forgive me, if I decline the trial in the case of my horse. But, if you will permit me, I cheerfully peril my glove against your favorite in behalf of 'Graystreak,' yonder."

"No, no, sir; your horse, your 'Ferraunt.' "

"You can't refuse, colonel," said Barry.

"No, Randall!" said Henderson.

"Impossible!" cried Nettles; who was anxious to see 'Ferraunt' take the field.

"A lady's challenge!" cried Mrs. Foster; "chivalry forbids that you refuse."

"I am compelled to do so, Miss Foster. It would give me pleasure to comply with your wishes, but I never run my horse, or any horse; I never engage as a principal in racing of any kind."

Nettles and Henderson both drew Hammond aside to argue the matter with him. They were followed by Barry, who was in turn followed by the jockey, Ramsey. Nettles had his arguments, which were urged in vain; and, when Henderson dwelt on the claims of the lady, Hammond replied, somewhat reproachfully:

"*You* know, Miles, that I shouldn't run a horse, were all the fair women in the world to plead."

"Well," said Barry, "what a man won't do for pleading, he may do for bantering. I'm here for that, colonel, and I'll double upon the hundred against your foreign horse."

"I must decline, Mr. Barry; I'm no racer, and will not run my horse; but, let me assure you, sir, that your mare, though a very clever thing, could not hold her ground for a moment against him."

"Easy bragging," said Ramsey, with a chuckle, "when there's no betting."

"And as easy to lay a horsewhip over a ruffian's shoulder, sir, when he presumes where he has no business."

Ramsey disappeared in an instant; a roll of the drum followed, giving notice of the approaching struggle; and the desire to see "Ferraunt" on the ground, gave place, among the few, to the more immediate interest which belonged to the known competitors. Barry instantly hurried off to his groom and stable; Nettles sauntered away to the starting-post, while Henderson and Hammond returned to the carriage. The latter felt that the manner of Geraldine was changed. Her eye met his, but there was a coldness in the glance, which his instinct readily perceived; but, true to his policy, he suffered it to pass unnoticed; was respectful without being anxious, and attentive without showing too much solicitude.

"*You,*" said Geraldine to Henderson, "you, too, I am told, ride a fine and fleet horse; do you not intend to run him?"

"If Miss Foster desires it."

"Of course I desire it! What do you call your horse?"

"Sorella!"

"Sorella! a pretty name. Well, how does she run? Is she fleeter than my namesake?"

"What say you, Randall?"

"Oh, don't ask him! He will say nothing that'll please anybody. What's your opinion?"

"That 'Sorella' is too much for the 'Fair Geraldine!'"

"I'll not believe it; and I transfer to you the challenge that your friend scorned, or feared to take up. Which was it, Col. Hammond?"

"Let us suppose *feared,* Miss Foster!" replied Hammond, gently, and with a pleasant smile.

"I don't know what to make of you, Col. Hammond. I wish I could make something of you. But I despair; I'll try no longer!"

"That you should have even tried, Miss Foster, is a satisfaction to my vanity."

"Oh, don't indulge it. It was not to give you any pleasure, I assure you, that I thought to try at all; only to please my fancy, and—"

"Still, I am gratified that I should, in any way, have contributed to this object."

"Nay! you are presuming; you torture everything I say into a compliment to yourself. But, hear me! if you won't run your horse yourself, let me run him. I'll ride him. I'm not afraid. I'm ambitious now of taking the purse from the whole field, and snapping my fingers at their Crazy Kates and Graystreaks, and even their Geraldines. Geraldine against Geraldine. How will Mr. Barry like it, I wonder; and that, too, at the cost of his hundreds. Cool hundreds, I think, he calls them; cool, I suppose, from being separated from their companions. Well! will you let me ride your 'Ferraunt?' "

"If you will suffer me to place him at your service when at home, Miss Foster!"

"No, no! I want a race-horse, not a saddle-horse; I want him here, not at home. Don't suppose I'm afraid to run him. I'm as good a rider, I know, as almost any on the ground, and—But say! shall I have him?"

"I dare not, Miss Foster; for your own sake, I dare not. But I feel that you are jesting only—"

"No, indeed! I'm as serious as I ever was. I don't know what you mean when you say you dare not, unless, indeed, you think—"

"Oh! don't ask Col. Hammond any favors, my child, he's so full of notions!" the step-mother again interposed, maliciously. Geraldine threw herself back in the carriage with an air of pique, and Henderson looked at his friend commiseratingly, as if to say: "You've done for yourself, forever!" The other seemed unmoved, however, and preserved the utmost equanimity. There was another roll of the drum; at this signal, Henderson held up a blue ribbon to Miss Foster, who drew from her reticule a crimson cockade with which the ingenious Mr. Jones Barry had provided her. This she fastened to her shoulder, acknowledging her sympathy with the colors of her namesake. Henderson, in another moment, disappeared, glad to have an excuse, in the commands of the lady, for showing off to advantage his equally fine horse and person.

CHAPTER VI.

THE RACE.—CROSS PURPOSES.

OUR preliminaries are all adjusted, and the moment approaches for the conflict. The eyes of all are now directed to the central point from which, at the tap of the drum, the contending horses are to start. The card-players desert their log beneath the shade-trees, the greasy pack being thrust into the pocket of one of the company till the more immediate object of interest is over. The rifle-shooters lean their implements against a tree, and seek the common point of attraction. The cooks leave their seething-vessels; the negroes hurry from their horses; all parties, high and low, big and little, crowd upon the track, pressing upon the ropes that guard the little space assigned to the running animals, and crowding absolutely upon their heels. The scenes that we have witnessed, in a few striking instances already, are in progress on a smaller scale everywhere. Bets are freely offered and taken, now that the horses are uncovered and in sight. The first animal that stripped for the examination of the judges, was a large horse of Jones Barry's, called "Glaucus," a great-limbed beast, that promised much more endurance than speed, and yet had the look of being too heavy to endure his own weight beyond a reasonable distance. His chances lay in the fact that the race in which he was to run was but a single mile, and his legs were quite sufficient for that. Yet "Glaucus" did not seem much of a favorite.

"An elephant!" cried one.

"Looks more like a gin-horse than a race-horse," said another.

"No go," said a third.

"Slow go," at least, quoth Tom Nettles, addressing Barry himself.

"Not so slow either; sure, rather."

"Yes, of the dust from other heels, if not of his own. I'll take 'Crazy Kate' against 'Glaucus' for a five, Barry; and the Mississippi mare against him two to one; say ten to five."

67

"I'm not to be bluffed, Nettles. I'm your man!"

"Grayshaft," a neat little creature of Dick Vose's, next vaulted into the space, and underwent the usual peeling. Light-limbed, clean-legged, and with a good glossy skin, "Grayshaft" won a good many favoring voices. "Estella," a filly of Ralph Biggar's; "Nabob," "Keener," and "Flourish," were severally brought forward, and had their backers. Each of them had some points to commend them. Some told in length and ease of legs; some in good muscle, in general carriage, in beauty of shape, in eye, head, and other characteristics. But the expression of admiration was much more decided, among the multitude, when "Crazy Kate" made her appearance in the space. Now "Crazy Kate" was remarkable for showing nothing calculated to persuade the casual spectator into a belief in her fleetness. She was, in truth, a very vulgar-looking beast, singularly unmeriting the appellation of "Crazy," as no creature could possibly have looked more tame. Her hair was coarse, confused, and rough, as if shedding; her mane was matted, and an occasional cockle-burr could be seen hanging among the bristles; but all these signs were regarded rather as the cunning devices of the old jockey, her owner, Lazy Jake Owens, than as at all indicative of her qualities of speed and bottom. The more knowing followers of the turf readily discovered, through all these unfavorable indices, the slender limbs, the wiry muscle, the strength and substance, which denoted good blood, agility, and fleetness. The contrast which the Mississippi mare presented to the ungainly externals of "Crazy Kate," was productive of a shout in her favor. "Graystreak" was the model of a fine animal; perhaps wanting somewhat in height, but possessed of immense capacity, great muscular power, fine color; in limb, action, muscle, exhibiting largely the characteristics of high blood, speed, and great endurance. Her skin was glossy, her eye bright and steady; and she showed, in her movement, so perfect a union of spirit and docility, that you felt, at a glance, that her training had done full justice to her blood. There was no resisting the impression which she made. Barry himself felt it; but he relied upon the known cunning of Lazy Jake Owens, and was confident that still greater merits lay beneath the unkempt, uncomely aspect of "Crazy Kate." Lazy Jake himself seemed as confident as ever; feeling sure in the private engagement with Ned Ramsey, which made *him* safe, at the expense of all his backers.

"You have now a good view of the horses that are to run, Miss Foster," was the remark of Hammond, venturing to arouse the damsel from something like a reverie. "They have already examined them, and weighed the riders. In a few moments, they will mount and be ready for a start. Suffer me to throw back the top of your barouche, when you can rise and see the whole field at a glance."

"Oh! do so, Mr. Hammond, if you please. Where do you say I shall look?" Geraldine eagerly rose as she spoke, and while Hammond threw back the top of the carriage, she scrambled forward upon the seat beside him, using his shoulder with the utmost indifference during the proceeding.

"Your favorite does not run this race, which is considered a less trying one than that which she will encounter. It is for a single mile stretch only, and repeat; and many a horse who would beat, in a longer conflict, would probably lose in this; while the winner, here, would be nothing in a contest which was continued for two or three miles at a stretch."

"And which of these horses will win the race; not that dowdyish-looking beast, surely?"

"She will do something towards it; more than most of them; for the rudeness of her appearance is due rather to the small arts of her owner, than to her native deficiencies of beauty. She is not a handsome creature, but, well dressed, would be far from ugly."

"Fine feathers make fine birds, you would say," responded Geraldine, merrily, with a smile and toss of her own plumes.

"Exactly: but this poor beast is carefully disguised for the purpose of taking in the simple, who look to externals only. She is probably second best of the horses in the ring."

"And the first?"

"Is that sleek and quiet animal that stands immediately behind her. She is a strange creature from Mississippi, and is probably the best nag on the ground for fleetness and endurance."

"Your 'Ferraunt' excepted?" said the lady, slyly.

"My 'Ferraunt' probably excepted," was the somewhat grave reply.

"I *wish* you *would* run that horse, Mr. Hammond. For *my sake* you might."

This was said in somewhat lower tones than usual.

"For *your* sake, Miss Foster, I would do much; but there is a reason—but, hark! they are preparing for the start. You see that rider with the scarlet jacket. He rides the horse 'Glaucus,' another of Mr. Barry's racers. You see there are several horses in front, with different colors. Stand upon the seat, and you will better see them."

She adopted the suggestion; rose to the prescribed elevation, he keeping his place on the floor of the carriage, while her hand rested, as if unconsciously, upon his shoulder. In this manner, shading her eyes with the other hand, she directed her gaze upon the points to which he severally drew her attention.

"They are now all mounted. The white jacket and cap is the Mississippian; the blue is 'Crazy Kate.' Hark, now! The word—they are off!"

A thousand "hurrahs" from the multitude. The excitement in the bosom of our damsel was scarcely less.

"They go! they are gone! Oh! mamma, do you see them? How they dart—how they fly! Where are they now, Mr. Hammond? I do not see. I cannot follow them!"

The start was a beautiful one, made at an equal bound, "Glaucus" and "Grayshaft" taking the lead; "Keener" and "Flourish" following close, and "Crazy Kate" and "Graystreak," with "Nabob," just hanging at their heels. Soon, however, the position of the parties fluctuated. "Flourish" made a dash, and flung her tail in the face of "Glaucus;" "Nabob" went forward till he locked him, and was, in turn, passed by "Crazy Kate;" the Mississippi mare breezing up with a gradual increase of velocity, evidently under the most adroit management of rein. "Glaucus" struggled bravely against this new adversary, and made a desperate push, which succeeded in throwing "Flourish" and "Nabob" out of the lead; but "Crazy Kate" still kept ahead, until her backers began to shout their exultation, when, to their consternation, the Mississippian flared up under a single application of the whip, and shot ahead as suddenly and swiftly as an arrow from the bow. She passed the string just a quarter of a length in advance of "Crazy Kate," who was just as closely pressed by "Glaucus" and "Grayshaft." These four horses seemed only so many links of the same chain, so equally close did they maintain their relationship at the termination of the brush. The other horses were considerably in the rear. The race was to the Mississippian, and the *flats* were feeling in their pockets. Lazy Jake Owens was somewhat scarce, and a long and dubious silence succeeded the wild shouts that relieved the suspense of the multitude.

"What horse has won, Mr. Hammond?"

" 'Graystreak,' the Mississippian, Miss Foster!"

"But not greatly. It seemed to me that all the horses were together. If he won, it was scarcely by his own length."

"It sufficed: but he might have quadrupled that distance. But it was not the policy of his driver that it should be so. He is modest. He looks rather for success than triumph. He prefers the money to the fame. But the greatest contest follows, that in which your favorite takes the field."

"Yet the Mississippian will win, you say."

"Yes! he will prove too much, I suspect, for your namesake. He will not win so easily, however. Besides, Miles Henderson will run his mare, and she's a bright creature."

" 'Sorella?' "

"Yes! he *may* beat her; but she comes of the same blood with 'Ferraunt,' and if managed rightly—"

"It depends upon the rider, then?"

"Greatly! and I will see Miles on the subject."

"Really, Mr. Hammond, that you should know so much about horses, and yet refuse to take part in the struggle!"

"I love horses, Miss Foster; I delight in their beauty, and their movements are grateful to me. Perhaps but for certain reasons, which concern me only, I should be passionately fond of racing, and frequently engage in it. But my objections are insuperable. I *dare* not! But for this you should have been the mistress, this day, of all the movements of my horse."

He disappeared in search of his friend. Mrs. Foster sniggered, as he went. Seeing her step-daughter looking seriously, while her eyes followed the retreating form of Hammond, she said:—

"It's nothing but his pride and arrogance; it was so always with him, and with all his family. They delight in being perverse. His mother is just that sort of person; a cold, formal, conceited, consequential, old, stiff-capped somebody, that would be like nobody else. As for Randall Hammond, every one knows that he's a tyrant. He thinks he can do as he likes with women; that they're all so anxious to get him, that they'd submit to any dictation. But he'll find himself mistaken yet. Now he loves you, Geraldine, quite as much as he loves or can love anybody; and when he finds he can't be master, he'll perhaps be willing that you should be mistress; but you'll have to make him feel that he's nobody first. He's a haughty, cold—"

"Oh! hush, mother; you know that you don't like him."

"No! I don't; not a bone in his skin, nor his old mother either. But what I say is true. You see for yourself, and you'll learn to see with my eyes before you see anything good in him!"

"I shall scarcely do so then. But the man's a man. He don't change. He's firm; and that's something. He don't flatter, either; and though that vexes me, yet I don't think the worse of him for it."

"Oh, yes! and he'll hear you singing yet—

'When is he coming to marry me?'"

"No, he won't! mother, nor any man. I don't care whether I marry or not. I don't see that marrying is so necessary; and I'm positively sick of hearing women talk of marriage, as if it was the only subject in the world to talk about."

"And so it is; a woman's nobody until she's a wife!"

"And then she's *one*-body's!"

"Yes! and then all's safe! But, if you're wise, you'll marry anybody sooner than a master."

"And when I submit that any man shall be my master, I shan't complain, be assured of it. But no more of it; for here comes your favorite, Captain Barry."

"I wish he were your favorite, too. He's the man; you can manage him like a feather."

"A feather, then, would be a good substitute for a husband!"

"Yes, indeed, if it adorns one's bonnet!"

"Hush!"

"Well, ladies! you see I've been unlucky," began Barry; "my 'Glaucus' just lost the race by a span. Jim Perkins rode him badly. He held in where he should have let out, and I saw him looking behind, and jerking in, just when he should have used the whip. But that's nothing. I didn't count largely on this race. In the next, however, I'll ride 'Fair Geraldine' myself, and then we'll see after this 'Graystreak.' You saw the run? You saw that the 'Mississippian' and 'Crazy Kate' were both put to their best? Now I know that 'Geraldine' can gallop round 'Glaucus' at his speed. We'll see!"

"Well, remember, Mr. Barry, I've a fortune in gloves on my namesake."

"Never fear! never fear!"

"But Mr. Henderson's going to run his 'Sorella.'"

"Yes; I see him busy. He stands no chance. 'Sorella' is sister of 'Ferraunt;' 'Geraldine' can beat 'em both. I only wish we could get Hammond to come out with his iron gray. We'd show him! We'd take the conceit out of him!"

"What can be the reason of his reluctance?"

"Reason!" exclaimed the mother; "why, there's no reason, but his pride. He thinks horseracing vulgar."

"That can hardly be possible. Indeed, I'm sure, from what he said to me, that it is not pride. Besides, I'm not so sure that I can't persuade him to it yet."

"Indeed! you may give up that notion," said Barry. "He particularly told Nettles and myself that he wouldn't run his horse for you or any woman breathing."

"Said he that?" demanded Geraldine, while her eye flashed sudden fires of indignation, and her cheek flushed with the feeling of a slighted pride.

"To be sure he did; not twenty yards from your carriage; and when Nettles and Henderson were telling him that he could no longer refuse, after you had asked him."

"It was like him!" said the step-mother. "I hope you're satisfied now!"

The daughter was silent; and Mrs. Foster, satisfied with the step gained, was prudent enough to say no more. Barry ran on for some time longer; but, finding that what he said was little heeded, he hurried away to the stand, and to make his preparations for the next great race.

Meanwhile, Hammond, unsuspecting the evil seed which had been planted in his absence, had sought out Henderson, in order to give him counsel in relation to the race. It may be said here, that Hammond was not only an excellent judge of the qualities of a horse, but that he particularly knew "Sorella." He had imported and partly trained her; and she had been his gift to Henderson, some time before. He now took the latter aside, and said to him—

"You are too heavy to ride 'Sorella' yourself, Miles, and can venture little against this Mississippi filly. I think that 'Sorella' can beat her in the long run, but only under a first-rate rider. Now, do you go over with me to the wagon of old Nathan Whitesides, whom I see here, and we will get his son, Logan, to ride for you. Logan is a first-rate rider, and has had frequent practice with 'Sorella.' He knows her, and, which is quite as important, she knows him. He is one of the most dextrous jockeys that I know, though he seems a simpleton. If any one, not myself, can beat 'Graystreak' with 'Sorella,' it is Logan Whitesides."

The boy was sought, found, and employed. A few whispers in his ear, and Hammond left the parties; returning to the carriage of Mrs. Foster, seemingly no more concerned in the race than the most indifferent spectator. He resumed his seat quietly on the box of the barouche, but not before discovering that a change had taken place in the manner of Geraldine Foster. She was constrained in her answers, and totally incurious about the race. Not so the stepmother, who seemed to grow good-humored in due degree with the increased reserve and *hauteur* of the damsel. Hammond was a politician; he did not appear to discover any changes, and spoke as quietly, and offered his services and his information as unpretendingly as he had done before. His manner was that of a gentleman who had nothing to gain, and is conscious of nothing to be lost; but who, in obedience to habitual training, defers gently to the sex, and shows

that solicitude for the graces of society which makes one always willing to contribute to its amenities. It is not to be concealed, however,
that he took advantage of the frequent provocations afforded by Mrs.
Foster, to make himself particularly interesting. Without effort, he
betrayed his resources of reading and observation. He was lively,
without levity; various, without painstaking; and copious, without
suffering himself to fall into tediousness. Gradually, the ear of
Geraldine inclined to his voice. She forgot, in his conversation, the
reported rudeness which had vexed her pride; and, by the time that
the preparations were completed for the main race, she was again
on the seat beside him. Mrs. Foster had not calculated on this result.
She was chagrined to find that her conversation had brought out new
powers in their companion, which could not fail to place him in
favorable comparison with his rivals; and she was too vulgar a
woman to know how to repair the evil unless by a positive rudeness,
for which she was unprepared, and for which she could have no
excuse. She sat silent, accordingly, leaving the field entirely free to
Hammond; who, finding Geraldine a somewhat pensive listener
beside him, adroitly addressed the sentiment which was uppermost
in her thoughts, and confirmed, still more profoundly, the impression
he had made. At moments, a recollection of the scandal which she
had heard came upon her with a twinge; and her brow was momently
clouded, while her heart sunk; but the cloud passed away, and the
heart grew lifted, as, watchful of every movement, yet without seeming to be so, Hammond took care so to direct her thought *from*
himself, as to make the most favorable impression of self through
media the most indirect. We will not attempt to pursue the conversation, which depended upon turns of expression, tones, and
glances, which mere description must always find indescribable.

The excitements of the race interposed to give variety to the
conversation between the pair. Hammond allowed nothing to escape
which seemed to belong to his duties as *cicerone*. Aware of the
preliminaries, he knew at what moment to direct his companion's
attention to the course.

"They are hastening with their preparations for the race, Miss
Foster, and if you will rise, as before, you will enjoy a good view
of your favorite. She is certainly a very pretty creature."

"Where? Where?" and the damsel rose in her place, and again stood upon the seat above her attendant. But this time her hand did not rest upon his shoulder as before.

"You see her there, just beneath the stand of the judges. She is certainly a beautiful little thing, and comes up to the stand handsomely."

"Then you think that she will win?"

"It is very doubtful. She has, at least, two very formidable competitors."

"The Mississippi?—"

"And 'Sorella.'"

"Is 'Sorella' a very fast animal?"

"She *was*, six months ago."

"But now?"

"All depends upon her rider."

"What of the ugly-coated beast—the dowdy, crazy something?"

"She may get the first heat, but will hardly do anything in the second. She wants substance. The danger to your namesake is of the same kind. She has spirit and fleetness, but not sufficient endurance. For a single mile, she might carry herself against either of these horses; but these are three-mile races, which her powers can scarcely undergo. That Mississippi mare is a model of training. I see where she stands, sleek, smooth, and so perfectly at home; so quiet; as if she knew her business thoroughly, and regarded it as done. 'Sorella' has work before her."

"Does Mr. Henderson ride 'Sorella?'"

"No. I have persuaded him not to do so."

Geraldine was about to ask the reason, when a nudge from her step-mother behind silenced her; and, just then, the tap of the drum, and the voice of authority, drew the eyes of all parties to the starting-post.

CHAPTER VII.

THE horses entered were but four in number. These were, our Mississippian, "Graystreak," "Crazy Kate," the "Fair Geraldine," and "Sorella." The former was now decidedly the favorite of the field, and odds were given in her behalf. Numerous bets were offered and taken, and the excitement on the turf was great, and momently increasing. The "Fair Geraldine" had her backers, and so had "Crazy Kate" and "Sorella." But the latter was little known among the regular jockeys, and, though a symmetrical and well-shaped animal, there were none of those salient characteristics in her appearance which are apt to take the spectator. It was seen that she was fleet; and that she was rather bony, seemed to promise something for her hardihood. Ned Ramsey noticed her with some anxiety; and the watchful Lazy Jake Owens observed that he had a whisper *en passant* for the gentlemanly stranger who had so freely taken the offers of Jones Barry. But neither Ramsey nor the stranger declined any banters against "Graystreak;" their confidence in that favorite creature being in no respect impaired by the presence of the new competitor. Of course, we do not pretend to follow and describe the varieties of feeling and interest shown by the spectators. How they perilled their money, in what amount, and upon what horses, noways concerns our narrative. We may mention, however, that Miles Henderson had a couple of hundred and a few odd *fives* invested in the credit of his mare; while our friend Tom Nettles was pretty safe in taking the field against the "Fair Geraldine" and "Crazy Kate," to the tune of two or three hundred more.

The examination of the horses showed them off to great advantage. "Graystreak" looked sleek, quiet, and confident, as before. "Sorella" was a meek animal also, with just such a twinkle of the eye as shows that there is no lack of spirit, with all the meekness. But the "Fair Geraldine" stripped to the survey with all the consciousness of a proud and petted beauty. She was restive and bright; a little too anxious and impatient, and carried her head with a toss which was not unworthy of her lovelier namesake. Her appearance compelled the admiration of all; and many were tempted to bet upon her beauty, who did not consider her heels. Her rider now was Jones Barry himself. He was really not satisfied that Sam Perkins had not done justice to "Glaucus;" but, whether satisfied or not, nothing could possibly have prevented him from doing as the Earl of *Tote*ham had been said to do at Doncaster.

"Your favorite is ready for the race, Miss Foster! you see Mr. Barry takes the field in person;" and Hammond pointed to the gaudy figure of that worthy, as the impatient "Geraldine" wheeled and capered beneath him.

"The white is 'Graystreak,' and the blue—"

"Crazy Kate!"

"But where is Mr. Henderson's rider?"

"He mounts now—that strange-looking urchin with a yellow-spotted bandanna, wound, gypsy fashion, around his head, without a jacket, with his shirt-sleeves bared to the elbow, and his suspenders wrapped around his waist."

"What a strange-looking creature! Who is he?"

"One Logan Whitesides; a knowing lad among horses, who is particularly well acquainted with 'Sorella.' He was her only rider when she was under training, and his whisper will do more with her than any other person's whip."

"Was it that he might get this boy that you counselled Mr. Henderson not to ride himself?" asked Geraldine, with some interest.

"Yes! I knew that 'Sorella' would need every advantage in a contest with the Mississippi filly, and that Miles was quite too heavy to run her successfully himself."

Unconsciously, the girl looked pleased. Hammond saw the expression, and mused upon it; particularly as a querulous exclamation, at that moment, dropped from the hostile step-mother. But the proceedings of the course drew all eyes thither. All were saddled, the word was given, and away they went, like so many ambitious heroes, into battle.

The start was a successful one. The four horses seemed to jump off together, running side by side for a while, as if delighting in the line and order of a platoon charge. But soon the "Fair Geraldine" led off, taking the track for a quarter of a mile; "Crazy Kate" laying herself close behind, and "Graystreak" and "Sorella" seeming to find their amusement in driving the two before them. Before the mile was two-thirds traversed, however, "Crazy Kate" showed symptoms of lagging, and "Sorella" dropped her with a bound, making even play between the "Mississippian" and the "Fair Geraldine." The latter continued well on, not needing any urgency of her rider, until the clattering heels of "Sorella" and "Graystreak," just at her haunches, impelled her to an effort. She bridled up at this forwardness, and a slight smack of the whip shocked her into a still more indignant determination to leave all vulgar companionship behind. She went off with a rocket-like impulse, but without obtaining her object. It was now evident that the "Mississippian" was resolved to cut her off from her triumph, and her rider was seen to apply the thong smartly to her sides. She passed, accordingly, between "Sorella" and the object of her ambition, and the next moment found her, lock and lock, in affectionate embrace with the high-spirited and aristocratic beauty. Vainly did the latter try to shake her off. All her efforts only served to keep the two in this position, when, to the surprise of both, a shrill whistle from the rider of "Sorella" brought that mysterious creature with a rush between them, and flinging the dust in both their faces, she passed under the string, leaving her tail hidden between the lifted heads of the two emulous competitors. "Crazy Kate" darted into the allotted limits quite in season to save her distance, having reserved her powers for another brush.

The race was a beautiful one. The several merits of the first three horses were now fully displayed, though the extent of their powers of endurance could only be conjectured. They had evidently been ridden with a due regard to their qualities; and the competition was such as to maintain the excitement of the multitude, and to keep them in suspense till the very last moment. A shawl might have lapped them at several points in the race; and an ell of ribbon might have circled them as they darted beneath the string. It was clear that judgments were to be revised. "Sorella" had been undervalued. "Crazy Kate" looked better than ever, and her rider was known to be a first-rate jockey; and "Graystreak" was under the teaching of the very Machiavel of the Georgia turf. The "Fair Geraldine" had behaved too handsomely to have lost any of her supporters; and, whether "Graystreak" had yielded the heat through policy, or actually lost it in spite of all his efforts, was a very doubtful question, even among the knowing ones. There was a whisper that she seemed to complain in one of her pins; but Tom Nettles, who examined her closely, made no such discovery. Ned Ramsey showed anxiety, however, and this was seen by "Lazy Jake Owens," as well as Nettles. His personal care of his horse was exemplary, and his efforts to enable her to recover and cool off, without effort, were so many studies for the youthful jockeys who were crowding about and emulous of his renown. Jones Barry was by no means dissatisfied with the doings of his mare. She did not seem uneasy or distressed; cooled off naturally and soon, and was ready for the second trial in the shortest possible space. But, to have seen the affectionate care of "Sorella," which was taken by her gypsy rider—how, in addition to the usual strippings and rubbings, he wound his arms about her neck, kissed her as if she had been a sweetheart, and whispered all sorts of pleasant nonsense in her ears; and how the filly turned to him with a knowing gesture; and how, when he stooped to rub her legs, her nose rested upon his shoulders with a sort of human interest, which drew crowds about the two in unaffected admiration! It realized, in some degree, the stories that we hear of the Arabian and his favorite steed. Logan Whitesides had first had his ambition lifted by his employment in the training of "Sorella." She was a first-love to him, and it would have come nigh to break his heart had he not achieved the victory.

"And so 'Sorella' has really won the victory?" said Geraldine to Hammond, as he returned to the carriage after a brief interview with Miles Henderson.

"The heat only—a third of the victory, Miss Foster. They are now preparing for the second trial."

"You are a witch in horses, Mr. Hammond. But pray what did you say in that short whisper which I saw you give to Mr. Henderson and his gypsy boy?"

Hammond laughed as he replied:—

"I simply instructed him that his policy was to *lose* the next heat."

"I don't understand you—lose!"

"That is, not attempt to win, but suffer it to be taken by the 'Mississippian.'"

"And why, pray?"

"That her strength in the third heat should not be perilled by an undue effort in the *second;* when, as most of the other horses will put forth their best ability, she might probably peril herself for nothing."

"I see, I see! But why lose to the 'Mississippian?' You say nothing of my namesake!"

"Your namesake has done her best already."

"You don't flatter, Mr. Hammond," said the step-mother; "I do believe you have a spite against that animal."

"O no, Mrs. Foster! I'm sure you believe no such thing. She is a sweet and beautiful creature, who will do all that is in her power. It is her misfortune that her powers are overtasked. Mr. Barry expects too much from her. He does not overrate her fleetness, but he overrates her endurance; and he will distress, and probably injure her, before the race is over. So far from a spite against her, I sympathize with her, and if I could, would gladly save her from the hard work which is before her."

"Well, I'll never believe but you have a spite against her. You believe in any horse on the ground but her. I'd like to see you run your own; but I suppose it would require something more than a woman's entreaties to persuade you to that."

There was something in the tone with which these words were spoken, not less than the words themselves, which grated offensively on the ears of the person addressed; but he remained silent, and in a few moments the preparations for the second heat enabled him to divert the conversation to another channel. At the signal given by the drum, Geraldine again stood upon the seat of the carriage, an eager spectator of the issue. The word was given, and the start was again beautiful; the four steeds seeming to lap each other, whirling away for a while, in a sort of linked movement, which showed them all as if locked together in mutual relationship. "Crazy Kate" and "Geraldine" were soon again in the lead, as if by mutual consent between "Sorella" and "Graystreak;" swinging forward by the groups of spectators, the wagons and the tables, east and west, as if waltzing with wings at both feet and shoulders. Merrily did they glide away, leaving a space of thirty feet or more between their competitors, who appeared perfectly content to jog on together at a pace which inconvenienced neither, yet enabled them to keep always within speaking distance of the lively things in front. Thus trailing for the first mile and better, they suffered the game to be played by other bands, only piping moderately to the music. But soon the "Mississippian" began to grow restive under restraint, and to put forth a much more ambitious leg than he had hitherto shown. He lifted away from "Sorella," and was soon upon the heels of the two ahead. A few bounds enabled him to separate the links between them, and to throw himself towards the back stretch of the second mile, between "Crazy Kate" and her fair competitor. "Sorella" made a similar push forward, and soon overcame the space which kept her from the embrace of "Crazy Kate;" but whether it was that the latter was less tempting than the beauty with the beautiful name, she did not prolong the *tête-à-tête* with her, but hurried forward to a more select meeting with the "Fair Geraldine;" perhaps it was a feeling of sympathy, which, at this moment, prompted the latter to forego her exertions, and loiter for the coming up of one who sought her so closely. Meanwhile, the ambitious maid of Mississippi darted ahead of all opponents, and, with so few tokens of civility, as to provoke the emulous efforts of the two nearest riders. Jones Barry was seen to apply the whip with unkind severity of hand, to the tender flanks of his favorite; while the gypsy boy who rode "Sorella" appeared to urge her forward with the utmost seeming anxiety, but without the use of any weapon. It was now perceived that the "Fair Geraldine," as if under a feeling of degradation, no longer lifted a hopeful and exulting head, nor tossed pridefully her luxuriant mane. That she began to droop was evident to the spectators, while the repeated strokes of the lash, from her rider, betrayed his own consciousness of a fact which he was quite unwilling to believe. These exertions still gave her headway for awhile, but it was at the expense of her heels. She gradually relaxed after these efforts, and soon had the mortification to find "Sorella" quietly working ahead, as they both stretched through the first quarter of the third mile. Hammond saw with satisfaction, that, while the boy who rode "Sorella" appeared to labor anxiously, he used no whip, or only appeared to do so, while the beast lifted her legs freely, and set them down as if on velvet. The crowd, who knew nothing of his game, now looked upon it that she shared the exhaustion of "Geraldine," and were quite deceived by the arts of her rider. Even Ramsey himself counted upon him as a horse "done brown;" and whispered to Lazy Jake Owens that the race was won. But Lazy Jake was no slouch at an opinion either, in the matter of horseflesh; and he answered, in the common proverb of warring in the South: "Don't whoop before you're out of the wood." But this heat was decided. The "Mississippian" had shown the cleanest heels, taking the track from all. It was observed that "Sorella," after once or twice yielding the lead to the "Fair Geraldine," now changed the figure entirely, and hastened forward so as to throw herself within a few decent bounds of "Graystreak," as the latter passed in under the string, the final victor of the heat. The native spirit of "Geraldine" did not suffer her to fall behind very far, though it was evident to all good judges that the game with her was up for the day; while "Crazy Kate" enjoyed to herself the Irishman's fun of driving all the rogues before her. Of the three winning horses, "Sorella" was the only one who had been economized, and the excellence of her jockey enabled her to keep this important fact a secret. A couple of lengths between her and "Graystreak," and twice the number between her and "Geraldine," left the minds of the multitude still in that condition of doubt in regard to the future which makes equally the interest of race and story. The betting parties were still hopeful; for, even where their favorites had not won, they came so near it, with the exception of "Crazy Kate," as to leave nothing certain in the chapter of coming events.

Well rubbed and groomed, three horses showed themselves for the third time upon the track. "Crazy Kate" has withdrawn in dudgeon, in consequence of the manifest neglect with which her companions have treated her performances. Her backers have sullenly yielded up their *tin* to the numerous friends of the "Mississippian;" while Ramsey, and the unknown gentleman, have been reminding numerous persons of certain fives, tens, twenties, and hundreds— including our friend Jones Barry—which they unwisely perilled on the heels of a feminine creature avowedly *non compos*. This pleasant little episode greatly relieved the otherwise tedious interval between the second and the last heat. The "Fair Geraldine" seemed to have recovered her former spirits, as she came once more upon the turf; and, with the word "Go," she led off, "solitary and alone," as she had been ambitious to do on all previous occasions. But, after the first half mile, both the "Mississippian" and "Sorella" seemed disposed to make play, and to show that both had heels of wing and steam when the exigency was at hand. It was clear, however, that the two latter waited for each other. They knew the real adversary, and knew exactly when to terminate that deference for the beauty who now led them which, it was evident, they had yielded rather through policy than admiration. As the first mile was overcome, they gradually swallowed space, taking the wind completely out of the sails of "Geraldine," passing on each side of her, and closing up, as if anxious for the track. Barry at once put on steam with a heavy hand, but no application to the flanks, in the case of one so tender, could possibly furnish the legs with the proper facility for flight. The beauty wanted age for endurance. "Send me no more boys," said Napoleon to the government at home: "they only fill the hospitals." The tender years of "Geraldine," her delicate training, were adverse to her soldier-ship. Famous at a charge, she could not stand the campaign. The two veterans, better fortified by muscle and training, of better bottom and not less speed, soon forged ahead, and left her painfully to struggle up the hill alone. "Graystreak" was evidently girdling up her loins for the last great effort. She felt the necessity of putting all her soul into her heels, as she felt that she had a sterling customer beside her, one who took a deep *shot*, and loved long *reckonings*. There were bone, and muscle, and speed, to be overcome, and she had a pride and reputation at stake, to say nothing of the hundreds which our friend Jones Barry no doubt found *cool enough* by this time. There was evident mischief in the "Mississippian." Her rider glared round, in his white uniform, at the queer little gypsy rogue who kept tenaciously with him, neck and neck, as if measuring their mutual strength for the last great struggle. It was neck or nothing with them both. Both were resolute to do, or die. The gypsy rogue seemed to crouch, at moments, in his saddle, as if to take the leap of a cougar on the fox, and his heels would sink slightly into the sides of his creature, as if embracing her with a love which found all its pleasures in hers. Side and side they rode, until, in the eyes of the distant spectators, they seemed to resolve themselves into a single man and horse. The struggle was desperately close. It was your purse or mine, as they darted eagerly towards the last quarter stretch, leaving the wind behind them, and seeming to whiz along through air, as a bullet from the cannon. "The bravest held his breath for a time." The multitude pressed forward along the track. Mouths were open wide with expectation; eyes dilating beyond their orbs, with delight and anxiety.

"How beautiful!" exclaimed Geraldine Foster, as she grasped the arm of Hammond.

"Beautiful!" said Hammond, naturally enough, as he gazed into her eyes. We dare not look with him while the struggle is thus at its height. The jockey on "Graystreak" now made tremendous efforts; his eye fixed on the stubborn little gypsy, as if to note the opening for an advantage. Neck and neck they still clung together, and but a few more bounds were necessary to the final achievement. "White-jacket" gathered himself up for the last issue, and, rising in his stirrups, with the whip keenly and rapidly administered, he raised the head of "Graystreak" for the final bound beneath the line. But "Nojacket," our little gypsy, knew his moment also. He gave no whip; he rose not in the saddle; but crouching, rather, and clinging upon her neck, he whispered a word, a single word, in the ear of "Sorella," and the noble Arabian went out of the lock in a way to make an arrow wonder. By a single head, she passed ahead of her resolute competitor; and, as her triumph was beheld, the big, swollen heart of the multitude relieved itself by a shout that shook the field. Then our gypsy-jockey dropped from his creature, and seized her about the neck, kissing her once more as passionately as the lover, for the first time successful. He felt the triumph as much more precious than he did the "cool hundred," one of the several that had been transferred on this occasion from the pockets of the wealthy Jones Barry to those of other people, with which Miles Henderson rewarded him for his riding. Then might the multitude be seen following the horses—horse and rider—with exultation and admiration. Our gypsy was, next to his horse, the wonder of the field. The boys scampered after him as *their* hero, while the negroes, everywhere exclaiming as he came, pointed him out to their grinning companions, as "Dat little Login Whitesides; da's a debble hese'f, for ride!" Glory is a thing of various complexions; and our little friend Logan was quite as well satisfied, no doubt, with the negro form of compliment, as with that which issued in rounded periods from more polished lips. Let us now look to other parties.

CHAPTER VIII.

THE GANDER TOURNAMENT.

THE excellent lady, Mrs. Foster, was quite dissatisfied at the result of the race. Perhaps she might have been still more so, had the victory been obtained by "Ferraunt," instead of "Sorella;" by the horse of Hammond in place of that of his friend. She did not conceal her mortification, which vented itself in expressions of strong sympathy with Jones Barry, even in the presence of his conqueror. He, however, either was, or affected to be, wholly indifferent to the result. He had various excuses for the defeat, which he could ascribe to any and everything, always excepting his mare's ability and his own riding.

"I'll go you a thousand any day, Miles Henderson, on 'Geraldine,' against 'Sorella.' I know what my mare can do. But she wasn't groomed properly. That little rascal Sam Perkins would give her water, though I told him not; and he girt her in so tightly, that the poor thing could hardly draw a decent breath."

"And you're a little too heavy for your mare, Barry," added Nettles; who, having pocketed a clever share of the money of the other, could afford to do the amiable.

"There's something in that," was the admission of Barry. "But, Tom, didn't I ride her beautiful?"

"You *can* ride," was the liberal acknowledgment of the other, with just the sort of emphasis and look, in the right place, to render the admission satisfactory.

Meanwhile, Henderson and Hammond had both been conversing with the ladies; though the latter could not but perceive that Geraldine manifested, in his case, a more than usual degree of reserve and distance. He was not long at a loss to what influence to ascribe this deportment, since Mrs. Foster, though outwardly civil, was yet not altogether capable of suppressing all shows of that spirit by which she was secretly animated towards him. True, however, to his maxim, he betrayed no particular concern, but was only the more studious to overlook none of the formal and becoming courtesies which society had established as proper from the one sex to the other. He was not only scrupulously polite and attentive, but particularly graceful and spirited. His conversation rose in force and animation with the consciousness of his equivocal position; and the vivacity and freedom of his dialogue and manner were only restrained by an overruling resolution to permit to himself no such liberties as might incur censure or provoke offence. He played the diplomate with a rare excellence; and Mrs. Foster leaned back in the carriage, heartily vexed with a person whom she longed to wound, yet who gave her no advantage; and who, in spite of all her malice, still contrived, seemingly without exertion, to win the ears, and compel the sympathies of her *protégé*. The carriage, meanwhile, was got in readiness; the horses were *geared* in, and the lady proceeded to invite the gentlemen to return with her to dinner. Hammond and Henderson declared their pleasure in escorting the ladies home; while Jones Barry and Nettles excused themselves by alleging that, with them, the business of the day was very far from being over. There were several races yet to be run. "Glaucus" was again to try his heels against some other nags, which were yet to be brought forward; and there was to be a "*scrub*" race for *sweepstakes*, in which more than twenty horses had been already entered. The interest of Nettles in these events, though he ran no horse himself, was not less great than that of Jones Barry, while his profits were likely to be much greater.

"Besides," says Barry; "there's the circus, Mrs. Foster, the circus;" and he rubbed his hands. "And I never saw the circus in my life. I'm told they do all sorts of things. There's a man there that jumps through the eye of a needle!"

"Oh, Mr. Barry, how can you believe such nonsense?"

"It's true, by the pipers! here's the advertisement; here's the picture itself; the man and the needle."

"As large as life!" said Nettles.

And Barry pulled out of his pocket one of those enormous bills of the circus, which one sees at times, in the South and West, covering the sides of a court-house. As he held it up, it fairly covered him from head to foot.

"I don't see why he shouldn't jump through the eye of such a needle, Mr. Barry; the needle seems a great deal larger than the man."

"So *it does*," said Barry.

"Oh! but that's only to show it to the people, Miss Geraldine; that's only the picture; for I saw the needle, the real needle itself; and I assure you that it's not much larger than those you ladies work with. It isn't exactly a cambric needle, I grant you; but then again, it's nothing near like a bagging-needle."

"You saw it, Tom?" asked Barry.

"To be sure I did!" was the reply.

"And you believe, Mr. Barry, that any man could go through such a needle?" queried Mrs. Foster.

"I don't see how he can," said the other, gravely; "it would break out the eye."

A roar of laughter from Henderson followed this oracular opinion, of which Miss Geraldine herself indulged in a moderate imitation. Mrs. Foster lay back in the carriage, frowning and mortified. Nettles continued:—

"But that's not all; the clown who goes through the needle uncorks a bottle with his eye, sets fire to a wheelrocket with his whiskers, and afterwards swallows his own head."

"Ah! Tom," says Barry, "that won't do! Nobody can make me believe that. It may be that he could draw a cork with his eye; and, as for setting off wheelrockets with his whiskers, that, I suppose, isn't altogether impossible; but I'll be d——d if I believe a word about swallowing his own head. Swallowing his own head! Why, who the deuce could ever think of doing such a thing? Oh no, Tom Nettles; that cock won't fight! It's likely he may make a show of doing something of the kind, by sleight of hand."

"Of mouth, rather."

"Well, mouth then; but I know it's all make b'lieve—don't you think so, Mrs. Foster?"

"I don't think about it, Mr. Barry. It's all trick and humbug. Circuses are all vulgar places. I have no interest in them."

"Vulgar! why, Lord bless you, Mrs. Foster, the whole country's to be there. Don't you see the carriages coming in already? There'll be a matter of three hundred ladies, I reckon."

"Ladies, indeed!" said the lady. "Perhaps so, sir. We sha'n't be among them, however. Scipio," to the driver, "are you ready?"

"All ready, ma'am."

"Well, Mr. Barry, we leave you. Mr. Nettles, we shall always be glad to see you at the lodge. Gentlemen," to Hammond and Henderson, "do you still keep your purpose of riding with us, or have the charms of the clown, as we have heard them described, persuaded you to think better of it, and stay for the circus?"

"If one could be sure that the clown would act honestly, and really make a gulp of his own head," mused Hammond, with gravity.

Barry looked up bewildered, his mouth wide open, as Nettles proceeded to assert that the thing was really done in a most lifelike and natural manner; though, as the clown reappeared always the next day with his head on, looking quite as well as usual, he concluded, with his friend Barry, that it was only "make b'lieve," mere sleight of hand or mouth, the clever trick of a clever juggler— "though," added the speaker, with admirable gravity, "it certainly takes in everybody—everybody believes it."

"Drive on, Scipio," said the lady, imperiously, as if anxious to escape from the confiding, yet dubious gaze of Barry.

The carriage whirled away, Hammond and Henderson taking opposite sides, the former beside the window near which Geraldine sat, while his friend was the particular escort of the mother. We will leave them on their homeward progress, and return to our companions, Jones Barry and Tom Nettles.

These two worthies at once proceeded with proper diligence to business. Under the counsel of the latter, Barry employed, as the rider of "Glaucus," the little gypsy, who had lifted "Sorella" so handsomely over the track; and the result was an improvement in the events of the contest. But it is not our purpose to pursue the history of the turf at Hillabee. Ours is not a racing calendar, and we must leave such histories to those who are more perfect in the history of the stud. It is enough that we say that the day continued one of great excitement to the close. Some small winnings, at the winding up, served somewhat to console Barry for his heavier losses; and he was rendered particularly happy, as Tom Nettles introduced him to a couple of the chief men of the circus, by whom he was invited into the hippodrome itself, and permitted, while yet the day lasted, to behold the vacant scene upon which such wonders were so soon to be enacted. He was particularly anxious to get a sight of the clown, but did not express his desire; as he felt that one who was destined so shortly to swallow his own head might very naturally desire to have all the interval to himself, that he might prepare himself for the impending catastrophe. Here, a table being spread *extempore,* some cold baked meats were brought forth from a curtained interior; and, with the help of a ham and a loaf, which Nettles gathered from the booths of one of his acquaintance, and a stout quart-decanter of French brandy, which the equestrians had brought with them, Jones Barry was very soon reconciled to the absence of the ladies. The decanter was soon emptied and replenished, and this in time disappearing, the place was occupied by a couple of bottles of tolerable wine. Nettles was fond of strong drink, but he had one of those indurated heads which could bear any degree of *soaking* without betraying their owners. Jones Barry was much less of a veteran, though he loved good liquors, after a gentlemanly fashion. Enough, however, that, before he left the table, he had become captious and somewhat unruly; and it was only by adroit management that Nettles could conduct him out of the tabernacle, so as to afford to the manager an opportunity for preparing for the performance of the night. In the open air, Barry was more manageable, though it required an additional supply of stimulus to keep his stomach from entire subjugation to the hostile power which he had thrown into the territory. Nettles was not unwilling to indulge him. He was a fellow of fun, and found his capital in this excellent subject. He had set out to enjoy a *spree,* and he was resolved to make a night of it. An hour's wandering about the encampment, for such had the racecourse at Hillabee become for the occasion, and there were a thousand ways for getting up and letting off steam, to employ the slang phraseology of the region. Wagons were to be upset, drunken men stripped, the tails and manes of horses cropped; these, with other practices, in which the humorists were quite as "rough as ready," served to beguile the interval between the close of the race and the opening of the circus. But it was the fortune of Jones Barry to make himself conspicuous in a more important enterprise. The wanderings of our companions in search of adventures led them, with a crowd of others, to an amphitheatre, about three hundred yards from the race-course, where they witnessed a sport in progress, to which it seemed that all they had hitherto beheld was mere child's-play, tame and spiritless. This was a *"Gander-pulling!"*

Reader, do you know what a gander-pulling is? If you do not, it is quite as well that you should form some idea of the sources of pleasure to the purely vulgar and uncultivated nature. Man is undoubtedly a beast, unless you contrive some process for making him a gentleman; and there is no question but that, as he has a natural appetite for recreation and pleasure, if you do not contrive for him such as will not be unacceptable to the Deity, the devil will more liberally provide with such as will make the man acceptable only to himself. *Gander-pulling,* accordingly, is one of those sports which a cunning devil has contrived to gratify a human beast. It appeals to his skill, his agility, and strength; and is therefore in some degree grateful to his pride: but, as it exercises these qualities at the expense of his humanity, it is only a medium by which his better qualities are employed as agents for his worser nature. Gander-pulling has been described as a sort of tournament on horseback; the only difference is that the knight has a *goose* for his opponent, instead of a person like himself. The man is mounted on horseback, while the goose is mounted upon poles. These poles, or saplings, are thrust firmly into the ground, some twelve feet apart; but they are united by a cord at the top, which hangs loosely, while, pendent from the extremity, the living gander is fastened by the legs. Here he swings his head, hanging downwards just above the path, between the two saplings, and just high enough to be within reach of the man on horseback. The achievement of the rider is to run his horse, at full speed, at the bird, and, grasping him by the neck, to wring his head off as he passes on. This is not so easy a performance. The neck of the gander has been previously stripped of all its feathers, and has then been thickly coated with grease or oil. Nothing can be made more slippery; and, shining and warming in the sun, the glittering neck of the unhappy bird looks like that of a young boa, for the first time practising from the bough, under which he expects the rabbit or the rat to glide. To increase the difficulty of the exploit, and to prevent any unfair delay in the approach of the assailant, four men are stationed, armed with flails of hickory, on each side of the track, and at proper intervals. These, as the horse approaches, lay their hickories upon his flanks; and so unmercifully, as not only to make him go headlong forward, but frequently to make him bolt the track in order to escape such unfriendly treatment. The course is laid out on the exterior of a circle some two hundred feet in diameter; which circuit the rider must necessarily make before reaching the goose, starting from a post which is properly watched by judges. He is not expected to go at full speed except when within twenty yards of the game. Thus guarded, the victim is not so easily decapitated. It is only the experienced horseman, and the experienced sportsman, who can possibly succeed in the endeavor. Young beginners, who look on the achievement as rather easy, are constantly baffled; many find it impossible to keep the track; many lose the saddle, and, even where they succeed in passing beneath the saplings without disaster, they either fail altogether in grasping the goose, which keeps a constant fluttering and screaming; or, they find it impossible to retain their grasp, at full speed, upon the greasy and eel-like neck and head which they have seized. Meantime, their failure is by no means sauce for the gander. The tug, from which he at length escapes, makes him feel excessively uncomfortable while it lasts. The oil without does not protect him from severe sore-throat within. His voice becomes hoarse with screaming; and, long before his head is fairly off, he has lost those nicer sensibilities which teach him exactly how the event took place. The beating and bolting of the horses, the emptying of the saddles, the failures of the "pullers," the screams, and wild wing-flapping of the bird—these constitute the glory of the entertainment; every point in the tilting being watched with eager anxiety, and announced with screams and yells from the multitude, which form no bad echoes to the cries of the goose.

So much for the sport in general. It had been some time in progress, when Nettles and Jones Barry drew nigh. The moment the latter beheld the scene, he at once declared himself the man to take the gander's head. Nettles was very far from discouraging him from an adventure which promised fun; the more particularly as his companion, if not absolutely drunk, was, as they phrase it in Mississippi, "in a state of betweenity," i. e. neither drunk nor sober. A dozen had already tried their hands without success; but, evidently, to the perfect disquiet of the gander. There he swung aloft; his wings flapping furiously at intervals, and, every now and then, his throat pouring forth a sharp sudden scream, the moment he became conscious of a horse in motion. Barry fixed his eyes upon the shining neck, and shook his hands at the bird, the fingers spreading out, like claws, as he cried to the victim: "Here's the claws that'll have you off, my beauty! You're shining there for me! Who goes a V against Jones Barry? Who, I say? Let him show himself, and be ——!"

It is to the credit of Nettles that, though willing to see the fun, he would not suffer his companion to be fleeced. He interposed, that his bets should be trifles only, though, in this friendly interposition, he incurred the denunciations of the person whom he saved. Already had he paid for his "matriculation," and little Logan Whitesides was dispatched for "Glaucus;" for, though fuddled, Barry was not prepared to employ the "Fair Geraldine," his favorite, for such ignoble purposes.

"Hurrah for Jones Barry," said Ben Burg; "He ain't too proud to jine in the pleasures of the poor man!"

"He's jest drunk enough for any sort of pleasure, poor or rich," was the comment of Lazy Jake Owens.

"I'll lay you a quarter, Jake," said Burg, "that he'll take the gander."

"That'll be because he's near kin to him, then."

"If he does," said a third, "it'll be owing to his liquor. He couldn't do it sober."

"Shall we go a quarter on him?" said Burg; a conscientious feeling prompting him to vindicate, to this extent, the ability of a person from whom he had contrived to borrow a couple of half eagles but a few hours before.

"Make it a half, Burg."

"D-o-n-e!" said the latter, rather slowly.

The vulgar look with respect, even while they sneer, at the doings of those above them in fortune or position. It was the fortune of Jones Barry to provoke a sensation always among this class of people. They watched and waited his movements. The gander obtained a brief respite, while the boy went for "Glaucus"—settled down into a drooping quiet, and hushed for a period his screams. Our sprightly little gypsy was not long before appearing with the horse. He was ready saddled and bridled for the heat, and it was with more ambition than agility that our hero contrived to vault into the seat. Then it was that the uproar grew.

"Hurrah for Barry!" cried Nettles, at the top of his voice.

"Who goes a picayune against Barry?"

"Done, with you, 'Squire Nettles."

"And here's another! He's no more the chap to take off a gander's head than I am to put it on."

"Hurrah for the captain!" cried Burg.

"You may hurrah till your throat aches, but that goose will never catch that gander," was the unseemly echo of Lazy Jake Owens.

A hundred voices joined in the shouting. The boys rolled, and roared, and tumbled, throwing the dust up fifty feet in air, as the knight of the goose prepared to make his passage at arms. The men with the flails did not need to use their hickories. Barry came on at full speed, and, amidst shouts of congratulation, he kept his horse steadfast along the track, and through the saplings, from whose united tops the gander was suspended. The bird flounced and shrieked, flapping his wings with immense violence. Barry, dropping his bridle in his excitement, threw up both hands, and grasped, not the goose, but the rope by which it was suspended. The horse passed instantly from under him, and, for a moment, he hung in air, the wings of the gander playing the devil's tattoo rather rapidly upon his face, breast, and shoulders. It was but for an instant, however. The cord, calculated to sustain one goose only, broke under double weight, and down came the pair together, the gander uppermost. Never had such a scene been witnessed before, in the whole annals of gander-pulling, even from the first dawn of its discovery among our European ancestors. The field rang with shouts of merriment;

a most royal delirium seized upon the republican. Some rolled on the earth in convulsions; some clapped their hands and shouted; while the boys shot off their guns, to the great confusion and disorder of horseflesh.

Barry rose half-stunned and throughly bewildered. The gander had revenged himself on our luckless adventurer for all the assaults he had himself sustained. His wings had been busy, from the first moment of their encounter and fall, to that when the parties were separated, and chiefly upon the face of our hero. His cheeks were scraped rather than scratched; his nose and mouth were bleeding. His shirt bosom was equally torn and soiled, and his hair was lifted in as much disorder as was Job's when he beheld the vision of the night. Nettles came to his relief, and had his face washed, while little Logan Whitesides ran after and recovered the horse "Glaucus." Ludicrous as had been the scene, and much beyond any that the multitude had expected, they were still, now that the first burst of merriment was over, in no mood to lose their usual fun. The gander was re-hoisted, newly greased, and set aloft, screaming with new disquiet as he rose in air. There were twenty gallant youngsters all ready to undertake the feat at which Jones Barry had so ingloriously failed; but a proper courtesy required that he should be permitted to recover his laurels. But when the thing was proposed to him, he shook his head. He had not quite recovered from the unavoidable confusion of ideas which resulted from the twofold influence of the cognac and the concussion.

"No, I think not," said he. "Goose, eh! Nettles; we've had dinner." Such was the seemingly inconsequential reply; in which, however, Nettles detected the latent meaning.

"Yes," said he, "and ate very heartily, both of us; why should we want the goose?"

"Shall we go, Tom?" asked Barry, sobering by degrees, and feeling rather shamefaced.

"No!" said the other; "here's Meredith's wagon. He keeps good liquor; we'll take a consoler." And they went aside together to the wagon, where they both obtained an apple-toddy, the saccharine property being derived from the best mountain honey, while the apple-brandy was as good as ever filled up the corn-rows at election time. Barry felt better after the beverage, and the two returned to the gander-tournament together. The game was already resumed and in full blast. Three or four assailants had been baffled. But they usually came up a second and a third time to the scratch, the only discouraging circumstance which finally arrested their efforts being the repeated charges for new entries. The gander was one of fortunate fates; his owner was delighted to perceive that the instincts of the bird enabled him to anticipate the moment of danger, and to exercise his most rapid movements, just as the grasp was made upon his neck. He eluded several fingers; but some clutched him, and the "scrag" paid severely from the jerk which followed, even though it finally slipped from the gripe of the enemy. But his voice was suffering, and his action was greatly diminished. It was then that Nettles found himself plucked by the sleeve, and drawn aside by our gypsy boy, Logan Whitesides.

"Well! what now, Logan?"

"Why, Squire, ef you'll only ax the capper to let me ride 'Gloccus' at the gander, I'm a thinking I can ease off that head thar, ef 'twas never done afore."

Nettles found it no difficult matter to persuade Barry, and almost the next assailant of the goose was our urchin. He certainly looked less like one to "ease off the head" than those who had preceded him. He was the smallest of all the adventurers; rode squat, with a stoop, doubling up like a frog or monkey on the leap. But if he lacked in size, he was possessed of rare agility. He was all wire and spring; and, a fact not generally known, he had been trained to the sport in another county, and when much younger. His ability in riding we have already seen. Nettles was a judge of boys as well as horses.

"Who covers an X against little Logan Whitesides."

"I'll do that same," cried Lazy Jake Owens, and there were other customers for similar amounts. Nettles soon found that he had nearly a hundred upon the fate of the gander. It was not long in suspense.

"Go ahead, Logan!" was the cry of Nettles.

The boy obeyed him. The boys rushed after their hero with a shout. He himself shouted, and the descending flails of the men of hickory scarcely grazed the haunches of the fleetly-hurrying "Glaucus." In a moment, he had reached the foot of the scaffolding from the top of which hung the victim. The bird uttered tremendous screams, and flapped his wings wide and heavily. Then could the gypsy boy be seen to crouch, then to shoot upwards like an arrow, and the next moment he was through the saplings, bearing aloft the head, windpipe, and all of the gander but his body;—the segregated throat continuing to pour scream upon scream, convulsively, as the urchin waved the head of the bird in triumph over his own. The field shook with the uproar of rejoicing, and little Logan Whitesides promised to become the hero of the county. He won not a little in more solid coin than praises. He too had his bets abroad, and was calling in his fips and picayunes, his bits and quarters, from a considerable space around him, while Nettles, with equal satisfaction, was reminding sundry of his neighbors of a certain handsome letter of the alphabet whose name was X. Barry, too, was in a high state of exultation, for was it not his "Glaucus" by whom the victory was won?

CHAPTER IX.

HOW THE HERO OF THE CIRCUS MAY SWALLOW HIS OWN OR HIS NEIGHBOR'S HEAD.

ALTOGETHER, the events of the day had not tended to soothe the humors nor satisfy the self-esteem of Mr. Jones Barry. The first excitement over, by which even the defeated may be temporarily sustained, he began to reflect upon his losses. His favorite mare had been discredited; and though "Glaucus" had retrieved in the sweep-stakes the honor which he might have been supposed to have forfeited in the first races, yet this could in no respect compensate for the defeat of the "Fair Geraldine," coupled as was this defeat with the loss of several "cool hundreds." It was in due degree with the increasing soberness of Barry, that he began thus moodily to meditate events. The conflict with the gander, which had left him with a head and neck quite as sore as his moral feelings, had somewhat subdued his vanity; and he really began to think, as people had long since begun to say, behind his back, that he had been making a great fool of himself. Reflections such as these, were they allowed to continue, would probably almost always result in the improvement of the individual. But, in the case of weak persons, who have been accustomed to avoid and escape such reflections, and whom fortune and circumstances enable to do so, it is scarcely possible for such a mood of mind to continue long. There are always some good-natured friends in every fool's circle, to assist in keeping him a fool; and, by interposing at moments when self-esteem is beginning to be rightly humbled, they succeed in silencing the officious monitor, either by well-sugared falsehoods and specious flatteries, or by doing what our excellent sportsman, Tom Nettles, conceived it proper for him to do on the present occasion. He saw, as the effects of the apple-toddy subsided, that Jones Barry was about to sink into sullenness, which he regarded as a sort of stupidity; and he knew but one specific in all such cases, and that was to repeat the dose which had been found already so effectual; they stopped, accordingly, at a wagon on which they saw conspicuous a pine sapling above a barrel, and were soon gratified with the beverage they sought. The spirits of Barry rose with the draught. The effect was so pleasant that another was called for, and, by the time that the two had reached the entrance of the hippodrome, our brave gander-puller avowed himself as expert a rider on double horses as any fellow in the circus.

"It's true I've never seen 'em, Tom," said he, "but I've heard of them often enough. Joe Smith used to tell me of what he'd seen in Savannah and Augusta. Now, Joe used to say of my riding, I was fit to be in the circus. For a cool hundred now, I'd ride against the crack fellow of this company, who, I suppose, is no great shakes, and by ——, if they give me a chance to-night, I'll challenge the whole kit and boiling of 'em."

"Oh, you be k——d, Barry," said the other, irreverently: "you are the greatest brag I ever heard. Let yourself alone, and don't be trying to be everything. You're quite enough as you are. You are a good-looking little fellow."

"Little!" exclaimed Barry: "By gracious, Nettles, I'm as good a man as you are, any day."

"So you are, but not as big!"

"Little! But I don't suppose you meant any insult, Nettles, for you said 'good-looking' too."

"So I did! I say, you're a devilish good-looking little fellow; you're rich, and have everything you want. You *can* ride, though you're quite too heavy for 'Geraldine.' "

"Yet you say I'm little."

"Yes, little and not light. You see, you're a sort of chunk of a fellow, with more girth than legs, and a leetle too ambitious for your weight, Jones."

"You're mighty plain spoken, Tom."

"Why yes; friends have a privilege, you know."

"O yes—to be sure; but look you, Tom, I feel monstrous like licking the best friend in the world, when he calls me little."

"Well, you don't lick me, for two reasons; the first is, that I won't let you, and the next is, that you won't let yourself. But look you, Jones, this is dry talking, and I see you're in bad spirits; let's look after some good ones. There's a wagon there; I reckon we'll find something. Let's take another drink, and we'll be fresh for the circus."

"Agreed," said the other; and, as they rolled over to the opposite side of the road, amid a confused assemblage of carts, carriages, and wagons, the unsteady gait of Barry showed but too certainly that the apple-toddy had been already too potent for his perpendicular.

"Ride!" said he. "By gracious, Tom, I could straddle a barrel of peach, and make it streak away as fast as them circus fellows make their horses."

"Humph! If you go on at this rate, your swallow will be as good as the clown's, who means to take in his own head, you know."

"And you, Tom, you a fellow of sense, to believe that cock-and-a-bull story!"

"Believe what you please, but here's the liquor. Ho! there, Gerdts—that you?"

Nettles knew the whole country.

"What's left of me, 'Squire. But what'll you have? Here's mountain-peach, and here's apple."

"The apple, then, with a bed of honey for it to dream upon. I stick to the apple, Jones; I never mix my liquors if I can help it."

"What!" cried the other, with a grin; "afraid! Tom Nettles; afraid of two liquors! Halloo! there, old Gerdts, you don't know me; never mind; give me both; peach and apple; who's afraid? Equal parts, old still, and no slow charcoal dropping. Ease my eye, quickly; it's strained by the heavy sunshine."

Barry was becoming pleasantly perverse, and was in the very humor for all sorts of cross purposes. When conducted with some difficulty by his friend, they entered the amphitheatre where they had taken their dinner that day. The scene was now changed as if by magic. The place was thoroughly lighted, a perfect blaze of splendor, which showed, conspicuously clear, the remotest parts of the pavilion. The seats, which encircled three-fourths of the area, were occupied almost entirely. Our two friends were compelled to

take places on the lowest bench, and within a foot of the small rim
of earth which had been heaped up around the ring, rather as a
mark than a barrier. There was no fence to keep the spectators from
the track, and to check the erring vaultings of a vicious horse and an
inferior rider. The seats were divided into two great and equal
sections, one assigned to the whites and the other to the blacks. They
were raised (a rude scaffolding of plank) to the very eves of the
tent, and the heads of the visitors were in close neighborhood with the
shaking canvas. Hundreds of showy damsels, with ribbons and
feathers flying, might be seen, all impatience and sunny smiles, their
several gallants being eager in describing what they knew, and what
they anticipated. Many of these had come a great distance to the
sports of Hillabee; as, in ancient times, they flocked to the amuse-
ments of the tournament; and for the same reason, the equal desire
for recreation and novelty, and the want of great cities, which afford
these habitually. The *dress circle* was eminently well filled. The
girls and boys had crowded in from all parts of the country. Ancient
ladies, who had heard vague tidings of the circus, or had probably
had glimpses of such a vision in their youthful days, came hither
to revive old memories, or to gratify long-cherished desires. The old
gentlemen necessarily accompanied their wives and kindred. The
farmer was curious to see the reality of those spectacles of which
great pictures had already been made to adorn his hamlet, and
jockeys naturally came wherever the heroism of horseflesh could be
made to tell. The negroes were not less curious. Hundreds were in
attendance, from all quarters. They had trudged or trotted on foot,
on mule, in wagon, for ten or fifteen miles the night before, to see
sights and wonders. Each was in his best. Bright calicoes flamed on
every side, to the very summit of their circumscribed domain; and
all was hope and expectation, as Jones Barry and Tom Nettles made
their appearance, and scrambled to a seat.

They were not kept in waiting long. The spectacle soon began.
Horses, pied and spotted, and of all colors, made their appearance.
Children rode, women rode, the clown rode, and it was all sorts of
riding. Of course, we shall not pretend to describe a spectacle with
which everybody is more or less familiar. Journeys to Brentford,
Gilpin's race, and several other pieces were enacted. The equestrians

had their share of applause; but, after all, the glory of the spectacle was in that comical fellow, the clown. Buried in a grotesque and monstrous Egyptian mask, his face thoroughly concealed, and so artfully that its location could not exactly be determined, his voice seemed to come from some vaulted and hollow apartment below the ground. His antics were indescribable. His jugglery alone must demand our attention, as it somewhat involved one of our acquaintance. It happened that the scene required our clown to take wine with an African magician. He was momently expecting him, and he was proceeding to show the audience how he should bamboozle the magician, and finally "swallow his soul."

"Swallow his soul!" exclaimed Barry, in horror, to Nettles.

"He'll do it!" said the other, gravely. "You'll see."

"Here, now," exclaimed the clown, "is a brandy-cocktail in which I've buried Mumbo-Jumbo's soul. It's the most beautiful drink in the world; perhaps you'd like to try it?" said he, and he very courteously presented it to our two friends. Barry saw, as he fancied, some of the fine cognac of which he had partaken freely in that very place, on that very day; and, being exceedingly thirsty, he innocently and incontinently exclaimed—

"I don't care if I do—thank you!" Speaking thus, he rose and put forth his hand; but, by an adroit movement, throwing the long bunch of streamers from his fool's cap full in the face of our hero, the clown gulped down the beverage himself, exclaiming—

"Perhaps you'll wait till you can get it!"

The audience roared with delight. Furious at his disappointment, and the ridiculous figure which he cut, Barry at once *mounted* the clown; and, at the first grasp, tore away what seemed to be the entire head and neck of the unfortunate jester. With this terrible evidence in his clutches, he looked around him aghast, scarcely daring to guess the extent of his achievement. The clown, meanwhile, had retreated at the first assault, and before Barry could recover his wits and equilibrium, for he could not well anticipate a renewal of the conflict from one whose entire *caput* he carried in his hand, the mountebank, squatting low, darted between the legs of our hero; who had, in some measure, straddled the little circuit of earth by which the ring was circumscribed. The face of Barry was to the audience, and the assault of the clown surprised him. He was lifted from his feet before he apprehended danger; and his assailant, rising under his burden, which he did not seem to feel, trotted with him quite across the arena. Barry was thus carried forward horizontally, his head addressing the white, and his heels the negro portion, of the assembly.

"Tom Nettles—Tom!" was all that the poor fellow could articulate, but he screamed and kicked tremendously. His efforts were wasted on the air. The clown had only attained his great flexibility by exercises which had imparted the most wonderful power to his muscles, and Barry was but a child in his grasp. His struggle only increased the fun. The audience shrieked and howled with delight, in proportion to the futile efforts of the captive; and when they beheld the captor hurry with his prey to the negro side of the house, and saw him pitch the unfortunate gentleman headlong into the arms of a great fat negro wench, one of the most enormous in the assembly, who sat trickling with oleaginous sweat, on the third tier, one would have thought the whole pavilion would have come down with the delirious shouts of the multitude.

"Here's an abolitionist for you, mother Possum-fat!" cried the clown, as he plumped poor Barry into her embrace.

"I no want 'em!" cried the woman, shuffling herself free from the burden. Barry, rolling out of her lap, continued to roll down the successive tiers, until he came plump into the soft bed of sand and sawdust, which had been prepared for a very different animal. Furious with rage, he rose to his feet, and, seizing a pole with which one of the equestrians had been balancing, he darted headlong at the offending clown.

"Hurrah, red-jacket! Hurrah, clown!" were the several cries of the audience. "Hurrah, Captain!" was the more cordial shout of recognition and encouragement from those who personally knew our hero: "that's being into him with a long pole, indeed!"

But the clown had no idea of meeting such an enemy, armed in such a fashion; and, eluding the tremendous blow and thrust with which Barry addressed his ribs, he vaulted clear over the shoulder of the latter and disappeared behind the screen which sheltered the actor from the audience. His enemy thus out of sight, the furious champion proceeded to wreak his vengeance upon the inanimate objects around him. The scene in which the clown was to have tricked the African magician out of his soul was a most exquisite garden of Bagdad. There were stands of beautiful flowers, vases of great magnitude, statues, and several rich things by way of ornament and decoration, which, seen through the medium of distance, or by the aid of flickering lights, looked to be very precious. There was also a sort of close bower, a framework draped with silk, in which the cunning clown had placed a sleeping beauty. She was not the smallest part of the temptations with which the soul of the magician was to be entrapped. Barry, with his pole, had already thrown down one or two of the wooden flower-vases, with their precious contents, and his pole now descended upon the bower, which a single stroke served to precipitate to the ground. To the surprise of the assailant, not less than the assembly, up sprang from the ruins a most beautifully dressed damsel; young, pretty, and habited like a Sultana. It was fortunate, indeed, that the weight of the pole had not fallen upon her. But it has grazed sufficiently close to arouse all her fury; not waiting an instant, she darted upon our hero, and, drawing the little stiletto which she wore as a part of her Oriental costume, he might have been made to pay seriously for his frolic; for the rage of the woman was apparent in her closely set teeth and her fire-gleaming eyes. But Barry seized her arm, as she struck, and dropping his pole stood only on the defensive. The farce began to look greatly like tragedy. The enraged woman now shrieked and struggled. Her husband rushed out from the interior, armed with an axe. The clown again made his appearance, followed by the whole *troupe,* each seizing whatever weapon offered as he came. There were sailors, and Turks, and magicians, and even little Cupid's urchins, two feet high, whom papa and mamma were thus assiduously training in the way they should not go. These all confronted our unlucky jockey with the most uncompromising fury in their looks. He had spoiled the proceedings, thrown the assembly into the most admired disorder, and it was justice only that doomed him to a condign punishment. But, if they were formidable, Barry now no longer stood alone. Tom Nettles was by his side, and the long pole which Barry had discarded was in his grasp.

"Hillabee boys," he cried aloud, "bring out your hickories!"

Twenty vigorous youngsters sprang out at the summons, and ranged themselves on the side of the amateurs. Great clubs of knotted hickories were already flourishing high; and, forgetting his late danger, Jones Barry already felt that he was a hero. He still maintained his grasp upon the Sultana, and seemed disposed to carry her off as the captive to his bow and spear, when the cool voice of Nettles commanded him to let her go. He did so; and the sleeping beauty, now wide awake, darted into the arms of the magician, who was her husband, upon whose bosom she sobbed convulsively, as at a providential escape from a great danger. Thus the parties stood, confronting each other; both looking firm and fierce enough, and threatening trouble. Not only did the whole *troupe* of equestrians range themselves for battle under the leadership of the clown, but one of the horses coolly marched in, covered with panoply, and, thrusting his head over that worthy's shoulder, seemed to promise him sufficient backing, and in truth looked very formidable. It was a scene; the clown, as a matter of course, opposed himself to Barry, who, armed with a pole, looked aghast at the twofold conflict before him, in the threatening aspect of both horse and rider. But Nettles fortunately knew the head men of the company. He said—

"My friends, this is altogether a mistake, which I can easily explain, and, I trust, easily reconcile. There's no fun in fighting, though we're by no means afraid, as you may see, to meet any number of men or horses. But there's no real cause of quarrel between us; and if you're agreed, we'll separate our forces. The boys of Hillabee will retire to their seats, keeping their hickories warm, lest we should want them again; and the gentlemen of the circus will go on with their exercises as before. In the mean time, Mr. Barry and myself will retire with the manager here, and we'll adjust the difficulty in private together." A suggestion so politic was acceptable to all parties, though, once on the ground, the Hillabee boys did not relish the idea of returning without having done something glorious by way of showing how well their destructive faculties had been developed. Barry was a little scrupulous about entering the mysterious sanctum to which the clown and the Sultana had retired, but, having great confidence in Nettles, and being assured by the great coolness and confidence of the latter, he followed him and the manager into the place of retreat. Here he found himself amidst a motley group. Horses were staring them in the face on all hands. Some of the equestrians were already mounted. Here in one corner was a trunk and box; there a table and chair; and there a chest; and there a bundle; and there the uniform of a giant; and there the dozen masks and jackets of the clown. There, too, recovered from the dust and danger of the arena, was the unlucky colossal mask and headdress which our hero had torn off from his enemy at the first encounter. Nettles walked in with the air of a man perfectly at home.

"And now," said he, "Diavolo," addressing the clown, "let us begin the work of peace, as you begun the war. Prepare us one of those excellent brandy cocktails with which you tempted my friend to desperation. Had you known the diabolical thirst that's been troubling both of us the last three hours, you'd have known 'twas quite as much as your head was worth to mock us with anything half so delightful. Quick, now; and let there be peace between us!"

The arrangement promised to be satisfactory to all parties. The cocktails were speedily prepared; prepared in a nice-looking, brass-bound bucket, of dimensions to guarantee a sufficient taste of the beverage for all the *troupe*. The bowls were filled; hands were shaken; eyes glistened; and, with the consent of the magician, his lovely Sultana freely bestowed the kiss of peace upon our hero. The example was gratuitously followed by the clown, whose embrace and salutation were distinctly stamped upon the front of Barry, in unequal decorations of vermilion and burnt cork. Their embraces seemed to affect the dextrous Tom Nettles with a serious delight.

"How beautiful," said he, "is it to behold brethren thus dwelling in amity together! What a spectacle! It is necessary that the audience should see it; that they should see that this is no mockery; but that the foes have freely exchanged forgiveness. Another draught from the bucket, gentlemen," said he, addressing Barry and the clown, "and then go forth that the people may witness those beautiful embraces."

Barry had no scruples about the dram, but he rather hung back at the proposal for the embrace in public. His reluctance disappeared with the draught. He swore that Diavolo was the best fellow in the world, and made the finest cocktails; and, with an arm about each other's waist, each bearing a cocktail in hand, they emerged from the canopy into the area, and drank to each other, and the audience. If war exulted in the previous scene, philanthropy was proportionally happy now. The audience were ravished. The old ladies wept. The old men thought it just as well; and the negroes were perfectly well satisfied; wondering only a little to behold a man drinking with such a capacious swallow, who had so recently been deprived of his head. All seemed perfectly well satisfied but young Hillabee, from whom some discordant hisses were heard to rise, while the unemployed hickories were made to clatter against the sides of the benches.

"There's a drop yet in the bucket," whispered the clown to his new comrade. The hint was not lost upon Barry. He returned to the sanctum, where he found his friend Tom Nettles. There they remained till the performances were over, and the crowd departed; when they were invited to a hot supper with the *troupe*, in the great area of the pavilion. The invitation was not to be disregarded. The equestrians lived well; and Barry and his friend were both hungry. But, were it not so, the wishes of the latter would scarcely have had any weight upon our delighted hero. He *had* been the hero of the night, though after a somewhat doubtful fashion, it is true; but he had been conspicuous, and had come out of the scene with applause. Of course, he could not doubt that it was his appearance which was so warmly welcomed when he had come forth in the embraces of the clown. The clapping and shouting seemed to him the most grateful sounds to which he had ever listened; and the brandy cocktails were the most delicious of mortal beverages. It was a night of glorification. The supper-table was spread. His friend was placed on one side of the manager; he occupied the other. Beside him, sat the lovely wife of the magician, whose graciousness never even provoked the frowns of her mysterious lord. At first, Jones Barry felt a little squeamish on this subject. When she gazed so tenderly in his eyes, and suffered her finger to rest so impressively on his wrist, he felt a dubiousness, and looked his doubts at the husband. But he knew not the indifference of professional magic to those mortal subjects. The latter saw everything without discomposure; and, after a little turn of hesitation and doubt, our hero delivered himself up, soul and body, to all the intoxication of a conviction that he had won the heart of this most beautiful of all the creatures of Faery. They drank together, and whispered together. The hours waxed late. Barry sang a comic song, at the instance of Nettles, and, at the conclusion, was more delighted than astounded, as his Sultana, throwing her arms about his neck, and seating herself in his lap, in the face of all the assembly, called him the finest little fellow in the world. He did not know how he should recompense such devotion, but by forcing a great ring from his upon her finger. She coyly suffered him, in a moment after, to transfer the diamond breastpin from his to her bosom. He put it there himself; and all this the magician saw without seeming to regard it as in any wise improper. The next morning, Barry found himself where he had supped, sleeping upon one of the benches, with a bundle of straw under his head, and one of the horse-cloths, green and scarlet, spread above his body. Tom Nettles, as he opened his eyes, was to be seen standing with the manager at a little distance, and mixing a couple of rosy anti-fogmatics.

CHAPTER X.

THE HUMORS OF THE CIRCUS.

BARRY was not the man to suffer from headaches; but his stomach was one that needed to be fortified by tonics. The sight of his friend, when he discovered the occupation in which he was engaged, fully aroused him. He was on his feet in an instant, jerking up his trousers, and approaching Nettles with the haste of a person who fears that he may come too late. But there were some particulars in which Nettles never abandoned his companion. He was emphatically what young people call "a good fellow," and good fellowship implies the necessity of assisting your friend and facilitating his ready attainment of all desirable indulgences. In making an anti-fogmatic for himself, he had not forgotten his comrade. There was a huge vessel before him, where the beverage stood in waiting, and Tom, Jones Barry, and the manager of the amphitheatre, were soon engaged in a hob-a-nobbing match that didn't stop at a single stoop. Barry declared himself quite happy. He had enjoyed a pleasant dream of the magician's wife, and he naturally inquired after her.

"Look in," said Tom Nettles, with a smirk to the manager which Barry did not perceive, while he pointed the latter to the sanctum where the reconciliation had taken place the night before. Without a moment's hesitation, our little hero followed the finger, and found himself in the lady's dressing-room, her toilet only begun, and she, in the most loose undress in the world, employed before the broken mirror which hung from one of the uprights of the tent. Barry was astounded, and would have started back; but she saw him in the glass, and, wheeling round, at once summoned him, though in the very sweetest accents, to approach.

"You are just in time," said she; "I wanted somebody to lace my jackets."

"Jackets!" exclaimed Barry, aghast.

"Yes, to be sure! Come now, you're a nice little fellow, I know. Let me see—you have small fingers. Show yourself diligent, and help me to fix myself. That man of mine never gives me any assistance. There he sleeps. Look at him. He will snore till noon, and never fairly wakens till it's time to dress for the performance."

She pointed to the end of a wagon that appeared under a corner of the tent, from which, sure enough, the ears of Barry detected a very decided snore. But this did not encourage him. He was utterly astounded at the new duty required at his hands. In all his experience, he had never before laced a woman's corsets—or unlaced them; and he scarcely knew how to understand the Sultana. But seeing his hesitation, Sultana-like, she stamped her little foot, and repeated her orders. She did not leave him long doubtful that she was in earnest.

"Come," said she, "what do you wait for? Is it because you're bashful? Well! at *your* age! But you needn't be, here! We know a thing or two! we've no false modesty here, I assure you. A leg's a leg, with us. We talk plainly, and are not the worse for it. We don't make a fuss about shadows as long as we keep the substance; and indeed, it's only those who have lost the substance that do. Come, stir yourself, and there's a kiss to begin with, by way of recompense."

A few moments found our hero awkwardly busy with the waist of the Sultana. While thus engaged, the manager and Tom Nettles came in.

"That woman," said the manager aloud, "has tired out every member of the *troupe* in lacing her. She will have her waist brought within the narrowest compass, and she breaks her cords daily in trying to make it smaller. There's not a hand among us that she has not made sore in the abominable work, and now she takes to our visitors."

"And why not?" said the Sultana, with the air of the orient. "Is he not rewarded? It is not often he is permitted to study a good model."

"A little too round, madame," said the manager.

"Too round!" screamed the Sultana.

"Not a bit," said Tom Nettles, coolly interposing to span the waist. "An exquisite union of symmetry and strength."

"Strength!" demanded madame.

"Yes, to be sure; strength is necessary to grace, even in a woman. It's the mistake of too many of the sex that an air of feebleness is supposed to imply delicacy. It is rather the reverse. I wish to see vigor with grace; and a woman ought to seem as capable of a fine wrestle as of a fine sentiment."

"I've a great mind to trip your heels for that," said the Sultana, pertly.

"And if I am to take a fall, I should wish for no worse embrace than yours. But I leave Barry to the danger. He's a better wrestler than myself, and it strikes me that his lacing begins to look much more like hugging. Beware, Jones, or I'll tell your sweetheart."

Barry blushed to the roots of his hair.

"Has he a sweetheart? Is he in love?" demanded the Sultana.

"The danger is that he is in love with more than he can manage. Yesterday he loved but one woman. What lessons you have taught him, since that time, may be guessed from the way he performs the present operation. His lacing is very like embracing; and, if he goes on at this rate, he'll be for a wrestle in earnest."

"And if he is," said the magician, suddenly thrusting his head upward from the tail of the wagon, "I'll engage that Nell can throw him, or any man in company."

"Nell! Oh, you wretch!" cried the Sultana. "Nell!" She was Madame Zerlina, in the bill of the performance. "Was ever such a monster! How he takes a woman's name in vain! Do some of you give him his dram, his phlegm-cutter, his antifogmatic, or whatever else he calls it, that he may sober himself to a civil way of speaking."

"Ay, Nell, bring it yourself."

The wife seized a tumbler that stood on a chest beside her, and held it to Nettles, who filled it from the flagon which had been brought in by the manager. She darted away the next moment to her magician, without seeming to remember that Barry, who, in his clumsiness, was still busy at the strings of her bodice, was compelled to follow after her, or lose the ends of the cord which had been confided to his care.

"There, you!" she cried, thrusting the drink into his clutches.

"Isn't she a beauty?" said the magician, with a leer to Barry, as he took the liquor. Barry could only smile and simper, and look silly.

"Beauty!" said she; "too much of a beauty for you. That's the way he flatters a woman, with Beauty! Beauty! on his lips, said half-asleep, and his mouth opening on the quart-pot, which alone made him waken up. You don't talk of my beauties now, but you feel them."

"Yes, indeed," said Nettles, "and he'll stay feeling them all day if you'll let him."

"Oh, Tom!" murmured Barry with a grin.

"Don't you mind him," said the Sultana. "Have you done now. There!" she exclaimed, wheeling about and grasping the unsuspecting Barry in her arms, giving him an embrace, before releasing him, that half took away his breath. "There, that's your reward. It isn't often a fine woman bestows a squeeze upon her sweetheart, and I only do it now to show you what your friend means, when he says that the beauty of a woman means vigor as well as grace. If you'd like to try the wrestle after the squeeze, say the word, and I'm ready for you."

"And I'll go a hundred on Nell against the field," cried the husband, from the wagon.

"Oh, beast there, with your Nell," cried the heroine, indignantly. "I've done everything, I've even thrashed him, to teach him good manners, but it's so much love and labor thrown away."

"But how about the wrestle? Who takes me up?" demanded the husband. The Sultana herself looked about her with the eye of a challenger. She was still only dressed in part, and her fine bust and figure afforded not a bad idea of Cleopatra. Her breasts seemed breaking through the very partial restraints upon them, and her arms, partly bare, were admirably white and rounded, revealing that equal union of muscular and flesh development which crowns the person with strength, without lessening its beauty. By this time, however, the admiration of Jones Barry had in some degree given way to misgivings and apprehension. His sense of the beauty of the woman was somewhat impaired by his disquiet at her boldness. The privileges to which he had been admitted had certainly shown no warmth or feeling on her part, and, in fact, she had treated him rather like a boy than a man. He was awed and abashed by her manners, rather than delighted with her charms; and the single squeeze which she had so gratuitously bestowed upon him was quite sufficient to satisfy him, without desiring the wrestle. He accordingly said nothing, while Nettles, with exemplary coolness, quietly re-marked that "he, perhaps, should have no serious objection to the trial, could he be sure of *fair* play, but as he had never found that from a woman yet, he was not disposed to incur any unnecessary risk."

By this time one of the subordinates made his appearance, announcing breakfast in the amphitheatre. Nettles gallantly assisted the lady in completing her toilet, and this affair adjusted, he gave her his arm, and conducted her into the temple. He was followed by Barry, who felt nothing but envy at the ease and readiness with which his friend performed the duties of the courtier. The equestrians played the part of hosts with great liberality and good-humor, and the meal lingered for more than an hour, in which, while the cates were various and ample, they constituted but a minor portion of the attraction. The coolness, readiness, great resource, experience, and anecdote of these performers furnished an unfailing subject of wonder to Barry. They seemed to know everything about the world, and some of them seemed quite at home on the subject of books. Zerlina, our Sultana, or "Nell," as the magician, her husband, persisted in calling her, was quite a dabbler in literature. She was read in the dramatic poets, and had an ambition for the stage, which some mysterious influence prevented her from seeking to gratify. She made frequent exhibitions, at the entreaty of Nettles, of her powers, while reading favorite passages, and thus increased the degree of awe and admiration which Barry already entertained for her. Her civilities were somewhat less free than they had been the night before, but they were still such as a matron might readily bestow upon a moderately grown boy. Poor Barry, though pleased with much of this sort of petting, was yet humbled by it! and it was with something of a feeling of relief that he received a hint from Nettles that it was time to depart. The *troupe* were to exhibit another night at Hillabee, as the multitude, though diminished, was still sufficiently large to compensate the performance. There were extem-porary races throughout the day, but generally with common horses. To these neither Barry nor Nettles greatly inclined, and their separation from their hosts of the hippodrome was pretty much a leave-taking of the field. Nettles had known the manager, the magician, and the fair Zerlina, some time before, and they parted as old friends. The Sultana squeezed Barry's hands with a frank earnestness, as she bade him good-by, telling him he was a nice fellow, and she should always remember him by his gifts, pointing to his ring and breastpin. It was with a twinge that our hero heard this speech. He thought sulkily of the half-maudlin tenderness of the night before, in which he had been beguiled of jewels that he would prefer to see on very different fingers. The thoughts of Nettles, in some degree, took the same direction with his own. As they rode together homeward, and when they had fairly emerged from contact with the multitude, the former, with a quizzical smile, said to Barry—

"I say, Jones, what the d——l would your sweetheart, the fair Geraldine, have said, could she have seen you sitting in the lap of our Nelly, eh?"

"I didn't sit in her lap, Tom; she sat in mine."

"So much the better for the sight! What would she have said, or what could you have said, had she suddenly plumped in upon you when Nelly was in your lap, her arm about your neck, and giving you that smack of the lips, which seemed to you like wine from heaven? You got drunk almost instantly after it. You hugged her like a hero, until she couldn't stand it any longer, and broke away, as if she feared some harm from her magician husband."

"Oh! I didn't, Tom. Now don't you be telling that nonsense about."

"How can I help it, Jones, my good fellow? The joke is quite too good to be lost. For the one smack, the moment you had tasted it, you gave her a dozen, till she gave in and cried ' 'nough! 'nough!' as fervently as the fellow whose sockets are filling fast with sand from his enemy's fingers; and such a squeeze about the body that she fairly heaved again, though pretty well used to tight bracing."

"Never, Tom; never!"

"But it's a true bill, Jones. Then, you sung a comic song; and, in trying to get on the table for a Virginny reel, you slipped over into the sawdust, and lay there with a gurgle in your throat, as if you were trying to drink and sing at the same moment. You don't know, I suppose, who laid you out upon the benches?"

"No, Tom, I don't."

"Who, but Nell and myself? She took your arms, and I your feet, and we swung you up, saying, all the while—

'Warn ye once, warn ye twice,
Warn ye thrice, and away,
And away, and away, ye go!'

She brought the horse-cloth and spread over you, and the clown delivered a sermon over you, in which he said that, though a small man, your skin and stomach were capable of stretching to a brandy cocktail as readily and extensively as those of any man he ever saw; and not one of us said a word against it. You were treated gloriously, Jones, and you were glorious; but what would the fair Geraldine say to it all?"

"By gracious, Tom, she musn't hear of it!"

"Had she only seen you lacing the jackets! Ha! ha! ha!"

"Tom, my dear fellow. Tom Nettles"—

"Looking for all the world like a great boy, with his big eyes spreading at the sight of an apple-tree filled with fruit, yet trembling to think of the steel-trap lying quiet in the grass below. Oh! Jones, Jones, if ever a man looked at a woman greedily, it was you, this morning."

"Now, Tom! Tom! Don't! Never!"

"I'll swear it! You did! Jones, I'm afraid you're a bad fellow among the women. You ought never to think of Geraldine Foster. She, at least, ought never to think of you. You don't deserve her. She's too good for you. You'll make a bad husband. And I can't think of suffering her to marry in the dark. She must know—"

"Tom, my dear fellow. Honor bright! But, I see you're only joking."

"Joking, indeed! No! no! There's only one thing that will prevent me from interfering, and that is—" He paused.

"Eh! What?"

"That there's no sort of use for it, as there's no sort of danger that she'll ever marry you."

"And why not, I wonder?"

"Why not! When you prefer to stay here at a horserace, to seeing her home. When you let her go off under the escort of your rivals, while you go a gander-pulling. When the circus is more grateful to you than her company; and when, not content with the performances of other people, you take another man's wife into your lap, and—"

"But, Tom, she don't know; she won't know—"

"These things are sure to leak out; and when it's known that you gave this pretty woman your ring and breastpin, and promised to remember her as long as you lived—"

"No, I'll be k——d if I did."

"And I'll be k——d if you didn't!" responded the tormentor.

"Tom, by the blazes, you're no friend of mine, or you wouldn't talk so. But, I know you of old. You only do it to worry me. You won't blab."

"Well, suppose I don't? What chance do you stand with the fair Geraldine when you neglect her so, and when you have such chaps as Ran. Hammond and Miles Henderson against you?"

"I don't care a curse for Hammond. She shows him less favor than all the rest. She's cross to him; and, for that matter, it don't seem to me that he cares a curse for her."

"Don't you believe it!"

"Well! let him come. It costs nothing, and it comes to nothing. She don't care for him."

"I'm not so sure of that!"

"She don't show it, at least. She's more shy of him, by far, than she is of me or Henderson."

"The shyness is in his favor. Was Nelly shy of you? No, indeed! She'd kiss you in sight of fifty people. But, you only be saucy, more than she is prepared to suffer, and she'd as soon dirk you as drink. This very shyness of Geraldine Foster shows a feeling that she wants to hide. It's the same as saying, 'This man is something to me.' He has an effect upon her, and let him but pursue—"

"But he don't pursue."

"He don't! You don't know Ran. Hammond; and I tell you, Jones Barry, that if any man of you three ever marries that girl, it's Ran. Hammond. I know something of him, and I know something of woman, and if he isn't already as deep in her heart as you were in your cups last night, though without getting drunk by it, then I'm not one of the Nettles family."

"Well! that's speaking sure; for you *are* one of the Nettles family, and make yourself known wherever you go for a real son of the bush, if it's only by the feeling you produce. But you don't raise my skin, Tom; for, between us, I feel pretty sure that the game is to be mine."

"Ah! Ha! well!"

"The mother promises me—"

"The mother! You're more likely to marry the mother than the daughter. But it isn't the mother, exactly; and Mrs. Foster has no such influence over her husband's child as to say how that cat shall jump. If ever there was a woman who had a will of her own, it's that girl Geraldine Foster. I'm thinking that the mother favors you; but I don't believe she can do much for you, unless the daughter is a weaker vessel than I think her."

"Well! only you don't blab about this circus business, Tom—"

"I don't know how I can keep in, Jones. It's too good."

"Oh, by gracious, Tom, you must! I'll be hanged if I wouldn't fight my own brother, if he told upon me."

"Yes, but you'd hardly fight me, Jones, for you know I'd kill you; and then you'd lose your fortune, your sweetheart, and everything else. No! you won't fight me, Jones; and if you talk in that sort of way, I shall have to come out with the story. I'll have to go to Mrs. Foster. I'll have to say, I must see Miss Geraldine. Then, I'll up and show her about the lap, and the squeeze, and the kisses, and the lacing, and the—"

"Tom, stop! By gracious, you must stop. Here's somebody coming after us!"

The conversation, thus interrupted, it is not our object to pursue. Nettles had no other purpose in what he said than to annoy his companion, though the opinions which he expressed with regard to the superior chances of Hammond in the pursuit of Geraldine Foster, in comparison with the two competitors, were honestly entertained. He dined that day with Barry, who kept bachelor's hall, and who recurred to the subject after dinner. Here again Nettles repeated his opinion. Barry did not seem satisfied that he should do so; and, in the course of the conversation, betrayed something of a hostile feeling towards Hammond, which the other was surprised that he should entertain.

"Somehow," said he, "he crosses me at every step. He bought that place of Wingard's, though he knew I wanted it—"

"But didn't he want it too?"

"I suppose he did, but—"

"But you overslept yourself, having been drunk at my house the night before, and didn't get to the sale in time."

"Yes, true! and the fellow got it for half the money I was willing to give."

"More lucky for both of you, perhaps."

"Then he gives Miles Henderson this bloody mare, that takes 'Geraldine' off her heels—"

"But you bought 'Geraldine' after he had given 'Sorella' to Miles—"

"That's true; but he advises him to run her, and tells him how to do it."

"He did one and not the other, and did only what any other might have done, and nobody have cause to be angry. The truth is, Jones, you are in too bad a humor to do Ran. Hammond justice."

"And if, as you say, he stands the only chance with Geraldine Foster, sha'n't I have good cause to be in a bad humor? Now, you see, though you prove to me that all his influence upon my successes comes up naturally enough, yet, somehow, when you find a man always in your way—taking the start of you himself—helping his friends to do so—crossing you at this, and beating you at that—the worse from his not *trying* to do so; it looks as if he were your born enemy. You can't help feeling as if he was. But, I tell you, I'll not stand much more crossing; and some of these days, if things get worse, Ran. Hammond and Jones Barry will have to ask the question, before witnesses, which is the better man."

"Pshaw! pshaw! You haven't drank quite enough, Jones, for a sensible judgment in this matter. A few glasses more will give you the right pitch for thinking. Now, let me tell you, I won't have you make a judy of yourself in this fashion. Hammond's a man whom you'll do well to have no quarrel with. He's an ugly customer. He'll be slow to take his gripe—won't do it, as long as he can decently help it; but when he does, he takes hold like a bulldog, and never lets go till his teeth meet in the flesh. You're a fool, Barry. You have fortune, and good liquors; enjoy yourself in all sorts of ways; keep blooded horses and run races; a fine parcel of gamebirds, and enjoy the cockpit like the Napoleon of Mexico. You keep the best of wines, and are not afraid to drink them; you can ride, run, and fight, and enjoy yourself in all three ways, in one day—now with a goose, and now with a clown; and have, besides, a devilish keen eye for the women, so that you'll be thinking of one seven miles off, while another's in your lap."

"No more of that, Tom; pass the bottle; and if you say so, we'll send out for a few larks and make a night of it."

"Agreed; a night of it."

CHAPTER XI.

LEAVING our good companions to make a night of it, let us follow the footsteps of the party from which we turned to pursue the more devious progress of the pair with whom we have so long loitered. We have seen that the ladies were well attended in their departure from the race-course. On this ride, our two gallants necessarily did their utmost to make themselves agreeable. Without being in anywise remarkable for his talent, Miles Henderson was a very pleasing and amiable gentleman. He could converse rationally and gracefully, but without ever rising into those subjects, or those portions of a subject, upon which, to converse well, most persons must first have learned to think independently for themselves. But, in the ordinary language of commonplace and society, Henderson could always be respectable; and, being an observing man, he had gathered a sufficient supply of material for chitchat to enable him, usually, to prove interesting to ordinary companions. We have seen him taking that side of the carriage upon which sat Mrs. Foster. This lady was comparatively young. She had succeeded to the arms and name of Mr. Foster at early womanhood, and when he needed a nurse rather than a wife. She had survived him, without altogether surviving her youth. A good natural constitution, vulgar health, a lively temper, and an exquisite feeling of satisfaction with herself, had served to keep her in good bodily condition. She was, in other words, a buxom widow, fair, fat, and forty; who did not wholly forget herself in taking care of the fortunes of her step-daughter. She was vain and giddy; and, though satisfied that the devotion of Miles Henderson, not less than that of Randall Hammond, was wholly given to Geraldine, she was not the less satisfied with the external homage which she incidentally received in consequence. Sometimes, indeed, she seemed to forget the claims of her step-daughter wholly, and exhibited a degree of satisfaction at these attentions of the suitors, and an anxiety to monopolize them, which frequently occasioned a smile among these parties. It was one of her causes of dissatisfaction with Hammond, that he never suffered her to misconstrue his attentions. Approaching her always with profound civility, his address and style of conversation, when directed to her, were never of a kind to suffer her to be in any degree forgetful of the fact that she had a daughter as well as Jephthah; and the way to have won the heart of such a woman was to have shared with her, in some degree, a portion of that devotion which most women value beyond all other possessions, even where they do not design to secure or keep the worshipper. Hammond, perfectly aware of her character, knew exactly what she wanted. But he was too proud a person to make any sacrifices to her vulgarity or vanity. He was one of those men who feel that the course of true love not only does not usually, but that it cannot, in the nature of things, often run smoothly; and felt sure that a portion of his triumph must ensue from the capacity of his future wife to rise, through affection, superior to the discouragements of prejudice and domestic opposition. He was, perhaps, not unwilling to be known to Geraldine through the medium of doubts which nothing but real affection would attempt to overcome; and some knowledge of her character persuaded him, indeed, that this was really the most politic course for the attainment of his object. Accordingly, we have seen him betraying what would seem a degree of indifference to the game, which he did not feel. He showed no anxiety to take or keep possession of the field; no feverish desire to hold his ground in the presence of rivals; but, on the contrary, a calm and courteous readiness to share all his opportunities with others; and, indeed, to forego them wholly on occasion, giving way to the advances of those who were notoriously his rivals. Mrs. Foster was greatly at a loss, for a while, to understand the policy of this seeming indifference; but her instincts enabled her to discover the truth, which her reasoning faculties never could have attained; the more particularly as she found that Geraldine Foster, flattered by the constant devotion of her suitors, was somewhat piqued by the dignified refusal of Hammond to engage in the common struggle. With a vulgar policy, the mother's object now was to impress upon our heroine an idea of the arrogance of Hammond; his pride, which refused the ordinary civilities which all lovers are prepared to bestow; and an insolent consciousness of superiority, which made him always anxious to deny the service which gallantry, and a sincere affection, would be only too happy to perform. His refusal to run his horse at Hillabee, as we have seen, was one of the instances which she found to produce the desired impression upon the mind of her *protégé*. To a certain extent she had succeeded in producing this impression. The proud and haughty spirit of Geraldine Foster, conscious of her charms, and accustomed to the devotion of the other sex, and the envy of her own, was mortified at the little seeming power which she possessed over almost the only man whom she had ever really desired to subdue. She felt his strength, his superiority. Her attention, when he spoke, acknowledged it; her anxiety for his coming declared it, even to herself; and the growing feeling of her dependence upon him made his apparent indifference only the more offensive to her vanity and painful to her heart. The step-mother had worked, not unsuccessfully, upon these feelings; but Geraldine was so much a creature of impulse that the work of months might be undone in a moment. A happy accident might bring the lovers together in explanation, and mutual sympathies, suddenly rendered active, and seeing under the influence of favoring circumstances, might render the determined will of Geraldine such an ally of her heart as to defeat forever the subtle designs of the hostile mother. It was the game of the latter, therefore, to provoke disgust in the mind of the girl, to annoy her pride into resentment; and, seizing upon some particular moment of mortification, to force her into engagements which should be fatal to the hopes of Hammond. Her labors to this point had produced pique only, and not disgust in the bosom of Geraldine; and this feeling, Mrs. Foster had the sense to understand, was rather favorable than otherwise to the hopes of the lover. It declared his possession of a power, already, in the heart of the capricious beauty, which felt his neglect rather as a loss and a denial, than as provocation of scorn; and the step-mother trembled as she saw that it was far easier for Geraldine to feel the alleged neglect and indifference of Hammond than to defy or to resent it.

If he was not altogether conscious of the sort of game Mrs. Foster was disposed to play and was playing, his own was one that tended greatly to overcome and baffle it. His plan of operations has been already sufficiently described. It consisted simply in the maintenance of the most dignified civilities, and in foregoing no courtesies, in performing them with a grace as perfect as possible, and in studying how to interest the object of his attentions, without seeming to be engaged in any such study, or to possess any such interest. If the plan was wisely conceived, it was as dextrously carried out. Randall Hammond was no ordinary man. He was a person, emphatically, of character; with a strong will and fiery passions; but a stern, methodical, and well-ordered judgment, which enabled him to subdue himself at the required moment, and reject from his eyes all the disguises of prejudice, and from his tongue all the impetuous resolves of passion. He was never more fortunate in his game than when escorting the ladies from Hillabee. We have seen with what temper both of them left the ground. Mrs. Foster, quite dissastified with the results of the racing—as they not only left her favorite beaten, but proved the correct judgment of Hammond in an exercise in which he did not himself indulge; and Geraldine, piqued and offended at the perverted language reported of Hammond, so conclusively confirming the representations of Mrs. Foster, and so disrespectful, seemingly, to Geraldine herself. Hammond soon discovered that something was wrong, and having sufficient clues to the character of Mrs. Foster, and perfectly aware of her feeling for himself, he readily understood that the mischief was in her. But there was no way to make a direct issue, and he was not one of that feverish race who refuse to leave anything to time. He was content to pursue his own game as if nothing had happened, and to make himself agreeable in spite of his enemy. His resources were all accordingly put in exercise, and even Henderson wondered at the exhibition of conversational powers which he never dreamed that his friend possessed. But friends are generally the last to appreciate the powers of one another, since they seldom recognize those feelings of mutual provocation by which alone they can be made to develop themselves. Gradually, Geraldine forgot her pique and disquiet, in the delight which she experienced at the racy remark, the keen point, the pleasant anecdote, contained in the conversation of her companion; and it was with feelings of vexation, at beholding a progress that she could not prevent, that Mrs. Foster threw herself back in the carriage, and surrendered herself to a protracted spell of silence and bad humor, answering Henderson only in monosyllables, and compelled, in spite of herself, to listen to the dialogue which seemed equally to show the indifference of both the parties to all her intrigues.

The cavalcade reached the residence of Mrs. Foster in this manner: Geraldine, if not perfectly reconciled to Hammond, forgetting for the moment all her causes of complaint; Miles Henderson a little dulled by what he saw of the success of his friend, but reconciled to his own apparent decline of fortune by the conviction that his fortunate rival was indeed his friend; while Mrs. Foster brooded over other schemes for fomenting anew the displeasure of her step-daughter.

"Foster Lodge" was a place of considerable beauty. The immediate approach to it was through a broad avenue, nearly a mile in length, guarded and overshadowed from each side by the stateliest elms and oaks. The dwelling stood upon a gentle eminence, with a broad and sweetly-sloping lawn of green on each side of the avenue, extending nearly to the public road. The house was half shaded by great trees, a modest dwelling of two stories, with a piazza fronting the avenue, the roof of which, concealed by a parapet, was sustained by six great columns, that rose up majestically from the basement to the upper story.

Dinner was in waiting when the parties arrived. Ham and turkey smoked upon the board, and there were birds and fowl, eggs and milk, and the usual variety of vegetables, so certain to be found in all good farmsteads. Mrs. Foster was an economist. She was a farmer's daughter; a poor one too; and had been early taught in lessons of thrift and painstaking. These she had not forgotten in her improved fortunes. Indeed, they were her virtues. Her estates thrived in her hands; and, if not a good tutor for the daughter, she was a very good nurse of her property. This was ample, if not large. It was the misfortune of Mrs. Foster that she did not esteem it ample. This was one of her reasons for preferring Jones Barry to either of her present guests. The fact of his greater wealth, and that feebler character which made him subservient to Mrs. Foster's humors, were the chief sources of that favor which he had found in the good lady's sight.

Dinner passed off pleasantly. Hammond continued in the same humor which had accompanied him from the race-course. Even Mrs. Foster, herself, was sometimes compelled to smile at his sallies; and when she did not, it was only from the annoying conviction that they were rapidly undoing all her work. It was night before the party rose from table, and a short interval was afforded for promenading in the piazza before tea was set. This was followed by music. Geraldine sang and played like an angel; this, at least, was the open-mouthed declaration of Jones Barry, in her own hearing; and both Henderson and Hammond were endowed with rich and tolerably well-trained voices. They accompanied the lady; while, at intervals, they resumed the conversation, either with herself or the step-mother. It was eleven o'clock before any of the party seemed to suspect the flight of Time, and then they were only apprised of the fact by Hammond rising to take his leave.

"But why not stay all night?" was the frank demand of Geraldine. Mrs. Foster addressed the same inquiry to Henderson. The latter looked to Hammond entreatingly; but, true to his policy, he declared the necessity for being at home early in the morning; and he had promised his mother, who would sit up and expect him, to return that night. He had five miles to ride.

"But you, Miles," said he to his friend, "you need not ride. You can stay."

This speech again worried both mother and daughter. It seemed strange that one who really loved a lady should encourage a rival to keep possession of her ear, and should give him opportunities. But Henderson felt ashamed of the weakness which prompted him to take advantage of the permission; and, somewhat desperately, declared his purpose to ride also. He had engagements also which required his early rising; and, in short, the gentlemen soon took their departure together; the ladies, one of them at least, sinking down upon the sofa with an air of sullen disappointment.

"A cold, haughty upstart!" was the exclamation of Mrs. Foster.

"Who, mother! of whom do you speak?"

"Of whom? Why Hammond. He is not capable of any feeling but pride. He is pride and ambition all over. He love! He has no more heart than a millstone, and seems to look upon women only as so many creatures made to wait upon man, and minister to his wants and pleasures."

"Well! I wonder how it is you can see things in this light. Now, really, Mr. Hammond seems to me to be equally a man of feeling and sense. He speaks like one. He doesn't throw about him his sentiments, and he wastes no professions on the air; but he gives to every subject the proper sympathy that it seems to require; and it can't be denied that he can discuss the greatest variety of subjects, and in the most interesting manner."

"Oh! he has subtlety, and wit, and cunning!"—

"Cunning! Well, that is the very last word which I should ever have used in speaking of Mr. Hammond. I see no proof of it. He is too frank, too bold a man, to be cunning; and is particularly free from it, I'm sure, in dealing with ladies. Who ever hears him compliment one's singing or playing, except, perhaps, by his attention?"

"That's his cunning!"

"Well, I confess, I like it better than that silly artlessness which, whether you play well or ill, rewards you with the same undiscriminating flattery. But he goes further. He has told me plainly, on more than one occasion, where I made a false note, or sung with false emphasis, or blundered in any respect; for his ear is quite as good as his opinion is honest."

"That's his cunning again! He sees that you dislike the common talk, and he changes it to suit you."

"Something more than that, mother. What did he say to both of us last week about gentlemen proffering themselves, as a matter of gallantry, to pick up a lady's glove, or handkerchief, running across the floor to do so, when it lies at her own feet, and she might pick it up herself?"

"Well, and he is only a cub for his opinions."

"On the contrary, mother, I think he is quite right. I quite agree with him, that it is enfeebling, and so enslaving, women, to do for them those things which it is proper for them, and easy, to do for themselves; that it makes us improperly dependent upon men, when we expect them to serve us in any besides substantial and weighty labors, which it is inconsistent with the nature of our sex to undertake; that it impairs the dignity of the man, and, while putting woman into a false position, renders him capricious, and makes her, in the end, the victim of a tyranny."

"All an artful notion to excuse his own cubbishness and want of gallantry."

"Well, now, mother, you certainly can reproach him for no want of courtesy and civility throughout the day. He has been with us, the only gentleman who never left us during all the racing."

"That's his policy. He stuck to *you*, as a matter of course."

"Yet, in the same breath, you describe him as lacking in the usual devotion—as being too proud and haughty, and—"

"I see, Miss Geraldine Foster, that your heart's set upon this match. I see that you'll throw yourself into his arms whether he will or no—"

"What you say, mother, let me tell you, is not likely to prevent me. But there's no danger of that. I confess, I think him a very superior man to any of my other suitors. You can't deny his superiority."

"By no means; he's a wit, and a colonel of militia, and they talk of sending him to the legislature or Congress; and, I suppose a young lady can't do better than to fling herself headlong into the arms of so promising a person. But I can tell you this, Miss Foster, that, when I was of your age, the man who swore that he knew no woman for whom he would run his horse, and that, too, when the young lady he was courting was entreating him to do so, would be courtesied out with a 'No, sir, I'm obliged to you, but beg to be excused.'"

"I don't know that Mr. Hammond is seeking me, mother, and it's very certain he is not courting me; but this I can tell you, that, if ever he should do so, he shall be made to swallow that speech. He certainly, before he gets this hand, shall run a race for it—he shall!"

"Will you stick to that?" demanded the mother, eagerly.

"Will I not! It's a vow; change it who can." And the elevated form, the flashing eye, and extended hand, lifted upward as she uttered this rash resolution, to which the keen cunning of the mother had goaded her impulsive spirit, presented a fine subject for the dramatic painter.

"Only stick to that, Geraldine, and you'll test his passion! You'll see which he thinks of most; this lady of his love, or his iron gray. I tell you, his soul is full of mule-pride; he's as obstinate in what he says as if the whole world was bound to give way to him."

"I sha'n't give way to him! He'll find me as firm and proud as himself. He shall run his horse; he shall race whether he likes it or not, if he has any hope of me. But he does not think of me, mother, I'm sure you're mistaken."

This was said with an air of despondency, as the maiden threw herself upon the sofa and covered her face with her hands.

"And what if he does not?" responded the mother; "you surely are not so badly off for beaux that you need care whether he cares or not. I don't think he cares much for anybody but himself. I tell you, he's too proud for love of any woman, as you may suppose, when he openly declares that he will not run his horse for all the favors of the sex. Only you stick to your vow, and you'll see what his love will come to."

"He shall do it, if he seeks heart or hand of mine. He shall do it, he shall!" We may add that the excellent mother did not suffer her to forget the vow.

CHAPTER XII.

TOUGHNESS OF THE TENDER GENDER.

WE must skip, without notice, the events of several weeks, in which but little apparent progress was made on any hand. The parties met frequently, now at church, now at evening assemblages of friends, and still, as before, very frequently at the dwelling of our heroine. Randall Hammond continued his policy, though with a misgiving, which gradually increased with the increase of his passion; and an eye less anxious, and a mind less excitable than that of Geraldine's, would have readily detected, at particular moments, the proofs of this strengthening interest. But what with her own feelings engaged in the issue, and the continued and perverse hostility of Mrs. Foster to the claims of our hero, she was kept in the same dogged mood towards him in which we have beheld her while taking the strange vow recorded in the preceding chapter. He saw and felt the influence, but was without any means to meet and to contend with it; unless by the exercise of the same patience which he had hitherto displayed, and the unwearied exhibition of those talents and resources which had rendered him still agreeable in her eyes in the teeth of all her prejudices. His mother, it may be mentioned in this place, had expressed her doubts of the propriety of his seeking in marriage the hand of Geraldine Foster. Of the young lady, herself, the venerable dame knew nothing, except from hearsay; and rumor rather exaggerated defects than acknowledged virtues. The objections of Mrs. Hammond lay to the step-mother, whom she knew as a pert housekeeper employed in a neighboring family, when she was promoted by Foster, then sinking with a feeble constitution, and equally feeble mind, into imbecility. She regarded her influence over the step-daughter as vicious and dangerous, and, whatever might be the individual endowments of the girl, she insisted upon their abuse and perversion in the hands of such a guardian. We have seen that she is right in some measure; but she overrated the influence of the one, and underrated the powers of resistance of the other. The girl, in reality, in many respects, controlled the woman. The latter, conscious of low birth and inferior education, though naturally clever, was submissive to the daughter in most social respects; and it was only where the latter was necessarily diffident, as in the case of her affections, that she exercised any influence over her sufficiently powerful to baffle the impulses of her own judgment. In affairs of the heart, or, rather, where young persons are called upon to decide between two or more favorites, the adroit suggestions of third parties have always more or less weight. The mind distrusts itself but too frequently when the affections are busy with its decisions; and it is because of this fact, that we find so many of that pernicious class called match-makers in the world. They interpose when the will of the interested person is at fault. They profess friendship, and it is at such a time that the poor heart longs for such a succor. They insinuate doubts, or suggest motives, and determine the scales, for or against a party, by such arguments or innuendoes as are most likely to influence the feeble nature which relies upon them. Mrs. Foster's hold upon Geraldine, in this matter, lay in the morbidly active pride of the damsel. This she contrived to goad and irritate by daily suggestions, in which the most innocent movements of Hammond were perverted. The fear of Mrs. Hammond, with regard to her influence upon Miss Foster, went still farther. She dreaded lest she should govern her in all respects; lest she should have tutored all her moods and feelings by the low moral standards by which the step-mother herself was influenced; and have made her equally selfish and presumptuous with herself; coarse in her aims, narrow in her opinions; jealous of the worth which she never sought to emulate; and ambitious of society, not for its real advantages of mutual training and attrition, but for its silly displays and petty ostentations.

We need not repeat that, in these apprehensions, Mrs. Hammond labored under error; but she did not the less entertain them. A long and serious conversation with her son, the day after his return from the races at Hillabee, was devoted to this subject. In this conversation, she freely declared her objections to the match with such a person, related all that she had heard of Geraldine, and told her son all that she knew of the step-mother, concluding with an earnest entreaty that he would look in some other quarter for the exercise of his affections. She was even good enough to mention the names of two or three young ladies of their acquaintance, whose charms were considerable, and against whom there lay no such objections as she entertained for Miss Foster.

But the son, though grateful for this counsel, as frankly told his mother that it fell upon unheeding senses; that he was really and deeply attached to Geraldine; that he was not blind to her faults, and knew her to be equally proud and eccentric; but her pride, he said, arose from a high spirit, sensible only of right purposes, and her eccentricities were the growth of a superior intellect, under an irregular education, and were due in some degree to a consciousness of independence, falsely founded, perhaps, of the circle in which she moved. Like other lovers, Hammond expressed the opinion that her eccentricities would certainly be cured by marriage, particularly under the admirable domestic system which he was prepared to establish. For the step-mother, he had nothing to say. He had certainly no defence to offer. She was pretty much the woman that his mother had described her. Besides, she was evidently hostile to himself. But her influence over her step-daughter was nothing. If exercised in any way, it was only in opposition to himself, and he could readily understand how she might operate successfully by artifices, particularly in dealing with a person who was herself truthful and unsuspicious, where she might never attain any influence by open authority. He continued by repeating the assurance to his mother that he felt too much interested in the lady to forego his attentions, but that he should watch her conduct narrowly, and not risk his peace upon any object to whom such objections could apply as those which she had urged. He concluded by expressing his desire that his mother would visit Mrs. Foster, and see the young lady for herself. There was no good reason why she should not do so. It is true she did not like Mrs. Foster, but if people visited only those whom they liked, society would be almost empty of individuals. Mrs. Foster had called upon her, and had invited her to her house. True, she might remember her as a pert housekeeper, but she was now a householder; and if pert in this capacity, it was a fault which could be charged upon a thousand others. At all events Mrs. Foster was no worse than her neighbors, so far as the world was permitted to see. And to recognize her as everybody else did, would in no degree impair the ancient position which Mrs. Hammond held in the public esteem. If any other reason were wanting, it was undoubtedly to be found in the probability of her son establishing an alliance with this very family, when, as a matter of course, all difference of relative position must be overthrown forever.

The worthy old lady sighed as she acknowledged the truth of these reasonings, and prepared to submit to them. At an early day her carriage was ordered, and Mrs. Foster was confounded when she heard that the equipage of the stately old lady was in progress up the avenue. This was a triumph to her vanity which would have been eminently gratified, but that it seemed to operate against her project of marrying her daughter to Barry. One of her favorite topics of denunciation, where Hammond was concerned, was his own and his mother's arrogance; and the neglect of the latter to return her visits was an argument for the truth of her assertions. But neither Geraldine nor herself was insensible to the compliment paid by this visit. Mrs. Hammond was at the very head of society in that neighborhood. Her position was unquestionable. Hers was one of the oldest families; and the dignity which she maintained, along with the virtues of benevolence and hospitality—to speak of no other of the Christian charities—all of which were eminently conceded to her, rendered her quite as much beloved as respected. It had been rather injurious to Mrs. Foster's pretensions in society, that Mrs. Hammond had not recognized them. That she did so now, at this late day, was undoubtedly something gained; but the perverse pride in her heart prompted a feeling of resentment at the visit so long deferred, and she suddenly exclaimed to Geraldine—

"We won't see her. She has taken her time about it, and we will take ours. Let Clara go and tell her we are not at home."

"No, indeed, mother! that won't do. You will gain nothing by it; for people will only say, you have done it for spite. Mrs. Hammond is not a woman to be slighted. However we may feel her neglect of us, she is a lady of worth and character; and I can't think of showing her any resentment. Besides, I feel none. I remember her when she used to visit my own dear mother, though I was but a child; and I have heard father speak of her as his friend, when he needed friendship. Indeed, I have heard that she lent him a large sum of money to save his mills; and, in the settlement of the affairs of the estate with Lawyer Griffin, I see the repayment only took place the year before my father died. No! she has had some reason, I suppose, for keeping away, and that she comes now shows that these reasons exist no longer. We *must* see her. I feel nothing but respect for Mrs. Hammond."

This was said in a way to silence opposition. But the step-mother had the last word, framed in a fashion that she had been too much accustomed to employ of late to forego very readily.

"It's just as you will, my dear. You have very good reasons for what you say; but I rather think that if your heart did not incline so much to seeing the son, your reasons wouldn't be half so good for seeing the mother. Take care now; I see what's coming. You will be overawed by the consequential old woman, until you submit to the consequential young man, and then good-by to all your freedom. I know you, Geraldine Foster; you'll be imposed upon by the high heads of these people, until you forget all your resolutions."

"And I tell you, mother, that you know nothing about Geraldine Foster, if you think she is to be imposed upon by anybody. I am—"

"Well, hush now, before the old witch hears you. She's coming into the parlor now."

Geraldine muttered something about the improper use of the epithet old witch, and Mrs. Foster sniggered at the rebuke. The affairs of the toilet proceeded in silence, and the daughter was the first who was ready to descend.

"She shall wait for me," said the mother, proceeding very leisurely. Geraldine left the room, and descended to the parlor. She felt a little awe, certainly, as she entered the room and encountered the tall, stately form of the venerable woman, with her dark dress, and her formal mob cap. But the benevolent manner, and the sweet tones of the old lady's voice reassured her.

"I know you, my child, by your dear mother. She was my intimate friend. She was a kind and loving person. You have her eyes and mouth. Your forehead and nose are your father's, and you are tall, like your father also. Your mother was rather short, but she was so well made that she did not seem so, unless when standing close to others. If you have her heart, my child, as you certainly have all her beauty—"

The old lady squeezed the hands of the girl, but failed to see the humid witnesses which were gathering in her eyes. Those of the speaker were already wet. The sympathies of the two were becoming active, and Mrs. Hammond had already reproached our heroine with having failed, since her return home, after a lapse of several years, to seek out one of her mother's most intimate friends; and Geraldine, who had been kept from doing so only by the perverse influence of her step-mother, was awkwardly seeking to account and apologize for the neglect, when the door was flung wide, and Mrs. Foster sailed into the room, blazing in her best silks, and making as formidable a show of trinkets as if she were the belle of the evening. At her appearance, the whole manner of Mrs. Hammond seemed to change. She drew up to her fullest height her tall, erect person. Her eye assumed a severe simplicity of gaze, which entirely changed its expression; and her reception of the new-comer, Geraldine could not but remark, was singularly unlike that which had met *her* appearance. The truth is, the absence of simplicity, the obtrusive ostentation of Mrs. Foster's manner, a mixture at once of dignity and assumption which was neither confidence nor ease, brought out all the native superiority of her visitor. Besides, she remembered her as the usurper, foisting herself by cunning upon the weakness of a dying man, and succeeding to a position in society for which her training and education had not prepared her. The first meeting between the two, already prepared to be belligerents, was productive of impressions which strengthened their mutual dislikes and distrusts. Mrs. Foster was boisterous and confident; talked recklessly, as if her purpose had been to show nothing but scorn of all the usual modes of thinking and feeling, all the forms and manners, which her guest had been wont to hold in reverence. The deportment of Mrs. Hammond was the reverse of this; but it was so full of a dignity jealous of assault, and resolute against intrusion; so cold in its stateliness, so stern in its simplicity, that our heroine, though vexed at the bearing of her step-mother, was not less chilled and offended by that of her visitor. We need not detail the progress of the interview. The call was a very short one, and the parties separated mutually dissatisfied. Mrs. Hammond, chafed with the impertinence of Mrs. Foster, and disposed to see in Geraldine (who had been very quiet) nothing but the susceptible creature whom the step-mother had fashioned in all respects to resemble herself; while the latter, though not exactly satisfied with herself, was yet confirmed in all her grudges and ancient hostilities, as she felt the cold supremacy of that bearing which she had bullied, without being able to forsake or overcome.

"There," said she to Geraldine, when her visitor had been bowed down the steps; "there you have her in full; the queen of Sheba, with her head in the clouds and her feet among the stars. She's as proud as Lucifer. You'd have a fine chance with her as a mother-in-law. She'd rule you with a rod of iron. Do you smile, it's a look; do you laugh, it's a scold; would you dance, it's a sermon; and so day by day, until you're broken down with the sulks and sours: no milk could keep sweet long under that face of vinegar."

Geraldine was silent. She, too, had been disappointed by the visit. She could see that there was something wrong in the carriage and language of her mother; but unfortunately, her ear had become too much habituated to the modes of speech and thinking of the latter to feel, in full force, the improprieties of her conduct; and she regarded the stern deportment of Mrs. Hammond as totally unprovoked by anything that had taken place. She was quite ignorant of that past history of the step-mother which their visitor knew too well, and it was really in some degree as the sincere friend of Geraldine's own mother that the soul of the old lady revolted at her substitute. But this the young lady was yet to learn. She, as we have said, was silent; while Mrs. Foster ran on in a strain cunningly calculated at once to express her own hostility and to alarm the fears of Geraldine. She painted the tyrannical mother of Hammond subduing all the spirit of his young wife, of any wife whom he should bring home; restraining all her innocent desires, chiding her sentiments, and keeping her in such a bondage to her antiquated notions, as would effectually quell all her sweetest impulses, and embitter all her youth with the mere caprices of authority. From the mother she passed, by a natural transition, to the son. He was the true child of his mother; cold, stern, unbending, despotic. She was eloquent on this theme; she recalled and dwelt upon, with perverse ingenuity, every incident that could serve for its illustration, and it was only when she broke down with utter exhaustion that she was content to stop. Poor Geraldine said nothing. She was certainly impressed by what she heard. The speech of Mrs. Foster was not without ingenuity. Yet the girl thought of Hammond with kindly feelings. It was only when her temper was roused that she was disposed to side completely with her cunning and dishonest counsellor. Somehow, she could not concur with her now, even in respect to the stately mother. Though chilled to the heart by the progress of the interview, she yet remembered the sweetness with which it had begun.

How different had been the deportment of the old lady before her step-mother made her appearance! How kindly had she spoken; with what affectionate remembrance did she seem to dwell on the personal appearance and the virtues of her mother; and, surely, she had seen the gathering tears in her soft blue eyes at the very moment when she felt that her own were filling. Whence, then, the change? how could the appearance of her step-mother have effected it? There was a mystery in this, and the aroused heart of Geraldine brooded over it; and daily, with an increasing pleasure, did she remember the sweet words and the sad tears which the mother of Hammond had shared with herself when the two were alone together.

CHAPTER XIII.

SOME TALK OF MARRIAGE.

But an event was now at hand which was calculated to divert the thoughts of Geraldine Foster into other channels. Her seventeenth birthday was approaching, a period of immense importance to all young damsels. It was destined to be regarded as such in the present instance. Already, for more than a month previous, the rumor had gone abroad through the neighboring country, of a great *fête* to be given at the "Lodge." Supplies for the occasion were already making their appearance. Wagons from Savannah and Augusta, laden with good things, were seen arriving, and public expectation was on tiptoe for the event. In due season our young men were all honored with invitations to the birthday *fête*. Mrs. Hammond was also included in this compliment, though Mrs. Foster was pleased to say, while her step-daughter was penning the invitation, that she knew "very well that the haughty old hag would never come again." She was mistaken, as we shall see hereafter. The truth is, as regards herself and her own feelings, it never would have been the wish of Mrs. Hammond to darken the doors of a lady like Mrs. Foster, for whom she could never feel esteem; but the case was altered in respect to Geraldine. She regarded the latter as the innocent, though perhaps misguided child of a very dear friend, and on this account alone she was prepared to treat her with solicitous consideration. There was yet a better reason. Mrs. Hammond had now satisfied herself that the affections of her son were really engaged to the maiden; too deeply engaged, indeed, to render prudent any farther exhortations and warnings on her part. She resolved, therefore, instead of discouraging with a vain importunity his pursuit of the object, to yield herself to his cause, and contribute, as far as it would be becoming in her, to the promotion of his wishes. She

138

distinguished, accordingly, between the girl and the silly step-mother;
and, while revolting at the offensive frivolities and forwardnesses of
the latter, was prepared to take the other, as the future wife of her
son, to her most affectionate embraces. This determination led her to
accept an invitation which she otherwise might have treated with
indifference. It must not be supposed, however, because we find
Mrs. Foster speaking in offensive terms of Mrs. Hammond, that
the visit of the latter had been disagreeable to her, or that she had
failed in returning it. This was very far from being the case. While
she disliked to meet with the old lady, from a real feeling of in-
feriority, and from a painful consciousness that Mrs. Hammond knew
more of her real history than anybody else; she yet felt the importance, in a social point of view, of appearing to maintain an
intimacy with one of a rank so unquestionable. She soon, with Geraldine, returned the visit in which she had behaved with so much
insolent familiarity; and was received with the sweet benignity,
mingled with dignity, which so becomes a well-bred lady in the
character of a hostess. Geraldine could not but feel the superiority of
bearing in this venerable representative of a passing age, to that
to which she was accustomed; and could scarcely reconcile the
gentleness and meekness of the old lady's manner and tone with
that which was so commanding in her carriage and so impressive in
what she uttered. True to her decision, and regarding the possible
relation in which the maiden might yet stand in regard to her son,
Mrs. Hammond was particularly anxious to please her younger
visitor. While the three ladies traversed the garden, which was a
very ample and beautiful one, she loitered with the younger of the
three, and again renewed the subject of her intercourse with her
mother. The garden itself afforded a sufficient reason for recalling
the subject. Mrs. Hammond's taste for flowers had been greatly influenced by the superior sympathies, for these lovely creations, of the
first Mrs. Foster; and it was in the power of the former to indicate
to Geraldine a fact, of which she was now for the first time made
conscious, that the garden at the "Lodge" had been laid out exactly
of the size and plan of that which she now examined. Its fate, however, had been very different. While the latter was blooming in full
perfection and variety, the former had grown into a waste with

weeds. Geraldine only resolved to make amends to the memory of her mother by restoring her favorite fruits and flowers. The judicious manner of Mrs. Hammond, the equal delicacy and adroitness with which she had again managed to speak to the young girl of her mother, and to show the tender interest which she herself felt for her memory, were by no means thrown away upon the daughter, who was sensibly touched, as well by the manner as by the matter of her venerable hostess. Mrs. Foster beheld this with some disquiet, and more than once contrived to divert the conversation to other and far less interesting topics. She herself was treated with the greatest deference, Mrs. Hammond being at pains, for the sake of the ward, to treat the guardian as if she fully deserved to be such a custodian. At the end of an hour, the visitors were prepared to depart, and Randall Hammond made his appearance just in time to see the ladies to the carriage.

A few days after came the invitation to the *fête*.

"You will go, dear mother, will you not?" was the inquiry of Hammond, uttered in pleading accents. She was disposed to plague him, and expressed herself doubtfully.

"I don't know. I am old. These night parties are not good for me, and I don't enjoy them."

"But, for my sake, mother."

"I don't know but that, for your sake, I ought to stay away. I am half afraid to give any encouragement to this pursuit."

"Oh, don't say so, mother; don't think so."

"Oh, but I must think so, Randall," said the old lady, with real gravity; "for I confess I am not satisfied that Geraldine Foster is the lady for you. That foolish step-mother has done her best to spoil her."

"But she is *not* spoiled."

"Perhaps not. Of that I can say nothing; but what does the world say?"

"Mere scandal, I warrant you."

"Nay, nay, Randall; we can't so easily dismiss the popular report. We hear every day of her eccentricities; of her riding wild horses without a saddle, leaping high fences, and even threatening John Estes with horsewhip and pistol."

"Pshaw, mother! How ridiculous!"

"Ridiculous, it may be, but not wholly wanting in truth. Our old neighbor, Jacob Barnes, tells me that he has it from Peter Estes, the brother of John."

"Be assured, a wholesale falsehood. This John Estes was the overseer for Mrs. Foster, and was dismissed by her for neglect and insolence. He no doubt revenges himself by all sorts of falsehoods. He is a worthless fellow, I know; but if I hear him at his slanders, let him but cross my path with them, and I'll—"

"Come, come, Randall! none of that. You are only too ready to take up the cudgels for other people. You are not yet authorized to be the champion of Mrs. Foster or Geraldine; and I'm afraid, as I hear the story, that the young lady can be her own champion, and will be apt to reject your assistance. Barnes says, on the report of Peter Estes, that, when John Estes demanded his full year's wages, Mrs. Foster ordered him from the house; and he, not seeming in a hurry to obey her, Miss Geraldine threatened him with the horsewhip, and seemed disposed to use it. At all events, as Barnes phrases it, John Estes, in fear of bodily danger, made off in double-quick time. There's no doubt something in it."

"Yes! no doubt he deserved the whip for his insolence; and in her indignation she told him so."

"But Estes reports that she got her father's pistols, and said she was not afraid to use them; and professed to be as expert with them as any man."

"Pshaw! another exaggeration, quite as easily explained. How naturally would a young woman wish that she were a man to pistol an insolent fellow who dared to bully her at her own fireside!"

"Still, my son, you would prefer that such a speech should be made by Mrs. Foster rather than the daughter?"

"I don't know! I don't see any harm in this expression of a strong and becoming indignation by a young lady. Geraldine is, no doubt, high-spirited and impulsive. Perhaps, too, she may be called and considered eccentric, as she undoubtedly possesses talents. But I have seen nothing in her conduct which can at all justify these stories; and I ask you, dear mother, whether you have?"

"You know, my son, that I have seen her very seldom since she was a mere child."

"Ah! mother, the long and short of it is, that you would rather see me married to that stately dowd, Miss Arabella Mason, or that cold Grecian, your amiable beauty, now rapidly becoming an antique, Miss Jane Hallett, or—"

"Randall, these are young ladies whom I very much esteem," said the mother, gravely. "Either of them, in my opinion, would make you a much *safer* wife, if personally less beautiful, than Geraldine Foster. But I have no prejudice against her. On the contrary, if I were not stunned and alarmed by what I hear of her wildness, I should prefer that she should be your wife in preference to anybody else. You have heard me speak of her mother, who was very dear to me. Had she been so fortunate as to enjoy her mother's guardianship, instead of that of the coarse, weak woman who succeeded her, I should have had no apprehensions. I offer no opposition to your pursuit. You are of age, and I only entreat that you do not allow the beauty, and the more piquant attractions of the young lady's wit, to blind you to her deficiencies. I will go to the *fête*, since you wish it; nay, I had meant to go before you spoke to me, if it were only to show how readily I can sacrifice my own scruples, whenever such sacrifice becomes necessary to my son's happiness."

"Thanks, dear mother, many thanks! You will not regret, you will not repent, your indulgence. You will see Geraldine in better aspects, the more you know her. These reports are mere silly exaggerations, easily raised upon a vivacity of character, and a freedom of carriage, which are not common to our country damsels. I think as little of the step-mother as you do; but I doubt whether Mrs. Foster can greatly influence Geraldine. She is quite too independent for that."

"No doubt, provided the attempt to influence is apparent, but this is very doubtful. People like Mrs. Foster, sprung from a low condition to one for which they are unfit, are very apt to exercise habitual cunning, and they operate their ends with secrecy; while persons of very independent temper, like Geraldine, particularly where they pride themselves on their independence, are very apt to be taken in by the very persons who affect to acknowledge their want of power. Art, in this way, operates, by successful subtleties, in blinding the judgment of superior will; and the more stubborn the person, the more easily deluded when in contact with such an agency. This I suspect to be the true relation between the two. Mrs. Foster I *know* to be artful in a high degree. She had never succeeded in becoming the wife of Henry Foster, but for the practice of her housekeeper-cunning."

"Mother, you are harsh."

"Randall, you are right! But it is in your ears only that I speak these opinions, and they are meant to guard you from mishap. If, as I suppose, you are resolute to address Geraldine, I warn you that Mrs. Foster is secretly working against you."

"Ha! how do you know it?"

"I know *her;* she cannot but work against you, being what you are; and the report goes that she openly favors this little person, Barry."

"You hear that too from this old chronicler, Jacob Barnes?"

"Barnes is a simple and an honest creature, who reports things just as he hears them. But his reports, Randall, and my opinions, are only to be valued as they teach caution. Pursue your object steadily, if you will, but with an eye open to the degree of influence which this lady exercises over her ward. By this you may judge whether you can succeed with the one, without regard to the prejudices of the other. I should be sorry to see my son rejected, even where I would not have him seek."

This concluded the conversation, which was interrupted by the arrival of Miles Henderson. He too had received his invitation for the *fête,* and he came over to consult with Hammond in regard to it. The two friends wandered out into the fields, and, under the shade of quiet trees, they conferred frankly about their mutual feelings and prospects. There were no reserves between them; and, without hesitation, Henderson showed his friend the draft of a letter to Geraldine, in which he had made his proposals. The letter he himself designed to give her, at some favorable opportunity, on the day or evening of the *fête.* This festivity contemplated a *picnic* in the woods, and by the banks of a small fishing-stream and mill-seat called Gushlynn; and at evening, music, dancing, and other sports at the "Lodge," and in the grounds, which were to be lighted up for the occasion. All these arrangements had already transpired, and were freely discoursed of by the multitudinous mouth of rumor. Henderson did not doubt that he should find more than one fitting occasion, during the day or night, on which to present his *billet d'amour*.

"It is very well, Miles; fairly and properly written. For my part, I have to move with caution. I am too decidedly the object of Mrs. Foster's dislike not to feel how doubtful are all my chances; for, though I sometimes fancy I have made a favorable impression upon Geraldine, yet her changes are very sudden, and she is yet so young as not to feel the importance of shaping her conduct consistently after deliberate resolve. I do not deceive myself as to the danger which I stand from this caprice, which may invite and beguile, only that it may deny and contemn; not that I suppose Geraldine the woman to behave thus with any previous design. But she is so much the creature of impulse, and is so likely to be governed, in some degree at least, by that spiteful mother-in-law, that I feel more and more dubious the more closely I approach the subject. It is barely possible that I, too, shall propose to her on the day of the *fête*. This will depend, however, entirely on the temper which she appears to be in, and upon the sort of opportunity which is afforded me. Of late, Mrs. Foster seems disposed to keep watch upon me, and, by her constant presence, to baffle everything like private or interesting conversation with Geraldine. I can only deal in common-talk and generalities, which lead to nothing."

"Which lead to a great deal, Randall. Your generalities have always a meaning in them. I see that Mrs. Foster watches you more closely than she does anybody else, and that only proves to me that she considers you the most dangerous. But you make more out of the restraint than anybody could beside yourself. It's evident enough that, though you talk generalities only, as you call them, they are such particularities to Geraldine that she gives them the best attention; and, if you don't seem to say anything meant especially for her ear, it's very certain she appropriates it all more eagerly than any other. The truth is, Randall, I'm more jealous of you than ever, and this is the very reason, that you get on so successfully in fixing the interest of Geraldine in spite of the clear dislike and the crossplays of the step-mother. I'm only going to propose now, to get my answer. I don't see that I've the least chance or hope. She treats me civilly, and Mrs. Foster is a great deal more kind to me than she is to you; but, after all, though I try hard to find a meaning in this civility, it amounts only to this, that I don't behave amiss, and the attention of a young fellow is never disagreeable to a miss. But the suspense and anxiety vex me, and so I'm going to make an end of it, and either make the spoon or spoil the horn."

"With such feelings, Miles, I should not propose; but the subject is one which I dare not undertake to counsel you upon. You will, of course, do as you please."

"Oh! I'm sworn to give in this paper. There may be more hope than I have reason for. A man, who is really in love, can't always see his chances for himself; and Geraldine Foster is the first and only woman I've ever seen that I really wished to marry. I'll try her, at all events; and if nothing better comes of the trial, it will at once put an end to my anxiety."

"Be it so, Miles. You hear what I tell you. I shall prepare no letter. I'll leave it to circumstances to determine. If opportunity offers, and she seems favorable, ten to one that I shall declare myself. If not, I have only to keep quiet and wait a better season."

"Yes; but you may wait too long. 'Spose she takes me?"

"My dear Miles, she couldn't take a better fellow. Next to myself, I should rejoice to see you in possession of the prize."

"But suppose, seeing no chance of you, and tired of waiting, she takes this beauty, Barry?"

"Then he's welcome to her, and she wouldn't be the woman for me. I should rejoice in my escape."

"Randall, you're a cursed sight too proud."

"No, Miles, I only put a proper value upon a wife. The girl who is in such haste to get a husband as to marry any that offers rather than lose a chance is worth no man's having."

"I don't know but you're right."

While upon this fruitful subject, let us pass from the two friends to another of the parties to our story, whose feelings, about this period, were similarly concerned with the fair Geraldine, and the approaching festivities. Sunday was usually chosen by our excellent acquaintance, Jones Barry, for his dinners. He was then apt to call in his acquaintance, to see his friends, and make a day of it. He never denied himself on these days. He was a bachelor, a man of wealth, and enjoyed a certain degree of impunity. He at least assumed that one, whose behavior was so uniformly good during the week, should be permitted his enjoyments on the Sabbath. Of course, we quarrel with no man for his opinions. We are indulgent, and only propose to show his practice under them.

Jones Barry had a cleverish cook, who could make mock turtle to perfection, and dress a haunch of venison to the equal satisfaction of epicure and hunter. He loved good things, and never stinted himself at any time; but it was on Sunday that he particularly laid himself out to be happy. The first day of the week had come in which the birthday *fête* of Miss Foster was to be celebrated. He had several guests that day, and an excellent dinner. There was our old friend, Nettles, among the former, to whom one end of the table was assigned. Joe Blake, Dick Moore, and Tom Lechmere formed the rest of the company. The dinner passed off gloriously. When the cloth was removed, the host, raising his glass, cried—

"Fill, gentlemen, and drink to the health of the fair Geraldine."

"Lady or filly?" inquired Nettles.

"Come, Tom, don't be disrespectful. She may yet be my wife."

Nettles repeated the question.

"Lady or filly, Jones?"

"You're a beast," cried Barry; "drink before I send the bottle at your head."

"Do nothing of the kind, I beg, until you've emptied it at least. But still let me ask. I drink, you see; for it matters not much to your friends whom you marry; but which is it, Jones? We know you love the lady, at least you say so, and it's very certain to everybody that you really love the mare. Now, if a Roman emperor made one of his mares a divinity, and fed it on silver *crowfoot* and golden ears, handsomely cracked in a marble basin, there's no reason why a Georgia planter shouldn't promote his filly by marriage."

"Pshaw! that's all nonsense about the Roman emperor."

"True, every bit of it, except that I have my doubts about the gender of the beast. But tell us truly. Out with it like a man. Are you to be married to the fair Geraldine?"

"To the lady, perhaps."

"Is it fixed?"

"Not exactly, but so nigh there's no fun in it."

"Ah! then you have proposed, Jones?"

"No—not to Geraldine herself, but the mother goes for me."

"But that's not the daughter."

"It's something towards the election."

"Don't believe a word of it, Jones," answered the reckless Nettles. "It's like your racehorse calculations. You'll be beaten when you're most certain."

"And who's to beat me, do you think?"

"Why Ran. Hammond, to be sure."

"He! he stands no more chance than my grandmother. Why, Mrs. Foster hates him as she does poison."

"What of that? I can tell you she wouldn't hate him long, if he was willing to marry her instead of the daughter. But her hate don't hurt. That girl has a will of her own, if ever woman had; and Madam Foster's dislikes won't help your likes, I can tell you."

"She as good as tells me I'm sure of Geraldine."

"Many a slip betwixt the cup and the lip. Now look you, Jones, my boy; I like you well enough; your dinners are excellent, and you keep the best wine decidedly in the country."

"Do you really think so, Tom? You *are* a judge."

"You do—only you keep it always too near your own plate."

"There it is—Blake, hand that bottle to the ox."

"Ox! well, I suppose it is because I'm an ox that you offer me a horn."

"Take two of them, that you may be finished."

"But I'll not finish there."

"Go ahead!"

"Well, as I was saying, I like you and your dinners well enough. You're a good fellow in your way, though you have too great fondness for women of the circus."

"Tom! Tom! mum! Honor bright, old fellow."

"Out with it, Nettles!" was the cry of Joe Blake, and the rest.

"Another time, boys, another time. Let's see, where was I? Ah! I was saying,—but, to begin fair, I'll give you a toast. Fill, if you please."

"Fill, gentlemen," said the host. "Fill to Tom Nettles, charged."

"Here's to Ran. Hammond; a stiff fellow, perhaps, but a real man and a true gentleman."

Jones Barry gulped and swallowed with the rest.

"I drink," said he. "I can afford it. I'm not afraid of anything Ran. Hammond can do in this affair."

"You're not! Well, mark my words; this girl's for him, and not for you; and better, let me tell you, that he should marry her, and not you. Better for *us* as well as you."

"And why, pray?"

"Why, then, let me tell you. She'd be your master in no time, and she'd rule you with a rod of iron. No more dinners on Sunday, boys. No more wine for good fellows; and, instead of our excellent friend, Jones Barry, presiding where he does—now running a fine horse, now opening a fine bottle, now jerking at a gander's gullet, and now sitting in a Sultana's lap—"

"Mum, Tom, mum!"

"I say, instead of this, look at the poor fellow, afraid to say his soul's his own! He gives no dinners, boys, for his wife finds no pleasure in our company; he opens no wine, my boys—his wife keeps the keys; he pulls no gander's neck, since his wife makes him tender-hearted by pulling his; and, instead of sitting, now and then, in the lap of a pretty woman at the circus, drinking apple-toddy, he hates the very sight of a pretty woman, as it tells him that, instead of a mistress, he has got a master. No, no, boys! I say the fair Geraldine to Ran. Hammond; he can tame her; and if our friend Jones must have a wife, let her be the fat, laughing girl, that serves the bar at old Hiram Davy's corner; who sweetens the toddy with her smiles instead of sugar; and when she says, 'Is it to your liking, sir?' makes it go down like a blessing. She's the girl, boys, for Jones Barry; and I drink the health of Susannah Davy, and may good fellow never get a smaller armful!"

"Armful, you snake in the grass! Why she's a houseful; she weighs three hundred if she weighs a pennyweight."

"Three hundred! Jones, that's a scandal. I was at the last weighing; two hundred and forty-five, and the stillyard on a perfect level—not a grain more. You couldn't get a better wife, if happiness is what you aim at."

All these sallies produced their appropriate merriment. But we need not pursue our good fellows through their midnight orgies. Enough that Tom Nettles floored his host, and, after seeing him solemnly laid out on the rug before the fireplace, he coolly took possession of Barry's own couch, which the latter did not seem greatly to affect. The rest of the company, towards the small hours of the morning, were similarly disposed of.

CHAPTER XIV.

THE BIRTHDAY FÊTE.

The decision of Miles Henderson was precisely that of Jones
Barry. He had prepared himself, under the special instructions of
Mrs. Foster, to make his proposals to the fair Geraldine, on the occasion of her birthday. That excellent lady, the step-mother, had
several private conferences with this favored suitor, without the
knowledge of the young lady. In these conversations, she particularly
encouraged his hopes, and enjoined upon him the experiment during
the progress of the festivities. She did not tell him upon what she
had based her calculations of success, probably with some just
apprehensions in regard to his prudence; but she might have trusted
him; for, in all his revelations to his companions over the bottle, he
never yielded up his secrets entirely. He still kept something to himself, following the counsel of Burns—which even Tom Nettles,
who wormed a good deal out of him without seeming to design it,
could never succeed in extracting from his tongue. It is probable
that the calculations of Mrs. Foster were not remarkable for their
profundity; yet they might have been sufficient, for all that, for the
purpose she had in contemplation. She probably designed nothing
more than so to vex the capricious pride and impulse of Geraldine,
with respect to Hammond, as to make her disgust him by her eccentricities; and the scheme was a good one, so far as it was founded
upon a pretty correct knowledge of the character of both persons.
But the *affaires de cœur* of young people are so much influenced
by chance and circumstance—some would say Providence—that the
nicest calculations of cunning are apt to fail at the moment of exigency; and, with some knowledge of this danger from casualties, our
excellent step-mother was more than usually careful in devising
the events as well as the picnic and the supper. How she did this,

or tried to do it, it is not exactly necessary that we should show; and we must not anticipate actual events by speculating upon their features and family likenesses while they are yet in the womb of the future. Enough that all parties had completed their arrangements for the birthday, which at length dawned to the awakening of many and conflicting anxieties.

The sun smiled brightly and beautifully that morning, without a cloud; and, as the purpose of the ladies at the "Lodge" was to make "a day of it," the company began to appear right early. They came from a considerable distance, Mrs. Foster having been at pains to invite the most remote acquaintances, in order that the display should not be thrown away upon few and inferior judges. Her preparations had been conceived on a scale which, however rustic, was unusually liberal for that region of country. Supplies, as we have seen, had been pouring in for some time previous. A number of violins, clarionets, and tambourines had been employed, and a volunteer drummer made his unexpected appearance with the rest, assuming that no musical noises were objectionable at a *charivari*. In one sense, it was a *charivari* that was in progress; but our opinion is, though no censure was passed upon his conduct, that the drummer was decidedly guilty of presumption. As if troubled with some suspicions of the same sort, he modestly withdrew his performances to a distance, and only within earshot of the house. Here, upon a small mound, which had probably been an Indian tabernacle, and which was surrounded with a clump of pines, he threshed away with his merry sticks to the delight of those who, in carriage or buggy, were passing up the avenue. The horses danced with delight as they heard the inspiriting clamor, and the attempts to run away only gave more life to the proceedings. The drum became, in a little time, too useful for dismission.

Mrs. Hammond arrived at an early hour. Her son did not then accompany her. He was governed in this delay by motives which we may conjecture from what we have heard him say, on a previous occasion, to his friend Henderson. It was his policy not to seem too anxious. His mother's motive for coming early was that she might not stay late. She did not come seeking amusement, and she designed returning home before the day was out. It was in compliment to the lady, who might yet be her son's wife, that she came at all. She was received respectfully by Geraldine, and civilly enough by Mrs. Foster. The latter was too greatly in her glory not to seem amiable that day. Her vanity was in full exercise, to enable her to play her part with suavity and grace.

Of course, we cannot pretend to describe the persons present. They were very numerous, not less than two hundred and fifty having been invited. All, certainly, did not attend; but there were some who came without being conscious of the necessity of being asked; and these were usually the most conspicuous and active in their attentions to themselves and one another. Our amiable friend Miles Henderson, and our humorous friend Jones Barry, arrived at the same moment; the latter accompanied by his Mephistopheles, Tom Nettles. It was with a slight shade upon her brow that Geraldine observed that Henderson came alone. She had looked, as a matter of course, that Hammond would accompany Henderson. Her mother saw the expression in her countenance, and remarked, in an under tone, as Miles rode up—

"So, his friend's not with him. I doubt if he comes at all. His pride would scarcely allow him to do anything which seemed to do us honor."

"But his mother's here," whispered Geraldine.

"To spy out the poverty of the land, and to go home and sneer. We havn't such a display of plate as the Hammonds can set out; and she will have her say about the difference between old times, when she was everybody, and now when other people want to be somebody."

"Mother, you are too harsh!"

"Too harsh! Well, you can make up for it by being too tender! We'll see yet if the soft heart of the woman proves too weak for the arrogant pride of the man."

The daughter felt the imputation, and turned away with an expressive smile upon her lips. The mother knew the meaning and the value of that smile, and she was satisfied. Pride was the weakness of Geraldine; and upon this characteristic the cunning woman played. She knew that while she kept this feeling sore and irritable, her schemes were in no danger; and she knew enough of Hammond's character, and suspected enough of his policy, to believe that he would be more likely to increase this irritability of her daughter's mood than to soothe or overcome it. We shall see whose politics were the wisest.

The greater portion of the company having arrived, the grounds began to be filled with groups, detaching themselves from the mass, each for the gratification of his or her peculiar sympathies. Some of the younger damsels might be seen swinging or skipping rope under the shade-trees, with a fair sprinkling of dapper young lads to devour, with greedy looks of love, their several movements and devices. Here and there, along the avenue, might be seen a whizzing ball, in the hurling of which the youngsters were the performers, and the ladies were lookers on; while tables, spread conveniently, offered cakes and lemonade as refreshments to the languid and exhausted. But anon, the drum gave the gratuitous signal, and the clarionet and violin led the way for a procession. The swing and rope were abandoned in a moment, the ball received its last cast. The youth of both sexes came together, and paired off, by a very natural movement, which showed how sympathetic were the instincts of both parties; and away they march in a procession which led through a beautiful avenue of oaks and cedars. It was at this moment, and while our young friend Jones Barry, being plucked by the sleeve by Mrs. Foster, was breaking away from the society of Tom Nettles, and rushing forward to offer his arm to Geraldine, that Randall Hammond was seen suddenly to glide from under a clump of shade-trees, near the avenue, and anticipate his intentions. Geraldine certainly did not, in her countenance, reflect the spite which was apparent in the visage of the mother, at this moment, to Tom Nettles, who muttered to himself with that sort of grin and chuckle which the man of mischief puts on when he sees sport.

"It sticks, old lady, does it? and so it should. Ran. Hammond is the lad to conquer both of you."

His sneer and feeling did not prevent him from playing the gallant with the very lady whose vexation had so much pleased him. While the anger was yet quivering on her lip, he drew nigh, and with the sweetest smile in the world, and the nicest compliment, he tendered her his arm; which, as he was a most comely person and a moderately young bachelor, the judicious lady at once frankly accepted.

"Really," said he, "Mrs. Foster, you are in every respect fortunate. The day is just the day for such a *fête,* and it is no discredit to the company to say that it is worthy of your arrangements. I need not say that they are worthy of any company."

"Oh, Mr. Nettles, you overwhelm while you delight me!"

"True in every respect, my dear madam. I never saw so excellent and large a collection of fine people before in the county. I could scarcely have thought, indeed, that the county could boast of so many fashionable-looking people."

"Nor does it, Mr. Nettles!" answered the lady, with a delighted smile. "In some instances, I have gone out of the county for my guests."

"That explains it," said he, quietly, as if assured and satisfied. "Miss Foster," he continued, "is a beautiful creature. *They* would make a noble couple."

The motion of his hand was in the direction of Geraldine and Hammond, who were just wheeling out of sight in a turn of the avenue. The remark, which he well knew was wormwood to his hearer, remained unanswered. Nettles was a man to dash his bitter usually with some sweet; though, perhaps, the bitter was apt, finally, to preponderate.

"But it is the misfortune of young persons, who have no guardians sufficiently their seniors to command their veneration, to be perverse in such matters. I should fear that Miss Foster is too decidedly your companion to be sensible of your authority."

"There is some truth in what you say, Mr. Nettles, though, as her proper guardian, I ought not to confess it. But, the fact is that, when I yielded to the entreaties of Mr. Foster, I was but a child myself."

The words passed through the brain, but did not find their way to the tongue of Nettles: "Pretty well grown, and honestly twenty-eight, if old grandmother Crowell knew anything about it." He did not suffer any pause for reflection, as he answered—

"The county proverb is a true one, I'm afraid, Mrs. Foster."

"What proverb, Mr. Nettles?"

"That which says that the mothers are only the elder sisters of the daughters, and that the widows are always in the way of the virgins!"

"But you don't believe it, Mr. Nettles?"

"At this moment, I have every reason to do so;" and the grateful lady was not unconscious of the slight contracting pressure upon her own of the arm in which it rested. The thought irresistibly forced itself upon her—

"How strange that Mr. Nettles shouldn't have thought of a wife. Certainly, it's high time for him to do so, if he ever means to get one."

Nettles was a famous mocker, but we must follow the company rather than the conversation. The procession continued through most delightful groves, all the way to the mill-seat of Gushlynn. On the route, the young people sported like so many kids. Conspicuous among these was Jones Barry; who, playing his antics directly in the sight of Geraldine Foster, might, if he had been sufficiently observant and sagacious, have seen upon her countenance a scorn quite as expressive as that with which Michal saluted David when she saw him dancing along the highways. Geraldine, in respect of pride, was no bad representative of Saul's daughter. Barry was the centre of a bevy of fat girls, whose dimensions somewhat reminded him of the barkeeper's daughter, whom Nettles had counselled him to choose for a wife. It was evident that he was not less a favorite among them, because he consented to play antics in their sight. He might have had his choice among them, without leaving the rejected any better satisfied, or worse off. Miles Henderson revolved near Geraldine, but as an escort to one of the Baileys, a quiet, dignified girl, one of the three or four whom Mrs. Hammond was not unwilling that her son should espouse. The procession passed forward, the music still vibrated along the groves, and soon the groups began to arrive at the beautiful place chosen for the picnic, the fine park of open pines which spread along at the foot of the falling waters of Gushlynn. This was an abandoned mill-seat, the great dam and floodgate of which were still maintained in repair; the former being a broad carriage-track, overgrown on each side and perfectly shaded by great evergreens, the water-oak, the cedar, and several other trees; while the floodgate afforded a pretty and picturesque fall of water, whose torrents were always making a pleasant murmur for the groves. Above the dam lay an immense sheet of several thousand acres, several feet deep, of water; while below, the falling surplus found its way, after passing the wreck of the old mill-house, into a sweet little lake, which was sufficiently deep for midsummer bathing. This too was surrounded by an ample shade of evergreens, and the *tout ensemble* presented one of those lovely pictures of united elevation, water, and shade-tree which, after all, present the most durable materials for the landscape painter. Here then, along the mill-dam, in the shade of the pine woods below, and at intervals around the *reserve* and the lakelet of discharged waters, our company dispersed themselves, each after his own fashion seeking pleasure. Here again the swing was found, as well of rope as of great grape-vines on which the young damsels reclined, and in which they were rocked occasionally by the eager hands of the dutiful young men. Here, too, the ball was again put in requisition among the more athletic, who darted through the wide green avenues in graceful flight, or hurried in pursuit, with good-natured fury. Some of the young ladies did not scorn to engage in the play, though it was observed that all who did so had previously taken the precaution of wearing short frocks and ample pantalettes. These nice little appendages of the petticoats, it was perhaps censoriously remarked by some of the elder maidens, were worn quite gratuitously by several who in no other way could be suspected of being still in miniature girlhood. But this matter does not concern us. It may be well, however, to state that Geraldine, whatever might have been the imputations upon her eccentricity, was not seen to participate in any of these wilder exercises, though her excellent step-mother frequently urged it upon her, and stoutly seconded the entreaties of our friend Barry, who challenged her to a match at rope-skipping. That the eye of Hammond and his mother were both upon her, all the while, with some curiosity, did not discourage Mrs. Foster from her object. On the contrary, somewhat stimulated by seeing that they watched the daughter, she was more than ever anxious to persuade her to the exhibitions of the hoyden. We have already some knowledge of her policy. It did not succeed in this instance, even though, stung by refusal, she said bitterly, as she turned away from the girl:

"Well, you are perhaps right. I see that the Queen of Sheba, and her wise Solomon, are both watching you. They would never countenance, I suppose, any such innocent practices."

The high-spirited girl was half tempted to whirl away upon the rope, or to seize, and wing, and pursue the ball, as she heard this imputation upon her courage, but she too had her reflections, and prudently forbore. Indeed, she now began to feel, not only that she had something at stake, but that her step-mother was neither the most wise nor the most disinterested of counsellors. Barry, sustained by her guardian, she began to feel was something of a bore; and she was conscious of a purpose, which she now perforce maintained, which would sufficiently try the sense of propriety as well in Hammond as his mother. But of this hereafter. It is certain that she refused to do the *graces* on the skipping-rope, or the *fairies* in pursuit of the flying ball. She conducted herself with a demureness which, while it vexed her mother, was quite satisfactory to other parties; and Mrs. Hammond returned home, at an early hour in the day, much better reconciled to the object of her son's admiration than she was before she came.

Meanwhile, the business of the day proceeded with pleasure, as it had begun. Dinner was spread under the shade of the great trees; a well-considered repast, in which the provision was ample, and in good taste. In this matter, Mrs. Foster received no small assistance from her daughter, who had brought to her knowledge the refinements of the ancient and elegant city of Savannah. When one of the plain country ladies of the past generation beheld, for the first time, a display of silver forks, and silver fish and butter-knives, she exclaimed, with looks of genuine apprehension, "I reckon the widow must have *broke* Savannah!"

The fruits of the West Indies had been brought to grace the repast. There were oranges and lemons, plantains and bananas, pineapples and cocoanuts. There were preserved fruits and foreign cordials, and a very generous supply of champagne; a beverage which most effectually entrapped, to their overthrow, sundry persons who had never drank any beverage of similar flavor more grateful than "persimmon beer." Our friend, Jones Barry, through the agency of Mrs. Foster, was a conspicuous person in the order of the exercises.

He was rather a volunteer, when the champagne-corks were to be sprung, his whole soul being surrendered to the happiness of seeing the young ladies start with surprise at a sound which was so unwonted from such a source. We must add that his practice was scarcely so innocent when he busied himself in decoying the same simple damsels to such free draughts of the liquor as rendered them scarcely less ridiculous than himself. That mischievous creature, Tom Nettles, was busy, however, in playing upon Barry the same game which he played upon the girls, and he watched with no little pleasure the uncertain strides which the latter took among the several groups which he haunted, while his voice equally increased in thickness and rapidity. These ludicrous proceedings, however, were about to undergo a change. There is scarcely any human pleasure, as we know, which can be considered certain for three hours together. Our hero, Barry, in the midst of his merriment, suddenly remembered that he had a serious business before him; a look and a whisper from Mrs. Foster drew his attention to Geraldine, who had wandered off with Miles Henderson to the ancient mill-site, and was now to be seen at the extremity of one of the remaining beams or sleepers. The torrent ran at considerable depth below. Beside her, stood Miles Henderson. He seemed about to leave her; and, with the words, "Now's your time," Mrs. Foster left Barry to pursue his purpose.

Barry, who was a creature of simple impulses, immediately started away, and, in his passage up the mill-dam, met Miles Henderson returning alone. Poor Miles had given in his petition, but without waiting or seeking for a present answer. He only implored that Miss Foster would read his billet at the first opportunity, and communicate her reply as soon as possible. He muttered something about anxiety and suspense; but he was rather unintelligible to himself, and he could not trust himself to be more explicit. He was crossing the mill-bank quietly, without seeking to attract attention, and was just about to descend to the plain, when Barry appeared below. The latter, however, perceiving the object whom he was pursuing to be still lingering at the end of the great sleeper which crossed the chasm, one end resting upon the bank and the other upon the opposite foundations of the mill-house, proceeded to take the shortest route for reaching her, and, instead of keeping the bank, he darted aside, and was in a few moments seen upon the sleeper. The height was a dizzy one, and so was the head of the daring suitor. Miss Foster, seeing his approach, hastily thrust the note of Henderson into her bosom. At this moment, and when he was half way across the passage, he began to fumble in his own bosom, and before he or anybody could conjecture his peril, he toppled suddenly, lost his balance, and went over, kicking and floundering with ineffectual struggles, into the boiling waters below. Fortunately, they were deep enough to break his fall, which was some twelve or fifteen feet, and he disappeared, headforemost, in the petty gulf. Geraldine screamed aloud, for she saw the accident instantly, and the scream was echoed by a dozen other pretty damsels on the opposite side. It required but a few moments to make the event known among the crowd, and twenty seconds had not elapsed before Tom Nettles and Randall Hammond had made their way to the edge of the lake, where Barry was now struggling with very ineffectual efforts, his wine being diluted, seemingly, to the entire defeat of his energies, by the disproportionate quantity of the inferior liquid which he had swallowed after it perforce. A couple of long-pointed poles happened to be convenient, and were seized in the same instant by Hammond and Nettles. With these they fished the poor fellow up by his clothes, to the bank, the mischievous Nettles contriving, more than once, by seemingly awkward movements, to thrust him down into the lake just when he expected to be out of it. It was in vain that Hammond honestly labored to get the gallant upon his legs. It happened, unfortunately for Barry, that his head lay nearest to Nettles; and the *wilful agitation* of the latter, with his pole thrust into the breast of Barry's coat, succeeded in giving him several severe dips before he was finally extricated.

"Whoo! Tom! What the devil, man! would you drown me in a mill-pond?"

"No, Jones, my dear fellow; but I'm quite nervous at your situation—quite."

And, as he spoke, the head of the unfortunate took another plunge, at the very moment when Hammond was drawing him ashore by the leg. He came forth looking aghast, shook himself like a water-dog, and it was then seen, for the first time, that he held a letter clasped in his hand.

"Why, Jones, what have you got there?" demanded Nettles.

"A letter!" and, with the words, he cast his eye up to the head of the mill-seat, as if still looking for Geraldine. But she was no longer in sight.

"A letter! Where the deuce did you get it?—at the bottom of the lake?"

"Don't ask me, old fellow. I'm no better than a heathen icicle. I'm chilled to the heart. Get me into the bushes, and bring me a bottle of champagne."

"A good brandy-toddy would be better," said the other, while he hurried off. Hammond then conducted him into the woods, while he summoned his servant to go off for fresh clothing.

"Won't you go home yourself, Barry?" demanded Nettles, when he returned, having first administered his drink.

"No; I feel better now. I shall be dry soon. Here, Tony—[*to the boy in waiting*]—kindle up a fire, and let me know what the natural feeling of dry breeches is. What a d——d affair it is!"

"Dreadful!" said Nettles. "But that letter, Jones?"

"Oh! if you must see it, there it is."

Nettles, reading the address—

"To Miss Geraldine Foster," &c.

At these words, Hammond disappeared, leaving the two friends together. It was night when they showed themselves again, Barry looking as happy as if nothing had happened, and ready for all the grateful intricacies of the Virginny reel.

CHAPTER XV.

Mrs. Foster was greatly discomfited at the disaster of her favorite. She contrived, however, to keep her countenance; an effort of which her daughter was not capable. She, as well as most of the young damsels, as soon as it was discovered that Barry was in no danger, laughed outright at his predicament, and were extremely amused and interested at the way in which he was fished out of the pond; the particular part taken by Nettles in this delicate operation being very intelligible to most of them. His disappearance in the bushes was followed by a movement of the whole party. The day had passed with great satisfaction to most of the company, and even this accident did not materially abate the general satisfaction. The dinner was excellent; the cates, viands, the wines and dessert, in especial, were equally new and grateful to the popular palate; and it was with heightened feelings of enjoyment, and heightened expectations also, that the guests listened to the signal of the drum, which announced the return to the homestead. With flying colors and triumphant music, the gay cavalcade moved forward; but in order very different from that in which they came. There was now more life and impulse, and less formality. People are more at home usually after the wine and walnuts; and the chatter was incessant, the laughter wild, and not a few pranks and petty excesses were practised on the return route among the younger people. Hammond did not now escort Miss Foster. He left that pleasant duty to other gallants, of whom the fair damsel had a liberal supply. Henderson also kept aloof, feeling quite too anxious and too much interested in the result of his application to risk himself near the person who held his fate in her hands. The return of the party was happily timed to bring them into the grounds about the "Lodge," just about dusk. A fairy scene greeted the eyes of the guests as they now drew nigh. A hundred altars seemed to flame, at intervals, among the trees and along the great avenue. Here rude elevations had been made of clay and sand, upon which piles of dry combustible pine had been accumulated, and which were now all blazing brightly, in sharp, upward-darting tongues of fire. The rich illumination lighted up the scene less softly and brightly, indeed, but even more picturesquely than the moonshine; and the happy groups wandered through various pathways over which the blazing brands cast a rich, red lustre, that eminently enlivened the rude forests, and made the particular trees stand forth, each like a frowning giant. The admiration of the company was unanimous, and Mrs. Foster exulted in a triumph which she did not inform any of her guests was due wholly to the fancy of her step-daughter. For that matter, the entire scheme of the day belonged to the latter. All that was fanciful and picturesque in the design originated in her taste and invention. Tea was served, as the party wandered among the trees in the park. The tables which had borne lemonade and cakes in the morning, were now covered with hissing urns and fairy-like cups of china; and here the pledges for partners were given for the dances which were to follow. After the pleasant fashion of the peasants in the south of Europe, gay squadrons prepared to dance under the shade-trees, and by the light of the pine-blazing altars. Others, more considerate of domestic forms and health, prepared to occupy the great hall, the parlor, and piazza of the dwelling-house. The music was already in full discourse, and the groups whirling in the dance, when Nettles and Barry made their appearance. The latter had been fortunate, taxing the full speed of his horse "Glaucus;" the "Fair Geraldine" being in too great esteem to be used for common purposes, in getting from home a fresh supply of snugly-fitting garments. His long-tailed blue, and shining gold buttons, made a conspicuous figure in the assembly, particularly when contrasted with his pantaloons, of the most delicate velvet buff. Mrs. Foster saw his return with delight. The good lady had begun to be apprehensive of the game. She was afraid that the ridiculous attitude in which he had been placed, his somerset from the sleeper into the lake, and the unhappy floundering which followed there, had disgusted her daughter. She was also by no means a satisfied spectator of the frequent, though brief and broken sketches of conversation which had taken place between Geraldine and Hammond. The reappearance of Barry, restored in appearance, and looking rather attractive, was refreshing. She drew him privately into an inner room, and, while she served him with a dish of tea from her own hands, she could not forbear breaking forth with—

"Really, Barry, how could you make yourself so ridiculous?"

"Ridiculous!" he exclaimed, sipping the beverage; "I ridiculous, ma'am?"

"Such a ridiculous situation, I mean!"

"Perilous, you mean?"

"Yes! it was perilous. But how did you come to fall? What carried you out on that sleeper?"

"I reckon the champagne had something to do with it; champagne and love together."

"Love?"

"To be sure! What else? Wasn't Miss Geraldine at one end of the log, and alone? Didn't you give me the hint, and wasn't this the letter?"

Here he showed the luckless epistle, which, full of fiery virtue, might be supposed to have been well tempered by its subsequent saturation, like a hissing blade of Damascus in the sacred waters of the Baraddee. Mrs. Foster seized the neatly-folded epistle in her hands.

"Give it to me! I will deliver it myself, this very night. Meanwhile, do you go out and make yourself agreeable with the young ladies. Don't be too particular with Geraldine. Only let her see you, and see that you can make yourself agreeable to others. Dance with that Miss Berrie; flirt as much as you can with Miss Dooly. Either of them would be glad to snap you up. Let her see that! There's several others, Miss Higbee, Ellen Mairs, and Sophronia Ricketts, all of whom will be glad to have you 'squire them. Only don't be rash, don't venture any strange thing, and all will go right. I'll deliver the letter!"

"Well! I thank you very much, for I was beginning to feel quite squeamish about it. I'm a little afeard that Hammond's getting on rather fast!"

"He! never fear. He has dropped too many stitches for him to take up in a hurry. Will you have some more tea?"

"I shouldn't care if I had something stronger."

"Oh! you mustn't think of any such thing now. I can give you stronger *tea*."

"Well; if there's nothing better."

"Taste that," said the hostess, spooning him from a cup which the servant handed; and the scene was a good one for the painter. Barry, like an overgrown boy, sitting back in his chair, while the fair widow—by no means old or uncomely—cup and saucer in one hand, and spoon in the other, fed him with the smoking beverage.

"Prime!" said he, with an air of satisfaction. Then taking the cup, he dashed it off with something less of appetite than resolution; and, abruptly darting from the chamber, hurried out to seek a partner. Mrs. Foster followed him with eager interest, and was at length pleased to see him sprightly whirling it with the bouncing Rebecca Floyd. It was with no dissatisfaction that she beheld Miles Henderson dancing with Geraldine. It was somewhat strange that she entertained no such fears of this young man as of his friend. He was quite a worthy and a very *lovable* person; tall, graceful, good-looking, very amiable, and tolerably well off in point of fortune. But, somehow, these qualifications never occasioned a fear; though they were in all respects, but that of fortune, very far superior to any of the possessions of her favorite. She kept the couple in sight till the dance was over; and then hurriedly summoned Geraldine, in a whisper, to the inner room, but not before Hammond had succeeded in engaging her for the country dance that followed; the silly and highly objectionable custom of securing partners for many dances ahead, not then prevailing as it does now—certainly not "in these diggings." When the two were safely together in the snug little apartment, where Barry but a little while before had sipped his tea, Mrs. Foster, with a very triumphant air, thrust the letter of that worthy into the hands of the young lady.

"There! There's something for you."

"What's this?"

"An offer!"

"Indeed! Here's a pair of them, then, I suppose," said the maiden, somewhat coolly, as, for the first time, she took from her bosom the billet of our friend, Henderson. "First come, first served," and she proceeded to break the seal of the latter.

"Who's that from?" asked the step-mother, with some anxiety.

"Miles Henderson. He gave it me at the mill."

"Oh, well!" and the good lady seemed relieved as the daughter proceeded in its perusal. This done, she laid it quietly on the table; Mrs. Foster taking it up and going over it as soon as she had laid it down. The perusal of Jones Barry's declaration followed, on the part of the person to whom it was addressed, and Mrs. Foster watched Geraldine's countenance with increasing curiosity, while pretending to examine Henderson's letter. But she gathered nothing from the face of our heroine. She read the one epistle, as she had done the other, with a singular calm, amounting to indifference; and, handing it to the mother, begged her to take care of both.

"But what will you say? What are you going to do? You accept?"

"There's no hurry! I'm not in the humor now to think of these things. The gentlemen deserve that I should think of their offers respectfully."

"Oh, certainly! But Barry?"

"Mr. Jones Barry must learn to wait as well as his neighbor," was the quiet reply; and at that moment Geraldine was relieved from further questioning by the entry of Miss Betsy Graystock, who bounced in to say that Mr. Randall Hammond was looking for his partner, the country dances being about to begin. It was with some chagrin that Mrs. Foster saw the promptness with which her *protégé* hurried out after this notice; and her disquiet increased as she watched the couple through all the mazes of the dance that followed. It was her endeavor to keep these parties continually in sight, while they remained together; but this was not altogether possible, consistently with her cares and duties as hostess. Her attention was finally called off to some domestic arrangements; and, while she was engaged in the inner room, the dance ceased. Returning to look after her charge, as soon as the confusion of shifting groups could possibly allow, she was a little displeased and distressed to find that they were now nowhere in sight. It was not her policy to afford to Hammond— whose influence over Geraldine she really began to apprehend—any unnecessary opportunities; and, seizing Barry by the arm, she sent him off, with a whisper, to look for Geraldine in one direction, while she set off herself, in another, to detect the whereabouts of her supposed companion.

Hammond, meanwhile, had readily persuaded Geraldine to a promenade under the shade-trees along the avenue. They were not alone in this measure. The gay groups, most of them, after dancing, had taken a similar direction; and, as the night was pleasant, they might be seen straying away through the various groves, glimpsing here and there through the prolonged vistas, their white garments gleaming spiritually under the flickering lights from the numerous blazing pyres of pine wood, which the watchful care of the negroes in attendance from time to time supplied with fuel. The search of Barry and Mrs. Foster was not an easy one, to examine these various groups and trace out the particular couple among the scattered flocks that wound about capriciously in every turning of the wood. It was still more difficult, when the object of Hammond—perhaps not unobserved by his companion—was temporary secrecy and seclusion. He led her away from all other sets, and, in the doubtful light of a half-decaying pile, and under the friendly shadows of a venerable oak which had lived long enough to know how to keep secrets, and was probably too deaf to hear, our hero made his declaration. He spoke in warm and touching language, evidently with a full and feeling heart, but still in accents of a firm and dignified character. The imperfect light did not suffer him to perceive the emotion which his proposals occasioned on the cheeks of the damsel; but he felt her hand tremble in his, and her reply was slow. For some moments, indeed, a profound silence followed his speech, and his heart began to sink with a feeling of dread and disappointment, for which, it must be confessed, he found himself very imperfectly prepared. But, with some abruptness in her manner, as if her reply was the result of a real effort, and was, indeed, foreign to the genuine feeling which was at her heart, she somewhat surprised him by saying—

"I am honored, Mr. Hammond, by your offer, and—"

There was a pause, when she again began—

"You have heard, no doubt, Mr. Hammond, that I am a very thoughtless, a very whimsical, a very capricious, a very eccentric girl, and, in truth, I am so. I have been very foolish, and my foolish resolutions sometimes trouble me, as they do in this instance. But the kind and complimentary declaration which you have made reminds me of one of my own, and I am half ashamed to tell you what it is."

"Indeed! But, dear Miss Foster, you cannot doubt that I will be the most indulgent of all judges—"

"Oh, surely, as far as it is possible; but your declaration makes you an interested one, and my resolve concerns this very declaration."

"Indeed!" with an air of some surprise.

"Yes, indeed!" and there was now some little pique mingled in with the lady's embarrassment; "but it concerns not only your proposals, sir, but those of other persons. You must know, sir, and I do not mention the fact except from the necessity of the case, that yours is the third offer of marriage which I have had to-day."

"Then, Miss Foster, I am to understand that I am too late?" This was said rather proudly.

"Not so, Mr. Hammond. You are, on the contrary, rather quick. I have as yet determined on neither, and a rash resolution—a foolish vow—makes it impossible that I should determine directly. I—I have been very foolish, sir."

The poor girl seemed really very much embarrassed. Her sympathies were all with Hammond; but her pride had been committed, and it was still watchful and resentful. Hammond perceived and felt for her embarrassment.

"If I knew what to say or what to do!" said he. "If I could only conjecture the cause of your embarrassment!"

And he hesitated. The pride of the girl came to her relief.

"I have been very foolish, no doubt; but that is no reason why I should be cowardly. I must risk the reproach of being whimsical and ridiculous; but you shall know all. Mr. Hammond, your horse 'Ferraunt' is, you tell me, the fastest horse in the country?"

Her companion was confounded. This question, seemingly so absurd, was put with all imaginable seriousness; nay, with something like a vehement earnestness, while the speaker looked directly up into the face of the person she addressed, as if anxiously awaiting his answer. He was bewildered.

"Really, Miss Foster, you surprise me. What can the speed of my horse have to do with the matter?"

"A great deal—a great deal. Only tell me, is it not so? Is not 'Ferraunt' the fastest horse in the country? In short, can't he beat Mr. Henderson's 'Sorella,' and the 'Geraldine,' my namesake, of Mr. Barry's?"

"Such is my opinion. Nay, without an accident, I am very sure of it. But really, Miss Foster, you must again permit me to express my surprise at the question."

"Oh, I know that you think me very ridiculous, and I am so—I am so," answered the girl, now laughing playfully and wildly, as if with a heart fully relieved of a burden.

"Forgive me, sir, I am but a child; seventeen only, to-day. Forgive me; but will you spare me to-night? Suffer me to convey to you my answer in writing."

She gave him her hand as she spoke. He seized and conveyed it to his lips, and the action was in noways rebuked. But it was witnessed. Mrs. Foster broke in, at this moment, with "Geraldine, Geraldine! my daughter, you are wanted."

"I am with you, mother;" and she whirled away with the intruder, who had barely time to say, "What do I see, Geraldine?" when Jones Barry came up to entreat the hand of the latter for the next cotillon, and to relieve her from the necessity of answering a very awkward question.

CHAPTER XVI.

THAT LAST DRINK AND DANCE, AND WHAT CAME OF IT.

WE must premise that, when dispatched by Mrs. Foster in search of Geraldine, Jones Barry did not proceed directly upon his mission. He was diverted from this object by his friend Tom Nettles, who appeared to have been seeking, and who, seizing him by the arm, drew him to the rear of the building with a look and manner of very mysterious confidence.

"Jones," said he, "champagne is an excellent creature, and so is sherry. I like them very well in their way. But they seem to me, in comparison with our good old Georgia drinks, like the dessert to the solid feast. The nuts are good, the raisins, cakes, and almonds; but, after all, my boy, give me a genuine haunch of venison, a good smoking ham, and a fat turkey, or a pair of ducks. So with these wines. I acknowledge champagne to be a fiery, well-bred gentleman; but he is too uniformly genteel and delicate. I want more solid argument than he can give me, and so I turn, when I can, to a sober whiskey-punch, a brandy cocktail, or a peach or apple toddy."

"But you can't get any of them here," said Barry, eagerly.

"Can't I? Leave Tom Nettles alone for finding out where the weasel sleeps. This fellow Abram, who serves as a sort of major-domo in the widow's household—By the way, Jones, the widow would suit you better than the daughter; she's a better armfull. Don't you think so?"

"She looks well."

"Ay, and would wear well, old fellow."

"She would, indeed."

"Think of it. It's worth a thought."

"It's too late now."

"What! are you engaged to the daughter?"

"I suppose you may say so. It's as good as that. I've handed in the letter."

"P-h-e-w! Don't halloo till you're out of the wood."

"But to the liquor. Abram—"

"Oh, Abram: yes! Well, that Abram's a fellow after one's own heart; and, whether you marry the daughter or the widow, I hope you'll give him to me. Feeling the want of the stronger spirit, I said to him: 'Abram, this is a pleasant fellow, this champagne, to say a word to at coming and at parting, but he don't seem to answer so well through a long visit. Now, haven't you something in the shape of a plain, homely, sensible old Georgia drink, that won't foam, and hiss, and sparkle when you speak to it?' Upon which the fellow whispers to me: 'Old master had a jimmyjohn of mighty fine peach in the garret, and, since he's gone, we never uses it.' 'Abram,' says I, 'your master was a sensible man when alive, and I hope was sensible enough when he died to go to a place of good spirits. God bless him, and us. Abram, my lad, can you get us a look at that jimmyjohn?' "

"Well?" demanded Barry, somewhat eagerly.

"Well! Here it is, and here's Abram, and here's a few fellows like yourself, ready to take a toss at the tankard."

They had now reached an apartment in the basement of the building, where a few rude tables sustained a world of crockery, cups, plates, and glasses, such as had already been used above stairs. On one of these tables stood the ancient demijohn, covered with antique dust and honoring cobwebs. Honey, water, cups, and tumblers were in readiness, and nothing was to be done but drink. Even the beverage—a sufficient quantity—had been mixed in anticipation by the judicious Nettles, and the beaker, that was thrust into Barry's grasp, glittered to the brim, with equal strength and sweetness. In the taste of the sweet, he did not recognize the potency and excess of the strength, and it was with a royal mind that he now broke away from the group of drinkers to continue his search after Geraldine. We have seen at what moment and under what circumstances he found her. As he left Nettles and his companions, a loud laugh attested the conspiracy.

"He has it," cried Nettles.

"A most mortal shot," said Dick.

"It'll floor him, sure," said Ned.

" 'Twould floor a bullock," muttered Peter; and, with these calculations, they all scattered in pursuit of their victim, with a view to watching the results.

Meanwhile, unsuspicious of danger, and with a confidence in himself gradually increasing as the peach began to "blossom" in his veins, Jones Barry led his partner triumphantly to the hall, where the dancers were rapidly assembling from all quarters. The company had begun to thin; the hour was becoming late; the old people had pretty much departed, except those inveterate appetizers who will wait through the tedious rounds of dancing in which they do not share, in order to partake of the supper, in which they never fail to insist upon something more than their share. It is not every day, with these, that Paddy kills his favorite cow, and they make the most of the event when he does. There they sat or stood about the room, waiting anxiously the close of the last cotillon. Meanwhile, the music sounded merrily, and the dancers began to vault and whirl. Jones Barry and Geraldine found themselves confronted by Tom Nettles and Polly Ewbanks—Polly being the most portly of all the fair people assembled—as ignorant of the dance as a horse, and as clumsy as an elephant. But Polly had a rather pretty face, and though she felt doubtful of the sort of display which her legs would make, she was willing to peril them rather than lose the chance of a market for her face. With rosy red cheeks, and a rolling, swimming motion, like a great Dutch galliot in a heavy, swelling sea, Polly went to and fro, very imperfectly steadied by the arm, and hand, and counsels of her partner. "Why the deuce," was the thought of Barry, "did Tom Nettles choose such a woman for his partner, when so many so much more comely and compatible could be had?" But Tom had his reasons. There was mischief in his eye, only perceptible, however, to his comrades, one of whom was in the same set with our couple, while the others were eagerly and anxiously looking on. But Jones Barry had neither the time, nor was he in the mood, to make reflections. The peach began to poach upon the territories of his brain. He leaped high, he vaulted, whirled, wheeled, clapped his hands, and at length seemed about to reach that condition of *extase* in which certain virgins under religious inspiration have

attained, by which they can stand upon the air and dance upon nothing, without the aid of any unseemly ornaments about the neck.
Geraldine began to be disquieted; but her situation admitted of no
extrication. She felt its annoyances the more as she beheld, at a little
distance, the grave, sedate, and circumspect eye of Randall Hammond
fixed upon the proceedings. But the confusion grew. First, there was
some little awkwardness in Tom Nettles himself. He wheeled to the
right when he should have gone left, and when the figure called
him to cross over, he sent his partner into the arena. She was
constantly blundering; but this Jones Barry was now becoming too
happy to perceive. Though a very fair dancer himself, his errors
soon became apparent. Yet he was correcting Nettles all the while.

"Wrong, Tom; to the right about! Now we go! How it blazes!
Whoop! She flies! Glorious, Tom; eh?" and he strove, while
speaking, to bestow a significant look with those eyes which were
momently becoming more and more small. Round he went, whirling
his partner with him. Round went Tom Nettles, with his nearly
round partner, her enormous sides seeming to sweep and force back,
at the same moment, every object of the circle.

"Wrong, Mr. Barry," said Geraldine, as he darted forward with
a bound after the leviathan beauty.

"Not a bit of it!" he cried, with a hiccough.

"Here!" said Nettles to Polly Ewbanks.

"There!" he cried, in the next moment.

"Now!" he muttered, as he wheeled her forward.

"Here!" as he whirled her back. Her face was as red as the sun
at setting, after a hard day's travel in hot weather. Her breath came
and went without leaving her very sure of its coming. Barry grew
more and more happy; made all sorts of movements, to all points
of the compass; and, at length, while all was buzz, and bustle, and
confusion, a terrible concussion was heard. He had come in conflict
with Polly, in one of his erratic moments, and the event was precisely
such as might be anticipated from the encounter of the earth with
the tail of the great comet. It was more than a comet's tail, comparatively speaking, that which overthrew Jones Barry; but down he
went, his legs passing completely from under him, and between the
uplifted feet of Polly, effecting that catastrophe which the mere

jostle with him had not occasioned. Down she went also, in the midst of the ring, which spread out on all sides to make the space which her dimensions rendered necessary, and with a squall that shook the house to its centre. There was no describing the scene—the terror, the screams, the disquiet.

"Back to back!" cried Barry, now fairly drunk, and sending out his legs as well as he could, with their movements somewhat cramped by the pile which the fair Polly still continued to present, as a sort of fortress against all his efforts.

"Help me up, for mercy's sake!" was the imploring entreaty of the fat unfortunate. Nettles tried honestly to do so, but his laughter deprived him of all his strength; and it was left for Randall Hammond; who, at the first signal of tumult, extricated Geraldine from the ring, to do this friendly office for the confounded maiden, whose hurts and alarm had not made her forgetful and indifferent to the awkward exhibition which she had made, particularly in falling, an event rendered utterly unavoidable from the fact that Barry's feet came between her legs at the moment when she was whirling upon a single pin. The dance broke up in the rarest confusion, Barry being borne out by Nettles, with the assistance of some other of the conspirators; having hurt his head, as it was fabled, with striking against the floor. But the blow came from the "peach" out of that antique "jimmyjohn," which Abram had so unwisely discovered among his old master's treasures. The unfortunate gallant was taken to an outhouse, and snugly put to sleep upon a straw heap; his last intelligible words being: "Back to back! back to back, Miss Polly!"

CHAPTER XVII.

SHOWING THAT, AS REGARDS HORSEFLESH, A WOMAN IS AS STUBBORN AS A MULE.

THAT night Jones Barry slept at the "Lodge." The excellent hostess, who but too justly suspected his condition, having made the proper inquiries after the departure of her guests, soon ascertained where his treacherous friend, Nettles, had bestowed him, and had him borne to a comfortable chamber. He himself seemed to have been unconscious of the transition. It is the tradition, which Nettles traced up to Abram, that the only words spoken by him, when disturbed for removal, were the same which he had last spoken in the ball-room: "Back to back, Miss Polly." The next day at a late hour, on opening his eyes, he found Abram in waiting. Coffee and toast were brought him in his chamber; for his offences were readily forgiven by his indulgent hostess, and no attentions were withheld. She gave him every opportunity. He came forth at noon, looking very much ashamed of himself, with only a confused recollection of what had taken place. He said not a syllable about the peach-brandy, but the good housekeeper had already extorted a confession from Abram. This she kept to herself; and, in conversing with him about the accident, she generously threw all the blame upon poor Polly Ewbanks.

"She's so monstrous fat, and so mighty clumsy, that I wonder she ever shows herself among young people at all. But how's your head now, Mr. Barry?"

"Prime! 'Twould be better, I think, if I had a little something to settle my stomach. I ate too many sweet things last night."

"Perhaps they put too much honey in your peach!" said the widow, slyly.

"Peach, oh! I do recollect drinking a little with Nettles. By the way, Mrs. Foster, a little of that stuff, it's a fine old liquor, wouldn't be amiss."

"On the principle," retorted the widow, "so well known among you gay young men, that the hair of the dog is always good for the bite."

"Ah!" said the offender, "I'm afraid you know everything, Mrs. Foster. You're quite too knowing; yes, you are!"

"We know enough to be indulgent, Mr. Barry. What say you to the peach?"

His assent was not hard to obtain, and while Mrs. Foster compounded the peach toddy with honey, she gave him the gratuitous information that "poor dear Mr. Foster was quite fond of his peach-dram. I made it for him regularly twice a day, Mr. Barry; once about this hour, and once just before he went to bed."

"What a dutiful wife!" was the reflection of Barry, as he heard these words, and followed the graceful movements of the widow. He remembered the words of Nettles: "Not a bad armful, indeed!" His further reflections were arrested by her presentation of the spoon, as she had administered the tea the evening before, but now filled with a very different beverage.

"How's that to your liking?"

"It's the very thing. Ah! you know the way to a man's heart!"

The answer to this compliment was arrested by the sudden entrance of Geraldine.

"You here, Mr. Barry?"

"I'm never anywhere else!" said he, quite gallantly. "How are you this morning, Miss Geraldine?"

"I should rather ask after your health!" was her quiet but sarcastic answer. "You were in the chapter of accidents yesterday. How's your head?"

"Much better, I thank you! If my heart were only half so well!"

"Your heart! bless me! what's the matter with that?"

"Ah! the pain—"

"A pain in your heart! Does it come and go, Mr. Barry?"

"No! It stays!"

"Then you ought, by all means, to consult a surgeon. There's nothing more dangerous. You may go off in a minute. If you will allow me to advise, I'd set out for Savannah, without a moment's delay. Nay! I'd go to New York, and see the celebrated Doctor Physick."

"No! no! Miss Geraldine, no physic for me. It's not a pain that physic can cure. You, Miss Geraldine, you can do more for me than any doctor."

"I! in what manner?"

Barry looked about him. Mrs. Foster had left the room. He drew his chair a little closer.

"You got a letter from me, yesterday?"

"Last night, sir, yes!"

"Last night, yes."

There was a moment's silence. At length Geraldine, throwing aside the ironical manner which she had been employing, and, without any disquiet in her air, said frankly—

"Mr. Barry, I'm very much obliged to you for the favorable opinion which you have of me." He bowed and smiled. "But," she continued, "I have made a vow that no man shall have my hand unless he wins it."

"Wins it?"

"Yes! Now, sir, you have a beautiful horse which you have done me the honor to call after me. You have said, a thousand times in my presence, that this horse is able to beat any in the county. If this be the case, sir, you are able to win my hand, and I put it upon the speed of your horse to do so."

"I did think, Miss Geraldine, that my filly could outstretch any other horse in the county, but you yourself saw that she was beaten by 'Sorella.' "

"Yes; but you told me that she was barely beaten, and only in consequence of previous fatigue and your own too great weight as a rider, in comparison with the rider of 'Sorella,' who was a mere boy. Now, I tell you, in the same day when I was honored with your proposals, I received those of Mr. Henderson and Mr. Hammond."

"And what do they say to this?"

"They have not yet been answered. My answer goes to each of them to-day. You will communicate with them. You will arrange with them for the trial of speed, and the day of the contest shall be the day of the wedding."

"Miss Geraldine, permit me to say that you're a most strange young person."

"I am afraid so, Mr. Barry, but I can't help it. I've made this strange resolution, and I can't break it. You're at liberty to enter the field or not, at your pleasure, and that you may freely enjoy this freedom, I beg leave to hand you back this letter."

"Oh! I'll try. I'm not afraid. If Miles Henderson has to ride 'Sorella,' I'll be sure to beat him on 'Geraldine.' I don't know what sort of a horse is that of Ran. Hammond's. They say he's a top-goer, but I'm not afraid. I'm ready. I'll try for it."

"Then, sir, you will see and confer with them. In this paper, you have my conditions, which I had drawn out to send you, not expecting to see you here. Suffer me now to wish you good morning."

"It's most deuced strange!" was the beginning of a soliloquy which the entrance of Mrs. Foster arrested. He immediately proceeded to unfold the answer which he had received; an unnecessary labor, since the amiable widow, from a neighboring closet, had listened to every syllable. He was surprised to see her looking so well pleased, and expressed his astonishment and his apprehensions.

"Fear nothing!" was the consoling assurance of the widow. "This requisition of Geraldine's, in fact, leaves the game entirely in your hands."

"How's that? That beast of a horse 'Sorella' has already beaten 'Geraldine.'"

"You'll be able to walk the course! They'll not run! This fellow, Hammond, is as proud as Lucifer. He will bounce outright at the proposition, as an insult; and if *he* didn't, his mother wouldn't let him run, for she's as proud as the devil's dam. Between 'em, they'll look upon Geraldine as little better than insulting 'em; I've managed that. In fact, I've put her upon the whole scheme; so that, if she really had any preference for either of these men, she might kill off her own chances in your favor."

"It does brighten," said he, "but what of Henderson?"

"He'll do just as Hammond tells him—just as Hammond does. There's no fear of him. Only you take care to say that you *will* run; say so from the beginning, and make your arrangements, and leave the rest to me."

"But when's the day?"

"That's to be left for those to determine who enter for the prize. The marriage is to take place on the evening of the day when the race is decided. In other words, you're to start from a fixed point at a certain hour, on a certain day, the competitors all together, and he who first comes up to the door of the 'Lodge' may claim the lady. I am to know the day, and the wedding feast shall be prepared, and the parson shall be in readiness."

"It's a new way of doing business."

"It's the way for you, so see to it; and don't let out to Nettles or anybody what I tell you of my calculations, for then they might come to other resolutions, if it was only to balk us. If they once thought I had anything to do with it, they'd most certainly do so; for then they'd think that Geraldine was directed what to do by me."

We need not linger with these parties. If Jones Barry was confounded by the answer received to *his* proposals, what was the astonishment of Miles Henderson and Hammond? The letter to the former was a simple but respectful one. It declared the resolution of the lady, and forbore all expression of feeling or opinion. He sallied off with it to Hammond. The latter read it, and mentioned that he had also received an answer to his application, the purport of which was the same. He did not show the letter, however, and it was with a secret pleasure that he remarked a material difference in the style and wording of the two letters. While that to Henderson merely declared her determination, in simple terms, as if written without an effort, showing the writer to be comparatively indifferent to the feelings which she might provoke, that to himself was distinctly apologetic in its tone. While her requisition was precisely the same in both the letters, she was here prepared to show something like a regret that it had been made. "I deem it right to say," was the language in one place, "if only in justice to myself, that it is rather in obedience to a resolution, perhaps rashly made, but which I must still hold inviolate, that I attach so singular a condition and qualification to my assent, particularly where, as in the present instance, the application, as I am well aware, does me so much honor."

This may have been ironically said, but it was more grateful to the self-esteem of Hammond to fancy otherwise: and though vexed and wondering at the absurdity of the requisition, it was somewhat grateful to discover such a decided difference in the language employed in Henderson's letter, and his own. Besides, he recollected with feelings of satisfaction the inquiries which the young lady had made the night previously as to the speed of his horse. All this made it sufficiently apparent to his vanity that she desired his success; and yet the requisition was not the less offensive to all his ideas of propriety.

"To choose her husband according to the legs of his horse!" said Henderson, with praiseworthy indignation.

"It is astonishing! there is some mystery about it," said Hammond.

"To put us on the same footing with that silly creature, Barry!" exclaimed the one.

"The mother is at the bottom of it," responded the other.

"What is to be done?" cried Henderson. "I'll be d——d if I'll run a race to get a wife. If it's in the heels of my horse that she's to find my merits, I shall be at a loss where to look for hers."

"Very well said, Miles, and quite spirited. But, as you say, what's to be done? that's the question. Now, I'll tell you what I think. I propose to go and see Miss Foster in person, and to talk the matter over with her, showing all the absurdities of this requisition, and the ridiculousness of the position into which it will throw all parties. I think she may be persuaded to hear reason, for I am disposed to think that the whole affair originated with the step-mother. What she proposes to effect by it, unless it be merely to astonish the natives— a thing grateful enough to her silly vanity—it is impossible for me to conjecture. Now, without pressing Miss Foster on my own account, I propose simply to argue the matter with her; to show her how it will appear to the public; and endeavor to impress upon her how uncertain will be the securities of domestic happiness where the tie is based upon such conditions. What think you, Miles? Such was my purpose before you came."

"Has your mother heard of it—have you told her?"

"No; and I don't mean to tell her; for I know that she would at once require me to withdraw my proposals. She would never forgive Geraldine for what she would regard as an insult."

"And so do I consider it. But, as you say, she may be led by that woman, her step-mother, who is as mischievous as a young puppy.

I don't know but your plan is the right one. You go to her. You can talk with her. I'll ride over to Nettles's during the morning, and meet you here again at dinner."

"Very good," was the reply, and off the parties posted. To Nettles, Henderson unfolded his troubles; but that quiz could afford no consolation. The mystery was entirely beyond his solution. He thought the affair comical in high degree, and concluded that the principle once adopted—that of running a race for a wife—would completely revolutionize the concerns of marriage.

"It would certainly discourage me from the attempt to change my condition. I prefer running rigs to running races; and if I thought ever so much of a woman, I shouldn't thank her for admiring the legs of my horse more than she did my own;" and, with these words, he extended the favorite limbs—showing a handsomely-turned thigh, calf, and ankle—and stroked them with the complacency of a bachelor whose frequent escapes from the snares of the sex have sufficiently shown his value.

Meanwhile, the eyes of the widow Foster beheld our hero, Randall Hammond, wheel into the avenue and come cantering gently up to the entrance of the "Lodge." She hurried to the chamber of Geraldine, whom she found already acquainted with the fact. She did not perceive that the countenance of the latter expressed something like trepidation. She was arraying herself for the reception of the guest.

"Well, you'll have to see him," were the first words of the widow as she broke into the room; "but what he comes for, unless to make you break your resolution, I can't see. And now, Geraldine, show your firmness; for no matter what man you marry, if you waver now, you'll never be your own mistress afterwards. He'll rule you without mercy, if you don't. I know something of men. They're all tyrants where you let 'em; and this man, Randall Hammond, is perhaps by nature one of the greatest despots I ever saw. His mother's educating has made his nature a great deal worse than it would have been by itself. He's too proud, mark me, to run horse or man for you. He's too proud, in other words, to climb the tree for the fruit. It's a sufficient honor for him to open his mouth and let the ripe grape fall into it. But I wouldn't be so ripe as all that, either. Now, I know that he loves you desperately; and only you hold out, and make no concessions, and he'll have to come to your terms.

It'll be a bitter pill for his pride to swallow; but swallow it he will, rather than lose his fruit. All your happiness depends on his being made to see that you are firm. To keep from being imposed upon, a woman has only to show that she won't yield; and it will be as it was with Mohammed and the mountain—if you don't give in to the man, he'll have to give in to you. Mark what I say, my child, and keep to your resolution. Beware of his fine arguments, and have but the one answer: 'It's a vow, Mr. Hammond, it's a vow; and if you truly love me, you'll run off your own legs as well as your horse's, and not find it so difficult or so unpleasant.' Stick to that, and I'll engage all comes out as you wish it. He'd like to have you without any trouble, for that's what his pride requires; but, sooner than lose you, he'll run a foot-race into the bargain, and not stop at a 'hop, skip, and jump.' "

Mrs. Foster was accustomed to rabble on in this manner. But there was a great deal that was artful in her speech, a great deal which she did not believe herself, but which she yet framed adroitly to impress upon the belief of her daughter. Thus, while insisting that it was only the pride of Hammond that would revolt at the conditions which she stipulated, she yet took care to insist that this pride was not sufficiently stubborn to risk the final loss of charms which he so earnestly desired. She had, by this time, discovered that he was Geraldine's favorite, and she felt the danger of suggesting that (as she herself believed) there was every probability of his taking so much offence at the requisition as to withdraw his application for her hand. To stimulate her pride, therefore, without making timid her hope, was the policy of her game; and she had just the requisite cunning to succeed. When the servant announced Mr. Hammond, with the further intimation that he called to see Miss Foster in particular, Geraldine was armed with certain high notions of feminine prerogative, and was prepared to give his pride a lesson such as would make it tremble with just apprehensions for her love. Not that she felt quite secure in her convictions, but that she felt quite wilful. People frequently are never more apt to be perverse than when they feel that they reason feebly and unjustly, and, working upon childish passions and foolish principles, Mrs. Foster had succeeded in rousing a temper in her *protégé* which made her imperious without making her confident. She was resolute in her purpose as she descended to the parlor, but her heart trembled with strange chills and apprehensions all the while.

The first meeting was one of comparative awkwardness on both sides. But manliness was the particular characteristic of Randall Hammond. He had a duty to perform, and he soon approached it. Having satisfied himself of his course, there was a simple sturdy directness of purpose in his mind that brought him at once to its performance. Gently speaking, and tenderly taking her hand—a proceeding which she did not resent—he spoke in those soft, subdued accents, which are supposed to indicate equally the presence of a warm feeling and of a proper taste.

"My dear Miss Foster, you have proposed a singular condition for us, as that on which your hand is to be obtained."

"I said and felt that it was so, Mr. Hammond."

"But surely you are not serious in the requisition? You cannot surely mean to peril your happiness on the heels of a horse?"

"You put it in strange language, sir."

"But in language the most appropriate, certainly. This surely is the fact. You tell the gentlemen who propose for your hand that there is no choice between them. This, of itself, might well stagger the affections of one whose self-esteem is as active as his passion."

"But I did not mean anything of the sort, sir."

"Then, permit me to say, the case becomes still more perilous for yourself, if less offensive to the suitor; since, if you have a choice, you wilfully subject it to all the chances of the dice by risking it unnecessarily on the speed of an animal which may fail, of a rider who may fall, of a will which may take offence at so unwonted a requisition, and withdraw from the pursuit even where his affections are most deeply interested."

"It appears to me, Mr. Hammond, you describe a very feeble passion when you speak of such."

"By no means, Miss Foster. The passion may be as warm and active as it should be—the love unquenchable and enduring; but the sense of propriety no less tenacious, and the wholesome laws of principle too stubborn to give way to any impulses of the heart unless they are found justified by virtue."

"Is it possible, Mr. Hammond, that the affections should be warm or devoted where the individual refuses to peril his horse to obtain them?"

"I would peril my life for this hand, my dear Miss Foster, should occasion require it; but have you forgotten that most famous passage in the history of chivalry, when the imperious beauty, conscious of her power upon the heart of a noble knight, threw her glove into the amphitheatre at the moment when an angry lion was stalking over it, and motioned to the brave cavalier to restore it?"

"And he?"

"Obeyed her, braved the lion, recovered the glove, and restored it to the lady."

"Well! Was it not nobly done?"

"Perhaps! In those days such follies had a significance and merit which they do not possess now. But there is a sequel to the story."

"Pray tell it."

"The knight who braved the lion for the lady, from that moment yielded the lady to other knights. He turned away from the reckless beauty who would peril the life of her lover only to exhibit her power over him; and the world applauded the desertion, and the beauty was abandoned by all other knights."

The pride of the maid was touched.

"In this fable, Mr. Hammond, I am to behold a warning, I suppose."

"A truth—a principle—is a warning, Miss Foster, to all mankind. In proposing for your hand, I was prepared to let you see into my whole nature—my feelings, opinions, and the principles by which I am governed. I am now dealing with you with the frankness of one who hopes to find a wife in the woman with whom he speaks. I speak with you unaffectedly. I would peril my life for you in the moment of necessity, and joy to do so. I might peril it, as a proud man, at your mere requisition, or your caprice; but it would be also at the peril of my esteem for you. There is no peril in bestriding a blooded horse, and engaging in the contest you propose; but it endangers self-respect, it offends public opinion, it degrades the suitor, as it admits no difference—except, perhaps, as a jockey—between him and his competitors, and—"

He paused.

"Go on, sir."

"I almost fear, Miss Foster."

"Nay, sir, you have spoken with little fear, thus far. You may surely finish."

"I will! It is only right that I should show the danger to yourself. It puts the lady in the attitude of one whose standard depends upon her caprice and whims, rather than her principles."

"You speak plainly—certainly without fear."

"My dear Miss Foster, I have perilled all my life in the offer I have made you of my hand. I have everything at stake which is precious. Pardon me, if this consideration makes me bold, where love, alone, would only make me humble. We are both young, but you much younger than myself. You have seen the world only through the medium of other eyes. It is easy with the young to err, and seeing thus, to see falsely even in the most important interests. I should almost be disposed to think that, in making this requisition, against which I beg most respectfully to protest, you have obeyed any but your own impulses. Let me entreat you to reverse it."

"Really, Mr. Hammond, you attach a singular importance to a horserace."

"Surely, not so much as you, Miss Foster, when you are willing to risk all your own happiness upon it."

"It is your pride, sir."

"It is, but I trust not an improper pride."

"I don't know, sir; but my pride too is concerned. You have been told that I have made a vow. I have said, *to you,* that I felt it to be rash, and feared that it was foolish, but the resolution was taken. I will not now say whether I do or do not regret it. Enough, that it is unchangeable."

"Do not say this, I entreat you, Miss Foster; for my sake! I entreat—But no! To you I may be nothing. For your own sake, then —for your future peace, and happiness, and hope—do not peril everything on a resolution so utterly unmeaning and without obligation. It needs but little effort of wisdom to show that truth, propriety, common sense, all agree to absolve you from such a vow. Beware how you persist! It will be fatal."

He rose as he spoke.

"Do you threaten, Mr. Hammond?"

"Warn! Warn only."

"I thank you for your warning, sir; but I doubt whether it is due more to your notions of principle than to your own feelings of pride, and—"

"My pride, Miss Foster! You do not know or understand me. I spoke not for myself in this matter, but for you. Not with regard to him who should be fortunate enough to secure this hand, but in regard to the happiness of that heart which you will permit me to say, I believe to be more misguided than wilful. The conditions which you couple with this hand will, I fear, greatly peril that heart, no matter who the suitor it shall win. Am I to understand that you will not, in any circumstances, modify this resolution?"

He took her hand as he spoke. His eyes were fixed upon hers imploringly, with an expression of the deepest interest in her reply. Hers sunk beneath them. The struggle in her heart was great, but the whisper of the evil genius was still in her ears.

"It is his pride that speaks, and you must humble it, if you would not have him your master. He will not give you up. He will yield to your terms, when once he finds that he cannot command his own."

She faltered forth a renewal of her resolution. Then he rose, released her hand, and said

"I leave you, Miss Foster; of my determination on this subject you will permit me to write hereafter."

He was gone, and she hurried to her chamber and flung herself in a fit of weeping upon her bed. The mother would have consoled her, but in vain.

"You have destroyed me!" was all she said. "He will never come again."

"And if he doesn't," was the elegant response of the mother, "there's as good fish in the river as ever came out of it."

A proverb that certainly fails in respect to the mackerel fishery. We never get half so good a mackerel, nowadays, as was common ten or fifteen years ago, though we pay as good a price for it.

CHAPTER XVIII.

HOW THE RACE WAS RUN, HOW THE RACE WAS WON, AND WHAT HAPPENED THEREUPON.

"She may whistle for it! I'll never marry a woman who chooses me on the score of my mare's legs and bottom."

Such was the elegantly-declared resolution of our now thoroughly indignant Miles Henderson, when Hammond reported how ill he had sped in his mission to Geraldine.

"She certainly pays us no compliment."

"Compliment! She treats us as if one man was just the same to her as another. Who'd marry a woman on such terms? What man who values his happiness at all will take a wife who don't prefer him to all other suitors?"

"Miles?"

"Well, Ran.?"

"Geraldine *does* express this preference."

"How?"

"She knows very well that 'Sorella' can beat Barry's filly. She has done so. Now, it seems to me that this must have been in the recollection of Geraldine when she made the requisition."

"Yes, but 'Ferraunt' can beat 'Sorella.'"

"True, perhaps; but if *you* will engage in the conflict with Barry, I'll decline it. I'll leave the field to you."

"No, no, Ran.; that won't do. I sha'n't run at all. If the lady don't like me sufficiently to answer 'Yes' at once, we're quits. I wouldn't have her now on any terms. I think she has treated us most outrageously."

"I'm disposed to think her foolish and vexatious mother's at the bottom of it all, though what she proposes to gain by it, I do not exactly see; yet a thought strikes me. It's very clear that Mrs. Foster has all along preferred Barry to either of us. Now, if we withdraw from the field, he walks the course and takes the purse. This, perhaps, will be just the thing that the mother hopes for. That she has blinded Geraldine by some artifice, is very possible. Now, I'm not willing that the mother should be gratified. I'm disposed equally to balk her and to punish Geraldine. I feel something of your indignation; and, though I'm sure she prefers either of us to Jones Barry, yet I fear she presumes upon what she thinks our passion for her, to coerce us with this humiliating condition. She seems to take for granted that we cannot but yield, however little we may relish doing so."

"What's your plan?"

"To accede to her conditions."

"How, accede!"

"Yes, apparently at least. We'll write her to that effect, see Barry, make the arrangements for the race, and get all things in readiness."

"Well!"

"It will be easy to throw Barry out—to beat him after the first mile—and thus defeat the calculations of the mother."

"Well!"

"We agree that the wedding takes place the very day of the race. Let them have the company, let them get the parson, let them make the feast, and let us —"

"Well! well!"

"Ride off as we came, leaving them to eat the supper, and marry as they can."

"Bravo! I like it! It will shame them to the whole country."

"They deserve it! What think you?"

"It's a sentence! They shall pay the forfeit. The idea is capital. It'll be a lesson to such people hereafter."

"Then let us proceed about it. What we do we must do quickly, so that the thing shall not be blown unnecessarily abroad. I shall keep it from my mother if I can; at all events, I must keep from her that I mean to put in for this prize. To do this, I'll go home with you, and we'll write and work from your house. To Barry we must send to-morrow, and have the race early next week."

The arrangements, as devised, were all made. Barry was invited to an interview, and readily came into the arrangements; somewhat

disappointed, however, to find so prompt an acceptance of the conditions, in spite of the confident predictions of Mrs. Foster. That
good lady was quite as much confounded as anybody else; but she
made the best of a bad bargain. She encouraged Barry to hope; and
it was with a confident face that she could now say to her daughter—

"You see? 'Tis as I told you—you have only to be firm, and he
submits. This is the way with men, always. Women yield too readily.
Let them only stick out to the last, and they'll rule in the end."

Meanwhile, the affair got abroad, and was the cause of no little
excitement. The subject is one which still, to this day, interests the
people of the surrounding country. They call it the "race for a wife."
Of course, it was the crowning event in the history of Geraldine
Foster's eccentricities. They little knew how small was the share of
the poor girl in the proceeding. Nettles was delighted with the
affair. Its novelty charmed him. He did not exactly expect that
Hammond would have engaged in the contest, for he had quite as
high an opinion of that gentleman's pride of character as was
entertained by Mrs. Foster; but he said nothing against it. He told
Jones Barry, however, that the game was all up with him; that the
"Fair Geraldine" stood no chance against either the heels of "Ferraunt" or "Sorella." "But," he continued, "I shall be glad to see
you beat, for reasons I've already given you. This girl is not the
girl for you. Better the step-mother, Mrs. Foster. She's neither old
nor ugly, and she knows what good living is. Besides, she's a widow,
whose gratitude to the man that will take her off her own hands
will make her tolerably submissive. But, better still, the fat girl,
Susannah, at Hiram Davy's corner. She's the good creature, the
sweet laughing armful of happiness, all fat and good-humor. Even
Polly Ewbanks, whom you overthrew at the ball, would be more
suitable, and, for that matter, she evidently likes you."

"Don't speak of her, the cow! I'll never forgive her for that
tumble. She threw me, thrusting her elephant legs between mine,
just when I was *cavorting*."

"The boot's on t'other leg, Jones. It was you that thrust your pegs
in the wrong direction, and you did the mischief. In truth, Jones,
I'm afraid it was more design on your part than accident."

"I swear to you, Tom, I never designed anything; but I'm willing to confess that that 'peach' was quite too much for me, after the sherry and champagne."

"Not a bit of it; but there was a sort of destiny that made you and Polly Ewbanks fall together; and, mark my words, I prophesy that, if ever you marry, it'll be one of the three—Polly Ewbanks, Sukey Davy, or the widow Foster—and I don't care much which; though Sukey or Polly, either, would make you the best wife. It's very certain that if Geraldine Foster is to be got by running only, you stand no chance against 'Ferraunt' and 'Sorella.' "

Mrs. Hammond at length heard of the terms of the conflict, and was shocked at its monstrosities. She at once appealed to her son in the earnest language of a mother, to avoid any such competition. He answered her evasively but satisfactorily, in calm but earnest language.

"Fear nothing, mother; there is no prospect of my ever being united with Miss Foster."

And here the matter rested until the day appointed for the trial. The three competitors had, in their separate answers, agreed upon the terms. They had also—using a discretion which had been conferred upon them—concurred in entreating that the day of the race should be that of the wedding also. The company were accordingly invited, and the Reverend Timothy Bindwell, of the Presbyterian Church, was entreated to be present, and made his appearance in his robes of office at the appointed hour. He was one of those to whom it was always agreeable to bring the young together in the blessed ties of marriage, particularly where the wedding-supper was apt to be good, and the marriage-fee a liberal one. His expectations, on the present occasion, were of superior magnitude. It was observed as an evil sign by Geraldine that Mrs. Hammond, though invited, was not present when the company was assembled. She remarked this to her mother, as something ominous; but the latter had her answer.

"Oh! she no doubt feels as bitter about it as she can. If her pride could have ruled her son in such a matter, he had never consented to the terms."

"I hardly think that he will consent now."

"How! When we have it in black and white, under his hands? But dress, my child"—this conversation took place in Geraldine's chamber—"dress, so as to be quite in readiness. I'll send Rachel up to help you."

"Send no one! I'll ring if I want her."

The mother left the room, and the poor girl, as if with a presentiment of the mortification to which she was destined, sank down listlessly before the window, looking out upon the long avenue up which the competitors were to ascend. How bitter were her reflections at this moment! How she deplored the readiness with which she had given ear to her mother's counsels! and with what warning solemnity did the words and looks of Hammond, in their last interview, when he came to expostulate, rise to her recollection! She probably would not have been dressed but for the reappearance of Mrs. Foster, who insisted upon her immediate preparations. She assisted her in making her toilet, taking care all the while so to speak as to fortify the pride of the damsel, and excite her spirits through the agency of her vanity. Pale, but—in the language of Mrs. Foster— "beautiful as an angel," the devoted girl was at length prepared for the conflict and the company. Meanwhile, let us look after the several claimants for her hand.

We need not detail the preliminaries, important to the parties, but not so to us, which were duly arranged among themselves. Time, place, distance, the signal for the start, were all agreed upon; and at the proper minute the several competitors, each attended by his friend, appeared upon the ground. Tom Nettles officiated on the part of Jones Barry, who had in fact become a sort of dependent upon the superior judgment of that humorist, and never failed to seek him on every emergency. Henderson and Hammond were attended by two young men, whom it is not important to introduce more especially to our readers. The word was given, and the three steeds leaped off most beautifully together, but had not run a hundred yards before the "Fair Geraldine," as if fearing the loss of her good name in such formidable rivalry, or frightened by some unusual object along the roadside, suddenly bolted into the woods, taking rider through bush and through brier, a formidable chase, which, but for his frequent practice as a fox hunter, would have certainly endangered his neck. When the unfortunate Barry succeeded in reining in his capricious beauty, who seemed disposed to emulate her namesake, he found his competitors clean gone out of sight, and himself hopelessly distanced. He gave up the chase entirely, and, cantering out into the open track, came forth just as Nettles, and the two other bottle-holders, were riding forward to the "Lodge." He joined them, and, putting the best air upon his defeat possible, he told them how it happened. The two friends of Hammond and Henderson condoled with him like men of proper gallantry; but Nettles openly congratulated him upon the event.

"The hand of fate is in it, Jones. You are destined for Polly Ewbanks, Sukey Davy, or the widow. I'm glad of it. This jade is too high-necked for you, and would have ruined you forever as a good fellow."

Thus talking, they wheeled into the avenue. Meanwhile, let us hurry to the "Lodge," and see how things are working there. Geraldine had not long descended to the parlor, and was in the midst of salutations and congratulations innumerable and inconceivable, when the cry rose from the piazza—"They are coming! They are coming!" This occasioned a rush. The bride was deserted, and with a strange sinking of the heart, she crouched, rather than reclined, on the sofa, leaving it to others to report the conflict, which she no longer had the courage to behold. Mrs. Foster was the first to bounce into the piazza as she heard the cry. Parson Bindwell placed himself along-side of her, and the several groups, according to relationship or intimacy, ranged themselves in near neighborhood. The banisters were thronged, two long benches were filled with crowding forms, and several stood upon chairs dragged for the purpose from the parlor. Poor Geraldine hearkened breathlessly to the murmurs and the cries from without.

"The sorrel has it!" cried one.

"And now the iron gray!" cried another.

"But where's Barry? Where's Barry?" was the impatient inquiry of Madam Foster.

"Distanced!" was the answer from one of the party, "as I always said he would be."

It was evident there were but two horsemen, and these were Hammond and Henderson. The race was evidently a close one. Approaching in front, the spectators could see no inequalities in their speed, and opinion was kept in a constant state of fluctuation as they advanced.

"Now they come! They come with a rush!"

"The sorrel has it!"

"No, 'Ferraunt!'"

"It's hard to say which!"

"They come! They come!"

At these words, Geraldine could bear the suspense no longer. She darted to her feet, rushed to the door-way just in season to behold the two horses, lock and lock, wheel before the entrance; while the riders, waving and kissing their hands to the company, and bowing their heads, darted away at the same speed in the opposite avenue leading up the road, and were lost to sight in a moment.

"What does that mean?" demanded the parson.

"They are off!" said another. "But who won?"

"The iron gray! Hammond was ahead by a neck."

"It was close work; neck and neck, and hard to say which had it till the last moment. Then it was that Ran. Hammond's horse came out a neck ahead."

Such was the verdict, gravely delivered, of those who had most closely watched the conflict. But where were the competitors? Where was he who had triumphed, and to whom the trembling prize was to be awarded? Geraldine did tremble, but it was with a joy which spoke out in her bright eyes, and played in a sweet smile upon her pouting lips. But why did not Hammond appear? What could be the meaning of that reverential bow, that wave of the hand, as the riders continued on their course; and of the long delay which followed? Meanwhile, Barry and Nettles, with their companions, made their appearance. The misfortune of the former was soon explained; and, in her grief and vexation, Mrs. Foster drew him in with her to the well-known little room where he had sipped his tea and toddy at her hands, to reproach him, as well as she could, for his accident and defeat. Here he could not help the reflection forced upon him by Nettles, that there was really something quite lovable in the widow. It was while they sat together that Geraldine rushed into the chamber, her face red, her eyes dilating in anger, her whole appearance that of indignation almost rising into fury. She held a crumpled paper to her mother, which had once been a neatly-folded billet.

"See to what I am brought by your counsel!"

The mother read. The note was from Hammond to Geraldine. It ran thus:—

"Mr. Hammond presumes that curiosity as to the respective speed of his and other horses, alone, prompted the singular requisition of Miss Foster, and that she had no serious design of making such performance the condition of a solemnity so vital to her happiness as that of marriage. Mr. Hammond has done his best to gratify her curiosity, and should be sorry to avail himself of the result to the prejudice of Miss Foster. He accordingly begs leave to release her from any supposed obligations to himself."

"Disgraced! Insulted! Oh that I were a man! That I had a friend! a brother!"

The widow pushed Barry, and, as Geraldine paced the chamber with face averted, she contrived to whisper him. He at once started forwards at the repeated words—

"That I were a man! That I had a brother! an avenger!"

"Give me this hand, Miss Geraldine, and I will be your avenger."

"Will you kill him, kill him?" she demanded, turning quickly. "Who?"

"Who but Randall Hammond? He has degraded me before all these people. Kill him, and you shall have the hand that he rejects with scorn."

"I'll call him out. I'll shoot him if I can!"

"Do so, sir! do it quickly, and I am yours, yours!"

CHAPTER XIX.

PISTOLS FOR TWO—THE DUEL.

Jones Barry was greatly elevated by his new commission. His vanity was immediately tickled by being adopted as the champion of the fair. He had heard something of the days and institutions of chivalry, and he felt all over knight-errantish. It was not that he desired to shed blood, for he was, in fact, rather a kind-hearted creature; but to be somebody, and to be moving always conspicuously in some one's eyes, was sufficiently grateful to make him lose sight of all other matters. Full of fight, he hurried at once to Tom Nettles, to whom he laid bare all the particulars of his situation.

"It's d——d strange!" said Nettles; "and yet I don't know. To touch a woman on that point is to run into the quick with a rusty gimlet. I suppose, since you've pledged yourself to the lady, you'll have to challenge; but Ran. Hammond will blow you into splinters. He's a dead shot at a shingle."

"A shingle's not a man; and I can shoot too. The question is, Tom, will you see to this business for me?"

"Oh, certainly!"

"Well, ride over to Hammond this morning, make the arrangements, and, after that, come and give me some practice at the distance."

"Very good. I'll ride round to your house from Hammond's in time for dinner, and we'll make a night of it. It's no time for practice after dinner, so we'll leave that for next morning at sunrise."

This being agreed on, Nettles at once proceeded with the challenge, which was peremptory, to Hammond. It must not be forgotten that the bearer of this letter was a great admirer of Hammond. Nettles only amused himself with Barry, and did not respect him.

"Why, Nettles!" said Hammond, "how can I go out with this foolish fellow? The thing is ridiculous. He is the laughing-stock of the country. A good-meaning, harmless creature enough, but one whom I should be sorry to think of raising to my level. As a general rule, I have resolved to fight anybody that makes a demand on me, if only to prevent annoyance from persons who are always to be found anxious to make for themselves a capital of courage out of your reluctance. But I should be afraid of the ridicule which would attach to a formal combat with one so utterly silly and ridiculous as Barry."

"Well! there's some danger of that, I confess; but we'll keep the thing as quiet as possible."

"You can't keep it quiet. His vanity will never suffer him to sleep until he succeeds in making everybody know that he is a champion for the lady."

"Some danger of that; but the truth is, Ran., the fellow is resolved on it, and when that's the case he can annoy you quite as effectually, and perhaps make the ridicule much more successful, than it would be if you were to meet him. If you say you won't meet him, why, I shall give up the business; but, in his present temper, he'll only seek somebody else, who will be very apt to follow it up, and vex you into it at last. Now, I have a plan by which to shift the ridicule to the proper shoulders."

He whispered his scheme to Hammond, who heard him with a dubious shake of the head.

"If I am to go out," said he, "I should prefer to do so with a serious resolution. I should never wish to trifle in such matters."

Nettles had his arguments, and, without being convinced, Hammond consented that his decision should be referred to Miles Henderson, whom he made his sense-keeper, as well as friend, on the occasion. The two rode over together to Henderson's, and the whole affair was submitted to him. Hammond, as in duty bound, put himself in the hands of his friend, and the subtle Nettles found it much more easy to impress the latter than the former with the propriety of his scheme, whatever that may have been. At present, its purport is concealed from us. Henderson, indeed, was greatly tickled with it, and Hammond, still doubting, was compelled to submit.

"It'll be rare sport, Ran. We shall have the laugh to ourselves. Let him get the lady if he can, but, at all events, give him a mighty bad scare. I know Jones well. He's got as soft a heart as anybody in the world, with all his bluster and conceit, and if we don't make him run for it, my name's not Nettles."

Hammond, it must be confessed, did not altogether relish the cool and philosophical manner with which the other was prepared to consign the lady to the arms of her champion. He still felt a deep sympathy with Geraldine, though she had greatly mortified his pride, and it was only with the conviction that her conduct had been dictated by a total indifference to his claims, that he was reconciled to yielding her up without a farther struggle. His mind was distracted by lurking doubts of this same indifference, and was continually recalling the numerous little instances in her conduct which had encouraged him in the belief that she really had a preference for him; but these impressions he had been compelled to discard, however unwillingly, in the more recent events which we have described. But her beauties were more deeply engraved upon his imagination than he had been willing to believe, and he now listened to her final surrender with a secret sense of pain, of which he was thoroughly ashamed. The plan arranged between Nettles and Henderson for the duel was such as he could not approve of, and he only submitted to it as one accustoms himself, in such cases, to submit to the conclusions of his friends, even where he deems them unwise. It is a matter of punctilio which decides many such affairs, in defiance of the deliberate judgment of nearly all the parties. But upon this head we need not dilate. Enough that Nettles went off with an acceptance of his challenge. In three days the parties were to meet. Time, place, distance, and all the particulars were fully agreed on between the two seconds, and they proceeded—one of them, at least—to put their principals in training. Barry, not a bad shot before, was practised every day, at frequent periods, until he could snuff a candle.

"You're now as good a shot," said Nettles, "as you need be; you can snuff a candle at ten paces."

"Ain't that famous shooting?"

"Yes; but I've seen Ran. Hammond divide a firefly upon the wing!"

Nettles had his own mode of encouragement, truly, and possessed the art, in high degree, of warming and cooling his patient in the same instant—as in Russia, they tell us, a fellow is taken smoking out of the vapor-bath and rolled over and over in a mountain of snow—and all with the view to reaction. Nettles was never more happy than when he could exercise the nerves of our friend Barry with such pleasant contradictions. As soon as the duel had been determined upon, and the preparations made, Jones Barry proceeded to report progress to the lady whose battle he espoused. Mrs. Foster, we are pleased to state, was now entirely opposed to the affair; but Geraldine's anger continued. She had few words; but these were all vindictive and wrathful. She thanked Barry for his zeal, and renewed the assurance that, with the fall of Hammond, he should have her hand. Nothing was said of his own fall; but, of course, in that event, the hand could be of no use to him. Before the parties separated, Geraldine drew him aside.

"Mr. Barry, I must be present at this meeting."

"You, Miss Geraldine?"

"Yes, I must see it. I must *see* him fall!"

"But how? We have but two friends on each side present."

"I care nothing for your fantastic forms. *I must be present.* I do not mean to be seen, but to see. You must manage it that I shall be hidden in the neighboring wood. None shall know."

"But, Miss Geraldine—"

"Oh! It's strange, it's unreasonable, it's unnatural. I know all that! But I must and will be there. Tell me, will you arrange it?"

His answer was a compliance, and he kept his word. Concealed in a neighboring copse, Geraldine Foster was present when the duel took place. She had contrived to get away from the "Lodge" without her mother's knowledge. The place of meeting was at a spot, about three miles off from it, well known to the combatants of the neighborhood as "Pistol Quarter." Here, on a pleasant afternoon, not ten days after the equestrian contest for our damsel, the same parties met to decide a more formidable issue. The preliminaries for a duel are usually very much alike in all cases, and they were not departed from in the present instance. Nettles, for once in his life, seemed thoroughly serious. He proceeded to his duties with the air of a man who anticipated the worst. To Barry he said, while placing him—

"You look quite too fierce and vindictive, Barry. I am afraid you have bloody feelings. I trust you will be satisfied with winging him only."

"I am sworn to kill him," was the stern response.

"Then God have mercy on his soul and yours! Should he entertain a like feeling, you will both be at 'Cedar Mount' (the graveyard) before to-morrow night."

Thus saying, he placed his man, and after the lapse of a few seconds, the signal words were given: one—two—three! The sharp fire followed, almost instantaneously. For a moment, both parties appeared erect, but, on a sudden, Hammond was seen to totter and to fall right forward.

"The bullet is through his heart!" was the hurried speech of Nettles to his principal. "To your horse, at once, Jones, and be off as fast as Heaven will let you. It's all over with him."

"Is he dead?—have I killed him?" was the demand of Barry in wild and husky accents.

"You've done that same!"

"Oh! God have mercy! I'm a murderer!"

"Begone!" and with the words he pushed the pale and conscience-stricken wretch from the ground, helped him on his horse, and saw him wheel about and disappear. He fled, looking behind him, with terror and vengeance dogging at his heels.

CHAPTER XX.

THE GHOST OF A BUGGY.

At this stage of our story, it is just as well that we should suffer our Tennessean to put in.* It is here that he claimed to be privy himself to the affair; and, though we despair wholly of being able to give his language exactly, and certainly shall not attempt to convey the slightest idea of his tone and manner, yet, as a witness on the stand, we conceive it only right that he should speak to those parts of our narrative which he himself beheld. "Tom hain't forgot," said he, "that when the Ingins in Florida, this Powell, and Wild Cat, and Tiger Tail, and twenty more smart red skins, was playing hide and seek with Uncle Sam's rig'lars, Old Hickory swore a most stupendious oath that Tennessee could find the boys who could clean them out. I reckon I was among the first of the volunteers that turned out when the Gov'nor said we was wanted. I won't tell you how we made out in Florida, for that's pretty much in the books and newspapers a'ready. It's enough to know, as I said before, that the Tennessee boys didn't do better than other people. Fighting we had, and fight we did, whenever there was a chance for it; but, Lord bless your souls, there was no more seeing your inimy till his bullet was in your gizzard, than there was swallowing it afterwards with a good digestion. And when you did see the red skin, it was on a smart gallop, on the other side of some etarnal swamp that you had to cross, belly-deep all the way, before you could get at him; and then you didn't get him no more than the man who hunted the flea. Well, it was on the 21st day of November, 1836—I keep all the dates in black and white—that we were ordered to push for the inimy into the Wapoo Swamp. We had had a smart brush with the red skins, and drove 'em famous only three days before. We charged

* See Introductory Narrative.

199

with a big shout into the hammocks—the swamp—and the Ingins gave us yell for yell, and shot for shot. They had a smart sight upon us for a good bit, while we were trying to get at 'em, and they popt us over, man after man, as they run from tree to tree, making every tree speak a bullet as soon as they could put the tongue behind it. Now, it happened that just when I and twenty others was wading through a good big bit of bog and water, with a pretty thick scrub in front, where the Ingins harbored, and jest when they were blazing away their hottest, who should we see, ahead of us all, but a man rather under the middle size—a white man—as ragged as a gypsy, without any hat, and with an old musket in his hand, pushing across, shouting his best, and full in the face of the fire of the red skins? Jest then, when we were all beginning to feel squeamish, he was going ahead, and whooping, without a bit of scare in him. Well, that encouraged us. We saw the Ingins aim at him, and I reckon his rags had the marks of more than a dozen bullets; but he didn't seem to mind 'em, and they sartainly never one of them troubled him. Away he went, shouting and shaking his musket, and away we went after him, and away the Indians went before us all. We drove 'em, and got the victory. We picked up some scalps, but nothing to speak of, and lost some good fellows. But I tell you that ragged volunteer went ahead of us all, and he was this same Jones Barry, about whom I've been telling you this long story. He had run all the way from Georgy into Florida after killing Hammond, without knowing much where he went. Never in his life had any man so bad a scare. He had run, as I may say, into the arms of the Ingins, without hearing their rifles; and I do believe, as I am a free white man, that he scared them a great deal worse than our whole Tennessee regiment. For, look you, he was a man to scare people. He was, as I tell you, in rags from head to foot. He had been living among the briers, running into them almost at every sound. He had no covering for his head. His eyes were bloodshot; his face scratched over, and bleeding on all sides; and his hair had grown half white in twenty days. He looked for all the world like a madman. He was a madman; and, though he fought with us, and marched with us, and did everything pretty much as he saw us do, yet his senses, I'm mighty sure, were, all the time, more than a hundred miles away. Somehow, the poor fellow got in with me. We marched together and slept together. I reckon he saw that I was a good-natured chap, and so he tuk to me. I soon saw that he was miserable—that there was a scare that was gnawing in him all the time—and after awhile I found out that he was haunted constantly by the ghost of Randall Hammond. One night he ran out of the tent with a terrible fright. Another time, when standing with a sentry, he fired his piece and gave the alarm to the whole army. Then he'd fall upon his knees and beg for mercy, and cover his eyes with his hands, as if to shut out some frightful thing he couldn't bear to look upon. Sometimes he'd run into the hammock at midnight, never fearing the Ingins, though we all thought it as much as one's life was worth to go near it. It was the dead he was afraid of all the time. Now, there was a sodger among the rig'lars to whom Jones Barry one night made confession and eased his heart of all its secrets. But it didn't ease him of his misery. The soldier came to me and told me all, and I ax'd Barry; but then he was shy, and swore that he never told the fellow any such thing. But it wasn't more than twenty-four hours after, when he come to me and said—

" 'I can't stand it much longer. I'm almost crazy now. Ran. Hammond comes to me every night. I'm his murderer, and he will have my blood. I must go back to Georgy, and stand trial. I'll go and give myself up.'

" 'Well,' says I, 'my poor fellow, if you'll only wait till we're mustered out of sarvice, I'll go along with you. I'm sorry for you, and I don't think you're so much to blame. You've got a heart a little too tender; and as you killed your man in a fair fight, I don't see as how he should haunt you. He had as much chance at you, as you at him.'

" 'Yes! but I thirsted for his blood, and he never did me any harm. He was a good man too! I must go back. I will deliver myself. I see him every night, covered with blood, and beckoning me, with his hands, to come. It's he leads me into the hammock, and there he leaves me. I must go back and give myself up to justice.'

" 'Well, only wait till we're mustered out, and I'll go with you.'

"He promised and did wait, and I kept my word. As soon as I got my discharge, I said to Barry, 'I'm ready.' We bought a pair of stout Seminole ponies, on a credit from our commissariat, and went off like gentlemen soldiers. I mustn't forget to tell you that he killed the mare that he made so much brag about, the 'Fair Geraldine,' in his run from Georgy, and tuk it on foot as soon as he got near the Ingin country. How he lived, God only knows, for I never saw a poor innocent eat so little. But I encouraged him, and made light of his mischief; and by little and little he began to improve. We got him some new clothes as soon as we struck the settlement; and, I think, when he got them on, his appetite came back a little to him. One night, the first night after we crossed the Georgy line, he ate a pretty good supper of bacon and eggs. I think 'twas all owing to his clothes. But that very night he gave me and the whole house a most outrageous scare. He broke out in his night-shirt, and dashed out of the room, and down the stairs into the hall, where he squatted under the table. We slept in the same room, and as soon as I could slip on my breeches I made after him. He swore that the ghost of Hammond squatted down at the foot of the bed, and looked over into his face, though he tried to cover with the quilt. I told him 'twas the hot supper that gave him the nightmare, and I made him take a pretty deep swallow of apple-toddy, that the landlord made for us, after we routed him up with such a scrimmage. Well, so we went; now better, now worse; now calm, and now stormy, till we got pretty nigh his county, where all these things took place. Then his scare came back to him, then his heart failed him; and just when the ghost stopped troubling him, he began to be troubled by the fear of the laws. But I said to him—

" 'Be a man. You've come so far, see it out. Better be hung and have it over, than to be scared to death every night.'

"He groaned most bitterly, but he said, 'You're right! I can't stand to suffer as I have suffered. I'm only twenty-six; and look, my head's half white! I'm an old man in the feel as well as in the look. The ghost of Ran. Hammond has done me worse than my pistol ever did him. He's given me a hell upon earth, so that I can't believe there's any half so bad for me hereafter. Go ahead!'

"And so we went forward. It was a most sweet and beautiful afternoon when we came into the very neighborhood of all these doings. We had passed several places that were famous in his recollection. There was Hillabee race-course, where they had the gander-pulling, and the circus, and soon we drew nigh to the great avenue leading to the 'Lodge,' where the young lady lived that had been the cause of all the mischief. But it wasn't there that Barry wanted to go. The first place he wished to strike for was the farm of his friend Nettles, and we were only a half a mile from it, according to Barry's calculations, when we came, by a sudden turn in the road, upon a buggy drawn by a splendid horse, and carrying two people. One of them was a tall and noble-looking gentleman, and the other was a most beautiful lady, *perhaps* about the most beautiful I ever did see. They were coming right towards us at a smart trot, and, the moment Barry laid eyes fairly upon them, he turned pale as death, and dashed his horse into the bushes and off the road. I followed after him as soon as I could get a chance, but not till I had taken a good look at the strangers that seemed to frighten him so much. They rode by in a minute, and the gentleman gave me a civil bow as he passed. Then I pushed into the woods after Barry. I found him off his horse and hiding in the bushes, all over covered with a sweat, and trembling like a leaf in the wind.

" 'Why, what on airth,' says I, 'is the matter now? What *has* scared you so?'

" 'Didn't you see him?'

" 'Who?'

" 'Hammond! 'Twas his ghost in the buggy!'

" 'And what has his ghost to do in a buggy, I wonder? and who ever saw the ghost of a buggy before?' said I. 'I don't believe much in such a notion, and if that was Hammond's ghost, I wonder what woman's ghost it was sitting along-side of him. If woman ghosts are so pretty, I shouldn't be much afraid of 'em myself.'

" 'Woman!' said Barry, mightily bewildered. 'Was there a woman with him?'

" 'Yes, as surely as there was a buggy and a man. Now look you, Barry; if that was Hammond in the buggy, he's just as much alive as you and me. The chance is, after all, that you only wounded him, and you and your friend took a mortal scare too soon.'

" 'No! no!' said he, very mournfully; 'haven't I seen him almost every night? hasn't he followed me everywhere?—into the woods, into the swamps, into the hammock of the Ingins? and ain't my head gray with his coming?'

" 'I don't know,' says I; 'but if that was Hammond in the buggy, he's no ghost; and it's your conscience that's been a troubling you. But let's push on, and see your friend Nettles; he ought to be able to tell us all about it.'

"And so, jest as I said, we pushed forward, and I reckon it all came out fast enough, as you shall see."

CHAPTER XXI.

SHOWING HOW HAMMOND'S GHOST WAS LAID, HOW BARRY
WAS HUNG, AND HOW JUSTICE WAS DONE UPON OTHER
OFFENDING PARTIES.

DISMISSING Tennessee for the present, we retrace our steps, and go back to the field of personal combat—that famous "Pistol Quarter," which has witnessed so many fearful and violent transitions from time to eternity. We resume our narrative at the moment when Nettles sent poor Barry in terror off the field. Hardly had he disappeared when a wild shriek was heard from the adjoining thicket, and, before the parties on the ground could conjecture what was the matter, who should rush out amongst them but Geraldine Foster? Never were people so much confounded. Randall Hammond was lying on the grass just where he had fallen, his body partly raised, and resting on his elbow. She threw herself upon him with a cry which betrayed the wildest sense of personal suffering.

"I have slain him—I have slain him! Speak to me, Hammond; dear Hammond, speak to me. Say that you forgive me. Forgive the madness and the folly that have brought you to this. I loved you only; I shall always love you; but they told me you were proud and tyrannical, and they provoked my childish vanity until I maddened. Oh! Hammond, will you not forgive me? Will you not? will you not?"

She clung to him as she cried. Her arms were wound about him, and her face was buried in his bosom.

"Geraldine! Miss Foster!" said Hammond, trying to rise.

"Call me Geraldine; call me yours; forgive me, and take me with you, Hammond! At this moment, I am yours only! I loved you only from the first!"

205

Nettles winked to the prostrate man, and made certain motions which, strictly construed, might be supposed to mean, "Take her at her word, marry her on the spot;" and the looks and signs of Henderson, now thoroughly cured of *his* passion, were equally significant to the same effect. But Hammond was superior to the temptation.

"Nay, Geraldine, you are deceived. I am in no danger; indeed, I am unhurt."

She started as if to rise, but he now restrained her, and, looking to his friends, motioned their departure.

"What does this mean?" she demanded.

"Hear me patiently, Geraldine, and let me plead in turn for your forgiveness. It means a foolish hoax, in which nobody ever dreamed that you would be a party. I am unwounded, and the object has been simply to scare the foolish person who, without provocation, has sought my life."

"Without provocation, Mr. Hammond? Do you forget the cruel insult you put upon me? Was it no provocation to shame a young maiden before all her friends and people? Oh, Hammond, how could you do me so—you, for whom I showed but too much preference from the beginning, in spite of all that my mother would say?"

"Will you suffer me to repent, Geraldine—to make amends?" And, by this time, the arm of the pleader was round about her waist, and his lips were pressed upon hers, and alone in that haunted wood, famous for its many murders, the two were betrothed with all the dearest promises of love. We need not follow the progress of the scene. Enough to say that the persons whom Barry and his friend from Tennessee encountered in the buggy, were Mr. and Mrs. Hammond. They had been fully three months married, and were living very comfortably together at the residence of Hammond's mother; while Mrs. Foster, vexed to the heart, was chewing the cud of disappointment at the "Lodge" alone. All these facts were gathered from Tom Nettles, who very frankly declared his agency in the proceedings.

"I'm blowed," said the Tennesseean, "if I was Barry, if I wouldn't have a real fight on the strength of it, and I'd make you my mark, my man."

But Barry himself shook his head.

"I've had enough of killing," said he.

"I can put you in the way of something better," said Nettles. "Polly Ewbanks is still alive, single, and fat as ever; Sukey Davy still keeps the bar at the old man's corner; and Mrs. Foster looks as well as I have ever seen her, and keeps a most excellent table. I'm willing to make amends, Jones, for what harm I've done you, by doing you finally 'for better or worse.' Now, if there's a man to manage either of these three pretty pieces of mortality, I'm that person. Shall it be 'back to back, Miss Polly—'"

"Hush, you Satan!—"

"Or, 'Is it to your liking, sir?'"

"Devil!"

"Or, 'Is it more of the honey or more of the peach, dear *Mr.* Barry?'"

The Tennesseean lingered a week among his new friends, and became so much enamored of Nettles that he asked him home with him. But the latter, born for the use of his neighbors, had a commission in hand for Barry that was somewhat urgently pressed. His hints had not been wholly thrown away, and Barry, among his latter-day reveries, was frequently and pleasurably entertained by the recollection of that cup of tea, and that bowl of toddy, by which the widow Foster had refreshed him in the little back room of her domicil. He remembered her round, well-proportioned figure, the sweet smile upon her face, the pleasant sparkle in her eye, and the grateful beverage in her hand; and he so earnestly pressed his ruminations and convictions on his friend Nettles, that the latter posted off one pleasant afternoon to the "Lodge," and did not return home until the next day. He was, as usual, received in the kindest manner by the widow. He had always been solicitous of her favor, on the score of his just appreciation of her dinners and evening parties. If Nettles had a weakness at all, it lay in his passion for the creature comforts. He had always taken care to please her accordingly, and she was always glad to welcome him. He was a good companion, who picked up all the scandal going, and was ever ready for any mischief. We will suppose that, when the hour came for the evening meal, he found and enjoyed a delightful supper. The widow was unusually fresh and attractive. She had stolen off soon after his arrival, leaving him to adjust his six-feet upon the sofa, while she consulted her toilet. She returned just as he was emerging from his *siesta*, looking like Cleopatra, except that her dimensions were not so great, her skin so dark, nor her jewels quite so magnificent as those of that famous queen of Egypt.

"Really, Mrs. Foster, you grow younger and more fascinating every time I see you."

These gallant words accompanied a graceful taking and squeezing of the fair lady's hand. "There is one thing, however, which I think faulty about you."

"Faulty!" in consternation.

"Yes, faulty! and the fault is in your mind, your feelings, your thoughts, your sentiments."

"Indeed, Mr. Nettles!" bewildered.

"Yes, madam! it consists in your contentment; in that cold disdain of humanity; in that scornful indifference to my sex, which makes you willing to sacrifice this youth, this bloom, this beauty—nay, you know I never flatter!—I say, to sacrifice all these possessions in seclusion, without sharing them with that most precious of all heavenly gifts, a husband."

"Really, Mr. Nettles, you have a most elevated opinion of the value and usefulness of your sex."

"Not more than the really wise of your sex have been always pleased to entertain. You remember it was the *foolish* virgins that were unprepared at the coming of the bridegroom."

"Yes, sir! but even were I to allow that, there is still another difficulty. The bridegroom does not happen so frequently in a widow's chances that she can change her solitary condition when she pleases; and, unless there is a prospect of his coming, what's the policy of her admitting that she finds her solitude unpleasant?"

"Mrs. Foster, many a man would woo if the lady would only coo; but men, you are aware, are naturally modest."

"Oh, Mr. Nettles!"

"They are, madam! they are! It is the woman always that is the tempter, and naturally enough. If we put a very high estimate on her value, we are apt to feel that we fall below it, and we approach her rather with a sense of her superior merits and position than of our passion, though it may burn us up all the while. Now, a case happens at this moment to my knowledge, and I must say that you are interested in it."

"Me, sir!"

"Yes, Mrs. Foster, you! I know a gentleman who feels for you a most profound passion, but who dares not—"

"Nay, Mr. Nettles! what have you ever seen about me that should repel or discourage any gentleman?" and the lady smoothed down the folds of her dress, and, smiling sweetly, inclined somewhat to the speaker.

"The beautiful crocodile!" thought Nettles to himself; "she evidently suspects me of being this bashful gentleman. What a harpy!"

But, though thus thinking, he never suffered his eyes to breathe any but an expression of tender interest and regard. Still, fearing that she might assume too much, as Nettles never deceived himself in the opinion that he was a very personable man and likely to prove quite too attractive for most women, he hurried forward to a full revelation of his object, and of the person in whose behalf he came. He had his own way of doing this.

"Mrs. Foster," said he, gravely, "you have certainly shown yourself to be the most remarkable of women. I have seen you for six months working busily to procure for another the devotion which was all the while overflowing for yourself."

"Really, Mr. Nettles, you speak parables. What are you driving at?"

"Let me explain. You will do me the justice to admit that if anybody knows the people of this county, man, woman, hoyden and hobby-de-hoy, it is myself."

"Granted, sir!"

"Some of these have been accustomed to consult me in the most important matters. Among these persons is my friend Jones Barry. You partially took him out of my hands, but you played your hands badly. You perversely tried to persuade him that he was desperately in love with Miss Geraldine—"

"Don't speak of that young lady in my hearing, I beg you, Mr. Nettles!"

"Pardon me, but I can't help it; it's necessary to what I've got to say. But I'll not dwell upon it. Well, as I tell you, at the very time that you were doing your best against nature and yourself, to force this belief into his heart, the poor fellow was devotedly attached to another."

"Indeed! You surprise me, sir."

"Such was your powerful influence over him, that you could persuade him to anything; and, yielding to your seeming wishes and opinions, he professed attachment to your step-daughter, while his heart was all the time ready to burst with a passion for yourself."

"For me, sir? Jones Barry fond of me?"

"To devotion—to distraction; and how you could be so blind as not to have seen it, passes my imagination. How often has he consulted with me on this very subject! How often have I told him, 'Come out like a man, and tell her what you feel!' His only answer was: 'No! She doesn't think of me. It's evident she thinks only of the marriage of Geraldine. She will never marry again. Her heart's in the grave with Foster!' Then he would weep, and say: 'I must marry Geraldine, if it's only to be near to her!'"

"Poor Jones! and how he concealed it!"

"Concealed it? No, madam, it was only from *your* eyes that he concealed it. It wasn't his art in hiding; it was your blindness in not seeing. Why, the night of the *fête*, he said to me that, when you fed him with tea from the cup, while he sat in a chair in your little back-room, he thought he should overflow with delight, and the next day, when you mixed him some peach toddy, he said, 'coming from your hands, it was the most delicious dram that ever his lips had tasted.'"

"Dear Jones, and he felt all this?"

"All this, and was silent!"

"And I was doing my best to force him upon one who didn't care a straw for him."

"Suicidally, as I called it; for, as I said to him, you are evidently made for each other."

"You said *that*, Mr. Nettles? Ah! you're a sharp-sighted person."

"Says I, 'Barry! Foster is young and lovable. She's scarcely older than her step-daughter. She's unselfish. She sees that you are the man to make Geraldine happy, because she feels that you would make herself so; and she ought not to be permitted to sacrifice herself. Go to her, tell her the truth, lay your whole heart open to her, and my life on it, she will then discover what, perhaps, she does not yet see, that you have taken a deeper hold on her own heart than she has any idea. At her, like a man; and, if she be the tender-hearted woman that I think her, she will not reject you.' "

The widow sighed deeply. "But he did not follow your counsel?"

"He did not believe me. His fears blinded him. He worshipped you too devotedly. Had he felt a weaker passion, he would have been more bold. But his heart failed him, and he would have suffered himself to be shot; nay, don't I know that he went out fully expecting to be killed by Hammond's bullet, even hoping it, that he might no longer be kept in such miserable anxiety?"

"Poor, poor fellow!"

"And now, that he knows my object in coming here, he is on thorns of misery. His horse is already saddled. He has raised all the ready money he can, and, the moment he gets my report, if it's unfavorable, he'll set off to join his fat friend in Tennessee. He will sell out, and leave Georgia forever. He even talks of joining the regular army, hoping to be killed in the first engagement."

"But he must never do it."

"It will depend on you. He is at my house waiting. I have agreed that, if I am successful, I am to wave a white handkerchief, and if not, a red one, just as I get in the avenue. His mind's in a most awful state, and it's for you, my dear Mrs. Foster, to determine his fate."

"Oh! Mr. Nettles, you see too deeply into the hearts of us poor women to doubt what must be my answer. Poor, dear Barry, I always was fond of him. But I never thought he had any feeling for me, and so I tried only to get for him that disobedient girl."

"What blindness! And so?"

"Oh! you do with me what you please, Mr. Nettles. It's a wonder you never married yourself. You're single only because you never wished to be otherwise."

"Ah! you flatter me, Foster! But I must resign my hopes and wishes to others. I live for my friends only. But, in giving them up,

I have my consolation; and when carrying off the heart of a lady to another, I am privileged, as a matter of course, to take her kisses for myself."

The widow did not struggle seriously against the spoliation which followed this pretty speech.

"Barry will be the happiest man alive."

"But have you a white handkerchief with you? I see that you use a red one," demanded the provident widow.

"Indeed I have not!" said Nettles, feeling in his pockets, and looking disquieted.

"Take mine, dear Mr. Nettles. Poor Barry, he must not be suffered to throw himself away!"

How Nettles chuckled as he left the "Lodge!" In less than a month, the widow became Mrs. Barry. We have no reason to suppose that her husband repented the proceeding, and we know that Nettles did not. He usually took his Sunday dinner at the "Lodge," and was master of ceremonies on all occasions. He himself never married. Why should he, when he could so easily persuade his friends to do so? Miles Henderson, in the course of the year, was caught by Henrietta Bailey, one of the girls of whom Mrs. Hammond thought so much; and he lived sufficiently happy with her to feel no repinings at the sweet and singular affection which existed between Hammond and his wife. He, it is true, remained the master, but she exercised, though she did not assert, all the authority of the mistress. There has been no duel at "Pistol Quarter" since the famous affair that terminated the tragic part of our comedy.

THE END.

"WOODLANDS", SIMMS'S HOME NEAR MIDWAY, SOUTH CAROLINA

From an engraving, c. 1852, by Thomas Addison Richards
Courtesy New York Public Library

PADDY McGANN;

—OR,—

THE DEMON OF THE STUMP.

"If thou be'est a man, shew thyself in thy likeness: If thou be'est a devil, take't as thou list." . . . "I defy thee."—SHAKSPEARE.

CHAPTER I.

"Now, my comates and brothers in exile,
 Hath not old custom made this life more sweet
 Than that of painted pomp? Are not these woods
 More free from peril than the envious court?
 Here feel we but the penalty of Adam,
 The season's difference."

                    As You Like It.

———

It was November, and the delicious season that we call the Indian Summer; when, after two or three smart white frosts, and possibly a little ice, the cool spell passes off; the winds grow calm, and modestly beseem themselves, the temperature becomes sweet and genial—neither too cold nor too warm; when, after a heavy fog each morning, the sun suddenly bursts through the vaporous sea, in a shower of golden light; when the whole circumference of heaven, and the whole broad plain of earth, the great forests and the little hills, seem to move together in concert, as at a feast or bridal; when the woods capriciously change their suits, day by day, and ever to a glorious motley; when the birds grow more elastic in the air; when the long lines of cranes are suddenly beheld trooping south; when the squirrels are every where to be seen in eager movement, plying rapidly between their groups of great green water-oaks and the neighboring cornfields, each with his mouth full of stolen fruit; when persimmons are rapidly ripening; when Cuffee, and Cudjo, and Sambo, and Cæsar take out the dogs nightly—Towser, and Teaser, and Tear'em, and Take'em—for coon and possum hunt; when the hogs, having had full range of the peafield and the potato patch, are about to be driven up to the fattening pen, and when, following the good old English rule, which forbids the hunt from the *spring* of the leaf to the season of its *fall*, the hunters begin to sound horn and summon the beagles every morning for the chase, and when, briefly, the harvest being good, the season delicious, no war in the land, and plenty on every board, our country seats are everywhere glad in themselves, and with gladness welcome their city friends to the sports and hospitality of the old plantation.

It was just such a season as this, and under just such pleasant circumstances as I have catalogued above, when I was entreated to *Desilla,* the fine plantation-seat, on the South Edisto, of my excellent old friend Wharncliffe, and it was just on one of the sweetest days of this delicious season, that, taking our cue from every bird of the air, and every beast of the field, we left a late dinner table and took horse for a canter to the river, about three miles from the dwelling.

The afternoon sun was just bright enough to be a charm to the sight, without being oppressive to the frame; and he flung his jewels about him with the gayest profusion, varying, at every moment, the bright motley of every hemispheric crown of the forest, to every color of the rainbow! In such weather, through such foliage, to dash off on free-going steeds, is to feel life in every vein and artery; and we went forward, absorbing, at every bound, from sun, and air, and woods, the sufficient aliment for a delicious stock of happiest reveries. In such a canter, the heart forgets its cares, the head its anxieties, the whole nature seems to cast off its burdens, and the soul wakes up to the pleasantest sensations, as a bird that feels its wings with the first glance of the morning sun over its shoulders in the nest!

Wharncliffe, though a good planter, was not the less a good dreamer, like myself, and in his moments of escape from the dull drudgeries of life, could give himself up, quite as readily, to the sense of the *dolce far niente,* which, by the way, does not, even in the Italian mind, signify merely the delight of doing nothing. At all events, if it implies the extremest measure of physical repose, it by no means implies the dormancy of the intellectual nature. On the contrary, with many, and the most superior minds, great mental activity is almost inseparable from extreme physical quiet; will, indeed, admit of no physical exertion, but seems to absorb, for its own uses, all the vital energies of the animal man.

It is Cowper who says, somewhere, "how various are the employments of those whom the world calls idle." Cowper was a busy man enough, and he too was a dreamer. But the difference between him and Wharncliffe was simply that he had bad dreams, while Wharncliffe had good ones. This was all owing to temperament. Cowper was a hypocondriac, a sad mixture of the nervous and the desponding lymphatic. Wharncliffe was nervo-sanguine, and while relishing field sports to excess, was yet capable of reverie. But his reveries were always hopeful, and tinted by a pleasant sunlight. He was well read in books, and had a good collection; had some skill in fiction, and was a pleasant *raconteur,* though a man of delicate sensibilities, was frank and free in his intercourse with men; and though, perhaps, a shade too old and quiet for the chase, as a frequent pursuit, yet relished it on occasion, and delighted in its details. So much for my host and companion. It will be enough said of myself when I report that we knew each other well, and so we rode together, enjoying equally the season, yet scarcely uttered a syllable during our canter of three miles. When men fully understand each other, they rarely have much to say in the matter of mere conversation. They know that they think together, and that their tastes and sympathies are mostly in common, and this is enough of course. Each, at times, has something to teach or to impart, and then indeed, with all such persons, the practice is rather to *discourse* than to *converse.* It is only the blockhead that will insist on putting in his oar when such people have any thing to deliver. So much by way of *caveat* to that large class who are for talking all the time.

And so, silent and thoughtful, but quite satisfied, rode Wharncliffe and myself, till we reached the river landing, some three miles, as I have said, from the dwelling. We passed through a two-mile tract of heavily timbered swamp, and came out, at length, on a noble headland, around which the stream made a broad sweep, leaving us on a promontory. Wharncliffe was expecting some rafts down the river, and we alighted to look after them. Seating ourselves at length upon the bluff, we both tacitly began to make pictures out of the scene, such as would have inspired the landscape painter with a score of subjects.

Very sweet and picturesque were all the surroundings. The noble stream, the Edisto, one of the prettiest rivers in our State, is neither very broad nor very deep; but it is very winding, and between avenues of the noblest shade trees; the waters, very sweet to drink, are as clear as crystal; the river winds mazily, but not lazily, in continuous bold sweep around jutting headlands, and travels to the ocean, some three hundred miles below, at the rate of four knots an hour. So bold are these curves at times, that you shall swim several miles in your *dug*-out (let us call it a gondola), yet find yourself (across the land) within two hundred yards from the spot where you first struck the paddle into water.

This is the great lumber river of the State, supplying Charleston, the sea islands, Cuba, and in days when there was peace in the land, largely contributing her stores of pine to the benighted cities of the North. It is great in its fish; and we are in the very neighborhood, which, in spring and summer, is so much frequented by amateurs of the Izaak Walton order, coming down from the precincts of Augusta and Columbia, to tickle their trout dexterously, and weave pretty sentiments out of their dying agonies. Here, with fashionable rods and lines, and painted flies, and *artificial* silver fish, they practice charms to wile the trout from his bed, and persuade perch, and bream, and rock, and pike, and cat, into their baskets. The bream and red-belly perch are great favorites, I notice, with the ladies. The trout and rock, not so delicate, but well flavoured and substantial, are commended by their portly dimensions to the masculine gender. You shall often capture a trout large enough to take a junk bottle into his jaws. The epicure specially rejoices in the *blue cat* of the Edisto, which is not only one of the largest, but the most delicate fish that swims in these regions. But beware how you subject him to vulgar treatment. Use none of your artificial and compounded sauces in *costuming* him for the table—nothing stronger than melted fresh butter, and fresh well-shriven parsley—no condiments! Here, too, if sport only be your object, you may take, in the proper season, and after a peculiar manner, the monster sturgeon of a hundred pounds and upwards. He, too, commends himself to certain tastes, and my friend, Jamison, vows that he is *much* more delicate, when on table, than many a politician when under it! But his dressing, like his person, has its own peculiarities!

Ah! pleasant are the memories, most delightful views, that crowd the brain of the grateful visitors, whom thou wast wont, in happy seasons, to beguile to thy green borders, and thy sweetly gushing streams. Sometimes there came the stately Englishman, and the canny Scot, and the free-handed son of green Erin, and the gallant Frenchman, and they shared the warmth of our firesides, and thou gavest them freely of thy finny inhabitants. But the memory is warmer of the sacred few among our own people who loved to seek us out in our rustic solitudes, and who came hither eagerly seeking thy treasures. There is Maxcy Gregg, now a Brigadier of the Confederates, doing brave service on the banks of the Potomac. Alas! thy perch and bream, thy trout and thy cat, content him no longer. He has become a fisher of men, and can already count his score of pitched battles, from Vienna to Sharpsburg, which may be called his pike-fishing; and his hundred other smaller affairs, all victories, which may be likened to his conquests over perch and bream in the Edisto. Thus has he gone on fishing to the Chickahominy, and to the James, and again across the Potomac into Maryland—"My Maryland"—Eheu!—until now, in pursuit of larger game, he probably despises our "small deer" of the Edisto. May he soon return to his earlier loves, and to our simple tastes and solitudes.*

*Alas! alas! of what avail are thought, and hope, and prayer, and precaution—the human preparation which provides, or the divine instinct which foresees?—and what a mockery is the fond calculation which counts on events of pleasure, and the possessions and prospects of the future. Even as I write the above passage—but a little week, indeed, after I had written it—came the mournful tidings of the death of my noble friend on the battle field of Fredericksburg. He died, as he had ever lived, a fearless, true man, and solely devoted to his country. His last words, addressed to the Governor of South Carolina, should form the only inscription upon his tomb. He would wish no other, and would rebuke our plaudits, even as he would rebuke our tears. Alas! and yet—

"Quis desiderio sit pudor aut modus
Tam cari capitis."

His last letter to me, post-marked at Winchester, Va., 11th Nov., is full of sanguine calculation for himself and country and deals in a variety of subjects, including a brief discussion of certain features of the Greek tragedy, in which he quotes, (from memory,) sundry passages in the original. He expresses the hope that his Brigade may be sent for service to the South Carolina coast, and prays that he may be there in time to engage in its defence, in the event of assault. He tells me that he has preserved all his official papers; but, under my suggestion, will henceforth proceed to keep a diary. He pleasantly commends to Gen. Jamison and myself the use of peach and honey, as a substitute for other unattainable liquors. "Let me exhort you," he writes, "and the friends in your circle, to cultivate native resources. Was not the honey of Hymettus famous for long ages that knew not sugar? And can any drink be better than the distilled juices of the peach, old and mellow?" He writes of the army and the prospects of the war, but the matter is not yet proper for publication. The snows are falling while he writes, and he adds—"our poor soldiers, with-

And there is Jones, who should be a Brigadier along with Gregg, and Jenkins, and a score besides, to whose companionship he would have done honor in the stricken field. He has not forgotten—will not soon forget—those pleasant tides and times when, floating down the North, and winding into South Edisto, from Orangeburg, he 'emerged into the vicinage of "Burwoods" and "Woodlands," Jamison at the helm of the "dug-out," as he has since been at the helm of the State in the hour of its greatest peril.

Ah! pleasant comrades, little did either of us think that all our waters were so soon to become troubled! No more happy sunshine—no more merry sport, or gay carolling, or lively repartee, or lively badinage—quip, crank and leer;—and no more "Hollands" for the manufacture of that famous beverage which your President knew so well how to compound. But be of good cheer!

<blockquote>
The darkest day,
Wait till to-morrow, will have passed away.
</blockquote>

Even as I write the thunder rolls westward from the east. There is storm along the heights of Virginia. The cry is havoc; the war-dogs are again unleashed! The tempest rages, and the bloody banner of the foe goes down in its own blood. We are victors, and this time the route is complete. Thirty thousand of the insolent invaders bite

---

out tents, many of them insufficiently clad, without blankets, and some of them barefoot, bear their hardships cheerfully; but in such weather they suffer much." Another extract— "The little town near which we are encamped, has Berryville for its proper name, and Battletown for a nickname. The latter is said to be derived from the numerous fisticuff encounters which General Morgan, (of the Revolution,) had there, before he had risen from the rank of a waggoner, to that of a general officer. One big bully, in particular, is said often to have worsted him." In a previous letter, post-marked Oct. 16th, and dated from Camp Barnes, Berkeley county, Va., between Martinsburg and Winchester, he engages in a discussion of Grecian history, which something of mine had provoked, in which he draws freely from the original Greek of the dramatists, making an amusing commentary of his own. At the close, speaking of the "luck of his brigade," he says: "In the three months following the 25th June last, it was engaged, more or less seriously, in ten pitched battles, besides minor affairs, and bore its full part in the great victories of Cold Harbor and Manassas (the second), as well as in the hard fought fight of Sharpsburg; where, &c."—"and in the repulse of the enemy's attempt to force the passage of the Potomac at Shepherdstown—regarded, by Gen. Lee, as one of the most brilliant affairs of the war, &c." Maxcy Gregg was one of the first to take the field in our State. His patriotism was ardent and his politics consistent. He was of the straightest school of State-rights politicians. He was an accomplished scholar, of high rank in his profession, a high-toned gentleman. *Sans peur et sans reproche!* His name, henceforth, is monumental in his native State.

the dust.* Our triumph is secure—our independence! and Peace, with her beautiful rainbow, plucked from the bosom of the storm, and spread from East to West, from North to South, over all the sunny plains and snowy heights of our beloved Apalachia,† sends our gallant sons back once more to the calm blessings of each hospitable home!

So mused and thought we both, as we gazed upon the placid waters. Our thoughts, Wharncliffe's as well as mine, were, I am sure, the same, for, even as I started up with a cry, almost realizing with my own eyes the vision of conquest in my fancy, he too rose and exclaimed—

"It is not all over—our happy life, my friend! We shall enjoy the old sports of our sweet little river once more, in communion with our noble-hearted companions. It cannot be that God will deliver us into the hands of these atrocious heathens. As between us and the Deity, there is no doubt a sad reckoning to make; but as between us and these accursed Yankees, no reproach lies at our doors, unless that single one of having too long slept within the coil of the serpent. I have faith in God, my friend.—He may punish us, and we must suffer, for this is the meed of our desert; but he will not let us sink. I have faith in his promise, in his mercy, and I know that, after this tribulation, our peace shall return once more—our prosperity—our friends; and the "song of the turtle shall be heard in the land!"

We grasped each other's hands in silence. Words were no more. The thought prevailed in the prayer which each heart silently felt to stir within him, covering each cheek with a glow, and making every pulse to tingle with a strange exulting sense of hope and delight.

---

* But a day after the passage was written, the great battle of Fredericksburg took place. As the events of that day become more distinct and better known, the prophecy seems to have been fulfilled to the very letter. The defeat of the abolitionists seems to have entailed upon them a loss, in killed, wounded and missing, of numbers scarcely less than those given in the text.

† The Apalachian chain of mountains, stretching from Virginia to Georgia, through the two Carolina's, and forming the backbone of the country, links together the whole South, the States equally, of the Atlantic and the Gulf. Apalachia should be the poetical name of the Confederacy. This native word, of the red man, cannot be surpassed in equal dignity and euphony.

CHAPTER II.

———

Our raptures were broken by an unexpected occurrence. Just then we heard a loud shout from the river, quickly followed by a merry peal of laughter, mixed up with a boisterous snatch of song. We had been about to turn away, but the sounds arrested us. Looking up the stream, we beheld the successive appearance of a score of rafts—"bull" after "bull" darting into sight, rounding a point of land, and plunging forward, in rapid progress with the current, for the opposite shore. At last came one containing the Pilot and his crew—the whole rafting party comprising a couple of whites, and a goodly gang of able-bodied negroes.

They were evidently equipped for what is usually a long journey. From a clay platform on the "pilot's raft," a goodly fire sent up a volume of smoke. One of the negroes was at the cook-pot. There was on board a caboose, a chest, a cypress "dug-out," or canoe, a pile of wood, on which one of the negroes lay asleep, with his nose bulging out eastward; and you might see, without too close a search, a pile of sweet potatoes, a barrel of meal, a box of bacon, and various edibles in the shape of peas and pumpkins. Evidently our raftsmen were on a voyage of some weeks.

It was a picture. John Brunson was Pilot, and carried his long rifle, ready for deer or turkey. One of the negroes, a jolly looking

222

dog, with a face as round as that of the moon,—supposing her lady-
ship to be veiled in an Ethiopian cloud—and mouth spread wide
with a grin that opened it from ear to ear, had his fiddle and bow
in hand, and began to scrape dolefully the moment he discovered us
on the bluff. In quick succession each "bull" bolted by; swept with
the current to our shore, where we exchanged salutations with
Captain and crew; rounded off, and darted down, down the stream,
till another sudden turn of the river took them out of sight. But
for many minutes after we could still hear the creaking of the
violin, broken by an occasional whoop to or from the shore. As they
sped from sight, I mused upon their probable voyage.

"We lack antiquity, Wharncliffe," said I; "or rather, we lack
youth. We have never enjoyed youth. Our people are all full-
grown animals, without having gone through the process of growing.
They have never known childhood, and lack all its fancies; else
such a life as this, passing day and night through such scenes, with a
progress among so much that is picturesque, in a country so sparsely
settled, would inspire them with such fancies as possessed the
Arabian, and these would elevate the intellectual and imaginative
nature, if they did not mature the social. With such skies, such a
climate, such glorious forests, overhanging such waters, forever murmuring their under-song to the sea which they are approaching, our
uneducated people should glow with wild and beautiful superstitions.
Romance should be the natural growth of such a life, in such a
region, under such conditions, and this would begin with the rude
art which prefaces the advance of barbarism to the first low hills of
civilization; then would follow the sense of the beautiful."

"Rather, the sense of the beautiful would precede and follow
the art."

"Perhaps you are right. At all events, our popular deficiency in
fancy is due, I take it, wholly to the fact mentioned: our people
have no past—no present memorials—which can excite; they have
had no youth! You smile."

"Only to think how much you remain an optimist, on the verge
of sixty!"

"My experiences of trial have robbed me of none of my dreams."

"And I, too, am a dreamer, and what is more, a *believer*. I see
the fancy in our people, however latent. Fancy and Imagination are

innate. They are the endowments of every people, in degree. They
are dormant, like most other intellectual faculties, until called into
activity by the pressure of external forces. Even the African possesses them, though in him they develop themselves hideously, or in
gross and coarse ideals. The dormancy of these faculties in our
people, is not so much the lack of the past, as the lack of *attrition*.
Our lives are too obscure and monotonous."

"Not more so than that of the Arab."

"Yes! The Arab may be nomadic, but he wanders *in groups* and
families—in tribes. He rarely passes out of the tribe; is rarely
segregated from it. The tribe is sufficiently large for variety, and
there is always a curious diversity of *gift,* as well as character, among
its inmates. As they hold together, and are forced on their own
resources, they have the necessary attrition for development. Each
brings his gift to bear in the common stock. One brings music; another
poetry; another contributes astronomy, perhaps; a fourth is seer and
prophet; a fifth is the ancient of the tribe, who remembers far back,
and can trace out the details of old adventures; he is biographer
and historian; another is the weaver of fiction—the tale-teller—who
mingles past and present, and out of the vague memorials of the
one, teaches and amuses the other. And so the traditions of the tribe
are perpetuated. The boy grows up *in* them, and transmits them;
adds to them with new material, which is duly reported by his successor. They make the most of their small resources, and the attrition of this sort, provocative of imaginative activity, is perpetually
going on. Nothing is lost among them, nothing forgotten; and a
tribe, in this way, will be able to repeat the same details, in the
same manner, through the lapses of a thousand years. It is so also
with our red men. The attrition among both these people, when
once you consider how large is the family circle in both, is a
thousand times greater than that of our poorer sort of people. Every
palm tree which the Arab has once passed in his wanderings, becomes
individualized and recorded among his people. Every star that has
been grateful to his sight, or a guide for his eyes, takes thence a
place in his household. The palm tree sheltered his great grandsire,
Abou Hassan, three hundred years before, when he made his last
pilgrimage to Mecca, and Abou named it after himself—and prob-

ably indicated it as under the special protection of a Djinn or presiding genius. So of his fountain—his Diamond of the Desert—it is a thing sacred; its histories, traditions, associations, are all on record; and whatever may be the leading idea in its connection, be sure that each successive part of the tribe will work upon it with a thousand fanciful variations. The tribal or patriarchal life may be wandering, but the *society* is stationary. If it moves, it moves together, and there is no loss of the common capital by any removal. On the contrary, every superstition is hallowed, and borne away with them, even as they bore away their *Lares familiares*. And so with our red men. But not so with our people. Their very individuality of character, which favors independence, and is the nurse of self-esteem, is a foe to attrition. Every marriage breaks up a household, in the formation of a new one. The young do not remain with the old people, or very rarely. Each is eager to be setting up for himself. They go apart—go into the solitude—and every such step is a loss of progress towards civilization. They lose not only what they had of old tradition, but the attrition which is necessary to the creation of new mysteries. Their invention is only taxed in material ways. They are never called upon for fancies."

"And what will remedy this? for if this be true, the evil is innate."

"Not so; it is still the effect of circumstance. Increase of population, or a stationary population, will supply the lack in season; and the process of acquisition is also a process of attrition. The *fiction* will come from the *friction*. The transition periods are those always most full of invention. The realm of romance is ever a debatable land. It is the unsettled empire between two great extremes, for which both parties are contending. In their conflicts they evolve the wondrous event, the daring heroism, the beautiful eccentricity, the curious custom, the wild, graceful manner, the flashing novelty, the piquant adventure, such as make the periods of Chivalry and Feudalism—periods dear to Poetry and Romance. It is the perpetual conflict between Valentine and Orson—between the ever hostile worlds of civilization and the savage. It is in the transition of a people from the one confine to the other, that developes the richest materials for art in fiction. And this is also the formation of society.

"But, without going into any argument, let me assure you that our people do not need a *past*, to be informed and stimulated by

Fancy. They have the innate faculties of Fancy and Imagination, and these are, in some degree, perpetually acted upon by the circumstances in which they live. I think I could show you many proofs of it, even in this precinct, where there is but little attrition, and very few provocatives to mental exertion, out of the beaten tracks of necessity. You are also in error when you assume that our backwoodsman has inherited, or retains none of those superstitions which belonged to the original European stocks from which he came. I have traced out many proofs of European fable and superstition in the meanest households. They retain old world *ideas* even as they retain old world *words,* with singular tenacity. Hardly one of the peculiarities of language, which the Englishman of to-day regards as an American pronunciation, but may be traced out in the old British drama. So, too, of peculiar phrases, including domestic proverbs. The very fact that their stock of language and literature is limited, and that they have little attrition, compels a tenacious hold of what capital they have. All the old British superstitions are retained, and you may trace them, in different sections, to an English, Scotch, or Irish source; to the Scotch, perhaps, more than either. There is still, for example, a lurking faith in witchcraft, and a belief in its spells, charms and conjurations. Wizards and witches, or, as they are called, 'Witch Doctors,' are still in demand. Dogs, cattle, and even guns are sometimes bewitched. Old women are still pointed at as suspects. Warts, and even cancers, are said to be cured by spells and periapts; and you may even now sometimes find the ancient horse-shoe nailed beneath the door-way, forbidding the witch to pass. I myself have been consulted by one in great distress from this supposed cause, and I have relieved by an *abracadabra,* sealed up and hung about his neck as an amulet,—aided by a potent dose of salts and magnesia."

"Good! You acquired, then, a reputation for a Witch Doctor."

"No! The patient had sufficient self-esteem to keep his secret from other persons. And here, by the way, lies the reason why so little is known, among the higher or educated classes, of the prevalence of the superstition. The people say little about it—much less than formerly. You get at it by an accident, perhaps, or in the excitement of their fears, or in the extent of their imaginary suffering—if it be imaginary. They are shy of all allusions to the subject, for several reasons. There is a lurking dread of the wizard himself, who does not like to be spoken of too freely, any more than did the Witch of Endor; and the common people are aware that the educated classes hold their superstitions in contempt. Their self-esteem, which is not powerful enough to fling off the superstition, is yet jealous of the sneer of the better educated. But the faith is present, is still active, and sufficiently shows the susceptibilities of the possessor in respect to fancy and the picturesque. In fact, I have found most isolated people—men who live by hunting and fishing; persons who lead a lonely life—to be superstitious; sea-faring men are usually described as being so."

"Our old friend, Commodore Berry, denied that to me."

"And I have had scores of other sea captains to confirm it. Berry was perhaps unwilling to make the admission for his class. His self-esteem, knowing as he did the general opinion of the highly educated classes, forbade that he should make an admission for his own which might render it ridiculous. And this is the process, whenever the self-esteem is excited, and which is always the case with the uneducated in any country, when they come in contact with those who are held to be superior in refinement. In this respect, our mountain hunters greatly resembled the red men. Besides, it is a part of the superstition, to believe that evil will come of the much talking of it. The spectre is said to resent every report made to the metaphysician."

"Of whom spectres are proverbially in dread."

"And the Devil himself, if old psychologists are to be relied on. Dunstan's metaphysics, by the way, were at the end of his tongs."

"Yes, when dealing with the Devil *in propria persona*. But, dealing with the people, his subtlety lay rather in the art of Cagliostro than in that of Faust. It is strange, also, that Martin Luther should have preferred a material defence against Satan, rather than a spiritual one. That flinging the inkstand at his head—"

"Was, I take it, merely figurative. It meant simply that he exhausted his ink bottle writing against his Satanic majesty, and might well fling away the empty inkstand at the assailant upon whom he had previously exhausted all his wits and ink."

How far we might have proceeded in this bald, disjointed chat, carried on while we were preparing to re-mount our horses, need not be conjectured. We had started a metaphysical subject which might well have kept better wits employed till midnight, and for which the midnight would seem the most proper hour; when we were, unexpectedly, interrupted, and in a way which startled both of us. On a sudden, a clear, manly voice burst out in a rough song from the thicket, not a hundred yards distant, which skirted the river in that quarter. The sound, and the singer were evidently approaching. Wharncliffe's eyes brightened:

"Now," said he, "shall I be able to verify some of the things that I have been saying to you. The man who comes is quite gifted in his way, yet is one of the most uneducated of our people. He is really a smart fellow, and a curiosity besides. You will find that he has not only fancy, but imagination; and with a sufficient supply of Monongahela on board, by way of steam, he will exercise your psychological taste to the uttermost. Hearken to what he sings. I have heard it before. It is all his own composition."

CHAPTER III.

———

Song and singer were rapidly approaching, and we could now hear
both with sufficient distinctness to make out the words of the rude
ditty which the stranger was carolling as, emerging fully from the
thicket, he strode towards us with the free majestic air of the mountain
hunter, who well knows what a long line of shadow his figure
casts from the hill-tops, in the rising and setting of the sun. He
had seen us, and saw that we awaited his approach. He began his
ballad anew:

> "Oh, would you hear tell of Paddy McGann,
> How he hit on a notable plan,
> To aise all his woe, by an aisy woman?"

"A bad rhyme, Paddy," said Wharncliffe, as the new comer drew
nigh.

"None better in the wide worrold, yer honour! Where's the
fault of it? Would you have W— O— WO," (spelling the word,)
"M— A— N, to mane any thing bether or worrse than *wo*-man?
That's the thrue pronouncyation, yer honour, accordying to all my
parts of spache. I knows very well that you fine people have their
own pretty thricks of pronouncyation, and you will say *wimmin,*
when it's written plain before all your eyes '*wo*-men;' and when the
very sinse of the thing itself, and the expariances of all the worrold
will tell you that the crather was intended, from the beginning of the
airth, as the very wo of man, even as the good book tells us; and so,

229

yer honour, I must sing it, with laive of your friend and acquaintance
—" (a bow to me—and then the next lines of the song, sung out as
if in broad defiance of all the devils!)

> "Be aisy yerself awhile, my dear,
> And the saddest intelligence soon shall ye hear,
> Of what befell Paddy last March was a year."

"And what befell you, Paddy, last March was a year?" asked
Wharncliffe, slily giving me a wink, which seemed to say,—"I know
all about it already, but Paddy likes to repeat his tale of grievances."

"Ach, shure, yer honour has no need to ax. Faix, ye knows all
about it already, as well as meself, or ye ought to know; and if ye
don't know, yer more onbeknowing to the thruth of the history
than all the good people—good and bad and middling, promiscus—
(that's to say, all the same, all's one)—along this most blessed
beauty of a river."

"Indeed, Paddy, what you say is the truth. I should know every
thing that concerns you, for we have been, and are still, Paddy,
the best of friends."

"Is it friends that we are, yer honour? And do ye ax it, Colonel,
of poor Paddy McGann, your obadyent sarvant to command? Shall
it be for yer honour I shall give my vote at the next turn-out for
Congress?"

"Many thanks, Paddy, but my ambition does not lie in that direction. You have great men enough always in the field."

"Grate men! Calves, yer honour; and sucking calves at that. It's
but raisonable that we should thry a man, and a raal gentleman, now
and then, if it's only to have a dacent feeling of respectability ourselves, once in a way. I'm clear for a gentleman next turn, Colonel.
I'm sarious. The cattle have had the kaping of the pastur for a long
spell of it."

"Let them keep it still, Paddy, so far as I am concerned. But let
me make you acquainted with my friend, Mr. Stylus—Stylus, Mr.
Bucket—Mr. Ned Bucket."

"Ach, and away! None of your jokes, now, Colonel!—

I'm Paddy McGann,
When over the can;
And Patrick McGarvin,
When doing the carving;
So none of your poking,
The ribs of poor folk in—
You're jibing, you're joking."

"What! you refuse to answer, then, to Ned Bucket. Perhaps I should be more respectful, and say Mr. Edward Bucket?"

"Say nothing about it, yer honour. I'd almost prefar that you'd kick the bucket; though I only says that by way of a joke, for am I not the very person that wants you to live a thousand years. I'm no Bucket, though sometimes a *dipper*, when there's another man's bucket that wants baling. No, Mr. Stylus—happy to know you, sir, and the fradom of a long acquaintance between us, sir, with a full table, a clane cloth, a nate decanter, that's parfection in every thing, except that it wants a stopper! Don't mind Wharncliffe's jokes. He likes a *shy* at the head of his poor friend, if its only for the humour's sake, and he does it with a bucket, if not with a shell. I'm Patrick McGarvin, at your sarvice; and, among friends—only among friends, sir—I shortens it to Paddy McGann. That's my drinking name, sir, and the Colonel gives it to me now, as he thinks I've been drinking; and he's right, in a *leatle* measure. I've had a pull or two with a friend on the river; but nothing to spake of—only a brush at the bottle with the cuff of my sleeve. As for that other name, Ned Bucket, I can't answer to that, drunk or sober, though I'm jubous the Colonel thinks I'm desarving of it."

"And very good deserving too, Paddy, as I've been told by some of my neighbors."

"Och! the neebours, is it? Well, there's only too many among 'em so neeborly that they will be putting a cold spoon into the devil's own dish. May he make it hot enough to scald their tongues. Now, don't ye, dear Colonel, be after desaiving Mr. Stylus with any of their d——d neeborly old woman stories. He's a new gentleman to me, and I want to be liking all your friends; and I would'nt have them to be taxing me with a crooked suspicion hanging on to my coat tail. Happy to be known to you, Mr. Stylus; more happy to be known to you, *agraably*. Stylus! By the powers, but that's a queerish sort of name! I've been given to calling it Styles, all my life. That's the name in all Barnwell, and Edgefield, and Lexington, I reckon. There's a dozen Styles's that I've known in my time, and they were all goodish sort of men, 'specially as I never happened to meet with them in the week days, only of a sundays, when they had on their long coats and long faces."

"Ah! but this gentleman's name is Sty*lus*—a very different name. Stylus means an iron pen—"

"Thunder and turf! You don't say so, Wharncliffe? He don't write, then, with a goose-quill, I'm bould to question. If he's a writer at all, *he* ought to be the Bucket. How he'd make the feathers fly!"

I need not say that we shook hands cordially—the genuine pump-handle shake. There was something so sly in the fellow's manner, so arch in the twinkle of his eye; and the twist of his mouth, and such a mixture of sharpness and simplicity in his garrulous speech, that I was more than once impressed with the awkward notion that he was quizzing me; but the manner of Wharncliffe re-assured me. He was evidently well acquainted with his man.

"Are you in charge of this *fleet*, Paddy," said Wharncliffe, referring to the raft.

"No, yer honour. But I stept on board at the call of my old friend and companion, Jack Brunson. He's pilot. We've had many an ixpedition together, from the freshes to the salts, and pretty much l'arned the river out of the same book—that is, from the same master. Both of us have had the tachings of one you know'd well on the river. I mane Britton Elzy. He was famous in these parts, whether for rafting, or turkey shooting, or fishing. I was a-bobbing for trout, and was doing very well, and catching a few pairch besides, when the 'bulls' came plunging down and spiled my sport for the rest of the day. So I went aboard when Jack Brunson sang out for me; and he pulled out his pocket pistol, (flask,) that he calls his 'blazing star,' and I took in a couple of heavy round shot 'twixt wind and wather—jist barely l'aving out the wather—before you come in sight. Then a third shot at l'aving the craft, and

I fale all the pleasant effects of it. It took me but one skip from the 'Bull' to the 'Bluff,' to make me fale that Patrick McGarvin was changed into Paddy McGann! But I caught some fine fish before I got the shot. Shall I be bringing 'em up for your supper, Colonel, 'specially caying that you've a friend with you? Did you ever, sir," —to me—"ate of the Edisto fish? If you hev, you're not now to be l'arning your grammar. If you hev not, ye'r come to as pretty a school for idication, in the taste of fish, as ye'll find in all the empire of South Carolina."

I assured him that I was not now, for the first time, to undergo initiation in the fry, boil and stew of Edisto fish; and he griped my hand with the grasp of one who says "You'll do! you'll do."

"Bring your fish, Paddy, and take supper along with us," said Wharncliffe.

"Supper!—and is it *me* you're asking to supper, Wharncliffe?"

"Why not? No one will be more welcome, Paddy."

"And I belave you, with all my heart and soul; and I *will* come! But, stop!—I'm not the dacentest looking sort of white man, jist now, yer honour, with these fisherman's duds, you see. Here's a hole, and there's a holy; and, at the knaas there's a patch of grane upon breeches that once was brown—"

"Oh! never matter, Paddy. We look at the man *through* his clothes, and in spite of them—"

"Ach, Colonel, and that's the very thing you must not do in my case. It's what I should'nt call the most purlite or daycent practice—"

"Pshaw, you booby!" with a laugh. "Come, Paddy, and don't mind your inexpressibles. You will see none of the family but myself. The ladies are all gone to Orangeburg, for a week. My friend, Stylus, and myself, are playing bachelors together. We are the only occupants. So, come up as fast as you can, that the fish may have a chance of getting themselves well dressed for supper."

"Faix and feathers! But they have a better prospect before them, in that way, than the Paddy that hooked 'em. I'll come, any how, yer honour; since its not more than eight days o' the week that Paddy has a chance of dacent company. I'll come!"

Shaking hands cordially with the strange fellow, we mounted our horses and rode off; but could hear, for a mile, his sharp breezy voice in song, the chorus of which saluted us at starting.

"Och! sorra the day for Paddy McGann.
Och! sorra the por misfortynit man.
But sorra be slaping,
Be aisy for waping;
Be aisy, take comfort whenever you can.
There's the *can*,
Pass it round,
And a drop will be found
To aise all the woe in the heart of the man!"

CHAPTER IV.

Evans.—Here is Got's blessing and your friend, and Justice Shallow; and here, young master Slender: that, peradventure, shall tell you another tale, if matters grow to your likings.

THE MERRY WIVES OF WINDSOR.

"Well," said Wharncliffe, as we rode homewards, "what do you think of our Paddy!"

"He seems a character."

"He is all that—an original, a natural man."

"No bad recommendation, when so little is fresh and so much artificial. Such a man is assurance of fidelity and saliency together."

"He deals in no commonplaces, you may be sure; and he is to be relied on whether at fight or feast."

"Is he an Irishman?"

"Only a part of one. His father was Irish—a regular bog-trotter—and Paddy inherits some of the brogue, which, as you see, he blends curiously with our native backwoods *patois*. But the brogue is only strongly apparent when Paddy has been rather free in his potations. At all other times it is unobtrusive."

"He is somewhat bitten by the bottle to-day."

"Moderately so. But he has a strong head, and can swallow an enormous quantity of whiskey without losing legs or tongue. I can always tell when he has been drinking; but I have never seen him drunk—never, certainly, to the loss of his wits. I am told that he takes a periodical *rouse*, and at such times he will disappear for a week, only to come forth a new man for two or three months following. When sober, there is no more energetic, industrious, hearty, intelligent, good-natured fellow in the world—prompt to do you any

235

service—will work for you, fish for you, fight for you, and fancy all the while it is you that are serving him."

"He should be a valuable neighbor."

"He is. I have always found him so. Perhaps I should qualify what I have said about his industry—industry implying regular habits of labor. Now, Paddy is a desultory sort of person; as perhaps must be the case with all persons who are famous as hunters or fishermen. But he works with wondrous energy, as we phrase it, '*at a spirt,*' as if the labor was a mere sport, especially if he be doing the work of other people. He serves; carrying wood for love, even as Ferdinand waited on Miranda—and finds that 'the labor love delights in, physics pain.' But, unquestionably, Paddy is rather an idle than an industrious fellow, though energetic when in performance of any kind. He has the reputation of being one of the best raftsmen on the river, and knows the sinuosities of it thoroughly. In this capacity he can always find occupation when he desires it."

"What local mystery lies under the *sobriquet* of Bucket, which you gave him?"

"Ah! you heard him disclaim it. But he is nevertheless strongly suspected of being the writer of certain anonymous letters, signed 'Ned Bucket'—a series of backwoods satires—which make their way through the post office, to unsuspecting parties. It is supposed that these are written by a score of hands,—that every village precinct, in our middle country, has its own 'Ned Bucket,' and that Paddy takes the charge of our little precinct."

"Indeed! Is there any merit in these things?"

"Yes, indeed—at times, and in certain quarters,—as shrewd, keen, coarse satire and rebuke of all pretension, wrong-doing and offensive vanities. Sometimes they seize upon particular instances of fraud, misconduct, vice, or usurpation, and the quarrels of neighbors as their topics; and thus supply a sort of rude censorship over the community, when judges, juries, and even clergymen are, perhaps, too forbearing or utterly derelict of duty."

"Why, these things may thus grow into a popular literature."

"Were there the facilities of a press, they would. But the labor of penmanship, and the failure in easy diffusion of the sheets, will necessarily keep the practice and its influence limited. It is, briefly, the *old English broadside*, in bad hand-writing rather than in clear print. 'Ned Bucket' writes equally in prose and verse, and you have seen that Paddy McGann has a talent for improvisation. As performances of art, the satires of 'Ned Bucket' are rude enough; but they exhibit shrewdness, observation, good sense, wit at times, seasoned with a little malice; hit off simple vices or follies with dexterity; twit one for his meanness or avarice, another for his hypocrisy, another for scandal-mongering, and do not always spare the tender gender."

"Verily, no bad beginnings of popular literature, even as the Oscan Attellanæ were of the Italian comedy."

"Yes, and the anonymous is simply the equivalent of the ancient mark."

"But the practice may become a great annoyance, and occasion much scandal and offence."

"No doubt, but the same thing may be said of the license of Aristophanes. Here, in some cases, it has done so, and been mischievous. It has brought dissension into families, disturbed the peace of some innocent people, and not unfrequently brought trouble, in the shape of a cudgel, upon the shoulders of some of the Buckets who did not wear their masks with sufficient caution. I have heard, indeed, of one or more duels which it has occasioned. Our friend, Paddy, has heard my opinion of the practice, and its dangers; and, as he fights rather shyly with me, when the subject is mentioned, I am inclined to suspect him the more strongly."

"Have you seen any of the things of which he is suspected?"

"Yes, several."

"Were they clever?"

"Enough to cause a laugh, at moments, and sharp enough, at times, to make a victim wince."

"And you think him clever enough for such things?"

"Yes, indeed, monstrous clever is Paddy—rough, unlicked, with scarcely any knowledge of books or letters—only a degree or two above the level of William of Deloraine; but he picks up from passing sources of information, has a wonderful faculty of absorption, and you shall not say a good thing in his hearing but he will probably re-produce it, in an original fashion, the next time you meet with him. But you shall hear him to-night. I will put him on the track of one of his own stories, which he verily believes, and from this you shall judge in what degree our uneducated rustics are endowed with the qualities of fancy and imagination. You will see, too, that their superstitions take a shape which the German and British muse have rendered classical.—His narrative, if I can get him to repeat it, will remind you strongly of the German Kobolds, the Scotch Brownies and the English Lubber-fiend; and I can assure you that I cannot discover in him, his life or associations, any clues to his indebtedness to any European sources. All seems to be due to his innate faculties, or to the local superstitions."

"And he has no knowledge of books?"

"Oh! he may have read Robinson Crusoe, Cook's Voyages, and the Seven Champions of Christendom—possibly a stray novel or history—which is too commonly a very dull fiction, wholly wanting in the art of the novelist. But education—reading—in any proper sense, Paddy has none."

"But his father—his mother?"

"His father was a poor Irishman of the humblest stock, who came from the North of Ireland when a boy, worked at the hod in Charleston, and became a ditcher in the interior. There he married, somewhere in Lexington, the daughter of a small farmer, who was something of a virago, and who was probably smartish. If our Paddy inherits any mental gift from either, it is probably from the dam. The sire was never anything but a hod-carrier or a ditcher—dull, heavy, laborious—who neither wrote, read nor thought. Paddy had some twelve months of 'old-field' schooling, scattered over a period of three years. Since then his only schooling has been that of the rather obscure world in which you find him now."

At this point of our dialogue we found ourselves at the entrance of Desilla, and had scarcely dismounted and taken our seats in the portico before Paddy McGann stood before us. By short cuts through the woods he had overcome space, afoot, almost as rapidly as we on horse-back.

He brought with him a string of very fine trout and perch of most appetizing dimensions. These were not all. He next displayed, from a bag, a pair of fine English ducks, which he had shot in the morning.

—As I have already said, Paddy was quite as great an expert with rifle and fowling-piece as with the angle. He carried with him an enormously long smooth-bore, of French make, a double-barrel, of whose marvellous virtues, in his hands, he was very boastful. He asserted that for six years (allowing one interval, of a dreary sort, of which we shall hear in season) he had won every beef that had been shot for in a precinct of twenty miles round.

As Wharncliffe beheld the fish, he exclaimed—

"Bless me, Paddy, this is a glorious sight for these starvation times. With such a choice mess for supper, we must make a night of it; and we must have others to share in our spoils. Ho! there, Satrap.—Get your horse; we must ask Jamison to supper. Say to General Jamison, boy, that he must come, and come soon, and not fail to come. Tell him I've got some foreign gentlemen to meet us at supper——"

"Furrain, Maussa?"

"Yes; he will understand—foreign, big men from over the big sea. But, my dear Stylus, do go to that table and pen for me a couple of notes. Say to Jamison that these foreign gentlemen are particularly anxious to hear whether we are really willing to make the Prince of Wales a King of Carolina, as Mr. Russell reports."

"The miserable cockney! Was ever such a whaler?"

"Oh! no solemn visage. The fool has been humored according to his folly. Write, my dear Stylus, to Jamison and my kinsman Frank Carroll, at Janina, in a manner to mystify them both. Tell them what you please, only have them to supper. Say to them, in Paddy's own style—

> The finest fish
> That were fried in a dish;
> And, to crown them with glory,
> A song and a story!
> We'll keep 'em from starving
> By fish of McGarvin;
> And, with help of McGann,
> Soon finish our can!"

"I'll be Dod-dern'd, Colonel, but you're making free with *my* song."

"Your thunder, Paddy!"

"By thunder, but some of it is."

"I confess it, Paddy. How could I help it—I've heard it so often, and like it so well."

"Ah! now you're greasing me before you swallow me, just as they say the big snakes do."

"Greasing reminds me that I must make preparation for the supper. I must see to the cook. Paddy, my good fellow, these fish and ducks are a treat for any prince in Christendom. Put *this* in your pocket," handing him a bank note.

"I shant put it in my pipe, Colonel, that's certain."

"Well, Paddy, my good fellow, only continue to bring us fish and flesh, bird and beast, such as these, whenever you can. Because there is war, shall there be no life in the land; shall merry-making cease; shall friends meet no more together; shall not the young assemble, as of old, for dance and music, and shall not the elders look on with hopeful smiles, and cherish a sufficient faith in the good God that he will protect their young ones from the devil and the enemy, in whatever devilish shape he cometh? So mote it be!"

I could see that Wharncliffe thrust a five dollar note into the hands of Paddy. No price had been asked for his game—no offer was made. Paddy knew with whom he dealt, and never made charge to a gentleman, but quietly took whatever was given him. Had nothing been tendered by Wharncliffe, he would have been equally well satisfied. So Wharncliffe told me afterwards.

"There are some of these people with whom I never bargain. Paddy, in fact, would not bargain with *me*. Sometimes I have no money to give him for his game. It matters nothing. I take the game, and neither party has a word to say about the matter. But if Paddy wants money, he comes to me and says so; and if I wish a service done, I send to Paddy and say so. He has the freedom of the plantation: gets powder and shot from me; comes and gets his iron work done at the blacksmith shop; gets mules, and wagon, and so forth; and, in return, I have the freedom of Paddy. We live in a sort of mixed patriarchal and feudal relation to one another. Were I assailed by an enemy, the first person who would rally to my succor and defence would be Paddy. At the first blast of the horn, he would be at my portico with double-barrel and rifle; would be moulding his bullets at my hearth; and go the rounds as a scout, or take his post as sentry, all as a matter of course. Such are our relations."

Enough on this head. And now fancy us all around the fire—we three: Wharncliffe on one side, myself opposite, and Paddy in the centre, occupying our host's snuggery—a sort of refuge reserved exclusively to himself and his masculine visitors, and in which he mostly dwelt during the absence of his family from home. It was his library; a good sized apartment, of twenty-two by thirty, containing some five thousand volumes, mostly English, with many good books, and some rare ones.

But the room was not exclusively a library. It had its own little beaufet, or side-board, with all the necessary fixtures of a country hall. Rifle and shot-gun hung in racks over the door, with large hunting horn suspended from a huge pair of antlers. You might see occasionally open (after practice), a case of fine duelling pistols; and there were various articles scattered about, which showed equally the thrifty planter and the Southern country gentleman. The reader may guess readily at the details, which had in them nothing extraordinary, but exhibited comfort, plenty, some show of taste and elegance, and a graceful hospitality. The chimney was large, and blazing vigorously with oak, hickory and lightwood. The servants were spreading the table in preparation for the supper; and already had we discussed a stoup of peach and honey, when we heard the roll of carriage wheels to the entrance. The next moment came General Jamison, and soon after, Frank Carroll—both from residences only a mile distant.

These arrivals rendered necessary a renewal of our peach and honey, and we soon resolved ourselves into a half-circle about the fire. Paddy was known to all the parties, though to none, perhaps, half so intimately as to our host. A half sofa was wheeled into the circle, and as all the other persons took chairs, Paddy subsided upon the sofa in an attitude to suit his person, which, now that he was seated, appeared to me much more massive than before.

A very large man requires not only room, longitude and latitude, but freedom for evolution. It is not easy to dispose of himself in a moment; and I could see that some time was required, on the part of our huge friend, to adjust his proportions to his sphere, however ample.

But Paddy showed no vulgar awkwardness. Though in an unaccustomed circle, he exhibited ease, and exercised the most perfect freedom, with some *nonchalance;* but there was no rudeness—no impudence—in his behavior or remark. All was respectful in his conduct and the way in which he uniformly addressed us. His bearing was even graceful, as his frame, though heavy, was tall and not cumbrous, his limbs wonderfully flexible, and his movements natural, and with a sort of native grace, the result of a well-proportioned person, of a frank mind, a strong will, and daily exercise as a hunter, afoot or on horseback. He was, in truth, a bold, brave, hardy fellow —none of your drowsy lymphatics; had no small share of the mercurial in his temperament, and was so restless of the staid, the even, the common-place and familiar, that, as he himself phrased it, he must, "plaise God, find something innocent and active for himself to be doing all the time; and if he didn't, there was the Devil, sure, to put him at his own occkypation, which always had a strong smell of the brimstone about it."

Supper followed, and went off magnificently, enlivened by a good appetite and a cheerful conversation upon fish in particular, and wild ducks in general, in which Paddy took part, modestly enough for one whose experience entitled him to authority. When all was over, and the table cleared, and we had resumed our seats about the fire, our host began:

"And now, Paddy, let's have plain dealing with one another. I have a design upon you, and will fiddle while you dance. But I am resolved to make you show off your good qualities to our friends. The General you know already, and Dr. Carroll, and my friend Stylus you in part know through his books, which I have lent you. But I want him to know *you.* As he is an author, he is glad of every chance of meeting with a *real* man, who speaks the truth, and is good for something in a way of his own. I have told him something about you already,"——

"Ach, faith, Colonel, but I'm jubous you've told him too much already. He'll be for putting me in one of his books"——

"And no bad figure would you make there if he did, Paddy; but, in truth, I have told him very little, and nothing but what I believe to be true. I have said that you are a smart fellow, an honest fellow, and a friend of mine"——

"You may take your mortal oath of that last particular, Wharncliffe."

"That you are a first-rate hunter, angler and raftsman; and that, unlike most other hunters and fishermen, you are good at many other things besides,—that you can handle your axe as well as your gun and rod—that you can split your two hundred rails a day; that you can make (when you please,) as many bushels of corn to the acre as any farmer in Orangeburg or Barnwell district; that you can run a ditch as straight, and dig it as wide and deep as ever your father could, and in half the time,"——

"That's true, by all the pipers!"

"That you can read and write, and pretty smartly; that you make verses actually—when the whiskey's free; and that you are very much suspected of writing many of the elegant letters which ride post in this precinct under the name of Mr. Edward Bucket—an otherwise unknown person."

"Ach, Warncliffe, you're a cow that gives good milk, and a plenty of it, but kicks the bucket over when it's fullest. You will be having your crack about all that"——

"Never mind now 'about all that!' Tell us nothing that you do not care should be known. We wish to pry into none of your secrets. I do not *know* that you write these letters, and do not wish to know, especially, Paddy, as I think the practice a bad one"—

"I'll give it up, Wharncliffe! I'll never write another! Ach, botheration, Colonel, but I'm trapped!"

"Never mind, Paddy, all's under the rose! We will say no more of Bucket, lest we too seriously wound your conscience. To come to the particular matter which I have in hand, I have been telling Mr. Stylus, here, that you have had certain strange adventures"——

"Strange enough, by the Powers! But did you tell Mr. Stylus *all* about them, Colonel?"

"No, Paddy, I left that for you to do. I prefer, and so does he, that you should tell them yourself. Nobody can do it half so well, and I have promised him that you will relate them."

"What, Colonel! all about my stump devil!"

"Yes, on sea and land."

"What! the v'yage to sea on a raft into the bargain?"

"All that—every bit of it."

"And the shooting, and the fishing, and the courting, and the marrying? Ach! By my faith, and St. Patrick's, too, you're for putting a sharp cross on my naked temper. It's too long a story, Mr. Stylus."

"I love long stories—especially when the Devil's the hero!"

"But, Lord love ye—you don't know what you're axing, Mr. Stylus. Let the Colonel tell it. He knows all about it, and will make short work enough of it. If I undertakes the telling, it'll be past cock-crowing before I've emptied my basket."

"Precisely. That is just what I expect, Paddy, and after eating so heartily of this fair supper of your providing"——

"My providing, Wharncliffe, but *your* paying for."

"The providing is all, Paddy! Had you not provided, there would have been no such provocation to eat. Having eaten, according to the provocation, I must not dream of sleep till the short hours. And all have eaten in like manner, famously—even the General, in spite of his dyspepsia. As for my friend Stylus, whether he sups or starves, he never suffers himself to sleep when in chase of a good story."

"Ah! but that's the question, Colonel.—*You* say it's a good story, but I say it's no story at all, but a most outrageous truth."

"Truth or fiction, Paddy, all the same. We are resolved upon having your adventures, from your own lips; and that you may not feel fatigued while telling them, see that black bottle on the side-board. It contains Irish whiskey that is probably as old as yourself. That sugar dish contains loaf-sugar—the last in the house. That kettle, which already simmers on the fire, will soon be boiling; and Mr. Stylus, here, makes a first rate whiskey punch. In that other bottle, so clear and white, is a quart of old Holland gin. In twenty-five seconds, should the punch fail to keep you up—"

"Or put me down!"——

"General Jamison, who makes a cocktail as ably as Mr. Stylus a punch, will be ready with that manufacture in time to help your speech. The tobacco and pipes are at hand. There is a warm fire and a good audience. It is not often, Paddy, that we have such good company, or a Ned Bucket among us."

"Honour bright, yer honour! You promised to say no more of that scamp of a scribbler! Plaise let him be quiet, if all this good company's consenting."

"Be it so, Paddy; and now for the story."

"Story! Lord bless yer honours, I have none to tell. It's my real life adventures, if any thing. I'm like the man at the dinner that was knocked down for a bumper, as they calls it, bekaise he could neither sing a song, tell a story or throw a summerset and a spache together. But, if you was to knock me down fifty times, I couldn't tell you a story. It's not in the nathur, Colonel."

"Call it what you please. You know what we desire. But I see what's wanting. General, pray compound for us a cocktail, all round."

"Shall it not be a whiskey punch, first? The whiskey and Paddy have a like origin, and the law of affinities would seem to require that, in Paddy's case, the poteen should have precedence."

"Truly the punch makes a solid foundation! What say you, Paddy?"

"Is it me, Colonel? Then I goes for the Punch. Poteen is the natheral mother of punch; and the wonder to me is, that no body, making the one, has ever thought of some beautiful invention to turn it, by the very same still into the other. Poteen *now—presto*, as they say, and in a minute—here the punch!"

"Ah! Paddy," said the General, "but we should then lose all the pleasure of making it. Were our pleasures to come, ready made to our hands, it would be the death of most of them. For what sings the poet—

> Love's *labors are his pleasures*—
> For what were love without
> The pain, the care, the doubt,
> While counting o'er his treasures."

"Faith, General, but I'm half thinking, then you're right. Them varses are sensible; but I can't say I have ever heard them before.

As for the love, General, where it's to eend in marriage, the less we say about it the bether. I've had the trouble of the courtship, and there the throuble was pretty much the pleasure. It was the great mistake that I ever eended the courting. If 'twas to be done over, I'm sure the love should never come to its mortal death under the hands of the parson."

"It's only after you've bought the article, paid your money for it, and carried it home, that you find it's not genuine."

"Pinchback for gold!"

"Topp'ed off with well-watered whiskey, when your stipulation was against all water."

"It's your honours that says it, gentlemen; all round, you're right. By jabers, many's the time I've had to pay for the adultherous article, and tote it home in a three gallon jug, when the river was all the while running, at my own door, with the very best water in the world."

"Fill Paddy's glass, Stylus. We'll warrant this article, Paddy."

"Don't I know the *House*, Colonel, tho' there's no bush at the door, and no pay ax'd at the counter. Ach! what a blessed world 'twould be if there was no body left in the land but gentlemen; and by that I don't mane your superfine gentlemen, who are too nice to know the uses of their own sowls and fingers; but them that knows that a clane conscience is better than a clane hand; that don't fear the dirt, as they knows always where to find the soap; and will clap their shoulders to a poor man's wheel, to help him out of the rut, without stopping to ax if he's a distant cousin. And so, gentlemen, I begs to drink to you, and to give you,—'Clane hearts in preferance to clane hands'—not that I don't like to see clane hands after the work is done. I'm for claneliness in general, but clane hearts in particular; and here's to a pure conscience, though it goes along with a poor head. Them's my sentiments, gentlemen, and here's to *you!*"

"A very sensible and discriminating toast; not too strong for good heads nor too rough for good society. Paddy, you don't drink!"

"I'm waiting on you, Colonel."

"Drink, man, drink—and don't let the milk sour!"

"Is it milk, yer honour! Oh, by jabers, but heaven send grane pastures to the cow that gave it. The blessed Saint Pathrick himself never cleared his sight with more beautiful eye-wather! It's a'most too good for the week o' days, though the very thing for the weak o' body. It should be kept for Sundays, and holiday times, and Christmas, and New Year's Day. Ach, them holidays was a bright invention! 'Twould be a good thing if we had a few more of them scattered over the fifty-two stupid wakes in the year."

Suppose the beakers duly filled and promptly emptied, with *gusto* and flourish; suppose the parties all disposed once more in their several places—the fire still burning brightly—the pipe furnaces all in full blast, and each man blowing his several clouds, in a half dreamy yet expectant attitude, and you may readily conceive that our night in the snuggery had fairly begun; the kettle, in the meanwhile, it must not be forgotten, continued to sing its contented under-song by the fire, waiting patiently the signal for a repetition of its marriage rites with the more potent spirit on the table.

Wharncliffe now resumed his appeal to Paddy for the peculiar stores in his keeping. But Paddy was not unlike the half-bred young lady in the parlor, who thinks mere reluctance a sign of modesty, and needs frequent entreaties to the piano.

"Ach, Colonel, why would you be afther making a poor man ixpose himself?"

"You're a rich man, Paddy."

"Would you prove it, yer honour, to the tune of a few thousands, you'd make me the happiest dog that ever lay on a carpet."

"You're rich in good feeling and good humour, Paddy; in good sense, good health, youth, curious experiences and pleasant fancies."

"Ah, Colonel, would you blarney a poor fellow, till he feels himself all over in a souse of treacle?"

"The naked truth, Paddy."

"Then, for the sake of a bashful father, put on the baby's clothes, or he'll take could from the ixposure. Here's Mr. Stylus, who's not knowing me at all at all, and he'll be afther thinking that you're poking a dry stick of fun into the vanity ribs of the Edisto raftsman."

"Never a bit of it! Stylus is a knowing person, who sees through a fool as clearly as a common man sees through a barn-door, and don't need help in making his discoveries."

"By jabers, Colonel, that's to say he's found a mighty grate hole in my body already. Oh! hokey! is that what you would say, Wharncliffe?"

"He will find the hole, Paddy, if you hang off like a conceited girl that needs a dozen askings before she consents to be made happy. So 'leave off your damnable faces,' as Hamlet hath it, 'and begin.'"

"It's good sense, yer honour, when one's got something to say, that he should say it, and not be making mouths for practice at his own image in the glass. And if it happens that he's got nothing to say, the sooner he gets *shet* of it the better. That was my argyment onst when I was driving the wagon with dad. He was pretty sleepy, and I driv mighty fast over a mighty fine piece of road—'So, ho!' says he—'what the flinders, Paddy, do you mane? Would you shake me to pieces, and drive the poor bastes to the devil, and with such a load on their haunches.' Says I—'It's a mighty good road, dad, and we ought to make the most of it.' 'Right, for you, Paddy,' says he, 'and there's raison in the argyment.' But soon we come to a mighty bad piece of corderroy, rough with the old poles, and with great roots and rutty holes, hopping o' both sides, in the way of every wheel in the vahicle! And here and there was a nice little bog to give the wheel a saft resting place after its throuble! And thar, in that very place, I whipt up the mules, and driv faster than ever. Then, when dad felt the jolting enough to shake the very liver out of his meat-house, he rose up, and cried out—'Soh! soh! Paddy, how's that? You driv *fast* in the *good* road to make the *most* of it, and thar's raison in *that*; but what the devil sort of raison kin you show for hard driving over the devil's own causeway?' 'The best in the worrold, dad,' says I, 'as you'll say yourself after you hears me.' 'Well,' says he, 'I'm a listening with all my ears.' 'It needs only one of them,' says I. 'Well?' says he. Says I, 'we drives fast in a good road to make the *most of it;* and we drives faster in a bad road—to git out of it as soon as we kin!' 'And thayre's raison in that, too, Paddy, my son,' says he, 'and you have the good argyment upon me. But I'd jist like you now to take the jidgment of them two poor

brute bastes of mules upon the question.' 'Well,' says I, 'they've
hearn my argyment, and they say nothing; and to say nothing's a
sort of silence, I'm thinking; and silence, as I've hearn a thousand
times, dad, from your own self, is only another word for consenting;
and consenting's agreement; and when all party's agreed, why, *drive's*
the word!' The old man said no more, but slipt back quiet into the
fodder heap, and fixed himself as aisy as he could for the jolting;
for the road, for a mile more, was a sort of devil's turnpike, more
holy than righteous! After a little while I heard him say, with a
mighty grunt: 'Ef I had only the money to idicate Pat for a lawyer!
He was born to be a lawyer! He's got all the natheral argyment and
only wants the ideation. He's powerful quick at a raison; and tho'
I knows all the time he's wrong, yet where to find the hole in his
argyment is the puzzle! He so beflusters me with the cunning of
the argyment, that I can niver git at the sinse of it.' "

Paddy was tickling his trout—playing off his lawyer dexterity
upon *us*. Wharncliffe knew his man, and gave me the wink. I rose,
and in a few seconds had refilled the tumblers with the smoking
beverage—taking special care to make that of Paddy more than
usually potent. At a signal from the host, I proposed a bumper, and
Wharncliffe a toast.

"Gentlemen," said he, "I give you our guest, Mr. Patrick
McGarvin, whose tongue, I'm sorry to find, is still under a spell!
May this bright beverage unloose it."

"That's to say, Colonel, I've been talking all the time!"

"Exactly; and not to the purpose, Paddy! And now, as it seems
that you are still bashful about your story, I propose that Mr. Stylus
should set you the example. He has a drinking song which he wrote
only the other night, and which will give you time to prepare your
ideas, and get your memory in order. Mr. Stylus, let me tell you,
writes poetry like an angel and sings like a nightingale in bad
weather. He has a bad cold usually which affects his ear, and being
hard of hearing, it affects his speech. But he is as bold to sing as to
write, and is not too bashful, Paddy, to make his friends happy."

"The top of the morning to his voice, Wharncliffe, and the sunny
side of the shadow to his poethry. I shall be happy myself to hear
Mr. Stylus sing—more in particular as you tells me that he made the

poethry himself. I shakes his hand with gratitude and consideration, since I looks upon a poet as, properly spaking, the man after my own heart."

"Bravo, Paddy, and many thanks. You shall have the song."

"And Jamison will find you the accompaniment on his flute."

I did not imitate the scruples of Paddy, but, in hopes that my example would cure his bashfulness, sang the following rough and terrible dithyrambic, for which the General promised an impromptu accompaniment. I took care to impart an Irish twang to as many words as possible, which seemed to me eminently proper in a song which set out to show the "Raisons in Law and Liquor."

"There needs should be reason for thinking,
To the eyes that are evermore winking,
  But, when eyes gleam with fire,
  What fool would require
A rhyme or a reason for drinking?

Leave books to the sages that make 'em,
And laws for the scoundrels that break 'em,
  But in wine we have saws
  That are better than laws,
And we're infidels if we forsake 'em.

These teach us that thinking's a trouble,
That your glory is only a bubble,
  And that study and care
  Do but end in a snare,
Making innocent students see double.

We have doctrines more genial and better,
Writ in crimson, and not in black letter;
  Madeira for ink
  Gives us freedom, I think,
While your thought only forges a fetter.

The devil take Blackstone and Vattel;
Here's the wisdom that's born of the bottle,
  And the student who drains
  The last drop, for his pains,
Shall never have pains in his throttle."

The readiness with which I had responded to the call made upon me at once silenced all the scruples of our raftsman. Besides, the punch was beginning to do its work.—Paddy was no longer bashful, if that had been his infirmity before; and, making no more feints, he now proceeded to deliver the required narrative. But we noticed that his familiarity had sensibly increased—that, dropping all respectful prefixes to our names, he soon dropped the Christian name also; and now, instead of General, Colonel, Doctor and Mister, as applied severally to the party, it was briefly "Jamison," and "Wharncliffe," and "Carroll," and "Stylus;" and, at the outset, clapping me on the shoulder, he cried out—

"Stylus, ould fellow, that poethry was capital—like the punch! Och, when such punch and poethry goes together, who's afeard? Ah! blessed St. Pathrick, it's like a drop of salvation on a burning tongue."

"Which, Paddy, the poetry or the punch?"

"Both, Wharncliffe, both! It is the *mixture* I spake of! I took them both in at the same sense; and the punch strengthens me, and the poethry inspires me, and if it's my adventures you are axing and waiting for, I'm your obadient servant to command!"

We all expressed our anxiety to hear; and, disposing ourselves in attitudes, he to speak and we to listen, he began. I shall re-produce his story in his own language as nearly as I can, omitting as much of his Irish and backwoods brogue as it is possible to do without impairing the individuality of the narrator.

CHAPTER V.

Her.—Come, sir, now, I am for you again: Pray you sit by us, and tell's
a tale.
Mam.—Merry or sad shall't be?
Her.—As merry as you will.
Mam.—A sad tale's best for winter: I have one of sprites and goblins.
THE WINTER'S TALE.

———

"And now, gentlemen," said Paddy, bracing himself up for the
occasion, "sence nothing better will sarve you but a poor raftsman's
story, I'm not the man to baulk you in what you wish, though I gits
no credit in the telling of it. And I'm the man for a quick beginning,
ef so be the devil will let me. A short horse is soon curried. It's aisy
to take the measure of a terrapin's toes! Well, it's no great shakes of a
story that I've got to tell; but Wharncliffe, who is a devil for
mischief, in an aisy way of his own, has put you up to hearing it,
and the poethry and punch together hev' put me up to telling it.
And now, before I fairly begin, I must give you a warning that you
must keep in ricollection as I travel. I know that Wharncliffe don't
altogether belave in my story——"

"Stop, stop, Paddy! I never said so. I believe, and have reported
you to be a man of veracity——"

"Och, to be sure you hev', and all that, and the rest of it! To be
sure you do, and if I thought you didn't, would I be afther saying
a word to the purpose, or dhrinking a drop in yer house, though the
blessed St. Patrick stood by with a full bottle of the an'intment ready
for his eyes and my own? I know, Wharncliffe, that it is not the
thruthfulness of Paddy McGann that you suspicion, but his sense
and judgment in the matter. You say that I dhrame—that it's my
imagination that makes it all—that I hev' what you call 'hollowcina-

tions'—which is as much as to say that I dhrame with my eyes wide
open! You rather think—for you hev' tould me as much—that when
I have heard and seen the adventures and things that throubled me,
I have always had a dhrap or two too much of the beautiful poteen
in my swallow. It's the misfortin of a man, when people know that
he loves the crather, to charge upon that everything that happens
to him, whether he be drunk or sober. Now, gintlemen, it may be
all true enough that I may have had some liquor aboard of me
when these things happened. Hardly a day has passed for a matter
of twenty years when I did not have some liquor aboard; and I
rayther reckon that a man must have something in him that makes
it aisier for the devil to take hold of him. It may be sin and a bad
conscience, or it may be the whiskey, which some people seem to
think is as bad as both of them. The Good Book tells us, and so
does the parsons, that, when a man has sin in him, then he is more
at the mercy of the devil than at any other time. Then is he nearer
to the devil and further from God. Now it may be that 'tis all
owing to my own sinful nather and avil dispositions that I have been
put at the marcy of the etarnal inimy!—That's raisonable enough.
All I am sartin sure of is that he *has* been at me, and putting it to
me with tooth and horns and tocnail; and it may be that the whiskey
has given him a better gripe of me then ef I had been quite sober,
and free from a sinful conscience! But whiskey or no whiskey, I
have all my feelings and senses, and can see and hear! Another
thing I beg leave to say before I begin, sence Wharncliffe says it's
my imagination, and that is that, drunk or sober, from the time
when I was knee-high to a turkey gobbler to the time when I stood
six foot in my stockings, I did not belave in the devil at all, at all!
I had no notion of the devil—no opinion of him——"

"What! no opinion of the devil, Paddy?" asked Wharncliffe
gravely. "Was not that being very disrespectful?"

"May be so, Colonel. I kaint help it! I was brought up so. It's
true, my good old mother used to tell me often enough, when I was
growing up, and mighty mischavius, that I was going to the devil
fast; but dad would tip me a wink, and whisper, 'all in my eye and
Betty Martin, Paddy! The devil's an ass—a scarecrow!' But, without
this encouragement of my father, I had no opinion of the devil,

anyhow, and you couldn't scare me with him the darkest of nights! I've slept in a churchyard under the ould trees, and between the graves, and niver had a bad dhrame as much; and I've been where the ghosts were said to haunt, at midnight, thick as hops, and niver seed the first shadow of one, or smelt sulphur anyway, ontil I was a'most middle age. So, you see, my imagination, if it's that, didn't begin to work in that way for a mighty long saison."

"But the whiskey *then*, Paddy?"

"Ah! Wharncliffe, you haint got me ther, neither; for I can't remember the time when I didn't love the blessed wather. I was nursed on whiskey, weaned on whiskey, and vaccinated with whiskey; and could take as big a drink of the crather at eighteen as I ever took at thirty-five."

"But not so often, Paddy, nor so strong?"

"Just as often and strong, Wharncliffe! But I'm not denying that the whiskey, and the fire together, put me at the marcy of the inimy, and made it aisier for him to get the gripe of me. I reckon a man grows on till he dies—grows into some new knowledge or ixpariance every day, that makes him wiser or weaker, and makes it aisier to hurt or to help him! Some men never grow wise enough to let you help them; others again ax only a little help, and then do wonderful things for themselves. Ef my blood's bad, then a cut of the finger makes an ugly sore; when the blood's pure, it heals amazing fast. So, as we grow, we get stronger against the things that would hurt us, or weaker and more liable to their power; and I rayther think that it's so with the heart and the soul, as with the body. What the Good Book calls the 'Powers of the air,' are powerful over us just as we are weak and wicked. I've been weak and wicked enough, the Lord knows, to be at the marcy of them powers of the air time and again; though I must say, gentlemen, that I'm not belaving that I was more wicked, or drank more whiskey at the time the Devil took hold of me, than I had always been and done before. For this matter, ef I was put on my Bible oath, I do think I could swear, with a good conscience, that I was rayther better, and bettering ever day, seeing that I was getting older, and I hope wiser"——

"And writing 'Bucket Letters,' Paddy, to prove it."

"Ach! Colonel, you will be emptying your bucket on a rheumatic shoulder. But that puts a body out, and spiles a story."

"Well, I wont spoil yours. I am only dealing with your argument. Go on. We fully comprehend your *caveats*."

"Caveats! What's them? Argyments, I reckon! Well, I'll go on; but, gentlemen, ain't you a *leetle* thirsty, after so much talking?"

The hint was duly taken; and, wiping his mouth, through the long beard of which the steam of the punch rose into a little cloud, Paddy began again. He was great at beginnings.

"Well, gentlemen, I 'spose you know my ockypation in life?"

"Which of them, Paddy?" asked Wharncliffe.

"Faix, Colonel, you may well be axing! The truth is, gentlemen, I'm a sort of 'Jack-of-all-trades,' and perhaps good at none; though I won't confess to that. I'm something of a farmer, and have a bit of a farm, as you, Colonel, and the General, both know, a few miles across the river; but I'm precious seldom there now, for though homely enough, 'taint much of a home to me. There's a Mrs. Patrick McGarvin in the case. Well, I'm something of a carpenter, too, and can frame a 16x18 house as well as any country carpenter I ever seed handle a hammer. Then I'm something of a hunter, and can strike a buck with my rifle at a hundred yards; and I'm good at the *bob*, and have taken as much as 60 pounds of trout in this beautiful Edisto of ours in one day, in mid-winter—though 'twas a mild season. But my chief ockypation is rafting, and I knows the river like a book. Well, what with farming, and carpentering, fishing, hunting and rafting, I lived a blessed aisy life. I lived in all my limbs, and in all my veins; in my heart, in my head; and was, I may say, as happy as a lord; though why a lord should be more happy than other people, the Lord only knows! I was never sick; I was at all the frolics; loved a dance, a camp-hunt, a horse-race—any fun that was a going; worked cheerfully; never felt lonesome on the river, or a fishing, but was always a doing; so that I had sound sleeps by night, and woke at day peep to walk out and hold my head up to the rising sun! I owed nobody money; I cheated nobody; had no schemes; was not a shop-keeper; and didn't so much as dhrame of getting to the Legislature; thinking that, considering the sort of animals we sometimes send there, it couldn't be altogether a dacent place for a full-blooded white man; and so, as I tell you, owing no man, and fearing no man, I was as happy as a man could be. I was a *free* man, had enough and to spare, and lived on the water, and lived on the land, in the best consate of myself, and without trying to take down any man a peg in the good opinion of his neighbors. My ould mother lived on my farm over the river, and sometimes I stayed there, and farmed it; at other times I slept, and stayed on this side of the river, in a sort of log house that Wharncliffe let me have, as a sort of Hunter's Lodge, as he called it. He built it just for that purpose himself.

"Well, just at that very time, when I was in my best feather, and in beautiful consate of myself, comes the Devil, or some of his angels, to take the consate out of me. All on a suddent, a change comes over my experience, beginning, now, some six years ago. I begun to have strange and oneasy feelings as I boated on the river, or hunted in the woods. I first felt as if somebody, not natheral to me or to the airth, was walking close beside me. After a while I could hear the footsteps behind me, as if some one was tracking me like an inimy."

"Had you no enemies, Paddy?" asked Jamison.

"None that I knowed on. I had no quarrel with any man."

"But might not such sounds be occasioned by dogs, or hogs, or deer?" was *my* question.

"Ach, Mr. Stylus, you're no hunter, or you wouldn't ax that question of an old woodman like me. Every sound and sight that's natheral to the woods, is natheral to me. No, sir—gentlemen—'twas a beginning that was to work on till it left me under no danger of making any mistake. Soon, I heard the sounds clearer than iver—close behind me—and soon I heard strange laughings, and whisperings, on the river and in the thicket. 'Twan't long after this when I heard v'ices calling me by name, and there'd be a laugh, as if the varmint, whoever 'twas, know'd he was making me oncomfortable enough,— and the laughing would be a sort of Ingin yell—a Ho! Ho!—like an owl's whoop, close to my shoulder."

"Why not an owl?" asked Carroll.

" 'Twan't any owl. I knows every sort of owl in the woods, and can make a whoop and halloo like his own. No, sirs, 'twas no natheral owl that was at my shoulder! Well, I used all my ears, and all my eyes; but looking and listening did no good—never brought the strange thing under my hand or gun; though I was ready enough to strike or shoot. I'd look about me, and hunt about like a keen fox-hound, who knows how to double on the tracks of the most cunning old fox that was ever started. But nothing could I see then, nor for a long time after. And so I went on for weeks and months, feeling all the throuble of a hunted baste myself! And day by day, the thing grow'd worse and worse, till I never set out of a morning without the full ixpectation of hearing them cursed steps behind me, —heavy and slow—or that whispering, talking, whooping, and calling of my name: 'Och, Paddy McGann! Och, Paddy McGann!' —and I would turn about, quick as a shot, with gun ready cocked, and knife aisy in the belt, and sing out, 'Who in blazes are you that make so free as to call Paddy McGann? Show yourself upright before me, dod dern you!' And then there'd be a great horse chuckle, as if the dern'd thing was going to split his very sides—'Ho! Ho! Paddy McGann! Ho! Ho! Paddy McGann!'—but nothing more. Now, gentlemen, you see when these things come to you, day by day, and last for months, it's not hard, and it's not aisy, to tell what a man's feelings may be! After awhile I could think of nothing else, and it troubled my sperrits mightily, I tell you."

"And then you troubled the spirits, Paddy," said Wharncliffe.

"Ef it's the whiskey you mane, Wharncliffe, you're right! I did take big drinks when the trouble was so constant upon me; but ef you mane that I got drunk upon it, you're onrasonable. I don't think liquor could ha' made me drunk. I was more like going mad. To be hunted down, day and night, by an unseen hunter, in them same woods where I had been always the crack hunter before, was a letting down of my consate that was cruel hard upon me. I lost flesh; I felt jubous of my footsteps; I was looking like a wolf out of my eyes, and feeling like a devil at my heart.

"But worse was yet to come!

"After awhile I began to find that something was wrong about my gun! I didn't get any game!"

"Wasn't that owing to your health and spirits, Paddy? You did not hunt, perhaps, with your wonted skill," said Jamison.

"Not so, Gineral. I did hunt, and as well as ever I did in all my life. Ef anything, I brushed up more game. But I didn't *kill* any more. The first time I got to feel this was when down in your own swamp, I made two clean misses, one afther the other, at a big buck, at not more than forty yards one shot, and fifty the other;

and this with my good old double barrel. And so, day by day, I went on missing, till at last I got so that I couldn't hit a squirrel on a water oak or fence. The same way with the partridges. I was no longer able to pick up a bird. By this time I got scared. Here was my favorite ockypation, where I thought myself most of a man, gone out from me! I trimbled when I thought of it. It was as ef old age, and palsy, had come upon me, in a single night. Oh! sirs— gentlemen—'twas a most terrible thing to have this feeling.

"Well, I examined my old gun to see if anything was wrong with *her*. I claned her out, and brushed her up, bright as a new pin, and sighted, and lined her, and laid her in a groove, and the poor old crather was as straight as an arrow to the sight and line. The sights was parfect. I tried it on a tree, and at eighty yards planted every pelter in a round of nine inches. Well that put me in heart again! But, Lord love you, the moment I began to hunt, the missing was as bad as iver!

"Well, my good friends and masters, I couldn't keep my secret any longer. 'Twas too great a load for one man to carry. So I went off to my old friend, Sam Hartley, and told him all about my throubles. I borrowed his gun, and for a week didn't miss a shot with that. But at the eend of that week I did no better with Sam's gun than my own. Then I cleaned up again, and got some fresh powder from town; but 'twas no use; and Sam Hartley said 'twas the gun that was bewitched. Well, I didn't belave in witchcraft, and I laughed at the idea; for I had no more opinion of a witch than I had of the devil, and up to that time of my throubles had no serious idea of any thing much—none to scare. But Sam shook his head. Says he: 'There's more things in this world than man has ever seed or ever will see; and there's powers that can work upon him through the air by night, and through the moon, and through the stars. We l'arn about them all in Scripter. And one man can work upon another from a distance, and put a bad mouth on him, and on his cattle, his horse, his dog and his gun; and thar's women that have not only the bad mouth, but the evil eye'—

" 'And that's true,' says I, 'Sam; I belave; but it's a natheral power.'

" 'Natheral or not natheral,' says he, 'it's beyond human onder-standing; and all we know is, that things happen without any cause that we kin fix upon. It's onaccountable.'

"I felt queerish in my own belief by this time, but I wouldn't let on to Sam that I did so, so I said 'well you may think as you plaise, but I snap my fingers at the devil and all his witches.' He looked dark at me, and says, 'Mind how you talk. You don't know who's listening.'

" 'Who?' says I. 'Why, the ould devil himself.' Then, says he,

" 'Do you belave in the Scripters, Paddy!'

" 'In course I does—ef it's the Holy Bible you mean.'

"And so, convarsing, we sat up the better part of the night in his cabin, talking over the whole thing; and he got down the Bible, and he showed me from the Scripters more than a hundred places, where there was wizards and witches in old times, and he said 'I belave there's witches now; and as for the devils, look sharp about you, Paddy, for instead of one devil, there's a thousand, and I kin prove it all from the Scripters. And some of these devils, I belave, live in the woods, and some in the waters and rivers, and some in the air, and some, as I'm a sober, christian man, I belave, lives in the very fire itself! and they're so made that, jest as they live, according to the place, or element, so they have a perticklar nather, for that same place or element. They breathes it, and it's nathcral to them as the air we breathe is natheral to us.'

"Then he went on to say that what was common in old times was jest as common now—that what had been, would be always to the very eend of time—for that men were jest the same now-a-days as in the Bible times, desperately wicked; rogues and liars; thieves, and murderers, and adulterers; extortioners, and cheaters, and swindlers, and sarcumventors; and that ef a Devil, and a thousand devils, was necessary among the Jews, even when the Lord himself was a-governing them, how raisonable to belave that they are jest as necessary now among the Christians, who are even more consaited than the Jews, and in their consate was for governing their own selves and also every body besides.

"And that seemed to be very raisonable of Sam Hartley. And so he argyfied the matter, as I thought, quite sensible from Scripter, and Sam knows the blessed volume a-most by heart, and could always find the text he wanted.

"Well, my good friends and masters, tho' you laugh, I will tell you. The upshot of the business was, that he over-persuaded me to carry my guns to a witch doctor, one Abe Miller,* who lived in Orangeburg District, and he give me a letter to him, and to another man, who was a witch doctor too, one W. P. Mills,* who lives near upon the skairts of Lexington. Well, I took the letters, and went to Abe Miller only, thinking that one doctor is, perhaps, more safe than two. Well, Miller spit down the muzzles of my guns, smoked 'em out with yairbs and tobacco, rubbed 'em with soot and ashes, run 'em up the chimney, and made a good many motions over 'em, and mumbled a sort of prayer; then told me all would be right, and I must take 'em and hide them away, the barrels, in a clear stream of running water, for jest seven days and seven nights. I paid him three dollars; he wanted to charge me five, but I was not willing to pay so much for an ixperiment I was so jubous about; and so he let me off with three. But I might as well have saved my money. The witch doctor did no good. They shot as bad as ever; and when I met Dr. Miller, some time after, he told me 'twas bekaise I beat him down in his price. I wasn't such a believer as to give him the balance. And now, Mr. Stylus, if you think the singing of that kettle means any thing, we'll try another little mouthful of that blessed biverage. We must all be a little tharsty after sich a long conversation. Here's your immortal health, gentlemen, and the devil take the witches!"

"And who shall take the Devil, Paddy?"

"Ach, ef St. Patrick could come back again, and play 'em the purty trick he put upon the sarpents, I'd refar you to him! Ach, ef he should but try this liquor, he'd not lave the counthry in a hurry."

* Both of these persons carried on the business of the wizard in the sections indicated, until within a few years. They were poor creatures, living in ignorance and extreme poverty —for the Devil seems to keep his agents usually on short commons—and both operated, I believe, by herbs and harmless potions. Witch doctors, by the way, and witches, are antagonist professors, and must not be confounded. I find that witchcraft, according to the common notion, is mostly confined to women, and these are generally remarkable for their age, ugliness and bad temper. The witchcraft practiced by the young and comely, though perhaps not more innocuous, is yet held to be more pleasant, and is not a penal offence.

CHAPTER VI.

"This isle is full of noises."
THE TEMPEST.

———

Paddy resumed his narrative.

"I said, my good friends and masters, that things were as bad with me as ever. They were worse. I not only couldn't shoot, but I couldn't fish. I could catch no fish. I had jest the same luck in fishing as in hunting. Either the fish wouldn't bite, or I caught nothing but pollywogs. Then my lines were constantly getting tangled and broken among logs, and brushes, and fallen trees that had never been seen in deep water before. It was every minute a break of hook or line. Never was such a losing business; and when I thought of what I had been and done, and of the nothing I had come to, I felt jest like throwing myself down upon the flat airth and tearing all the hair out of my head. From the fishing I went back to the hunting. But 'twant no better. Sometimes I would knock over a squirrel or a partridge, and I'd tickle myself that all was coming right with me again; but, Lord love you, the moment I got a chaince at bigger game it was all Dicky with me as before. The gun would go off, it is true; but so too would the deer or turkey; and shot and powder went for nothing. And now, gentlemen, if you will consider what it is for a man suddenly to find himself good for jest nothing, at them very things which used to make him so proud before, you will come to a right understanding of the misery of my life, and my constant thinking and feeling, night and day. I had to hang my head in shame. I couldn't sleep for the thinking, and couldn't eat for the misery, and what, with night-waking, and trouble-thinking, and loss of appetite for my food, I got to be thin of body and weak of spirits, and down-hearted in all my sowl. I had spent my money and my time for nothing, and I had to live and to support my poor ould mother. It's true, we had something to go upon. She was in the dry, with a good roof over her head, and we had a small stock of brood-sows and pigs; and the ould woman raised a little poulthry, and I had worked a small crop and made enough corn and potatoes to do her and me for the year, and feed our negro, one mule, a couple of cows, and my own good horse, Black Sam. And the old woman did some knitting, and weaving, and spinning, keeping us in clothes and from wear and tear; but we had no money, and she must have her coffee— breakfast, dinner and supper; and she must have sugar. And she had so loved to eat wheat flour, that she was never satisfied onless she had a good barrel in the house. And all them things I had to think of, and a good many more. But where to git the money, since my right hand had lost its cunning, and my eye had lost the seeing, and my poor sowl had lost all the luck. I had a good many customers, like Wharncliffe, here, who had only to look at my fish and birds, or venison or turkey, to hand me out the cash. But now, I could no more bring supplies to my owld customers. No more hard money for an aisie day's work. It was the hard work now, and the money harder to come at. Well, I had sometimes to borrow, and the more's my shame to say it. I was in such throuble and sorrow, that the money I borrowed was pretty much spent in whiskey and tobacco! Wharncliffe, here, has sometimes helped me out, and if the truth was known, though he wont allow it, I am something considerable owen to him now."

"Not a dollar, Paddy."

"Well, you says it, Wharncliffe, but I think it's all your benevolence and good failing, and ginerosity that makes the friendly spache in a poor man's hearing."

"And out of it too, Paddy, and at all times. You have long since paid me, in fish, and flesh, and fowl, for all the money you've ever got from me."

"I am not the less owen to you, Wharncliffe, in sperrits and affection. Yes, gentlemen, my good friends and masters, he and other kind persons let me have the money when I ax'd for it; and too much of it went for whiskey and tobacco.

"Och, the curses and the blessings—the whiskey and tobacco. The curses, because they wrap up a man's conscience with his brains,

and put them to slape so soundly, that he doesn't dhrame of the
devil at his elbow; and Och! the blessing, sence thcy brings him slape
and forgetfulness, though his only bed may be in an old sow's wallow.

"Yes, my friends, whiskey and tobacco may be curse enough, but
them's pretty much a poor man's only consolation in his time of
throublc—considering how the world goes—how people happen to
fale, and think, and suffer, and want to fly from faling and thinking
and suffering! You who have fine parlours, and fine society, big
collections of books which you know how to read and onderstand—
and some of you to write—who have da'ters who can play for you
on the piana, and who kin intertain your friends in a hundred ways,
to say nothing of a plenty to ate and drink—you kain't exactly
onderstand the difficulties of a poor man in his hour of trouble—you
kain't *begin* to onderstand 'em. He has no fine house to go to when
the night sets in, may be with storm; and no fine family and friends;
no books, no music; no closet and cellar stuffed with meats and drink;
no nothing; but cold and lonesomencss, and desolation, and the dying
out of all hope in his heart. And when he kain't slape for the dreadful
thinking, Och! sorra my sowl, it's like as ef he was in a dunjon,
dape down in the airth, the walls growing in upon him, and the kay
lost, and niver a window to entrate him to break his bones or his
neck by a jump, rather than suffer from the suffication that's sure to
come. He jest feels as ef God had given him up altogether, and tould
the ould Devil to take his will of him, jest like another Job! And jest
so, night a'ter night, did I feel, setting by my lonesome fireplace,
here in the swamp, for I stayed here a'most constantly, faling
ashamed to go home to the ould mother, having nothing good to
carry her. There did I set, not caring to ate, having nothing much to
eat but hominy and pertatoes; no meat, no fish; and with no money
to buy, only enough to git the jug filled as fast 'twas empty; and
nothing to be done a'ter, 'cept to cram the tobacco into the pipe and
smoke on, 'till the tharstiniss came to call out for another and
another dram. In course, I knows all that you may say about the
sinfulness and the foolishness of looking to sich supplies for the
consolation and the strength. But there's a time when a man gits
beyond the rasoning, and let no man spake of the want of wisdom in
another, ontil he has passed over the sunny country of hope and
comfort, and sees nothing before him but the great black bog and

swamp of disolation and distress, with no end to the marsh, and no way to get round, and nothing to do but to plunge in and go for'ard, though he goes as deep as for'ard, at every step.

"Yes, there did I sit, smoking and drinking—drinking and smoking —the more's the pity!—Och! wirra sthru! Och! wirra sthru!— looking at the poor old gun and the rifle, now of no count in my hands—the things that used to be my pride and my glory and salvation; and in the black sorrow and green bitter in my soul, I cried out to the poor spacheless, unmaning innocents, 'How kin you desart me a'ter sarving me so long!' And there was hooks and lines, that used to bring out the biggest trout and pairch in the Edisto, now all broken and tangled at my feet; and when I would begin to mend 'em, and work awhile at 'em, I'd throw 'em down with a dreadful sort of heart sickness, and cry aloud, 'What's the use!' And there I let 'em lay—nothing but break and tangle. I couldn't find the heart to mend 'em!

"And so things went on day by day, and niver got no better! But I didn't give up, though I drank the more whiskey—spending three times as much for the potheen as I did for the pertatoes. I had some stores put away for the ould woman, as I reckon I told you; and some to sell—about sixty bushels of corn, as many of pertatoes, and some twenty bushels of pindars. And bushel after bushel went for a little meat, a little coffee and sugar, and a good deal of whiskey! I wasn't in debt yet, that was one comfort; but I saw plain enough that the day was a-coming when I'd have to borrow or stale. And so thinking and feeling, I'd keep in my cabin for a week at a stretch, niver once wanting to go out! For I said—

" 'What's the use? I can neither shoot like an honest man, or fish like a happy one!' And then, them whisperings and talkings and walkings just behind and about me, whenever I went into the woods, they worried me to pieces! But as I tell'd ye, I wouldn't give up! The feeling of shame and cowardice would go off. I would look at the old gun agin, and the old dog, and I'd say, 'Can Bark and Bite be all wrong in sight and scent?' And the gun would look all the same to my eyes, as straight as an arrow—for all the world as it looked when I used to plump the bull's eye, off-hand, at every shot! And the poor old dog would look up at me with his sorrowful grey eyes, as ef he know'd my sufferings, and wanted to help me

all he could. And when I thought this, I said to myself, 'My friends
ain't all gone. Luck's all—let's try again, good dog!—let's try
again, old rifle!' So I'd pick up the old gun, whistle the dogs, and
put out for the swamp thickets. The beast was true, and he'd start; and
the deer would come to me—always a fine buck, with good head of
horns—but I might as well have swallowed the bullet as sent it
after him. And I'd get home after night, only to sit down by the
fire, and ax myself if 'twas worth while to live in sich a fashion, all
the keenness gone out of my eye, and all the sleight out of my hands!
And then I ax'd myself ef the gun would miss ef I was to pull trigger
with the muzzle at my own head!

"Oh! my masters, gentlemen—I tell you—that ugly thought
came mighty often into my head in them days of my tribulation;
and one night, in pertick'lar, after I had missed the prettiest chance
in the world—an old buck not forty yards off, coming on me quartering; and when I dash'd down the gun upon the ground, and a'most
tore the hair out of my head, then to hear the most infarnal spell
of laughter, jest at my elbow; and to catch my knife out of the
belt, and turn round ready to kill, and—nobody thar, but my own
self! I was mighty nigh, that minute, to driving the we'pon down
into my own throat. But the devil had'nt got a full gripe o' me yit,
and I took up the gun, though I thought 'twould never be of any
use in my hands agin, and calling in the dog with my horn, I put
out for home! But sich a home!"

"Stop one moment, Paddy," said I. "Pray tell us one thing. When
you heard those noises, the chucklings, whisperings, yells of laughter,
how did your dog behave? Did he appear as if he heard them also?"

"That he did! He looked jest as wild, sometimes, as I felt. He'd put
out and get on the *slot*, and he'd hunt, and his cry would be good;
but oftentimes he'd run back to me, in the middle of the hunt, and
lie down, and whine as if he'd seen a snake! I wonder I did'nt tell
you of that afore: for the strangeness of the dog made me feel the
worse, and feel sure that there was something in the wind jest as
hurtful to his sense as to my own. But he's first-rate blood, and even
in his scare, it took only a few words from me to encourage him;
but when he got a scare of this sort, he did'nt run with his old
sperit. Dog and gun both failed me, and fishing tackle, too. Why,
sirs, on the river, I've seen the trout a-pushing my bob about as ef

'twas only a play-thing for their noses; and never a one could I take in all that time of my tribulation! Yet, with a bait hook there was no eend to the *polly-wogs* that I drawed out of the water, only to fling 'em back again with a curse. Nothing better could I take for wakes and wakes at a time.

"Well, as I was telling you, I went home a great deal more in the humor to go dead at once, than to scuffle on with the life any more —sich a life! and I flung the gun down in the corner; and threw the lightwood on the fire; and got out the whiskey,—and that 'minds me, Wharncliffe, that convarsing together as we've been doing, makes the throat dry and tharsty—"

[Paddy always assumed that we had been doing our full share of the talk. It was one of his idiosyncrasies.]

"Yes, Stylus,—by the way," said Wharncliffe,—"we have been letting the glasses stand—

'So let the cannikin clink.'

Am I right, or is not rather—
'So let the can *again* clink?'

"Besides cannikin means *little* can, and we must do nothing to-night on the small figure. Does your water boil?"

"It knows when it's wanted."

Paddy waited patiently. The glasses were soon refilled,—and he grappled his with the air of one about to do a magnanimous action—

"To the ever blessed memory of the Holy St. Patrick. May his riverence never be wanting for a drop of sich eye-wather."

"Would you have him with a drop in his eye, Paddy?"

"Ach, if he had the same taste for it, as his poor airthly namesake, it would'nt be a drop but a dakanther. It's a most beautiful invention, this same whiskey punch, and does credit to the janious of ould Ireland! Wharncliffe, I drinks to your better health and sperrits, and better onderstanding of the world of sperrits! Amen! General, to you sir; and may the public kettle always afford you enough to fill your own! Stylus, my boy, you desarve a blessing, and a golden wish:—May you always have the right sperrit to put into your books; and may your books always kape you in sperrits, for yourself and your friends! Ach! Wharncliffe, this is no common whiskey! You're the clever chap that has a nose for the genowyne, anyhow, whether in man, or beast, or bottle! May the good sperrits befriend you always, and forever more. Amen!"

"And now to our conversation, gentlemen," said Jamison.

"I think I had the word, Wharncliffe?"

"The floor, Paddy."

"Ah! when I takes to the floor, there will be an eend of the argyment, General; but as I aint ready for the floor jest ylt, and don't expect to be this blessed night, even at the short hours of the morning, I'll go on with my raisoning."

"While we prepare ourselves to answer it, Paddy."

"Answer it! It's not in you to do it, Wharncliffe, sence the thruth is solid like a mountain, and high as the blessed sun in the heavens, when it's doing its very best to shine for the benefit of the poor people of the airth. You may answer with a mighty pretty argyment in your metaphysics, but where it takes a mighty long argyment to choke off a strong witness, the case is as good as lost before it gits to the jury. I've known a lop-sided Judge's charge to hang fire, when he tried to shet up the muzzle of a straight up and down witness."

CHAPTER VII.

"Look you, I will go pray."
HAMLET.

———

Some further chat succeeded, however, before Paddy resumed his argument. Wharncliffe and Jamison, who were both sceptical, had a good many questions to ask, and subjected the narrator to rather a searching examination. Carroll had some questions, also; but it seemed he was more curious about the sorts of timber in the swamp— questions that may have had their source in the fact that he owned a saw mill at Janina, and was a contractor to supply government with lumber for gun-carriages and gun-boats, and so forth. I, too, had some questions; but was far from sceptical, my organ of the marvellous being large, according to Spurzheim, who once examined my head. At length Paddy resumed as follows:

"Where was I? Ach! it was after the hunt by the 'Willow Slue,' where I missed the old buck at forty steps, and had the Devil at my elbow laughing at my tribulation! Well, you see, yer honours, I went home to the lodge, and threw down the poor old gun, and made up the fire, and got out the little jemmyjohn—a single gallon —and didn't wait for the warming of the water, but filled the pewter mug a'most half full, and swallowed it naked, without so much as winking; then set down and looked at one place in the fire, till I seed in it all the houses and churches of Charleston city in a blaze! And then I seed no fire, and only a great red eye staring at me out of the back of the chimbley; and I shivered all over, as I looked, and, with the cowld, I got up and threw on some more lightwood; and then I swallowed another cup of the raw liquor! Jest then, Bark and Bite give tongue, and ran to the door; and the next minute I heard a knocking; and says I to myself, 'Who kin this be? but Paddy

McGann is so miserable a man, that he's afeard of nothing, though it be the very black Devil himself that's a knocking to come in!'

"So I went to the door, and unbolted and threw it wide open, and stood in the opening and looked out with all my eyes. But there was no body to see or hear. And I banged the door to and bolted it, and took a third drink, and sat down by the fire, and the dog crawled to my feet and whined most pitiful, as if he knowed all of my throubles and tribulation. But I looked into the fire and said nothing; but through the blaze I could see into the black darkness of the swamp thicket, and I could hear, out of all the terrible silence of the woods, a long yell of laughter that seemed to put out the fire at onst.

"But I threw in another chunk of lightwood, and I took up my gun and laid it across my lap, and looking at it, yer honours, I fairly cried like a baby to think that, after serving me so well, so long a time, it should turn out to be good for nothing in the eend! And I was jest for flinging it into the fire, as if it was only a pine knot, when the same knocking rattled the door again, as if 'twas going to shake it down; and this time my flesh was creeping, and my hair standing up from the roots as stiff as young corn growing in a clay field, and by that I know'd that it was only another trick of the Devil at the door! I felt sartain he was there; and tho' I didn't care a button if he come in or not—I was so far gone in misery—yet I wouldn't rise from my seat to let him in, but jest threw another lightwood knot on the fire. But he didn't rattle again, jest then; and I reckon it was a full quarter of an hour before I heard another knocking at the door. Still I wouldn't git up, but kept looking straight into the fire; and the knocking went on, and then I heard a voice, and, listening, I made it out to be the voice of Sam Hartley. So I opened and let him in.

"He had come to see me and spend the night; and I was glad of it; for, though I wan't afeard to be alone, I felt the lonesome bad enough. We took a drink together, and he ax'd me how things was going on with me; and I told him all.

" 'Well,' says he, 'it's curious enough, Paddy, and mighty bad; for, you see, next Saturday old Stephen Potter is to put up a mighty fine steer to be shot for. The beast is as fat as he can go, and must weigh a good 500 weight on his legs, and I want you to win it. I'm nothing of a shot myself, and you air, or waur onst.'

"I jest groaned and pointed to the gun!

" 'I kin do nothing now,' says I. 'I kaint depend upon gun, or sight, or aim, or dog! They all fails me now!'

" 'The thing is on you yet?' says he.

" 'Bad as ever,' said I; and I up and told him all the doings of the week, or, rather, the *not* doings; for I hadn't bagged even a bird or fish, and was jest eating up my corn and bacon without gain or profit.

" 'Well,' says he, ' 'tis mighty strange, and there's no telling what's to be done for you, Paddy. It's either you, or it's the gun, that's cl'ar. Now which? You've tried Abe Miller for the gun, and you say he haint helped you.'

" 'Not a bit.'

" 'Then I reckon it must be in *you*. Do you find any thing the matter with your eyesight?'

" 'I sees you as straight before me as a p'int-blank. I sees your eyes, nose, mouth, and the wart on your chin jest as plain and cl'ar—bating the bad fire light—as I ever seed 'em in all my life. I sees dog, and deer, and turkey, when I'm about to shoot, jest as free and full of size as I ever seed 'em; and I ranges the gun, from bush to sight, as smooth and even as the time when I was always sure of my shot. But I haint got the assurance now. For that matter, I'm only sure now-a-days that I must miss.'

" 'It's mighty queer! I tell you what, Paddy, it's what the Doctor calls your "narves." It's something the matter with your narves.'

" 'Narves,' said I, 'Sam! Narves! Why, man, my narves is like an iron vice. Kin you feel *that?*'

"And I gin him but a single gripe about his wrist, and it made him squeal again.

" 'Stand up,' says I, 'and jest try one hug.'

" 'No,' says he—'thank ye, no.'

" 'Oh!' says I, 'I shan't hurt you. I jest wants to let you see and feel that it's not the narves, or the strength, and I don't b'lieve it's the sight, that's the cause of my trouble.'

"And he stood up, and though he was a big man like myself, I doubled him up, like a side of leather, and laid him upon the bed, and without a strain of back or arm, or body.

" 'It's cl'ar,' said he, 'you're strong as ever. Well, if 'taint the sight, or the strength, or the narves, then it must be the devil.'

"And jest as he said that, the door got a mighty rattle from the outside.

" 'Jesus!' he cried, 'What's that?'

"And I laughed out, almost like a devil myself.

" 'Go and see, Sam,' said I.

" 'Go yourself,' said he. So I went to the door, threw it wide open, and steped out. There was nobody to be seen. I called him, and we both looked together, all round the house. Then I called out the dog, and set him on, but after giving tongue, once or twice, he came back with a pitiful whine, and sneaked back into the house.

" 'What could it be?' said Sam, as we once more seated ourselves aside the fire.

" 'The devil,' says I. 'It's no human, be sartin. Come, Sam, take a drink.' He didn't wait for the second axing.

"Well, gentlemen, we two sat up till pretty late talking over my affairs. Sam tried his best to put courage into me, and try the gun again, and try for the beef the coming Saturday, and I agreed. I was to use his gun, or he was to try and borrow a famous gun from somebody in Orangeburg that had one. But I was jubous. My heart was weak, if not my body; but I promised him to do my best and to defy the devil and all his works. But, Lord love ye, my masters, and very good friends, it was a pitiful, a most comickle sight, to see us two full-grown, middle aged men, sitting over that lightwood fire, drinking whiskey, argyfying how to sarcumvent the devil! We talked over the powder and shot, and the strength and the sight, and the narves and every thing; and we examined the gun and the rifle, and we could see nothing to blame in anything, so we agreed the devil was to blame. And then we took another drink, threw some lightwood on the fire and went to bed. But I couldn't sleep a wink till near upon daylight, and we both lay abed 'till the sun was two hours high.

"We then put out together; he went home, but I went to Midway, to Carson & Whetstone, to see if they had any first-rate powder.

Captain Whetstone was a good hunter himself and a good shot. I know'd *that;* but I didn't tell him my particular troubles, only that I had been mighty onlucky in my hunting lately, and I put it on the powder. So he show'd me some Kentucky Rifle Powder, three F. F. F., and said he could warrant that. I took a canister of that, and told him if there was any vartue in the F. F. F., I should prefer to have some of six F. But he said that was the best, so I went off, trying to think that after all it might be the powder.

"Well, with my gun and dog, I went up to see my old mother, who was on a month's visit to my cousin Betsy Sykes. She said I was looking worse for wear, and told me, as she had told me a hundred times before, that I ought to git married, and she mentioned a dozen young women that she thought would be glad to have me if I'd say the word. But I was thinking more of the beef to shoot for, than of any woman; and of the rifle and shot gun; for if they failed me any longer, of what use was any woman to me, and how should I be feeding her? In good times, when I had the skill in my right hand and my eye, I could always provide. But now, I found it no easy matter to find even my old mother in provisions. She was a good old mother to me, and took it mightily to heart when anything was the matter with me; and she said she seed for some time past that something was the matter. But, of course, I never tell'd her a syllable about the particular raison of my trouble, and what I was feeling daily, and what I was fearing nightly, and what kept the sleep from my eyes, and shut out all the peace and sweet consolations from my heart.

"Well, I staid with her and Cousin Betsy Sykes till the app'inted Saturday, and jest kept hanging about the house like a lazy hound, lying about, and trying to sleep and to forgit. When Saturday came, I put out without a word; took Sam Hartley in my way, and found him ready and waiting for me.

" 'And now,' says he, 'Paddy, how are you off in wind, and limb, and eye-sight? How's your narves? Let me have the feel of you.'

"And he jest examined me all over, as ef I had been a broken-winded plough-horse.

" 'All's right,' said he. 'You look and feel steady enough. Hold out your rifle at arm's length.'

"I did so, and held it steady as a rock.

" 'Now,' said he, 'take a shot at that *blaze* on yonder pine. Thar's a black spot, jest in the middle, to my eyes, and I reckon it's about eighty yards.'

" 'It's all that,' said I, 'and ten more to the back of it.'

"But I up rifle and took aim, and without being long about it, I cracked away. We stept off the distance. It was ninety-three yards exactly. And there, plump in the black spot—in the very centre of the blaze—there was my bullet! Lord! how Sam capered and danced.

" 'You'l do!' says he. 'All's right agin, Paddy! The charm's gone off somehow. You'll take that steer, I'm sartin.'

"This put me in heart and hope. I felt like a new man. I wiped out the rifle carefully, and measured my charge closely for the hundred yards, and put on a fresh, bright, thick London cap, of the best quality, and off we started for Stephen Potter's, where we was to shoot for the beef.

"There was a big gathering of people, and more than fifty of the boys put in as candidates for the beef. We paid up our dollars, and had all our names counted off and set down, to shoot in the order of our payments. They all know'd that I was a good shot of old, but somehow it had got about that my gun was bewitched; that I could do nothing; and they came about me, several of 'em, and begun to ax questions, and to worry me. When Sam Hartley seed that, he took me off to the edge of the woods, and says he—

" 'Now, you keep here, till your name's called. They'll only worry you, and be ixciting your narves, so as to make you onsteady. It's the narves, I reckon, a'ter all, as the Doctors say. I'll jine the crowd, and answer questions in my way, and keep 'em off from you.'

"So he went off and left me by myself; and I went a leetle ways into the woods, out of sight but not out of hearing, and it suddenly come to me to pray to God to help me out in the shooting. We prays to God before meat, that it may do us good, and why not pray for help when we are about to do any thing that aint positively wicked? I hopes, gentlemen, my good friends and masters, you don't see any meanness or cowardice in a man's praying for help at a time of great weakness and oneasiness, though he does pray with the hopes of gitting something by it."

He had our approving assurances and proceeded:

"Well, as I was on my knees, and in the middle of my prayer, I heard, on a suddent, a great yelling and laughing jest behind me; and then a voice that I know'd to be that of Isaac Clymes, a great bullying and fighting fellow. He had no love for me, nor I for him, though we never had much to do with each other at any time. Now, it seems that he had hearn that I had been up to the witch doctor, to take the charm off my gun and rifle, and jest came at that time to worry me about it; and he said the very thing that he thought would worry me most.

"'Oh! ho! on your knees, a praying. You first try the witch doctor and then you try God. Well, for a man of your girth and strength,—a man that's so proud and boastful, I should never have ixpected to see you so much scared and down upon your marrow-bones, Paddy McGarvin.'

"I heard every syllable; but, though I felt the hot blood rush up to my face and head, I was in the middle of my prayer, and I wouldn't let any thing break me off, so I went on till I finished my prayer, and he went on talking, all in the same fashion, and very provoking, I can tell you, to a man of my temper. But I said to myself, before I got up:

"'I'll keep down the temper. I'll stand a good deal. I'll try, for the sake of peace, and my own comfort, and I'll show Sam Hartley that my narves aint to blame. I must git the beef of it if I kin, since my own hope, and my heart, and all that's dear to me seems to depend upon that one shot.'

"So, when I got to my feet, and I was rather slow about it,—a'purpose—I jest said to him; 'Good morning, Isaac Clymes, I hope you're well,' and he answers blunt enough—

"'Well, that's queer speaking for what I've been saying to *you!* I'm pretty sure, Patrick McGarvin, that's not what you would *like* to say!'

"'Why, what should I like to say, except to wish a man good morning, when I meets him?'

"'But you've heard what I've been saying to *you*, I reckon. Hev' you had convarsion, that nothing but praying will do you, even when you come on a shooting match? or do you calkilate that praying will take the witch pison off your rifle?'

" 'I'm praying, Isaac Clymes, bekaise I feels the want of it, jest as I'd take a drink of water when I felt tharsty—'

" 'Or whiskey?' said he.

" 'Yes, or whiskey,' said I. 'If it suits you to laugh at a shooting match, it suits me better, perhaps, to pray. It's a blessed thing that we live in a country where a person kin suit himself so aisily, without treading on his neighbor's toes.'

"I was keeping in, gentlemen, I tell you, mighty hard, for the man was quite impudent, and wanted to be so; and more than once, I felt the devil gitting up a breeze in my blood, till I was forgitting the very prayers I had jest been making. But I answered him peacefully, and moved off towards the gathering, where the shooting was now begun. But he came along close beside me, and kept on talking.

" 'Well,' said he, 'I reckon there's to be no eend to the wonders! I do think the man's got religion.'

"I made no answer to that.

" 'I wonder if in getting religion, he's left off whiskey!'

"Still I said nothing, but went for'ard. I could see that he had been drinking pretty freely himself; and I could onderstand that nothing but that would have given him the impudence to come and talk to me so sassy; a thing that he had never dared to do before, bully as he was! This aisiness of mine rather encouraged him, and he went on more boldly than ever. Still I kept down the devil, though he turned and twisted in me like a sarpent with a bruised tail. At length he said:

" 'Well, I never could have believed, unless I seed it myself, that a big fellow like you, and one who used to be counted upon in a free fight, could lose all his sperit by a scare! And who, but a person wanting a man's heart, could be made to belave that his gun was under an old woman's bad-mouth. To think that such things should frighten a stout fellow into religion! And ef 'tis religion you had got, I don't see why that should take away a man's sperit. If you goes on so, why every body will be after kicking you as you walks the high-road.'

"To all this I only made answer—'No they won't. Only let 'em try it! But, Issac Clymes, you had better be walking your way, and I'll walk mine. Whether it's religion I've got, or what, is no man's business but my own. I'm not for quarreling or fighting to-day, and I'm not fond of it at any time, but I've got enough of the devil in me to show my teeth, if a hard file is set against 'em; and I kaint stand too much pushing agin the wall, from any man.'

" 'Ah! now you talks a *leetle* like a man; but 'taint talking only that's to get a man credit for having a big heart for his friend or inimy; and if he gits to saying his prayers, only bekaise he's going to shoot for a steer, then I wonder what sort of a d——d long prayer he'd be making before he gits into a raal fight!'

"I stop'd short, and jest measured the fellow with my eye; and I dropt the butt of my rifle on the ground, and set my teeth hard, and was jest about to say something—what it was I kaint say now, but it was something to bring on a fight, when Sam Hartley came up, and, knowing Clymes well, draw'd him off, telling me, at the same time, that they were gitting pretty close upon my name, and that I must be ready. So I jest sauntered back to the woods, and tried to git my mind aisy, and my blood a little cooler. After a little while Sam came back to me, and looked at me quite curious, and said 'that drunken fellow's been *riling* you. Don't mind him, but git yourself right. How's your narves?'

"Well, he felt my arms, and found them firm; and he looked at the cap of my rifle, and said:

" 'All's right; and now come up to the scratch like a man, and shake a bold fist at the Devil and all his works!'

"I went up to the target, which was a broad blaze on a big pine, and the ace of hearts—a card—nailed on the blaze. There were some eighteen shots in the blaze, and not one had cut the paper yet. I saw there was no harm done, and that ef I shot as well as I had done, coming on with Sam, I was pretty certain of the steer. So, when they called my name, I stood out and took my place, and Sam come and stood beside me; and I felt just as firm and strong as ever in my life. I felt as cool and saw as straight, and when I sighted the rifle and pulled the trigger, I would have bet my head against a pumpkin that I should plant my bullet in the very ace-spot on the card. But what do you think? I missed the tree altogether, jest as if there had been no bullet in the gun!"

CHAPTER VIII.

Charles.—Come, where is this young gallant that is so desirous to lie with his mother earth?

Orlando.—Ready, sir; but his will hath in it a more modest working.

Duke.—You shall try but one fall.

SHAKSPEARE.

———

"And now, gentlemen, if you're all consenting, and Mr. Stylus kin say that his kettle sings to a good old tune, I'm for trying another kiss from the mouth of that beautiful sperit that looks so smiling on the table. Ah! Lord! when I thinks and talks over that shooting match, and the disapp'intment for me and poor Sam Hartley at that time, I feels that I needs every drop of consolation I kin git."

We felt for Paddy, and imbibed our consolations also from the same fountain he so much eulogized.

The bowl having passed round, some little conversation ensued, in which Paddy was asked to explain certain passages in his narrative; and this done, he was allowed to resume it:

"Well, gentlemen," says he, "before I know'd that I had altogether missed the mark—for I could hardly belave it when they tell'd me I had missed—there was a most infarnal yelling, and whooping, and shouting, and hallobalooing, from all the fellows that run up to look for the shot. I couldn't make it out; but it was a gineral rejoicing; for you see, from what they all know'd of my shooting in past times, they waur all afeard of me. Well, that shouting didn't help my temper a bit,—preticular after I know'd of the miss—and when they come up, a dozen of 'em, rolling, and capering, and yelling, who so happy—I felt like pitching into the crowd, and driving my mutton wedges right and left. But poor Sam Hartley, he come up and drew me off. He was mightily cut down, poor fellow!—more so

277

than I waur meself, and didn't know what to say to please me or
satisfy himself. As for me, I said nothing. But I felt jest as ef I had
a thunderstorm inside of me, ready to burst out at any moment! As
I walked off with him, I suddenly took my rifle and dashed it agin
a tree—my poor old rifle! I broke the stock off at a blow! Just then,
who should come up to us but Isaac Clymes, agin, and more in liquor
than ever, and says he:

" 'That was a fool's doings, Paddy McGann! as if the rifle was
to blame.'

" 'That's true enough,' said I, 'though a beast said it.'

" 'Do you call me a beast,' said he, breezing up to me, bold and
blustering enough.

" 'No quarreling—no fighting, boys,' says Sam—'it's all nonsense.'

" 'Let him say,' then, says Clymes, 'ef he means to call me a beast.'

" 'Don't mind him, Paddy,' says Sam—'the boys have been putting
him up to a fight, and provoking him. They tell'd him that he's
afeard of you.'

" 'Let him not cross my path,' says I, pushing Sam aside and standing up, with my eyes looking as straight as an arrow into the eyes of
Clymes. By this time the whole crowd had got around us, some pulling and talking to him and some to me, and all saying them very
things that they know'd would provocate us both. I could see they
wanted to see us hitch, and I reckon'd they had some bet upon it.
But, tho' I looked steady enough at Clymes, and show'd him, from
my looks, that it wouldn't take much to make me pitch into him
with a short hammer and a heavy drive, yet, as I'm a living sinner,
gentlemen, I didn't want to fight. I rather felt as ef I could go into
the thicket and cry like a baby. So, I didn't say a word, but kept
steady; and he was, I reckon, encouraged by my look, for he
grow'd bolder and bolder, and pushing through his party, he at
once put himself right before me, and squared off, with his fists
doubled.

" 'I ax you,' says he, 'Paddy McGarvin, does you mean to call me
a beast?'

" 'Stand out of the way, Isaac Clymes, I don't want to hurt you.'

" 'Hurt be d——d!' cried he. 'I ax you again, and if you're an
honest man, you'll give me an honest answer—does you mean to
call me a beast?'

" 'I *think* you one!' said I, 'since you will have it; and a d——d dirty beast too—something of a cross between a polecat and a skunk!'

"With that he let drive at me, with all his strength and fury; but I had my eyes close set on his'n, and was ready for him. I parried his blow—closed in with him, and gave him one fling,—but one—and down he went; and thar' he lay—couldn't get up to the scratch—his thigh bone was broken! I had pitched him down over an ugly stump, that neither of us had seen, that lay close beside us, and, whether his leg had got twisted or not I don't know. I sartinly didn't mean to brake a limb for him, tho' I wouldn't have cared much, at that time, ef it had been his neck! my blood was b'iling over; and I then turned to the rest of the crowd that had been belling him on, and I said:

" 'Now, come on, d——n you, any two of you, and let me see ef I kaint break some scoundrel's neck, to-day. As I'm in for it, I may as well go through the whole kit and b'iling of ye!'

"But none of 'em were so drunk or so foolish as to tempt the devil in me. They could all see that he was powerful strong, and hearing Clymes a-groaning upon the ground, they had no more curiosity to see if I could fling another into the same heap.

" 'Stand aside,' said I, as I pushed through 'em—'and ef you're onsatisfied, any of ye, say the word, now, or forever a'ter hold yer peace.'

"And they did stand aside. But ef I had not a-had so many strong fellows, who were friendly to me, on the ground, they might have tried to git me down, with a rush all together, but for every fellow among Clymes' party, there was a stout chap in my own. None of 'em offered to stop me, but began to bissy themselves making a sort of cradle to carry Clymes off, and Sam Hartley and myself went our way without any farther obstruction. He picked up my poor old broken rifle. I sent it down to Wappoldt, in Charleston, afterwards, and got a new stock for it; and now it's as good as ever, as you may see. It a'most broke my heart when I seed what I had done to it in my passion. But it was all the Devil's doings, gentlemen; he caused me to miss the tree; he put the ugly stump in the way that broke Clymes' thigh bone, and 'twas him that worked me up to smash the poor we'pon that had sarved me, like a most faithful sarvant, now going on twenty years. It was the Devil that had the strong gripe of me through all that season!

"Well, it was a most doleful walk, that of Sam Hartley and myself, on our way home. He went home with me, and I was glad of it, for, Lord love you, there was my poor old mother, she had got home before me, and was all eagerness, waiting for the beef! You ought to have seen her poor old withered up face when Sam told her that one of the Zeiglars had won it!

" 'How could Paddy miss?' she said, wondering; and so she went on wondering for more than a week a'terwards, putting me into a fever every time she talked. She had been so sure of me and my gun, that she had come home to make preparation for curing the meat; and she had the barrel ready, and the salt, and the trays all cleaned, and the chopping-block, and the big pine table, and we were to kill the steer that day, and, the Lord knows, what a fine supper she had laid out to sarve up, to me and my company. 'And how could Paddy miss?' was every now and then the word. At last, she said:

" 'Paddy, my son, aint something the matter with your gun? I've noticed now you havn't brought home deer and turkey, or even birds, for some long time past.'

" 'Powder's bad, I reckon,' says Sam Hartley. *I* could say nothing; but jest snatched up my hat and pushed out into the woods; and when I was gone, the ould woman up and told Sam that something *was* the matter with me—that I looked as ef I had some secret throuble; and she went on to say that she wouldn't leave the house again, for I must be lonesome. Then she told Sam that she was thinking of a wife for me. Only think—a wife for a man that couldn't airn his own meat—that had lost the sight of his rifle—that could catch no fish! And how was I to live? Our poor farm would never do it for three, hardly for more than one, now; for the poor ould woman was too weakly to do any thing about a farm, except raise her few ducks and chickens! Oh! 'twas a most miserable, redickilous idee!

"That night Sam slept with me; but we did not get to bed till the small hours. We sate up over the Bible; he looking out all the parts that told of witchcraft and the Devil, and how he tempted men, and worried them, and possessed them, and blinded them all for his own purposes. And Sam and me together read through the whole book of Job; but not that night. He came again and again, and was very friendly, and whenever he came we made a night of it. We read the Bible and drank a good deal of whiskey; and whenever Sam was in liquor, instead of fighting and quarrelling, he was for preaching and praying. He was a main good fellow, Sam, and stuck to me in all my troubles.

"But he couldn't be with me always; and when he was off, and I was alone, with my poor ould mother, her tongue, talking all the time with a good feeling for her son, kept me always in a sort of fever. 'What's the matter with you, Paddy?' she'd say. 'You never bring home any meat now, any fish, or birds. What *air* you doing with yourself?'

"Then I'd seize my shot-gun, whistle the dog, and put out for the woods; or, if the day was warm, I'd try the fish; and at night, when the season favored, I'd go a trouting; but gun and line and bob waur of no use in my hands. And ef 'twas a misery to hunt and fish to no eend, it was doubling the misery to go home, and hear the ould mother's wonderings, and see the bacon going fast, and the corn, and the peas, and the potatoes, and nothing in the world coming in! I was gitting more and more desperate every day, and drinking more and more whiskey—and that, too, seemed to have no more effect on me than so much water!

"And all the time of my hunting or fishing, the throuble at my ears and elbows was going on. Why, gentlemen, I'd sometimes hear a boring like an augur at a tree jest at my very ears; then a sawing, like the sawing of blocks; then a splitting, for all the world jest like the wedge driven into the block for rails or clap-boards; and this in the deep woods, miles away from any plantation and workmen; and the sounds coming up under my very nose! At other times, I'd hear heavy footsteps behind me; and sometimes I'd feel my arm or shoulder brushed, as ef somebody was passing by in a hurry.— Then there was a confused talking jest at my very ears; and every now and then, a shout or yell, not thirty yards off, and nobody thar! Every day these throubles got worse and worse, 'tell I was half the time in a trimble and a rage! I got so used to it, at last, that I got desperate sassy, and would cry aloud, 'Ef you're the devil, whoever you *air*, stand out and let me look at you.' Then I'd hear a chuckle, a sort of dry, husky laugh, at my very elbow. Wheeling about, quick as a shot, I'd see nothing! And so it went on for weeks longer, ontill I fairly prayed on my bended knees, that ef it waur the Devil sent for my tormenting, he should come out boldly and look me in the face! I was desperate enough now to face any devil, no matter what the length of his horns, or the blackness of his face.

"But the answer I got to the prayer was nothing but a horse laugh; so sassy, so provocating, that I fairly danced agin with the rage, that I could see nothing! It wasn't time to show himself yit. I reckon he had his own reason for keeping off a leettle longer!"

CHAPTER IX.

"Take any shape but that!"
MACBETH.

————

"That night I went to my lodge in the swamp, and thar I staid three days, day and night, hardly ever laving the house, and seeing nobody. I hadn't the sperrit for any thing; and I confess to you, my good friends, that I did nothing but drink whiskey and look at the fire. I hardly cared to eat. Thar lay the gun, and thar the lines and hooks, but I niver touched 'em onst; and it made my very soul sick within me, whenever I looked on 'em. The fourth day Sam Hartley came to see me, and brought with him a gun that he had borrowed from one of the Felders, of Orangeburg.

" 'Now,' says he, 'let's put out, and try for partridges. Thar's a plenty on 'em in and about the swamp fields.'

" 'What's the use to try?' says I.

" 'What's the use to be a man?' says he. 'A man's got to try, and try on, and try agin, spite of all disapp'intments, till he gets through the swamp. You're in a swamp now; the timbers thick, the briars sharp, the water high, and the mud and clay like so much pitch. I put it at the worst,' says he, 'not to flatter you. It's a hard row, and maybe a long one; but you've got to work through it, and you will work through it, Paddy, if so be you're a man! Here, I've brought you a gun I borrowed for you. You shall take that—it's a mighty fine gun—and I'll try yourn; and we'll see where the mischief lies.'

"Well, he talked so that he worked me up, and off we went, I taking Felder's gun, and he mine. Now, Sam was nothing of a shot, and he know'd it; but luck's all, and Sam got all the luck. He didn't hit every time he shot, for he niver yit had done so; but he bagged a dozen partridges, more or less, a pair of woodcocks, one rabbit, and some six or seven doves. And this was all done with my gun! While, with Felder's famous piece, all I made out to do was to kill a couple of fox squirrels, and tear the fur out of a rabbit. I missed every shot at a partridge.

"We got home at night, and then he began discoursing about what had happened; and he says solemnly—

" 'Paddy, it's *you*, not the gun.'

" 'I knows it,' said I.

" 'It's you that's bewitched, ef anybody, or anything.'

" 'I knows it.'

" 'Well, thar's a raison,' says he, 'for everything. How came you to be bewitched? You've laid yourself open to the devil in some way.'

" 'I knows it,' says I.

" 'And now, the question is, who has bewitched you? Hev you had any quarrel with——'

"And he went on to mention two or three old women that he had suspicion of.

" 'No,' says I.

" 'Hes the ould woman, your mother, had any quarrel with any of them?'

" 'Not that I knows on.'

" 'We must find out, ef we kin,' says he. 'I'll see the ould lady to-morrow, and ax her myself.'

" 'Then,' says I, 'ef I'm bewitched, it's the ould Devil himself; and if thar's any ould woman in the business, she's only a sort of ripresentative of the devil.'

" 'That's true enough,' said he; 'and the best way, perhaps, for you to get *shet* of the ould varmint and the ripresentative, is jest to git religion.'

" 'Git religion,' says I. 'But how am I to do that! Ef it won't come to me, I dont see how I'm to git it.'

" '*You must go to it!* You must read your Bible, say prayers regilar, night and morning, and go to Church whenever thar's preaching. Let us pray now, Paddy.'

"So he down'd on his knees, and I did the same; and Sam prayed a mighty good, strong prayer—for Sam was strong in Scripter reading and talking, and I only wondered he had niver once thought to take to preaching regilar. But he only now and then exhorted,

when there waur a few neighbors gathered together. After praying
—and he wrestled with the inimy for a good hour, tell my knees
ached agin—we got up and tuk a drink, and then he set down to
reading the Bible, all pretty much out of them parts that talked
about witches, ould Beelzebub, and the other devils. In the middle
of his reading, quite loud, for Sam liked to hear his own v'ice, and
thought a good deal of his reading, we heard the door give a
thundering rattle. I set quiet.

"'Somebody's at the door,' says Sam.

"'It's the ould Devil himself,' says I, 'come to hear you preaching.'

"'Don't talk in that way, Paddy,' says he. 'It's not right. But I
reckon it's some human body come to see you.'

"'Only him,' says I, quite coolly, 'ef it's any body.' Then the door
rattled agin.

"'Go and see,' says he.

"'Go yourself,' says I. 'I *know* it's him.'

"Then Sammy squatted down upon his knees, agin, all in a
shiver, and he begun to pray at the top of his v'ice; but, by this time,
he was so frightened that his ideas all run together in a heap, and
you couldn't make out what he prayed agin, or what he axed for!
I niver moved, but sat down in the chair looking at the fire; and
the door rattled agin; and that stopt Sam's praying in the middle!
He got up and come close to me, holding up the big Bible jest as if
it was a cover against a bullet.

"'Paddy,' says he, 'this is dreadful!'

"'Take a drink,' says I.

"'Oh! don't speak of it,' says he; but he swallowed the drink,
and a pretty big one, too.

"'Who kin it be,' says he, 'this time o' night.'

"'I tell you,' says I, 'it's that same raging lion you've been reading
and praying about, seeking what he kin devour! Ef I thought he'd
stop to let me take a look at him, I'd open and see.'

"And with that I ris up, and was going to the door.

"'Oh! don't, for your life, Paddy,' says Sam.

"'Yes,' says I—'now that my blood's up, Sam, I'll open to him
though he comes in the very shape of the great Dragon himself.'

"And as I went for'ard to the door, Sam backed to the further eend of the room, squatted down upon his knees, behind a chair, and jest held up the open Bible in front of his face as a sort of defence.

"Jest as before, there was no body; and as I shet the door agin, seeing how skeered he was, I said, 'I reckon, Sammy, 'twas nothing but the wind.' As I said it, we could hear a 'hoo! hoo! hoo!' right over the chimney; and Sam dropt the Bible, and cried out, 'the Lord presarve us!'

"Says I, 'Sam, it's nothing but an owl.'

" 'It's the Devil's own v'ice,' says he.

" 'Do you think so?' says I—'Then I'll give it back to him!' and I gave a screech, and a yell, and a 'hoo! hoo! hoo!' jest as loud as the Devil's own;—'till Sam seized me by the arm, his eyes ready to pop out of his head, and begged me, for the Lord's sake, to stop and not provocate the beast! Och! how I laughed—but it warn't a laugh of fun, my masters, but the laugh of a man grown desperate to fight agin any odds, of any beast that ever rampaged in the woods!

"We heard nothing more that night, but it was a long time before I could git Sam out of his staggers; and only after several good drinks of whiskey."

"Which gave him another sort of staggers," said Jamison.

"No, Sir-ee, not a bit of it. Sam was stronger in his head than in his heart, and could carry, without spilling, as much liquor *in* his head, as you could carry water on the top of your'n."

"But the cause of his scare, Paddy? Of course, it *was* the wind rattling the door, and it *was* the whoop of an owl you heard."

"No, S-i-r-r! 'Twas what I said first according to the best of my knowledge and belafe! 'Twas the Devil, and not any wind, onless from the breath of his infarnal mouth; for the night was jest as calm as a baby sleeping; and as for the whoop, it was beyont the throat of any scrache-owl in our swamps to give out such a dern'd sharp, thick, monstratious halloobaloo! 'Twas the Ould Beelzebub, that was jest laughing to hear us two poor backwoods blockheads trying to sarcumvent him with Bible reading and praying!

" 'Twan't aisie for Sam to sleep that night, and he waked me more than onst before morning, as the skear came back to him. We finished the jimmyjohn that night!

"Next morning, he was more bold and sassy. As he seed the sun shine in at the windows, he begun to talk big, and say—

" 'To think, Paddy, that we should let ourselves be skeard by an owl!'

" 'An owl!' says I. 'Ach, Sam, ef that owl iver gits the picking of your feathers—and he may do it yit, spite of all your praying—he'll give you sich a dressing of brimstone, as will cure you of all skin diseases for ever a'ter! He'll so purify your blood with sulphur as to make you sweet enough for his own table.'

" 'How kin you talk so—it's onrespectful and ondecent! But I'm not to be skear'd; and now, let's put out for a deer hunt. Hev you niver a drink left in that jimmyjohn?'

" 'We'll squaze it for your sake; but I'm jubous there's not enough to clear the eyesight of a sand-fly.' But I made out to git him a wineglass, and then he began to sing, by which I know'd he warn't altogether cured of his last night's skear.

" 'It's no use, Sam, for me to go hunting,' says I.

" 'Yes,' says he, 'you must! Never say die! Don't give up! I tell you, you've got to work through the row—through the swamp— that's the long and short of it; so be showing yourself a man. The harder you work the sooner you come to the eend of it.'

" 'And what's the eend?' says I.

" 'You might as well ax me what's the eend of any man's life! Who knows but the Lord God of the univarsal world! But this, I think, I kin say: ef you work through, like an honest man, with a brave good heart, feeling your troubles like a man, but standing up to 'em with determination and pluck, then the eending will be good. You'll work through it, I tell you, and though I'm not much of a man myself, and not a strong one, nor an over brave one, yet I'll stick to you, though all desarts you, an' I'll see you through, and pray for you, and ixhort you, and try to do my best to make *you* do *your* best, and help keep your courage up.'

"I catched his hand in mine, and gin it a squeeze; and says I— 'Sam, you *are* a good fellow, and what's more, you're a good friend and a good man, and a braver man than you think for! Any man that sticks to his friend, thro' thick and thin, and does his best to help him out of the wallow, when all the rest of the world desarts him, is a brave man as well as a good one.' "

"But," said Wharncliffe, somewhat reproachfully, "you were not in that condition, Paddy. You were not deserted."

"No, Wharncliffe, I warn't—the Lord be thanked for that marcy. I had many friends, and you one of the best among 'em; but Sam didn't know *that*; and I hadn't then let on to you, or to any other friend, but Sam, the preticklar throuble that had me yoked in the mill of tribulation!

"Well, Sam, coaxed and argyfied me into the deer hunt. He had brought two dogs, and I had two, so we could make a pretty merry cry. I loaded my double-barrel double careful, and we set out o' horseback. You know my Black Sam, Wharncliffe, and know that he's as fleet as the wind, and with bottom enough for any thing, from a month's hard journey down to a three mile heat. As we rode, I got in better sperrits. I thought of what Sam said, which was sensible, and I had my own thoughts too. I said to myself, 'this thing kaint last forever. It came on me suddently and will go off suddent, and as I don't know when it *will* go off, I must jest hunt on, ontell it does! In the meantime, the worst of it is only a little starvation— eating dry—giving up whiskey and tobacco, and feeling mean when I used to feel so proud! When I've lost the meat, and the pride, and the vanity, the whiskey and tobacco, it's hard to see what the Devil kin strip me of next! It'll be a small business for sich as he, when he's onst taken off a fellow's clothes, to be taking off his skin besides.'

"Well, we put in at Hop's thick, and had a *drive* thar. I *drove*, and Sam took a *stand* at the old First Crossing, at the Big Lake, on the 'Woodlands' plantation. 'Twant long before the dogs got on trail; and in about an hour they started. I soon heard Sam's gun, and then his horn; and riding out to him, I found he had dropt a fawn, jest at the crossing. Sam was for pushing down to 'Burwood'—'twas Dewitt's then, long afore Jamison bought the place. But I said to him—'Sam thar's more deer in that *thick* yet.' So we put in agin, after rounding the thick 'till we got upon the uplands. Well, you see, the dogs, jest as I said, started agin, and Sam got another shot below, at a fine doe, but missed her. He got back the dogs, however, when they were straight pushing for the river, and was bringing them up to me while I was pushing through the *thick*. By this time I thought I had cleared it out, and was riding quite easy, looking out for nothing, and jest thinking over my condition, when, all of a suddent, my horse *shied*, jest as if quite frightened. I looked up, and jest before me, not forty steps, was the biggest buck I ever seed in all my life, going at an easy lope. In a minute, I giv him one barrel, and then the other, two plain shots, a-most p'int-blank, both times; but they waur both *blank* shots, I reckon, from what I seed of the behaviour of the buck. He didn't seem to feel or mind any thing, but jest as ef he know'd that I hedn't another barrel, he kept on the same easy lope, and actially turned and doubled upon me, onder my very eye sight, taking the back track for 'Desilla!'"

"*Old* Bucks will do such things," quoth Wharncliffe.

"Nothing strange in that," said Jamison.

"I knows it, Wharncliffe! I knows it, Jamison; thar's nothing strange for an old buck, that's been hunted for three years, to double like a fox, but this one was so dern'd cool and aisie doing it, jest onder my very eye sight, onder the bead of my gun, a'ter two shots had been fired at him, and jest as ef he know'd I hadn't another barrel to give 'em!"

"Well, Paddy, ef you missed him, it was natural enough for him to think there was no need of hurry, especially, as a buck of any experience must know that two barrels are all the best guns carry."

"How should he *think*—how should he know? But it's sartin that he acted as ef he both thought and know'd all about it as well as myself. I watched him for a minute—then jumped down and loaded up both barrels, and double-careful as afore. Meantime I could hear the dogs coming back, jest as ef going over the old trail. He seemed to hear 'em, too, for he was now out of sight. When I last seed him his tail was up, and he was going it, asily enough, for Desilla, and right towards the railroad. Sam came back with the dogs and told me of the doe, and how he had missed her. She was across the river by this time. But I didn't mind her. I told Sam about the big buck, and we made our calculations for him. We made a pretty smart circumbendibus, and pushed for Desilla, meaning to take them woods, and brush through 'em from the railroad culvert, at the 'Woodlands' and 'Desilla' corner, down as far as the hunt would carry us. Something made me mighty eager after that buck. He was so sassy, and took it so cool, I determined to give him a good heating, ef 'twas in the dogs, and horse and gun to do it. I was fairly mad after him, and when Sam proposed that we should take another turn in the woods below, I swore a most tremenduous oath, that I'd hunt nothing but that buck that day! and I didn't.

"And so we pushed on, and put in the dogs close upon the Little Lake, and by the 'Woodlands' and 'Desilla' corner, though there wasn't thick enough thar to keep us long in a straight drive. I put in the dogs, but Sam wouldn't take a stand, but said he'd *drive* with me, and we'd have a better chance at him, four barrels in place of two, ef so be he was still willing to run slow and double upon his tracks. We hadn't been in the *drive* twenty minutes before the dogs were on a hot scent. Soon Sam got a sight of the beast and cracked at him, he says, at not more than forty yards; but he didn't seem to raze a hair of him. He doubled after the shot, and fairly dashed between the dogs, giving old Teazer an ugly wipe of the shoulders, with one of his horns. It was soon my chaince, for he come thundering upon me with a rush. I blazed away, but he went on, but this time with a big bound, that took him clean into the air, going over a harricane track at a jump. I reckon my shot was throw'd away, the same as Sam's. Well, would you belave it, the cussed brute kept a-doubling in this leetle piece of woods—not more than a hundred acres—jest throwing the dogs out, now running to the main road, now back again to the '*thick*,' now into the bay, and now again upon the hill side—going slow when we warn't ready, and fast enough when he giv us a chaince—for a good hour at the least. We got long shots at him, loaded up agin in that time, and went in for killing him; more mad than ever for his hide! Sam was jest as crazy, now, as me, to kill!

" 'Gallop round,' says I to Sam, 'to the *first* crossing of the Little Lake, at 'Woodlands,' and take your stand! you'll git a chaince at him thar.'

"So, Sam went; but he lost his chaince, as you will see, by not minding what I said. He went down to the *second* crossing of the Lake, at the old 'Beckalee Place,' and took his stand thar; for, as he told me a'terwards, he thought the old brute would skairt the Little Lake, and not try to cross where the land was so open.

"Well, he missed it. When we started the beast agin, and we did mighty soon—for that matter, he jest seemed to be throwing himself in our way to laugh at us—what does he do, but, after doubling a leetle, push into the big bay of the Lake, between the railroad and the 'Woodlands Settlement,' close on to the spring, then dash across to the hill where the family burying-ground is; that he skairted along the edge of the hill, close by the old rice field, and dashed down into the road, over the first crossing, with a full head right upon the railroad.

"And I after him at every step! I kept the spur in Black Sam's side till he was red with blood, covered with sweat, and foaming, like a wild beast, at the mouth! One minute the buck was dashing through the water, and the next minute a'ter, Black Sam! I was only waiting to git a clair sight on him, and had both barrels ready cocked. The next minute he was dashing past the brick-kiln, head full on the railroad. I know'd I'd see him then, pretty soon, and I put the spur deeper into the sides of my horse. We waur both, horse and deer, going at full speed. Jest then, when there was no stopping horse, or man, or beast, I heard the steam-whistle blow, and the rolling of the wheels. It was the down train coming up, *lated,* and going as hard as it could drive. I might run into it or not; but I couldn't stop, and wouldn't ef I could! I was mad enough for any thing! On I went, and there, coming up like a harricane, was the *ingine* and a mighty long train of cars; but there was the old buck, too, going at the top of his speed across the railroad track, and never once looking to the right or left. He didn't mind it, and I didn't mind it! I driv in the spurs, and the next minute I was over, too, but with the hot steam of the *ingine* blowing full in my face! The buck went on headlong, and I felt I was losing him. I could hear the whooping from the cars, for every body could see the sight; and och, my masters, it was most infarnal beautiful! But I seed I was losing ground; and, dropping the bridle on Black Sam's neck—he going his best, at a run, but falling off—I took dead aim at the beast, and blazed away, at not more than fifty yards! But, just as I pulled trigger, I could see that the cursed buck had *shied* out of the line of sight about five paces. Then I gin him the other barrel, and as I'm a human sinner, when I pulled trigger agin, the rascally beast had *shied* back again to the first line, and both barrels was throw'd away! And away went the buck, and the dogs limping after him. We were all dead beat—dogs, and horses, and men; and the scoundrel buck, as ef he know'd it all, let us see him for three hundred yards more, going for the big lake woods, at an easy lope for him.

"Now, Wharncliffe, you will remember the time, for that same evening both Sam and myself come to you to git you to jine us with your whole pack in the morning. We staid with you that night, and I told you all about the hunt and the big buck, and how he had sarved us out; and you did jine us the next day, and with all your dogs, the same cunning old buck sarved us all out agin, in the same fashion."

"I remember, Paddy. It was certainly a most extraordinary hunt."

"Warn't it."

"But, Paddy, you will remember I then told you that I saw nothing in it that could be thought unnatural. I think it was then, for the first time, that you told me of your suspicions."

"Edzactly! But you wouldn't belave me then, and you kaint be made to belave me now; but I've got more to tell that I never let on to you, nor to no body else, even to Sam Hartley, though I hev told you both a great many things besides. We had the hunt the next day, and most extrornary it was, as you yourself considers. We had, if you 'members, more than fifteen dogs at his heels—your'n and ours; and they might jest as well been at home in the kennel, for the good they waur in the chase of that devil buck. I went home to my loop, with Sam, in worse heart than ever, though I felt now that I had to work through the swamp jest as Sam said; and I made up my mind to do it, luck or no luck. I kept away from the ould mother, and read the Bible mighty often, considering; and I took the woods every day, sometimes with Sam, but more often by my own self. But the luck warn't with me, tho' I'm thinking the Devil waur, all the time. And for weeks I had no body with me, of human, only that same onseen Devil that was a hunting me to my eternal ruination! Even Sam, I thought, begun to feel shy of keeping company with a man so onfortynit as me, in spite of all he had promised; and I didn't blame him; for who could blame a man who wanted to eat his hominy in peace, without the human sartinty of finding the Devil, all the time, dipping his spoon into the dish! But the more friends kept off, the more I got strong in the determination to stand up to the rack, fodder or no fodder! And the more I felt that the Devil was a watching close beside me, did I git the wilful feeling to let him see that I was a man to defy him to the worst! I seemed to myself to git prouder and prouder every day, to stand up to the fight; and when I was praying to the blessed Lord for help and strength, I felt myself a wishing that the beast would only stand out, and show himself face to face! I was so desperate of heart that I felt sure I could face any Devil, let him be never so black! It's true, I thought I'd already seen him, plain enough, in that same old buck, but I felt agin that that warn't his *natheral* shape, tho' what that was I couldn't think, onless by reading about the ould Dragon in the Bible. Sam sayd the Dragon figger was much like an alligator, or a big sarpent, only that it had great wings, much like a bat's, but as big as a cloud, as they must be to carry such a body. Of course, it was only his Devil way of disguising himself, when he took the innocent figger of the buck."

Here a pause! Paddy looked significantly at the boiling water, and the water comprehended; and the whiskey leaped to its embrace; and the sugar subsided gently in the arms of both; and the whole party imbibed of the compound thereof, in pure sympathy with the wants of Paddy!

CHAPTER X.

"What new Roarer is this."
BEN JONSON.

———

After a pipe and some little conversation, Paddy resumed his narrative in the following fashion:

"Well, my good friends and masters, you've hearn what sort of prayer I made, and you see from that, that ef I was in tribulation, I had lost none of my pride and sperrit. I was strong of heart and proud of stomach, and I reckon it was my pride and sperrit that God was determined to bring down. I prayed and called for my inimy, jest the same as if he was a common man of my own heft and inches —yes, even ef he was a great deal bigger! When I walked the woods, all alone by myself, I would cry out to him to come out and face me. I warn't afeard. I shook my fist as ef 'twere in his very face; and when I'd hear the steps behint me, and the voices in the thick, and the cussed 'hoo! hoo! hoo!' jest in my ears, I'd stop and square myself about, and say—

" 'Oh! dern and blast you for a beast that has a v'ice but no body. Dern you, jest show yourself, full in front, with all your horns, and see ef I don't clinch 'em, without axing any favors!'

"Well, I reckon, my friends, that warn't the right sperrit for a human man, heving to deal with sich an inimy.

"Now, whether it waur that the Devil hearken'd to my prayer and challenge, and wan't onwilling to oblige me, or whether he thought I was now brave enough—seeing I had got more used to him—to stand a closer acquaintance, I kaint say; but he now sartinly did begin to draw nigher. The talking, and the cussed laughing and whooping, got to be worse, and more constant in my ears than ever; and I could see the shadows go in and come out from the woods with a

294

sort of rush, but without any noise—jest a glimpsing by me, as it were,—as ef going with the wind. But there was no wind! Ginerally these things would happen when there was a dead calm—when the woods seemed to be sound asleep—no birds—no singing or chirping —not even a squirrel's bark or jump to be hearn; and when all was so still, that it seemed to you as ef the whole wide airth was at a grand funeral, where nather herself was to be put in the ground! And jest then the skies would seem to be of a thick lead colour, hanging down closer to the tree tops, and making an etarnal vault for the burial! It was ginerally a most awful stillness, and made your heart ready for any expectation.

"Well, it was jest such a day as this, all so still and onnatheral; not cloudy, but lead like and solemn; not a breath in the woods, not a sound. I had my two dogs with me, and my double-barrel, and had put out before day, thinking to do something in the swamp by an airly start. My dogs waur both trained to run slow, and as I couldn't git that big buck out of my head, I kept constantly thinking of what way to sarcumvent him!

"Among the things I had hearn about witches and the Devil, they said you could only hit 'em with a silver bullet. Well, I cut up two whole silver dollars into heavy slugs, and charged both barrels of my gun with them. I was willing to try any thing, and not mind the ixpence, carrying on the war agin sich an enemy!

"But I seed no more of the big buck. I started nothing all the morning, and it was noon afore I give it up. Jest then I found myself pretty nigh the river, and as I always carried my fishing tackle along, I thought I'd try for fish. So throwing off my coat and shoes, I laid 'em down on the bank, and told the dogs to mind 'em. Then I took the dug-out, and pushed up stream, taking my gun along with me, for I didn't know but I might have something to shoot. A gun is always handy to carry, and I always like to have my we'pons ready—gun and knife! I pushed up from Jamison's 'Moonbend,' up by the 'Turtle Cove,' above the 'Woodlands' landing, and shot over to t'other side of the river; paddled up, for a mile, to a piece of the swamp where I know'd I could find plenty of worm-bait; got a gourd full; then put out to the 'Horn Cove,' near 'Desilla' landing, and began to fish.

"Well, my masters, to my great happiness and astonishment, I had fine sport. I caught more than fifteen pairch in an hour; and I began to feel happy as a lord, thinking the charm was gone off, and my good luck come back to me. But, all on a suddent, I heard a great rush in the water jest above, and the leatle waves spread down to where I was, and shook my dug-out, jest as ef 'twas an egg-shell in a b'iling kittle. But I could see nothing—a'ter that I didn't git a bite. I reckon'd 'twas an alligator splurging among the fishes and scattering them off to their hiding places. But I kept hoping on, and thinking, with my line in the water, for, may be, half an hour a'terwards.

"Every thing was most awful still; the skies looked thicker than ever; all the birds that hopped about, when I first paddled up, waur off; and the cypress trees, overhead and around me, looked gray as ghosts in a church-yard. I begun to feel right sorrowful, if not skear'd. The stillness seemed so awful, as if an airthquake was going to happen. So I pulled out my bottle—only a pint flask, and that's a small day's 'lowance to a tharsty man—and took a pull. 'Twas the second I had drunk that day. Jest then, when I had hardly got the flask back into my bosom, the whole woods seemed to be alive with noises; and sich noises,—'twas as if all the frogs, and all the owls, and all the alligators were in full bellow. Then it fell suddenly still, and niver a sound agin along the whole river.

"What was I to make of that? The stillness, on a suddent, was as awful frightful, as was the uproar jest afore it. While I was a thinking, I heard another rush, and something, big as a horse,—dark, and without any figger, that I could make out,—rushed along the very edge of the river,—through the bushes and long grass,—and was gone, out of sight, in a minute!

" 'What in the world,' says I, 'is that? What's gwine to happen now?'

"Hardly had I said the words, when I heard a great bellowing a mile below, jest like an alligator-bull in a passion; then the bellowing grow'd into a roar; and sich a roar: as if the beast was hurt in his tender ribs. I had heard of lion's roarings, but I niver seed or hearn the beast; and Sam Hartley says there are none of 'em in this country; but, from what I'd hearn of the lion and his roaring, I thought it couldn't be anything but him, and that Sam must be mistaken! So I dropt line and tackle into the bottom of the boat, picked up my gun, and got her ready for anything to happen.

"Another grand roar come after this, and then I heard my dogs giving tongue, very sharp and angry; and soon it seemed to me, from the roaring, and the barking, fast and furious, that the poor brutes waur a fighting with some strange beast! So I laid the gun acrost my lap, and paddled down the river, fast as I could, to where I left the dogs to take care of my coat and shoes.

"When I got there, and jumped ashore, my coat was torn to pieces, my shoes scattered fifty yards apart, and the dogs waur gone! I could hear them, in furious cry, a full half mile off, with every now and then a monstrous great roar between. The place where I had left the dogs, the airth was all tore up, as ef a big fight had gone on there; the brush was scattered wide; and it seemed as ef twenty horses had been jumping and trampling all about!

"Yit, though I looked with all my eyes, I could find no track of any sort of beast, but only of the dogs; and they could never have so torn up the ground by themselves.

"All this time, I could hear the noise of fighting in the woods beyont. I pushed for the place, gun in hand, as fast as I could drive. I followed along the big lake. The hallabaloo seemed to come from the swamp thick, close on to the 'Woodlands' 'Sand Field,' nigh by the 'Holly Thick.' And as I went, you could hear the sharp barking and snapping of the dogs; then the roar of the beast; and then a yelp, and then a parfect storm of bark and roar!

"So it kept up till I was only a hundred yards from the place. Then I heard a mighty rush, through woods and water; no more roaring—only the dogs in full cry! And when I got to the place, there was all the signs of fighting, jest as I had seen it at the 'Moon Bend,' on the river—the brush scattered; the airth tore up; but no signs of dog or beast! I could hear the dogs, now, a full quarter off, on the other side of the big lake, nearly upon a west course.

"I set out to follow; was pushing across the lake, which was tolerably full of water; and, when I was in the middle of it, and everything quite still, on a suddent, I hears a mighty rush, jest as ef 'twas a herd of mad cattle; and, for a minute only, I could see something dark and big, but without any shape or figger, shooting by me, not fifty yards off, and going back across the lake, as ef pushing for the very place of fighting I had jest come from! I up gun, but before I could cock and sight, the thing was gone.—'Twas jest a twink I had of it—a sort of glimpse—and no more sight but that! 'Twas quick as the lightning, and jest as black as the cloud! But I could hear it breaking through the cane and brush, and trampling down the dry leaves and sticks, for all the world as heavy as the biggest bull that ever run at a scarlet hankercher!

"In five minutes after, I was so happy to see my pups pushing on the back track after him. I had been afeard that he had torn or trampled them to pieces. On they went, keeping their breath, and only giving out tongue at slow times.

"I cheered the poor brutes on, and pushed back a'ter 'em, first taking a heavy pull at the flask; for I was detarmined to push that beast to his haunches, and be in at his last kick, ef 'twas in the power of mortal bones and sinews to keep up with sich a skrimmage as that.

"It seemed as ef I'd niver git to the place: so much bog; so many trees to *coon*, and so wide was the swamp; and all the time the thick beyont seemed fairly a-fire with the fighting! Sich a roaring, sich a barking, sich a tramping, I niver heard the like in all my life before. I was a'most mad. I whooped and holler'd to the dogs: 'Hurrah, Teaser; hurrah, Towser; at him, good dogs; take him by the throat—by the snout; pull him down! I'm a coming with knife and gun!' And jest after that I could hear the dern'd 'Hoo! Hoo! Hoo!'—a sort of hoarse screech, answering to me across the lake!— Though I was pretty much out of breath, I roused up for a last push; and down thro' mud and water, and over cypress logs and cane-thicks, and across alligator holes, as ef the devil was a pushing behint me, instead of in front; and when I was nearing the bank, I heard another great rush. The beast was off agin, heading along the edge of the lake, and going it like a streak of lightning! And the dogs after him! When I got to the place, there was all the signs of the fight, jest as in the other places—the airth tore up, the brush and leaves scattered. Twenty horses, in a stampede, couldn't have made more show upon the ground!

"I was dead tired by this time. It was onpossible, on my two legs, to go further. So I took out my flask and tried another pull, for the strength. I warn't afeard. It was only the strength was wanting.

My legs gave out, and I laid down jest where I was, listening to the dogs afar off, down the swamp; and the roaring, jest for all the world as ef they had clinched the beast agin, and were making the teeth meet in his flesh!

"After I had been rested a leetle, I got up, and looked all over the ground for the track of the strange beast. But there was no track! It was all broken up a'most as ef it had been ploughed ground. The only tracks I found were made by the dogs! And there was no sign of blood or hair, which I would ha' swore would ha' been in plenty, seeing as all the sounds from the dogs waur sounds of a bloody skrimmage, and both of 'em were powerful and sharp, and could fight like *mastives;* and one of 'em was a cross of mastiff upon hound.

"Well, I lay down agin, in wonderment, not knowing what to think, or what to do.—Hunt after the dogs any more that day was onpossible. They must take their chaince. I couldn't hear 'em now. Either the fight was over, or they had gone pushing the beast lower down the swamp, into Patterson's.—After I had rested a while, I took another drink, and that emptied my bottle! I then got up, threw the gun on my shoulder, and pushed for the boat, after my fish, and then for my cabin. I was dead beat out, and so tired that I had to stop and rest a dozen times before I got home; and then I felt ashamed of myself for giving up the hunt, and leaving my poor brutes to all the danger! It was a'most sundown when I reached the cabin, thairsty as a sinner, and wanting a drink above all things. I soon got one, made a fire, and sat down by it to clean my fish. I'd ha' brought 'em to you that night, Wharncliffe, but I was so tired, and then I was afeard you'd laugh at me about the beast that worried me,—for I'd hev to tell you while the thing was fresh on me—and you'd be after calling it only a wild hog!"

"Well, I suppose it was a wild hog, Paddy,—some fat sow fighting for her pigs."

"Thar it is, now! As ef I hadn't hunted wild hogs by the hundred, an didn't know the difference! A sow!"

"It might have been a wild boar, Paddy," said Jamison; "they squeal like thunder."

"As ef I could mistake a wild boar's squal for that infarnal roar!"

"Possibly it was a bear," said Carroll. "Only a year ago there was a report, you will remember, of a bear being seen to cross the main road near 'Desilla,' and just below Midway."

"I've hearn of that report, but I've niver seen a bear in these parts, and I reckon no body else. But there's another wonder agin, that I've got to tell you. Soon a'ter night the dogs came in, dead tired, like myself; and as they laid by the fire, too much used up to eat, I s'arched their bodies, thinking they must ha' had some severe bites from sich a fight, with sich a beast! There warn't a scratch upon 'em; and they had sartinly done *him* no harm, for their mouths and noses hadn't a sign of blood! Now, what do you think of that, after sich fighting?"

"It doesn't seem, Paddy, that there was any fighting at all."

"Och! Wharncliffe, a'ter all my evidence?"

"You heard the sounds, no doubt Paddy; but did you see the fight?"

"No, I didn't! But listen to me. Though they hadn't a scratch that I could find, what'll you say when I tell you that both of the dogs was stiff and stark cold and dead, by next morning?"

"They died of apoplexy, being heated, and drinking too much cold water on an empty stomach!"

"Och! Wharncliffe, you're a most onbelaving Thomas! But that's not all. That night, when I had my fish a frying, what should I hear but that infarnal 'Hoo! Hoo! Hoo!'—right over the chimbly, as ef the old Devil was a chuckling at what he had done; and jest after that, down comes a peck of soot, right into the pan of fish, and spiles all my pairch. The etarnal beast begrudged me the very supper that had cost me sich a day's work!"

"Clearly," says Wharncliffe, "Paddy is distinguished by Providence. Like Socrates, he, too, has his Demon!"

"With a difference," said I, "since the Demon of Socrates was a loving counsellor, and that of Paddy, a most consummate bore!"

"Talking of boars, in connection with this curious history of Paddy," says Jamison, "I am reminded of a similar story in Feudal History. Get down your Froissart, Wharncliffe, and let me see if I can find it."

"I think I remember something of it, too; the more impressively, indeed, as Philip Pendleton Cooke, one of the most sweet and graceful of the poets of Virginia—the author of 'Florence Vane'—has made it the subject of one of his 'Froissart Ballads'—a beautiful volume of fresh and spirited poetry, published only a few years ago. Philip Cooke has left us; but his mantle has descended upon a younger brother, John Esten Cooke, one of the best of the young novelists and poets of the South—a noble gentleman and pure Christian!"

"Well," said Jamison, turning over the huge volume, in Johnes' translation of Froissart, "if I can find the passage, you will see in it a beast exceedingly like that vague monster which has so baffled Paddy and his dogs!"

"But don't you think, Paddy, while Jamison is looking up Froissart's devil, that a good bumper of whiskey punch would do something towards *laying* your own?"

"Ach, Wharncliffe, you'd be the wisest man I knows, ef so be you were only a belaver."

"I am a believer, Paddy—in *good* spirits, not in *bad* ones. Come, Stylus, are you ready for us?"

"Ach, fathers, may we niver swallow worse doctrines than this. Here's your blessed health, gintlemen, all round."

And we hob-a-nob'd, and filled our pipes, and were soon ready for Jamison.

CHAPTER XI.

"Ever since the Squire related it to me, I have much thought upon it, and shall do so as long as I live. It is a fact, as the Squire assured me."

SIR JOHN FROISSART.

———

"I have found the passage, gentlemen;" said Jamison, "but fear to read it, lest it should confirm our friend Paddy's faith in the demon that troubles him."

"Och, niver fear, Jamison; I'm too far gone in the belafe of my own ixparence, to make it of much difference what I hears about other people's divils."

"There is so much similarity in the two stories, as to tend very much to the strengthening of your opinion, Wharncliffe, about the universality of all superstitions. They seem to have a common origin in the instincts of our nature."

"Well, it will do no hurt, I fancy, to any of us. Read away."

"I will condense a long chapter into a short one. It seems, that, according to the belief among *his* people, the celebrated Gaston Phœbus, Count of Foix, had his familiar, or Demon, as well as King Saul and Socrates, and the Count's Demon, like that of Socrates, was a subservient one. He brought him the news, much faster than the mails and couriers of that day could have done.—He was a sort of spiritual telegraph. For example, he, the Count, was advised of the battle of Aljubarota the very day after it happened, though he was in Béarn, and the battle took place in Portugal. Enough, that his people were generally impressed with the belief that their lord had a familiar, who reported everything, of any importance, to his ears, almost as soon as the event took place.

"He was not alone in the possession of a familiar. It seems that a certain Lord, Raymond de Corasse, was fortunate enough to obtain

302

the services of a Demon, who happened to take a liking to him, after first alarming and annoying him, his wife and servant, by hideous noises of one sort or another. This Demon, taking a liking, as we have said, to this lord, served him with intelligence, even as the Count de Foix was served by his. But he did not show himself; only spoke to him, would wake him by pulling the pillow from under his head, and by other modes. When the knight was awake, Orthon, for that was the name of the Demon, would tell his news; the lady of the lord, meanwhile, covering her head with the bed clothes, terribly frightened. 'Then,' quoth good old Sir John, 'did the Lord de Corasse know, by means of Orthon, all things that were passing in different parts of the world.'

"This connexion between them lasted *five* years; and the lord found, in all that time, that Orthon's reports proved invariably true, and that he was a most dutiful servant, and *all for love.*

"But the Lord de Corasse seems to have been something of an ass, since he let his secret be known. A secret, the existence of which is known, is already half revealed.—But there was some danger in the discovery of this, since it involved the loss of a faithful servant. Orthon, had told his lord, that, if ever he should anger him, he should lose him.

"Well, vain of his secret, and the power which it gave him, Lord Raymond boasted of it, and was persuaded to demand of Orthon that he should show himself in his proper shape, precisely as our friend Paddy challenged his familiar to do. Well, the Lord of Corasse made the demand, and now we shall let Sir John Froissart tell the story in his old simple fashion. It will be found, by the way, at chapter 18, vol. 2, of Johnes' Froissart, in the beautiful 2 volume 8vo. edition, recently issued from the London Press of Henry G. Bohn."

"Read it, Jamison," said Paddy, impatiently.

"It fell out when the Lord de Corasse, as usual was in bed with his lady, (who was now accustomed to hear Orthon without being frightened) Orthon arrived and shook the pillow of the knight, who was asleep.—On waking, he asked 'who was there?' Orthon replied, 'It is I.' 'And where dost thou come from?' 'I come from Prague, in Bohemia.' 'How far is it hence?' 'Sixty days' journey,' replied Orthon. 'And hast thou returned thence in so short a time?'

—'Yes, as may God help me. I travel as fast as the wind, or faster.' 'What? hast thou got wings?' 'Oh, no.' 'How, then, canst thou fly so fast?' 'That is no business of yours.' 'No!' said the knight. 'I should like exceedingly to see what form thou hast and how thou art made?' 'That does not concern you to know,' replied Orthon, 'be satisfied that you hear me, and that I bring intelligence you may depend upon.' 'By God,' said the Lord de Corasse, 'I should love thee better if I should see thee.' 'Well,' replied Orthon, 'since you have such a desire, *the first thing you shall see to-morrow morning, on quitting your bed, shall be myself.*' 'I am satisfied,' said the knight, 'you may now depart. I give thee thy liberty for this night.'

"When morning came, the knight arose, but his lady was so much frightened she pretended to be sick, and said she would not leave her bed the whole day. The Lord de Corasse willed it otherwise. 'Sir,' said she, 'if I do get up, I shall see Orthon; and, if it please God, I would neither see nor meet him.' 'Well,' replied the knight, 'I am determined to see him;' and leaping out of his bed, he seated himself on the bedstead, thinking he should see Orthon in his own shape; but he saw nothing that could induce him to say he had seen him. When the ensuing night arrived, and the Lord de Corasse was in bed, Orthon came and began to talk in his usual manner. 'Go,' said the knight, 'thou are a liar; thou ought'st to have shown thyself to me this morning, and thou didst not.' 'Ay,' replied Orthon, 'but I did.' 'I say no!' 'And did you see nothing at all when you leapt out of bed?' The Lord de Corasse was silent, and having considered awhile, said: 'Yes, when sitting on my bed-side, and thinking of thee, I saw two straws which were turning and playing on the floor.' 'That was myself,' replied Orthon, 'for I had taken that form.' The Lord de Corasse said: 'That will not satisfy me; I beg of thee to assume some other shape, so that I may see thee and know thee.' Orthon answered, 'You ask so much that you will ruin me, and force me away from you, for your requests are too great.' 'You shall not quit me,' said the Lord de Corasse; 'if I could once see thee, I should not again wish it.' 'Well,' replied Orthon, '*you shall see me to-morrow, if you pay attention to the first thing you observe, when you leave your chamber.*' 'I am contented,' said the knight, 'Now, go thy ways, for I want to sleep.' Orthon departed. On the morrow, about the hour of eight, the knight had risen and was dressed. On leaving his apartment, he went to a window which looked out into the court of the Castle. Casting his eyes about, the first thing he saw was an immensely large sow———."

"Paddy's lion!" quoth Wharncliffe.

"Don't you be afther stopping the gineral, Wharncliffe."

Jamison resumed:

—"But she was so poor; she seemed only skin and bone, with long hanging ears all spotted, and a sharp-pointed, lean snout. The Lord de Corasse was disgusted at such a sight, and calling to his servants, said—'Let the dogs loose quickly, for I will have that sow killed and devoured.' The servants hastened to open the kennel and to set the hounds on the sow, who uttered a loud cry, and looked up at the Lord de Corasse, leaning on the balcony of the window, and was never seen afterwards; for she vanished, and no one saw what became of her."

"And, so the Lord de Corasse lost his best servant! The old moral, Paddy, from the days of Eve, the dangers of idle curiosity. Beware how you call upon your Orthon to be showing himself in his true shape."

"Ach, Wharncliffe, but I *will* call and defy the baste. *My* Orthon, as you calls him, has never done me a hand's turn of good yit, and the sooner he quits kaping my company, the sooner I'll respect him as a dacent gentleman, kaping his proper distance. But it's curious like, aint it, my masters? What sort of book is that, Jamison? It's a mighty big one. Jest let me look at it with you. Ach! an' it's to the full of pictures? And that's what they calls a Castle? Them's towers? Ach, an' that's the way they fight, is it?—like our Ingins, with their bows and arrows. What's the name of them peoples, Jamison?"

"French, mostly—Italians, Spaniards, English—a mixture."

"It must be glorious to rade about 'em. And what sort of man was the one that wrote the book—a man of credit—to be counted on?"

"Very much so, Paddy. In fact, we owe to him a very important portion of our French and English histories."

"I'll rade it, Wharncliffe, some day, with your lave."

"You shall have it whenever you want it, Paddy, and reading it will be apt to keep the Devil from troubling you. A good book is the Devil's worst enemy. And now that we have translated your lion into a sow, suppose we try the swill."

"I'm agrade!"

"And you shall then go on with your story, Paddy. I know you have a great deal more to tell."

"Faix, almost a history meself."

We drank to Paddy's future successes.

"And how long after that chase, Paddy, did you keep your bed?"

"How do you know I kept it at all? But I did! I was all over black and blue with bruises, for three days after, jest as ef I had been in the fight meself. Then I was broke up by the loss of my dogs. I cried over the poor pups—they were my own raising—the poor dumb crathers,—and I buried them under the big oak in front of the house; and ef dogs have sperrits, then I knows that the ghosts of Towser and Teazer will see that no thieving scamp will ever daur break the lock of my door when my back's turned.

"Well, for three days I niver went out. But I thought of what Sam Hartley said—'niver give up! niver say die! Try on, and try till you work through the swamp!' And so I buttoned up, and buckled on, and took my gun and went to see Sam, to beg a dog from him, and then I took to the woods as hot as iver, thinking of that strange baste, and praying all the time to git a shot at him. But, after going the rounds for a week, and not a sight of him or any other big beast, I drew the silver slugs out of my barrels and loaded up with turkey shot. It was high time to look for meat. I had got out of the last rasher of bacon, and the starvation was beginning to stare me in the face. I was a'most out of powder and shot, too, and there warn't a drop of strength left in the jimmyjohn. Now, in hunting for the strange baste, I had found out the roosting place of the turkeys, and I started one morning, long before daylight, and was in the thickest of the swamp before the first gray peep betwixt the trees. Well, I treed my birds, sartin, and had draw'd aim on a most monstrous big gobler—I reckon he'd a weighed full thirty pounds. In idee, I had seen him drop, so heavy with fat as to burst his breastbone. In idee, I had him fast, with a nice piece of buckskin tied round his neck, and a hanging on my shoulder. But as I spread out, taking the deadest aim, and was pulling the trigger, a dern'd ugly log, the very picture of the one that broke Isaac Clymes' thigh, rolled from under my foot, and I lost my chaince. The gun went off, and so did the turkeys! There waur three on 'em, all roosting and fast asleep in the tree, though the daylight was peeping through the branches.

"Now, as I'm a living sinner, I niver seed any log lying in my track when I set my foot down."

"Well, what of that. You were staring, with all your eyes, into the tree-top."

"No I wern't. Jest the contrary; for as I was afear'd of making any noise, by the cracking of brushes under my feet, I looked careful to see whar I should set them down, and I could take my bible oath, that jest where I set my foot there wern't the least sign of snag, or stump, or log. It was clean as my hand."

"No doubt that, in your eagerness, you made several other steps forward, and without looking, and indeed without even knowing that you were in motion."

"Lord save you, Wharncliffe, for a most onrighteous, doubting Thomas—as ef I was so green in the business, jest like a new beginner—an overgrown forgitful boy—as ef I didn't know my own business—as ef I should forget the only thing that was needful to remember. Why, Wharncliffe, in hunting turkeys no man ever seed my two legs astraddle. I laps one over t'other when I creeps towards my game, and let the old sentinel gobler look up when he pleases, he will see no more legs to me than a pine sapling. No, my very good friends and masters, I knows my business, and this time was mighty partic'lar about it; for I wanted meat and money dreadful bad, and a pair of thim goblers I was sworn for. They waur worth three dollars at Branchville, and here at Desilla. I sticks to the mention of that log now, bekaise I had mighty good reason to belave, and think and knew, a'terwards, that the said log was not put there for nothing; that it put itself there, and wern't there when I put my foot down; in fact, I tell you my raal belafe, when I says it was no log at all. I verily belave that it was the Devil himself—that preticlar Devil that hed set out to throuble meself. He either tuk its shape, or harbored some whar; but I rather reckon he took its shape, jest as the Orthon of the book took the shape of a straw, first time, and then of a sow, when it was, all the time, nothing less than an evil sperrit."

"You see, Jamison, that old Froissart begins to work. You have confirmed our friend, Paddy, in his faith. Now, Paddy, confess—you never thought that your Devil harboured in that log till you heard about Orthon. You may have thought that he put the log there; but that he was the log itself, or had got into it, you never suspected before."

"Wait till you hear me out, Wharncliffe, and then let's hear you.

"Well, not three days a'ter this, hearing that the ducks waur pretty thick in the river, as the weather was mighty cold and dry, and all the ponds waur dried up, I put out to a place where I know'd they would crowd, that is, at the old mill cut just above Turtle Cove, at 'Woodlands' landing. I got there just before sun down, and went to work to find myself a place for squatting close, and covering the largest spread of water with my gun. Well, what should I find but the snuggest sort of hiding place in the worrold. There was a thick of cypress knees, and in the middle of 'em was an old cypress rotted down and pretty much rotted out, making a hollow, full breast high. The chunks from the tree had filled up the inside of the hollow so that I could stand in it and keep dry feet, though jest outside, the water was over four foot deep. I got into this hollow, and when I squatted down you couldn't see a sign of me from any where round. I had only to raise up quiet and blaze away, whenever I seed there waur a good chaince. And so I set myself down patient awaiting for the ducks. Well, about dusk thar they come down with a rush from every quarter of the heavens; and you could see 'em spreading out in long lines, up and down the river, now flapping their wings, then paddling off and on,—running this way and that, a mighty consider-able of a crowd, and most of them the biggest English ducks I ever seed, and I said to myself, 'now if luck would sarve,—ef the Lord would only be good and gracious to me—ef that infarnal Devil would only make himself scarce, wouldn't I bag a bushel of them beauties! And so I prayed, and so I watched—watched and prayed— waiting my time for a mighty haul. More than a dozen times I had scattering chainces at three or four of 'em at a shot; but as they kept a coming down, the flocks, I waited on 'em, knowing that I must git better chainces after a while. At last, when it was gitting too darkish, I laid out a line of more than twenty, all in a row, and blazed away; and in the same second of time, I found myself over head and ears in the river—my gun gone, I blowing like a porpoise to git the water out of my throat and nostrils, and every duck in the river gone. I could niver see the first one that I hit, and I reckon I didn't hit the first one, seeing that the very moment I pulled trigger I went over into the swash.

"And how do you think the thing happened. Why the derned stump of the old cypress that I rested the gun on, when I fired, give way onder me as ef it niver had a foundation, and thar was I scuffling in the water, then beginning to freeze, in one of the coldest nights in about the coldest spell of weather that we've felt for twenty years. Och, sorra my sowl,—the very memory of that wather, and of that night, of them ducks, and that freeze, sets my whole body in a shiver; and ef you'd be doing a sarvice to a drowning and a freezing man, Mr. Stylus, you'll be filling this tumbler out of the pitcher with the ixpedition of a steam ingine.

"Ach! the Beauty my Darling! but it does swaten the bad memory of an avil disposition, from the crown of my head to the sole of my feet. Here's to you, gentlemen! in my freezing recollections I had a'most forgot my good manners and rispicts! Here's to you, my friends, and may you niver have the luck of Paddy McGann, when he took lodgins, for duck shooting, in the corner of a cypress stump, with the Divil beside him as he pulled the trigger!"

CHAPTER XII.

"Hath this thing appeared again?"
                                        HAMLET.

———

"Now," says Paddy, resuming his narrative, "You'll be afther supposing that, in that business of the duck shooting, it was all nothing but an accident; that I leant too heavy on a rotten stump, and it give way onder me."

"Certainly," says Wharncliffe, "it could be nothing else."

"I know'd you'd say so, but I now knows better. Be sure it was that same dern'd old stump that broke Isaac Clymes' leg, and that rolled from onder me when I cracked away at the turkeys; for when I raised up in the river there waur no sich stump to be seen floating about me."

"Well, it sank; it was water-soaked."

"Och, Wharncliffe! tell that to an old raftsman. But wait a bit, and you'll hear further. I'm a coming pretty fast on to another transaction, which, I rether reckon, will make all the other ones clear enough.

"I said the devil that was a troubling me, was getting more free and sassy; was coming nigher to me every day; and carrying it on step by step, leettle by leettle, ontill, at last, he made a stand up, square to me, and let me see a leetle more of his inches, jest as I had axed and prayed him to do."

"One thing, Paddy; after that sousing in the river, did you take cold?"

"No, I didn't."

"How did you escape? Had you not a leetle bottle of whiskey along with you?"

310

"Well, Wharncliffe, I confess I had."

"Very well; and you took a good drink as soon as you came out of the water."

"It stands to raison I did."

"Very true! But Paddy, didn't you take a drink *before* the sousing?"

"Well, you see, my masters. It was one of the coldest days in the year. I tell'd you so at starting, and I was pretty well frozen up about the feet and ears; and for what should I carry the bottle, ef twarn't for the drink? To be sure, I tuk a drink before I fell over."

"Well, Paddy, you can't be surprised if folks say and think that too much whiskey is apt to make a man fall over."

"But who says I tuk too much?"

"The falling over will be apt to prove the fact."

"Niver a bit, Wharncliffe! I knows what I kin take, and what I kin stand; and I put it to these gentlemen here, ef, looking at my inches, they calkilate that I am a man to be upsot by a poor pint of whiskey in cold weather, when it lasts me six or eight hours in a freezing sitivation."

"Surely not," we all agreed.

"And on the honour, gentlemen, my good friends, I didn't take a drap more; and half of that was drunk afther the accident. Don't you mind Wharncliffe, he's always afther bedivelling me, a'most as bad as my stump divil. But jest you listen to me. Afther all the sousing and soaking I got, I walked home mighty brisk, and had a drink left in the bottle, to warm my innards, when I got to the lodge. But one thing I must not forget to tell you. The very minute I tumbled into the river, I haird, jest above my head, that infarnal screech, that 'Hoo! Hoo! Hoo!' that seem'd to tell me what sort of sperrit was at work for my ruination."

"Oh! clearly, Paddy, that was an owl!—The river swamp is full of them, and such a great bulk of a man as you are, tumbling headlong into the river, must have scared up the owls for a mile around!"

"And how often must I tell you, Wharncliffe, that I knows the v'ice of every owl in the swamp, and that this v'ice was like none that I iver heard? It was the v'ice of that beast that throw'd the soot down my chimney and spiled my fish; it was the v'ice of the same beast that skeer'd Sam Hartley when he was a praying with me;

the same v'ice that crowed over me when the beast had got the better
of me, in all my hunts, and chases, and fishing, and shooting matches.
—Twan't no owl, twas the divil's own infarnal throat, and nothing
better, that sent out that same dern'd impudent 'Hoo! Hoo! Hoo!'
when I was a-rolling in the freezing wather!

"But ef you'll wait on me, you'll see that I'm coming to the p'int
to prove it."

"Very well; proceed, Paddy."

"Afther that sousing, you may suppose I didn't sleep comfortable
that night, and feeling bad next morning, I didn't go out. In the
a'ternoon I rode over to see my ould mother, and I spent the night
with her. She said that I warn't in good sperrits, and she was at me
agin to git a wife, telling me of some young women, the da'ters of a
fellow a few miles off, named Pogson. He had a half a dozen young
women, but I know'd very leetle about 'em. In fact, I didn't go much
about among the women, and only know'd them when I seed 'em at
the meeting house. But Pogson had the character of being a poor
mean shoat, as lazy as any possum, and mighty tricky. So I put off
the ould woman, saying I'd think about it. I was purty doleful all
night, but I never let on to her what was my trouble. The next
morning I canter'd over to Sam Hartley, and I warn't in any good
humour when I met him, for, you see, I thought that Sam had been
fighting shy of me, not liking to keep company with a man that the
divil made so free with. Sam felt oneasy, when he seed me. I could
see it in all his looks and motions and he begun by making his
excuses for not coming to see me, by telling me of work he had to do,
mending up his wagon and going over to Orangeburg sale day, and
buying cattle. I said nothing to all that, and as neither of us seemed
to talk so free as in old times, I soon buttoned up and rode off. I
reckon the poor fellow was glad to get shet of me; perhaps he was
afeard that ef he seed me too often at his own house, the divil would
be a coming there a'ter me, and making as free with him as with me.
I know'd edzactly where his shoe was a pinching him, and, poor
fellow, I didn't blame him, for he warn't over strong of heart,
though he was so deep in the Bible, that he had a better chaince
than me in a fight with the beast; and he ought to have hed the
heart for any scrimmage!

"When I went back to the lonesome cabin in the swamp, I felt worse miserable than ever. My luck was gone, my skill of hunting and fishing—I hed no family and no friends—and a'ter thinking over all my sitivation, I jest concluded I hed to work out the row, through the swamp, and ef I couldn't, why I hed only to drop down in the bog, and let them that pleased cover me up where I lay! I cleaned up my gun, but without any heart or hope. But I shet my eyes against what was to happen, and jest worked on. When daylight came next morning, I tuk the dog that I had got from Sam, and pushed for the swamp, ready for anything, but not heving a plan for anything. A'ter a while the dog started a rabbit, and run off on her track, and I niver seed him any more that day. The mean beast, a'ter he tired himself down, quietly slipt back to the lodge and laid himself down in the doorway, jest waiting for me to come and feed him, I reckon. Perhaps he too was skear'd by something in the woods! who kin tell? I didn't blame him. I hadn't the heart for it. At another time I'd ha' given him the whip.

"But seeing the dog was gone, I turned in to hunt for turkeys, down by Patterson's peafields. But I seed none, and the day was half wasted. I then flushed up a smart flock of partridges, but wouldn't shoot with the turkey shot in my gun. So I drew the turkey shot, put in squirrel, and went to look a'ter the partridges. I hed watched and seed 'em where they lighted, and so I pushed on, making a leetle sweep to get round 'em, under cover of a bit of woods that lay close on to the Little Lake. I thought I could sarcumvent 'em. You may guess how mean I felt in sperrit when I could give up hunting buck and turkey, and turn in to sarcumvent sich small birds as partridges.

"Well, sure enough, I did sarcumvent 'em. I creeped up softly enough, and got upon 'em without rumpling a dry leaf or breaking a stick. There they waur, a long string of 'em on the ground, busy feeding, and never smelling or suspicioning me a bit. I had a great chaince at 'em, all along the corn row, in a straight line upon the ground.

"Well, twarn't the sport I was a'ter; twaur the birds! I know'd I could only git one shot, and my poor ould mother was now a wanting meat. She had a great liking for birds. So, ranging the whole flock pretty nigh, I up gun and cracked away, and I tumbled 'em over in all directions! Maybe I didn't make the feathers fly! I picked up as many as nine birds, and my heart was jist in a most 'O, be joyful' condition, for it seemed to me as if the charm was taken off the gun, or off me, at last, and I was free of the divil and all his liberties. I fairly shouted out for joy, as I begun picking up the birds, most of 'em dead, and only one or two that I hed to wring their necks. But Lord love you, my good masters, jest when I was picking up the birds, when I was most joyful, thinking now that all was right agin, I heard the same etarnal screech—'Hoo! Hoo! Hoo!' and I started up and began loading the empty barrel of my gun. 'Hoo! Hoo! Hoo!' agin, and this time it seemed almost at my ears. I set my teeth fast and went on loading, and as I wadded the powder, I poured in a dozen good pelters, thinking I might have the very black beast himself upon me. I hedn't quite done wadding, when I heard a v'ice crying out to me, and, Lord love ye, what was my feelings when I found I made out the very words. All before this, I could hear the sounds of talking and voices, but niver the words, 'cept the infarnal 'Hoo! Hoo! Hoo!' ef them's to be considered any human words at all. But now come the words to my ears, plain enough."

"And what was said, Paddy?"

"I remembers every word edzactly. The v'ice said—

" 'Ho! Ho! Paddy McGann! will you niver be a sinsible man?' "

"Why, Paddy, he was rhyming. He was fighting you with your own weapons."

"I reckon he didn't mean that, for he went on without any rhyme or raison. He said next—

" 'What are you doing here—a killing my birds—my pets—the little darlints of my children!'

"I looked up and around and all about, to see for the spaker. But divil a figger could I see! and the v'ice worn't a natheral v'ice—twarnt like any human that I iver heard. Twarnt like Patterson's v'ice, or Dewitt's v'ice, nor your'n, Wharncliffe. 'Twas nobody's v'ice I had ever hearn afore. 'Twas a hoarse, thickish v'ice, as ef the speaker hed a bad cold, or spoke through a shingle, or out of a hollow, and it was followed a'ter by a sort of snort and a chuckle, more like the dern'd 'Hoo! Hoo!' than like any laugh. I didn't know what to say, but kept staring about me on every side, but I could see nobody, jest nothing at all, at all, 'cept the thick woods at the edge of the lake, and a great big ugly dead blackened stump, that the fire seemed to hev gone over, and that was a standing out in front of the green bushes. At last, says I—

" 'Who the divil can that be?'

"Then says the v'ice—'Who are you axing a'ter? Ef it's me, l'arn to be sinsible.'

"Then says I—'Whoever you are, stand out and let me look at you!'

"Then there was a dern'd cry of 'Hoo! Hoo! Hoo!' agin, and then the v'ice said—

" 'As ef you wasn't looking me full in the face now!'

" 'Where?' says I.

" 'Here!' says he.

" 'I don't see! Show yourself clear, and ef you're a man of my inches, then, dern you, I'll take hold of you, though you're all soak'd in brimstone.'

" 'Hoo! Hoo! Hoo!' he answered. 'Look agin, you beetleeye?'

"I looked with all my eyes, but I couldn't see a mortal, or a human, or a divil, or anything that had a right to sich a v'ice and sich a spaking!

" 'Who are you?' said I, 'and *whaur air* you!'

" 'I am the owner of them birds, I say. I raised 'em for my own children!'

" 'Children!' says I to myself. 'It can't be the divil, for I niver heard of *his* having any children!'

"Lord love you, my masters, I didn't think of the large family of divil's children in this world; I've sence thought of it many a time, and I conclude, though the Holy Writ don't tell us so, when I see the world so full of 'em, that the Devil has jest as large a hand in the business of making men—and women too—as the Great Lord of the Univarse himself! But, not to trouble you with my thinking, I made answer pretty quick.

" 'Your birds—you the owner! Let me look at you, then, and see what right you hev to them more than me.'

" 'I raised 'em, you dirty fellow, jest as an old woman raises chickens, by good usage and good feeding. And for you to come and murder 'em. Murder, I calls it,' says he, 'to take 'em in a line upon the ground! To give 'em not the shadow of a chaince! You a sports-man! you a hunter! Sorra's the day when you got a gun into your clumsy fists. But I'll punish you for your murdering acts, you dirty villain. I'll see that you get no more meat! You a hunter. Hoo! Hoo! Hoo!'

"And the v'ice eended with a sort of screech owl whoop that made the woods ring agin! By this time I was frocious. I could have faced twenty devils as soon as one. I cried out:

" 'Who *are* you? Come out, dern you, and show yourself!'

" 'Who em I! That's good!' says he.—'Well, ef iver you know'd a body, you ought to know *me!* I'm your master! I've bought you, body and soul, so you know who you've got to sarve, you dirty crathur!'

"Then I fairly splurged! I raged, and dashed about!

" 'Och,' says I, 'ef you're my master, come out, face to face, and show yourself, and only let me see the turn of your mouth and the color of your gills when you're a giving your orders! Come out of yer hiding place, my beautiful masthur, and I'm your humble sarvant to command.'

" 'Oh! you blind turkey-buzzard!' says he. 'Kaint you see me straight before you? I'm a looking at you now, and you looking at me, full in the face!'

"And jist then, as I'm a living sinner—I seed—'twas jest like a flash, all suddent—I seed a big red eye looking full out at me from the very breast and body of that big, ugly, black stump I tell'd you of before. 'Twas but one eye, that seemed to shine out from a dark hollow, and it 'minded me of the eye that I had seen so often a watching me in the fire. The moment I seed it, without stopping to think, or spake, or another question, I up gun and let drive pint-blank at the eye!—Then he hollowed—

" 'Hoo! Hoo! Hoo! and you've the consate to be a hunter, and to shoot for the bafe and kaint hit the bull's eye at twenty steps! You've only bruised my shins, you buzzard!'

"I could see the red eye blazing at me bigger than before; and says I—

" 'I'd do better next time;' and so I up gun agin, and let fly, with as dead aim as I could take, with the other barrel that hed small shot in it. Then he give another

" 'Hoo! Hoo! Hoo!—oh! What a shooter! You've burned my eyebrow, you buzzard!—Two shots at your master; and what'll you do next, I wonder!'

"By this time I was biling over with the fury I was in—and as I hed no more loads in my gun, I made a rush at the stump, charging with the gun as ef it was a bay'net, full at the eye itself, and it looked to be larger and redder than ever it did afore. I took dead aim!

" 'Stump or divil,' says I, 'I'll try a push with the muzzle, ef I've got no more shots!'

"And I never tuk better aim in my life; and no bay'net ever made a straighter plunge; for I drove the muzzle right into the socket (which was a round hole in the stump, where a knot hed fallen out) and jist where I hed seen the eye a minute afore.

" 'I reckon,' says I, 'I've darkened your peeper!'

" 'Hoo! Hoo! Hoo!' cried the beast—'you've only shet up my front window, you blackguard! and what'll you be thrying at next, I wonder.'

" 'That you'll see, pretty soon,' says I, as I was pulling at the gun to pull it out of the hole; but it stuck there for all my pulling, jest like a wedge driv' in, and fastened there o'purpose.

" 'Hoo! Hoo! Hoo! Why don't you pull away, you blackguard. Do you think I wants my window shut up. Put your marrow into it and pull. You've not the skill to be a hunter, or a fisherman. You ought to have the strength for a ditcher like yer ould daddy that's gone afore you, and I wont say whaur.'

"With that, I was jest like a madman, the fury was so strong upon me. I let go the gun, finding I couldn't pull it out, and, Lord bless you, the moment I did so, the gun dropt out of its own self. But I didn't mind it. I hed no load in it now, and I jest let it lie whaur it dropt, and I rushed upon the cussed stump, and grabbed it with both my arms. I was thinking to hold it tight, slip round it, and find the cussed varmint, whoever he was, a hidin' behint it; but Lord save your honest souls, my good friends and masters, what do you think? The stump giv way with me, the moment I clinched it in my arms, jest as ef it had been rotted off at the ground—jest as the cypress stump did in the river—and down we come together, and we rolled over together, I on him now, he on me the next, and so we kept a rolling down the slope of the hill, I holding on all the time, and as it did seem to me, the blasted thing holding on to me, for all the world, jest as ef it had hands and arms. It stuck to me somehow, even without my holding on, and even a'ter I was willing to let go; and I reckon we must ha' rolled down the slope, over and over some ten or fifteen feet, 'till we got to the very edge of the lake. Then I shook myself loose, and backed off from it a leetle, trying to git back my wind and sperrits; and then I ran back to git my gun, determined to load up and see what my pelters could do, for ef I could bruise the shins of the beast and burn off his eyebrows, I thought it only raisonable to hope I might, a'ter awhile, put some shot into his body. Lord love you, my masters, when I came back, gun in hand, there waur no log—the airth was smooth—but as I stood, ready to crack away, and was s'arching about, I haird, right over my head, a mighty 'Hoo! Hoo! Hoo!' and the rush of the biggest pair of wings, not like the owl, that makes no noise in the air, but a rattle and a rush, jest as ef an eagle was a coming down from a mighty pine, straight for the back of a fish-hawk!"

CHAPTER XIII.

"First, let me talk with this philosopher."

———

Here Paddy paused, much heated and excited, and took a drink without any preliminaries. I should mention that no one could be more animated than was he, in his telling of this story. He suited the action to the word, with all the play and passion of a born actor. He kept his seat but little in his narrative, but rose to his feet at all the exciting parts, strode the floor, confronted us, used hands and arms, while his face was full of intelligence, and every feature was made to express the several emotions of anger, astonishment, rage, vexation, disappointment, mortification and terror, in turn.

"And now," says he, "gentlemen, axing your pardon for helping myself without waiting for you, but hoping you'll do the same, ef only to keep me from being bashful—now, what does you say to that? And what was I to think and belave, after hearing what I did, and having sich a scrimmage with sich a beast, without any more figger than a burnt stump? Answer me now, my good masters, all—you, Wharncliffe, you, Jamison, you, Carroll, you, Stylus."

For a few moments there was no answer. The truth is, all parties seemed dumbfoundered. The man was so earnest, so natural, so solemn even, and appeared so religiously to believe everything himself which he had reported. At length Wharncliffe said, bluntly enough:

"Had you any whiskey along with you that day, Paddy?"

"Thar it is! I know'd what was a coming. You, Wharncliffe, air always putting down the curous and strange to the whiskey account, and you've as good as towld me, many a time before, when I was a telling you of my curous ixparience, that I was only, 'I wonder how

319

you come so!' You hain't got the right faith in men, no how, Wharncliffe; and I reckon a right faith in men brings us pretty much to a right faith in God! What is it you sees in me to make you suppose I hevn't got a right judgment for things? You knows I wouldn't tell you a lie! You knows I tells you what I belave! Now, I ain't sich a fool as to belave in anything without good cause for it; and you knows that my hearing is good, my eyesight good, my limbs good, my narves good; and that, ef I belave, it ain't the skear that makes me belave. I wasn't skear'd in this business. At first, I was jubous, and tuk by supprise. But I niver backed a foot from the throuble, and I always tried to face it full! And it tain't one thrial only that I've had, but a thousand. Look at the whole history, as it runs through a'most five years—and thar's more of it yit—and it's all of a piece—sarcumstance upon sarcumstance; from the time of my first feeling that my luck was gone, in everything, to the time that the woods grew to be so strange; then, after that, the sounds and noises; then, the whisperings and v'ices; then, the infarnal 'Hoo! Hoo! Hoo!' in my ears, jest whenever I was most miserable and onlucky; then, the strange doubling of the old buck; then, the adventure with the beast, and the dogs dying; then, the sousing in the river; and then, the fight with the stump,—and thar's more yit to come."

"But you have not answered me about the whiskey, Paddy. Your argument is very fair; but I have my own way of thinking about your case. Will you now tell me if you had any whiskey with you that day?"

"In course, I had! I hardly niver goes without it, ef I hev it to carry. I tuk a bottle out with me when I started, for I was to be gone all day, and the wind was pretty sharp in the morning, and the ice was upon the ground. But that one bottle lasted me all the day, and I had more than half of it to go upon in the afternoon."

"Did you finish it, then?"

"Not till a'ter I got home!"

"Had you eaten anything that day, Paddy?" asked Jamison.

"Not a mouthful!"

"Ah! And what was the size of the bottle, Paddy?"

"The size of the bottle? Why 'twas an o'rnary quart bottle—a pink bottle. But ef you thinks that I'm a man to be flung by an or'nary pink bottle, lasting from sun to sun, you're not knowing to the man that's talking to you! I've done bigger things than that in the way of drinking, when the meesure would have swallowed up more quarts than one. I don't brag of it, mind you, it's only my confession."

"But not on an empty stomach, Paddy."

"Faix, yes, and on a pair of empty stomacks, by the Holy Pipers! No! no! gentlemen, my good masters and friends, I worront drunk that day, I tell you; and hadn't the slightest squint towards upsetting. I was sober, as I am jest now, when I sees no divil of a stump, but only sarten good liquors that might well stump the divil!"

This hint was too broad to be mistaken, and I promptly filled the glasses. With a lordly nod to all the company, head in air and eyes bright as a wild cat's, Paddy tossed off the bumper without a struggle; and, spreading his shoulders wide, and bracing his large figure to its utmost erectness, he was truly a fellow of magnificent proportions.

After a pause, while we drank to him more slowly, he said—

"I'm a truthful person, my very good friends, and know, too, when the liquor trips me. It didn't then; and that little quantity couldn't begin to do it at any time! No, it's the fault of you wise men, and l'arned, to be always trying to find out a raison for every thing, and when you fails to do so, you belaves in nothing!

"But I tell you, gentlemen, that you're not expected to find out raisons for everything; in fact, ef you were able to find out the raison of everything, you would niver be seeking God at all—you would'nt belave in God, and, what's more, you wouldn't need a God! Men don't git their faith in one another by their raisoning, but by strange and secret feelings of their own,—they don't know why or how—but it comes to 'em nevertheless. Yet they will try to make or find a raison for every faith. Here, only 'tother day, I heard one of our great men making a spache at a public meeting, and he begun by saying that 'an impenetrable wale had fallen between him and the subject before him'—them's the very words; yet, would you belave it, he went on, afterwards, to raison for a half an hour about the whole affair, and what was to come of it. Now, when he said the wale was impenetrable, don't you see that he was guilty of a sin in trying to break through it or lift it up. God made it impenetrable a-purpose, that it should *not* be penetrated!

"Since my throubles begun, I've been a thinking over all these things—about mysteries and miraculous doings, in past times; not a day, not an hour, that I haint thought of 'em, after the fashion of a poor man without any book-larning; and I conclude, gentlemen, that God has a way of speaking to men, and acting upon 'em, either by himself or by his agents, in a way to *pervent* their raison from taking any liberties with his argyments; for, as sure as a gun, ef he didn't then their raison would be always popping up out of their self-consate, and putting him out of sight! And so he confounds their raison jest as often as he kin, even as the Good Book tells us! He will find a way for himself to make them *feel* him, and *fear* him, and *know* him, though he says not a word to their raison or common onderstanding."

"All very well, and very well said, Paddy," replied Wharncliffe; "but, for the benefit of the company, I wish to ask you a question?"

"Ax away, Wharncliffe; but I reckon I knows what's a-coming."

"Perhaps so, but we'll see. Tell us, then, did any of your friends or companions ever see these sights, and hear these sounds, besides yourself, and when you heard them."

"None, I think, but Sam Hartley, and I've told you about his ixparience when he was with me."

"Ah! and did he hear them at *first?*"

"How at first; when?"

"When you first called his attention to the subject."

"No, he didn't; but he heard them a'terwards."

"That is, after you had repeatedly told him of them, and desired him to hear."

"That's true. I tell'd him first about it."

"Well, Paddy, there are numerous cases in the books, I think, quite as remarkable as yours. Men have seen spectres—ghosts— stalking about their rooms and sitting in their very chairs, when nobody else, though in the same room, could see anything! Now, if one's eyes could see, why not the eyes of two? if one pair of ears could hear, why not all? That they do not see and hear, seems conclusive that the seeing and hearing person is under some diseased condition of his own system, the nerves or brain, or both, just as your friend Hartley conjectured."

"Well, you're not far out, Wharncliffe. I said, from the first, that I had no doubt, that bekaise of my sins—and they were enough, I reckon, to put me at the marcy of the devil—I had very likely put myself further from God, and nearer to Satan; and he took advantage of it! That's the very thing I've been trying to tell you; that jest as in the condition of the body, there's a preticklar liableness to disease; so there is a preticklar condition of the sowl when there's a preticklar liableness to the powers that act upon the soul. God chooses his prophet, I reckon, from a preticklar sort of man, preticklar by raison that his sowl is aisy to be worked upon as God plaises; and so the Devil, he acts his meracles upon them that's laid themselves open to his arts and temptations. Two men from our parts shall go down to Charleston in mid-summer; one of them shall take the yellow fever and die, and the other shall come away without a touch of fever. And why? Only bekaise the one shall be in sich a condition of body as to catch anything that's going; and the other not! One shall be taken and the other left; yet both shall be in the same outer sarcumstances; both in the same house and air; doing the same business and liable to the same exposure to the sun and night! and jest so of the sowl of man! Ef, by my doings and thinkings, I lay my sowl open to the Powers of the Air, they can take the gripe of me, and hold on, jest so long as my heart is foul, and my feelings, and thinkings, and doings, is agin the natheral laws of God. It's jest so much law. I puts myself under a steam ingine and am crushed. Ef I didn't put myself there, no harm's done. I put my finger in a vice, and it squeezes it to pieces. I had only to keep my finger away and be safe. Every power works according to law, and don't axe whose body, or whose finger it is that's under the wheel, or in the vice. It works on, whether it's got a body to crush up or not. And the law, for the powers of the air, is the same law as that for the wheel and the vice. They work on, all the time, jest as the winds do—regular like the sun, moon and stars—and we humans pass on under 'em, or not under 'em, jest as we happen to be doing, thinking or feeling. Ef I happens to be feeling bad passions, and have a liking to the 'Seven Deadly Sins,' one or all of 'em, I come under the operation of these powers, jest as much as I should under the wheel and vice, ef I went deliberate to them, and throw'd my body down, or stuck my finger in, and prehaps, gentlemen, there's a preticklar nather that's always more liable than another nather. Some men don't sin much, bekaise they don't do much of any sort of business. I knows men who are harmless as rabbits; that jest sit down, feed and sleep; and hardly say anything. Other men are always a-doing and talking, working in some way; restless and oneasy ef they aint a-doing; and I'm one of them. Ef I ain't a-doing good, you may be sure I'm doing bad; for I'm sure to be doing something. And them's the kind of men that's always in danger. And them's the sort of men that Providence, or the Devil, will always be choosing out for their work; for the idle, aisy sort of men, that do nothing, I don't count them altogether as men at all! They come into life, and go out of life, and nobody axes for them while they stay, and nobody misses them when they go! I reckon they ha'nt got sowls at all; for it's sartin they never makes any use of 'em; and tho' they may do nothing bad, they do nothing good; and who shall tell what their thinkings and feelings may be; and how vicious they might have been, had they only manhood enough to be anything. Now, whether it's for good or for evil, I bless the good Lord that he made me a man! I aint too lazy, or too scary, to do my work, and to face any danger; and though I was sore bruised all over, after that tussle with the infarnal stump, yet I felt a sort of pride, that I had wrestled with the Devil, and had him onder me, though he did fling me off, and roll over me, and made me sore; and I don't suppose I hurt him much; yet, d——n him, I was atop of him more than once, and after that I rether wished for the chaince to mount him again!"

"But, Paddy——"

"Stop a bit, Wharncliffe! I aint done answering you yit. You tells me of a person seeing a sperrit setting in his chair, or walking all about the room, and no body else able to see him; and you argy that that's proof enough that there was no sperrit, and that it was only the diseased narves or brain of the man that sees it. Now, that's the strangest sort of human raison, that a man that can't see or hear, should be a judge for him that kin; that the better the seeing and hearing, the worse the judgment. It's jest as ef you should call in a man that couldn't read, to say whether another man is reading right out of the book. All that kin be said for sich persons is that they couldn't see and could'nt hear. The human raisoning goes too fur and don't go fur enough; and it don't touch or come nigh the argyment that I makes to you. A sperrit is not sent, or meant to be seen in any or'nary way. It's a thing oncommon. We reckons that it comes for an oncommon occasion. Ef it's sent to one person, and not to another, I kin asily onderstand how the Lord should so make the law that it shall be seen and heard only by that one person. Well, he sees it bekaise of a preticklar power given to him to see it, and the other man, or men—twenty prehaps in the same room—shall, onder the same law, be made to see and hear nothing. Why, even among common humans, a man shall contrive his v'ice in a whisper, so as to tell me any thing, and you, nigh as you air, shan't hear a syllable, prehaps not see even that he speaks to me. It's either a gift in the man to see and hear the sperrit, or it's a preticular condition of his sowl and body, which makes his sight and hearing better. I knows a case of a man who was very sick, and we all thought him gwine to die, who riz up in his bed and said, 'my brother is coming; I hear his horse coming down the avenue.' And he was in a close room, the avenue half a mile long, and none of us, three in the sick room, and all of first rate hearing, could hear the sound; and yit the brother was at that very minute riding into the avenue. The sharpness of sight and hearing may come from disease, but it's a mighty great sharpness, greatly stronger sometimes, than when a man's well-doing; and the Lord may make use of the condition of the patient to put the sight before him, or the words in his ears; or it may be by a preticklar dispensation of his own, there being some need for it, that no body could see. Now, the sight of a ghost, or a sperrit from the dead, or an angel, is all put down to merac'lous accounts; but no body will say that it's merac'lous or onnatural, ef the angels and sperrits are about us at all times, day and night. Ef we belave in the immortality of the sowl, then they may be anywhere and everywhere, having their habitation in the air. The mirac'lous is in our seeing or hearing them talk, as ef 'twas not according to God's law that any mortal living man should see the dead, or the sperrits and angels of the Lord. Now, then, ef this be the law, that or'nary human sight shall not see, why, then, clearly no one kin see the sperrit 'cept the one person it is sent to."

"This, Paddy, is what we call a begging of the question."

"I don't know rightly, Wharncliffe, what you mean by that. It would seem more raisonable to be begging for an answer. But, don't you stop me in my argyment. It may sound very foolish in the ears of you l'arned men of books; but it's been a long thinking for me.

"Well, God has sent his angels, and his sperrits,—and, according to Holy Scripter, has come himself when he has had something preticklar to tell to man; and I reckon whenever the same thing needs to be done over agin he does it or has it done; and I reckon there's many a thousand in this poor, foolish world that needs it now jest as they did a thousand years ago. I reckon there's not much change in man's actions, though he now has a greater consate of himself, with his raisoning and philosophy. I reckon he sends his angel to the person who, by his daily living, and feeling, and thinking, puts himself preticklarly nigh to him; and so I reckon the devil kin make himself felt by any person who acts in a way to incourage him to take liberties with him. I belave the Lord, to this day, chooses out his agents among men—prehaps without their knowing it themselves—and they go blindly to the work—and he fits them for the things they are to do, by working upon their sowls in some way, their feelings, their minds, their hopes and their fears; and so he sends them visions, which, I reckon, are something like drhames, though clearer, and he teaches them too in drhames; and sometimes there are cases, I reckon, where a man kin only be saved by some preticklar and powerful tratement; or converted to better uses, from sinful ways; or be made to know that he has a sowl at all. So we know that Saul, afterwards Paul, was converted from his parsecution of God's people, by light from Heaven, which blinded him, and a v'ice which cried to him and told him what evil he had done and what good the Lord now wanted him to do; and though the people who were with him, saw the light, *yet they did not hear the v'ice.* And yet, in a court of law, according to human raison, Paul would be considered a parjurer, by raison of the people who were with him, who would all swear that they heard no sich speaking v'ices as he had sworen to. That's the very nather of God's merac'lous doings; that they aint common, that the v'ice and sight are for one and *not* for many, and that sperrits shall be seen and v'ices shall be heard by them that's either in the way of it themselves, by raison of the preticklar condition of their sowls, or by raison of God's preticklar merac'lous will to make them fit for his uses and purposes. As for one seeing, and the others not, I count that as no evidence of much credit, even in common affairs. There's my excellent old acquaintance, Barnaby Flint, of Lexington,—he's near-sighted, and kaint see a squirrel on a pine sappling to save his life. That's his bodily infirmity. How could he swear agin my seeing it? And so there's a sort of sowl *near-sighted-ness,* when it's not given to a man to see any thing beyond his bowels or his money box; where a man's taken up all his life, all his thoughts, and feelings, and sentiments, and affections in filling his belly; eating, and drinking, and stuffing; or, with the lucre of gain —hungering a'ter money, starving for money, thirsting for money, and delivering up his whole sowl to the mammon of onrighteousness! Why, how should sich a person see or relish any of the things of God? He's got an eye only for the one appetite. So men put themselves, by their appetites, out of the way of God and into the way of the Devil! And the Devil has his merac'lous doings too; and he works upon them, jest as they put themselves into his vice or under his wheels. As for this seeing of sperrits, gentlemen, it's curious, but a good many people in our parts belave, to this day, that the poor, innocent, dumb beasts of the field, kin, and do see sperrits; that dogs sees them constantly, and so they accounts for their howling and barking at night.

"It were more raisonable to suspect that thieves were at the hen-roost, or breaking into the meat-house.

"They barks at *them,* too, but in a different fashion. Well, I've known men to anynt their eyes with the humor that comes out of the dog's eyes, saying that would make them see sperrits too. But there's a curious account in the Holy Book of a beast seeing a sperrit when a man couldn't, and giving his evidence upon it. It's when Balaam's ass saw the angel blocking up the highway. And there was a double meracle then when the ass spoke."

"Showing that Balaam was more of an ass than his donkey."

"Don't you be talking so, Wharncliffe! 'Taint proper in you or any man. But I reckon I've said enough on this p'int. I don't count the valley of a button all the argyments I've hearn from wiser men than myself on this subject of sperrits. I find them answered in Holy Writ, and I find them answered in my own sowl and conscience, and I find 'em answered in the secret fears of the very men that spakes them. They belave and tremble, with the hair standing on an eend, like Job's, when the midnight sperrit passes over 'em. They don't see it, but they feels it, and they shiver in every limb; and then, bekaise the feeling is very oncomfortable to them—as it was meant to be—they try to argyfy themselves out of it, and to argyfy their friends too, ef only to hide their own secret fears. I tell you, my friends, there's a secret something in all your sowls, that when the proper hour comes and the clock strikes, it may be in the deep midnight, when you're all alone in the darkness, that will jest knock all your daylight and human argyments into higgledy-piggledy and bosh! I've known many a good fellow who would make all the fun in the world of ghosts and sperrits, when he was in company and the bottle gitting lighter every minute, who was the greatest coward in the world at night; but you couldn't get him to go into a grave-yard after dark! I've gone into 'em, and slept in 'em; and onst upon a time, I've helped some young doctors to dig up the bodies for desection. It was their business, and they waur right; but it worn't mine, and I was wrong for doing it; and I was sorry for it a'terwards, when I had time to think of it! And a precious deal of thinking I've had to do upon this same matter of ghosts and sperrits, and witchcraft, and God's workings upon man, and the Devil's workings! Many and many an hour I've set down in my dug-out, when I could catch no fish, and tried my best to catch the right idee of what I was in this world, what I hed to do, and what the Lord was doing to me, or letting the Devil do; and the more I l'arned from the thinking, the more mean I felt; the more I felt that there waur a thousand mean as well as devilish things that had power over us, and the more I felt that we waur too full of consate about our mortal wisdom, trying to find a human raisin for the very things that God has put above all raisin and beyant all s'arching out, I'm sartin that he has thrown what the orator call'd the impenetrable wale over a thousand mysteries, and that we kaint lift that wale till He pleases. But we must belave that there's a great deal behint it that's working for us and upon us, whether for good or evil, the Lord only knows! and I belave it's for the good! I knows this, that, in spite of all my throubles and sorrows and vexations, I'm a better man this last five years than I was before, when nothing was a-troubling me!"

CHAPTER XIV.

"Some heavenly power guide us
Out of this fearful country."
THE TEMPEST.

———

Here was a pause. It was evident that Paddy needed some rest. He filled his pipe, took his seat and puffed away for awhile in profound silence. This silence nobody seemed disposed to break. What we had heard was calculated to require some reflection, and Paddy appeared to think so. A little by-play between Jamison and Wharncliffe, touching superstitions generally, did not move him even to look up, but he puffed away at his pipe very strenuously; meanwhile the short conversation died out, and another pause of expectation succeeded. We were all resolved to hear Paddy out, and to make a night of it.

A signal from Wharncliffe, and I filled our cups from the steaming kettle. We all drank, and Paddy was, at length, called upon to resume his narrative. I may remark, that we only occasionally offered any interruption to his progress, and this was only by a brief question or two. I have not thought it necessary to note the instances. In fact, whatever our commentary or opinion might be, such was the stern earnestness of the narrater, such his vivacity and rapidity, his animation, rising at times into bursts very like eloquence, and that the most natural in the world, that none of us felt any disposition to interrupt him. He might have been an orator—would have made a great jury pleader. That he solemnly believed every syllable of his own report none of us could doubt—that he had reasoned himself into a full faith, also, in his peculiar pneumatology was equally unquestionable. He resumed,—still upon his "argyment," and not his narrative.

"Well, now, gentlemen, you see that I went on a-thinking; and I asked myself, why, if it was the devil, and he wanted to try a wrastle with me, he didn't come in his own shape and figger, and not put himself into the rough sides of a half-charred stump of pine? But I answered that—'The Devil knows his own business best! He kin take what shape he pleases! Besides, what is the devil's shape and figger? Who kin say? One time, we hears that it's a sarpent; another time, a dragon—which, I reckon, is a sort of alligator, with wings; and sometimes, so they tells us, he comes like an angel of light—which, I reckon, is jest as ef he looked like the prettiest woman in the world!' But I soon come to think that, whenever sperrits do take the throuble to consarn themselves with men, they takes always the most natheral shape in the world! Job sees a shadow in the night—and a shadow is natheral to the night; it was only a deeper and a darker shadow. Now, in all sitivations, when I've seen, or fancied I've seen sperrits, they've gone by me like a cloud or a shadow. Sometimes, a flash seems to cross me in the woods; and when I looks, it's an opening in the trees, and that sometimes looks like a mortal figger. Then, when I hears a sound in the woods that startles me, it's like the rush of a wing; and what's so natheral to the woods as the rushing of a bird's wing? But though 'twas like, 'twas onlike! And why should it startle me? I hears the *raal* sound, and it don't make me jump or look round. I sees the *raal* tree, or the *raal* shadow, or the *raal* natheral stump, but no v'ices come from them; and I passes on. But jest when I ixpects nothing, and fears nothing, I feels something—a wing brushes acrost me—a hand presses upon my shoulder—something goes by; and then I hears the v'ices, near or far, that sound jest enough like human v'ices to make me *feel* that they're *not* human! It's a mystery of the sowl, gentlemen—a mirac'lous something— to keep the sowl alive in itself, and watchful; and keep our hearts from gitting too proud and insolent about worldly things; and keep us from all greediness, whether it's food, or drink, or money!— Them's my thinkings, my friends, on all them subjects.

"But to begin again. I went home after that wrastle with the stump, or the devil, and didn't feel much the hurts till the next morning. Then I found myself sore, and black and blue all over! But I got up and went about, trying to do something about the farm, patching up the garden fence for my ould mother, and putting up a pen for the pigs. She seed my face scratched and bruised up, and axed me how I come by it.

" 'Honestly,' says I, 'rolling over a crooked log.'

"The partridges, that had been the first cause of that trouble, she had cooked for breakfast, and mighty fine and fat they waur. If the devil had raaly raised 'em up like chickens, he had plenty of cow-peas to feed 'em on! The ould woman and myself ate two a-piece, and we had the other five for dinner; but I couldn't help thinking, while I crunch'd the bones, of what the beast said to me about the meanness of knocking over the birds squat upon the ground! I know'd 'twas right what he said. 'Twarn't the sportsman's way of shooting partridges; but 'twas the meat I was a'ter, and not the sport; and the truth is, I had got so jub'ous about my own skill in shooting, that I mistrusted my chaince of doing anything with 'em on the wing.

"But all that's neither here nor there. I worked about the farm all day and put up a few shoats for fattening. I suppose I needn't tell you—Wharncliffe knows—that I hev quite a smart farm in the Forks. Smart, no! it's poor enough—the land—and there's no great deal of it—only about 160 acres. But we've got a good log house, with a broad gallery in the middle; two good rooms, 18 by 20, and two shed rooms, a leetle more than half as large. I've an acre garden, and we raise enough to do us. We've got but two niggirs: one an old fellow, that works in the field, and raises corn, peas and potatoes; and one a gal, that waits about the house. My poor ould mother—rest her sowl—she did the spinning and weaving, and made all the cloth even when she was over seventy. We had one mule for work, and I had my saddle-horse, and a fine one, a colt of Reliance's. Two cows gave us milk and butter, and we had a few brood sows that found us in bacon. It was a God's marcy that the Devil wasn't suffered to light upon cows, and pigs, and poultry, and field or farm! I reckon 'twas my preticklar sinning that sent down the throuble upon me one! The farm kept the ould woman from want and cold, and, as long as my luck lasted, I kept her in good sperrits, with all the comforts I could git—sugar, and coffee, and tea—she liked 'em all; but I needn't go into them preticklars!

"Well, I staid at home for a matter of two days, and then, feeling the soreness of my body passing away, I went off, on the third day, jest a'ter dinner, and pushed down into the swamp, and I went straight to the place where I had the wrastle with the stump! I looked all about, but could find no sign of any sich stump, either standing or lying down! I had armed myself, the best I could, for another fight—tooth and toe-nail—if it pleased the Devil to come up to the scratch. I took my gun along, my bowie-knife, and a pocket pistol.

"In course, I know'd that all them waur carnal we'pons; but I considered that ef the devil plased to put on a mortal shape, or one of wood, why he must take the chaince of suffering something in his mortal or wooden shape. I could hurt *them,* I know'd; though it mout be I couldn't do no harm to a sperrit! But I must tell you, that for the two nights gone, I took to the Bible like a young student. By the fire light, after the ould woman had gone to bed, I laid myself down on the hairth, and spread the Holy Book out before me on the floor, and read, and read till my eyes ached. Whether any good come to me of the reading, I kaint say; but I got up and said my prayers, and preticklarly pray'd for help and wisdom from the Lord. Ef he tried me, I axed only that he should give me the strength needful to bear up under the trial; and I then jest left it to him to say whether I should be beaten down by the Etarnal Enemy, or git myself free from his gripe forever! I was willing it should be a last fight, and a death grapple between us; and I felt that he could only kill my poor mortal body! I went into the fight as the Lord's soldier—a volunteer,—and though a poor sodger enough, yet I was full of faith, and I felt bold enough to say to myself that I wouldn't show the white feather, even to the devil incarnate! And so I went to bed and slept soundly till next day, when, as I told you, I took the field with bowie-knife and gun, and s'arched the place over, looking about for the inimy. But, as I said before, he was no whar to be found. I marched up to every ugly old, odd-looking stump I could see, and rammed my gun agin it, and kick'd it, and ef I could ha' found a nose on it, I'd ha' pull'd that! —done any thing, I tell you, to provoke a fight! But 'twarnt no use; and I pleased myself with thinking that the Devil had got some bruises, too, in his wooden body, that did not heal up so soon as my own!

"I staid in the swamp two good hours in the night. I heard the owls scream, and jump'd a buck in Jamison's field, but he was too quick for me, and I warn't in the humor to throw away my loads— five pelters and a bullet in each barrel—upon any beast's jacket but the one I had set out to hunt! At last the moon rose, and I was gitting tired; but before I went, I kneeled down, thar, whar I was, in the darkest part of the swamp, and said my prayers over agin! and I vow'd to make myself a sodger of the Lord, ef he'd take me into his company, and never to desart his command for any temptations of his inimy or mine! I felt easier after the prayer, and stronger, and, as it was late, I pushed off for Saunders' farm and stayed with him all night. The next day I went home and there found Sam Hartley, who had jest come to see me. Better late than niver!

"He brought me a message from Captain John S. Jennings, who had a great fleet of rafts he wanted me to take down the river. The rafts was all gathered together at Cannon's Bridge; and waiting for me. I took but little time for preparation, and went off to see the captain and get his orders, and lay in supplies and provisions. I was to have about seventy bulls and about a dozen 'hands' to take care of—a purty large fleet. I wasn't long in gitting ready. I was in a hurry to be off: so I stowed, fast as I could, supplies for a six weeks' v'yage; plenty of bacon and meal, peas and potatoes, not forgetting a good three gallon jug of whiskey, and I carried rifle and shot gun, and bowie-knife and pistol, jest as ef I expected to meet the etarnal inemy at every turn. I fixed up the pilot raft very comfortable; made it strong with pegs and well boarded over; for I goes for being comfortable even in camp. I had a good caboose, and my river chist was a big one, with good padlock. Every thing was right and fair and square, and when I set off, Sam Hartley went down the river a few miles with me, and got out at the rail-road bridge. I think Sammy was glad to get me off, and a leetle sheepish for kaping off from me so long, preticklarly as he know'd my throubles. But I couldn't blame him much. I know'd him to be saft-hearted and skeary, and I don't blame a man who likes to keep the whole river, ef he kin, between his ribs and the Divil's pitchfork. And so I begun my v'yage, and I warn't sorry, my good friends; for you see I had a sort of hope that going off from the old range, I'd git shet of the old company, and I might git back the ould luck. In course, I didn't think that the same marciless Divil would take a'ter me and worry me in another destrict. I had no raison to belave his love for me so great as to make him travel so far from home!"

CHAPTER XV.

———

"Now comes the voyage, Paddy, I suppose!"

"Now it comes. You've niver been down the river in a raft, my friends and my good masters? Nor in a boat?"

"Never, Paddy."

"It's a mighty sweet and purty river—clear and sweet for drinking, and the trees shade you pretty much all the way till you get upon the salts; and you may do some fishing and hunting as you go. I've headed a deer in the stream, and got him by his horns. I've shot and fished sometimes every day going down. 'Twas by shooting at an eagle that Britton Elzy first l'arned to know that the shad run up the Edisto. He was going down with a flat onst, upon a time, and he seed a fish hawk dash down into the river and take up a big shiny fish. Well, a minute a'ter, he sees a mighty eagle dash down at the fish-hawk, from a mighty cypress, and as the fish-hawk seed him, he gin a scream, dropt the fish, and flew off as fast as his wings would let him. The eagle caught the fish before it fell into the river, and flew off agin to his cypress. Britton landed with his rifle, creeped up, and got a crack at the eagle. He missed him, and the eagle flew, but so skear'd that he drapt the fish. Britton pick'd it up and found 'twas the shad. That was the first that people ever know'd of shad being in the river, and that must ha' happened more than forty years ago. Britton told me himself. And now, my friends, you see a sort of picture of the way man works on man in this mean world of our'n. One robber robs the other. The fish-hawk starts the fish first; the eagle robs from the fish-hawk, and the man takes the eagle's breakfast out of his very mouth. That's the way!

335

We're a doing it from morning to night, and no body's quite sure of his pottage till he gits it fairly down his swallow. I reckon that's the raison some men ate so fast, hoping to make sure; and they use the swallow, leaving the teeth to do nothing! and from that, they says, comes dyspepsia and disease of the liver.

"Yes, it's a most beautiful fine river, and I love it, and shall love it always to my dying day; and you'd all love it, as I do, ef you know'd as much about it. But, Lord presarve you from sich a v'yage as I made, when I took down Captain Jennings' fleet."

"What! you had some adventures, then, on the voyage?"

"I reckon you may call 'em adventures! Why, I was shipwreckt and lost at say."

"Shipwreck'd and lost, Paddy! Why, is the v'yage dangerous?"

"Not a bit of it, ef you mind your eyes and keep the Devil from your elbow! As innocent a leetle river as ever swam down, singing its death song, to the say. There's no harm or danger in it tell you git upon the salts, and hardly then, if you knows your business and does it in a manful way, with a bright eye to the winds and tides and to the openings and intries. There's some danger to the rafts, from hanging on snags and harricanes."

"What do you call Harricanes?"

"Trees throwed down by Harricanes and lying secret in the river, with jest a snout and a horn riding up and hooking your timbers. But let me tell you my own way.

"You must know the whole distance from the head of navigation to Parker's Ferry is about three hundred and thirty miles. When you git to Parker's Ferry, you're upon the salts."

"What are the salts, Paddy?"

"You don't know that? Why, tide water. Well, a'ter you git thar, you count the distance, not by miles, but by the ebbs and flows of the tide. One ebb will carry your raft from Jacksonborough to Willtown Bluff; another to Black Island Cut; you pass the Cut into Dawboo river; then another ebb takes you to Peter's Cut: pass the cut and you are in Slana's River; one ebb takes you to Slana's Bluff. Here's one of the places where a head wind gives trouble, keeping you sometimes for days before you kin make White Point; from Slana's Bluff to White Point, is but one ebb, with a fair wind; and this will carry you through Hop's and Long Creeks. At

White P'int, you have the jining of White P'int and Slana's River, and here you may look out over the bar, and see the great sea—the big ocean itself, spread out and tumbling about in all its glory.— From White P'int you run with the flood tide, and this will drift you to Deadman's Cut: in this you pass Little and Big Ingadoo and Alligator on your left, and Reynold's mud-flat on your right. Well, the river from White P'int to New Cut is counted dangerous, for, you see, there are large creeks and sounds on both sides, and your rafts are apt to be drawed in by the suck, and when this happens, you've got to git bac' by the ebb, into the main channel again; and should you miss to make your rafts fast at this place why then you stand a most beautiful chaince of being carried out to say, and ef so, it's pretty much all dicky and the divil with you, as 'twas with me. The rafts kaint run from White P'int to New Cut ef the wind's a-blowing. You will be into the marshes at high wather, and thar you'll be apt to stick forever, onless a spring tide comes to help you; and even ef you gits off thar, when you pass the P'int, the wind may blow you ashore on t'other side, and thar you'll stick agin, unless you get the spring tide to come in to your help; and even then, ef the wind should chop about, it may blow you out into the etarnal jaws of the say! Well, to go on. From Dead Man's Cut, one tide will take you to the Narrors; one more through New Cut and into Church's Flats; and here you are at the head of Stono.—From this, one ebb will take you to Rantowle's; another to Wappoo; you pass then, through Wappoo, with the flood, and thar you are at Ashley river, with the ould city of Charleston before you, lying like a great tarrapin in the water, with a world of steeples and churches and houses on her back.—With one ebb you crosses the Ashley to the city—that is, ef the wind's fair—but I've know'd many a fleet that could'nt get across for ten days and two weeks. And so we run the or'nary v'yage, ef nothing goes wrong with the machinery. I've drawed a sort of map of the river, for Wharncliffe, years ago, and I reckon he's got it yit."

Wharncliffe nodded his head.

"That was done when he was in the Legislature, and, wanting to git a canal cut from Edisto to Ashley, so as to cut off all the dangers and difficulties of the navigation; but I suppose it'll take a few more ginirations to git our Legislature to the working of that measure out—it's too wise a measure for or'nary times and men to take hold of. We must wait upon men just as we wait upon God; and ontill he sends 'em, with the right sense of what they've got to do, we may be waiting forever. It's mostly the business of them people of Charleston to git this thing done, for they gits all the trade of the Edisto, and it's the great lumber river for the city. Ef an inimy now was blockading the Stono, and running up North Edisto, they could'nt git a log or a plank from the quarter 'cept by railroad, and then it costs more than it comes to. But I must leave that to our Legislators, them wise men that say yea and nay and eat ground nuts by way of studying the argyment.

"Well, you may consider me fairly started, and feeling better and in more sperrits than I had done for some time past. Sam Hartley travelled with me down to the railroad crossing, and then bid me good-bye and jumped ashore. Poor fellow! he was fond of me, but mightily afear'd of my Divil! He giv me a good deal of advice about rigilar saying my prayers, and he left with me a pocket Bible to read in, and he seemed to think that now I was off the ground and going into another destrict I would be let alone. But hardly had he got out ashore before I haird a big 'hoo! hoo! hoo!' jest beyant me, in the tree tops ahead, by which I know'd that the beast was a watching me! I only prayed that he had jest come to say 'good-bye.' But that warn't his idee, as you'll hear a'terwards.

"It was good weather and a good river; pretty full, and the chaince small for snags and harricanes. I had got things pretty comfortable on the pilot raft, hed a caboose, as I told you, and my kit full of everything that was neecessary to eating and drinking. There was a bed made of clay for fire. The niggers had a good supply, too, of bacon, meal and potatoes, and one of them played the fiddle, and all of 'em were sprigh, active fellows, and purty well behaved, according to color. We had a jolly time of it going down, and lived together like a well rigilated family that hed enough; where every one knowed what he hed to do, and was willing to do it; and we had time enough for fiddling, and singing, and dancing. All went on smooth enough for the first few days.

"When we got into the big river, we harnessed the fleet and got the bulls together. We met several other rafts that come in from the north Edisto. I know'd pretty much all the people. Among the white men was Kiah Clarke, a queer leettle fellow, with a bald head, and a big bump on the top of it, that I reckon he got in some night scrimmage from the butt of a hammer. He never could say a word, but he must begin with a 'blast me!' So he says, 'Blast me, Paddy, is that you, agin' on the river?' 'Blast me, Paddy, hev' you niver a drink for a thairsty swallow?' and so on to the eend. And there was Bill Barrs, a leetle old chap of sixty-five, with a small, sneaking, drawling, droning sort of v'ice, who was always a talking uf 'Sally and the children, and Pompey, my horse.' He was mighty consated of all of them, and prehaps, Pompey, as much as any. One day, on the river, I seed him jump ten feet from the bank on to the raft, and cry out, when I axed what skeer'd him, 'May I niver see Salley and the children, ef thar ain't an alligator as big as Pompey, my horse.' They were in his mouth always, and I reckon the poor ould fellow hed 'em in his heart too. And then there was Solomon Johnson, the half-breed; but you all knows him as fisherman, and hunter, and raftsman; and ef he's good for any thing, he's good for all three of them trades.

"Well, we all got on together without any trouble. I needn't tell you how we passed 'Walker's Suck,' and Silliman's Ferry, near to Jacksonborough. When we got to Graham's reaches, we tied up there; heard the fiddle going at Nelly Miller's, and we all pushed ashore, white and black, to have a leetle fun. Night had set in, and 'twas pretty dark. But there was a big blaze at Nelly's, outside the house an' in, and we could hear the shuffling and tramping of the feet, all a dancing. You must know Nelly Miller and her gals didn't keep the most respectable house on the river; but it was a mighty pleasant place for a frolic among the rough fellows of the rafts. She got her money by accommodating them handsome.

"Well, when we got to the house we found some thirty people, men and women, white and black, all in full fun and feather, capering, dancing and singing, with a black fiddler playing all sort of tunes, all in a jumble. There waur lots of liquor, drink a plenty, and a good number of the men and one or two of the women waur already 'How come you so?' Our party made the crowd a good deal more crowdy. We hed hardly room to turn; but we all turned in—who but we; and, I confess, I was about as ready for a *blow-out* as any of the company. As the liquor sarculated the room got smaller, the company

bigger, and so half of the party pushed out in the yard, and they
begun dancing out there and in the peazzir. Then there was a quarrel
for the fiddler, as to who should hev him; but this was soon stopt
by my fiddler putting in and satisfying both parties. We were at it
all night—one fun a'ter another; and what with dancing and drinking, one or two small fights, and a good deal of cussing and swearing,
we waur all of us troubled with 'big head' in the morning. It was
in May, and the next day set in with cloud and rain. But we went
on. When we got to White P'int, which we did, all safe, we were
fairly wrapt up in thunder and lightning. We fastened all safe at
White P'int, and then went ashore to Mother Jordan's, to have
another frolic. The last one, at Nelly Miller's, had jest given us
one heat and a most tremenduous appetite for another.

"Well, a most tremendous frolic we made of it, drinking and dancing, cussing and swearing, whooping and fighting. I had a little
skrimmage with a sailor fellow, Ben Blower, who, I reckon, hed
run away from some coasting schooner. He was a big boned chap,
mighty strong and active, and full of quarrel. Like all sailor fellows,
he wanted to hev his own way on land, and he capsized my fiddler,
with a side wipe, bekaise he played to my orders, and not his'n.
I wouldn't stand by and see any nigger in my command knock'd about
like a foot ball, so I clipt my sailor under his ear, and downed him.
But he soon got on his legs again, and made at me, and then I found
him a purty tough customer. But, in the eend, I thrashed him till
he couldn't stand on his feet or see out of his eyes. I didn't git off
myself without a sore nose and my right eye in mourning. The
fighting stopt the dancing for awhile, but didn't stop the drinking.
I made free with the mouth of the bottle, and so did all the rest;
but the fight did a good deal to sober me; and then I thought of the
rafts, and 'membered I was at White P'int. So, taking another drink,
I slipt out to get into the cool air, and look at the night. It was cloudy,
and mighty dark. There warn't a star to be seen. I was a-going back
into the house, meaning to set down quiet by the fire to a long pipe,
and wind up by a mouthful of the naked eye-wather, when jest over
my head I heard that dern'd 'Hoo! Hoo! Hoo!' loud as thunder,
and shrill in my ears like the screaming of a jackass. I felt a cold
shiver go through me, for it seemed to say, 'I hevn't let you off,

my boy; I've got you yit; I'm following you, and I'll follow you to
the eend!'

"It meant mischief, that hellabaloo! I felt that; and it made me
more skeary and more sober! I wasn't onsteady from the drink, but
I felt a sort of oncertainty of sperrit. Then I began to raison with
myself, and I said to myself—

" 'Here we're at White P'int, looking out upon the big say: the
wind's a-rising, and the place is dangerous for a raft to be in. Here,
I've got Capt. Jennings's fleet of more than seventy bulls; and I've
got a dozen of his niggers to see a'ter and take care of. 'Twont do to
drink any more liquor, Paddy McGann. 'T'wont do to be fighting and
capering any more, Paddy McGann. You must say to your business,
Paddy; say to your rafts, Paddy; say a'ter your niggers, Paddy;
and the sooner you say to them the better for all hands.'

"With that raisoning, I began to call for the niggers—Primus,
Dick, Ned, Peter, Sam, Bob, and the rest; but not one of the
scamps would answer; and every one slipt off, I reckon, with some
gal, into the woods. I then seed twarn't of no use to hunt 'em up
then; that they waur in for the frolic, and out for the night; and
all my hunting and whooping would be to no purpose. So I considered then, 'twas the best I could do to go down to the rafts, and
see ef all was right thar! So down I went, and I tried the rope of
the head raft on the stump I had fastened it to, and I found all
right. Then I went aboard and looked about and into every thing.
All was right. I belave there warn't a human aboard any one of the
long stretch of rafts, far up as the eye could say, 'cept meself one.
So I walked up and down, mighty lonesome. The night was a-gitting
chilly. I reckoned it was two hours from daylight. I could hear
the big say groaning outside, jest like a great monster that feels
some throuble in his sleep. But a thick gray wale seemed to hang
before me, wherever I turned my eye, 'cept back in the one quarter
where you could see mother Jordan's fire a-burning—the flame
fighting with the thick mist, that seemed trying to smother it up
all the time. I could hear all the time the whooping, the fiddle, and
the shaking of heavy feet. I had a strong itching to go back and
work out the night along with 'em; but I felt a sort of jubousness
that something would go wrong ef I did. So I kept walking the
raft till I began to feel chilly; then I thought of the caboose, where

it was warmer, and of the whiskey, which I always found to have a pleasant warming in it.—Well, with me, to think of a thing is to go at it: so I went to the caboose, and got myself a drink! Then I come out and walked my decks agin. It was getting darker, and I could feel the fog pressing upon me. It was so thick I could ha' cut it with my knife. I could see nothing but the grey fog; but where it jined the water I couldn't tell, and what was fog and what was say, was onpossible to make. I could hear the moaning of the wind and say out at a distance—moaning like a suffering sperrit— that was all; the only sound, 'cept, now and then, the scream of the fiddle and the whoops of the people at mother Jordan's. After awhile they got to be more and more fainter; I reckon bekaise more and more of the dancers were stretching off, pretty well drunk, to git what sleep they could in that mighty hubbub, and without any exartion a'ter it. I couldn't sleep. I paid another visit to the caboose, tuk another drink, and felt myself stretching my jaws a-yawning. But still I didn't feel sleepy, only oneasy and restive, and I don't remember lying down. I must have done so, half asleep, for while I was drinking, I could feel my eyes a-shutting too, heavy and slow, like some big gates that move slowly on rusty hinges. I reckon I jest dropt down whar I was, as soon as I hed swallow'd my liquor.

"I don't remember any more of what happened while I was awake. But in my sleep, I had a most tremenduous drhame, of the biggest owl in the world, taking me off the top of my chimbley, on his wings; I riding on his back as ef he was a horse; and he carrying me, full speed down the river, fast as he could fly, whooping, all the time, with the most infarnal 'Hoo! Hoo! Hoo!' that had iver shivered my senses.

"Now, whether it was the drhame only, or that I did sartainly hear that 'Hoo! Hoo! Hoo!' I kaint altogether say for sartin. I'm thinking that I did hear it, and, from what I tells you, a'terwards, I reckon you'll think so too. But niver mind that now! The drhame, or the scrame, may have waken'd me, one or t'other, or it mout be, both. But I wakened, and found it broad day light. In the next minute, I felt an oneasy motion of the raft, as ef 'twas riding on a heavy wave. Then I jumped out of the caboose, and Oh! Lord, what do you think? I *was* riding on a wave; and thar was another one jist afore me, and to mount; and another; and another! I looked where the fog was a-lifting, and I felt myself shiver to my very shoes, and my heart a sinking to the very bottom of my stomach! I was out at say, me one,—one alone,—on my one poor pilot raft; going out fast as I could drive, and the land already far away behint me, and sinking at the starn!

"I drapt down, all at onct, upon my knees. I prayed to the Lord, that is, I tried to pray, for my deliverence and salvation! But I had a'most forgot how! The words wouldn't come. They stuck in my throat. I was fairly choking with 'em!

"Then I remembered poor Sam Hartley, and all his prayings and exhortings for me, and his last advice to me to be always a-praying for myself, and I had forgot all as soon as we parted! Jest as soon as I had got mixed up with other company, I was divarted from all other thoughts. I was jest led off, like a redic'lous boy, thinking only of my sports and pleasures, sich as they waur! Oh! what a fool I was!

"And now where was I? Jest swallowed up in the great deeps, and the says gwine over me!

"I reckon'd it must be so pretty soon. Ef the wind and says waur to rise, what could save me? Nothing but the strong arm of the Lord, and his etarnal marcies!

"I looked out upon my condition. There was I going, on, on, on, fast as the says could drive me, on for the big gulf! The gulf! What a name! Enough to terrify of itself! I might be drifted on the coast of Cuba. I might be tore to pieces by the winds and waves, long before I got there. Any sort of a say would sweep over me and wash me overboard, and then I might be tore to pieces by the shirks, long before my eyes were sot fast in death! I might feel 'em, a dozen of 'em, may be, pulling me to pieces, this way and that; and, as I thought, I pulled up my legs, drawed in my arms, and jest set down a shivering all over.

"Oh! Lord, for a leetle piece of dry land! Anything in the shape of a solid, if only a foot square to stand upon. A bank of raccoon oysters would ha' been to me a sort of Paradise; and I looked all round me with a feeling of desperate hope to see something to catch at. There was the shore gitting lower and lower—and everywhere nothing but the etarnal say. I threw myself flat on my face, and groaned to pierce the skies!

"But I felt, a'ter a little while of desperation, that I was bound to be a man—that I must try—that I must do all I kin, to make the danger less, and keep myself safe as long as I kin! The longer the better! It mout be that some ship going along would git a sight of me, and pick me up before it was too late. So I jumped up to my feet and begun to consider. It was a need 'cessity to think quick, and I did think as rapid as a steam ingine!

"I ran to my caboose where I had my chist. I had a hammer, hatchet and some twenty-penny nails. There was a dozen loose plank lying across the timbers of the raft. I laid them level, and across, and nailed 'em down fast, a good big nail in every stock. I floored the raft over, and strengthened it in this way, and knowed that, unless the winds came on to blow hard, making a heavy sea, the raft would hold together for a month. Then I tuk the tiller pole, onshipped it, and stuck it between plank and timbers, and fastened one of my shirts to it as a sort of flag of distress. It was one of my new shirts that I was to wear when I got to Charleston. Then I nailed down the bottom of my chist, itself, to two of the stocks, so that no say could wash it off so asily. I then got a rope and slipt it round one of the planks, and made it fast; the upper ends I left loose, and long enough, to tie round my body and make myself fast, ef the seas began to roll over me. Then I tuk my raft pole and sounded; but, Lord love you, I was a mile beyont soundings, I reckon, before I opened my eyes in the morning!

"The next thing I had to see to was after the provisions. For me one, the potatoes would sarve a month; the bacon, the meal and the whiskey. But I had'nt a spark of fire to cook with, and what was the chaince of my keeping up a fire with the seas a-washing over me? But I longed for the fire, seeing as it is a cheerful companion; and then I thought the smoke of it might draw the eyes of other voyagers that waur too far off to see my signal flag. I then suddenly ricollected that I used to carry matches in my chist. I run to it, and found no less than three boxes, half full each, and some loose ones scattered in the chist. Finding these, I felt stronger in the sperrit. There was the clay fire-place, too, pretty thick laid on, and the water had'nt got to it yit! It was made on a bed of thick slabs, and right in the middle of the raft; and there was a pile, a'most half a cord of wood, with several big sticks of lightwood. I begun to make a fire at onst, and soon had a big blaze, and a great smoke rising up from me in the middle of the say! In the water kag, I found a plenty of water, more than enough for a month's v'yage with only one man to drink. Of the whiskey, I reckon I had about two gallons left in the jimmyjohn. Things looked brighter to my eyes; I got to walk my deck like a man; and, feeling better, I felt now that I could say my prayers. I downed on my knees and made as farvent a prayer as I iver made in all my life. It was from the bottom of my heart; and jest as I was done praying, the sun came out to shine with a flash, and I felt in a sort of glory, jest as ef I had taken a pull of sich fine punch as we've got here now. I felt now as ef I could go through a big fight, and ef I had to die, why I'd die like a man, looking up, not down, and not sneaking to my grave with a liver whiter than my shirt. After that I tuk a drink, and then walked my deck, looking out upon my sarcumstances.

"They wasn't raally any better. It was only as I felt that I made 'em out so. I was driving on, I know'd by the course I took, further and further out into the big say. Low down as I stood, I had, by this time, quite lost all sight of the land. Was I iver to see it again? my own home—my old river—my friends and people! Och! would'nt I have taken my chaince, with all my trouble, from the divil of the swamp, to be once more knocking about in these here etarnal swamps, though I niver hit my mark, or caught another trout from the river!

"And so things looked bright, or dark, jest as my sperrit, come and went; jest according to my feelings. It's so with man. The color of his feelings makes the sunshine and the cloud, makes the happiness or the misery; and so it's of much more consequence to him to hev' a clear world in his own heart, than to hev' a bright one out of doors.

"Well, by this time, I thought it high time to take another drink! I did so! I had no desire after food; but I put a peck or two of potatoes in the fire to roast, thinking that ef the seas washed out my fire, I could still have a supply in the locker. Meantime, I was rolling and rocking away. Fortynit for me, the seas was smooth enough, and there was little wind. My raft was pretty tight and strong, now that I had nailed the plank down upon the stocks and I felt that it would stand a pretty hard blow. My worst danger was from heavy seas breaking over me, and sweeping off everything that was loose. Well, I exercised myself in making all as tight as could be. I had some rope, and nails enough, and I sarched all about where to tie a rope or drive a nail. I find that's the only way in this world, to be always a doing, ef you wouldn't go mad, or turn into something meaner than a nigger's dog.

"Well, as I was looking about, and stirring to do, and find something to do with, on a suddent, I sees, floating astarn, the rope that I had used to make fast the raft to the shore, the night she broke away and went adrift; and, at the eend of the rope, there was the identical stump which I had tied it to.

"The rope was a first rate one, and quite new, and I seed a use I could put it to, in strengthening the timbers of my raft, or in tying down some of the things that might be swept off. There was my meal barrel, my meal and potatoes, all wanting to be made fast.

"Well, I went astarn, took hold of the rope and began pulling in, but 'twas just as ef I had set to pull in a man of war, or a brick house; the cussed log hung so heavy at the eend. That seemed strange to me, for how could it float so, ef 'twas so heavy. I pulled and pulled, ontill my very hands and fingers began to feel stiff and sore.—Well, I reckon I must have got considerable weak from wanting food that day, for I hadn't had the heart to eat a mouthful. So I let go the rope, and took another good pull of whiskey; then I turned in, and eat a couple of good sized potatoes, and I washed all down with another drink of whiskey. That was four drinks, gentlemen, my very good friends and masters, that I had tuk that day—"

"Don't forget, Paddy, that you were at it pretty nearly all night."

"I don't forget, Wharncliffe; but you remember I had very sound sleep after that drinking, and the effects was pretty much done off by this time, for it was now after 12 o'clock by the sun. In fact, I rether reckon'd it to be about 2 in the a'ternoon."

"But the size of the drinks must be taken into consideration, Paddy."

"Only two fingers deep, Wharncliffe, in a horn cup with a narrow bottom."

"Still, pretty good, I fancy."

"And these, Paddy," said Jamison, "were also taken on an empty stomach."

"That's true, Jamison; but that wouldn't make a difference, onst you consider the mighty desperation of my sarcumstances.—Drunk isn't so aisy to come, my friends, when death is a grinning in your very face! It's enough to tell you that I warn't drunk then, and warn't likely to be drunk. I was steady as a rock; and a'ter swallowing my potatoes, and drinking my whiskey, I felt myself strong as a horse. So I begun again at pulling in the rope, putting all my strength into it, and, Lord presarve you, would you belave it, the rope came into me as slick and easy as a young creathor, when she tells you to ax her mammy. There was no pulling or straining needful. All went slick as grease, and I got the rope up, till the log lay along-side of the raft.

"Now come the hard work. I laid down upon the raft and tried to loose the knot, but some how it had been made so fast, and was in sich a tangle of knots, that I couldn't start it no how. I tried to slip it over the stump, but it was fastened about the middle, and pretty close to the wood. After I had worried my fingers to no purpose, I thought of cutting it loose with my hatchet, but when I seed the long piece of rope, a'most three feet, that hung on t'other side of the knot I was onwilling to lose it; so I thought, at last, I'd try and raise the log itself; it would do for firewood, for it was a lightwood stump. How it ever come to break off, or git out of the ground, I wondered for awhile; but I did not wonder long. The explanation come, of itself, mighty soon a'ter.

"Well, I squared myself off as well as I could, and, on my knees, I bent over, and got a good grip of the cussed stump. On land, with a fair footing, I knowed I could lift it mighty aisy. But, in the fix I was, on the eend of the raft, and kneeling besides, I knew 'twould take all my strength and skill to do the business. Well, I tried, and got up one eend, and rested it on the but-eend of the string-piece of the raft. Then I tried it at the other eend. But when I got that up, the first eend slipt off; and when I got up that again, and tried the other, then was another slip; and so it went on tell I was almost wearied out. At last, I caught up the cussed thing in the middle, with both arms, and was bringing it up, though twas a mighty hard strain, when, all on a suddent, without my knowing the why or wherefore, I went over into the big say—head over heels! It seemed as ef the cussed stump had pulled me over, but that you won't belave. You'll be saying I only lost my balance. But, what'll you say, when, as I caught the log to float by, the cussed thing went down straight as it could drive, for the bottom. You'll say agin, bekaise I was too heavy for it. Well, I let go soon enough, and struck out for the raft, which was now good twenty feet off. But, thanks to the Lord, I was a first-rate swimmer. But, Lord love you, I was so skeard at the idee of being soused over in the wide deep say, that I hedn't half my strength or half my skill. And then, again, I thought of the bloody shirks, and I thought I could see a dozen of 'em coming at me with open mouths. Then I was desperate mad with the fright, and, hardly knowing how, I got to the raft and caught the rope; and what do you think? It was now altogether loose of the stump, and the dern'd stump gone! That made me sartin who my inimy was, and how my raft come to drift away with the ebb—it one—leaving all the rest of the fleet behint.

"I was soaking and shivering. I feel all the sensations now, and ef so be, Stiles has got any of that punch ready, I'd be for axing you, my friends, to jine with me, ef only to take the cold chill off my stomach! I tuk it then soon as I could get at the whiskey, and I wants it now, ef only to take off the memory of the transaction."

CHAPTER XVI.

The Voyage—Night—The Devil in the Wood-Pile—A Narrow Escape.

———

"Well, my friends, you've all been to sea, I reckon, and know something about it. I rather think that every man feels a leetle skeary or skeamish, when he first goes upon the great deep; but how do you suppose I stood up onder my skear—at sea—on a raft—me one, alone—with nothing to steer by, and nothing to catch a wind, or to make steam—just drifting about at the marcy of the winds and waves? Och! my masters, but it was a powerful strange skeary feeling that took me betwixt wind and water; took the very breathing from me, when I thought of it; jest as a fellow, driving a heavy fist into your breadbasket, takes the wind and the sense out of you both together. I don't pretend to be above a skear, when I'm onused to the danger, and havn't got any we'pons to fight against it. I was, I may say, like a man gwine into a fight, with his natheral we'pons all cut off. It's true, I hed arms and hands, but how to bridle the wind and ride the sea, and steer the raft, without sail or oar, or rudder! What I could do, with hands and arms, I did, as I told you already; and I kept on doing, jest so long as I could see where I could drive a nail, or plant a blow; and that done, why, down on my marrow-bones to prayer!

"But prayer aint easy to a man of my temper, that's always trying a'ter something to do. In the very middle of the prayer, I'll be thinking of something to be done, and then I forgits the proper eending of the prayer, or huddles it all up in confusion, so that the eend is pretty apt to forget the beginning. But, I prayed as well as I know'd how, for my heart was in it. I know'd that I was in the hands of the great Lord of the etarnal univarsal world, and no eye

349

seeing my sitivation but his own! And ef his arm warn't stretched out to save, or ef he didn't send the human help, in good season, why there's no saving in a case like mine!

"I know'd all that, and felt it; and so I prayed, and, having prayed, I looked out upon the say, East and West, North and South, with the biggest eyes of ixpectation that ever stared out of a poor mortal's head! And so I saw the great sun go down. He sot for awhile on the very edge of the waters, a-looking into my very face. And he seemed to me as ef he had a mortal eye in the face, and was looking at me in sorrow! Soon the face looked like a great bushy head, with human hair, but of the very reddest gould color. And it was the beautifullest, terriblest sight I iver seed—that great sun—so parfect and so big, looking so human at me, as ef he would like to stay longer, but going down at last with a suddent rush, that seemed fairly to set a-fire the big waters that were burying him. And over his burial place, there was a sort of goulden and purple crown; and it was as ef onseen sperrits waved an army of bright beautiful flags over him; and then, soon a'ter, came the black pall—Och! how black it was!—of the etarnal night!

"I niver seed sun set so fast. I niver seed the dusk last so long, onlighted by any stars. All around me, the sea looked black; and there was no telling, for a time, where the waters eended and the sky begun? Black and solid—a solid black wall—was built all round me in an eye-twink; and the winds seemed to me to howl the louder, and there was a great sighing over the waters, as ef the sperrits of the dead were beginning their sorrows at the burial of another poor human sinner!

"I sot squat upon my raft, in the very centre, and throw'd fresh pieces of lightwood on the fire. I hadn't the heart or the strength to cry or pray. I jest sot quiet, frowning back at the sea! But it niver minded my looks. It rolled on, and the little waves broke over my raft at every surge. Fortynit for me, there was not much wind, and the clear sunset was a security for a good day to-morrow. But that security didn't help my sperrits much! And so I tried the whiskey! A'terwards, I ate a couple of potatoes for my supper. My fire was burning well, and putting up a big blaze, that could be seen from a ship, I reckon, more than ten miles, so long as the sea kept down. That was my only chaince to be diskivered at night, and to keep myself from being run down in the dark by some passing vessel. Life was very sweet to me, my masters, as it is even to this day; and I did, and tried all I could, to keep up strength and sperrits, and heart and soul, and to make sure agin accidents of every sort.

"But 'twas hard work to keep from sinking down, and giving up, a'ter that thick darkness came on. But I recollected what Sam Hartley said to me so often—

" 'Niver give up! Niver say die!'

"So I braced myself up for whatever was to happen, thinking it jest as well to give in a'ter I had gone down.

"Well, my masters, it's supprising how a leettle thing lifts us up, jest as a leetle thing can throw us down. On a suddent, a most beautifullest star shined out before me. I couldn't tell which was the p'int of the compass, but it looked like the star in the East—it was such a beautiful gould color, and so big, and so bright. And soon a'ter, I seed another jest above it; and while I was looking at them two, both in a line, up and down, out come a third, jest below it, and at equal distance. And the three seemed to me like a staff put into my hand for support; and I says, 'This is a staff from God.' I couldn't lay hands on it, but it seem'd as ef my soul grasp'd the idee; and I said agin:

" 'I will hold on to this staff of God. It is a sign to me, He will not let me sink.'

"A'ter that the stars come out broadcast, thick as white bolls in a prime cotton field; and I lay back on the raft a-watching 'em; and some seemed to gather into diamonds, and some into squares, and some into sarcles, all round, and I found they all lived in families, and had relations—a thing which I had niver seed in all my watchings of the Heavens before. And I thought, these are God's watchers for the night, over the poor blind airth, wrapt up in the mouth of darkness. Now, you wise men, who read everything in books, you say these are all so many worlds, perhaps like our'n, having their people—men and women and children; and having governments and laws, maybe as good, or even better than our'n. But I *prefars* to think not. It's a more beautiful blessed idee, to consider them sperrits— angels set there to watch over us and guard us in the night. And when we thinks so, it forces us to think that the Good Lord has a care for us, since he has made sich beautiful watchers to have an eye to our consarns; and then I 'member'd a p'int in the Bible, where it tells us that He sees to every sparrow that tumbles to the ground; and so I consider'd that He would see to me, and help to keep me from tumbling, and being washed down by the mighty wathers! I was worse off, then, I reckon, than any sparrow, and need more help; and my consate told me I was bigger and worthier to save than any sparrow! Was all *my* strength and sperrit, my limbs and sinews, to be washed out etarnally, when there was so much good in me, to be worked out on the blessed airth? I couldn't and I wouldn't belave it, and I tuk heart and hope from considerin' it; and would you belave it, I tried to sing a sailor song that I partly 'member'd; but I couldn't git on fur with it, and broke down in the middle, and found myself, on a suddent, fairly a-crying, like an overgrown baby as I was! But that fit didn't last long. I felt ashamed, and got up and dash'd about, and threw more wood on the fire, and whistled, and looked into my caboose, and, at last, tuk another pull at the whiskey!

"Then I come out stronger, and 'Och!' said I, 'ef I had some fellow to whip now!' I thought of Isaac Clymes, and longed to git hold of him; and I squared off for a fight, and doubled my fists, and threw out my arms, and practised jest as ef I was in the thick of a scrimmage, till, in the midst of it, I found myself tumbling over my wood pile! Well, I was ashamed of that nonsense; but you see, my masters, I had jest nothing to do but to think, and thinking was about the sorrowfullest business I could be at!

"But I had to do it, and I sat down agin the wood pile, and leant back upon it, and thought how happy I'd be ef I was jest back agin quietly where that wood come from!—And I watched the stars as they swum along in the sky; and I watched the bright flashes of the wathers, as they surged along with a jump by me, and spread out in silver over the eends of my raft; and, in the midst of my looking, the moon come up out of the sea, and looked full into my face: looking so sad, as ef she, too, was a sorrowing over my sitivation. And all before her, she spread out a thousand leetle white clouds, soft and white as any silk, and she turned up all their edges and eends with melted silver; and then she walked up, and through 'em all, as ef she was a walking on her own natheral carpet! I niver seed sich beautiful soft clouds before, nor sich a beautiful moonshine. It's true, I niver watched the skies at sich a rate, or prehaps they'd have looked jest as beautiful a thousand times before!—But then it was the first chaince I ever had to watch them by themselves, without feeling the land onder me, and seeing the woods all about me! And then agin, the beautifullest thing of all was that broad streak, like a straight road, made of silver, in a straight line, right towards me, from the moonlight in the sea! It seemed to me as ef she was getting all things ready to march to meet me. Och! sartinly, my masters, the moon, and the skies, and the seas, were all made for one another; and you niver kin feel parfectly their beauty ontil you git them all together.

"Well, I watched the moon till my eyes got weary. She seemed so friendly that I begun to talk to her. She was my company. I said to her:

" 'You see my sitivation! Kin you do anything for me? You're so beautiful, you ought to be good! And you look so sad, with all your sweetness, you ought to be marciful! Have pity on a poor devil that's lost all his tracks, and ef some good angel don't come down to his help, the places that know'd him will know him no more!'

"And that prayer brought me to think of the poor ould mother, who had nobody to do for her but me. And I thought over all the friends and acquaintances that I hed—you too, Wharncliffe—and I thought how they'd none of 'em be axed to my funeral! And then the moon looked more sorrowful than ever; and I got weary to look at her, and hear niver a word in answer to my prayer—niver a sound, 'cept the moaning of the wind across the sea, that was surely the v'ice of a sperrit! And then I threw a few more lightwood knots on my fire, went into my caboose, tuk a pull at the whiskey, and laid down to sleep with my head and shoulders in the caboose, to keep my eyes from the moonlight—put my legs outside, to be ready for anything that should happen in the night.

"I slept mighty soon, for I was wearied out with the watching and the thinking. But I slept very miserable, and had the most distrestful dreams. I woke, I reckon, about two o'clock in the morning, with a very bad skeer. Whether it was the dream, or the thing itself, I can't say, but the cussed 'Hoo! Hoo! Hoo!' rung in my ears like thunder; and I dashed up, and worked myself out of the caboose, and stood up on my feet, hearing a great tumbling about in my wood pile.

"I thought, at first, that I had been run down by some vessel; but the moon was bright and shining over me, and I could see nothing besides but the mighty ocean, and that was jest as smooth as when I went to sleep. But there was still a tumbling about of the wood; and I begun to think some strange beast of the sea—the sea sarpent, perhaps—had jumped upon my raft, and was looking about for the owner! I run straight to the chist, and got out my hatchet, and armed with this, I went to my wood pile; but everything there was quiet, all on a suddent! Yet it was sartin that only a minute before the logs and knots was a tumbling over one another. Well, I picked up one or two small knots, and lighted up my fire, which had purty well burned down. I felt chilly besides, and tuk a pull of whiskey; then, as I didn't want to do any more thinking, I went and laid myself down agin in the caboose.

"Hardly had I done so, when I heard the logs a tumbling in the wood pile, jest as ef somebody was a rolling 'em one over the other. I went back, and jest as soon as I did so, all was quiet agin, and they all lay together as close and innocent as fifteen young pigs in a litter, sticking close to the side of the sow in a right line. Ef 'twas any strange baste among the logs, it must be a small one, and he must lie pretty close and snug at the bottom. I was jubous about the pile, but didn't ixamine close, thinking I'd leave it over till broad daylight. I was jubous of some trick of the divil iver sence I heard that infarnal 'Hoo! Hoo! Hoo!'—no matter whether it come to me sleeping or waking, in a drhame, or in reality. I jest contented myself with walking round the pile two or three times, keeping a sharp eye on it, and with my hatchet ready in my hand. All that time things kept quiet. But no sooner had I gone back to the caboose, and spread myself out for a sleep, than the trouble and tumbling begun agin. And so it kept up, off and on, for the rest of the night. Whenever I'd get up and come out, all was still as a mouse-trap; the moment I had eased myself off for my rest, why all was a rolling and a tumbling in the wood pile.—By this time, I know'd who was at the bottom of the trouble. It was my old inimy, at me agin, having desarted the swamp, it was cl'ar, to hunt me down upon the say!

"Well, you kin asily consider what sort of feelings I had by this time. Hunted down from the swamp to the sea—from the thick woods to the big waters—no peace any where! This new trouble and torment begun to lighten my load of skear. I wasn't now so skearful as angry. I felt more like fighting than anything else. I remembered the fight with the stump on the Big Lake; and I remembered the souse in the sea the day before; and I felt that another fight was before me, to come off before the day was another hour older. But I waited for broad daylight. I waited for the sun. I got my hatchet ready—my knife—my gun. I stuck the hatchet in my belt. My gun was loaded already with twelve pelters each barrel. I looked up my axe, and tried to sharpen it with an old file; and, all ready, and b'iling over with anger, I stood at the door of the caboose looking out for the sun to rise.

"And on a suddent, with a rush, he came up surging through the great watteray wilderness, jest like one of them mighty warriors of old times, with a flaming spear in his hand, a goulden target on his arm, and a crown of gould upon his head. I thought, when I seed him ride up from the waters in his fiery chariot—I thought of the great Pharoah pursuing the Israelites; and I thought of Sennacherib, with the Issyrians; and of Darius, with the Medes and Persians; of Alexander the Great; and all the mighty soldiers and heathen warriors you read of in Scripter and other books, from Goliath down to Gen. Washington! And my sowl got powerful strong within me, and I felt powerful to face the Divil, and King Beelzebub, and all his dern' Dagons of Philistines. And then I remembered David's fight with Goliath, the giant, and I put down my gun! Says I to myself—

" 'I'll take it with sling and stone—that is, I'll trust eentirely to my hatchet and knife!' And so, full in the face of the sun, I pushed out to the lightwood pile, and there it lay before me, looking at first innocent enough. But I walked round it, feeling quite jubous that all wasn't right. And sure enough, I seed the eend of a log sticking out that I niver remember'd to hev seed there before. It look'd monstrous like the stump that I had hed the fight with on the big lake; and then agin, it looked mighty like the one that I had fastened to at White P'int. But thar it lay, quiet as a mouse-trap; but, thinks I to myself, thinks I, it's jest as likely to be a take in! All the other logs was atop of it, and how it hed worked itself down thar was the question.

" 'To git thar,' says I; 'that accounts for all the tumbling!'

"And says I, to myself, I must work sly to get at it. I must ease off the other pieces first, before I begin. Wood, says I, has three inimies, dry rot, axe and fire. Dry rot is too slow for me here. It must be axe and fire. Ef the Divil takes the shape of a log, he runs the chaince of the wood; and darn his liver, if I kin only git a few good chops at him, and then give him a hoist into the fire, I reckon he'll feel his eyebrows worse burn'd than iver before, and he'll walk off with more bruises on his shins!

"So I said to myself. I then picked off from the top of the pile, a few of the fattest lightwood knots, and threw 'em on my fire, ontill it begun to burn famous. Then I squared myself off to git at the stick I was jubous of. I walked round it, and pulled off, and kicked off piece after piece, till I got him a'most separate from the rest; but jest when I was pulling off one of the last pieces, with my left hand—for I kept my right ready with the tommy-hawk—it tilted up, first one eend, then the other, and as I tried to fix it with my foot, the cussed thing rolled fairly betwixt my legs, and a'most tripped me up. I got clear of the staddle, and struck at the jubous log with my hatchet— 'twas a fair stroke, well aimed—but the hatchet glanced from it, as ef 'twas so much iron, and I had a narrow chaince of its grazing my leg. I saw 'twas a needcessity to be mighty careful, having to deal with sich an inimy, and I stooped to it; and, as I struck again, both logs got to rolling onder me; and they fairly pushed me over the pile; then the whole pile got a rolling and tossing about, and there was a general scatteration. But I set my eyes fast upon the jubous log; and I followed him up; and, being purty desperate now, I showered my blows upon him, fore and aft, not kearing ef they glanced or not, and I gin him five or six chops, he rolling at me, and onder me, and about me, all the time, and whenever he got among the other logs, making a scatteration among them too.—But I worked a trivance, and got between him and the rest of the pile, and followed him up with cut after cut. Now, I cut at one eend, for, says I, the fellow's head may be thar; and then I cut at the other eend, for it might be thar too; and then I hacked away at the middle, thinking ef the beast had bowels at all, I'd try and give 'em a short cut out; and so, lamming away, fast and furious, I am a thinking I worried the beast; for he backed out fairly, rolling away from me at every stroke, tell I got him close to the very eend of the raft where I had hauled him in. Then he tried to roll forward again, but I hacked away the faster, and stood twixt him and everything else; and says I—seeing I had got the better of him—'now I'll split you, you beast of Babylon!' and as I said, I staddled him, and cut up and down his whole length, as ef to split, when he fairly made a bolt, up and down, half opset me, and nearly carried me overboard with him. He went off with a big plunge, and was clean out o' sight in a twink."

"A very curious fight," says Wharncliffe.

"Wasn't it?"

"But, Paddy, haven't you somehow forgot to mention the drinks you took before going into battle?"

"There you are again, with the same ould talk, Wharncliffe, and thar's no sense in it. I'll tell you, I tuk but two drinks up to the time the fight finished, and both of 'em before it begun. After it begun, I had no time for thinking or drinking—"

"Or winking!"

"No! nor winking. No! not a minute; for, as you says, it was a very curious fight, and left you no time to wipe a nose, in case it got bloody. It was all confusion, and a tumbling and a tossing, a jumping and a rolling, from one log to the other—now one, now t'other—and sometimes all together; for, I seed that whenever the divil stump touched the other ones, they all seemed to catch the shaking agy, and that was the raison I fought so hard to keep 'em separate.

"I then—after he was overboard—got my wood into a pile agin; for it was scattered fore and aft, and when it was all done, and I could see no more of my inimy, I *then* went and tuk a drink, for I tell you fairly, I think I desarved it."

"That you did, Paddy."

"I'm sure I did. But I was the weakest crathur after the fight was eended that ever you seed. I had jest to throw myself down on the raft, and try to forgit that I was a breathing man."

"Well, what of the rest of the day, Paddy?"

"Och, for the rest! Well, 'twas peaceful enough. Oh! too peaceful! Nothing to be seen—nothing to happen! Sea and sky, and hot bright sun, and not a cloud in the sky, and not a speck on the sea, save and 'cepting my own poor speck of a raft. It was a day that seemed to be *oneending*; and yet, when the sun went down, bright and grand, and wrept in gould and purple, jest like the evening before, my heart seemed to drop down in my bosom, my hope went out jest like the sun, buried in the deep sea of my sitivation, and then came the night, dark as before, tell the stars come out, and the moon, and began telling me, one arter the other, how there was a God in Heaven, looking down upon me with his million of eyes, watchful of the very meanest of his mortal sparrows. And so I watched and thought and prayed, tell I got too weary, and then kindling up my fire, to last tell morning, I turned into my caboose for a sleep, with my legs out as before."

"But you didn't forget to take a drink, Paddy, before sleeping?"

"That I didn't, Jameison, and a pretty stiff drink too—a regular stand-up-to-the-rack drink—water or no water!

"I was mighty soon sleeping, and then come on a set of the most infarnal drhames, of all sorts of torments, and I wakened up with a skeer, hearing a most infarnal 'Hoo! Hoo! Hoo!' in my very ears, and that same tumbling of my wood, jest like the night afore. Well, I wouldn't git up. I had no idea of another fight with the divil, and I wouldn't try it sartinly till broad day light. But sich was the tumbling and tossing of the wood, that I soon began to be afeard that the dern'd thing would be scattering my lightwood knots overboard, ef I didn't see to it, and that fear carried me out."

"Well, what happened?"

"Why jest nothing. The moment I showed myself at the wood-pile, it was all quiet. But, when I went back, to try to sleep agin,—for I felt the monstrous tire of the day's work—the tumbling begun agin, hard as ever! Well, I got desprit agin, and taking another pull at the 'Oh! be joyful,' I went out, and what do you think I did?—I jest laid myself down on the wood-pile itself, right across it, though I know'd the divil, my mortal inimy was a lying snug onderneath! What do you think of that? I calls it a desprit action."

"It was certainly a bold one, Paddy. But what came of it?"

"You shall hear. First, let me tell you, I took kear, before lying down, to have my tommyhawk ready, and my knife snug in my belt. Well, when I throw'd myself down on the pile, I didn't stop to think. I was desprit, I tell you, and I said aloud,

" 'You bloody beast, ef you air determined that I shan't sleep in thar, (meaning in the caboose,) I'll see ef I kaint do my sleeping out here, and on yore ugly carkis.'

"And with that I stretch'd myself off across the pile. All was quiet. It was a rough enough bed, and I got up and got my over-all, and one of my potato sacks half full. I spread the over-all for lying on, and put the potato sack for a pillow. Then I laid myself down snug, and looked out at the moon, that was shining down, like the Queen of Sheba, when she went to see King Solomon. I reckon it was about 3 o'clock in the morning. There was hardly a breeze at all. The sea was smooth as a looking glass, and stretching out over it, in a long reach, was that grand highway of sparkling silver which the moonlight made, as ef jest to make a man dhrame of swate and aisy travelling in a happy country. I watched and thought for awhile, tell I found myself beginning to think strange things, and to feel as ef I was wrapping up warm in a beautiful cloud. But jest then, it did seem to me as ef I felt a soft rocking motion in my wood-pile. It seem'd to work up onder me, but so aisily that it never made my ribs give. I lay quiet, but a leetle more wakeful than before. And sure enough I felt the motion growing stronger, but 'twarn't onpleasant. It was jest a sort of rising up of the whole bed onder me; and I didn't feel the roughness of a single timber. Then agin, it begun to seesaw, from head to foot, as much like the feeling of a rocking cradle as anything in the world. Well, strange as you may think it, I found the motion so pleasant, that I wanted it to keep on; and all my thoughts and feel got to be pleasant; and I felt myself in a sort of dhrame-waking—not asleep, and not awake, and having a pleasant dhrame, with the thinking jest strong enough to keep the dhraming raisonable; and still there was the same sweet, aisy motion —a sort of swinging, with your head in a fine woman's lap, and a beautiful gal child a pushing you. I raaly felt all over, wrapt up in a beautiful garment of dhraming and moonlight!

"But, all on a suddent, without knowing why myself, for I remember no sound, I jumped up in a terrible skear, and had raison, a moment a'ter, to thank the Lord for givin' me the skear; for, would you think it, with that dern'd delightful dhraming and swinging—that rocking in the fine woman's lap—I jumped up to find myself, and my pile of wood, all on the very edge of the raft, and another three minutes of delicious dhraming and rocking, would have carried every stick of us overboard!

"But I got to my feet and senses in the nick of time. I hadn't five minutes, no—nor three—to spare! I was saved by the very skin of my teeth! Nothing stood betwixt me and the drowning sea, but my own shadow; and as I seed that in the water, I jumped back, and was safe; but with the cussed wood all in motion onder my feet.

"I jest stopt and look't at it, not knowing edzactly what to say or do! But I determined to do nothing at all, but jest leave it to nather to fix and detarmine. For you see, I was getting quite weary of keeping up a fight with the divil—a mortal inimy that I couldn't sarcumvent, and that come to trouble me only onder God's permission, and, perhaps onder his direction. So I jest left it to him. Ef I was to be manslaughtered, without giving me a chaince, well, let the thing have its way. As I said before, I was pretty much tired out.

"But Stilus, my dear fellow, do you 'member what the sun said to the sea; and what the sea said to the rivers—and what the rivers said to the hills; and what the airth said to the leetle clouds?"

"No! What did they say?"

"It's a long time between drinks!"

"And a very logical speech," said Wharncliffe.

"Stylus, I'm surprised at you!"

"And I at myself; but my interest in Paddy's narrative was such as to make me forgetful of his health."

"That's the right saying. A man's health depends on his having the right refreshment at the right time, whether it's to feed or liquor! We're in for the night, and mustn't let the sun, moon and stars go to bed thairsty. Here's to you, gentlemen."

CHAPTER XVII.

Still Half Seas Over—Day and Night—Sombrous Sights, and Thoughts—
Dreams and Visions—Long Struggle, and Final Despair, in which the Devil
gets up a Ballet.

———

Paddy soon resumed his narrative, the discussions in regard to
which, I may say, still went on, *par parenthèse*, among the party;
but I forbear these as hardly necessary to the story. It does not much
matter in what degree our faith, in Paddy's experiences, was enlisted.
Enough, that none of us doubted his own full faith in the spiritual
or demoniac character of the influences by which his fortunes were
affected.

"Well, gentlemen, my good friends and masters, I need not
trouble you or myself to tell, over and over, the same sort of
ixpariences, day and night, which I had to throuble me. Enough, ef
I say to you that for three days and nights more, I had the worry
and flurry with the dern'd beast in my wood-pile, ontil I gin over
fighting with him. I jest let him hev his own way. I hadn't the heart
any more to keep up the countervarsy, pretick'lar with a crathur that
come back agin to the scratch jest as often as he was throwed on his
back. In the same time, however, I felt myself growing weaker and
weaker, day by day. And my sleep was full of bad dhrames; and I
haird terrible noises, and seed visions that were fiery and red; and
when I waked, it was with the feeling of a great sinking of sperrits.
My sleep did me no good, and my days passed over, and I was sort
of stupid like, looking out upon the same etarnal sea, and feeling the
sun as hot as blazes, like a grand furnace covering the top of my head.
And about the fifth day I reckon—for I had begun to forgit the
count of days and nights, I jumped up in a suddent passion, and I
cried out aloud—

" 'What's the use to try any longer? It's only death at last, and there an eend; and why not death at onst, and put an eend to the dreadful ixpaience that seems much like hell itself! I'm jest now a-dying by inches, in a torter all the time! and there's no hope for me, not a sign of it! nothing but the sea that soon must swallow me up, and why not at onst? I'm not afeard to die! It's true, I'd rather die a fighting, in hot blood; but who to fight?'

"And jest as I said that, I seed the etarnal devil stump poking one eend out of the wood-pile, and I thought I seed an eye looking through the wood,—the same great red eye, I had seen before; and at the sight, I jumped at the pile, and I tore my way into it, determined to have a last wrestle, and tumble the beast into the sea and go with him myself! I grabbed the log fairly in the middle, and would ha' picked it up bodily, but it never moved a peg! I put my whole strength to it; and never stirred it no more than ef I had been only of a musketer's muscle! Was my strength all gone? I let go, and tried another log almost as big; and that I lifted up as aisy as if it had been a feather's weight. Twan't any loss of my own strength, and I was desprite; and that made me stronger in fact, for a spent at the least. What was it then that kept me from h'isting the infarnal stump into the sea, and going along with it? I jumped at it agin, but it stuck to my planks jest as if it had been bolted down with iron! I tried at it till breath and strength was gone, and then I cast myself down, flat on my face, and sent up the bitterest groan in the worrld. It was the bitterest ixparience, and I fairly cried like a child; and, in the midst of it, on a suddent, I heard the roaring 'Hoo! Hoo! Hoo!' that seemed to roll all around me from the very jaws of the sea!

"I jumped up and shook my fist at the infarnal log; and gnashed my teeth at it; and cursed it from the bottom of my heart. But it never showed no signs of life; and I jest spent my strength in groanings and cursings."

"That was the time to take a drink, Paddy."

"I did take it, Wharncliffe. But it didn't help me much; and I took another, and another, in that same hour; and then I felt all over like I was dying. I had a cold shiver run all through me, and a cold sweat broke out over my face, and head, and hands; and I laid myself down in the caboose, ixpecting to die! And in that way I suppose I fell asleep; though, it did seem to me as ef I was a-knowing all that went on, all the time. I thought I could see the sunshine, and hear the sea. But I reckon I was in a stupid sleep, for when I rose up and looked out of the caboose the sun was a-setting. And when I seed him going down, so grand, to his etarnal big bed, I said to myself:

" 'And why shouldn't I go down too, and have out my etarnal sleep? What's waking to me in this world? It's only a waking to the worst misery.'

"So I jest watched the sun tell he was fairly buried, and then I walked to the west eend of the raft, determined there to put an eend to my sufferings! And when I looked into the water, it opened with a surge, and looked so beautiful, blue and soft, with the beautifulest frosty white foam on the green edges, that I said to myself,

" 'It's the beautifulest sort of a grave for a poor suffering sinner!'

"And jest then the sun seemed to flash out once more over the sea, and I said:

" 'It's a'most too beautiful a world, in spite of all one's trouble, to cut loose from.' And I thought of the old woods and swamps, and our own beautiful river, and I thought of the old mother, and then it came to me that I might be saved yet, and that it would be always time enough to die when the time come for it; and I thought I heard the voice of Sam Hartley, whispering in my very ears, 'never say die, Paddy!' and, jest then, looking into the beautiful wather, I felt the chill creep over me like a wet cloud, and suddenly I seed a speck on the wather! Och! didn't I shudder and shiver all over, as the next minute a most powerful shirk, a dozen foot long, surged up, with his white sides, close to the raft; and I could see his eye aiming at me, sharp as a dagger, as ef the infarnal beast was ready to jump at me on to the very raft itself! May-be, I didn't back into the middle of the raft in the coward's double-quick. I was all over in a shiver, and, from that moment, as long as I could see, that day and the next, there was the big black fin of the beast to be seen whichever p'int of the compass I turn'd my eyes. The Great Etarnal Governor of the Univarse sent that beast there in the very nick of time.—From that moment, in all the misery of my sitivation, so long as I had my human raison and parfect senses, I never once again thought of eending my life by drowning. That shirk was sent as a watch upon me; and I know so long as I could see myself, that his ravenous eye was never once off of me.

"I laid myself down a groaning, and most sorrowful wretched, but I couldn't sleep.—The same feeling of stupid, half-waking half-sleeping dhrame, froze up all my limbs and a'most my senses, and when I'd wake up a leetle, it was only to see that great back fin of the shirk upon the top of the water, and see his white sides as he coursed around the raft.

"I felt myself gitting sick as well as stupid, and I tuk more freely to the whiskey than ever. I was hot at one minute and chilly the next. I had no appetite for food, and my head ached me terribly. It seemed to me as ef everything was getting of a bright red color, like the sun at his setting, and this, too, after the sun had gone down, and the stars were all out. When the moon rose, she looked as red as the sun. At midnight, the noises begun again in the wood-pile, but I didn't notice them any more. I hadn't the sperrit to strike a blow, and I felt that the strength was going out of me. I suppose, in the whole of that twenty-four hours, I hadn't eaten more than two potatoes. I made it up in whiskey. Suddenly, another change come over me. My skin got burning hot, and I felt that I had fever. I felt myself unsartin in the way of thinking; and, every now and then, I'd feel as ef I was in the woods, and I stopt myself more than once, a-whistling for the dogs, or saying something as ef my ould mother was a listening to me.

"That sort of thing gave me a mighty bad skear. I was afraid I was going to lose my senses. Only think, to be a raging madman—me one—alone, on that poor raft, a-drifting far and wide on the etarnal sea, shouting to the winds and skies and waters—to the sun, moon and stars; shouting, like a poor crazy fool; and, not onlikely, in the thick of my brain's confusion, jumping headlong overboard into the jaws of that infarnal shirk.

"There he was yit. I could see his black fin on the top of the wather, steady at his post like a sentinel, waiting for the madness to git the better of me, and send me jumping headlong into his very jaws. Well, what better could I do in my misery, than to drink and drink, and shut my eyes and senses to the misery of my sitivation?

That was my only consolation left; and though I felt the fever burning in me, I went to my caboose, and got my cup and stooped down to the jimmyjohn to pour, when, only think, my dear good friends and masters, there wasn't a drop left. The jimmyjohn was tumbled over on its side, the stopper gone, and every drap of the liquor had run out into the sea!

"Think of my misery! It was complete disperation; and I jest dropt down where I stood, and gin myself up to the eend! Who but the dern'd inimy that had hunted me down from the woods to the deep sea—who but he had done the mischief? He tuk from me the last drap of consolation; and I jest sat squat on the floor of the caboose, and gin myself up to the bitter death! A'ter a while I staggered out and went to the wood pile, and I looked at the infarnal log. It was quiet enough now, but jest afore, it had made a most riotous racketting; and I shook my fist at it, and said aloud—

" 'You've done for me at last! You've got me here in a starving and dying sitivation, and I don't keer how soon you make an eend of me! Human nature kaint stand no more!'

"And jest as I was done, there come out of the sea, all around me, more than a dozen yells of 'Hoo! Hoo! Hoo!' jest in mockery of my sitivation. It didn't provocate me at all. I hadn't the sperrit; and I jest shook my head and said—

" 'Yes, you may soon make an eend of it, and the sooner the better!'

"But, saft as a whisper in the ears, I thought I heard the v'ice of Sam Hartley—

" 'Niver say die, Paddy!'

"And says I, in answer—

" ' 'Taint what I kin say, Sam! It's for the Great Lord of the Univarse to say whether it's to be death or life! The eend of it is in His hands, for Him to cut the string or draw it out.'

"And that was, I recken, the last sensible word I had to say; for my head was raging with the aches, and the blood was surging through my veins, hot as the blast of a furnace; and all about me everything looked redder than before.

"Well, I remember creeping a'ter a while to the side of the raft, and I knelt down, and scooped up the water in my hat, and poured it over my head. And on a suddent, while I was a dipping the second hatful up, I haird a rush; and in a minute, the beast of a shirk, all his body fairly on the top of the water, surged up to me with a sound of thunder, and dashed past me, not half a foot from my hands. I drapt the hat, and it was gone, swallowed up in a twink; and after that one shirk, there came a rush of twenty more, I reckon; and they raged round and round the raft, as long as I could look. I could see their black fins and their white sides upon the wathers, and I could fairly see the red grin of their eyes, as ef they had got a taste of me a'ready! I staggered back, and was so weak with fright, fever and starvation, that I fell agin my caboose; and there I lay, I don't know for how long, but feeling worse and worse every minute, and without the heart to rise up and try to do something for myself. But what could I do?

"Well, my good friends and masters, what I'm now gwine to tell is maybe pretty much my dhraming, though it did seem to me all true and airnest raal at the time; and it was the last thing of my remembering. You will say that 'twas all a vision of a man out of his head at the time; and it may be so, but it looked mighty natheral and true, all the time, to my bodily eyes and senses—what was left me of seeing and onderstanding!

"Well, while I was a laying there, agin the caboose, feeling more dead than alive, on a suddent, I seed the moon come down from the skies, and stand up on one corner of my raft. And it was like a picture, all in silver; but in the middle of it sat a great gray-bearded man— his beard reaching to his middle, and of a shining silver white; and his face was as sweet as a girl's, yet it was grander and stronger than the face of any mortal man! And in his hand he carried a staff, that looked to me as ef you had jest caught and fixed solid a streak of lightning; the gold fires was a-flashing from it, from top to bottom. And suddently he lifted this golden staff, and touched the rock he sate on—and that looked to me to be made of some solid metal, but not exactly gold or silver—and at the touch the water spouted from the rock, like a beautiful rain, and sprinkled me all over, and kept sprinkling me; and I opened my mouth and caught it as it fell, and it seemed to cool me delightful! And as I kept drinking and feeling the coolness, there was a great flashing of light all about me; and when I looked, I saw three other moons, on each of the other three corners of the raft; and they were all like pictures, but with different figgers; one had a beautiful young woman, all in whitc, with a lcctlc baby in her arms; and she looked on the baby very sweet, but sorrowful too. And in the third, there was a strong man holding up the head of an old woman, who had her eyes shut, and looked to be dead or dying; for I could see the tears dropping from the strong man's eyes!

"But what was my supprise, when I saw in the fourth moon a parfect image of my own self, dressed up handsome, in my old hunting shirt, that seemed to be as good as new! I had on my belt, and pouch, and knife; but my rifle seemed to lean agin the frame of the moon. And what do you think I was doing? Why, drawing figgers in the air—nothing better than drawing figgers in the air! Now, what could that mean, whether I really seed that vision or only dhramed it? I tell you, my good friends and masters, that drawing figgers in the air had some meaning, though it's onpossible for my poor onderstanding to see the clear of it.

"Well, after I had seed and stared my very eyes out of the sockets, looking at these strange, beautiful and grand delightful sights—the water streaming out from the rock all the time—on a suddent, there was a great hellabaloo—sich a 'Hoo! Hoo! Hooing,' from so many v'ices, as I had niver haird before! And at the sound, up jumped every stick out of the wood pile—that divil stump of my mortal inimy among them; and each one stood upon eend, and they all begun a rigilar dance together; all over the deck of my raft; all round me; coming nearer to me at every jump; and at last wheeling right about me, in full blast, dancing away like mad, with the stump of my infarnal inimy right in front!

"Then I was filled with a desprit passion to jine in the dance; and I jumped up, strong as a bull, and I caught the dern'd stump about the waist; and it did seem as ef he caught me about the waist too; and quick as lightning we whirled about, and cavorted, and went for'a'd and back, and crossed hands, and changed sides; and Och! it's no use to be telling—there's *no* telling! I niver haird of sich dancing; sich jumping, whirling and wheeling, leaping and tumbling, in all my life! And when the dern'd stump sang out his 'Hoo! Hoo! Hoo!' I gin it back to him as loud as he; and we tossed each other about as hearty as ef we had been the best friends in the world. But all on a suddent the four grand big moons went out, and every log of the wood pile tumbled right back in his place, and jest lay quiet where it fell; and I fell down too, flat as the rest; and all was darkness! The last that I knowed, or kin remember, is that the rain was pouring down upon me in a flood from every window in Heaven."

CHAPTER XVIII.

How Paddy is saved from Wreck—How he gets into a better Craft, and is "Riled," and how he visits, perforce, the great City of New York.

———

"And now, my friends, what do you say to all that?"

A great deal was said, especially about brain fever, as the cause of all his visions of suns, moons and stars, the fever being produced by exposure and excitement. To all this, Paddy made only a gesture of dissent. He did not seem to think that the "argyment" needed any more formal answer. He shrugged his shoulders, and said, almost in the language of Hamlet, "that there were a good many things that we knew, no doubt; but that there were a good many other things happening in this poor devil world of ours, for which Human Philosophy had no explanation, and which were not meant for explanation."

Briefly, this was his philosophy. Mysteries are meant to be mysteries, and if they were not, there would be no need of faith. Reason might answer well enough. But to argue against the possible, simply from what we could prove, was a business in which Reason was apt to make herself very ridiculous. Paddy did not use these words exactly, but this was the substance of what he did say.

"Them shirks," says he, "was sent by the great Lord of the univarsal world to keep me from drowning myself; and that whiskey jimmyjohn was opset and spilt out to keep me from drinking myself to death."

"But," says Wharncliffe, "you believe that was done by your enemy, the Devil of the Stump?"

"To be sure I do, and with the permission of God; but I don't doubt but the dern'd devil thought, all the time, that he was doing

369

me a great dissarvice, seeing that the whiskey was all I hed for consolation in my misery and shipwrack."

"You have been a sort of Job, Paddy; but I observe that, so far, your persecutions have not resulted fatally."

"I'm alive and kicking! I'm here, that's sartin, and no bones broke, and no great loss; but it was a most miracklous preservation."

"Go on with your story," said Jamison. "I gather from what you have said that you lost all consciousness after your vision of the moons."

"And that dance with the Devil of the Stump!" said Carroll.

"Edzactly so! I 'member no more a'ter that ontil—och! Lord, it's no use to calkilate, how long I was on the raft, in that sickness, before I was picked up. But it was a God's marcy that I lost all the feeling of my throubles, jest at the right time, and when the madness was gitting fast ahead of the raison. I was, prehaps, two or three days jest drifting about on the raft, like a corpse, and in mighty bad weather. But to go on rigilar with the argyment:

"The first thing I know'd—the first feeling I had, when I did wake up out of my stupid sleep, was a dreadful rolling and tossing of the ship. For I was in the bunk of a ship, and the ship was in a storm, and pitching headlong and sideways and rolling dreadful. I could feel all that, and I know'd my sitivation edzactly the moment my senses come back to me. But I woke with a sore feeling in both my arms, and a sore feeling in the back of my head. I soon found that I hed been bled and blistered; they hed shaved off a part of my hair behint and stuck a blister there; and when I tried to move my head, I found a soreness in the back of my neck, and there they hed stuck another blister. But when I begun to move, a man riz up from a seat beside me and show'd himself. He had been my nurse and pretty much my doctor. He was a small, red-faced person, who answered to the name of Ellick Thompson. He was, as he told me, only a passenger in the ship—for I was in a ship —what they call a Brigantine, called the Adele, or Adela, and her captain was a Scotchman, named Wilson. Thompson was a Scotchman too, and both treated me well. Thompson told me how I was found on the raft, looking like dead. How they tuk me on board, and saved my chist, and my gun, my hatchet, and even my grits and pertatoes. How they found as I was in a swoond and with a fever; how I was soaked with water, and they thought the rain hed helped to save my life. How they doctored and bled me and blistered me. How a gale took 'em from the northeast, jest after they hed picked me up, and driv 'em into the gulf; and how I hed been then four days aboard of the ship. They didn't know, and I couldn't rightly tell 'em, how long I hed been aboard of the raft. I hed forgot the run of the days in that dredful sitivation.

" 'You'll do now,' says Thompson. 'Your fever's gone, and you've got back your senses; but ef you hadn't been a mighty strong man, you'd ha' died and gone to the devil.'

" 'No, I wouldn't,' says I, quite bold and sassy; ' 'twas Providence, not my man strength, that saved me. As for the devil, I'm beginning to think him a better fellow than people suppose. I ought to, seeing how I hugged and danced with him last night.'

" 'Last night?' says he.

" 'Yes,' says I, 'the last night I was on the raft.'

"Then he up and told me how I had been in a sort of dozing sleep, only starting up at times to roar and rave and talk onpossible things—how I had sung out like an owl, startling 'em all at a great rate. By that, I guessed that ef he hadn't haird me, he must hev haird the devil's own 'Hoo! hoo! hoo!'

"Well, he went on to say that I must hev been in bad company.

" 'For,' says he, 'you're our Jonah! We hed good weather till we picked you up, and just after we tuk a north-easter that's been driving us into the gulf, and it's jest now blowing harder than iver. Had the gale tuk you, on your craft, you'd hev been swept off in half an hour.'

" 'Well,' says I, 'I'm afraid I'm something of a Jonah, but don't, I beg you, fling me overboard agin. I've hed enough of that! Tell the Cappin to hev faith! I'm strong in faith now, since I hed that last bout with the devil;—fore and back two; right and left with your partner; and then the Mississippi double shuffle.'

" 'What air you talking about?' says Thompson, looking oneasy and beginning to feel my pulse.

" 'Och,' says I, 'it's only a dhrame I had. A dhrame of a dance with the devil.'

" 'Well,' says he, 'you musn't talk any more. Drink this stuff, and then try to go to sleep. Don't be talking—it'll hurt you.'

" 'Och,' says I, 'ef that's the only danger, don't be skeared. Talking niver hurt me yet! It agrees with my constitution powerful well.'

"But he wouldn't listen, but went out of the leetle room, where I was and locked the door a'ter him.

"A'ter a few hours, I trying to spell out the whole history and argyment of my sitivation, he come back, and the Cappin with him; and they both talked to me very kind; and the Cappin said—

" 'You're a proof of providential marcy. No man, without God's help, could suffer what you did and live. I only wonder you're not a raving madman now.'

" 'It's God's marcy and etarnal Providence,' says I. 'You're right; and onder God, my friends and very good masters, I'm owing to you for my living still on this blessed airth.'

" 'Blessed airth!' says the Cappin, with a loud laugh, 'it's precious little of the airth that you've got here to hold on to! We're a'most five hundred miles from any land, and we're in the thick of a northeaster. But, by God's blessing, that has saved you so fur, you'll git to shore yit.'

"Both him and Thompson was very kind to me, and though both of 'em talked as ef they thought I was a raal Jonah, and brought bad luck on 'em, that niver made 'em alter to me. They gin me the best of everything; hed broth made for me, and tea; and a good many things besides that was comforting to the stomach; and I got to bettering day by day, and as both of 'em said, 'twas astonishing how I picked up. They said that what I'd gone through would ha' killed a'most any other man. They talked a good deal about my case, but I niver let on to 'em anything about that privit history of my throubles that I've told to you here. When I told 'em about my feelings and sickness, and then the opsetting of my whiskey jimmyjohn, they said that was the best thing that ever happened to me in my sitivation; and between the loss of my whiskey and my soaking in the rain, they both concluded I had saved my life. But for them two things, they said, I'd ha' gone mad and throw'd myself overboard for the bloody shirks to devour! and I reckon there was some truth and raison in it. But still, I had a hankering a'ter a dram. The broth and tea were very good, but I reckon better for a woman's infarmities than for a man's; so, one day, when Thompson was axing me ef thar was anything I'd like to hev, I up and told him:

" 'Ef you hev some good whiskey now, and would put a leetle sweetening in it, and a leetle hot water, I think that would do me more good than any broth you could make.'

" 'Why,' says he, 'that's punch! I'm afeard it'll be too strong for your head jest yit.'

" 'But,' says I, 'don't be afeard, I've been nursed on whiskey, weaned on whiskey, fed on whiskey, and have lived all my life on whiskey! It kaint hurt me!'

"So he axed the Cappin, who was a sort of doctor, too, and he laughed out, and said:

" 'Let him hev it.'

"And Thompson made me some, as good as Stylus here, but not quite so much of it; and that was the first time that Scotch whiskey iver entered my swallow. I mended after this mighty fast, and in two days more they tuk me to dinner in the cabbin. There was the Cappin, Ellick Thompson, and two other gentlemen; and a very good dinner we had, and plenty of liquor. But the Cappin had an argyment with the other two men, and they come purty nigh to a sharp quarrel. The Cappin, who was a Scotchman, was pretty hard upon the Amerikin charackter. At last he said:

" 'It's a nation of rogues and swindlers. Their only idee of vartue is *smartness*, and they uses their smartness only to take a fellow in! The only difference between 'em, any whar, is that one man is a *smarter rogue* than the other. They're all rogues, and mean to be rogues; but one set is too cunning for the other—*too* smart—and so the other set goes for fools. And that,' says he, 'so far as my ixparience goes—and I've been knowing to the country for thirty years—is the charackter of high and low, rich and poor, big and little, man and woman, for all that time.'

"I wasn't in strength and sperrit to jine in the argyment, but I felt monstrous riled, and I couldn't help saying:

" 'Look you, Cappin: you've saved my life and doctored and nursed me as ef I was your own son, and I owes you an etarnal debt of gratitude; but, cuss me, ef I aint riled by what you says of the Amerikins. I'm an Amerikin myself.'

" 'Oh, pooh!' he says, with a mighty laugh. 'You're a Southern— you're one of the *geese;* the *fox* is in your feathers! The Amerikin charackter,' says he, 'is made by the North. The people of Europe knows nothing about *you*, 'cept that *you* keeps the niggers and the Yankees keeps *you*. Why, man,' says he, 'they'll cheat the very eyes out of *your* head, and you niver see 'em! They're too smart for *you*.'

" 'I' faith,' says I, 'that's what our people in Carolina thinks; but I'll be derned ef I likes to hear you say what you does about the *gineral* charackters of the nation. It kaint be true of all, and I knows it's not true of our people. Look you, Cappin, ef you was in our pairts and was to talk so, I'd hev to mount you myself, and try the measure of your girth and inches!'

"And he laughed agin, and said—

" 'We don't talk so of any people that'll fight for honor and good name. We only talk so of a people that will stand any amount of kicks, ef they kin only git off with your coffers. In a few days you'll be in New York, and then, mind you, keep your eyes bright. They'll soon find out how much *green* is in 'em.'

"Well, the other two men jest sot and tuk it all, though I haird that both of 'em was residents of New York. After dinner, I talked to Thompson about the matter, and what the Cappin said—and he answered me:

" 'The Cappin's right, but not wise in saying what he did. Them two men he talked at are jest the men to do him an evil turn. They'll jest as like as not set the mob upon him. For they're a people that's jest as bitter and revengeful as they are cowardly. Them's raal blue-bellied Yankees, both on 'em!'

" 'Well,' says I, 'ef they brings the mob on the Cappin, I'll stand by him!'

"And that very day, I looked at my gun and knife, and seed that they were in good order for sarvice—both had been saved and most of my things—and then I told the Cappin what Thompson said, and he said—

" 'They are too dern'd cowardly even for that!'

" 'Well,' says I, 'Cappin, I'll stand by you in a skrimmage.'

"And says he—

" 'You're a good fellow, Paddy, and a man! But, onderstand me: I considers you of a different nation from these people, and I didn't mean to give you any offence.'

"And there that matter eended; but I could see the two passengers go apart together, and they cut sly, sharp eyes at the Cappin whenever he passed. But he passed 'em mostly like a man who was jest then ready to spit. He would ha' clipt 'em in a twink!

"A few days a'ter, we had a talk on the same subject; and the Cappin said:

" 'Look ye, Paddy, you're a good fellow, but you've got to cut your eye-tooth yit. These Yankees are a-trying to cheat me now. You'll see! But I've got my finger on 'em, and they'll look mighty blank, I tell you, when I put it down. You'll see! Say no more; but jest look on and watch. I knows what I'm about.'

"That nor'east gale lasted us a'most seventeen days.

" 'You're the Jonah,' said the Cappin. 'But you're safe from the shirks! The gale's blowed over, and we'll make Sandy Hook by daylight. It always gives me satisfaction to save a fellow, and you're safe.'

" 'And I'm mighty obleeged to you for it,' says I. 'I've got a good deal of good livin' to do yit.' "

CHAPTER XIX.

Paddy in New York—His Virtuous Experiences in that Place—What He Sees of the Great and Good—The Philosophers and Statesmen of that City—A Literary Sponge.

"Well, the next day we took a Pilot, and by dinner time we come in sight of Sandy Hook, and soon we seed the two passengers that the Cappin had the argyment with, a talking together private with the Pilot.—Then Thompson said to me, 'Look at them fellows. They're a-telling the Pilot what the Cappin's been saying of their people.' And I seed the Pilot look grum, and cast sharp eyes at the Cappin; but nothing was then said. But Thompson warned him to keep his eyes wide awake for mischief. But the Cappin jest lifted a handspike, and he says to me—

" 'Paddy, that's a heavy argyment to be laid on a Yankee scull.'

"Says I, 'It's an argyment that will force its way into any onderstanding.'

" 'Now,' says he, 'Paddy, you'll jest please to make the ship your home while you're in New York. Ef you likes the lodgings, you shall hev 'em cheap. You shall pay me in love and friendship. I reckon,' says he, 'you've got precious leetle money to go upon, and you'll want all you kin git to go home with; for I kain't take you back, or I'd do so. I've been to Charleston afore, and likes the place and the people. I'd be willing to take a cargo there now, ef the owners was willing; but I reckon they'll send the ship this time to Greenock. But that don't matter to you. Only, while you're here, and I'm here, in New York, jest you stick to the ship and git your grub with the rest.'

"Well, I thank'd him, you may suppose, the best I could; and I shall always remember his kindness. And Thompson, too, was so good as to say to me—

376

" 'Paddy, I kin give you a bed in my room, and you kin git your meals at a "Restoorynut" (or some name like it). You'll be wanting to see things about town, and you must walk with me and see 'em. I have time, and know all the sights. I suppose you've got no money, but I kin spare you some leetle.'

"Says I, 'I've got fifteen dollars in South Carolina money, that was to answer my wants in Charleston. I reckon it won't go very fur here.'

" 'Quite as far,' says he, 'as in Charleston, provided you know'd the ropes in one place as well as in 't'other. But you don't, and you'll be swindled at every corner of the street. Keep your eyes bright, and I'll see you through. Ef your story gits abroad,' says he, 'they'll make a lion of you. They're fond of lions here, but sometimes make a mistake, and choose a beast with mighty long ears in place of him.'

"Well, I thanked Thompson, to the best of my ability, and shall always 'member him with love and friendship; though, in his talk, he was rather sharp and snappish, and didn't seem to be on the best tarms with the world. A leetle while a'ter this, the mate comes up to me, and most of the sailors arter him: and he makes me a rigilar speech.—The argyment was that they had a great regard for me, seeing as I had gone through a most mirac'lous trial, and most extr'or'nary sarcumstances; and how they had been delighted to hear my long yarns,—for, you see, I had to tell 'em all my story —and how, in testimony of their regard, and for the help of a brother sailor—for they said, tho' I was a fresh water sailor, yet I had show'd myself worthy to go among the salts all my life;—and, to eend it short, the mate offered me a purse of money, all in gould and silver, which he had collected among the crew.

"Well, I was dumbfoundered for a while, for there was the Cappin, and Thompson, and the Pilot, and them two Yankee marchants, and all the crew, waiting on me for the answer. The first thing I did was to try and scratch my head, forgitting that I had been wearing a blister there, and my head was sore and tender. But I soon left off looking there for the sense to answer. But answer I did, in my own poor way; but what I did say, the Lord only knows. Only I jest refused the money, telling him I was obligated to 'em jest the same, but that I had money enough to sarve me till I could git help from home. But says the matc—

" 'Look you, my hearty, ef you don't take the money, it goes chuck overboard. Jack,' says he, 'has parted with it, and won't have it again.'

"So says the Cappin, 'Take it, Paddy, and set the lads' hearts asy. You will find out what to do with it.'

" 'Well,' says I, 'I'm consenting, Cappin, ef so be you'll let me have the boys jest one night ashore, for a spree.'

" 'Very good, Paddy—you shall have 'em.'

"And all the lads gin a shout, and went off very merry. Meantime, I made an agreement with Matey to help me manage the frolic in the town, where, in course, I know'd nothing of the ropes. But I was a good deal usen to seamen, and as I always carried with me Good Humor, as a travelling companion, I made friends jest wherever I went. How them tarny fellows did fondle me! Even the Cappin offered to carry me to Greenock or Liverpool, and back agin, free of expenses, jest to have me with him. As for the sailors, they wanted me to jine as a hand; but, Lord love you, our woods jest then seemed to grow out like a beautiful pictur to my eyes; and then agin, I had tasted enough of the sea in my shipwreck; and as I thought of that, I shivered with the very idee of another v'yage.

"Well, we got safe to New York that very night, but didn't haul up to the wharf, but lay out in the stream, and the Cappin went ashore, taking me and Thompson with him. I went off with Thompson to his lodgings, and he showed me his room, and said whenever I wanted a bed I could git it there, and ef I wanted to write to my friends and family, there was pen and paper, and so forth. So I sat down and wrote a short letter to Wharncliffe, the only one, putting a letter inside for my poor ould mother, which I know'd Wharncliffe would send to her; and I axed him, bold, to let me have fifty dollars on the strength of my promise, as a man of honor. And he sent me a hundred, and he drove out to see the ould mother himself, and sent her a wagon load of corn, and a lot of bacon—"

"Pshaw, Paddy," interposed Wharncliffe, "who the devil wants to hear these petty details? Go ahead with your own doings, and let mine alone."

"And so I would, Wharncliffe, ef you'd tell them yourself; but seeing as you won't, I'm sworn to do it for you! Yes, my friends,

Wharncliffe jest doubled what I axed him, and wrote me the kindest and beautifullest letter in the world, offering to help me as far as he could, to see me safe home once more."

"Enough of that now, Paddy. It only remains to me to tell our friends here, that you paid me back every copper that I ever advanced for you."

"Yes, indeed, but taking my own time about it, and you taking your pay in game and fish—and only for the money lent,—not taking anything for the corn and bacon! Och! Wharncliffe, as the Holy Bible says it, 'Ef I iver forgits you, may my right hand forgit its cunning!' "

And here the poor fellow grasped Wharncliffe's hands, and squeezed them passionately, while you could see the big tears swelling in his eyes.

"Take a drink, Paddy," says Wharncliffe. "You are an affectionate fellow, and make too much fuss about a trifle."

"Friendship and good sarvice, in the nick of time, is no trifle, Wharncliffe; and that friendship that sends comfort to a poor ould widow, is sich a blessed vartue, that it desarves to be wrote down by an angel with a gould pen made out of the beams of the blessed sun himself."

"Bravo, Paddy, you are poetical."

"No, sirree, only raisonable and sinsible. But I reckon you wants me to go on with my story. Well, a'ter I wrote the letter to Wharncliffe and my poor ould mother, Thompson said to me, 'now let's jine the Cappin and go aboard; I've got some things to see after, and must sleep aboard to-night, and I reckon you'll be willing to do the same.' So I agreed, and we put out, and got to the wharf jest in time for the Cappin who was waiting for us.

"We had a good supper aboard, Thompson and me, and the mate, the only ones at table. The Cappin was in good sperrits.—He had seen the agents of the ship, and they waur mightily tickled, for he had brought a big cargo to a good market, and he had been so long at sea, that they waur beginning to feel skeary, thinking the ship was lost.—Next morning I slept pretty late, and was waked by Thompson and the Cappin, both coming to my bunk; and the Cappin said:

" 'Es I told you, Paddy, they've made a lion of you in the news-paper.'

"So he up and read from two or three papers, what they called the sing'lar adventures of the Edisto Raftsman, Patrick McGarvin, the name all in full, jest as I had tould the Cappin and the others. He had to put down all in his log-book. They said many things about me, some true and some not true.—They called me a brave, and even a handsome fellow, and mentioned how I hed suffered, and how they hed found me shipwrackt and insinsible, and a great deal besides.

" 'Now you'll see,' says the Cappin, 'by nine o'clock, some of these chaps of reporters will be coming aboard to see Paddy, and pump out of him all they kin git to fill up the newspapers, and what he won't or kaint tell, they'll fill up with their own invintions.'

"Well, sure enough, here they come, three on 'em together, and they pumped me till I was tired. They axed me every sort of question, even to how I lived and worked on the Edisto; all sorts of questions as to the length of the river, and its rifts and snags, and sawyers, and haricains, and how I hunted and how I fished. But I took kear to tell 'em nothing of my secrit throubles with the Devil of the stump. I answered quite civil, jest as Thompson and the Cappin told me, but I wan't eager to please 'em; for, you see, I hed been reading over the papers, and one and all of 'em had some impudent talking about South Carolina, and how they were for wiping her out, and crushing her, and sowing Charleston with salt; and a great deal besides about South Carolina being the great throuble of the Union; called her rebellious and insurrectionary, and can-tankerous, and I do not know what all. It was jest about the time when South Carolina was talking about seceding from the Union, now more than ten years ago.

"Well, them chaps axed me about all that too, and preticklarly wanted to hear from me that all that secession was only talk, and preticklarly to know ef our people was willing for that. They didn't stop to let me speak quick, for they went on to say it was only the talk of our ambitious politicians, who were desperit bekaise they couldn't git fat offices for themselves. Says I—

" 'On that subjic', gentlemen, I hev only to say that all my neighbors are agreed.—There's no disagreement among 'em. I've been ready for ten years to carry my rifle whenever the Governor of South Carolina tells me to draw a bead on an inimy, and I belave all our people are willing. *We* don't belave in the Union, any how. *We* don't see the good of it; and whenever our politicians say the word, we are ready to take the swamp.'

" 'Well,' says one of the chaps, 'that's bold talking for a leetle State that kin only bring twenty thousand men into the field against the glorious Union.'

" 'Sixty thousand' says I, 'upon a pinch, and I reckon every one of 'em's a man, to stand up to the rack, fodder or no fodder! Gentlemen,' says I, 'I knows precious leetle about the controvarcy, and kaint do much in the way of argyment, but I stand up for my native country, jest as I would stand up for my ould mother; and I'd fight for her grave in our ould Providence burying ground, whenever God shall please to send her out of the world, jest the same as ef she was a living woman!'

"Thompson and the Cappin stood by listening, and not saying a word all the time, 'till then, and then the Cappin slapt me on the back and cried out:

" 'That's the right sperrit, my good Edisto raftsman—stand up for your native sile!—'Tain't every man that kin hit the right of a argyment; but it's a clair case when a man's native airth is the question—it's his own—and when it's in danger, he has only to plant his foot square and ferm, and shake the fist of defiance at every inimy.'

"Then the three chaps went off.

" 'Now,' says Thompson, 'them three papers that talk so big about fighting and crushing your State, and use sich sevagerous languidge, are all edited by three of the arrantest cowards in all New York. I knows 'em all. The man who writes this,' p'inting to one of the papers—'I've seed him horse-whipt on the steps of the Exchange for insulting another man's wife; the fellow who wrote *this*, calls himself a *philosopher!* A fiddle de dee! In his paper, he is one of the worst bullies in New York. Yet, he, too, has been kicked about the streets a dozen times, and niver lifted his hand in defence of his head'—

" 'Or starn!' says the Captain, with a laugh.

" 'No; and he says it does him good, and I belave it, tho' it don't make him any better. He says that patience, onder a kicking, only proves the vartue of his philosophy! As for the dirty fellow that writes in *this* paper, he, too, has been kicked a dozen times. He's the very worst of all these fellows; a liar, a swindler, a whole-sale inventor of scandals, and a levier of black mail.'

" 'What's that?' says I. He told me, and explained it to mean——"

"Never mind, Paddy, we know it already, and know all these fellows."

" 'Well,' says Thompson, 'the worst of all is, that them three newspapers are pretty much the rulers of these people. They lead 'em back and for'a'd as they please. Here are three notorious poltroons, notorious rogues, notorious liars—stock jobbers, swindlers, and leviers of black mail—everybody in New York knows it—and yet the papers make their way and rigilate the politics of thousands and thousands. They flatter the people, in every way, at the expense of the best citizens; and the people are daily tickled—to their ruin! They are jest hurrying them on to the Devil!'

" 'And the sooner they git to him the better!' says Cappin Wilson. Then he goes on and says—

" 'My friends, I belave in God! I belave that He governs the world, jest now, as He governed it in the time of the Jews. I belave that He has His eyes upon all the peoples of all the nations; that He lets 'em hev full swing for a season; for, as the Bible tells us, He is slow to destroy a great city, and is willing to give 'em time for repentance. But, in that city, where it's onpossible to find ten men honest—ten men willing to face the truth and stand up to their raal principles—and who wont skulk when the danger comes—why, you may look for sartain, that such a people is doomed; and it's the natur' of doomed people to be always restless, fidgetting, oneasy, ontill they do something that brings the judgment down upon their heads! And it will come, as sure as thunder, onless we belave there is no longer a God in Heaven! Now, this people is the most vicious and the most impudent people in the univarse. Talk of London and its crimes and vices and vanities—talk of Paris and its vices and vanities. I know 'em all, and I tell you, my friends, that New York, for crime, vice, vanity, and all sorts of meanness, beats both London and Paris put together all hollow. They hev all that's bad in both places; and they are crowded with the scum of Europe; and they haven't got what's respectable in Europe; the old families, and old charackter, and the good manners and decencies which come down, through father and son, for a hundred ginerations! That's where you people, Paddy, hev the advantage of these! You kin look back to your grandfathers, and not feel dirty and ashamed! But most of these darsn't look back! They all looks for'a'd, satisfied that everything that kin come a'ter is better than what's gone before; and even better than what they hev in hand! Take you care of 'em! They'll swindle you! Ef a man helps you out of a ditch, in New York, feel your pockets before you let him go! He'll lift you up with one hand and pick your pockets with the other! They'll cheat and rob you in some way; and ef you git in a row with 'em, look to hev a scamp stick his knife onder your ribs, while he's axing you a saft question, with a smooth face, and looking all ciwility.'

" 'Great Gimini!' says I. 'Why, Cappin, it's a sort of hell on airth, 'cording to this charackter.'

" 'You'll find it so, ef you stays long enough, and has much to do with 'em.—There's good people, here and there, but only ax them what they knows of one another—of this one and that one—this politician or that—this banker or that—this milliner (millionaire, we suppose,) or that; and you'll soon come to your own judgment upon all. Jest study them. Ax Thompson here, he's knowed 'em thirty years.'

"Thompson jest grinned with a bitter sort of look, and said:

" 'Let Paddy try 'em for a week, with his fifteen dollars South Carolina money in his pocket. Better let him try the ixparience. He'll hardly belave in our'n.'

" 'Well,' says I, 'I'll begin the threat pretty soon. I think I'll set out as soon as the ship hauls up to the dock. I'll go ashore and look about me and see what's to be seen; and I'll try it a leetle by myself.'

"We waur hauling into the docks jest at the time we were talking.

" 'But,' says the Cappin, 'you'll lose yourself.'

" 'Lord,' says I, 'lose myself in the streets of a town, when the Divil himself, trying to mislead me, would niver lose me in the woods of the swamp!'

" 'But,' says Thompson, 'hev you niver a coat more like the cut that's common here? That coat of your'n, Paddy, is not the fashionable cut.'

" 'No! but it's one I like, and it's the only one I've got.'

"Now, my coat was a rigular hunting shirt, with great capes and heavy fringes of cotton. It was the ould revolutionory fashion, and I always fancied it. My poor ould mother made it a'ter the cut of her father's coat, and she thought it about the greatest coat in the country.

"Says Thompson: 'The boys will be running after him.'

" 'Niver you mind,' says I. 'I aint afeard.'

"By this time we hauled up to the dock. The moment we did so, up jumped a smooth, smiling gintleman from the wharf, and says he to Thompson:

" 'I wants to see the Edisto raftsman, so miracklously presarved from the raft.'

"Says Thompson—

" 'That's the man.'

"Then he comes up to me and says:

" 'I'm Mr. Cook, or Clark, or Park,'—I don't remember which—'and I'm editor of the New York Niggerbitcher'—some name like that—'and I want to hear of your marwellous adventures, in order to do you proper honor in my periowodical.'

"Says I—

" 'I'm the person; but I'm jest going ashore now, and I kaint stop.'

"Says he—

" 'I'll go 'long with you. I knows all about New York—that great city—and I'll be most happy to p'int out to you the remarkable things as we go.'

"Well, I was pretty well tired out by the other reporters, and says I:

" 'Don't trouble yourself, my friend. I'd rether *feel* my way.'

"But nothing I could say could pervent him, and he stuck to me; and I confess I found the chap useful; for he seemed to know everything and everybody, and he was so smooth-spoken, I couldn't think him a Yankee; but I made bold to ax him the question, and he spoke up bold, and said:

" 'Yankee, sir; no! God forbid; I'm a New Yorker.'

"Lord bless you, spite of all this impudence, I found out he was one of the blue bellies. I a'terwards found out that every editor in New York a'most was a Yankee, all but one or two, and they waur Englishmen and Scotchmen.

" 'And,' says I to Thompson, 'where are the natyves?'

"Says he—

" 'The sons of the old Dutchmen are nowhere. The Yankees over-run New York, like the frogs of Egypt.'

"Well, the editor of the 'Niggerbitcher,' or whatever 'twas, he walked me about everywhere, showing me, as he said, the 'glories of New York.'

"And he tried to surprise me, every now and then, showing me some big building, or some great thing. And he showed me Wall street, and he said in this street they settle all the affairs of the world.

"Says I—

" 'All, prehaps, 'cept my pea and pertato patch in South Carolina.'

"Then he carried me to the 'Museum' of a man named Barnum. Says he:

" 'It shall cost you nothing. Barnum's my friend. He's got here all the curiosities of the world.'

"And he tuk Barnum aside and hed a talk with him, then brought him to me, and said—

" 'Barnum, my good fellow, let me introduce you to my friend, the sylibrated Edisto Raftsman, Paddy McGann.'

"Then Barnum squeezed my hand, and begged me to walk around with him and see everything. And he showed me snakes and bears and panthers and maremaids and figgers in wax, and hundreds of queer things; and then, what do you think, he ups and offers me to come there, in my dress, as at present, and exhibit so many hours every day; and he offers me five dollars a day! I could hardly keep my hands off of him! But Cook, or Clark, come in, the editor, and tuk me off, and said, 'his friend, Barnum, was a good fellow, but was mistaken in his man.'

" 'I rether think he was,' says I. 'Exhibit! Dern his buttons, I'd like to thresh him!'

"But Cook said 'better not.'

" 'The truth is,' says he, 'he's been riled lately in exhibiting his maremaid, and he wanted to make up for her, and didn't think.'

" 'So,' says I, 'he wanted me to be a prostitute for his maremaid; the derned ——! I'll lick him yit!'

"But Cook tuk me off, with argyment, showing I was a stranger in the place, and not usen to New York customs. He carried me off to other places, and, at last, he said:

" 'Aint you snappish? Don't you think a bite would be agreeable?'

"I agreed, and he said:

" 'Here's an excellent house—a "Ristorynut"—where you kin git oysters and steaks and anything you want.' So in I went with him, and we went to a leetle table in a corner, and says he, 'now what'll you have?' Says I, 'oysters,' and he called out, 'oysters for *two*.' 'How will you have 'em?' Says I, 'naked as they were mother born—in the shell.' And he called out, 'two dozen oysters—naked—in the shell!' We soon devoured these. Then he said, 'what do you say to a beef-steak, or a mutton chop?' Says I, 'a beefsteak for me;' and he called out for two beefsteaks and potatoes. Then he axed me what I'd drink, and I tuk whiskey. He tuk brandy. A'ter that, I thought I hed done enough, but he thought of more; and he proposed to me—what *do* you think? 'Milk and mush!' 'Jesu crimini!' says I, 'mush and milk! a'ter oysters and beefsteak? I'm afeard it 'ud rile my insides! No,' says I, 'thank you, I'll take no more. I've got my satisfaction.'

" 'You've got no appetite,' says he, and he called for a platter of mush and milk, and Lord! how he swallowed it! 'Now,' says he, 'it's needful to wash down our Grecians. Will you stick to the whiskey or try a leetle of my favorite, brandy?'

" 'The whiskey for me,' says I. And he ordered both, calling out loud, though in a sort of whining voice, through his nose—

" 'One whiskey—one brandy,' and when the sarving boy come, he says, 'Gasson, bring us a dozen of your very best Cabannas,' by which I found he meant cigars. He offers me the cigars, on a waiter, and I tuk one of them. 'Take another,' said he. 'I don't kear if I do,' says I; and a'ter I had sarved myself to two, he puts one in his mouth, and claps all the rest into his pocket. And as we smoked, he got at me with a string of questions, all about my v'yage down the river, and how I broke loose, and about my feelings in my werry pekoolia sitivation, and I answered free enough, and felt bound to do so, where a man had treated me so handsome. And, by this time, the liquor had loosened my tongue, and I told him a dozen yarns about bear hunting and deer hunting, coon and possum hunting, and several of our backwoods stories, and I'll be hanged ef the rascal didn't put 'em all in his book, and pretty much too in the way I talked 'em. Wharncliffe showed me the book months a'ter, and laughed hearty at the way the cunning fellow picked my teeth.

"But that wan't all. A'ter he hed got out of me all that he could— enough to make a big budget in his book, he gits up and says,

" 'Wait for me a few minutes, and I'll be back, and walk with you down to the ship. I've got a pleasant supprise for you.'

"Well, I waited and waited. A'ter awhile the sarvant comes in, and says—

" 'Did you call, sir?'

" 'No,' says I, 'I didn't, but, now that you're here, I'll thank you to bring me another drink of that whiskey, and two or three more of them cigars.'

"Well, he brought 'em, all on a waiter, and I sate and smoked and sipped, till I was tired waiting. The liquor gin out, and I then called the sarvant, and says I, 'kin you tell me what's the time of night? It must be lating.' He went out and come in and told me. Says I,

" 'It's getting late, do you know where the gentleman's gone that I'm waiting for?'

" 'Home, I reckon,' says he.

" 'Home?' says I, 'how kin that be? He told me he'd be back in a few minutes.'—The fellow laughed a sassy laugh, and said,

" 'Ef you wait for him, you'll may-be wait a month of Sundays. You'll not see him in a hurry.'

" 'How's that?' says I, 'ain't he a gentleman of his word?'

" 'He! why, I suppose we must call him a gentleman, but I kin tell you he's a sponge. We knows him.'

" 'A sponge?' says I, 'what's that?'

" 'Why, you don't know what a sponge is?—he's a suck—he squeezes his supper out of a green horn, sucks it dry, and then makes himself skearce.'

" 'The devil he does,' says I. 'I kain't belave it. He tould me to wait a few minutes.'

" 'And,' says the gasson, 'he's been gone more than hafe an hour. Why, where *did* you come from?'

" 'From South Carolina,' says I.

" 'You're *sold*,' says he. 'He's *done* you! He seed the *green* in your eye, and he's tickled you in the ribs. You'll hev to foot the bill, stranger.'

"Says I, 'I kain't belave that the fellow would play me such a dirty trick. I'll wait for him a leetle longer.'

" 'Will you call for anything more, sir?' says the chap. That was just a hint.

" 'Well,' says I, 'as I'm setting at your table, it's only raisonable I should. I'll take another sup of your whiskey.'

"When the whiskey come, the chief man of the house, he come too with the waiter, and ax'd me some questions; and then he up and told me that the editor fellow was a dern'd cunning Yankee sponge. 'Why, dern him,' says I, 'he told me, right up and down, he warn't a Yankee at all—that he was a New Yorker.'

" 'So they all say,' says he, 'for the charackter don't ricommend any of 'em even in New York; and when a chap wants his supper out of another man's pocket, he'll deny his own mother ef it's needful. You're stuck,' says he—'you'll hev to pay the damage.'

" 'Well,' says I, 'ef it's got to be done, the sooner the better. A short horse is soon curried. Let me know how much I owes you. I'll pay, and would be willing to pay twice as much to have a good chaince at that fellow's oozen*.'

"Then the landlord counted up 'two suppers of oysters; two steaks; one mush and milk'—

" 'Dernation,' says I, 'I ought to ha' known that a fellow who takes a platter of mush and milk a'ter a dozen oysters and a steak, must be a skunk.'

" 'Two brandies, three whiskies, fifteen cigars—twenty-eight shillings is what you hev to pay.'

" 'And how much is that in dollars and cents.'

" 'Three dollars and a half.'

" 'So much' says I, 'for my first lesson in New York society,' and I tuk out a five dollar bill and gin him.

* Weasand.

" 'South Carolina money,' says he. 'It's at a discount; I must take out two shillings more for the broker.'

"I didn't well understand what he meant, but I said: 'take your pay; take what's right, and let me be off.' And, as I went off, I could hear the head man and the sarvant, with two or three others in the big room, a laughing, fit to split, over the business. I hed half a mind to go back and thrash somebody; and ef I hed my full strength, and any body to stand by and see fair play, I'd ha' done it. I hed some work to find my way to the ship, and when I got there, I found the Cappin and Thompson both oneasy about me. When I told 'em about my adventures with the editor, they laughed hearty.

" 'Why, Paddy,' says the Cappin, 'you're double green to be taken in by such a suck as that. He's a sneak as well as a sponge. Couldn't you hear it in the whine of his v'ice?'

" ' I didn't like his v'ice, I confess, from the first, but he was so humble and civil.'

" ' I would ha' warned you,' said Thompson, 'when you went off with him, but I thought you'd see through him, and then agin I tuk for granted that he'd want nothing more than to git out of you some stuff for his magazine. The other papers here call him 'the snapper up of onconsidered trifles.'

" 'It's no trifle of a supper he's got out of Paddy to-day. Two dozen oysters (Shrewsbury), two steaks, and the mush and milk, brandy and cigars. Why, Paddy, the rascal hasn't had sich a meal for twelve months.'

" 'Dern him! I'll look him up to-morrow and give him his pudding too. I'll wring his neck. Jest you go with me, Cappin, and see how neatly I'll squeeze the sponge.'

" 'No, no, Paddy, laugh at it as we laugh at you. Any attempt to thrash the fellow, will get you into the Tombs or Penitentiary. Here they don't punish the rogue or the slanderer, or the swindler, or the sponge; they only punish those who punish them. Cunning, Paddy, is the law here! Why, man, everybody laughs at the victim. It's considered quite a good joke to take a simple fellow in.'

" 'Dern the puppy! I didn't care about the cost, but to be tricked by sich a sneak.'

" 'Very mortifying,' says he, 'but the best sense in this part of the world, is never to let anybody see that you suffer! Grin and bear it.' "

"I never told Paddy," said Wharncliffe, "but the same rascally editor of the magazine, which Paddy elegantly denominates the 'Niggerbitcher,' once played the very same trick upon my noble and able friend, the late Hon. Richard Henry Wilde, the able lawyer, the accomplished debater, the graceful writer and the sweet poet. The Yankee sought out this unsuspecting gentleman, beguiled him of certain beautiful poems for his magazine, conducted him to a fine dinner at Delmonico's, with wines and cigars, and after they had eaten, excused himself for a few minutes, precisely as in Paddy's case, and disappeared, never to return. Wilde waited, like Paddy, with exemplary patience, until notified by the landlord that he would be required to foot the bill. For months after, the magazine was publishing his verses, with complimentary notices of its distinguished friend, the Hon. R. H. Wilde. Wilde never forgot the yell of laughter at the 'Restaurant,' when he was settling the bill. The proprietor, servants and all, seemed quite prepared for the event. They knew the 'suck' and 'sponge,' and fully anticipated the sequel. If it be any consolation to Paddy, I will tell him that he got off at about one-fifth of the amount which the eminent Georgian had to pay."

"Restaurant," says Paddy, "well, I always called it 'Ristorynut' before. I reckon you must be right in the name, Wharncliffe."

"Take a drink, Paddy!"

CHAPTER XX.

Paddy's Further Adventures Among the Wits, Philosophers and Philanthropists of New York—The Scrimmage—Paddy Takes a Ramble, and Discovers that all are not Profligate in Gotham; that there is at least one Generous Samaritan along the Highways, who is willing to Share his Good Fortunes with his Neighbor.

———

"The next day Cappin Berry, of the Steam Packet Line, come aboard to see me. I know'd him before, but we were not close acquaintance. I had jest seen him some three years afore in Charleston. But he was very friendly, and come to offer me help, in money, or any way, whatever I wanted. He offered me a free passage in his ship, and I thanked him, and told him plain, that ef I could git home in no other way, I would take passage with him; but I told him fairly, I was pretty sick of sea voyaging.

" 'You've raison to be,' said he; 'but remember, ef you kin do no better, come to me.'

"Well, I had other visitors, and got letters, some in a nice hand, from women. The first of these I got I showed to Thompson. Says he—

" 'That's an assignation.'

" 'What's that?' says I.

"He showed what he meant. Says he—

" 'There's thousands of women in New York that runs after every man that makes any sort of figger. There's thousands more who would pay any money to have people p'int at 'em. And there's thousands more that'll perjure their souls to get a new dress. Don't you pay any attention to them *anonymormon* letters.'

"And I didn't. Wilson said the same thing to me. All the letters praised my bravery, and courage, and that sort of thing; but, Lord

391

bless you, I don't see where I showed any bravery and courage. I jest had to grin and bear it, so long as life would last; and that was all!

"Well, that day I went out only a leetle way, for I was tired, and strolled over and about the wharves, and talked to the sailors, and got as far as Fulton market, and follow'd a crowd into a place where we got oysters. When I come back to the ship, I went to my bunk, and took a sleep. Then we had dinner; after dinner I took another sleep, for I was weak and drowsy. In the evening, about sundown, Thompson come aboard, and come right up to the Cappin, who was a-talking with me jest at that time.

"Says he—

" 'Cappin, these Yankees hev been hatching trouble for you, I'm a thinking. The wharf is full of rowdies, and a good many of 'em are firemen. And I could hear, as I come through the crowd, that you hed been talking agin the Amerikins; and there'll be a row; and so, you jest get ready for mischief. Ef I was you I'd hawl out of the docks, and drop anchor at a safe distance in the stream.'

" 'Well, perhaps, ef I was you,' said the Cappin, all spunky and fiery, 'I would do so; but being the man I am, I'll see 'em d——d before I give back an inch to any thousand of the blue belly rascals. They shan't scare me out of my ship; and shan't drive my ship out of the waters, while I kin raise a marlin' spike, or shoot a blunderbuss.'

" 'Well,' says Thompson, 'don't be rash. Keep off from blows as long as you kin, and meanwhile, I'll go ashore, slip through the crowd, go to the Mayor, and see ef he won't send a police force to quiet these rowdies.'

" 'Well,' says the Cappin, 'you may do so, and I reckon it's only right and proper. I won't do anything violent ef I can help it; but they must keep hands off of the ship. But I'll get ready for any sort of customers.'

"So, while Thompson steps off to the Mayor's office, Cappin Wilson gives a whistle, and calls up all hands. Says he—

" 'What do you think, my lads, there's a swarm of blue-bellied Yankee firemen—you see 'em gathering on the wharf—and I'm told they want to hang me out to dry at the yard-arm, and to lay you out, my lads, right and left, to the tune of "knock down and drag out," and "who shall pay the piper?"—Now, my lads, ef there's any among you that's oneasy in the stomach, let him stow himself away in the hold.

But the true lads will git their we'pons, from a marlin' spike to a mallet, and see that no infarnal Yankee shall put his dirty foot across this ship's gunwale, onless he comes here hat in hand, and with as smooth a face of civility as he kin put on. What do you say, my lads? Don't cheer now, or make a noise. Ef you're ready to back me, I mean to give the inimy a blasted big supprise. Jest you git ready, as I know you kin. Meantime, matey, run up the British flag, that the scamps may know the sort of animal they takes by the beard!'

"Well, in a minute a big British flag was flying over our heads, and the Cappin says:

" 'We'll see who'll take that rag down in a hurry.'

"The sailors scattered, and a'ter a while, I could see 'em tumbling up from all quarters, all in their red shirts, and bringing their marlin spikes and knives, long bars of iron, and even armfuls of heavy chain, and buckets of tar and pitch, that I seed were smoking. They clept them all down, here and there, ready to the hand, and jest stretched themselves out upon the yards to watch, and upon the deck to be at hand and convenient. Thinks I, it's time for me, too, to be getting ready for the scrimmage; so I went down into my room, and the Cappin called me into his'n, and there he was a-loading the biggest sort of a hand gun I ever seed. He called it a Blunderbuss. It was solid, shiny brass, and he was jest stuffing it with the biggest handful of buckshot and slugs. Says he—

" 'Paddy, no d——d Yankee shall ever walk my deck as a master. I'd sooner sink the ship.'

" 'Well,' says I, 'Cappin, count me down as one to back you. I'm here!'

"So off I goes, gits my rifle, wipes her out clean, measures my load, and drives down a tight ball. I hed six more bullets left. I buckled on my knife—

" 'And now,' says I, going back to the Cappin, 'now, Cappin, count on me to do the best long shot you iver seed! Jest you p'int out the preticklar fellow you want marked out, and I'll score him down one —and one agin—as fast as I can load and fire!'

"And he slapped me on the shoulder, and says—

" 'You're true blue; I knowed it from the first, even though I caught you napping, and without a sign of daylight in your peepers!'

"Well, as the sun went down, we could see the crowd a-growing bigger; and they got sassy and begun to hiss and throw stones. But the Cappin wouldn't let me fire, though it was gitting darker, and I was afeard I wouldn't hev a good light to sight my rifle by. Says he:

" 'Niver you mind. There's no need of a rifle or blunderbuss in this business; except, prehaps, jest to show 'em. I know these rascals. It's only the bully game they're at; and as soon as the police appears, they will be off! We'll jest keep the we'pons ready, *and let 'em see 'em!* and that, I think, will be enough! There's no fight in all that crowd! I've taken its measure!'

"I didn't think he was right.

" 'What,' says I, 'sich a crowd gather together and all to eend in smoke?'

" 'You'll see,' says he.

"Meantime, the stones began to fly purty thick and fast. The vessel was at the eend of the wharf, right across, and she covered the whole eend; so that the inimy could only attack us on one side, onless they come in boats. So fur they kept at a distance, and the stones would hit the side of the ship, only a few coming over; but seeing that we did nothing, you could see 'em gitting bolder and sneaking up closer; and some of the closest would fling a stone and then dodge back ahint a post, or retreat ten or twenty steps; but the crowd would push 'em for'a'd agin, and then come another shower of stones. Pretty soon they come among us, and one of 'em tuk Cappin Wilson right by the ear and cut him a leetle, but not to hurt. He was standing high on the quarter deck, and the mob could see him as he shied when the stone struck him, and they hurrah'd and cried—

" 'Give it to the d——d Scotchman! Hi! hi! Pitch it into him!'

"The Cappin kept steady. But I could see his eyes a sparkling and his mouth shut close, and I knowed from this and the paleness of his face that he found it hard to keep down his passion. The big blunderbuss was covered with an old cloak and lying at his feet. I saw him look down at it more than once; and then I said to him—

" 'Dern these yelling rascals. Say the word, Cappin, and I'll draw sich a bead on that white-coated fellow yonder, standing on the pile of stones and setting the puppies on, as will work sich a button hole

in his coat as no tailor will ever sew up. He thinks himself safe at
that distance, but only say the word, and then ax him how he feels.'

"'Don't lift your we'pon, Paddy! Be cool—be cool. It'll all blow
over ef we give it time.'

"And jest so it did. The Cappin was right. The mob had no head
and no great deal of heart. It was all tail. For, jest seeing me lift
my rifle, there was a tremenduous backing—some eased off gradual
—others turned about fairly for a run—and as the crowd pressed
this way and that way, one fellow was tumbled over into the dock and
likely to be drowned; and then, as they trampled each other, they
got to fighting among themselves. Jest then, and in the nick of time,
up comes a force of about thirty of the police, and they bangs away
with their clubs right and left, and collared and carried off a half
dozen of the noisest—and there was an eend of the great scrimmage!
All the damage done to us was a sharp cut of the Cappin's ear, and
one of the stones clipt a cabin boy across his nose, that spiled it for
beauty. As the Cappin said, 'the bridge of his nose was no longer
passable.'

"The officers of the police come aboard, and we all tuk a drink
together; and they waur very civil to me; axed for me; and offered
to show me all about, and carry me to the 'Five P'ints.'

"Says I: 'And how did you come to know that I was given so much
to liquor as to want so much at a time.'

"But they laughed, and made it clear to me that the Five P'ints
was a place—a dern'd rascally place—and quite a curiosity to strangers, from its being provarbially a place for all the Seven Deadly Sins,
all in a huddle, and trying which could outdo the other.

"Well, the Cappin wouldn't let me go ashore agin that night; but
he had a fine supper aboard, of birds and oysters, and Thompson was
there—he slept aboard,—and there were three other gentlemen, all
Scotchmen, and big drinkers. How the whiskey-punch sarculated.
The Cappin made it in a great wooden bowl, and we had roundish
wooden spoons to dip it up, and precious fine liquor 'twas—about as
good as Stylus's here. Well, I only remember one thing that was
said particular that night. 'Twas about the strength of an Irishman's
head agin liquor; and the Cappin said the Irishman couldn't drink
agin the Scotchman; that the Irishman's head could stand a shillaly
stroke better than Scotch whiskey; and he gave as a raison that the

Scotchman drank rigilar, and the Irishman only when he could git it!
—And from the drinking that night I'd put them Scotchmen's heads
for strength agin any heads in creation. But the Cappin said to me:

"'Don't you try to keep up with us, Paddy. You kain't stand it.
We ain't been shipwrackt and sun-struck, you remember.'

"He had raison for stopping me, you see, for I was thinking not
to be outdone by any one—for the honor of old South Carolina.—
And then agin, the punch, you see, was mighty temptatious. But I
seed that what the Cappin said was raisonable, and I didn't git
obstrop'lous. Nor did any one of 'em; for they got singing, and the
singing seemed to carry off the liquor like smoke out of a chimney.

"Next day, I went out with Thompson, and a'ter we got to Broadway, he left me to go see about some business, and I walked on by
myself, watching the people, and looking at the shops.

"Och! it's a great sight to look down a long big street like
Broadway, and see a matter of ten thousand people, for miles, going
this way and that way, scattering to right and to left; and then to
remember that every man of them has an objec', and is pushing for'a'd
on his own business.

"Well, as I was walking, and looking the eyes out of my head,
on a suddent, I sees a well dressed gentleman stoop down jest before
me, and pick up a bank bill. I seed it, I reckon, as soon as he, and
know'd it was money, but he stopped at once and picked it up; and
he turns right to me, and he says:

"'My friend, *we're* in luck to-day.'

"Says I, '*You're* in luck, my friend.—You've found money.'

"'And it's *your* luck, too,' says he, 'for you seed it as soon as I did;
only I was a leetle quicker to pick it up! And now,' says he, 'we'll
divide. The law is to go shares.'

"'How's that—the law?'

"'Yes,' says he, 'the law amongst gentlemen. When one finds
money, and another one's walking with him, or close by, the rule is
to divide and go shares. So,' says he, 'ef you have a *five*—this is a *ten*,
you see—give me the five and take the ten.'

"'No, sir,' says I, 'thank you. But I hev no right. You found the
money, and it's none of mine.'

"'But, my dear sir,' says he, 'you must submit to the law among
gentlemen. I should feel disgraced ef I did not share with you this

good fortune. You *must* take your share, and we will then go and drink together to our good fortin hereafter. We've niver seed each other afore, and we'll maybe niver see each other agin; but we'll take a cup of good fellowship together, and it'll be a pleasant thing to remember this acquaintance, that's come about so singular.'

"Says I, 'My friend, I'll take the drink with you, cheerful; but I kain't think of taking your money.'

" 'I tell you half of it is yours,' said he, 'and you mustn't be so ill-natured as to refuse your share. We'll drink together, and we'll share together.'

"As I still held back onwilling, he says, 'then we'll take the drink together, and d——n the bill, ef you won't want to take your share, I'll tear the d——d thing to tatters!'

"And he began to tear it.

" 'Oh!' says I, 'rether than you should tear up good money and waste it, I'll do what you say.'

" 'Ef you didn't,' says he, ' 'twould burn in my pocket. I'd never feel myself a gentleman agin.'

"So I gin him one of my two five dollars, of Charleston money, and he pushes the ten dollar bill into my hand. Then we went into a 'Restoryant' and gets a drink, and the gentleman stands treat, and we take a cigar together, and he axes my name, and when I tells him, he cries out—

" 'What, are you the remarkable man that had them astonishing adventures on the raft?'

"When I tould him I was, he gript me by the hand, and shook it almost off, saying he was the happiest man in the world to make my acquaintance, and in so remarkable a way. Then, after walking with me a bit, he says—

" 'I'm so sorry I hev to leave you now, but I jest remember an important engagement. Where kin I see you at another time?'

"I told him, and he promised to come to the ship next day; told me he was named Smith, George Washington Smith, and made me promise to wait for him at the ship till ten o'clock next morning. So, shaking my hand almost off, very affectionate, he went off, and turned out of sight into the next street.

"Well, what do you think was the upshot of that adventure?

"Why, when I told the Cappin, for I was full of the stranger's liberality, he burst out into a horse laugh, and jest then, Thompson come in, and he tells him the story, and he laughed fit to split!

" 'Why,' says I, 'what's there to laugh about? He's a gentleman who is so ginerous—'

" 'Ginerous!' says the Cappin. 'Oh! Paddy, let me look at your eyes. I didn't think you waur so green as all that.'

" 'Green!' says I.

" 'Yes, green as little Red Ridinghood.—Why, man, you're done.'

" 'Done?'

" 'Done, doubled up, laid out, sold, squeezed, sucked! George Washington Smith is a swindler! He's come over you worse than the "Niggerknocker" fellow. Let me see that fine ten dollar bill.'

"When I showed it to him and Thompson, they both said, 'It's a rigilar polecat bill—it's a counterfeit, Paddy, and that fellow would give you sich a ten for one of your Carolina fives, every minute in the day, and treat you to a drink in the bargain.'

" 'Now, dern his liver,' says I, 'kin it be true?'

" 'To be sure it is. The trick is one of the most common here in New York, but it only takes with a green-horn. The fellow knew by your dress that you waur a stranger, and from the way you stared about in the shop windows, he took you for a "saft," from the back-woods of the South! We must try to get you another rig, Paddy; that hunting shirt will cost you all your money. How much have you got left?'

"Well, I counted out, and found I had but five dollars Carolina money left, a one dollar New York paper, and a few ten cent pieces.

" 'And this ten,' says I.

"And they laughed agin.

" 'Needn't count that, Paddy. 'Tain't worth the paper it's printed on.'

" 'Dern the fellow,' says I, 'but he's engaged to come here to morrow.'

"And the Cappin laughed agin.

" 'Paddy,' says he, 'Paddy, how dernably they've neglected your education. But it's a sign you've lived among honest people all your life.'

"Well, as the Cappin said, the dern'd swindler, Smith, niver came to the ship, no more than Clarke come back to the 'Restoryant,' and Thompson tuk me to the bank, and asked the people there to look at my ten dollar bill; but they looked sharp at me, and said—

" 'How did you come by this bill?'

"Then Thompson told 'em all my story.—They know'd *him* well. But for that, I do believe they'd have tuk me up for passing counterfeit money. They took the bill and cross'd it all over, and told me to git the green out of my eyes as quick as I could; and that's all the satisfaction I ever had from that transaction.

"No! I mustn't say that. You'll hear a'terwards of something further of Mr. George Washington Smith, and how I indorsed his paper with red ink, though I hed nearly got into throuble for it. We was to have another meeting when he didn't quite expect it, and when he got *boot* to his share; and wasn't quite so elegant a gentleman as before. But this is to come a'terwards.—Meantime, my friends, ain't you thirsty after sich a long conversation?"

CHAPTER XXI.

Paddy is witness to an elegant Business Operation—He sees how two heads brought together suddenly may help an Argument—How he prepares for a blow-out—Takes a walk, meets an old Acquaintance, and gives him *boot* in his Bargain—What the Newspapers said.

———

"Next morning, I was thinking to go ashore and take a stroll, when Cappin Wilson said to me:

" 'Paddy, don't you go ashore jest yit. Wait a leetle. It'll be time enough a'ter 12 o'clock, and then I'll go along with you. I want you here, as a witness to a leetle matter which is curious. You remember them two blue-bellied Yankees that come passengers with us in the ship? Well, you thought, when I riled the Amerikins, that I was too hard upon them fellows; and, prehaps, you thought me a leetle too hard on you and your people. Well, I've tould you a'ready that I didn't mean *you* or your *Southern* people; so *that* boot is eased from *that* foot! But when I tell you that, I knowed all the time that them Yankee marchants, as they call themselves, was a-trying to cheat me, barefaced, you won't wonder that I talked out so freely! The fact is, I could hardly keep my passion down. I felt, all the time I was talking, like gitting up and taking them both by their noses, and leading 'em on deck, and jest kicking them from stem to stern. But you'll see me ixpose 'em to-day, and then you'll see how mean a Yankee can look when he's caught in his own trap! They're to be here at ten o'clock, bringing with 'em a lawyer, I reckon, and other off'cers. Now jest you stand by and see the ixposure, for I've got 'em onder the deadfall, and only wait to let 'em see the danger before I pull the string.'

"Well, sure enough, the fellows come, and they brought with 'em a lawyer, a mighty sharp, cute fellow by his looks, and a President of one of the banks, a mighty swelling, pompous sort of person. And the Cappin met 'em mighty civil and genteel, and he showed 'em all into the cabin, and he winked to me to come along. In a few minutes a'ter come two of the Scotch marchants that hed taken supper with us, and showed us how a Scotchman's head could stand whiskey punch and be niver the worse for it next morning! And *they* brought with 'em a lawyer too. Now, these Scotch marchants were the agents of the ship; and when we were all gathered in the cabin, the Cappin axes all, very purlite, to take seats around the table, and hardly had we done so, when the President of the bank, he rises up, very red in the face, and with a swell like a turkey cock, and he says, blunt and sassy:

" 'I must say, Cappin Wilson, this is a very strange and onaccountable proceeding. I cannot see how a box of specie should be missing from your ship; and I must say, sir, that you and your owners will have to account for it!'

" 'In course, sir,' says the Cappin, very smooth and saft in his discourse, 'in course, sir, we'll have to account for it.'

"And then the two Scotch agents, they said, in a breath:

" 'We doesn't ixpect, sir, to escape the responsibility. The ship's liable, and must pay for all losses.'

"Well, this seemed to be clear enough, but the lawyer of the bank, he got up and made a long speech, full of big words, laying down the loss. I couldn't make head or tail of it; but, when he got through, I found out that all he meant to say was the same thing, that the ship was liable, and that he should proceed to make her lawfully so without any loss of time.

"Then the lawyer for the ship, he got up and made answer. He hed a long speech, too, but when he had done, it appeared that he only said what they hed all agreed on—that the ship was liable to make up all losses, and in the most lawful manner! So I couldn't well see what needcessity there was for sich long talking, where all the parties waur agreeing. But they went on talking at each other, the two lawyers, and spoke of costs and charges; and then they had a laugh together; and, at length, Cappin Wilson, he put in, and he says:

" 'Gentlemen, the case is very plain, and my agents here aint going to make any difficulty about it. They've got to pay the loss and the sooner they set about it, the sooner the trouble's over.'

" 'That's right,' says the President, 'that's all we want! But' says he, 'the damages must be impressed. Specie is ruling high in the market now, and the per centage will be considerable. I have the opinion of three of the best dealers in exchange in Wall street, on the subject.'

"And he then laid down a paper.

" 'Well, well,' said one of the Scotch agents, 'there will be no difference about trifles.'

" 'You'll find it no trifle, sir,' said the President of the bank; and his lawyer put in, making a speech, and telling what the ixchange dealers said, and he went on to speak of the loss by delay in delivery of the specie, and a good many things besides.

"But Cappin Wilson put in coolly, and he says—

" 'There needn't be any 'casion for long speeches. We've got to pay you for a box of specie, in silver, valley ten thousand dollars.'

" 'Ten thousand devils!' roared the President. 'Ten thousand dollars—and in silver. Ha! ha! You'll find it no sich easy sailing, Cappin Wilson. You'll find my demand to be for seventy thousand dollars, in Spanish gold, shipped in Havana, by our agents,'—and he p'inted to the two Yankees—'and here is the affidavy of these two gentlemen, that when they shipped the box, it held jest that seventy thousand dollars, in gould specie, Spanish gould; and that's what you've got to answer to! They've got proof, by other witnesses, to the amount put up in the box!'

"And so he put down the affidavys of the two Yankees, and his lawyer took 'em up and read 'em for the good of the company; and he looked round, mighty consekential, as ef to say:

" 'What do you think of it now?'

"By this time, I begun to feel mighty skeared about Cappin Wilson; but when I looked at him, I could see the smoothest sort of grin on his mouth, and he looked as cool as a sarpent in December, and jest as quiet.

" 'What do you answer to that, Cappin Wilson?' says one of the Scotch agents.

" 'I kin only answer, sir, by these two papers, written and signed by these two shippers at Havana. Here, you see, they tell you, in this paper, that they deposit with me, as so much freight from Havana to New York, a box containing ten thousand dollars, in silver; these are their own signatures, and here is the freight list, where you will see that they have paid the freight on one box, containing ten thousand silver dollars. Ef they have shipt another box, with seventy thousand dollars in gould, they haven't paid the freight on it, and it don't appear any where in the freight list.'

"There was a great laugh a'ter this, and the lawyer for the ship took up the papers, and he said, laughing:

" 'My learned brother, this is a very pretty case for the jury.'

"And the other laughed, too, and he said to the President:

" 'Our Yankee friends have been a leetle too sharp! They've cut their own fingers.'

"Then the President blazed away at 'em with forty-two-pound speeches, and you niver seed two poor, mean skunks look so cussed cheap. But one of 'em had the impurdence to say, that 'the freight of specie was so high, he thought it only a fair business transaction.'

" 'And to save the cussed freight, you scoundrel,' said the President, 'you risked all the money.'

" 'That he did,' said the ship's lawyer. 'As I said, Brother ————, it would make a very fine case for the jury!'

"Says Cappin Wilson, who was a mighty smart fellow, as well as a good one:

" 'I 'member, gentlemen, when I was last down at Constantinople, a law case among the Turks, and ef Turkish law was good in New York—and it wouldn't be bad anywhere—then, by that, you'd lose every cent of this money! There was a rich man that lost a bag of a thousand pieces of gould. He give public notice by the crier, that he would give a hundred of the pieces to the person that would bring it back to him. A poor, leetle ould fellow, a porter, found the bag and carried it to him. He tuk the bag and wouldn't give him a copper. The poor man went to the Cadi and made complaint. The Cadi had both parties brought before him, and made the rich man bring with him the bag of gould—and he asked the rich man what he had to say. The other answered that the poor man had taken a hundred pieces out of the bag. The rascal had tuk 'em out himself. The Cadi set down and counted out the money. Sure enough, there was only nine hundred pieces. He put 'em all back and said:

" 'You lost a thousand pieces. This has but nine hundred. It is clearly not your bag at all!'

" 'And he give the bag to the poor man, and said:

" 'My good fellow, you must keep this bag ontil you find the right owner!'

" 'Now,' says he, 'ef I had been disposed to match roguery with roguery, all I hed to do, in this affair of our'n, would be to empty the gould out of the box, put in ten thousand dollars in silver, and on the strength of the freight list and the paper, signed by both these rascals—and I made 'em give me the mimorandum to be sure—you niver could ha' got a sixpence of that gould! All their after affidavys would ha' been no use agin their own written evidence! For the transaction proves 'em to be rigilar liars and swindlers.

" 'But neither me nor my owners are willing to play rogue, or do any mean thing for money. Here is your box of gould, all safe, and the only difference will be, you'll have to pay the freight on $70,000 instead of $10,000, and pay our lawyer all his raisonable charge.'

"Well, the President was too glad to git his money anyhow, and he made no bones of doing what was axed him; and he was quite civil, and got off his high horse mighty quick—but, in the midst of a great argyment between the two lawyers, Cappin Wilson, seeing that the two Yankees were edging off to the stairs, jumped up and said:

" 'Excuse me, gentlemen, there's one satisfaction I *must* have.'

"With that he made a spring and caught the two Yankees, each, with one hand by the nape of his neck, and he bumped their calabushes (heads) together till I thought he'd ha' smashed 'em both. I offered to help him and take one off his hands, but he said:

" 'No, Paddy, I'm good for both of 'em, and besides, ef there's any trouble to come of it, let it fall on my shoulders. These scamps have tried to bring the mob on me, besides, and I owe 'em something for that!'

"And all the time he talked, he was pummelling 'em: and they tuk it like holy martars. Then he kicked 'em out of the cabin, and as they got on the ship, one of 'em cried out—

" 'Your pocket shall sweat for this!'

" 'Try it, you rascal,' says the Cappin, 'and I'll indict you for swindling. I've got your own handwriting for it. I know enough of law to know that.'

"Then, as they stood on the steps threatening him, he jumped at 'em and begun kicking them, ontil he fairly kicked 'em over on to the wharf.

"We went back to the cabin, all of us, all laughing quite merry to see the sight, and there we had a good drink all 'round. The President got his gould, the Cappin his freight, the lawyers their fees; and everybody got in good humor over a luncheon, which the Cappin had on table in a twink. I niver seed or heard of the two Yankees from that day to this.

"Well, the Cappin and me went ashore, and rambled about the streets, and seed a good many sights and people; and when we both got hungry, we went to Fulton market and got a fine dinner of oysters and some good brandy. A'ter that, we went back to the ship, and in the evening he tuk me to the theatre, where we seed Forrest, the great Amerikin actor, and a fine sight it waur. And the next day, we did pretty much the same, and seed a good many sights, but had no adventure fit to speak of. The day after that, says the Cappin:

" 'Now, Paddy, ef you want the lads of the ship for a supper and a spree, better take 'em a Saturday night,'—that was jest two nights off—'that will give you time enough for priparation; and as you don't know much about the ropes here, why you must git the mate to make the needful arrangements.'

"So I did. I went to the mate right away, told him what the Cappin said, and put all the money in the purse that the sailors had made up for me, into his hands. I offered him, besides, the leetle that was left me of my own, ixpecting soon to git the money I hed wrote for to Wharncliffe (and it come the very next day), but the mate wouldn't have my money at all, but jest took what was in the purse. I don't know how much it was, for I never counted it, but 'twas all in gould and silver.

" 'And now,' says matey, 'we shall have a grand blow out, Paddy. We'll make the streets jump agin for joy. We'll hev a night of it that you'll remember.'

"Well, I left him to see to it all.

"Next morning, I went ashore, the Cappin saying to me as I went off—

" 'Sorry I kaint go with you, Paddy; only see that you take care of yourself.'

" 'Don't be afeard,' says I. 'I've got too leetle money to lose much.'

" 'Don't lose your head or your way, and see that you make good headway back; I want you to dinner. I'm to hev some friends aboard.'

"So off I goes, taking this time another path, and making off in a direction to find the Five P'ints by myself. Somehow, strange enough, I did get a leetle sort of lost. It's sartin I didn't find the Five P'ints, though I got into places that I thought very much like 'em. Lord, what sorts of people! and then the niggers! I got into a sort of nigger quarter, and ef I hadn't seed it with my own eyes, I never could have believed there was sich a dirty and ridiculous mean quarter in the very heart of sich a big, grand city. The houses were about the queerest, meanest, raggedest, tumble-down and tumble-up rookeries I ever did see; worse than anything in Charleston. Houses stuck upon houses, and houses stuck into houses, houses back of houses, and sich filth, and sich a stink everywhere, and sich a reskally set of niggers! I got out of it as soon as I could, and hardly hed I got out, and into a leetle better sort of street, when, Lord love you, who do you think I seed? Why, the very same beautiful, ginerous gentleman, Mr. George Washington Smith, who forced me to go shares with him in his findings! He was jest ahead of me, going it pretty fast, and not seeing me at all. I knowed him by the cut of his coat and the set of his hat, which was on one side of his head.

"Says I to myself—'I'll hev the change out of you now, my pretty fellow.'

"So I mended my pace, and pushed a'ter him. But he walked mighty fast, and I was afeard I'd hev to run a'ter him, and that might hev skear'd him, and made him take to his heels too; and I was jubous that ef he run he'd leave me behind, his legs being as long as mine and his build so much lighter. So I kept on as fast as a walk would let me, watching him mighty close; at last he stopt and spoke to another man, but the man jest looked at him and niver said a word, but passed on, as ef he didn't care to make his acquaintance.

"Says I to myself, 'that other chap's more sinsible than Paddy McGann. He's not to be caught for shares, that's sartin.'

"But that minute's stopping gin me a better chance, and I gained on him. Something made him stop agin, and I pushed up fast. At last, when he least ixpected it, I slapt him on the shoulder, and says I:

"'Glad to meet so fine a gentleman, so fine a day.'

"He jumped about, as ef he hed been shot, and when he looked 'round and seed me, he started for a run without a single word. But I was up to him, and before he could git the spring of me, I clipt him with the sharp eends of my knuckles over his cheek bone, and made as pretty a mark for beauty as a meat axe would like to see; but for his dodging, it would have been a knockdown argyment! Then he roared out 'murder, murder,' as hard as he could holler, and tuk fairly to his heels, I following up close enough to give him *boot* at every plunge for about twenty steps!

"By this time there was a rush of people that got between us. But the fellow kept on at high top speed. The crowd begun to ax questions, and to call for the police. I could see that some of the people looked threatening at me, so I cried out:

"'Stop that fellow! Dod dern you, you've helped him to git off, and he a passer of counterfeit money!'

"Jest then, two of the police come up, and I begun telling them of the swindler. Several in the crowd begun to tell of my assaulting and booting a citizen without provication, for they had seed the first attack; and says I—

"'That's true; I hed to come behint him, before I could git up to him and front him, for it was a stame chase!'

"Before I hed done, one of the policemen says—

"'Why, it's the Edisto Raftsman, Paddy McGann! Why, Paddy, old fellow, what hev you been about?'

"The policeman was one of them that hed come to help the ship agin the mob, and he had drank with me and the Cappin in the cabin a'ter that affair.'

"Well, I ups and tells him of the counterfeit bill, and he and the other police and the crowd, they all laughed heartily, and when I named Mr. George Washington Smith, they said he was a famous 'thimble rig,' and that they waur a'ter him then.

"'Ef he hadn't seen us, Paddy, he'd ha' hed you tuk up for assault and battery with intent to rob. He'd ha' brought the people upon you. You mustn't think to take the law into your own hands, Paddy, or you'll maybe burn your fingers.'

" 'Well,' says I, 'for that raison, I mostly used my foot.'

"The police laughed, and we all went off together and got some oysters and a drink; and, as they seemed good fellows, I told 'em of the ship's party for Saturday night, and axed 'em to come, and they said they would. I then went back to the ship, and got there in time for dinner; and when I tould 'em of my second idventure with George Washington Smith, there was a broadcast laugh round the table, and says the Cappin:

" 'Why, Paddy, you're born for idventures! Why, your idventures would be the making of your friend, the "Niggerbotcher" editor, and he ought to find you a mighty supper ef only to pick your teeth!'

" 'And pocket,' says Thompson. 'He rarely does one without doing the other.'

"Then the Cappin tells the company the story, and Lord! how it did tickle them.

" 'Well,' says the Cappin, 'you may be sartin to see the editor paying you a visit, ef he onct hears of this last idventure.'

" 'Ef he comes in my way agin,' says I, 'he'll git his pudding; and I'll make him find his own claret.'

" 'Give him *boot*, Paddy,—give him boot! Don't sile your fingers with sich a spalpeen!'

"We drank pretty late that night; and next morning, in comes Thompson, and says:

" 'Paddy, you're determined to be a lion. See, they've got you agin in the papers.'

"And sure enough, there they hed the whole affair, with Mr. George Washington Smith down in the newspapers onder the head of 'Police Report.' Two of the newspapers hed it tolerable correct; and they spoke of me quite civil, as the 'Edisto Raftsman,' whose sing'lar shipwrack and rescue from the raft they had already recorded; and they told me of my being something of a greenhorn, and how I hed been tricked by a notorious 'thimble rig' and 'note dropper,' and how I hed kicked him through the streets; doing sich justice, as they said, would save the ixpense of a police altogether, ef every honest man would take the matter into his own hands in the same way.

"But there was one paper that told a very different story. He headed it, 'Another Southern outrage upon Freedom and Civil Liberty'; and he went on to describe me as a brutal fellow from the South, who had been unfortunately saved from drowning, probably because there was another fate, by hanging, in resarve for me. He didn't say a word about the counterfeit, but mentions that, on being civilly entreated at a tavern by a generous citizen, a Mr. Smith, a member of the Republican Party, who had sympathized with my distress and was disposed to befriend me, I hed quarrelled with him in a discussion about the rights of man, and that, with the habitual brutality of a slave-holder, I hed assaulted him with violence and blows! How that I was a strong and sturdy villain, and Smith a feeble and infirm gentleman of advanced age; and the Lord knows what besides. But Wharncliffe seed all the papers; I brought 'em home to show him.

"Lord! what a rage I was in! at first, I was for going right away and giving that newspaper man as sound a thrashing as one man iver got from another; but the Cappin and Thompson wouldn't let me budge. They said—

" 'Don't you mind it, Paddy! Nobody minds the newspapers here in New York. Their business is lying, that's what they goes for. They do nothing else. You must know, Paddy, that the people here live by ixcitement. They're in a constant spasm for news. They'll run about from street to street seeking things to talk about. Look at the streets. You kin git up a mob in twenty minutes of twenty thousand men. Why, I've seen 'em mob a poor devil singer bekaise he said the Amerikins knowed nothing of music! and they mobbed an English actor here only a few years ago bekaise he warn't civil to an Amerikin actor! and you see they wanted to mob me on the strength of the say of those two dern'd blue-bellied Yankees! and ef you or I was to go in Broadway and jest stand in one place, look grave and p'int up with a finger to the sky and take care to say nothing, there'd be five thousand men stopping and straining their eyes to see what we waur looking at, and the business of these newspapers is jest to find the ixcitement and tickle the mob. It's all a mob; and they live by feeding as fast as they kin, devouring all they kin, going as fast as they kin, and singing out to one another as they go, 'How we makes the world spin!' and the newspapers have so tickled their vanity that they really b'lieves that the whole world goes on only onder their favor and permission. This paper that has so riled you talks the same way, every day, of the Southern men and Southern people. That's the hobby horse it rides, and there's a whole party that runs at the tail of that hobby! Ef you was to catch that editor and jest face him, you'd be supprised to see what a mean sneak he is! But he won't let you catch him. Ef you was to go to his office you'd niver see him. He is only a human throat, that does nothing but vomit agin the South! He's not a human at all. No! no! Paddy, no fighting here. Nobody ixpects you to fight, and you must l'arn to laugh at the blackguarding of the newspapers jest as everybody else laughs. Ef you attempt to whip these fellows, they've got a whole party at their backs, and they'd clap you up in the Tombs or the Penitentiary, and hev you cracking stones for six months, and nobody could get you out. You'll only hev to grin and bear it, and jest let your grinning look as much like laughing as you kin.'

"Well, I hed no idee of cracking stones, or going into the tombs before my time, or mounting a tread-mill, so I give ear to what the Cappin and Thompson said, both together agreed, and determined to let the dern'd newspapers say what they pleased; but I prayed, in my secret soul, for the time to come, nobody to cut between, when I might jest have a chaince for a clip at the infarnal editor, who was ividently inspired by the divil."

CHAPTER XXII.

Paddy McGann goes to a Tea Fight—Falls in with a strong-minded Woman, who overwhelms Him—A new idea of Oysters and their Sensibilities—His tastes and affections equally subjected to an Extreme Trial.

———

"That night," says Paddy, "the Cappin tuk me to a tea fight over at Brooklyn. Some lady friends of his'n wanted to see me. He said they were mighty fine people, a Scotch family, and I should have a good supper and hear some fine music.

"When I haird they were sich fine people, I didn't want to go; so I up and told him I hed no decent clothes for fine company. I hed only the one old hunting shirt, and that was of blue homespun, and pretty well wore, and my breeches waur monstrous shabby, the blue dye being pretty much washed out by the salt water.

" 'Niver you mind, Paddy,' says he, 'you've got a clean shirt, and for the coat and breeches, they suit you so well, and you look so well in 'em, that you couldn't go in better. Besides, them's the very dresses they wants to see you in. They want to see you nateral, jest as you look at home. Don't you bother about your clothes, so long as they don't gape anywhere. You're a man, and a mighty good looking one; and ef the clothes are shabby, what of that—"a man's a man for a' that!" The true man will always show through his clothing.'

"Well, that encouraged me, and we went along. Says he—

" 'You may lave your knife behint you,' seeing that I had it strapped on, onder the hunting shirt.

" 'But,' says I, 'I don't like to go into the woods without my knife.'

" 'But,' says he, 'there are no woods here.'

" 'No,' says I, 'but a great many varmints, as bad as any we've got in our thicks!'

411

"He laughed and says:

" 'Very well, as you please; and perhaps it's better, as you'll now be in pretty full costume. Don't you think of taking your rifle too?' —with a laugh.

" 'No,' says I, 'there's no *sighting* it by night, else I don't know but it might be safer.'

"The tea fight was over in Brooklyn, and we crossed in the ferry boat. We had a walk of half a mile, when the Cappin stopped and rung the bell at the door of a very fine house. The sarvant—a pretty white gall—opened the door, and didn't ax a question, but jest said, 'Walk in;' and in we went, first into a narrow gallery, and then into a big room full of pictures and looking-glasses and big chandeliers.

"A gentleman and lady both met us at the door, and we found the room was already full of people, all dressed in tip-top iligant fashion, with breastpins and bracelets, and shiney ornaments in the hair of the ladies; and the men, too, seem'd to come fresh out of band-boxes. They waur all spick and span, brand new. I was the only shabby looking person among 'em, for the Cappin, he, too, had put on his best shiney blue coat, with brass buttons, and a yellow westcote and plaid cloth breeches.

"But I warn't skear'd or ashamed. Ef they would hev me there, they must take me as they find me, only a plain man, out of the backwoods; and *to be a man,* I know'd don't depend on one's breeches, but on his behavior,—though many a man's apt to lose his behavior, ef he thinks his breeches ain't the right cut and color and fashion, or ef his cravate stands crooked on his neck!—I know'd a nigger onst, of Col. Dick Perry, of St. Paul's, who niver had his right senses about him ef you didn't let him wear his hat. All his sense was in his hat; and ef you tuk that off, he'd niver give you a straight answer. Old Col. Dick used to 'pologize for him, and say:

" 'Gentlemen, 'scuse Cuffie's hat. He'll niver wait on you sensible ef I make him take it off.'

"And so I reckon it is with many a white man. They only feel their consequence so long as they've got their new hats and coats and breeches on! But this ain't to the business.

"Well, the people was very gracious, and preticklarly the ladies. They come about me and was mighty curous with their questions.

While they were axing we haird a bustle in the passage way,—or, as they calls it, the hall—and then we haird a sharp, screaming woman v'ice say, loud enough for every body to hear—

" 'I come oninvited! I couldn't keep away! I haird you had the famous "Edisto Raftsman" here to-night, and I'd ha' died, ef I couldn't git to seeing of him!'

"And a minute a'ter, the gentleman of the house brought in a great fat, fine woman, all over feathers and necklaces, with her neck and breast a'most naked to the waist, though it was pretty coolish weather; and she come in like a queen, sailing away like a great ship, with all her sails spread, and all her flags a flying; and her eyes glanced quick around the room, till she seed where I waur sitting, and then, without waiting for any introduction, she comes straight up to me, and cries out,—giving me her hand to shake:

" 'Oh! I'm so delighted to see you! It is so great a happiness to see a true, brave man now-a-days, and one who has gone through sich an interesting ixparience!—How I should be delighted to be shipwrack'd—to be on the wide, wide sea alone—no! not edzactly alone! I should there prefar to have one fair sperrit for my minister —one dear, delightful companion—that I might say to him, "How beautiful is solitude!" Waur you not in a state of icstacy, Mr.— (what is the name? I always forgit names, and though the name's nothing—it's enough, ef the man is true and brave,) but still, it is a vulgar needcessity to know edzactly how to address the noble crathers we are talking to!'

" 'My name is Patrick McGarvin, ma'am, at your sarvice,' says I, quite humble, for she come down upon me like a thunder clap!

" 'Among his friends, Miss Anne Statia,' says the Cappin, coming up with a laugh, 'we knows him better as Paddy McGann.'

" 'I will be your friend,' says she, quick as a shot, 'and will claim the freedom of a friend! You shall be Paddy McGann with me!'

"Then she says to a young woman setting beside me, 'Give me that seat, my dear, for a-while, till I prefects my intimacy with Paddy McGann.'

"The young thing gits up, half skear'd, like myself, and then she bounces into the seat with a great squelch, and she was so spread out with her flounces and silk dress, and sot so close to me, that I was half covered with her garments. I tell you, her frock spread pretty much over one whole side of me. I was jest about to back my chair a leetle, but she was too quick for me; for in another minute, she half wheeled her chair about, so as nearly to front me, with her back pretty much to all the company, and then she begins to talk agin:

" 'And now, Paddy, my friend,' sticking her face close to mine, and looking into my very eyes, with the eyes of a hungry sarpent— 'Now, Paddy, my friend, tell me of your feelings when you were alone on the wide, wide sea, without a friend or comforter—without a consolation—with no fair sperrit for your minister.'

" 'Oh!' said the Cappin, putting in, 'he had some consolation—he had some sperrit for his minister, ontill his dimijohn of whiskey got upsit!'

" 'Oh! monstrous!' cried Miss Anne Statia. 'And am I to suppose that you found any consolation from sich a vile liquor as that, Paddy —a vulgar drink!'

" 'In truth, ma'am,' says I, 'I must confess I did! It was pretty much all I had for consolation.'

" 'But you had your longings, Paddy,—you longed for something besides. Say, was it not so?'

" 'Oh! yes, ma'am, I longed for a good many things that I couldn't git; but most preticklarly for a leetle spot of dry ground, where I could rest the soles of my feet, and think of the salvation of my body.'

" 'But had you no longings of the soul, Paddy—no grand hopes and inspirations—no great imaginations—no prayers for wings to fly to that beautiful sphere—to soar away from this lowly orb, and bask in the etarnal light of moon and stars!'

" 'Well, ma'am, I kain't say that I hed!—Ef I longed for the wings at all, it was to fly away to my native woods, and my poor cabin, and my poor ould mother!'

"Then she clasped her hands together, and cried—

" 'And them are longings of the soul, Paddy—your native woods —how romantic—the grand ould woods—the majestic trees—the beautiful groves, and vines, and meandering pathways, of your lovely Southern forests! And your home too,—how natheral sich a wish, and how delightful! "Home! Home! Sweet Home!" as dear Howard Payne sings it! Ah! for a home like yours, Paddy, in that beautiful Southern land! Oh! the land of the South forever for me! There you have feeling, and hospitality, and geniality. Here'—and she fairly seemed to shiver—'Here—

"The cold in clime are cold in blood,
    Their love kin scarce desarve the name;
But mine is like the lava flood,
    That biles in Ætna's heart of flame!"

Ah! beautiful Byron! He, too, longed for one sweet sperrit for his minister! Alas! he never found one! But there are women, Paddy, who *have* souls—warm and fond and powerful and passionate—who could hev answered to his prayer—to his flame!'

"Then she turned to the company and said—

"'Yes, there are souls, not fettered and tied up by your could convintion, who kin see, even in the obscure "Edisto Raftsman," the genial and passionate sentiment which our Northern world cannot feel or understand—who kin, like him, feel happy in a Southern forest, in an obscure log cabin, and make the flowers of poetry and love twine themselves about the rude porches, and be happy in the possession of one kindred sperrit; bold, hardy, courageous and manly! I am bold to avow that I am one of these same souls—alas! doomed to pine beneath an onfriendly sky, in an ongenial atmosphere—lacking that one sweet sperrit for a minister, which has been ever the want and the craving of onselfish love and inspiring genius!'

"And then she turned about and fired away at me agin, worse than iver. I niver was in sich a fix before; and I could see that everybody in the room was a-watching us. She fairly squared away at me; down fronted me; leant over to me; looked right into my eyes with all of her'n; and put her mouth so close to me that I thought she was going to kiss me outright, whether I was willing or no! Her hot breath come into my face, and 'twan't a breath from any ile of roses, I tell you! I was on the p'int of telling her that ef I hed any longings jest then, it was for a good full pipe of the strongest Kaintucky tobacco! But I didn't.

"There's no telling you all she did say, and no sinse in telling it; but it's enough to tell you, that she jest let out upon me like a mill-race; there was no eend to it! There wasn't a moment's rest for her tongue! She didn't give silence a chaince to recover hersilf. She drowned everybody's v'ice, even the pianner music and the singers; though I could hear enough to feel that two of the young gals present played and sung like beauties. But she niver listened, but kept on talking, with a sort of little shriek and scream every now and then, whenever she was gwine to take a fresh start! and it was all the same sort of nonsense like before—the biggest words for the biggest nonsense; like a great hoop-skairt over a crane body.

"At last we hed a call to supper, and a fine supper of oysters! Lord! how she did eat, as ef she hed been famished for a month. We all stood round a table to eat, and went into another room for it. Well, the moment supper was mentioned, she says:

" 'Git up, Paddy; we sup together as sworn friends, you know!'

"And she stuck her arm right through mine and bolted straight ahead as ef she knowed the way. When we got to the supper table, she says:

" 'Now you shall sarve me! Git me some oysters, some celery, and some sand-witches.'

"And so I got her the oysters and the celery, but the divil-a-bit I iver haird about sand-witches before. I only knowed about one sort of witches. So I axed the Cappin, and he showed me a large platter of 'em. Well, I thought I'd try some of 'em myself, and, Lord love you, they turned out to be nothing but bread and ham, cut mighty thin, and the slices laced in together, as it waur, between one another; now the ham and now the bread; now the bread and now the ham! Well, I sarved her three times, and a thundering chaince each time, and all the time she was eating she went on talking. How she could do it the Lord only knows! When we waur all done, she stuck her arm into mine agin, and we went back, in a drove, to the parlor; and the music struck up, and the young ladies begun to sing agin some mighty pretty Scotch songs. But she niver gin me a chaince to hear no more than before. Says she:

" 'Set you down *here!* I shall niver tire of hearing native eloquence from the lips of a gallant Southron.'

"She jest spoke as ef 'twas me and not she that hed been talking all the time! But now she didn't talk quite so loud and quick as before. I reckon the supper hed made her a leetle lazy. She spoke softer, and, as ef she was telling me a secret, she put her mouth close to my ears.

" 'Oysters!' says she; 'Paddy, did it iver strike you that oysters are the food of sentiment? They're onlike all other food. They provokes sentiment and tenderness!'

"Says I—

" 'They're quite tender for eating, but I niver thought about the sentiment in oysters.'

"Says she—

" 'Judging from the effect they has after eating them, one would think they hed a great deal of sentiment themselves; that they could feel—hev affections of their own, and no doubt passion. They kin love, Paddy!'

" 'The divil they kin!' says I, breaking out. 'How, in the Lord's name, kin *you know* that?'

" 'By raisoning,' says she. 'Have you niver haird of the "Loves of the Oysters"?—a divine poem, full of sentiment.'

" 'Kin there be a poem on sich a subject?' says I.

" 'Indeed there is, a most beautiful poem, which shows that an oyster may be onfortynit in love—may feel the pang of mortified affections—may ixparience denial—may love in vain!

" 'Ah!' says she, with a great sigh, looking deep into my eyes, and pressing her hand on my wrist, 'What a terrible thing, Paddy, to love in vain!—to give up one's whole heart to another, and he not know — not heed—not care! "To let concealment, like a worm in the bud, feed on her damson cheek!" Paddy, have you iver loved in vain?'

" 'Why, to tell you the truth, ma'am,' says I, 'I don't think I've iver loved at all!'

" 'What! and do you still carry a free, pure heart—a maiden heart —cold and clear as the moon—in maiden contemplation, fancy free? It is not a subject of pride, Paddy! and hev you niver seed the woman you *could* love, Paddy?' looking straight into my eyes.

" 'I kaint say that, ma'am,' says I. 'I niver thought much about loving or wiving at all, though my poor ould mother's foriver at me to git a wife. I thought more about hunting deer and wild turkey— catching fish and galloping a fine horse.'

" 'Manly ixercise,' says she; 'and to them you owe your noble limbs and manly strength. *You* hev not been tied down to the desk or the shop. You've hed room to grow and you've growed wonderful! But that's no raison, Paddy, you shouldn't have a heart and sweet affections. To love and to be tender, is as much a vartue in a man as to be brave and strong; and you must l'arn to love, Paddy,—you must larn to love!'

"And with that she stared closer than iver into my eyes, with both of her'n, so bold that I was fairly ashamed and afear'd! But I picked up courage, seeing her look so bold, and says I—

" 'Well, I think I must try ef so be even an oyster knows how to love and is so tender-hearted as you say. But an oyster's courtship must be quite comickle! I reckon ef an oyster-gentleman was about courting an oyster-lady and the sich, he'd be apt to say to her, by way of popping the question—"Will it please you to shell out, miss?" '

" 'Capital!' says the lady. 'Why, Paddy, my friend, you're a wit.'

" 'Not a bit of it,' says I; 'thank you! I'm only a plain backwoodsman of South Carolina, that's lost his way and finds himself in mighty strange diggings!'

" 'And you are longing, no doubt, to return to your beautiful cottage, in your genial, hospitable home, and when you're gone there and in the blessed enj'yment of your lovely forests, you will forget the poor, desolate hearts you leave behint you!'

" 'Well,' says I, 'ma'am, I kaint say that my cottage, as you calls it, is very beautiful, seeing it's nothing better than a log cabin—'

" 'A log cabin! How romantic! But the vine trails over it and the flowers wanton in the sun above it and great trees encircle it; you are embowered in the solitude, whar "transport and security entwine!" Oh! how delicious! Oh! that the forest waur *my* dwelling place! Beauty and profusion, glow and geniality; plenty, prosperity and peace.'

" 'Yes,' says I, 'for that matter, there's peace and peas in plenty, and potatoes too.'

" 'Oh!' says she, 'how I do relish those delicious Carolina potatoes, as far as I kin hev a taste for any more mortal food! You hev a log cottage—it's rustic, rural; not vulgar; and you hev peace and plenty! —what besides is necessary for human happiness, but the congenial friend, the one dear companion with whom to share your thoughts, feelings, sentiments and affections. No wonder you long to return from this cold calkilating, selfish region, where Ishmael stands at

every corner, his hand agin every man, and every man's hand agin
him, and no doubt, Paddy,' with a deep sigh, 'you are looking forward
to a meeting with some beautiful rustic in whom you ixpects to find
what every man's heart should be looking a'ter, the one sweet sperrit
to be your minister.'

" 'No, ma'am,' says I, 'not a bit of it! I've niver once looked at a
mortal woman to think of love and marriage.'

" 'Marriage!' says she. 'Ah, there, my noble friend, you name
the cruel word that is fatal to our sex. It is the invention of tyrants.
It is the bond and yoke that they fasten about the neck of woman
to keep her a bond-slave forever. But for that, how free and happy
she would be. Then there would be no impediment to the union of
true souls. Oh! hateful necessity——'

" 'Why,' says I, quite astonished, 'are you agin being married,
ma'am.'

" 'No! I suppose I must submit to the yoke, as it is imposed upon
my wretched sex. But it is no less a hateful necessity. It is the death
of love. Love, itself, is a sufficient bond for the heart, and, when
that is broken, marriage is only the yoke upon the neck of the poor
bondswoman and slave. Still, I must submit to that horrid tyranny
which keeps down the noble energies, and crushes the soul out of my
sex. My only security will be in the union with one who will usurp
no authority onder the kiver of law—who will make me free as your
own fresh breezes of the South, and will so love me as to make me
forgitful of my chains!'

"And, all the time she was talking, she was looking close into
my eyes, with a softness and a fire mixed together that would
have melted the bowels of an alligator. Oh! how I longed for a
good whiff of tobacco in self defence agin that breathing, that, as I
telled you before, wasn't from any ile of roses. Lord! that a woman,
with a bad breath, shouldn't hav' the sense to keep at a respectable
distance!

"Well, she talked of everything, and jest in this way. In the
middle of her talk, she pulls a note out of her buzzom. I hed seen
the eends of the note sticking out before.—For that matter, there
waur very leetle room for it, for the buzzom was so large and the
dress so low down, that you couldn' hide much in the hollow.

" 'I mustn't forget. Here's an invite for you to the swarray of Miss Pinch (or Clynch—I forgit now which edzackly—but it was some name like it) you must come. Miss Pinch's swarray's are all the fashion. There you will meet all the choice sperrits of New York, all the poets and authors, and artists and musicians—everybody that's famous.—The "swarray" is a special one, meant for your benefit. Be sure and come!'

"But, I'm sure, I needn't tell you any more of this stupid sort of talk atween us, though there was a great deal more of it—You've hed enough of it, I reckon. I told Wharncliffe all about it before, and when I repeated to him some of the varses she spoke to me, and I thinking 'em her own writing, he showed me the books that hed 'em in, Lord Byron and Shakespeare, and somebody else, and 'twas this foolish woman's talk that put me to reading them books, and I got a great deal of 'em by heart.

"Well, to make a long story short, the Cappin come up and said to me:

" 'Paddy, it's time for us to be off, or we'll lose the last boat for the night.'

" 'What!' cries she, 'you tear him from me before I have ixtracted from him the *hole* of his curious history!'

"As I'm a living sinner, I've tell'd you everything she axed me! She wasn't thinking of gitting anything out of me; she was only thinking of letting me hear how fine she could talk herself. Well, the Cappin 'pologizes very pretty—for he was a smart fellow, that Cappin Wilson—and he pays her some smart compliments which seemed to tickle her mightily; but he says to her: 'We have duties, my dear Miss Anne Statia, aboard ship and must be aboard by a sartin hour.'

"But this, he told me as we went, was only an ixcuse to git me out of her hands; 'for as sure as thunder, Paddy,' says he 'ef I hed let you stay, 'tell she was ready to go, she'd ha' stuck her arm into your'n, made you see her home and kept you there the rest of the night, making love to you.'

" 'Not to me, sure,' says I.

" 'Yes! to you, and to anybody that she kin pick up. She'd marry you to-morrow and ax no questions. She's past forty ef she's a day.'

" 'You don't say so. Why, she looked as bright and fine, and stared into my eyes with her own so big and bold, I thought her a sassy young woman of twenty-five.'

" 'Forty, ef she's a day, Paddy. But fine feathers make fine birds, Paddy, and what with her painting and that sort of thing, she makes out to keep down the wrinkles. She takes care niver to set too near the light.'

" 'I thought I seed some chalk or flour on her cheeks, but there was the bright red shining through it.'

" 'Paint and powder, Paddy. She's a made up thing, and as impudent as the divil.'

" 'I seed that!' says I. 'Lord! how she confluster'd me, and what big words she has, and what a harricane of a tongue! and the strangest idees about things, 'specially about marriage. She says—would you belave it?—that marriage is a bond of tyranny, for the destruction of womankind!'

" 'She's a Fureyite!'

" 'What's that?' says I.

" 'Why, she preaches the doctrines of a Frenchman named Furey, who denounces marriage.'

" 'The divil! Is that the idea?'

" 'How did you like your supper, Paddy.'

" 'What I ate of it was prime good, but I hed to do so much helping for Miss Anne Statia that I hed hardly a chaince to do anything for myself.'

" 'Yes! what a feeder she is! Why, Paddy, she'd eat a poor fellow out of house and home, even ef he waur a hunter. She's supported by a very good sort of brother, who is only a clerk himself, and how he finds her in all them feathers and furbelows, the Lord only knows!'

" 'What! aint she rich?'

" 'Poor as a church mouse, and consaited as a belfry pigeon! But let's go in here and git a dozen oysters and a good drink of brandy. These fine suppers, where the women eat so much, jest vex a man's appetite. They leave so leetle! and champagne, a'ter oysters, aint so wholesome as a leetle brandy.' "

CHAPTER XXIII.

Paddy's Southern Sympathies are played on to the amount of Ten Dollars—Suddenly becomes transformed from a Jemmy Green to a "Captain Drawcansir"—Goes to the "Swarray" of a Miss Pynch, or Miss Clynch, and sees a collection of the strong-minded Women of New York—Is perfectly satisfied.

———

"The next night we were to hev the great supper for the sailor lads; but in the morning Matey told me they hed to postpone tell Tuesday night, as they couldn't git things fixed in time for Saturday. Well, Monday night was fixed for Miss Pynch's 'swarray,' and the Cappin, he got an invite too, sent him Saturday morning. But I said I wouldn't go, tell he said I must.

"Says he—

" 'Paddy, it's the right raison for a young person to see everything that's to be seen, while he's young. It'll do to think over when you're old. At this "swarray" of Miss Pynch you'll see a queer set. They all pretend to be smart people. The fashionable, *they claim* to be the *cream* of society. But these people, poets and philosophers and artists and musicians and wits and what-nots, *they claim* to be the *wine* of society—some of them are only vinegar—some pepper-vinegar, and a smart chaince of them may be put down as skim milk and well watered at that. Each of 'em has some leetle capital of a sartin sort to go upon. But the most of 'em are downright fools. But they all contrive to git talked about, for half of them are editors or connected with the press; and they kaint do the littlest or the poorest thing in the way of writing, but they has some cussed little editor and newspaper to give 'em a horn-blowing. They work together in little sets or parties; they call 'em "clicks," and each puffs up his "click," with a clack, from day to day. You'll meet here, at Miss Pynch's, all them people you've read about in the newspapers.

Reading the newspapers about 'em you'd think that sich great writers niver lived before. But jest you go from one set to another and you'll hear a different story. What one "click" praises another abuses. What I want you, in preticklar, to see is the very persons themselves; and hear 'em talk; and in three minutes, only give 'em rope, and they'll hang themselves before your face, and believe all the time they're playing Cappin Grand over you. You've got sinse to see through a fool onst his tongue gits running. You must go, ef only to see how very little come of our biggest newspaper-people air.'

"Well, he persuaded me, and I agreed, when the night come, to go.

"'But,' said I, 'Cappin, I'm thinking to leave you next week and put out for home. I've been away long enough, and I'm gitting tired. I must go back and see how the old woods look, and feel myself once more on my native airth! I don't feel altogether like a free white man any whaur else; and I must go home, ef only to give my poor ould mother a chaince to scold me for letting myself be shipwract. I've got my money, all that's needful, from my friend, and I haint got no ixcuse for staying off longer, and what's more, I don't want none.'

"Says he—

"'That's all right, Paddy. It's your duty to go home and set your ould mother's hairt at aise. But you kin stay till the supper and "swarray's" over. The "swarray" is Monday night, and made so special for your sake. Friday night, I belave, is the rigilar night for Miss Pynch. On Tuesday you have the supper, and a'ter that a good rest for one day, and then you kin set off on Thursday.'

"And so we fixed it.

"A'ter that I thought to take a long stroll all the way through Broadway, and I was jest going over the ship's sides when I met Thompson coming up.

"'Paddy,' says he, 'when do you go home?'

"'Thursday,' says I, 'is the day we've fixed for.'

"'Wait till Saturday,' says he, 'and go with me in the Jeems Adger. I'm going to Charleston a Saturday—a sudden call. I'm going to see about some wracks on the coast of Florida. I'm agent for the onder writers, you know.'

"'Go to sea agin?' says I.

"'And why not?' says the Cappin, 'why not, Paddy? What did the newspapers say of you?—that you warn't born to be drowned.'

"'Dern the papers!' says I; 'but the truth is, I've hed enough of the sea to last me a year of Sundays.'

"'Pooh! pooh!' says Thompson. 'You'll hardly see or feel the sea in the good ship, the Jeems Adger. We'll make Charleston by Monday night and be thar Tuesday morning. It's a rigilar run, with these steamers, of only sixty hours. Then agin, I knows the Cappin well, and I'll git you a free ticket; and then I'll be company for you.'

"'It's a great temptation, Mr. Thompson,' says I, 'a very great temptation; but I fairly shiver at the idea of the sea and think of my shipwrack.'

"And I was skeary; but he and the Cappin together, they over-persuaded me, and I agreed; and Thompson tuk me along with him to Cappin Dickson, of the Jeems Adger, and introduced me, and he told the Cappin how I was thinking to go home by land and was afear'd of the sea after my late shipwrack. And the Cappin seized my hand, and says he—

"'Don't be afear'd! You shall go with me! I've hearn all about your shipwrack. It was a hard time, sure enough; but, as you've seen the sea in all its terrors, I'll now show it to you in all its smoothness. You'll see her as a sleeping beauty. You'll hev no shipwrack this time!'

"And he invited me to be his guest, and then he had a lunch, and I drank a glass of porter with him and Thompson. After that we went ashore, and walked up to the city; and when we got to Broadway, Thompson said he'd l'ave me to go and see the onder-writers, for he had work to do. So I went on my walk up Broadway, looking at every thing, and making my way through the crowd, with every now and then the people p'inting at me, and I could hear some of 'em say—

"'That's the famous Edisto Raftsman, that had the wonderful shipwrack!'

"Well, on I went, till I come to a place where the crowd was so thick I could hardly squeeze through. And says I to a man—

"'What's the to-do here?'

"'To-do!' says he, 'to-do?'

" 'What's the matter?' says I.

" 'Oh! only an auction.'

"When I haird that, I considered that I must buy some things to carry home to my ould mother. I knew 'twould tickle her to be able to show things and say, 'My son brought 'em home with him all the way from New York city;' and I thought that I might buy some things at the auction that would jest do, and prehaps git 'em a bargain. So I pushed my way in with the crowd, and got up to the eend of a long table. It was a very large hall, and 'twas full of people, all crowding close to the table. At the other eend of the table there waur three men and two boys, and one of the men was the auctioneer. Jest then, when I got up to the foot of the table, the auctioneer had a darkish box in his hand—I couldn't see well, as there wasn't much light, but I haird him say—

" 'Only nine dollars, gentlemen, for this rich and costly dressing case! Why, it couldn't be made in Paris onder fifty dollars. It belongs to a fine young gentleman of South Carolina, now lodging at the Claryndin House, who has been robbed of his money, and is now compelled to sell his chamber furniture to pay his tavern bill.— And only nine dollars!'

"When I haird of the distress of the young man, and that he was from South Carolina, I cried out, 'Ten dollars,' jest to give him a lift, and niver onst thinking that it would be sold for sich a price; and as I said the words, quick as a meat axe, the auctioneer cried—

" 'Gone—ten dollars—send up your money!'

"And with that he pushed down the box. I pushed up the money, and took up the box, and opened it; and, Lord bless you, the thing was all humbug and a catch-penny, and was brand-new—had niver been used by any gentleman at all. So I sings out to the auctioneer—

" 'Look you, mister, this box ain't worth a copper—it's all ginger-bread work!'

"And he makes answer, with a grin—

" 'That's none of my business. You bought it with your eyes open!'

"And with that there was a gineral laugh all round the room, as ef everybody was delighted to see a poor backwoodsman tuk in! That laugh riled me to the quick, and, with one spring, I jumped upon the table and drawed my bowie-knife; and, with the box in one hand, and the bowie-knife in the other, I jest rushed upon him, crying out like thunder—

" 'Yes, you bloody, desaving villain, I did buy it with my eyes open, but you, blast you, sold it to me with a lie in your mouth! And now, dern you, pay me back my money, and take your box, or I'll break it over your dern'd head, and cut off your ears in the bargain!'

"Lord, you should ha' seen how the crowd give way on every side, as I pushed up and flourished my knife. There was a cry round the table—

" 'It's the Edisto Raftsman!'

"The auctioneer was skear'd out of his seven senses, and he jest dashed down my ten dollar bill on the table, and I flung the box at him! I picked up the bill, and jest flourishing my knife at him, said:

" 'You try agin to cheat a South Carolinian, by playing upon his tender feelings, and dern you, nothing shall save your ears!'

"With that I walked out. There was no laughing this time, for I jest looked round upon the crowd, savage as a meat-axe!

"Well, would you belave it, even that got into the newspapers. A'ter that I got Thompson to go with me when I went to buy the things for my ould mother.—I got her a good warm shawl for winter, and two mighty pretty frocks, and some handkechers, and a few other leetle things. But I got nothing for myself, except a good knife for cutting a deer's throat, or a sapling.

"That night I went to the Bowery Theatre with the Cappin. He ixplained to me everything; but, on a suddent, in the midst of the acting, there was a man cried out in the pit, 'Hooray for the Edisto Raftsman!' and 'Three cheers for the Edisto Raftsman!' And then there waur a gineral uproar, cheering and hooraying, and every eye was sot upon me! I felt as mean as a possum pretending to be dead. But the Cappin says:

" 'You must git up, Paddy, and make a bow, and a speech, if you kin.'

" 'But,' says I, 'no speech, I thank you;' but I got up and made a perlite bow, and the Cappin said 'Forrest, the great actor, couldn't ha' done it better!' A'ter that there was another hooray, and then they let me alone.

"Sunday I went to Church with the Cappin, and haird a very drowsy sort of preacher. A'ter he was done they tuk up a collection. I got a silver quarter ready when I seed the waiter coming round, and, Lord love you, when I put it into the waiter, it was the only silver shining in the waiter.—All the rest was nothing but coppers.

"Thinks I to myself, I reckon all that goes for the poor, and not for the parson; he'd hardly be for pocketing that sort of kine!'

"Monday night we bucked up, the Cappin in his long tail blue, with shiney buttons, and his yellow waistcoat, and me with a clean shirt, and went to the 'Swarray' of Miss Pynch, where there waur a large company, and we waur sarved with lemonade and cake. The Cappin called it 'Literary Die-out' [diet, I suppose]. Miss Pinch shook my hand, and thanked me mightily for coming—said she wouldn't ha' missed me on any account—and then begun to introduce me to all sorts of people, gentlemen and ladies.

"We hadn't been ten minutes in the house, when we haird a v'ice in the hall, that I very well know'd, crying out, loud enough for every one to hear—

" 'Has he come—my friend—the Edisto Raftsman?'

"And then in bounced Miss Anne Statia, and jest shook hands with Miss Pynch, when she found me out, and was beside me in a twink.

" 'Oh! my friend, how are you? How happy I am to meet you agin. I'm out of breath gitting here. I wouldn't lose a moment of your precious conversation. And now tell me who you'd like to know among all these iminent persons? I knows 'em all, and will introduce you. That's the beautiful Fanny Osgood. She writes the most delicious varses. And she's a beauty; an angel; the wittiest, gayest, best-hearted creature in the world—all soul—all heart— spiritual quite, and writes like a fairy! The gentleman you see paying her sich attention is Eddy Poe, the author of "The Raven."—You've haird of Poe's "Raven"—the beautifullest bird of night—a bird of the graveyard, the mosslem and the steeple—who sings but one word —the saddest, blackest, midnight word—"Nevermore!" Eddy is a dangerous fellow among us women. We all worship him. He is so divine a poet; and so handsome! Did you iver see a finer face? What eyes! What a nose? What hair! What a mouth! Oh! he is parfect!

" 'And there's Mrs. Kirkland—look at her, how huge and fat a woman, and going on to sixty; and yet, would you belave it, she's

had herself engraved, like a slender young girl of seventeen, reclin-
ing in a bower!—Oh! the vanity of some people. She writes dull,
decent books, and has a miserable set here that puffs her all it kin.

" 'That tallow-faced woman,' says she, 'looking so demure and
sour, is the famous female metaphyscian, Margaret Fuller.—What
a figger! Jest you watch her as she walks, and listen as she talks!
When she speaks to you she does it in a way that seems to say,
"young person, listen! you now hev an opportunity of listening to the
words of wisdom for the first time in your life."

" 'That dull-looking person you see alongside of her is Mr. Henry
Tuckerman, the famous essayist. I kain't say but he writes a very
respectable essay, which always makes me sleepy; and when I meet
him, his mouth is always greasy, as ef he had jest come out of an
eating house.

" 'There's one of your Southern women now—that large fat
person in black—that's Miss Maria McIntosh, of Georgia; and she,
let me tell you, is one of our best and most sinsible writers.

" 'And there, you see that man jest come in, that has sich a smirk
on his face, and sidles along like a lame crab, that's our Bishop—
Bishop Grizzy, as we calls him. But he's no Bishop—only a Parson—
that's the Rev. Dr. Griswold. He is our famous Editor of authors,
and knows the name and risidence of every Yankee girl that iver
wrote varses in an Album. He's jest married his third wife, and has
his second living.'

" 'Why how the deuce kin he do that?' said I.

" 'Oh! very easy—by divorce! Our laws are very easy for good
people who don't draw well together. There's a good story about
Grizzy—but not now—here he comes. Bishop, let me introduce you
to my friend, the famous Edisto Raftsman, Paddy McGann.'

" 'Happy to meet you, Mr. McGann,' said the gentleman, with
a sort of sniffling v'ice, and taking my hand. 'I've haird of your
very wonderful escape!' And then he began to tell to us of several
wonderful escapes he had on the railroads and steamboats; but in
the middle of his talk, he looked up, and says to the lady, 'Isn't
that the villian, Headley? I'll not suffer myself to stay a moment
in the same room with sich a wretch!'

"With that he slipped into the crowd, and was gone in a twink.
Hardly a minute a'ter, and a thin, sharp faced, dark-complexion

man come up, and Miss Anne Statia introduced me to him as the Rev. Mr. Headley—'the author,' says she, 'of the famous histories, "Napoleon and his Marshals," and "Washington and his Generals."'

" 'Don't name 'em,' says the Parson.—'How do you do, Mr. McGarvin? I've haird about your perils by sea, and your marwellous escape.'

"Then he turned to the lady and said:

" 'Waur Mr. McGarvin to give me the materials, Miss Anne Statia, what a graphic, vivid and ixciting narrative I could make! On the broad ocean, in a miserable raft, hardly above the water, seas rolling over him, the storm howling, the lightning flashing, and he calm amidst the scene, like a hero in the storm of battle, bidding defiance to the elements of terror, and rising to the attitude and altitude of a God controlling the tempest!'

" 'Lord,' says I to myself, 'that beats Miss Anne Statia all hollow.'

"But immediately after, he said, 'warn't it that scoundrel, Griswold, I seed speaking to you a minute ago? How do you suffer such a dirty wretch to speak to you at all? Where is he now?'

"Says I, 'He don't seem to like you any more than you likes him, for he said indentically the same things about you, and said he couldn't stay in the same room with sich a wretch.'

" 'No wonder!' says he; 'the scoundrel dare not meet the flashes of this eye!' And with that he looked as fierce as any razor.

"But soon, Mr. Poe and Mrs. Osgood came up together, and she said:

" 'My dear Anne Statia, I kain't suffer you to monopolite the famous Edisto Raftsman all to yourself. I've brought Eddy up to know him. I've been telling Eddy that his adwentures would make a glorious subject for one of his grand, dark, imaginating poems—the wild, the waird, the inscrutable—mystic and supernateral—like his "Raven," or his "Conquering Worm," or his "Haunted Palace."'

" 'Oh! yes, indeed. What a grand idee!' says Miss Anne Statia; 'and he could call it "The Man of the Wrack." Wrack, alone, is a grand idee; but the *man* of the wrack—alone—in the storm of the elements—and he a true man—what a wonderful grand poem, Eddy, you could make of that!'

" 'Yes,' said he, 'but I kin make grand poems without the man and without the wrack. I kin make wracks enough, and men enough for myself. I don't need the actial, to make the idee. The idee makes the actial, and the concrit is born of the onessential?' And so forth—I kaint remember!

"This was going it a huckleberry or two above Miss Anne Statia. But she looked delighted, and cried out:

" 'What a grand conception!'

"And then Mr. Poe went off and took a seat by himself in a corner, and a'ter a leetle Miss Osgood went and sot down by him.

"The next person that come up was a young woman about twenty-five, I reckon, with a smooth and rather pretty face, and Miss Anne Statia introduced her to me, saying—'This is our grace—Grace Greenwood'—I a'terwards haird that her true name was Clarke—'the writer of all those beautiful poems of sentiment that make goulden light for the magazines.'

"And then Miss Greenwood smiled, and looked sideways, and said:

" 'Oh! Anne Statia, you will be a flatterer still. My poor varses——'

"But before she could finish—ef she iver meant to finish—up comes a spruce, buckish, short, red faced person, in a bright blue coat, with shiny buttons, carrying his hat in one hand and smoothing it down with the other.

" 'Ah, General,' says Miss Anne Statia, 'I'm rej'iced to see you. Let me introduce you to my friend, the famous Edisto Raftsman!'

" 'I came up for that purpose. I am happy, my dear fellow, to make your acquaintaince. Come aside with me a moment; I wish to speak with you on a matter of the greatest importance to yourself and country.'

"And he carried me off to a corner of the room, made me set down and then took a seat beside me. He then smoothed his hat and laid it on his lap, and deliberately tuk one of my hands into his'n, while he put his other round my neck. Says I to myself—'This is a loving person, to be sure.'

" 'My dear fellow,' says he, 'the "Home Journal," which I have the honor to conduct, with the assistance of "mi boy," Willis—I am the *Brigadier*, you know, and Willis is "mi boy." Well, the Home Journal is now the 'stablished orgin of the great people of this western world. It sarkilates throughout the civilized world;

it is the orakil of the fashionable; the maker of the fashions; the ruler of taste; the teacher of the arts and graces. This is the orgin for you. Your marwellous adwentures desarve to be presarved for the admiration of futur' ages, and what orgin so popular as the "Home Journal." I will give you notoriety; you shall hev fame. Your name will be sarkilated wherever the English language is spoken; and the same orgin which conveys my songs to millions yet unborn, shall also convey, to the same ears, your most marwellous adwentures. Yes, my dear fellow, you must suffer me to put your adwentures on record. You must come to me to morrow, to my office—here is my address— and suffer me to hear the pretic'lars of your wonderful adwentures. We hev a writer of short hand who will take down your story from your own lips. Myself and "mi boy" will dress it up with all the graces of art and fiction. You shall wake up, my dear fellow, like Lord Byron, and find yourself famous; and I will see that you hev a copy of the "Home Journal" sent to your iddress.'

"Before I could answer him—and I didn't know what answer to make—I spied a man enter the door, and I recollected him in a minute. It was the same dern'd scoundrel, the editor of the 'Nigger-knocker,' or whatever his cussed paper is called, that swindled me out of a supper and ate mush and milk after steak and oysters. I jumped up, the moment I seed him, and begun pushing through the crowd to git at him. Miss Anne Statia hed been watching me; and she called out to me, and she pushed for me. One fat woman I shoved aside a leetle too roughly, seeing she couldn't onderstand an easy push. All eyes waur turned upon me, seeing my hurry; and on a suddent the scoundrel editor seed me making right towards him. The moment he did so he crushed his hat down on his head and bolted right through the door and into the hall. It tuk me only a few seconds to git there too; but when I did he was gone through the street door and up the street! By the time I got to the street door, Cappin Wilson come up and cotched me in his arms.

" 'Stop, Paddy,' says he, 'don't be foolish. Don't be making a Judy of yourself. I sees what you're a'ter; but you'll niver catch that fellow to-night. Let him alone.'

"Says I—

" 'I'd give five dollars to hev a lick at him.'

" 'Save your money,' says he; 'the fellow aint worth kicking. Stay where you air; I'll go in and git your hat quiet and bring it out to you.'

"I could hardly keep in; but I didn't know where to turn after the rascal; and so I only cussed him and waited.

"Wilson staid mighty long, I thought, before he come; but said he was looking a'ter my hat, which had tumbled onder the hall table. But the truth is, as he tell'd me a'terwards, he was telling to the company all the story of the Niggerknocker fellow's swindle. Says he—

" 'I come off to bring you back, for everybody's delighted with the story; but, instead of carrying you back, I'll make off myself. We've hed enough of these people, Paddy, I reckon, and that cake and lemonade won't do for sich a long siege of an evening. We must git something more substantial as we go along. And,' says he, 'do you know what I've saved you from?'

" 'No!' says I—'any harm?'

" 'Harm enough,' says he, 'that fat fool, Miss Anne Statia, hed made sure of you to iscort her to the Ferry Boat—a long two miles walk—for it's a'ter twelve and all the omnibusses are stopt running for to-night. I saw what the crathur was a'ter from the way she followed you. She's wore out all the Jemmy Greens she could pick up, and would soon wear you out too!—Ah! here's an oyster house. Let us go in and git some consolation, after this long three hours in a house of fools——'

"There he stopt! We soon got our oysters and brandy, and in half an hour's good walking, were once more safe aboard ship."

CHAPTER XXIV.

Paddy's Great Supper to the Sailor Lads—Grand Dance in Broadway—"Hoo! hoo! hoo!" once more—Newspaper Immortality—Paddy's last Experiences in New York—He goes Home—Captain Wilson visits him, and has a chance at Deer, Coon, and Possum.

———

"Tuesday night, ef you remember, was app'inted for the great supper to the sailor lads; and next morning Matey told me everything was ready for the night, and no further postponement. The Cappin he says to me:

"'I'm sorry, Paddy, I kaint j'ine you to-night; but I must keep the house and watch close when I let the mate and most of the hands go ashore for a spree. That's the time for a Cappin to keep a sharp look out on all p'ints of the compass. But I'd like to go, Paddy, ef for your sake only. Thompson kaint go either, as he's to stay aboard and keep watch with me. We've agreed upon it, so don't think nothing of it.'

"Well, I tould him I was mighty sorry, but ef it couldn't be helped there waur no more to be said about it. Meantime, I give the Matey the purse of money which the sailor lads made up for me, and I offered him ten dollars more of my Carolina money, ef the other wan't enough, but he pushed 'em back and said he hed a plenty, and ef more was wanted he could find it.

"You should hev seen how fine Matey made himself when we waur ready to go. He hed a spick-and-span blue suit, as fine as the Cappin's, with big brass buttons to the coat and a yellow waistcoat; and he hed a big chain and bunch of seals to his watch, and a great gould chain about his neck besides; and all the sailors waur brushed up and looking as clean and sweet as ef they niver hed known the smell of tar. We marched up to Broadway, Matey and me, and

433

tuk an omnibus. The sailor lads they followed behint, but they got into omnibusses too, taking up two or three for themselves; and so we rode up to Canal street, where we got out and pushed up Canal street tell we came to a big, ugly house. Then, says Matey—

" 'Here's the place;' and we went into a large hall, where the table was spread for supper. The room was grandly lighted up, the gas blazing on all sides; and there were two big chandeliers over the table, head and foot. The table was spread for fifty persons, and we hed that many and more too. There were three police officers and mates and sailors from other furreign ships in port, and we sot down to a splendid supper. Lord, what we hed! There waur fish and fowl and flesh and birds; there waur pigeon and pies and oysters and liquor; brandy and whiskey and wine! Matey tuk one eend of the table, and he made me set at his right hand. There was another mate or Cappin of a vessel named Colman, who tuk the other eend of the table, and soon the boys come popping into seat after seat, tell the whole table was full.

"Then the business begun, and, Lord, how the fish and flesh begun to fly. Well, a'ter we hed pretty much quieted the wolf, my Matey, he leaned back a moment in his chair and pulled a little paper from his pocket, and he said:

" 'Messmates and fellow-sailors, hear what I've got to say. I'm not gwine to spin a yarn or to make a speech, but I'm gwine to give you a toast, and it must be a bumper, so see that you fill your glasses.'

"Then the mate at the other eend of the table, he sings out:

" 'All ready, Mr. Chairman, at this eend of the table.'

"With that, my Matey rises up, and he reads from the paper:

" 'Messmates, I give you long life and grate happiness to our friend and brother sailor, Paddy McGann, the Edisto Raftsman, who showed that he hed the pluck to hold on in the worst of weathers, when everything hed gone by the board, and when there wan't a plank left between him and Davy Jones. May his brave ixample sink deep into the heart of every brave and honest Jack Tar, so that, whativer may happen, he will niver give up the ship while there's a spar to hold by or a rope to climb; may it teach all true sailor lads that to stick to the ship in all weathers is a sign that a man will stick to his messmates; and when that's the case, that a pull, a long pull, a strong pull, and a pull altogether, is almost sartin to pull out of danger and bring the ship to her promised port in safety.'

"Lord, how the lads cheered and hammered the table! When they got quiet, Matey pushed me, and he says:

" 'Paddy, no backing out! Give 'em a speech, my lad.'

" 'Lord,' says I, 'I kaint speak. I don't know what to say.'

" 'Git up,' says he, 'and talk what your own heart tells you. Jest let your feelings out, man; fer whaur a man's got the right feelings, all he's got to do is to let 'em hev full swing; and they'll sharpen his tongue and ile it and make it saft, or make it strong, jest as it's needful.'

"Well, I gits up and makes a bow and makes a sort of speech. And I *did* let out, for my heart *was* full; but, Lord love you, what I did say I kin no more remember than I kin fly. But I made a speech and was a good while about it, and when I was done, there was a great cheering and uproar. They all got up on their feet and lifted their glasses and clinked 'em together, and cried: 'Hurray for the Edisto Raftsman!'

"A'ter that, the toast drinking and speech making went on till midnight. Never waur boys so merry, breaking out of school. The mates, they made speeches, and the sailors, and some of them very funny ones too; and, I confess, a'ter awhile, I got over my bashfulness, and got a speaking more than once too often. But the lads always cheered me. Then they called upon me for a back-woods yarn, and I gin 'em a snake story; and they called upon me for another, and I gin 'em a bear story; and one story brought on another, and no one missed Time from the back of his chair, until Matey got up, and said solemn enough:

" 'Past one o'clock, boys!'

"Then they all cried out for a *spree*, and setting the town to rights, the two police officers jest as ready as the rest. And so we moved out into the street, and, I do belave, that a'most every one of them picked up the nearest bottle, and stuck it into his pocket. We marched out two by two, matey and me at the head, and went up to Broadway. —There we found two sailors busy in a fight. We surrounded them in a twink, and set 'em on, and saw the fight out; and, when one of 'em was knocked down, we gin both of 'em a drink, and made 'em friends forever. Then we jined hands, and begun dancing in the middle of the street, and everybody that come along, we pressed, and made him jine in the dance. Lord! how we caper'd and kicked up our heels, jest like wild colts in a pasture. But, jest when we were capering the wildest, what should I hear, but, right above my head, the same infarnal 'Hoo! Hoo! Hoo!' that used to worry me at home. 'Twas like suddent thunder. I hedn't haird the cussed sound once, since the last time at sea; and I begun to think I had haird the last of it then. But it didn't tarrify or worry me now. What with the hot supper, and the strong liquor, and the good company, I felt myself the man for any devil. So, jest as I heard the dern'd screech, I screeched it back again, 'Hoo! Hoo! Hoo!' at the top of my v'ice; and it was catching. Every fellow in the ring caught it up, and the street rung again with the hundred 'Hoo! Hoo! Hoos!' louder than iver. Then we danced more furious than before, and every man brought out his bottle, and we clapt the bottles to our mouths, and drank healths in the street, and soon the two policemen went down, and we rolled 'em a-one side to the pavement, and went on singing and dancing madder than ever. After that, some other police officers come, and wanted to quiet us, but we showed 'em their two brethren, laid out by the gutter, and we made them drink too, and they got pretty soon corned. I reckon they had been drinking before, and one of 'em got quarrelsome, and we kicked him, and broke his rattles over his head.—Other policemen come up, but we made 'em dance and drink with us, and they found it aisier to do that, than to go into a rigilar skrimmage. Lord love you, but there's no telling all! only I know it was broad daylight when we got back to the ship, and then I confess, I don't edzactly remember how we did get back—we were both pretty much 'how come you so!' The last thing I remember, was Matey keeping me from climbing up to the rigging to the mast head, to prove that I was a sailor like the rest of 'em.

"Well, would you believe it, all that affair got into the newspapers. 'Great Sailor Supper to the Edisto Raftsman.' They made a-most two columns of it in some of them, and reported all the toasts and speeches —my own among them—though I'm sure I niver spoke sich etarnal nonsense as they made me speke; and this brought up agin the whole story of my shipwreck, and they painted it a thousand times worse than it was. They said as how the shirks were raging all round me to devour me, and how I shot 'em by the hundreds with my gun, and how I stabbed 'em with my knife, when they put their noses too close, and the Lord only knows what all they didn't say. One paper called it 'A Maracklous Preservation,' another, 'The Finger of Providence;' and each paper had a different name, and a different story, and not one of 'em true. Then they told the story, and made it quite funny, of the 'Editorial Supper Swindle,' as they called it; and they spoke of the New York editor, as Jeremy Diddler, when I had been calling him Park or Clark. Then they told of the 'Share in Counterfeit money,' and how I had kicked the rogue; and then they had the cheeting transaction at the auction, where I had made the rogue of an auctioneer give me back my money and take his box. This they made into a funny story too; and the whole finished with the great supper and the spree. It seems they had reporters—as the Cappin called 'em —at the supper table, and these fellows clapt down everything; and as the company called upon me to tell of my cur'ous adwenturs in New York, so the rascals got everything out of me. But they furbish'd it up in a way of their own, and put in a hundred things that warn't said, and warn't true. But they all praised me up mightily, for my coolness and courage, and constancy, and all that sort of thing—except one of them, who said that 'ef the police had done its duty, this Southern ruffian would be locked up fast in Sing Sing, and not be allowed to show his brutality at the expense of our citizens.' But, it went on to say, that, 'having escaped drowning, there can be no doubt that this brutal wretch is resarved for a dry death'—meaning that I was to be hung.

"Oh! I was in a passion! But the Cappin and Thompson wouldn't hear to my going to the office and licking all consarned.

" 'It'll do no harm, Paddy,' said they; 'everybody understands these things. But, ef this one paper makes a beast of you, Paddy— and it tries to do so bekaise you're from the South—the other papers make amends. They have made a lion of you, as I tould you they would.'

" 'But,' says I, 'how ridickilous! Full of lying and nonsense! Why, I'll be ashamed of it forever a'ter! People in Carolina will think I've been telling lies here. I must go to these papers and make 'em alter it.'

" 'Well, they won't alter it, and ef they did 'twould do no good. People wouldn't read the alterations. Don't you know a proverb we hev—that a lie will travel a hundred miles while Truth is putting on its boots. Maybe they'll promise you to alter and be very smooth-spoken; but they wouldn't do it! They won't spile a good story, and the people don't want 'em to alter it. They prefar a funny lie to a dull, sober truth. It's jest like our sailor lads here, when they calls upon a fellow to spin 'em a long yarn. They knows he's going to lie and they don't ixpect anything else but a lie. But they want a lie that will tickle 'em, jest the same as these people; and they look to these papers for their yarns jest the same as the crew looks to the foremost man. As for contradicting and altering, Paddy, be sartin ef they once try to do so, they'll make the matter worse. Ef you was to go to 'em and say, "I didn't kill a hundred shirks—I only killed five——"'

" 'But, Cappin,' says I, 'I didn't kill one.'

" 'Makes no difference,' says he. 'You go and tell 'em you want the thing corrected—that you didn't kill one shirk, let 'lone twenty, do you know how they'd correct it?'

" 'No. How? Tell the truth, I reckon.'

" 'Catch 'em at it! They'd say, "we find we were in error yesterday in mentioning the number of shirks killed by the famous Edisto Raftsman. Instead of twenty, he killed but five shirks, but each of them was thirty feet long; the other ten were alligators of the largest size and the most ravenous species." That's the way they'd correct one lie, only by telling a bigger!'

"Well, the long and short of it was, that the Cappin and Thompson put me out of the notion of gitting the newspapers to speak the truth; so I made myself as aisy as I could, only hoping and praying that nobody in South Carolina would iver read the nonsense and lying they wrote about me.

"While we was a talking, a young fellow come aboard and brought me a leetle letter and a big bunch of flowers, from Miss Anne Statia. In the letter she axed me to come and see her at her house in Brooklyn; and the letter was stuffed full of her big words and ridickilous sentiments. I tould the young man I'd see about it, and sent my respectful compliments to the lady, and thanked her a thousand times for her beautiful flowers; but I niver let on, for a minute, that I was a-going home on Saturday.

"Well, the rest of my time was spent in walking about the streets and seeing what I could see. I rode in the omnibusses as fur as they'd carry me, and went to the Park and to Jarsey City and Hoboken and Wehawken, and wanted to go to West P'int, but I hadn't got the time.

"One day I seed the police carrying a mighty purty white woman on a cart, and they tied her on there by her arms and body, but she struggled hard, and her feet dragged along upon the stony ground. There was a great mob following after. What she hed done, I couldn't tell, but some thought she'd been stealing; others said she waur drunk; but 'drunk or a thief,' says I, 'the woman's a woman, and they might hev the decency to carry her in a carriage.' Lord, ef the Abolitionists should see a nigger treated so in the streets of Charleston, what an uproar there'd be!

"Well, jest a'ter that I met two men a-standing by the corner of the Park and Broadway, and as I come up I hears one say—

" 'There's a coat now was the fashion in the days of Methuselah.'

"Then he looks into my face, and he says—

" 'My friend, where did you git that coat of your'n?'

"Says I, looking full into his eyes:

" 'Where I got my bowie-knife.'

" 'Oh!' says he, 'I don't mean to give any offence.'

" 'Well,' says I, 'it's not what you mean to give, but what I'm like to take!'

"Says I, agin:

" 'This coat, or the pattern of it, my grandfather, by the mother's side, sarved in at the battles of Eutaw and Cowpens, and he once threshed a man out of his breeches for laughing at it.'

"As I said that, the two fellows wheeled about and marched off, but they looked behind 'em as they went.

"A leetle while a'ter, I come up jest as a leetle rascal hed knocked over a woman's basket of apples and was helping himself as they rolled about the pavement. I gin him a clip and he tuk to his heels; when I helped the ould lady to pick up her apples. She thanked me mightily and offered me one; but I tuk a dozen and paid her what she axed, jest a cent apiece.

"I reckon it warn't a quarter of an hour a'ter that, when a drunken man, swearing dreadfully, run at a leetle gal that was sweeping the streets. She wern't more than twelve or thirteen years old, and she was half naked. Her coats hardly come lower than her knees, and she hadn't shoes or stockings. And the poor little thing, she jest run fairly into my arms. I caught her safe and put her behint me, and met the cussing fellow face to face; and says I:

" 'What do you want!'

" 'I'll lick that little divil,' says he.

" 'No you don't,' says I.

"With that, he up stick and come at me.

"But I hed my knife out and flourishing in his eyes in a minute, and he dropt his cudgel, and backed and I a'ter him, till he went over into the gutter; and though the whole thing went off in a minute, there waur a crowd of more than fifty people about us, curious to see what was gwine to happen! When I looked round for the leetle gal, she was gone.

"And them was pretty much the whole of my adwentures in New York city. Saturday soon come, and I tuk leave of Cappin Wilson and Matey, and all the sailor lads, with a full heart; and I could hardly keep dry eyes! And they waur all sorry to part with me! The Cappin gin me a beautiful shot-bag and powder-horn; and Matey gin me a beautiful brand new pipe. They waur good friends to me, and did all they could to make me comfortable, and to please me; and may thunder strike me to shivers if I iver forgits them!

"I may as well tell, at this time, how, two years a'terwards, Cappin Wilson, in the same ship, come to Charleston with a cargo. He writ to me the very day he come, and that very day I went to Wharncliffe. He will remember! And I said to him I wanted to git Cappin Wilson to come into our country, as he spoke so much about longing to see it, and see how we hunted deer, and turkey, and coon, and possum. And I told Wharncliffe as how I hed no place of my own fit to ax the Cappin to. And Wharncliffe said:

" 'Bring him to me, Paddy. He must be a fine fellow, and I'll be glad to hev him here, and you kin stay here with him all the time he's here.'

"And Wharncliffe wrote a letter to Cappin Wilson, saying as how he'd be glad to have a visit from so good a friend of *his* friend, Paddy McGann. Och! I'll niver forgit a word of them letters!

"So I tuk the cars next day, and went right down to Charleston, and pushed right for the ship; and the Cappin he fairly hugged me, and so did Matey; but they hadn't all the same sailors. What they had left of the old lads, they crowded about me, and we talked over the grand supper, and the awful big midnight dance in Broadway. And the Cappin made me stay with him for three days aboard ship, ontil he could git his business done. Then he put on his best blue coat, and plaid breeches, and yellow waistcoat, and one bright morning, airly, we tuk the cars, and got up before nooning to Midway; and there we found Wharncliffe's carriage a-waiting us; and we waur soon at Desilla. And Wharncliffe, he met Cappin Wilson at the door of the house, and he shook his hands like an old acquaintance.—And we went in, and had some glorious liquor; and he soon made the Cappin quite at home; and he spent three days with us.

"That night we made the boys take out the dogs, and had a coon and possum hunt; and ef iver you seed a man happy 'twas the Cappin, when the old coon fought the dogs! He fairly danced round the animals, and clapt his hands, and screamed, and could hardly keep from taking a hand in the fight himself.

"Next day we had a deer-hunt, and we got the Cappin a gun, and put him at the best stand, where I was sure the deer would come out.

"And so he did come out jest there; but, would you belave it, the Cappin, that had niver seed a deer in his life before, when he seed the old buck rushing out of the thick, with his tail straight, and his head in the air, he forgot he hed the gun in his hands, and jest flung up his arms, and cried out, 'Lord! what a beautiful critter!' And he only remembered the gun when the deer was out of sight; and then he shot off both barrels the way the buck hed gone! Och! he was so ashamed. He was jest like a boy, though not one of our backwoods boys, iver so leetle, would ha' done so.

"The next day, we tuk another hunt, and I driv' agin; but this time Wharncliffe himself went out, and he tuk a stand with the Cappin, and we started a buck and a doe, and they both tuck the crossing by the willow *sluo*, where Wharncliffe and the Cappin waur, and Wharncliffe and the Cappin both fired, but I reckon 'twas Wharncliffe that did the business. Both deer drapt in their tracks; and Wharncliffe made the Cappin belave that he hed shot the buck, as he said he fired at that one. Niver was so happy a man! He went down the next day, carrying me and the buck along with him; and he sat with the buck in the nigger car, and niver tuk his eyes off of him. And he tould ivery body how he hed shot him. And when he got to the ship, there waur a great palaver; and the mate could ha' almost cried bekaise he hedn't hed the same chaince! And the Cappin gin a big dinner, and he ax'd every sea Cappin in port; and, Lord! to hear him tell of the deer-hunt, and the coon and possum hunt, would ha' done your heart good. He was so happy!

"I staid with him three days more, and when I come off, he gin me several presents, and he sent up to Wharncliffe a Scotch cheese, and a barrel of ale, and a barrel of potatoes. He was a ginerous fellow, and I'm bound always to think well of Scotchmen after him. He was onwilling to let me leave him, and agin offered me a free passage back to Scotland. But, Lord! that sea! We had a most affectioned parting, both with him and Matey; but, it hed to come, so I left him, and, in a week a'ter, he sent Wharncliffe a letter, with one for me. He was to sail next day, and he did. Sence then, I've niver haird a syllable of him. I hope he's living and doing well, and that the good Lord has him always in his holy keeping; for, ef ever there waur a raal honest, opright, working Christian, then that man was Cappin Wilson. What ef he did swear a little when he was in a passion, and did like his liquor when he was thairsty, I tell you, my friends, he hed the heart of a true man in his buzzum, and every beat of it was a sort of signal for friendship.

"I needn't tell you, a'ter all that, that I got home safe from my v'yage with Thompson to Charleston. We hed a pleasant time of it. Thompson and me both went off the day of our coming into Charleston, he for Flurrida, and me for Midway, where I found all well, even to my poor ould mother, whose first words, as I know'd they would be, waur,

" 'Och! Paddy, how could you go and git shipwrackt, and treat your poor ould mother so!'

" 'But,' says I, as I hugged the ould lady, 'niver you mind mother, I'm here agin, hearty as a buck, sound in wind and limb, and, ef God will permit, I'll niver suffer myself to git shipwrackt agin!'

"Says she—

" 'Sae that you don't Paddy, for I could niver stand another shipwrack.'

" 'Nor I neither,' says I."

CHAPTER XXV.

Paddy resumes his old avocations, and the Stump fiend resumes his old parsecutions—But, in spite of all, Paddy prospers in the world, makes money, and his friends and neighbors persuade Paddy that he should marry—They select a wife for him, but he is "jubous" about the breed.

———

Wharncliffe good naturedly confirmed all Paddy's statements in respect to Captain Wilson, and, after drinking the Captain's health and Paddy's, the latter resumed his narrative.

"And now," says he, "my good friends and masters, you'll be after thinking that, afther I hed gone through sich a sea of tribulation in my shipwrack, all by the parsecution of that stump devil, I hed got enough, and would now be let off from further parsecution. You'll be thinking, that, afther seeing and hearing nothing of him but onst, in that one 'Hoo! Hoo! Hoo!' in New York, I was pretty much done with him, and he with me. But, when the Devil gits a fair gripe on a man's shoulder, t'aint so aisy to shake him off, and he begun agin, almost as soon as I got back to the old diggins, jest as ef he felt himself strong on his ould ground.

"I needn't tell you that, soon as I got home all my ould friends and acquaintances come about me to hear the news; and I hed to tell my story over twenty times. I went to see Cappin Jennings, and he treated me well and didn't blame me for the loss of the raft, seeing that it was an accident that might happen to the best pilot. Fortynit we hed a black fellow on board, a pretty good pilot too, and he got all the fleet safe to Charleston, 'cept the one unfortynit hull that I was on. So I got out of that scrape without loss of charackter or credit; though Wharncliffe, private to me, tould me that 'twas all owing to my overdrinking at the dancing match. But I swore 'twas all owing to the dern'd divil, in the shape of a stump that I hed fastened to! But the whole thing blowed over.

443

"I set to work about the ould mother's farm like a good fellow, and was soon working like a horse. Everything was out of gear, but I soon brought it right; and after some three weeks, I tried the swamp for a hunt and tried the river for fish. But I very soon found that I hed come back to my ould luck and to my ould tribulations. I hed no luck, and the same ould game of the divil begun upon me agin. There was the v'ices in the woods and the strange sounds and the feet walking behint me, and at night, over my chimney, the same etarnal 'Hoo! hoo! hoo!' louder than iver, as ef the ould divil was rej'icing that I hed agin got back into his claws. I needn't go into preticklars, sence you hev haird the same before. There worn't no difference now. Deer and turkey hunting, partridge hunting, fox and coon and 'possum hunting, and fishing, I was still hunted myself by the same miseries tell I got usen to them agin and they didn't skear me and I wouldn't ha' minded 'em so much ef 'twan't for the bad luck that was foriver sp'iling my sport.

"When I was at my rigilar working, I diskivered that I worn't so much parsecuted. I got a conteract from the railroad to furnish them with dry pine, and Wharncliffe ginerously let me cut down his dead timber and lent me a cart, wagon and horses to haul; and I cut and hauled hundreds of cords, at two-and-a-half a cord and made some money, enough to pay off ould scores, all round, and to furnish bacon for the ould mother and myself.

"While I was away, on my adwentures, the rascally niggers had stolen and eaten ivery brood sow and pig that the ould woman hed, and I hed to buy all the bacon that we eat.

"Well, I got some other jobs that paid me well, seeing as how I got the stuff for nothing and only hed to give my labor. I made another conteract with the railroad for cypress *caps*, and Wharncliffe, he let me cut in his *bays* all that I wanted. That gin me a few hundred dollars more. Then I got out several thousand cypress shingles for Wharncliffe himself, and for Roach and other people; and that put a few hundred more into my pocket. Then I made three wagons for Wharncliffe and other people; and what with one thing and another, I made more money in two years than I hed iver made afore."

"Paddy, you perceive, my friends," said Wharncliffe, "was beginning to realize the fruits of celebrity. His adventures made his fortune."

"Precious little of fortin was it," said Paddy; "but I confess 'twas more than I hed iver airned before, and sot me and my ould mother completely up agin. I bought a mule and some good young hogs and two milch cows, and made a cart for myself and hed my horse. And I found that, in all the time I hed rigilar work, I hed less and less trouble with the divil. I'd hear him when I was splitting shingles or hewing caps or working in any way in the woods. I'd hear him walking about and whispering, and now and then his cussed 'Hoo! hoo! hoo!' right over my head, and specially when anything happened to me. Once I cut my foot with the broadaxe—'twan't much of a cut, but it made me limp sore for months a'ter—and then I haird a terrible 'Hoo! hoo! hoo!' jest as ef the bloody beast was skear'd himself. Another time, a pile of wood fell down upon me and bruised one side of me purty bad, and then he howled agin. But he didn't worry me much, I tell you, when I was at any *rigilar* job. But let me go fishing or hunting, and then come the parsecutions and the frettings and bad luck, jest as ef the beast hed tould me true when he said the partridges waur his chickens! It jest seemed as ef he was determined that I shouldn't kill bird or beast in that swamp any more; as ef he thought I hed killed more than my share a'ready. And so 'twas with any shooting match. I niver had a chaince; as ef he hed determined that I should hev no more sport; but nothin' but hard work foriver a'ter. That was curious, worn't it?

"And so things went on, for, I reckon, three years; more than two years after Cappin Wilson's visit—so I waur jest haunted and parsecuted by that villainous beast, sometimes on a cold scent, sometimes on a hot; sometimes every day, sometimes every hour; ontil I naturally come to look for bad luck and disturbance."

"Stop a moment, Paddy, while I put in a few matters which you seem disposed to overlook. In the meantime, my friends, Paddy was never more prosperous in all his life. He made more money, improved his house and lands, furnished his stock, had ample supplies of bacon and provisions, pigs and poultry; his mother made butter to sell, and lard, and he himself was never more healthy. And his prosperity began when he was no longer successful as a hunter and fisherman, but addressed himself to tasks of regular labor. His demon, if he had a demon, was a blessing to him! Before he was troubled, as he tells you, he had a score of other demons at his heels; the worst of all, such as accompany the idle life of hunter and fisherman in our country; not one of whom did I ever meet who was not worthless in all other respects. The moment Paddy ceased to lead a desultory life he prospered."

"Maybe so, maybe so, Wharncliffe!—There's some truth, maybe, in what you say. The argyment is good as to the fisherman—but och! I've not done yit. See what the prosperity led me to."

"Proceed, Paddy," said Jamison, "I see you're coming to the pathetic!"

"Yes, indeed, pathetic enough, and emetic too!—Well, people seed I was prospering and doing well, and Sam Hartley piped up: 'You've got a plenty; you're nearing the middle of your life; you've got a good house and a farm well stocked. Paddy, you must git a wife!'

"Now, Sam hed got a wife jest three years before, and he hed two fine boys, and says I—

" 'It's the way with all people, their vanity makes it, to try and git other people to do what they hev gone and done!'

"Then he talked of his consolations—the company he hed—he worn't any more lonesome; and how his wife loved him; and then he p'inted to his children, and he cried out, as ef in prayer:

" 'Oh! Lord God! what do you see in Sam Hartley, that you should bestow sich blessings on him?—sich a fine house and farm! sich a good and beautiful wife, and sich fine, beautiful children, the very image of their father!'

"And my ould mother, she sot up the same cry:

" 'Git a wife, Paddy! Bring home a da'ter to me, and let me hev the grandchildren in my lap before I dies. I'm so lonesome here, and there's no raison why you shouldn't. You've got a plenty now to live upon. You're young and strong and hearty. You git plenty of work, make plenty of money, and you've got the most ixcellent friends to find you work every day. Git a wife, my son; bring home a da'ter to be company for your poor ould mother in her ould age. I kaint see well now how to make your shirts and knit your stockings, or do anything that axes for a fine sight. You must get somebody to be doing for you a'ter I'm gone; and who but a wife, that'll be a da'ter and a companion for me when you're off a-hunting or a-working in the swamp?'

"Well, the constant drapping of the wather will wear away the stone; and though I didn't want a wife, and hedn't much thought of it sence I was a youngster of nineteen—when I did think of it, and hed my eye, too, on a mighty fine gal in Orangeburg; but she died, and I was mighty much cut up, and I niver thought of any woman a'ter her. Well, as I say, though I didn't want a wife and didn't think about any, what with the talking of Sam and my poor ould mother, they driv the idee into my head, and says I—

" 'But where's the woman—who am I to git? I knows mighty few women that I would hev, and them that I might like to hev, prehaps wouldn't hev me; and I'm too old and strong a man now to be running about seeking whose hankchcr I kin pick up. I want to be sartin about the woman and then pop the question.'

"Well, the ould mother and Sam, they would set by the chimney corner for hours, argyfying the question; and Sam's wife, she hed a say in the matter; and I'd l'ave 'em at the argyment and clear out; only jest saying—

" 'When you're all agreed let me know, and ef I likes the physic well enough, I'll take it!' I confess, gentlemen, my friends and good masters, I would hev got clear of the argyment ef I could. But the others were all the time at it and at me, tell they worried me jest as much as my divil of the stump; and I would hev married pretty much anybody they pleased, jest to be let alone.

"But there's a kind of people that won't let you alone. They're for making you take the pretickler physic that they've got usen to. They're always for making you comfortable in the tight clothes they wear themselves; and for pouring happiness down your throat tell it chokes you. And so 'twas with them, my poor ould mother and Sam Hartley and Sam's wife.

"Well, they at last agreed.

"There was a poor skunk of a fellow named Pogson, that lived a few miles off, and hed a poor sort of farm of his own, mighty poor land and he a poor manager. He niver made a crop, and was always borrowing or begging. He, too, was a sort of fisherman, and about as lazy as Solomon Johnson. But he hed a wife, one son and five well-grown daughters, all tall and scrawny-boned, 'cept one, the youngest, Susan—or, as they called her, Susan Heffernan—Heffernan being her middle name. She wan't so tall and she was plump and rather pretty, and she seemed about the best-tempered gal of the flock. Nene of 'em was chickens, and she, Susan, was at the least twenty-five, so I was told; though I haird, a'terwards, that she waur thirty, ef she waur a day. Well, they settled upon her for me.

"'I don't like the breed,' says I.

"Well, Sam and all agreed that Pogson himself was a poor shoat, and that his wife was a mighty long-tongued, scandalous ould woman; and that the brother was a worthless fellow that did nothing but ride about to barbecues and horse-racings; and that the other gals were crabbed and cross-grained; but Susan, they said, was like none of 'em; she was a beauty, and so young and so tender and good-natured and quiet and easy, and so fond of home and so quick to work.

"'And she was so good to me when I was sick,' says my ould mother. 'She come and sot up with me and made me nice things; and helped me on my quilt; and helped me in my sewing and knitting. I tell you, Paddy, she's a mighty nice, fine gal, and will suit you edzactly!'

"'Well,' says I, 'ef she's been good to you, that goes a good way with me; but I tell you I don't like the Pogson breed.'

"'Oh!' says Sam Hartley and his wife, both in a breath, 'you aint to marry the whole family! Susan Heffernan aint like the rest. She's onlike the whole of 'em, and ef one didn't know to the conthrary, you would suppose she was the child of other people intirely.'

"I was jubous. The truth is, I always looked upon marriage as a thing that must mean love and warm feelings and affections—you must hev an inclining that way—and for the preticklar woman over all others that you hed iver seen; so that you think of her only in preference; and you're all the time thinking of her; and you're glad to see her come and sorry to see her gone; and you long for her to come again, and you niver feels tired, let her stay niver so long. There's no telling what love is edzactly, but I always counted it a sweet sort of oneasiness; a kind of pleasant fever, where you hev mighty pleasant dreams and fancies, and all mixed up with the one image of a preticklar young woman. I hed them feelings onst upon a time,—but they waur all gone from me when that young gal of Orangeburg died; and I niver seed the woman afterwards that iver made me think and dream in that sweet sort of oneasiness agin. As for Susan Heffernan, I hed seed her several times, but only onst or twice to spake to her; and she only looked to me like a hundred others, a smooth-faced young thing, with round, rosy cheeks and a sassy bright black eye and a plump round figger and a still tongue, which is undoubtedly a great vartue in a woman. But as for thinking to bring her home and put her on one side of my fire place and hev her all the time about me, I niver should hev dreamed of sich a thing in a thousand years, ef my poor ould mother hed only let me alone.

"But, as I tell you, nothing would sarve the ould lady but that I must marry and bring home a da'ter; and as I couldn't run about the country to look up a woman that would plaise me better, I jest thought 'twould be as well to let my ould mother hev *her* ch'ice. I don't think she iver would ha' thought of Susan Heffernan ef Sam Hartley's wife hadn't put her up to it; and I don't think Susan Heffernan iver would ha' come to see or work for my ould mother ef Sam Hartley's wife hadn't put her up to *that*, too! The two young women hed been knowing to each other long before, and they put each other up to a good many things besides that didn't make either on 'em look too beautiful in my eyes!

"One night they waur all at me, my ould mother and Sam Hartley and his wife; and Sam he prayed for me and read to me parts of Scripter, all going to show what a blessed thing is marriage life; and they all j'ined in the same tune tell my very ears got weary. It so happened that I was reading jest then, by the firelight, in an old magazine that Wharncliffe lent me, and as I turned over the pages, looking for something short, I seed a heading of a piece of poetry that come pat to the very matter they waur all talking about.

" 'Stop,' says I, 'here's something in poetry about marriage.'

"And so I read the heading. It was in big letters, and the editor said 'twas writ by a British poet more than two hundred years ago:

" 'HOW TO MARRY—OR NOT TO MARRY—1640.'

" 'Oh! read it,' says Salley Hartley.

"So I read it, and I liked it so well that I got it by heart, which I always do when a thing pleases me, and without trying for it.

I.

Marry not an ancient crony,
Nor a shrew, for love nor money;
　　Such a wiving
　　Were a hiving,
To bring comb, but never honey!

II.

Rather marry books or pleasure,
Sport or labour without measure;
　　Or, in drinking,
　　Without thinking,
Save your time and waste your treasure.

III.

The best pleasure is, when able,
To throw leg across free table;
　　Come and go, and
　　None to know, and
Question why you cut your cable.

IV.

Knowing neither wife nor master,
To curb speed, or spur it faster;
　　Goad your leisure,
　　Check your pleasure,
Break your head, yet bring no plaister.

V.

Wisely wait, nor fret to tarry,
Long, before you will to marry;
　　Then consider,
　　Maid or widow,
Which is worse to hound and harry.

VI.

If, at last, in desperation,
You *will* change your sitivation,
　　Marry any
　　But a zany!—

For a fool for a wife, to be with all your life, my poor ridickilous friend,—

> Is a constant vexation,
> A heart burning irritation,
> A perpetual agitation,
> A sore, and a boil, and a
> Blister of tribulation,
> The worst evil in creation,
> And a foretaste of d——!

And so I leave you to Miss Pandora and her box, for she, I take it, was only a pretty fool, and nothing but a fool; and there's no cure for a fool! It's almost the only human disease that's not to be cured by any human surgery!

> Hear to the reason and take the rule,
> Marry the fiend, but never the fool!"

Paddy delivered these verses, and the singular finale, with the greatest unction. None of us remembered them, and Wharncliffe suspected Paddy himself of the curious conclusion given to the sixth stanza, but he himself would give no explanation, but proceeded, with due rapidity, in his narrative. I must add, that a subsequent search among Wharncliffe's collection of old magazines, failed to discover the verses quoted, and Paddy's statement was made with every appearance of candor and simplicity.

CHAPTER XXVI.

———

"Gentlemen, my good friends," said Paddy, resuming his narrative, as he was wont to do, with his reflections, "ef I hed one bit of idvice, more than another, to give to a young man at the beginning of his active life in the world, 'twould be jest this:

"Niver you marry before you want to, and niver marry to pl'ase other people. You must feel the need of a something that you kaint find in victuals or drink or dress or sport or work; and that maybe you'll find it to be the want of a wife; and when you feel that want, why then you must try and plaise your own fancy, and not jest lie quiet while somebody else looks up a wife for you. It's a bad sign for marriage when you hev to be tould what you want; and it's a worse sign when you hev to git the eyes of other people to look out the thing you're ixpected to fancy; and ef the thing be a woman, and she's willing to be choosen by any third party, it's the worse sign for you that could happen, and maybe the worse sign for her.

"Now, I icknowledges that 'twas a most onreasonable thing in me, to live on till I was a-most of middle age, without once thinking that a wife was needful to me. I thought of it sometimes, myself, as mighty strange, that, when all the young fellows about, were going a courting, and getting married, I didn't feel any inclination to go and do likewise. I axed myself ef I was a-wanting in all natheral feeling—ef I hadn't any tender place in my heart—ef I was cold-blooded like a sarpent, and couldn't take pleasure in the innocent things of this life—in the company of women and children—in the things that was beautiful—in play and fun, and innocent divarsion.

452

"Yes, I thought I could; I was fond of play; I was fond of children; I could take the leetle crathers upon my knee, and dance 'em in my arms for hours, and swing 'em over my shoulders; and I loved to do it—that is, whenever they were leetle, and hadn't grown to be sassy—that is, ef they know'd their place, and hadn't, by spiling, been made impident and troublesome.

"And I liked women too, mighty well—that is, when they waur *settled* women, and waur quiet and sinsible, and didn't make fools of themselves, by consate and vanity; and, when I was a young man, jest eighteen, there *waur* a young person—I told you about *her* a'ready—that I used to like mightily to see and to go with; and, when the day's work was done, I was jest as often at her house, as my own, taking supper thar, and walking out with her in the evenings, and in the moonlight; and 'twas mighty pleasant to go a huckleberrying with her.

"Och! but she was a bright, beautiful crathur; and, so easy and tender, she wouldn't ha' trod the life out of a worm. I don't belave she'd ha' killed a fly, though it kept a worrying about her eyes and in her hair.—And she hed the sweetest brown eyes, and the longest, softest, brownish yellow hair. It shined jest like the sunset hiding in the autumn bushes; and she'd answer so sweet, with her head drooping to one side, and her eyes only looking up to you, sideways, slanting like, and them hafe shet in by the lids. Och! she was as modest as she was sweet, and so I always said she was sinsible, though she niver hed much to say.

"But, even with her, I niver thought about loving, though I mought have felt it; and as for marriage, it niver onst entered my head till the dark day, when I seed her stretched out, and covered with white garments for the grave; and then, och! my friends and masters, then, when it was too late, I thought of her for a wife, and, it then seem'd to me, as ef I hed lost my one chaince for happiness in a little dwelling of my own. And I never onst thought of marriage a'ter that, but jest took to the woods, more airnest afther the birds and beasts, and fishes, than I iver hed been before; and so, I reckon 'twas, that I grow'd to be a great hunter and fisherman.

"My sorrow for that sweet young thing got, in time, to be a sweetness, and I thought of her for long years after, but without any pain of feeling. I always felt it to be more pleasant to be remembering her, that I could see no more, than to look at all the finely dressed young women that I seed. And, ontil now—the time I tell you of—only two years ago—the idee of marrying or going a'ter any woman a courting niver come into my head.

"As I tell you, I begun to be afeard, seeing that iverybody was a-courting and marrying, 'cept me one. I begun to be afeard, I say, that I was hard of heart, cold as a sarpent, and wanting in the natheral feelings. So 'twas, when my ould mother and Sam Hartley, and his wife, all got at me to marry, and kept a dinging it into my ears, morning, noon and night, I jest said to myself, prehaps they're right, and I'd better give in.—It's true, thinks I, I don't feel the want of a woman, and I don't see any myself that I'd care to see too often, but, how's it with other people. Why, to my sartin knowledge, hafe the marriages are made up for men and women by their mammies or their friends, and they seem to git on, all of 'em, after pretty much the same fashion. They live together, and eat together that's sartin; and, ef they're satisfied with that, I reckon I ought to be; and then, my poor ould mother, she hed so set her heart upon it!

"One a'ternoon, there waur a grand counseltation at my house, between the ould lady, Sam Hartley and his wife, and me, all setting together, a'ter dinner, round the fire, and eating pindars. I didn't hev much to say, while all of them waur a-talking at me, but jest sat, drawing heavy clouds from my pipe, and they cracking and eating the nuts, and argyfying the question. And says Sam's wife:

" 'I don't know what to make of Paddy. He don't consider women, and he don't consider himself, and he don't consider you in your ould age.'

"This she said to my mother.

" 'I don't see,' she goes on, 'what's the good of a man, to reach his time of life, and niver hev a family of his own. It looks bad. It ain't decent and respectable, and people will hev their thinking as to his conduct. I tell you, Paddy 'tain't decent, and folks will say something's wrong.'

" 'As to that,' says I, 'who cares what people say. Let ivery man —yes, and every woman, mind his and her own business.—That's what I calls living dacent and respectable.'

" 'Well, but,' says she, 'it's only dacent, and a sign of friendship, when we secs a friend not doing what's right, to jest help him to a little idvice now and then.'

" 'That's the question—what's right in this matter? It waur right, I suppose, for you and Sam to marry, bekaise you both wanted to, and bekaise you liked each other; but, it's a different thing altogether in my case, who hevn't seed the woman yit that I kear to marry, and, perhaps, there's no woman that would kear to hev me.'

" 'There's the sin of it,' says she. 'How's it that you hain't seed the woman? 'Twas bekaise you ain't willing to look for her.—When a man wants a thing he looks for it, don't he?'

" 'There's the stump in your road, Salley Hartley. It's bekaise I don't feel the want of the thing, that I aint in a hurry to look.'

" 'It is sinful and onnatural, at your time of life, not to feel the want, Paddy McGann. People will think—'

" 'Och! the divil take the people, and all their thinking. Let them think what they d—— please. What's it to me? Why, ain't you satisfied to git married yourself, without wanting to box me up too.'

" 'Oh! don't git to cussing and swearing, Paddy,' says Sam. 'It's only raison what the women's says. You ought to git a wife, for your own sake, for the sake of dacency and religion, and for your ould mother's sake.'

" 'Well,' says I, 'Sam, that last one is the only one of all your argyments that I think's sinsible; and I've already tould you that I'm willing, ef so be I kin find the right woman to please me.'

" 'Well,' says Salley Hartley, 'I'm sure we've tould you of one, a mighty fine young woman, purtty enough for any man, and good enough too.'

"Says I—

" 'That's jest where I'm jubous. I tould you I didn't like that breed. I've been hearing, sence we hed that last talk, a good deal about ould Pogson, and, from all I kin hear, he's as mean a shoat as ever wallowed in a mud hole.'

" 'Well, but,' says Salley Hartley, 'you ain't ax'd to marry Ephraim Pogson—It's his da'ter,' and she turned up her leetle turn-uppy nose, and grinned like a badger out of his hole.

" 'No,' says I, 'but ef I'm looking after stock for my farm, pigs or poultry, I always prefars a good breed; and, when I hears that Pogson is a mean shoat, and his wife a parfect spitfire—'

" 'Who tells you that?' says she, looking fierce as a tom cat in frosty weather.

" 'Everybody,' says I.

" 'Then,' says she 'everybody is a liar.—I've known Betsy Pogson sence I was knee high. She's a good woman, I tell you, and hes got religion, and takes the sacryment every time, and she's got a fine family of young people.'

" 'What do you say,' says I, 'about Billy Pogson?'

" 'What! that boy! he's nothing but a boy—a wild, harem scarem chap, and I knows nothing more about him.'

" 'Well,' says I, 'to make a long argyment short, I've nothing to say agin any of 'em, from what I knows myself. It's all hearsay. But if a man's got to be consulted, in the case of his own marriage, he's got the right, I reckon, to ax a few questions, and see what sort of company his wife'll find for him to keep. I only wants to plaise my old mammy in this business, and ef she's plaised, I think I kin make out to be satisfied. I'll go and see the young woman, and ef she'll do, I'll say nothing about the ould people.'

" 'Why,' says Mrs. Salley, 'you talks as ef you was going to look out for a horse. I reckon you'll be axing Miss Susannah Heffernan to let you look into her teeth—'

" 'I reckon, Mrs. Sam Hartley,' says I, 'that there's no harm in a man's being as pretick'lar in taking a wife as in taking a horse; and I'll jest tell you, by way of finish, that I must not only have a woman of good teeth, but of dacent tongue and temper. There's one thing over all that I must see or find in a wife—she must hev a dacent common sense.'

" 'And what do you mane by common sense, I want to know?'

" 'Well, I'll tell you. She must know her place. Ef I puts her into a house, 8x10, she must learn to live small in it. Ef I gives her only three acres of ground, she must fit her idees to three acres and no more. Ef there's but six plates in the house, and three spoons, and but one pot, she must be so well content as to keep them clean always, and ready for use; and ef she's got but two frocks, and three pair of socks, she must think that she's got so much to wear, that she'd better put up one set for Sundays, and keep the others well patched for week o'day work. Good common sense means only to do what you've got to do, and fit yourself as closely to your place as to make the most of it. One thing, I beg leave to tell you, is, that I'll niver marry a *fool* ef I kin help it.'

" 'And what's a fool, I wonder?'

"Says I:

" 'It's a poor beast that won't let herself or anybody else alone. It's a wriggling beast, like a snake, with a sharp tongue and a silly one, that will be saying the thing it oughtn't to say. It's a beast that worries peace out of every household—a beast of impudence, and consate, and noise, and confusion; and when it happens to be a female beast, it's a sort of divil-snake—the very one, I reckon, a'ter which the wife of Adam—Mrs. Eve, I reckon we must call her, to be respectful—took her pattern. Now, anything for a wife but a fool! I could niver stand that!'

" 'I thinks, Mr. McGann,' says Mrs. Sam Hartley, 'I thinks you means to insult me—I *knows* you means to insult me; and I won't set here and be insulted by any man. Ef I had a man for a husband, he wouldn't set there, mumchance, and let his wife be insulted.'

"And she looked pitchforks at poor Sam. Says he:

" 'My dear Salley, Paddy don't mean to insult you. He'll tell you so.'

" 'Who cares for his telling, or for yours, I wonder. Ef you waur hafe a man, you'd stand up for your wife!'

"Poor Sam tried his best, and my poor ould mother tried her best, to quiet the tiger-cat; but on she went, like a great ingine with all her steam up. And the more she went on, the hotter she grew, jest heating herself by her own motion. I niver give her a word more, but she wheeled her chair about and downfronted me, while her tongue went, a hundred to the dozen! At last, her passion got so raging, that, on a suddent, she seized the paper of ground-nuts and shells she had in her lap, and dashed them full in my face, crying out, as she did so—

" 'Take that for calling me a baste and a fool, and ef I was only a man, or hed a man at my back, you'd git worse than that, I reckon.'

"Then my poor ould mother blazed up, and was gwine at her, full pitch, with tongue first, and finger nails a'ter, I'm thinking; but I got up, quite cool, shook off the pindars and shells, and went to the ould lady, and give her an asie squeeze down agin in her chair.

" 'Set you down, mammy,' says I; 'fighting and quarrelling's not the business for women. 'Member what the song says:

"Your little hands waur niver made
To tair each other's eyes."

" 'But,' says I, 'men kin and ought to settle these affairs for the women. Now, Sam,' says I, turning to where he sot, all in a heap and a shiver, 'now, Sam, I niver stand an insult like this when I kin help it. And as your wife is a woman, jedging by her garments, it's but raisonable that you, her husband, should pay all debts of her contracting. We've been friends a long time, ould fellow, but marriage is apt to break off the best friendships, especially whar the gray mar' proves the better horse! Ould friends though we hev bin, I must make you pay your wife's indebtedness! and now, tho' I'm sorry to do it, I mean to take you out here, and give you the dod-dernedist threshing you iver got in all your born days!'

"With that, I tuk him by the collar first, and then by the nape of his neck, and I gin his collar a twist which he found tight squeezing. He tried to hold back and to talk; but he could only bring out of his throat a sort of dry choking rumble. Says I—

" 'Come along out into the yard. I'll give you fair play.'

"But he was monstrous skear'd, and was for holding back, when I raised him up bodily, on my shoulders, and says—

" 'I'll put you through the window first, ould fellow, jest to show your wife how a poor husband goes down in the world bekaise he's got a fool for a wife!'

"By this time the she cat was upon me with all her claws. I got a scratch or two, but as she found me bent on flinging Sam out of the window—for I made b'lieve I waur in terrible airnest—she got him by the legs, and kept pulling back, while I waur pretending to be desprit for pushing him fora'd. Then my ould mother puts in, and she catches my arms from behint, and holds on with all her leetle strength; and all the time Sam was a twisting, and a trying to git loose, ontil I whispered him to take it asie, and not be skear'd for I wouldn't hurt him. On a suddent, I whirls him away from the side window, where I hed got him, and carries him to the front, which looked out on the piazza, and when I made the suddent whirl, it whisked Mrs. Sam over upon the floor, flat, sprawling, and my poor ould mother, she tumbled down on top of her.

"When I got Sam to the other window, I says to him, loud enough for all to hear—

" 'Sam, old fellow, as a ripresentative of your wife, you hev a divil of a temper of your own, and needs a cooling. Your blood's all in a fever, and I niver seed a man work himself in a passion so suddenly; and so, Sam, for your health's sake, and to keep you from going off in a fit, I'll cool you off in a tub of water.'

"And with that I rushed him through the piazza window, and stuck his head and shoulders souse into a large washing tub that stood on a bench jest onder the window. I gin him three good dips into the tub, full of soap lather, before I drawed him out, and sot him down upon his feet on the floor.

" 'Now,' says I, 'Sam, that's a warning to you niver again to get in a passion with your best friend, and fling your pindar hulls in his face!'

" 'But I didn't do it,' says he, with the look of an injured lamb, while his wife was a-wiping the suds and lather from his face and hair. She give me the look of a hungry tiger; but she said nothing.

" 'Well, 'twas your wife did it, and you and she by law are one, and now I give you fair warning, that for every crooked word, or look, your wife gives me, I'll take it out of you. You has to settle all debts of her counteracting.'

" 'I think that's mighty hard,' says he, looking at me pitiful.

" 'Hard or saft, make up your mind to bear it, for I've as good as sworn it on the Holy Volume. I kaint fight, or whip a woman, but I'll punish her through your bones, and ef iver she gets in a passion with you, and wants to hev you well threshed, let her jest say a crooked thing to me, and you'll get it: so I'll take for granted whenever she's out of sorts with me, that she wants to have you put onder the hammer, or in the vice.'

"They did'nt stay long a'ter that, but went off quarrelling, somehow, with one another. We could hear the woman's tongue—and she hed a mighty sharp and quick one—all the way through the avenue to the main road. A'ter they waur gone, my ould mother, who hed been trying to smooth off the bristles of Salley Hartley, she gives me quite a scolding for what I hed done. Says I:

" 'Ould lady, what would you hev? The woman's a tom-cat, and jest puts her claws into poor Sam's wool whenever she happens to be in a bad humor. I did'nt mean to hurt him, poor fellow; I'm as good a friend as he iver had, and I'm sorry he's got into the same pen with a bird that's got sich claws. One thing I've got to say, ould lady, and that is, that what I've seed of married life, in Sam's case, haint gin me any stronger liking for it.'

" 'Ah! Paddy,' says she, 'he's only made a mistake in the woman. Sally hed always a hot temper.'

" 'But she was always a great crony of yourn, and you thought the world and all of her.'

" 'So I did; and, putting out the temper, she's a mighty fine young woman.'

" 'When you put out the temper, you might as well put out the woman herself. It makes pretty much the most of her. And you say she always had this temper.'

" 'Yes, but it seems to me to hev grow'd much hotter since she's married. She worn't hafe so bad as she was to day.'

" 'That's not bekaise she's got a bad husband. It's not Sam's fault—and yet, I don't know but tis his fault. Ef a man won't be the master in his own house, the woman will be. His good natur, letting the poor young fool's head be turned by consate, and helping to turn it, that's what's made her such a tom-cat. He's a good crathur, but a leetle too much of a chicken. The worst of it, ould lady, is this: she's the fast friend and companion of your favorite Miss Susanna Heffernan—'

" 'Oh!' says my mammy, mighty quick, 'but Susan Heffernan ain't nothing like *her*. She's the sweetest, saftest—'

" 'And yet,' says I, 'what's the old say—

> Birds of a feather
> Flocks together.'

" 'Now, Paddy,' says she, 'what sort of woman would you be heving for a wife; for I reckon nothing will plaise you—not even an angel from heaven.'

" 'And hev I showed myself so hard to be plaised, mammy, that you say so? Don't you do here pretty much what plaises you?'

" 'Yes, that's true, Paddy; but I'm your mother—that makes a difference.'

" 'No! no!' says I; 'where a person's hard to plaise, nothing makes a difference. They don't mind the ould mother no more than they do the young wife. They turn back the hair and p'int the ears at everybody. Now, you're the first person that ever thought Paddy McGann hard to plaise.'

" 'Yes, Paddy, ef you had'nt been, you'd been married long ago.'

" 'And so I would, mother, but for a raison that you remember long ago.' And then I jest named the name of that sweet young girl of Orangeburg.

" 'Yes,' said she, 'poor Kitty! But a'ter that, Paddy—now more than fifteen years.'

" 'Ach! mother, ef I hed thought of marrying at all, I reckon, I should'nt be hard to plaise in the woman; and you may see that I warn't hard, when I gin up to your wishes so quick, and let you and that tom-tiger hev the choosing of a wife for me. Now, sence this evening, I think I ought to be a leetle more hard to plaise; and I'll take my time, and see ef I kin find out Miss Susan Heffernan. I won't take any woman's word for it. I'll watch her myself for awhile, jest as I'd watch a pretty sarpent a-sliding quiet along through the green bushes. I was jubous from the first about that Pogson breed.'

" 'But Susan is mighty handsome, Paddy.'

" 'Handsome is that handsome does, ould lady.'

" 'And she's young and saft and tender, and jest like a kitten, she's so innocent and so full of her fun.'

" 'Kittens hev claws and a kitten grows mighty fast into a cat.'

" 'Now, what do you want in a woman?'

" 'Well, ef you'll let me alone, I would'nt want her at all; and I warn you now, that ef by constant dinging it into my ears, you force me to marry this young woman—ef she'll hev me—'

" 'Oh! she'll hev you!'

" 'How do you know?'

" 'Oh! I don't *know*, but it stands to raison. I don't think there's any gal in the fork, that ef you onst say "snip," would'nt say "snap." She'll hev you for sartin.'

" 'May-be so—may-be not! I'm not so foolish and consated as to think that I've only to ax, and to hev. But I tell you, I feel sure that you're a-hurrying me on to do a thing which may be very good for me, or very bad! I reckon the company of a good wife and daughter would be a great deal for me, and for you too; but, Lord be marciful to me ef she's like this tom-terrible of Sam Hartley.'

" 'Oh! Paddy, she's an angel to her.'

" 'Well, I'm not onraisonable enough to ixpect an angel for a wife. In fact, I'd rather not. An angel's good enough, I reckon, in a climate where we don't need to get breeches mended, and sausages made up; but for our poor country, a good woman's the only crathur that could be passable as an honest man's wife.'

" 'Well, and what do you call a good woman, Paddy?'

" 'I've tould you all that before. She must jest know her right place, as a woman and as a wife, and, perhaps, as a mother; and stick to that place, and make the most of it, and be satisfied though it's only a 6x8 pole house, and a tin pan to eat out of. I could'nt stand a woman whose tongue was always a-going. Lord deliver us! here you women will set down by the hour, your tongues a tinkling all the time, you and Sally Hartley, from the moment you set down to table till the moment you git up, from morning to night— no eending—no rest for your own tongues or my ears! And what do you talk about? Nothing, as I'm a living sinner, but smoke and soot, and suds, and nonsense—dribble, dribble, dribble; spit, sput, spat; wish, wash, wush; prittle, prattle; pribble prabble, ding dong bell; the dipper's in the well! Lord deliver us! It's terrible! It's awful! One would think you felt it a sort of obligation to be talking all the time!—not an idee; not a business; not a work; not a matter of so much substance as to take between thumb and finger. Here, when I come in to-day—here waur you and Sally Hartley disputing about who 'twas that crossed the avenue jest before I come, going on to Cannon's Bridge. First *you* said:

" 'I seed Joe Evans crossing the road, a-gwine to Cannon's Bridge.'

"And says she, 'I reckon it warn't Joe; it was more like Mike Waters.'

"And says you, 'I'm pretty sure 'twas Joe, Salley.'

"And says she, 'I'm sure 'twant Joe; 'twas a taller man; I'm sure 'twas Mike.'

"Then says you, 'I ought to know Joe, Salley, I'm sure; for I seed him in his cradle.'

"And says she, 'I ought to know him, too, for I seed him at his marriage.'

"Then says you, 'Joe rides a bay horse, rawboned, and he wears blue homespun. I showed his wife how to made the dye.'

"And says she, 'Mike rides a bay horse, too, and he wears blue homespun, too; and this was Mike, I'm sure, for he's a taller person than Joe.'

"Then says you, quick, 'This man was short, Salley.'

" 'No,' says she, 'he was as tall as Paddy.'

"Then says you, 'Tall as Paddy! Very like it, indeed, Salley, when you know there's hardly a man in all the fork that's as tall as Paddy.'

"And jest so you went on, till both got as red in the face as turkey cocks, and began to quarrel, and you went on so, all through the dinner, till I throw'd down my knife and fork, and jumped up, and cried out—

" 'Sam Hartley, this is too terrible! I kain't stand it. Let's have a drink!'

" 'Well, 'twas very onmannerly of you, Paddy! Women have a right to talk, I'm sure, what plaises them.'

" 'But it did *not* plaise you! It made you both vext as blazes! And what gives you a *right* to talk? Nobody has a right to talk, that hasn't something sinsible to say; something good and useful to be know'd; some proper answer to give; or something fine and beautiful to be haird and to plaise the onderstanding. When you've got nothing to say, say nothing! Neither God nor man ixpects you to be talking all the time. It's the vanity, and no brains, that keeps the tongue so etarnally going; and what was the difference, whether 'twas Joe Evans or Mike Waters? Nara one of 'em is worth his salt.—It's this sort of talk that drives a husband out of the house; drives him to other company; and to drink and smoke; for if there's drinking and smoking among young men, they mixes with it some good sense generally and some fun; and 'bating now and then that you find a silly tongue in a younker's head, none of 'em iver drives you to disperation with sich infarnal gibble-gabble stuff. I tell you, mother, ef I'm to marry a woman with sich a tongue as this Sally Hartley, I'm a ruinated man foriver. 'Twill kill me, or I must curse and quit.'

" 'Well, don't you be afear'd of Susan Heffernan. She's the quietest, sweetest spoken'—

" 'Och! don't be talking any more. You've told me that a hundred times over. I don't want to hear. I must see for myself.'

" 'But will you go and see her, Paddy?'

" 'I suppose so—you says it—and I've promised. I see your heart is set upon my gitting a wife, and you've sot your idee upon this one. I'll go and see.'

"And thus eended the talk for the night. The next morning, bright and airly, I set off to do some wood cutting; but I found out, a'terwards, that the moment I was off, the poor ould mother was off too, and spent all the day with the Pogsons. She was jest priming the gal as to how she should behave; jest telling her all I'd been a-saying, and what I ixpected. Lord! Lord! that one's ould mother should so set her heart upon heving a thing done, as to take pains for the desaving of her own son, to his ruination! She and Salley Hartley, I found out a'terwards, were both in close confab with Miss Susan all day, and the gal had her lessons, for keeping down the fool ontil my head was made fit for wearing the cap and the bells for iver."

CHAPTER XXVII.

Paddy's Philosophies—His Courtship begins—progresses—His chief difficulty in not being able to see his sweetheart in "a state of nathur"—He goes to Church—A Dinner Party—He receives a message from the dead, and, as he thinks, through the Devil.

————

"Gentlemen, my friends and good masters, I warn't agin marriage. Marriage, whaur the parties suit each other edzackly, must be the most blessed condition upon this airth—a peg above friendship. When there is friendship, then the parties onderstand each other, but, the onderstanding between man and wife, must be closer and warmer, though it's still a sort of blessed friendship. They knows each other's want before the mouth kin open to speak it. They knows each other's feeling even before the eyes kin look it, and they go to do the thing that's wanted, and to meet the want, before there's any craving felt, or suffering begun. They speak to each other's thinking, and to each other's feeling, though, perhaps, with niver a word to say on either side.

"For there's sich a likeness between 'em, that what one feels, is only a sign that the other's a feeling it too; and they thinks so parfectly alike, that it's only needful to ax what one thinks to be sure of t'other; and so it's a sort of pleasure to be doing for one's self the very thing that the other's most eager a'ter. It must be a most blessed condition.

"And whaur there's two sich parties come together, living together in one house, having the same ockypations day by day, the same interests, and heving the care of the same things, the two hands working together, and not in cross-grain, agin each other, it's supprising how much good work is done, and how pleasant it is in the doing. It's this pleasant working together, onder one law, that makes marriage sich a pleasant sitivation and condition; and, ef this working together be wanting, then all its other pleasures are only so much husk and shuck, that burns up in a rush, and gives out no good heat, and lasts but for a minute.

"Often, and often, hev I considered how beautifuler than the spring and summer, is the sight of two young people, going side by side together through the world, or sitting side by side, or working side by side, living in each other and for each other, tending to their own leetle and humble habitation, and not bothering themselves about it, though they air pretty much all alone in the world, shut in by deep thicks from all the world, away from the great highway, the great people of the world passing by, without seeing or knowing, or caring to ax, ef two fond, loving young people lived anywhaur abouts.

"I've dreamed of sich a people, and sich a life, here, in our Edisto thicks, and, in my dreams, I've seed a tract of prehaps fifty acres, shut in on all sides by the river and the woods, and, in the middle of it, is a pretty leetle box of a house, what they calls a cottage, with prehaps only two rooms, and a neat little piazza in the South, and long vines, with green leaves and purple flowers running up the pillars, and trying to git a-top of the roof, and you reach the place through a long avenue of great trees, live oaks and water oaks, till you come to a yard, and there the avenue opens upon a nice leetle garden full of flowers, and you see the young people together planting out shrubs, and trimming the orange hedges, and counsultating together where to put this rose bush, and where to put this creeper. Och! it's the prettiest of my dreams, when I go to bed, a'ter a good day's work, heving hed no quarrel with man or woman.

"I warn't onwilling to be married, I say, ef I could find the one person who would be sich a friend to me. I could ha' given up all other friends for sich a one as that. But, when I looked round on every side, and seed no nice cottages, no fine walks, no avenues, no flower garden—all rough and dirty, and no vines running up the porch, no clean scrubbed floors and shiny windows, no two cheerful and good humored people working together—when I looked round and seed wives, instead of making things purty and sweet to the eye, not even keeping clean and dacent houses, but jest gathering

together in a corner, their tongues going twenty to the dozen, spit-
ting at each other and everybody else, and squabbling, like Mrs.
Sam Hartley,—and I've seed too many sich people in my time—
I was jubous about every step I tuck in the way of marriage.

"And it's no use for a man to say and think, he'll *look* out for
himself, and watch close, and be sharp, and not let himself be taken
in. He kaint do it. He's got no chaince. He niver kin git a fair sight
of things tell he's married, and then it's too late, for, you see, you
kin niver catch the young women in a state of nathur."

"How's that Paddy? What the devil are you driving at? You
want to catch the young women in a state of nature?"

"To be sure I does! But, none of your fun, Wharncliffe, you
knows what I mean. I wants to see 'em in their natural state."

"Pretty much the same thing, Paddy.—Really, old fellow, your
desires here are very unreasonable."

"No, they ain't! only you don't onderstand me rightly. I don't
mean what you think."

"Then, what *do* you mean?"

"Well, I'll try to make you onderstand.—When I comes to see
you, Wharncliffe, or Jamison, the moment I knocks at the door of
your library, you sings out:

"'Come in,' and I come in, and thar you air, jest as you waur
before, in your leettle green roundabout, or in that old ragged,
flowered and figered morning gown, jest as you waur before I came,
and you says, 'welcome, Paddy, come take a seat,' and you stick
out your feet over the fender, and there's the old slippers on, and
there's the pipe in your mouth, and all's free and aisy with you,
all *natheral*. You don't stop to change your dress a bit, and I sees you
as you air—a *natheral* man!

"But, when I goes to see a young woman, she's niver fit to be
seen! She keeps you a waiting at the door, or in one of the rooms,
till she kin fix up, and—"

"Why, Paddy, she's got to lace her corsets, and put on her hoops,
and comb her hair, and make her toilet."

"That's the mischief! Why does she wear them things? Not for
the comfort, that's cl'ar; for it's bekaise she wants to hev the comfort
of free breathing and aisie, natural motions, that she l'aves them
off 'till the visitor comes. This is what I calls the onnatural about

her. Why kaint she do as the men does, dress herself up for the day and be done with it?"

"But, Paddy, she's got household affairs to attend to. She must wash the cups, and wipe the tumblers, and see to giving out the dinner, perhaps make pies and pastries; and for them performances she has to roll up her sleeves, and tuck up her skirts, and clap on a long apron, and she'd feel very awkward if you should catch her in that state of nature."

"But why should she, any more than you, or me, or Jamison, or Carroll, or anybody else? You niver cares. The last time I was down at Jamison's, he come out to meet me at the door, in his slippers, and an old coat that had been in the wars, I reckon, for there waur a hole onder the arm, and one at the elbow, and I hardly think there waur a button left on the face of it; and don't I see Carroll—who is pretty much a boy to us, and jest married, too—don't I see him working at his mill, and in the shabbiest clothing; sometimes the pine gum from his logs sticking both legs of his trowsers together, so that he has to give an almighty jerk, when he wants to walk, to git the two legs onhitched. Why should a woman be ashamed to be seen, jest as she is, at her nateral ockypations?"

"Because she *is* a woman, Paddy, and not a man. She obeys a very different law. A large part of her power, to persuade and please, lies in her personal attractions. Men love beauty; and you remember what the young French Princess replied to the reverend Abbé, who asked her, 'What are women made for, my daughter?' 'To please the gentlemen, Father.' There you have the whole philosophy. When the lady keeps you waiting, in order to prepare her toilet, she does so in order to give you pleasure by her attractions. It is a compliment she pays you when she keeps you waiting. Now, as the gentleman does not seek to please you by his personal charms, he pleases you in another way, by not keeping you waiting. The lady is like the new moon, or a bright star, that never come till they are ready, and then come with all their beauty, and gladden you the more because they have so long delayed to come."

"All that's very pretty, Wharncliffe, and prehaps there's some raison in it, too. But when the woman gets a habit of living only for show, then the whole nater of the crather becomes a sort of desaiving. Ef a man happens to be in a passion when you comes upon him, he don't kiver up his passion suddent, in a sort of blanket. He goes on; you see him as he is, blazing away like thunder; he lets you see that he *kin* git in a passion; that to be in a passion, when there's good raison for it, is natheral, and very proper.—But it's not so with a woman. She kin kiver it up in a minute. Ef she's roaring like a wild bull before you heave in sight, the moment she sees you, she smoothes down; and that v'ice that was only a minute ago the rigelar shriek of a steam-car whistle, why, in a twink, it's as saft as a baby's whisper. There's no catching her in a state of nather, and no finding out what she is, till you're fairly strapped down by the parson."

"I see, Paddy, you are approaching the pathetic," said Jamison. "Come, we mustn't let the punch grow cold. Mr. Stylus has been busy in our behalf, and the company waits. When you have taken another cup of consolation, you will be in better trim to develop a progress which I see grows tragic.—Your air and deportment show it. You are beginning to look like Kemble, when he hears the voices ringing through the house at midnight, crying, 'Sleep no more' to all the house! 'Macbeth doth murder sleep!'"

"Ef he'd say, 'Marriage doth murder sleep,' 'twould be more to the p'int. Lord love you, but it's no subjec' for joking. But I must git on. So, here's to you all, gentlemen, my friends —here's to you all; and may you niver git into the hands of sich a Mrs. Macbeth as will keep you from your honest sleeps by night."

"Amen!" in full chorus. Paddy resumed:

"When the next Sunday come round, I haird that Parson Ballinger was going to preach at Providence meeting-house, and I know'd that everybody would be thar. So I determined to go, onbeknowing to my ould mother, jest to see how Miss Susan Heffernan would look and behave in Church. I seed that the ould lady waur a-gitting ready, and Mrs. Sam Hartley was to come for her in Sam's buggy. She axed me to go, but I put her off; hed my horse got, and talked about riding down into the swamp, or over the river, to Wharncliffe's. She sot off, onsuspicious; and I waited till she was out of sight; then I mounted, and made a sort of sarcumbendibus, by a bye-road, and got to the meeting-house purty nearly as soon as she did. I hitched my horse in the woods, out of sight, close upon the widow Parlow's fence; and then walked upwards to the road, but keeping myself kivered by the trees, to a p'int where I could see the people pass.—A'ter a while, there comes on the whole Pogson tribe of women, in their old Jarsey, draw'd by one lean-bodied, spavined old work-horse, that had all the bad signs, besides being as poor as carrion."

"You speak of the bad signs of a horse, Paddy," said I. "Pray tell me what they are. I'm on the look-out now for a pair, and want to choose wisely."

"What, Stylus, you niver haird the old rhyming about horse-buying? Well, there's no saying how true it is, for the jedging of a horse is jest about as great a puzzle as I knows on; that is, a'ter he's nine years old! The rhymes, ef I kin remember, go this way:

> One white foot, and you may *buy* him;
>   Two white feet, and you should *try* him;
>   Three white feet, you'd best deny him;
>   But with four white feet, and a long white nose,
>   Pull off his hide, and give him to the crows!

"Well, Pogson's horse had all these bad signs; every leg was white to his knees; and his whole nose, all the way up and down, was as white as Wharncliffe's hat—the one he wears when he goes to town. The Jarsey was pretty well wore out—a most rickety, tumble-down consarn; and 'twas chock full as it could hold. The ould lady was a driving, and at every step you could hear her flapping the reins down upon the raw bones of the beast, to make him go. Alongside of her was Miss Salley, and in the hind seat waur Miss Polly and Miss Susan Heffernan. 'Twas no small load for a mane beast, and as mane a wagon. The whole harness and establishment was so agy shaky that the ould woman darsn't let the horse stop a minute, for every new start was a danger to the whole consarn of going straight to pieces.—The ould woman, and all the gals, waur dressed up mighty smart, in fresh calicoes, with big red and yallow figgers, and their bonnets were kivered with the same colored ribbon. Thinks I to myself, thinks I, ef you was to put a leetle of that ribbon and calico money into that harness, you might run much less risk of having the whole spiled in the road mud some of these fine Sundays.

"I let them get on, and get out, and go into the meeting house before I went up. When I did go in, sarvice waur begun, and they waur all singing. I worn't much of a church goer, and everybody stared when they seed me—my poor ould mammy worst of all. She, and the Pogson's, and the Hartley's, all sot together, taking up a whole seat to themselves. Sam, he was dressed in full black; and he carried a Bible and psalm book, and niver tuk his eyes off the Parson. When my ould mother seed me, she pushed Sally Hartley, and *she* pushed the Pogson gals, and they all scrouged up together; and the old woman she then made signs to me that there waur room for me, jest atween her and Susan Heffernan. But I shook my head. I thought that waur coming to close quartering a *leetle* too soon!

"Well, I watched, and I listened. I could see that the gals waur on their best behaviour. Miss Susan, she niver once looked round at me, but sot up square, looking at the preacher when she did look up, but mostly carrying her eyes in her lap. A'ter a while I could make out her singing from the rest; and jest as my mother tould me, she hed a good v'ice and knowed how to let it out at the right time. For a girl that hed no idication in singing, she did mighty well. But her sister Sally had a sort of cane-whistle in *her* v'ice, and that was sharp as a brier; and Miss Polly, she had a sort of snort! The ould lady was dacent enough to sing only with her eyes, and they waur a warbling all round the meeting-house all the time, and fixing upon me, ivery now and then, mighty preticklar, with a pleasant sort of a smile, that seemed to sing—

'Come, little ducky, come out of the pond,
And have a warm welcome from good Mrs. Bond.'

I didn't much like the sort of music in her face, seeing that her nose was mighty sharp, and as red as her nag's was white.

"Parson Ballinger, he gin us a sharp, biting sarmon, very s'arching and sinsible; and he prayed hearty for the country and the people, and dismissed us with a farvent blessing. My poor ould mother didn't wait for the blessing, but, all the time it was going on, she was making signs to me to wait for her, as ef she fear'd I'd be off without axing for the blessing. Well, as my objec' was to know the young woman, and see what I could, and find out all thet they'd let me, I waited, and jined 'em in front of the meeting-house, where I hed to shake hands with the whole kit and bi'ling of the Pogsons, and a good many other people. And Mrs. Pogson was mighty scrumptuous and bottle-full of civility. It came out like sharp cider, out of a tight stopper, with a sort of foaming burst, that tuk away her own breath, ef it didn't your'n. The gals were all mighty smiling. Miss Susan Heffernan, when I spoke to her and shook hands, looked sideways at me, out of a leetle corner of her eye, as ef she *know'd* something, and I thought thet one of the white feet of the horse— rether a bad sign! But, otherwise, she was well enough, perhaps, as pretty and well dressed a young woman as any in the meeting; a leetle too fine, perhaps, in the ribbons and the feathers, but looking mighty pretty. The ould lady axed me to come and see 'em, and there waur a good deal of such talk before the church door, Mrs. Pogson being one of those persons who thinks it a binding duty to be talking all the time. She hed *all the white feet* of the horse, in spite of a very red face, and a very sharp *reddishy* nose. As for my poor ould mother, she was as happy as an ould hen, with one bare-legged chicken!—Sam Hartley's wife grinned as ef she knowed everything in the world's lock-up; and Sam, with his hands clasped on his breast, kept a bowing to Parson Bollinger, without a word to say to anybody else, till the Parson waur fairly out of sight, when he turned to me, and made a sort of thankful prayer that the Lord had given me so much grace as to see the needcessity of trying, at the eleventh hour, for the salvation of my poor soul.

" 'You'll be a brand plucked from the burning, my friend,' says he, 'ef you'll come rigilar to meeting, and ax the prayers of the congregation for an onlucky sinner.'

"Well, thar we all parted, my ould mother going off with Mrs. Sam, while I rode home to eat my hoecake and bacon like a bachelor. The rest of the day, I hed peace, though I waur pretty much taken up with thinking of marriage and the Pogson family not forgetting the break-down consarn of jarsey, harness and old horse.

"So much for the beginning of my courtship. A'ter a few days, I got an invite for myself and the ould lady to dinner with the Pogsons. So I went over to Wharncliffe to borrow his old buggy that he didn't use, and he ginerously gin it to me. It was sound in hub, and wheels, and tire, and, now that I've got it painted up, it's a'most as good as new. As I hed a horse a'ready, and as fine a crether as any in the country, the buggy was no ixpense. I've got it yit, though it's not likely I'll ever drive in it agin.

"When the day come for the dinner, I driv the ould lady, who was jest like a child, giggling to pieces over a new play thing.—Och! she was the most consekential poor foolish ould body, over the idee of my going a courting. I was afear'd she'd be for bouncing out of the buggy a dozen times by the way, she was so full of the idee of what she waur a-doing. I hed my own misgivings all the time, that what waur giving her sich pleasant fantidgits, waur going to give me chicken fits, or worse in the eend; but I held on, only saying—

" 'See you, mother, you don't git me hobbled with a fool! Remember, I'm a visiting this gal only bekaise you wants me to, and ef I marries her, 'twill be to please you, and not bekaise I'm at all wanting of a wife.'

" 'Niver be afraid, honey,' says she, 'I knows the gal, and I says it bould, Paddy, if you waur to look from the Edisto to the Savannah, you couldn't find a better crather for a wife.'

" 'I hope so; but remember, I hain't got my foot into it yit, and it's may-be, I'll keep out of the trap altogether. I must look out for myself, and see and larn all I kin; and so, don't you, bekaise you want the marriage, do anything to blind my eyes, and git me into a hobble from which you kain't git me out agin. See to that, and don't lend yourself to Sally Hartley, and jine with her and other people for the desaiving of your own son to his ruination.'

"When we reached Pogson's, we reach'd about as mean a sample of farming as iver eye could see. The fences waur hardly more than knee high; the houses waur going to ruin; the fields waur badly broke up, badly laid off, and iverything show'd, what iverybody said, that Pogson was a poor crather, that either didn't know his business, or didn't attend to it. The yard and the house all looked the same way. One of the pillars of the piazza was gone; one of the shutters was swinging on one hinge; the boards were gaping and rotting on the floor. There warn't a bush, nor shrub, nor flower, near the house—no sign of a woman's hand, or woman's neatness, or love of what was purty and sweet. I p'inted all out to my ould mother. Says I—

" 'I jedges of women, not by how they *look* themselves, but by what they *do*. They may show themselves as fine as a peacock's tail, spread out to sun and wind, but ef they don't let me see what they've been *doing*,—ef I sees about the house no signs of woman's doing at all—I kain't look with any pleasure at their purty faces, or their fine clothes and ribands. What I wants to see is the proof of a lady that's got feeling and sense, and neatness and industry, and a purty taste and grace, and a love of beautiful things outside of themselves. Now, you see, here ain't a shrub or flower, but I'll bet a picayune agin a pin, that you'll see a big looking-glass in that ere room, that they'll show us into, and, ef we could look, we'd fine one or more in every room in the house, be it iver so leetle.'

" 'That ain't the fault,' says she, 'of Susan Heffernan. She ain't the mistress here, and she takes a'ter none of the rest, Paddy. Och, Paddy! but the child does love the flowers, and would hev 'em ef she could; ef you'd only see her, how she fixed up my flower pots—'

" 'What's to prevent her, at home? Ef the old people didn't do it themselves, they wouldn't *objec'* to her doing it. They wouldn't be sich brutes as to refuse her to make things look neat and purty.'

" 'Yes, indeed, Paddy; they'd say she meddles with what don't consarn her, and the other gals, I know that they laughs at her whatever she tries to do. You see that palmetto bonnet that she wears; it's as purty as any bonnet I iver seed—purty as any that them gals at Bamberg make—well, she made it with her own hands, and niver hed a pattern.'

" 'They didn't laugh at her, did they, for that?' says I.

" 'Yes, they did,' says she, 'ontill it was done, and then nothing would sarve the other gals but she must show them, and help them make their bonnets too.'

" 'Well, she made it in spite of their laughing. Why did she mind their laughing when she wanted to plant the flowers, and lay out the garden here in front? Why you see the bonnet was to make *herself* look purty.'

" 'Och! Paddy don't be so hard upon the young thing. It's natheral that the gal should try to make herself look purty. Besides, where waur she to get the het ef she didn't make it? Them gals has to make everything that they wears. The ould daddy niver gives 'em a cent. He drinks up iverything, or gambles it away.'

" 'Does he gamble too?'

" 'That's what they says. But stop, there's Mrs. Pogson at the door.'

"Och! how glad was Mrs. Pogson to see us, and what a botheration she made. I thought she'd niver be done kissing my ould mother, and then I was afear'd she'd begin on me; she squazed my hand to pieces.—Then she dragged us into the room, and sure enough, the only sign upon the walls, was a big looking-glass. The room warn't sealed or plaistered. The tables waur of common pine. The floor hadn't been scour'd in a month, and the chairs waur of oak, with white oak plaited bottoms. A'ter awhile the gals come in, one by one, Miss Susan Heffernan the last; and they were all dressed up, fine as Peter Martin's widow, the Sunday after he was buried. Soon a'ter, come Sam Hartley and his wife, and then old Pogson rode in from the fields on the same poor, mane, white legged beast that they drove to meeting in the Jarsey.

"Pogson, Hartley and myself sot out in the piazzer smoking our pipes, while the table was a laying in the hall. The women kept in there; and, Lord, how their tongues went, Mrs. Pogson and Salley Hartley going it as if they had just newly oiled their machines.

"Pogson was a tall, lank-sided varmint, with keen black eyes, hair black as a coal, and long, bushy eyebrows, and skin as yellow as ochre. He was sharp-faced as an Ingin's hatchet; and his skin draw'd so tight over his cheekbone, that it was beginning to show cracks all over it, or with big creases as to look like cracks. He spoke with a long, saft voice, like a hungry hawk in the air over a field of brown straw, looking out for rabbits, of a warm spring a'ternoon. I didn't cotton to him any more than to his wife. He talked cunning enough, while his wife talked fool! As for the gals, the two oldest and tallest, they seemed to have the daddy's face and the mammy's tongue. They had sharp, shrill v'ices, like a whistle blown with water in it. As for Susan Heffernan, the good sign, so far, was that I hed hardly haird her v'ice at all. But she was the youngest; and my ould mother said they all kept her down. Ef so, twas a good thing for her and no harm done.

"They give us a good dinner of meats; roast pig, ham and a pair of ducks; there waur bacon and greens besides, but no other vegetables. Pogson had some whiskey and drunk pretty free himself. At dinner they sot me betwixt my mammy and Miss Susan Heffernan;

and the young lady behaved herself quiet, and didn't overeat herself. But the other gals they stowed away, as ef they ixpected their dinner to last 'em till next Sunday.

"But I need'nt tell any more of the preticklars of that day; nor of other days and evenings; for I made it a p'int to pay a visit two or three times a week, my objec' being to catch the young lady in a state of natur, ef I could! Onst I took through the woods; wouldn't come by the avenue, where they could see me a full quarter off; and I hitched my horse in the woods, and kept under kiver till I got to the yard, all onseen. But just as I opened the gate I was attacked by a great bull-dog, and the beast would have bitten me, I do believe, but that I was lucky to pick up a stick and crack him right across the nose. But the rumpus brought out the old lady, and with a long pole she ran at the dog, and the nigger come out and tuk him off and chained him; but I niver seed the young women till they waur all in full dress, and fine as redbirds. The ould lady *was* caught and looked mighty shabby.

"To make a long story as short as possible, I come to the conclusion that, in marriage a man had to risk something—yes, a good deal—and take pretty much everything on trust! My mammy was at me all the time, and Sally Hartley sot her husband on me, and so I had two witnesses, the best I could git, on behalf of Miss Susan's good behavior; so I pretty much determined to pop the question.

" 'Don't be afraid,' says my poor ould mother, 'she'll hev' you! I'm sure they is all ready for it. It's only to ax and to hev'. The gal loves the very airth you tread on!'

"But I hed my misgivings, and must not forget to tell you that all the time this courtship was a going on, my troubles in the woods waur greater I think than iver. The v'ices haunted me whenever I waur on the river or in the swamp. I could hear footsteps and breaking branches, and talkings all about me. Sometimes there'd be a screaming, and then the ould owl hoot, 'Hoo! hoo! hoo!' and once in a way I'd hear—

" 'So ho, Paddy; so whoo, Paddy!' 'You're going too fast for comfort, Paddy.' 'Be aisy! Dont hurry, Paddy!'

"And things like that; and one day a man, a stranger like, meets me near Cannon's Bridge, and says he to me—

" 'Air you not Paddy McGann?'

"Says I—'I'm the indentical man.'

" 'Well,' says he, 'I've got a message to you from a friend of yourn.'

" 'Who's he,' says I.

" 'He told me his name was Rafe Moore!'

" 'Rafe Moore,' says I, all in a sweat, 'why man, Rafe Moore's been dead and buried fifteen years! I seed him put in the ground with my own eyes.'

" 'The devil you did,' says the stranger. 'Well, it kaint be the same, for this person who calls himself Rafe Moore, is as live and hearty a man as you or I. I seed him in the swamp only this morning, and he said to me—

" ' "Stranger, do me a favor. You'll meet a man when you ride out named Paddy McGann." And he 'scribed to me your person and your horse, so I knowed you just as soon as I sot eyes on you.

" ' "Tell him," says he, "that his friend, Rafe Moore, sends you; and I'm mighty sorry I kaint git to spake to him myself. Tell him not to hurry in that business he's on; 'twont suit him. It's a bad business, and it'll bankrupt him! Tell him to do his own *seeing*, and jedging, and not use other people's eyes, and listen to other people's talk. The consarn wont suit him at all." He told me to tell you them very words. I ax't him what the business was; but says he, "never you mind; jest tell him that. He'll onderstand." Them's the very words he said, and with that he told me good morning, and went back into the swamp, where I reckon he had company, for I haird great shouting and whooping a'terwards. I would'nt hev thought of it again, I confess, but for meeting you and seeing that you answer'd edzackly to his 'scription.'

"I was fairly 'mazed! Says I—'and what sort of looking person was this Rafe Moore?'

" 'Well,' says he, 'he was a tall young fellow, not more than twenty-five, ef that; with light hair, and full, round, rosy face, and he wore a hunting shirt like yourn; and I marked one thing, he had a big mark of a strawberry on one side of his cheek, and a long red hair growing out of it. He had no beard.'

"That 'mazed me more than iver. 'Twas a parfect picture of my old friend, Rafe Moore, the brother of the young gal I used to

think so much of, and he tuk yallow fever in town, and come up and
died of it in the country; and, poor fellow, I helped to put him in
the ground! I was fair skeared!—But the stranger did'nt seem to see
anything queer in the message; and a'ter I got out of him all I
could, he went off and I niver seed him a'ter; and I niver got no
other message. But wasn't that enough? What could I make out of it?
Here's a plain message from the dead! and what hed my old
friend, Rafe Moore, as good a fellow as ever lived, and as true a
friend, what had he to do with all these troubles of mine? Could he
come back to the airth? The 'scription given by the stranger was
edzact! Why did'nt he come to me himself. Ef he could show
himself to another man, that did'nt know him, why not to me that
did? How I worried myself with all them questions, to no use.—At
last I come to the conclusion that it was the divil himself that come
and spoke to me in the person of the stranger. He told me he was a
nigger-trader from Alabama. But I reckon he was the ould divil and
no other, and his trade was in souls and not in niggers."

CHAPTER XXVIII.

Courtship and Marriage—The Wedding Supper—Impudent Behaviour of Col. Jim Meredith's Monkey—the Devil takes Formal Leave of Paddy, and Paddy takes Leave of the Reader.

———

"Months went over," resumed Paddy, "and found me still a-courting—that is, I was visiting the Pogson family every now and then, and trying to find out all I could about Miss Susan Heffernan. The ould people give me every chaince, and so did the young woman herself. The two sisters waur sometimes in the way, and seemed a leetle onwilling to git out of it; but I obsarved that the mother always contrived to call 'em out of the room, and put 'em at something to do, l'aving me and Miss Susan pretty much together. There waur a stout young cub of a brother, an idle chap, that tuk a'ter his father. He had a horse of his own,—how he got it, the Lord only knows,—but with his horse—a mean, scrawny boned critter, with only twenty hairs in his tail—he kept galloping about the country, going to every horse-race, muster-ground, barbecue and camp meeting that he could hear of.—Though not more than eighteen or twenty, he swore like a trooper, drunk like a fish, chaw'd any quantity of tobacco, and was a surly, quarrelsome chap, as sassy as a black snake in May. I didn't see much of him, and when I did, he fought shy of me, and looked sulky.

"Well, there warn't much to plaise me in the family, but there waur nothing in Miss Susannah to displaise me, and as my ould mother said, 'You ain't ixpected to marry all the family.' 'The Lord forbid!' says I—I could find out nothing agin Miss Susan. She was always neat in her dress—a leetle too fond of colors—but she was quiet, and hedn't much to say. I told you she was the prettiest of all the gals; in fact, she was quite purty. When I talked with her she was quite bashful, and would look down and answer as leetle as possible. But I could see that she was mighty pleased to hev me waiting on her. Sometimes, of an a'ternoon, I'd ax her to go and walk with me in the woods, and she'd do it, not onwilling, and then I'd let myself out and talk to her quite free, jest to git her to talk and show herself; but precious leetle she'd let out. And then she talked so low, almost in a whisper, that hafe the time I couldn't make out what she was a-saying.

" 'Well,' says I to myself, 'it's no harm in a young woman to be bashful; and not talking much is a good sign; and a saft, low v'ice, is an ixcellent thing in a young woman. Ef she ain't smart, thinks I, she ain't sassy. Ef she has little to say, she says it to the p'int and knows when to stop.' So, jest studyin' her day by day, I thought better and better of her; but still I felt, as I come nearer and nearer to the objec', that twarn't any sich love I was feeling as I ought to feel, before I made up my mind to marry. Dozens of times I remembered that sweet little Orangeburg gal, that I used to be so fond of; and in the midst of my walking and talking with Miss Susannah, that poor gal used to cross before my sight, as it were, like a thin mist among the trees, and look upon me as she past, as ef there waur a thickish sort of sorrow in her eyes. I did love that young crather; and while I thought of her, I axed myself ef I could be content to marry Miss Susan. But then agin, I thought and felt that I could niver agin have sich feelings for any woman as I hed for that young thing, going down to the grave when she was only jest seventeen. Ach! when I happened to think of her, I wished Miss Susan at home, and myself far away down in the deepest shadows of the swamp.

"But I hed to shake off them thoughts and feelings. My ould mother was at me all the time, and Sam Hartley was at me; and when I begun to hev misgivings, he said:

" 'You've gone too fur now, Paddy, to stop whar you air. You must go on further. The gal ixpects it—the family ixpects it—and everybody's talking of you and her. You kain't find a better gal, I reckon, in our parts, and the sooner you come up to the scratch the better.'

" 'Scratch is the word, Sam,' says I, with a groan. 'Twas no laughing matter to me then; and nothing but the divil—the trouble

I hed—and the worrying of my poor old mother, brought me to the scratch at last.—So I determined, as I couldn't find out any thing more of Miss Susan, to take my chaince, and bring the matter to an eending. And the truth is, another raison I hed for it, I begun to find myself over-lonesome at my work and in the swamp. When I hedn't rigilar work, and went for fishing and hunting, my luck was as bad as iver; and the sounds now that worried me begun to chainge. Instead of v'ices and whisperings, I'd hear cryings like a child, close beside me; and sometimes a sobbing and a moaning, as ef the person waur in pain, and wanting help. Then I had stranger dhrames than iver—and they waur always strange enough,—and now, in my dhrames, I'd constantly see that young gal of Orangeburg, and her brother Rafe, and they'd look at me very sorrowful, as ef they wanted to do me help, but didn't know how.

"Having determined to bring the matter to an eending, and consenting to marry Miss Susan, I was jest the man, onst my mind was made up, to go to work about the thing in the most ixpeditious manner. I warn't like Ben Rowell, who was at his courtship for three years, and then had to be helped out of it. You niver haird of Ben Rowell, I reckon, Mr. Stylus?"

"No, Paddy, I can't say that I ever did. What about him?"

"Jamison know'd him, I reckon, and Wharncliffe, too. He was a good-natured, poor sneak of a fellow, who fell in love with Araminta Grymes, and he went to see her night after night, for a matter, as they say, of three years. He was the laziest white man I iver did see; but he hed some property, enough to keep a good overseer; and he made pretty fair crops, and being close-fisted, he spent nothing. The Grymeses waur willing he should marry Araminta, and gin him ivery incouragement. And thar he'd go, night a'ter night, night a'ter night, as they say, for three years; and the ould people, they'd leave him with Araminta, he one side of the fire-place, and she t'other. And thar he'd sit, dewouring her with his eyes, and with niver a word to say. And so he'd a kept on for years, keeping other people off from the nest, without trying to git in it himself. The poor gal, she was a smart, clever, active leetle body—she was wore out with him. Thar he'd set, twirling his thumbs, and staring at her, 'till 'twas time for him to go, and then he'd git up with a groan,—he groaned from laziness, and niver wished to exart himself—and he'd say,

'Good-night, Miss Araminta,' and go sidling out to git his horse. He'd a' kept at that all his life, I reckon; but a'ter three years, night a'ter night, the gal couldn't stand it any longer. She waited for him to speak all the time, as she thought it sassy for her to begin. At last, one night she says:

" 'Mr. Rowell, do you always keep turning over your thumbs in that way?'

"He had a trick, you see, of lacing the fingers of his two hands together in his lap, and then twirling thumb over thumb—so."

Paddy showed us how the thing was done.

"Well, he kept at that all the time. When she asked him the question, it was by way of beginning the conversation. But what do you think he answered?

" 'Why, no, Miss Araminta. When I'm tired that way, I turns my thumbs back, this way; you see it's jest as asie.'

And Paddy showed us the reverse movement.

"Well, thar the conversation stopt for awhile. Ben kept a twirling his thumbs and staring in the poor girl's face with eyes full of famine. At last, the gal says:

" 'Now, *you* ax *me* something, Mr. Rowell.'

" 'Me?' says he.

" 'Yes, you,' says she. 'It's *your* time to ax *me* something, now.'

" 'Y—e—s! I reckon 'tis!'—a long stop.

" 'Well?' says she.

" 'Y—e—s!' says he. 'Miss Araminta—'

" 'Yes, sir.'

" 'I'd like to ax you, Miss Araminta—'

" 'Yes, sir. Yes! ah!—'

" 'To ax you—'

" 'Well, yes. Ax away'—all in a flutteration.

" 'Ef you iver seed an owl?'

"This was too much for Miss Araminta. She ixpected something very different. So she blazed up, and spoke out:

" 'I'll tell you what, Mr. Rowell, ef you've got nothing better to ax me, than ef I iver seed an owl, the sooner you clear out to the woods and turn owl yourself, the better. Only to think that you should ax me ef I iver seed an owl!'

"Well, the passion of the girl seemed to wake Ben Rowell up. He was hafe skear'd, and onbuttoning his fingers, and stopping the twirling of his thumbs, he said, gitting courage from his very skear:

" 'Well, Miss Araminta, I *hev* got something better to ax you.'

" 'Well, ax, and be done with it.'

" 'Well, will you hev me, Miss Araminta?'

" 'To be sure I will; and ef you'd hev ax'd me that years ago, I'd ha' said the same thing.'

" 'Would you!' said he. 'But how was I to know that?'

"And so Ben Rowell got his wife; and a mighty good one they say she made him; but she could niver bear to hear him tell of an owl, and they always hed a quarrel when she seed him twirling his thumbs. She made something of a man of him in the eend.

"Well, my good friends and masters, as I had determined upon the thing, I worn't going to play the game of Ben Rowell—to set twirling my thumbs and axing about owls. So I mounted my horse and started to go over to Pogson's. But, I thought I should niver git thar. My horse, that niver did sich a thing before, shied with me a dozen times, as ef skeared by something on the roadside, and came pretty nigh to fling me more than onst—a thing it's purty hard for any horse to do. Well, as I begun to enter into the avenue to Pogson's house, on a suddent I haird a crying and a mourning, most like that of a gal child, as ef she had been lost in the woods, and was tired out with fright and walking. All this seemed to make me jubous of what I was gwine to do; but I was in for it, and hed made my determination, and I was ashamed to back out. But I hed my misgivings that all worn't right, and more than onst something seemed to whisper in my ears, and to say, 'Turn back, Paddy.'

"But I went on, and soon found myself alone with Miss Susan in the sitting-room. I then thought of Ben Rowell and his owl; so I made short work of it, and ax'd his *last* question *first*; and Miss Susan said 'Yes,' modest-like enough; and a'ter a leetle stay, I left her to report the transaction to the family.

"As I rode home, I haird the crying and moaning worse than iver and it followed me for a mile. When I got home, I tould my ould mother what I hed done, and she throw'd her arms round me, and blessed me, and made a long prayer of it. Says I:

" 'Well, mother, you've got what you wanted, and ef things don't turn out right, the blame's on you! I tell you plain, I niver thought of a wife, and don't know that I want one. I marries only to plaise you.'

" 'Oh!' she said, 'it'll all be right, Paddy. Don't you be afear'd. Susan Heffernan is an angel—she's my favorite—she'll be a da'ter to me—she'll be a God's blessing on my ould age!'

" 'The Lord in his marcies grant it jest as you says. But I ain't so sure! I feel mighty queer and jubous about it, and how it's to eend.'

" 'Why, it's to eend in marriage, to be sure, and the sooner the better; and no long putting off, Paddy, my son. Ef 'twas to-morrow, I'd be the happier for it.'

"With sich a feeling on the part of my ould mother, and no onwillingness among the Pogsons, you may guess 'twas no long time a'ter that the wedding was app'inted. The women waur all busy for a month—my mother, Mrs. Sam Hartley, and Mrs. Pogson—who but they, and what a dint of a fuss they made. They met together a'most daily, and they waur all full of big preparations. I was for heving the affair very quiet, but nothing would suit 'em all, but they must hev a great supper and a dancing party. I grumbled, but it all eended in their heving their own way. As the time draw'd nigh, my poor ould mother, she says to me:

" 'Paddy, we'll hev to help out the supper. The Pogsons won't hev much. They've got mighty leetle bacon, and, would you bel'ave it, Mrs. Pogson aint got fowl, or goose, or duck, or turkey, in the yard. We'll hev to send 'em all them things, for it's as needful to us as to them, to see that there's a plenty. So I'll send over two of my ducks, one of my turkies, a pair of my young geese, and you kin let me hev a couple of hams, kaint you?'

"Says I—rather sharp: 'With man and woman, both strapping strong, three da'ters, and one son a'most grown, it's mighty strange they've got no meat and poultry. It's a *bad sign*, ould lady.'

" 'Oh! Pogson,' says she, 'is no manager.'

" 'But there's his wife,' says I, 'and three big daughters. Pogson need'nt see to the poultry. What are all them doing? It's a *bad sign*, I tell you.'

" 'Well, shill I send the bacon, with the other things?'

" 'Yes; jest as you plaise. I suppose you must.'

"And so they waur all sent. Well, the time come, and all things waur ready. I axt a few friends, Colonel Jim Meredith, the Napoleon of the railroad, among 'em; and I tuk him in my buggy from the cars at Midway, and he went home with me.

"He brought with him a great big box, or something kivered up with canvas, and tightly strapped, and I hed to git a cart from Wharncliffe to carry it. Col. Jim would hev it carried. Says he:

" 'That's my wedding present for your wife.'

"But he would'nt tell me what it was. He brought with him a dern'd sassy pet monkey; he said, to help make fun for the young ladies. And with him and the monkey, I driv off to my own farm, whar we hed dinner to ourselves, the ould lady being gone, by day peep, to help the Pogsons fix up.

"At dark I took Col. Jim and his monkey in the buggy, and we driv off for Pogson's. But my horse was mighty obstropolous all the way, shying, starting and dodging, and I thought we'd niver git thar. But we did safely at last, and found a good big company already gathered together. I did'nt know hafe of the people, and I reckon, from their looks, that some of them got there without any invite. They hed all the rooms well lighted up with lamps and candles, and in the front yard there waur two great fires of lightwood, so that everything was in a blaze. In the passage way the tables waur spread for supper, running the whole length of the passage-way. The two biggest rooms in front were lighted up for the company and the dancing; but it was hard work to git round the tables—the passage was so narrow—to git into the rooms, and half a dozen times the great hoops of the women waur sweeping the knives and forks and plates off the table. For sich a company, and sich a long table, I did'nt see whar Pogson was to git the victuals to put on it. But he hed bought a quarter of beef at Bomberg, and a couple of kids from Gardner Gess, as I afterwards found out: and I reckon he aint paid for them to this day! But that was no business of mine. I only seed that my two hams, and my ould mother's powltry wouldn't go hafe far enough for sich a crowd. In the front piazza, the men waur all got together, and the drinking waur already begun, Pogson and his son being busy all the time, axing the people. They had a sideboard at one eend of the piazza, and the men waur coming up all the time. Pogson and his son were *hafe cut* before we got thar, and when Col. Jim Meredith and I arrived, the old fellow hugged us one a'ter the other, and hugged the monkey. The little beast scratched his face for him. They hed lots of whiskey, and some sweet wine for the ladies. When the cart come, bringing Colonel Jim's present, Pogson wanted to open it right away; but Colonel Jim would'nt let him. 'Twarn't to be opened tell a'ter the marriage ceremony was over.

"Very soon the parson come—Parson Bellinger—and then we all went into the setting-room. It was fixed up with green bushes all over the fireplace and windows, and looked quite purty—the green hiding the rough plank everywhere. Then, on a suddent, Miss Susan Heffernan, she comes in, with the bridesmaids, all dressed in white. My ould mother come up to me, and says in a whisper loud enough for a dozen to hear—

" 'Don't she look like a blessed angel!'

"And, to speak nothing but the truth, she did look mighty purty, with her eyes drooping and cast down, as ef she darsn't look up for the bashfulness! Then Parson Bellinger, he got up, and we all stood up, and Col. Jim Meredith, he made me take Susan Heffernan's hand, and git the ring, and the Parson, he went on with the sarvice, and I could see he was determined on hitching us together as tight as he could.

"Well, jest as the sarvice was over, on a suddent, we haird the most tremendous owl-schreech right over the chimney, as suddent and awful as a suddent roll of thunder out of a clear blue sky in April.

" 'Good Lord presarve us!' cried my poor ould mother. 'What's that?'

" 'It's the divil!' says I, out loud.

"Then the Parson he gin us a mighty sarching prayer, agin the divil, that must hev hurt his feelings mightily; and then we all riz up from our knees, and the ladies, they sot down; and the men stood up; and there was a dull silence in the room, till Jim Meredith's monkey jumped out of his pocket, I reckon, right upon the shoulders of Mrs. Sam Hartley; and before Jim could git hold of him, he had his fingers in her fine head-dress, and her red hair, which warn't so fine, and it was all hanging about her ears in a minute. Lord, how she screamed—

" 'Take it off! Take it off! The dreadful beast!'

"Oh! she was roaring mad; and it made her furious to see ivery-body laughing fit to split! Jim run up to try and take the wicked beast off, but the leetle wretch, he sot squat, straddling her neck and shoulders, with his claws fairly fastened in her head-dress, her fine ribbons and her wool; and he stretched himself up, and looked over her head, grinning and barking, as ef he had his rights, and wouldn't let go.

" 'Take him off! Take him off!' she cried.

"And Jim tried his best; but he had to try it aisily, for fear of the head-dress; and the cussed beast had got his nails so fastened in the hair that it was no aisy matter. Jim, ready to split, coaxed him, then cussed him, and threatened him; but divil a bit would he mind. And the woman herself was bobbing her head from side to side, and dodging, and screaming all the time. But 'twas no use. At last, Col. Jim got in a passion, and knocked the beast over his nose, and gin him a pull, and with that the leetle wretch give one spring, and jumped away; and made all worse than ever, for he pulled off the whole head-dress. But that warn't the worst of it; for, to the supprise of everybody, the hair come along with it—the whole shock.—Nobody —not even Sam Hartley himself—iver know'd, till that minute, that his wife wore a wig!—for who would think of a woman gitting a wig of red hair?—her scalp was as bald as a pumpkin!

"Sich a scream! And off she went, kicking, into a fit of screeching hystericals.

"You should ha' seed Sam's face at the diskivery. His eyes a'most popped out of his head at the skear—his jaws drapped down, leaving his mouth jest half a yard on the stretch; and he jest stood so, never onst moving—with his hands clasped together, staring away his eyes, while his wife was stretched out, kicking and screaming, on the sofa, and showing more hair on her legs than she had on her scalp.

"The women got her out of the room.—Jim chased the monkey all about, from chimney place to window, and at last got back the head-dress and the wig.

"When Mrs. Sallie come back agin into the room, she gin him the look of a tiger-cat, with his teeth sot upon an edge! Says Jim to me;

" 'Paddy, I kain't go home to that woman's house to-night. She'd eat me up!—You must find me some other place to sleep at.'

"You see, Sam Hartley had ax'd Jim to stay with him that night, so as to take the cars convenient in the morning. I seed that what Jim said was right. She'd niver bear the sight of him agin! So I called up Isaac Bamberg, and he offered to take Jim up to Lowry's, and find a bed for him at his house!

"It was a long time before we got things quiet agin. In the meantime, however, the sarvants handed round the cake and wine to the company, and one of my friends slipt the Parson's fee into his hands, and he then went off, as he seed the preparations making for the dance. The fiddler was a tuning his fiddle in the piazza, and the Parson riz up to go. But here, old Pogson, who was drunk as a coot already, he got hold of him, and winding his arm round his neck, wanted to keep him to supper; but the Parson wouldn't stay. And when he was gone, then there waur a great gathering round the table to see the bridal presents.

"Thar they waur all spread out to be seen. There waur silver spoons, and silver knife and fork, and salt cellars, and pitcher, and basin, and pretty cups and scent-bottles, and a dozen other things; some for show, and some for house-keeping; some for dress, and some for use. At last old Pogson dragged in the big box that Col. Jim had brought, and he soon got off the kivering. And Lord! what do you think it was? A baby's cradle, with mattress, kiver-lid, and all, jest ready for use! You should have hearn the tittering and giggling among the women, and the big 'Haw! Haws!' among the men.

" 'Why,' says I, 'Jim, that wont be of any use for a year yit!'

"He laughed with a sort of side chuckle, and p'inted to a paper pinned on the pillow. Old Pogson snatched it up, but he was too boozy to read it; so Sam Hartley read it out.

" 'This cradle is made out of *native* wood, of our swamps, by a *native* workman of Augusta, and is intended only for the use of *native* productions. God save the State!'

"How ould Pogson danced over it! He hugged Jim and he hugged me, and a'most everybody. I reckon he had niver seen sich a gathering in all his life before. Says he—

" 'Colonel Jim, what *kin* be the use of that strange looking thing you've brought thar?'

" 'Oh! says Jim, 'it's always of use in ivery well rigilated family. One don't know how soon it may be wanted.'

"And Jim chuckled in his sly way, making his handsome face look twice as handsome; and Pogson, he roared out, and danced, and clapped his hands, and kicked the fiddler till he struck up for dancing; and to dancing all parties went; and who but they:—and what with dancing and drinking, the men were all in a fair way to lose their heels; and the women tuk lemonade, and used their tongues more than their throats. Sich a hubbub!

"At twelve o'clock we hed supper, and as soon as that was over, and the young people hed got to dancing agin, I sneaked off to my bed room, seeing that Susan Heffernan hed gone. We hed one of the shed rooms for our chamber, but whar they put the rest of the family, I kaint tell. As I entered the bed room I found hafe a dozen ould women thar, and so I told 'em they might go. I hed no use for 'em: but as they kept hanging on, I begun to ondress myself at onst, and that clared 'em out, Mrs. Sam Hartley being the last one to quit. She kept a running back and for'ard to the bed, whispering her last words to Susan Heffernan, till I fairly tuk her by the shoulders, turned her out, and locked the door.

"Well, the bed-room was dressed up mighty fine, with curtains and green bushes, and all sorts of ribbons. There was a tall looking glass on the t'ilet, and two candles burning. The ould house was fairly shaking with the dancing in the hall; and every now and then I could hear ould Pogson scream out between his happiness and liquor. There waur noise enough to drown the fiddle a'most, though it was the loudest and screakiest, I reckon, in all the district. I know'd the men waur hard sot on drinking.

"Well, while I was ondressing, taking off my cravat, before the glass, I hears, over all the fiddling and dancing, that same crying and moaning that hed been a troubling me so long. And when it stops, all on a suddent, the window shutter was pulled open wide, with a jerk, jest as ef the wind hed done it; and when I looked round I seed through the opening—for thar was no glass—a great big red eye looking full at me; and jest as I seed it, I haird a v'ice —the same v'ice of the swamp that I had hairn before—and it said—

" 'Oh! Paddy! So Paddy! Whoa Paddy!'

" 'What's that?' says Susan Heffernan.

" 'The divil, I reckon' says I. Then she screamed out.

" 'Oh! don't be skeared,' says I, 'I'm used to him!'

"But she kivered up her head. Then the v'ice said, plain as I'm talking now—

" 'So, Paddy, you've gone and done it, and I'm done with you! I'll trouble you no more; and now you'll find, ould fellow, you're in worse hands than mine iver waur!'

"With that the window was slammed to; and then I haird the crying and moaning agin, getting softer and softer, as ef 'twas going off; and in a leetle while I haird nothing more! And I've niver haird it sence; and for two years I've been free of all trouble in the swamp, and on the river, and in the woods; and my luck has come back to me; and I kin shoot as well as iver, and ef 'twant for one thing I'd be the happiest man in all creation!"

"What's that one thing, Paddy?" I asked.

"I'M MARRIED, Stylus and oh! Lord, gentlemen, very good friends and masters, after all my kear, and painstaking, and watching, and inquiring, I MARRIED A FOOL! A FOOL! A FOOL!

"But that's enough! I wouldn't hev' said it, but I could'nt help it. It jumped out from atwixt my teeth by the force of my feelings. That's enough!

"My ixcellent friends and masters, I'm done! I've kept you a long time listening to the ixparience of a poor backwoodsman and Edisto raftsman, and I'm in hopes I aint tired you out. You've got pretty much ivery thing I hed to tell of any consekence; and ef it plaises you I'm thankful; ef not, I beg you'll ixcuse a fellow that means no harm, and nothing but civility; and who's got too long a tongue in an empty head! I'm done! There's no more to tell you, 'cept only that to this day Mrs. Sam Hartley abuses Jim Meredith, for an infidel and monster. She says no good kin iver come of a man that keeps a monkey and rides a donkey. She goes so fur as to say that she believes the monkey is a sort of pet divil; and she shakes her head as ef to say the divil's got a tighter hold on Jim's soul than iver he hed in her wool. As for Jim, the story goes, that wheniver he happens to see Mrs. Sam at Midway, he shuts the door of his car, makes the ingine go faster, refuses to stop for passengers, and is mortal skeared till he's full a mile or two past. He may well be afraid of her. I do believe ef she iver gits a chaince at him she'll tear the eyes out of his head! And that eends. That, I belave is about all, my friends, that I hev' got to tell you."

"Oh! no, Paddy," said Jamison; "we cannot let you off so easily. There is surely more to tell, you end quite too abruptly. We must at least have a picture of the Honeymoon."

"Not a word more, general."

"Well, Paddy, I must only say, speaking entirely with regard to art, if you leave off so abruptly, you have conducted us to a most lame and impotent conclusion. Your devil of the stump has been at too much pains-taking surely, to be content to wind up only with a joke or a sarcasm! There must be surely something more of this history."

"Not a bit, gentlemen. No more that _I_ hev' to tell! As for the art, Mr. Stylus, I've only got to say, as I said before, that I warn't going to tell you a _story_, but a _history!_—There's no art in what I've been a-telling you; and nothing less than the sober, settled-down, etarnal fact! But ef you come to speak of the art, I've only got to ax you ef, in all the stories you iver read, they don't always eend when you comes to the death or the marriage? That's the case, I know, in all _your_ stories. As soon as you gits the two parties fairly hitched, you winds up the story. You knows that nobody cares to hear any further, when the man and woman are married, or when the man's knocked on the head, or goes dead somehow; and then you winds up jest with a leetle pictur' of the poor widder, disconsolate, in her mourning weeds, and gitting, as fast as she kin, out of the sight of the worrold! That's the way you does it always, so far as I've iver seed. Ef it's a happy eending, why it's marriage! At least, you stops short when you gits the couple married, and leaves the reader to suppose that all's smooth sailing with 'em foriver a'ter! Ef you wants a sad eending, why you knocks one or both of 'em upon the head; the man gits killed in a duel, or a skrimmidge, and the woman breaks a heart, or a blood-vessel, and goes off in a galloping consumption; and one way or t'other, you makes the reader happy at the eending. And jest so I finishes my history at the marriage, and you've then only to suppose jest what plaises you, as to the happiness coming a'ter. What more would you have?"

All our pressing availed nothing. Paddy was obstinate; and as we continued to urge him, grew restive and somewhat churlish.—Seeing this, Wharncliffe gave us the wink; the cups were filled, and, drinking all round, we forebore all further calls upon our Raftsman—

contenting ourselves with warmly thanking him for the satisfaction he had given us.

"And now," said he, "my friends and very good masters, as I shall l'ave here to-morrow, and long, I reckon, before any of you gits out of your blankets, I had better take my far'well of you this very night. It may be we shall niver meet agin, for I've volunteered and am going to j'ine the army. They've made me a sargeant of our 'Edisto Swamp Scouters,' and I'm to j'ine at camp next Saturday. So I've got to hurry and git ready as fast as I kin. I shall niver forgit you, or those happy nights I've spent here, listening to your conversation! As for Wharncliffe, he's a'most the only close friend I've got left, and I kaint l'ave him with dry eyes. May the good Lord of all peoples have marcy upon him, and all of you, and forgive you your sins and misdemeanors! God bless you all!"

The poor fellow seemed much affected, and we grappled hands with a degree of warmth which was gratifying to him, and entirely unstrained on our parts. Briefly, whatever might be thought of his narrative, the degree of interest which it possessed, or the probabilities which it involved, we were all pleased with the frank, masculine character of the man, his genuine simplicity, honest passions, and Doric intellect. When he left us, which he did after a hearty stoup all round, Wharncliffe retired with him to his chamber, and was an hour absent. When he returned—but we must reserve something for another chapter.

CHAPTER XXIX.

Mr. Stylus, *loquitur*—Wharncliffe's summary, showing what sort of a fool Paddy married, and what happened thereupon—The Pogson Brood—The Robbery— The Fight—The Stabbing and Kicking; and how the parties are left to the *status quo*.

———

And now, dearly beloved reader, having suffered our amiable backwoods friend to speak for himself, with few interruptions, the better to present you with his own unbroken narrative, in his own Doric style, it is but proper that I should say that this narrative was by no means contracted within a single night, although, to avoid unnecessary breaks in the story, I have suffered you to suppose so. Paddy was a week with us, at Wharncliffe's, hunting and fishing for us throughout the day, and talking for us nightly, from supper time till midnight.—Our other companions assembled nightly, enjoyed a good supper, of fish, game and venison; and listened, I think, as patiently to the narrator as I did myself. He was personally known to Wharncliffe and Jamison, as I have already shown, and their testimony in his favor, was warm, strong, and highly appreciative, as well of his mother wit and simple honor, as of his personal character.

In the course of this week, our circle was increased by the sudden arrival, from town, of the somewhat celebrated Father Abbot, of the well known "Lemurian Brotherhood," of Charleston, bringing with him two young men, lately initiated as members of the Brotherhood, and now in their first novitiate.

These young men, by the way, have already made their mark on society, and acquired reputation, which, no doubt, succeeding labors will greatly augment. They were Messrs. Paul Hayne and John Dickson Bruns; the former, receiving for his conventual name, that of "Brother Paulo," the latter "Brother Bruno."

493

They were all received with warm welcome by Wharncliffe, who was also of the "Brotherhood;" and they partook freely in the frequent discussions, political, social and psychological, to which the narrative of Paddy naturally gave rise.

I have foreborne, as much as possible, any reference to these discussions, since they led to no definite conclusions; all the parties maintaining their several opinions at the close. It may be as well to mention, however, the discussions in respect to the psychological experiences of Paddy, were singularly copious and discursive. Wharncliffe having affirmed the perfect integrity of Paddy—as, indeed, none of us could doubt it—the only question that remained was as regards the sort of influence, whether physical, or mental, or spiritual, to which his singular hallucinations, or experiences, were due.—But the discussions and their conclusions we may safely suspend for the present, waiting a more auspicious moment.

After Paddy had taken his departure, which he did the next morning at daylight—he left the neighborhood for his regiment in the course of the week—Wharncliffe assembled us together the very next evening, and, in compliance with our wishes, proceeded to give us the sequel of Paddy's narrative, from the period of his marriage. I will, as in the preceding pages, endeavor to make my report, as nearly as possible, in the language of the narrator.

"Paddy McGann, or Patrick McGarvin, my friends, is, as perhaps you have seen, a *natural* man; frank, fearless; open as day; carrying his heart in his hand, without sophistication or art; as generous as light; and buoyant of spirit as the air. Fraud he has none; his integrity is beyond all question; he is free from guile and falsehood; and whatever you may think of the supernatural of his story, of one thing you may rest certain—he himself fully believes it—he is the victim of his own delusions, if such they are. How they originated, it is difficult to say. I have already, more than once, indicated my own notions that they are due to an excitable imagination, a desultory and wandering, and half solitary life, and to the too free use of ardent spirits. For some four or five years he drank prodigiously. He still drinks, but not to the same degree. He drinks frequently, but you will observe that his potations are always of moderate dimensions; and, with a strong constitution, an ardent temperament, a good skin, and free, manly exercises in the open air, the liquor is measurably innocuous passing off through the pores instantly. Still, I suspect, that the period of his imaginary troubles, was one in which too much use of the liquor determined it to his brain, worked upon an excitable fancy, and produced the supposed psychological effects which he reports.

"I am aware that many of his details are such as we cannot account for, unless by straining greatly the probabilities of my theory; but, perhaps, were they reported by any other than himself they would be easier of solution. His mind, in an excitable condition, has a natural tendency to exaggeration; and this without any purpose, on his part, to color or distort the truth. I repeat my belief, that he honestly thinks that he has told us nothing but the simple fact.

"Of his mind I need say nothing. I think that he has said and shown enough to satisfy my friend, Stylus, that our simple forest population, of which he is a good, though *fine* specimen, is not naturally lacking in the gifts of fancy and imagination; and that they only need the *attrition* of society, the provocation to enterprises, and a growing passion for more various enjoyments and luxuries, to become a thoughtful and producing people; as much so as any peasantry or rustic population in the world. *No purely rustic population, by the way, has ever yet been known to achieve what is called a high civilization*—that is, as shown in the development of letters, science, and the arts. These must always come from the great marts and the densely packed communities of States.—The individual genius, emerging from such a population, would make no show, would find no audience, would perish among them, unless it threw itself, for attrition, audience and stimulus, upon the great city. But I will not digress into discussion.

"There is no use to say more of our sturdy friend, prior to the period of his marriage. That event was encouraged by myself in more than one conversation, in which he consulted me as to his mother's wishes. I told him that the old woman was right; that he had reached middle age, and required the companionship of a wife, and the comforts of a settled abode.

" 'Ah!' said he, 'Wharncliffe, but the woman! Now, I know no women hardly. I have not been fond of their company. What I've seen of them don't altogether please me. The fact is,' and he continued, 'as you know, my condition of life does not justify me in looking in the quarter where I *might* suit myself.'

"Such was the tenor of his speech, and I understood him. Paddy is not only a fellow of shrewd understanding and talents, but he is, by nature, a gentleman—having proper tastes, fine sensibilities, generous sentiments, above all meanness, and, as you have seen, with a certain loftiness of courage, which, among the common people, seems like *hauteur;* and even among the higher classes, though his speech and conduct are usually modest enough, his bearing is elevated, and at times, very noble and graceful. Certainly, his carriage and deportment might afford the best examples to persons who have been born in the purple! Of books he knows little; his schooling has been nothing; his language, unless when he becomes lifted by his subject, is a curious *patois;* yet his letters are all in very fair English, very well expressed, while his verses, of which I have seen a good many, show that his ear is harmonious; his mechanism being quite as good as that of hundreds of small poets who find their way into the newspapers and magazines.

"In counselling him to take a wife, I had no notion of his choice, or of any object that would suit him. I took for granted that he had a sufficient circle of acquaintances from which to choose. I simply told him to choose a good one. I well remember his reply—

" 'Yes, indeed, colonel—*anything but a fool!*'

"He could not endure the small talk of women—the endless prattle about trifles, and the perpetual disposition to prattle in what Wordsworth calls 'personal talk.' It must be confessed, that, on this subject, his tastes were rather despotic. He is an earnest person even in his play.

" *'He did marry a fool at last!'* as he said himself—a declaration which burst from him in the vehemence of his emotion, when closing his narrative. He felt ashamed of it afterwards, as he told me in his chamber; for said he, 'after all, she's my wife;' and it was because of his delicacy in regard to her that he refused to report the griefs and troubles which finally compelled him to quit her. I am in possession of the facts, from his mother, rather than himself. She, poor woman, bitterly repenting, when too late, of the influence she had exercised over her son, in prompting his marriage and choosing his partner, came to me in frequent consultation; but I could do little to soothe her, and nothing towards remedying the evil which she had brought upon herself as well as upon him.

"He had, indeed married a fool, and one of the silliest, spitefullest and most troublesome character. The girl was plump, and pretty, and—cunning. The match was brought about by the wife of Hartley. She knew enough about Paddy to prompt the girl, and give her all the cues for her behavior. Between them they contrived to delude the old woman, who, in her great desire to see her son married, and to one who was perpetually trying to please her, became an unconscious agent for his deception, and was easily imposed on herself. The family of Pogson was all bad—worthless, idle, vicious, silly, and unscrupulous! It was a bad breed, as Paddy himself had strongly phrased it; and the youngest girl, described to him as an exception, was probably the worst, having low cunning, but little mind; no will of her own, except in obstinate hostility to her husband; and, seemingly, a mere tool in the hands of her mother, who is about the saddest sample of a worthless jade!

"In a little month after marriage the mask was pretty much thrown aside by all the parties, and old Mrs. McGarvin, as well as Paddy, soon discovered that his wife was no angel. She exhibited a spiteful temper, and was aggressive and usurpative. Every day found some one of the Pogson family at Paddy's, where they made themselves very much at home. In a few weeks he found that his bacon had given out, and he then discovered that not only were the Pogsons great feeders, as guests, but they never left his house without carrying off a ham or a shoulder, with, perhaps, a sack of grist or of potatoes.

"Paddy expostulated with his wife, alleging, what was very true, that his means would not allow him to support the whole Pogson family! Six months' provisions of meat had lasted but five weeks! His wife surlily answered him, that it was very hard if she could not give her mother a piece of meat now and then. To this Paddy answered mildly, that if meat were plenty with him, and he rich, he would cheerfully give it himself; but that, under the circumstances, it was for him to say what they could afford to give.

"Finding his wife soured, and feeling that he had no other means of security, he possessed himself of the keys of his meat house and store-room, and gave out, himself, the daily allowance for the wants of his own family. When absent, he left the keys with his mother.

This brought the storm down upon the old woman's head, and there were constant quarrels in his absence. When he returned, it was to encounter a sulky slattern sitting in a corner, chewing the cud of spite and bitterness, and scarcely answering to question or entreaty. His labors, carrying him continually abroad—now working for the railroad, for the wealthier neighbors, or rafting on the river—he was for a long time uninformed as to the degree in which anarchy prevailed at home.

"Returning, however, on one occasion, after a two weeks absence, he found the two Pogson girls established in his mother's room, and the old woman turned out into a shed room. He sternly inquired into the reasons for this change, and insisted upon the old woman's restoration; but she, unwilling to encourage the discontents, and to confess the shame which she felt, at the blindness which had brought all the mischief on the house, assumed all the responsibility of the movement, assuring her son that she preferred the shed room, as more convenient for the management of her poultry.

"The Pogson girls appeared to have established themselves as regular tenants.—Paddy raged in secret, but submitted. His wife continued sulky, and showed no gratitude for any of his concessions. He found it necessary, in the meantime, to repossess himself of *all* his keys. During his absence, Pogson and his son both were in the habit of visiting the house daily; and on these occasions the wife displayed Paddy's whiskey and tobacco, of which these self-invited guests partook *ad libitum*.

"The robberies and vexations were endless. On one occasion, returning home from a three weeks absence on the rafts, Paddy discovered that the lock of his rifle was broken off, the brother of his wife having taken the gun away for a shooting match, and, getting drunk, was thrown from his horse, when it was broken. Paddy had to lock his weapons up in his mother's room, or take them away to his own lodge in the swamp.

"Meanwhile, his mother had her tribulations also. Her ducks and turkies disappeared in a night; and it was shown, afterwards, that Pogson himself had sold them to passengers on the railroad cars.

"The old woman and the fair Susan Heffernan, meanwhile, had got to 'daggers drawn,' and the squabbles were incessant between them; though, for a long while, the elder Mrs. McGarvin kept her own secret.—She shrank from the task of confessing to her son the full extent of the mischief she had so unwisely brought upon his head and house.

"Meanwhile, under the spoliation to which he was subjected, provisions grew scarce with him. He borrowed money from me to supply them. The waste went on. He had bought a valuable tool chest, for which I advanced the money; and before the year was out he was in my debt some seven hundred dollars. He owed other persons a few hundred more.

"He was now meditating the sale of all his property, for the satisfaction of his creditors; but I paid his debts, and took a mortgage of his lands, horse, negro and cattle.

"His domestic distresses became worse than those which vexed him when he was tormented by his imaginary foes. As his demon had told him, he had fallen into worse hands. He had neither peace nor comfort in his family; no rest, no security, no satisfaction; and he finally took up his abode in the lodge in the swamp, only visiting his mother once a week for the purpose of giving out supplies.

"On one occasion, when he had been absent a couple of weeks, he returned to find the whole Pogson family quartered upon him! Pogson's property had been seized and sold by the sheriff; and though the quarrels had been bitter and inveterate between the parties, yet they had not scrupled to trespass upon the son-in-law in their hour of trouble. Paddy would not have objected to this, however, much as he disliked it, but from the fact that they had again dispossessed his old mother, and contrived to turn her out, from the shed room to an old corn and provision house in the same yard with the dwelling.

"The old woman, who was now breaking fast, endeavored to persuade Paddy that the new change was made with her own consent; but he now saw through the amiable imposture, and, without scruple, expelled Pogson and wife from the room which they had taken, being the same from which the girls had formerly driven his mother, and the best in the house. Here he reinstated the old woman, Pogson taking possession of the outhouse.

"The consumption now of meat and bread was fearful; but the miserable wretches were destitute and had no where else to go; and Paddy, with many groans, submitted to his fate. Meanwhile, the old woman, Pogson, had prompted her daughter, Susan, to a further mode of distressing her son-in-law.—She had secretly opened an account at certain shops at Orangeburg, Midway, and Bamberg, and had not only run in debt, largely, for gaudy calicoes and flaunting shawls for herself, but had actually clad her mother and sisters in similar garments, at Paddy's expense. The facts were discovered only after large bills had accumulated against him. He was now compelled to give public notice, at these and other places, that he would pay no bills of her contracting.

"This, as you may suppose, increased the horrors at his home. Such a nest of fools and brutes was hardly ever known; and it is difficult to conceive of such stupidity, on the part of the wife and her family, even though you deny them all credit for principle and feeling.

"Returning home on one occasion, Paddy found his mother very ill; she had been declining for some time before, and he had expressed his apprehension to me about her condition. He at once rode over here, and stopped a few minutes, on his way to Dr. Sweat, at that time the ablest physician in the neighborhood. I gave the poor fellow a couple of bottles of wine for the use of the old woman, and subsequently provided him with quinine, arrow root, and other matters and medicines, which her condition needed. But she sank rapidly, and died literally of a disease which the novelists and poets have rendered quite too common—a broken heart! She was miserable, and mortified perpetually with the thought that her weakness and blindness had brought her son to wretchedness. She reproached herself continually with what she had done; but Paddy himself, generously spared her. He had no reproaches, but, like a dutiful son, he watched her bedside to the last, and nursed her with a vigilant fondness, which seems usually to be the office of woman only. The poor old creature had no other nursing. The Pogsons kept aloof from all attendance, as did Paddy's wife, who nursed nothing but spiteful and sullen humours. Yet, it will hardly be believed, that, as soon as the old woman was put into the earth, the wife applied to the husband for money to purchase mourning clothes. He told me of the answer he made her:—'Roll yourself in the ashes, woman!' I attended the funeral, and, for the first time, saw the wife and the whole Pogson brood together. They made an ostentatious exhibition of pious veneration at the grave of the poor old woman, at whose dying bed they had no ministry. Paddy told me that they never brought her a cup of water.

"When this event was fairly over, Paddy, for the first time, unfolded to me the full history of his mistakes and miseries.

"It was difficult to advise him. I had the mortgage of all his property; but he was required to leave its use to the wife. He was quite satisfied to do this, but he naturally revolted at the idea of supporting the Pogson family. Yet, how to do otherwise? It was difficult to say! Unless he himself lived with his wife, it was impossible to keep them off the premises. It was just as impossible that he should live with a woman who cheated him of his goods, who was the mere tool in the hands of those who robbed him, and who met him with unwearied sulks, silence, sullenness and spite. To a man of his hasty, passionate, frank and eager temperament, it was not only a perpetual pain to see her, but a perpetual danger. His passions were easily roused—sudden thunder-storms soon blown over—but terrible while they endure.

"Nevertheless, I advised him to make another trial of the temper of the woman, and, by the exercise of equal firmness and forbearance, endeavor to give her morals a gradual shaping to his own; to endure the Pogson tribe with patience, but suffer not the slightest usurpation. I thought it possible, that, by the due exercise of his own character —using the utmost prudence—something might be done towards her improvement. It was difficult to conceive of a wife being so utterly a fool, as to endanger all her own securities, by continuing in the track of wilfulness which she had heretofore pursued. It struck me, also, that Paddy's mother might have had something to do, involuntarily, in producing the mischief. At all events, all jealousy of the step-mother, if any had existed, would now be at an end. To afford him a sufficient motive to stay at home for awhile—the better to regulate his house-hold by his personal presence—I gave him a job in wagon-building, which would employ him for a few months, and had the lumber hauled to him at his farm.

"He took my counsel, confined himself religiously at home, and wrought at the wagons within twenty steps of the house. Here, he discovered that Mrs. Pogson had taken charge of the housekeeping, his wife, being lazy and a slattern, having quietly surrendered the control to her mother. Paddy simply requested Mrs. Pogson to let his wife attend to the house, upon which the old woman bounced, and Susan Heffernan sulked worse than ever.

"One day, young Pogson undertook to flog the one negro that Paddy owned, and showed himself quite insolent when Paddy arrested him, saying that he suffered no one to flog his negro but himself. The younker replied impudently that he would flog any negro that gave him insolence. Paddy rejoined by telling him to seek his lodgings elsewhere, and he disappeared for a season.

"Meanwhile, Paddy's wife, her mother and sisters, with sometimes the father, were in daily and secret consultation. Paddy had taken possession of all his keys, and gave out the daily allowance of food. Having rebuked Mrs. Pogson for usurping the housekeeping, Mrs. Susan refused the trust, or so grossly neglected it, that, in order to be sure of his own dinner, at least, Paddy was compelled to become his own housekeeper. The wife attended to nothing, did nothing, and suffered everything to go to ruin. He could not get a stocking darned, or a jacket mended, and for all repairs of his clothes, he was compelled to employ a poor woman in the neighborhood.

"Meanwhile, he spent his money on the house-hold as fast as he made it. Never were such feeders. It seemed as if the whole brood were striving to waste what they could not consume. I paid him weekly, for the work done for me, and he worked well, rapidly, and earned considerable sums, all of which were consumed as rapidly as realized.

"At length, one Saturday, coming over to see me as usual, to get his wages, and to pour forth his sorrows, a rain storm came up, and I made him stay all night, and to dinner the next day. In this visit, he gave me such a chapter of details as I will not repeat.—Enough, that I was disgusted enough only to hear it. But, I could counsel nothing.—Nothing short of entire escape from such a connection could prove remedial; and our laws afforded opportunity for the victim.

"He returned home in the afternoon to a scene which had nearly resulted in a tragedy of itself.

"It appears that his goings and comings were duly watched by all the parties, and a system of telegraphing established, by which his absences were promptly made known to the absent scapegrace of a son. It was ascertained that Paddy's departure was always a signal for the arrival of Tom Pogson. On this occasion, the fact that Paddy was known to be with me, and the intervention of the thunder-storm, gave the parties some security. They took for granted that Paddy would be gone all night, and, as naturally guessed, that he would take his Sunday dinner with me, as had usually been his practice. They proceeded, father and son, at least, to make a night of it themselves, and did so, with no little energy and effect. When, next day, Paddy returned home, he found his cupboard broken open, and literally sacked. In this place he kept his liquors, his powder, shot, private papers, a few books, and his little store of money. The keys were in his pocket. The brutal appetites of these wretches, were not to be foreborne. The temporary security, the continuance of the storm, and probably some previous drinking, had encouraged father and son equally to the burglarious act. The liquors were all consumed, the money drawer was rifled, a bag of buckshot, and a tin canister of powder, were carried off, and Pogson and his hopeful son were just recovering from a fit of drunkenness which had evidently lasted for twelve hours or more. They sate or lay in the dining-room, half dressed, when Paddy entered the house. He took all parties by surprise.

> One stupid moment motionless he stood,

and then turned to his wife for satisfaction.

"He had soon discovered the extent of the mischief done, and the violence used; for, seeing the state of the two men, he naturally turned to his cupboard. It had been prized open with a chisel, which still lay near it. His wife was sullen as usual, and, except by an impudent grin, made no answer to his questions.

"Pogson rose as he saw Paddy enter, and would have made his way from the room, but Paddy intercepted him. The son, still foggy, only raised his head and glared savagely at the brother-in-law.

" 'Stop,' said Paddy to Pogson, 'and give me some account of this! A man don't come into my house, break my locks, drink up my liquor, and rob me of money and goods, without giving me some account, though he happens to be my wife's father.'

" 'Who says I robbed you?'

" 'Who did it, if not you? There's the fact.'

"This met with a furious volley of abuse from the father and the son, wife and mother all engaging in the outcry, and all fastening upon poor Paddy, as if he had been the serpent spoiling their Paradise. He answered little to the abuse; gave his wife one look of scorn, mixed with loathing, and said quietly to the father—

" 'Mr. Pogson, it's no use trying to make a decent white man of you! I've tried my best to stand you, but I kaint. You must quit my house to-morrow. As for you, young man, you will please clear out at onst. I kaint stand *you* any longer.'

"The chap answered him insolently—

" 'I'll go when it suits me! It's my sister's house.'

"With that Paddy took him by the neck and shoulders, thrust him through the doors, and with a sharp, quick application of his boot-toe to his rear, sent him out of the piazza. He had hardly done so, when old Pogson assailed him with a heavy blow from behind. As he turned upon this new assailant, the youngster rushed in upon him, and with a bowie-knife, stabbed him in the left shoulder—fortunately, not severely, the knife penetrating only the fleshy part of the arm, without touching artery or muscle, and wholly missing the bone.

"Paddy, who is wondrous agile for a heavy man, needed but a moment to wheel about, and plant a blow between the young fellow's eyes, which made its mark for all time, and stretched the ruffian upon the ground, insensible for awhile. It was easy, after that, to deal with the father-in-law. Paddy soon had him by the throat, and, in the first impulse of his passion, was about to subject him to the severest treatment; but he had time to pause and reflect that Pogson was an old man, and his wife's father.

" 'I won't hurt you, Mr. Pogson, but I'll see that you don't hurt me!'

"He took him tenderly to the door, and firmly, but without violence, thrust him out.

" 'Never let me see you here agin,' said he, 'unless to carry off your family. You must do for them as you can.'

"You may guess the details—the clamor of wife, mother and sisters; the gradual recovery of the young cub, and the temporary separation of himself and old Pogson. Briefly, Paddy has now abandoned the wife, and she has again got the whole brood back with her, except the brother, who has gone as a conscript to the army, where it is to be hoped that he will indulge his bloody propensities in a legitimate way, and upon proper objects.

"I have charge of Paddy's farmstead, have hired a man to work it on shares, and take charge of the property; and he makes provision for Mrs. Paddy McGann, according to a weekly rate of allowance which I have given him. She is not allowed to interfere in the business of the crops. When sales from the farm are made, the money is paid to me, and I give her a monthly allowance. The Pogsons are not allowed to meddle with the business of the place in any way, nor to employ negro, mule or cattle; nor to cultivate a fraction of the land. The fast Susan Heffernan has been to me frequently since this arrangement, prompted by father and mother, to get an increased allowance in meat, bread and money; but I have yielded nothing. Pogson has applied to me for the privilege of planting and working some of the land, but I have rejected every application. But they still continue to pester the manager in every possible way, and have so annoyed him, more than once, that he has been compelled finally to threaten Pogson with a thrashing, if he does not keep out of his presence.

"This manager, by the way, occupies the out-house in the yard, within twenty steps of the dwelling; and, as I give him half of the profits of the farm, he is sufficiently vigilant. His selfish interest secures the property against the Pogson spoliations.

"Thus stands the case at present. Paddy, as you perceive, has volunteered for the war. What the poor fellow will do when it is over, is a problem; meanwhile, he suffers much more than he shows, and is so wretched when he thinks of his condition, that I verily believe he will cheerfully seek and encounter more risks in battle than are required for any degree of bravery. He keenly realizes, in his domestic experience, how far inferior is the grief and misery of being haunted by the Devil, than of being married to a Fool!"

Having dismissed Paddy to the wars, it is but becoming that I, the reporter of his story, should say a few words at parting, to the reader. He must not suppose that the curious details of our hero's experience, so strenuously asserted by himself as true, called for no question or analysis on the part of those who listened so attentively to the narrator. Many were the arguments that ensued among the several parties present, even while the story was in progress; and some of these have been glimpsed at already, in the way of simple caveat. When the hero had finished and gone, the discussion was resumed, and continued for several nights, among the party; but as this discussion led us far away into the subjects of illusion in general, hallucinations, the metaphysical and the supernatural, it evidently opens a field quite too spacious for any simple summary. Wharncliffe evidently ascribed all of Paddy's experiences to a lively imagination, under the impulse of an excess of blood in the brain, stimulated thereto by too frequent potations of rye or Jamaica. Jamison avowed himself naturally incredulous on the subject of the marvellous. His general opinion ran against all faith in the supernatural; and he based his incredulity on his own deficient experience in this province.

"Whatever may be the reason," said he, modestly enough, "nothing has ever occurred to me, from boyhood to the present hour, which I could not account for by those well ascertained general laws which regulate man's existence on earth. I confess I snap my fingers at all goblins, and utterly defy the whole spiritual world, whenever it undertakes to meddle with sublunary affairs."

Brother Bruno concurred with Jamison in his conclusions; but being a professional man, he argued the matter on scientific grounds, ascribing Paddy's experiences to his hallucinations, of which he gave a curious history, not dissimilar in kind and character.

Brother Paulo was inclined to believe that the subject of hallucinations was entirely too abruptly disposed of, by professional and scientific men, and inclined, as a Poet, to a much more generous faith in the details of the supernatural.

Carroll beheld an ingenious argument on the one side, and a plausible narrative on the other—clear, consecutive, and from a man of admitted integrity, who, drunk or sober, exhibited as active a reasoning faculty, and was quite as ingenious in his way, as any of the professions. He preferred giving himself time for reflection on a matter involving such a variety of interests, and in a field which he had never been permitted to explore.

"You are right, my young friend," said the venerable Father Abbot, "the province of the spiritual is one into which *you must grow*, but upon which you cannot reason *until you have had your growth*. I confess, my friends, I differ from all of you who fancy that our friend, McGann, has labored under his own delusions. And suffer me to say, that the province is one over which what we call science has no claim to control. Science can only argue or reason upon arbitrary facts, certainly known, and admitted without contestation. In all others, she is a child, groping absolutely in the dark. My notion of the spiritual is, that it is *individual*—that its developments depend purely *upon the growth of the individual*. To reason at all, is a very unusual thing among men. A large majority of mankind never reasons—a still larger, reason through their passions only. This is the case mostly with the young. To reason well, or justly, in youth, is a rare thing; only seen in the instance of a *very precocious intellect*; and, of these, it is commonly observed, *that they rarely ever grow*. Extraordinary boys—that is, extraordinary from the premature appearance of the reasoning faculty—rarely *grow* into extraordinary men. They are as remarkable at twenty, as at any period in their after lives. Now, it is one of the beautiful laws of the human world, that the proper growth in man is *serial*—in order—step by step—as in the natural world. Childhood, youth, manhood, age—all these are so many several steps in a regular progress, each of which steps argues an advance, and each advance develops new characteristics and powers. A large portion of the life of the child employs what mind he has, chiefly in the development of the physical nature, in order to the perfection of limbs, muscles and sinews, and their proper use and exercise.—Mentally, we tax only his memory, and his imitative powers. As he grows into youth, the passions become active, and lead to further developments, at once of mind and body, but chiefly to the increased exercise of his energies. Manhood applies these energies to use, in such pursuits in life as the particular individual nature or genius inclines to.—Middle life constitutes another stage in which the passions yield to thought, and thought takes a bolder stand, and a more independent attitude, and then it is that we first find the individual making his own laws, and shaking off the bondage of routine. This is the period when the gifted man invents, originates, broaches new philosophies, embarks in daring speculations, begins to compare or contrast his teachings with his experience, tests both of them by a thought made confident by practice, and just enough supplied with the motor power, by his passions—which no longer excite or delude, and only feed and sustain—as to feel the requisite degree of courage to shake off conviction, and to say, fearlessly, 'I believe,' or 'I deny.' In other words, to shake off mere external authority, and assert his own mind and moral independently.

"To this stage, after a few years, succeeds the *contemplative*, and so on, step by step, to the end of the chapter.

"Now, our medical men make a corresponding division of the several *physical* developments of the man. They say that his whole animal nature undergoes a thorough, if not a radical change, every *seven* years—that he is not, in fact, the same identical man.

"It is curious that the Poets have made a similar division of periods, in the development of his moral nature. They say there are seven stages. It matters not much about the number; but, assuming that the man lives to the period when all of his faculties have reached comparative perfection, then the division made by the Poets is exactly that of the Physicians, and without any concert between them. Seven times seven gives you forty-nine; and, at fifty, a healthy man is in the prime of his intellect, without the properties of the physical man being in any way disparaged. Now, these seven stages are so many periods of successive growth, in which, step by step, one step preparing the way for the other, in regular gradation, the man attains the full and final development of his powers, and this implies that he has reached the full measure of his individuality. Upon the degree in which he is individual will depend the discoveries which he makes, his susceptibility for discovery, the extent of his vision, and—"

Here the venerable Father came to a sudden and full stop. There was an audible interruption of his discourse, which he traced to the nostrils of one of his young novitiates. The Father was forbearing to the Brotherhood, and felt that he was unconsciously subjecting them to a penance, when they needed an indulgence. With a look of great benignity, he smiled upon the offender, and gracefully waved to the rest of the party his farewell for the night.

"Another time," said he, "and we will discuss the psychological involved in Paddy's case. For the present, it is enough that we see that the *spiritual* has done its work. The *physical* evidently succumbs. —But I, too, have revelations to make, quite as extraordinary as those of Paddy, and not ending, like his, in marriage with a fool!— There shall be other evenings, my brethren, and other Legends, and we shall prepare for them in future chapters. Enough for the present. I assure you that I fully believe in the truth of Paddy's revelations. To repeat the often-used quotation from Hamlet—

> 'There are more things in Heaven and earth,
> Than are dreampt of in thy philosophy.'

But these must keep. In the language of Lady Macbeth to her husband, 'To bed, to bed, to bed!' "

Part II

EXPLANATORY NOTES

TEXTUAL APPARATUS

1. The epigraph on the title-page is taken from Ben Jonson's *Epicœne, or The Silent Woman,* IV, iv.

2. The dedication is to Henry Placide (1799-1870), the celebrated comic actor, whom Simms had known in Charleston and New York.

2.11 philosophy of Sancho: See Cervantes, *Don Quixote,* trans. Thomas Shelton, London, 1740, III, 28: *"Look not a given Horse in the Mouth."*

3.12 Sessa! let the world pass!: Simms misquotes Shakespeare, *The Taming of the Shrew,* Induction: ". . . let the world slide: Sessa."

3.19-20 Goldsmith's first comedy: The reference is to the first performance of *She Stoops to Conquer,* which is described in Richard Cumberland's *Memoirs,* London, 1806, pp. 269-70. Simms is wrong, however, in calling it Goldsmith's first comedy.

5.16-17 the Wild Horseman of Bürger: Both "Lenore," and "Der Wilde Jäger," ballads by Gottfried August Bürger (1747-94), feature wild rides by spectral horsemen and were widely known during the "Gothic" phase of the Romantic movement.

6.34 nine: Since there are ten passengers, not, as the narrator says, nine, we may assume that Simms is playing a game with the reader. The author is playing two roles—those of the South Carolinian and the New Yorker, with the latter a disguise for the former.

7.14 Ashland: The home of Henry Clay, near Lexington, Kentucky.

7.16-20 State repudiation . . . Union Bank: In 1832 President Andrew Jackson had vetoed the bill for the rechartering of the Second Bank of the United States and the following year he had the government's deposits removed to the state banks. The western states—here represented by Simms's Mississippian—had opposed the Second Bank, on the grounds that it was too powerful and was operated in the interests of the commercial Eastern states—here represented by the Pennsylvanian.

9.1   the Irish Giant: The tallest human skeleton known is that of the Irishman Charles Byrne (1761-83), whose height was 7 feet, 6¾ths inches.

9.21-22   hanging of the Yazoo rogues: More than twenty members of the Murrell gang of highway robbers and murderers were caught and hanged in 1835. Simms had already used them in his fiction in *Richard Hurdis* (1838) and *Border Beagles* (1840).

9.26-27   set-to . . . with certain abolitionists at New Haven: Probably the reference is to the *Amistad* case of 1839-41. Negro slaves aboard a Spanish ship, the *Amistad*, mutinied and killed all but one member of her crew. Taken into custody at New Haven, the slaves were defended in court by abolitionist leaders.

12.2   St. Omer (595-670), Bishop of Thérouanne, was a notably successful evangelist to the Morini in Artois.

13.30   Andrew Jackson himself was involved in war with the Seminole Indians in 1817 and 1818. He was President when the Second Seminole War began in 1835.

15.10   The Withlacoochee River rises in central Florida and flows into the Gulf of Mexico. It was the scene of battles between Federal forces and Seminole Indians, December 28, 1835; February 27-March 5, 1836.

16.9   Shakespeare, *Hamlet*, III, ii: "leave thy damnable faces, and begin."

21.26   Benzoni's *Historia del Mondo Nuovo* (1565) is the source of the apocryphal story that Columbus stood an egg on end by crushing it at its base to prove that after a deed is done everyone knows how to do it. See Samuel Eliot Morison, *Admiral of the Ocean Seas*, Boston, 1942, II, 361.

31.37   Hillabee: No racecourse by this name has been located.

36.26   Switchel: A drink of molasses and water, often seasoned with vinegar and ginger, and sometimes with rum.

37.5   "blood-o'nouns": A corruption of "blood-and-wounds," a species of large bull-frog known for their loud bass sounds that suggest their name.

50.13   Mexican: A Mexican dollar.

50.34   fip: Short for fippenny bit.

57.11   Although there is no Earl of Totham in the peerage, possibly Lord Bruce of Tottenham (1804-78) is intended.

72.23   When is he coming to marry me?: Probably an American variant of the song "When shall we be married,|Billy, my pretty lad?" See Iona and Peter Opie, *The Oxford Dictionary of Nursery Rhymes*, London, 1951, pp. 74-75.

83.25   Irishman's fun of driving all rogues before her: not identified.

85.14-15   The bravest held his breath for a time: Simms misquotes a line from Thomas Campbell's "The Battle of the Baltic." See *The Poetical Works of Thomas Campbell*, ed. Rufus W. Griswold, Philadelphia, 1846, p. 188: "And the boldest held his breath,| For a time."

96.12-13   Job, . . . vision of the night: See Job 4:13-15.

100.17   k——d: Simms probably intends "knocked" in the slang sense "to have sexual intercourse with" here and at 117.8 and 117.9.

102.36-37   Journeys to Brentford, Gilpin's race: The first of these circus entertainments is derived from Oliver Goldsmith's description of a race from London to Brentford in which a turnip-cart, a dust-cart, and a dung-cart compete; see *The Citizen of the World*, Letter LXXXVI, in *Works*, London, 1854, II, 375-76. The second derives from William Cowper's poem "John Gilpin's Ride," in which the rider loses control of his horse; see "The Diverting History of John Gilpin," *The Works of William Cowper, Esq.*, ed. Robert Southey, London, 1836, IX, 306.

109.18 anti-fogmatic: A drink taken on the pretext of counteracting the effects of fog.

120.3 Napoleon of Mexico: President Antonio Lopez de Santa Anna (1794-1876) called himself "Napoleon of the south" after his capture by Sam Houston in 1836. His favorite sport was cock fighting. See Frank C. Hanighen, *Santa Anna, the Napoleon of the West*, New York, 1934, pp. 177-78.

144.16 mother-in-law: An obsolete synonym for stepmother.

146.32-33 Roman emperor . . . divinity: According to Suetonius, the Emperor Caligula gave his horse a stall of marble and a collar of precious stones, and was said to have planned to make him a consul. See *The Lives of the First Twelve Caesars*, trans. Alexander Thomson, London, 1796, p. 366.

150.13 See "Epistle to a Young Friend," *The Poetical Works of Robert Burns*, London, 1839, I, 170-71.

155.17 Michal saluted David: See II Samuel 6:16.

157.14 graces . . . fairies: In nineteenth-century dances, routines to promote grace of movement.

163.22 Baraddee: The standard spelling for this river near Damascus is "Barada"; but a compositorial error here seems less likely than Simms having followed an obscure source.

180.11 running rigs: Simms is playing on words. "Rigs" meant prostitutes in addition to its application to horse-drawn vehicles.

186.6 the imperious beauty: See Leigh Hunt, "The Glove and the Lions," in *Rimini and Other Poems*, Boston, 1844, pp. 122-23.

192.13 lock and lock: Forelock and forelock, i.e. neck and neck.

199.8-9 Powell, Wild Cat, Tiger Tail: American names for Indian leaders of the Second Seminole War. Osceola was known as Powell because his mother married a white man of that name. Wildcat was Coacoochee; Tiger Tail was Thlocklo Tustenuggee. See John K. Mahon, *History of the Second Seminole War 1835-1842*, Gainesville, 1967, p. 91.

199.23 The man who hunted the flea: not identified.

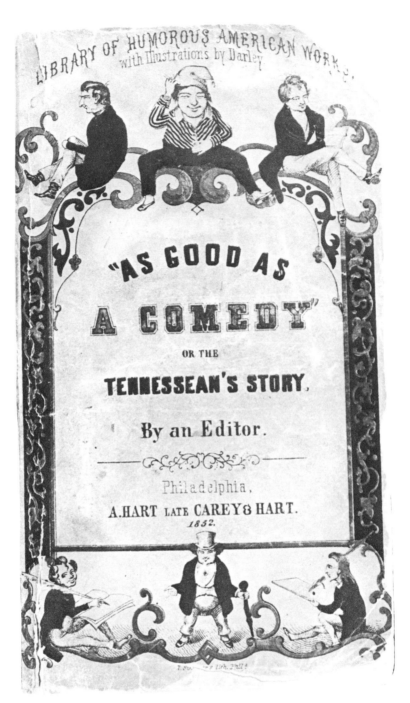

FRONT COVER OF ORIGINAL EDITION

Courtesy South Caroliniana Library

Textual Introduction: As Good as a Comedy

As Good as a Comedy was published in March, 1852,[1] by the Philadelphia firm of A. Hart, successors to Carey and Hart. It was issued in the decorated wrappers of the "Library of Humorous American Works" (see Introduction, p. xi), with an engraving by F. O. C. Darley, who illustrated nearly all of the works in this series (see plate 2). The book collates, 12° in half-sheets; 1-21⁶; 126 pp., [i] title-page, [ii] copyright and printer's notice, [iii] dedication, [iv] blank, [v]-vi Advertisement, [vii]-xxiii Proem, [xxiv] blank, [25]-251 text, [252] blank.

Despite the popularity of the series in which it appeared, apparently *As Good as a Comedy* was never reprinted, for no copies examined show evidence of reimpression. Because of the rarity and fragility of the book, it was impossible to bring together multiple copies for machine collation. But the identity of the physical makeup of all known copies of the book, plus the comparison of photocopies of sample pages, particularly those upon which textual problems occur, indicate that probably there was only one printing of the original edition of the work.

Two scenes from the novel (pp. 92-98 and 101-107 in the Centennial edition) were reprinted in the *Southern Literary Gazette*, N.S., I (May 22, 1852), 243-244 and I (June 19, 1852), 291-293, with only minor and obviously non-authorial changes. A typed copy of these variants is available in the Simms Collection of the South Caroliniana Library, University of South Carolina. No manuscript of the work appears to have survived.

The first edition of the novel, then, is sole authority for the text of *As Good as a Comedy*. Printer's copy for the Centennial edition was a photocopy of the Yale University Library copy. Proofs were also read against the copy in the South Caroliniana Library, and against microfilms of the copies at the Harvard University Library, the University of Illinois Library, and the Library of Congress.

On the whole the original edition appears to have been set in type and proofread with reasonable care, and few emendations were necessary for the Centennial text. In Table I below are recorded all

---

[1] *Letters*, III, 105n. It was deposited for copyright at the Library of Congress May 1.

changes made in the copy-text, along with all textual notes, including notes on refusals to emend.

Proofs of the text of *As Good as a Comedy* were read at least five times against copy-text (original or photocopy). All members of the Editorial Board of the Centennial edition read proofs at least once. In addition, the following graduate student research assistants of the University of South Carolina English Department read proofs and assisted with various editorial tasks: Karen Boyle, Thorne Compton, George Ellison, Carl Ficken, Eileen Gregory, Lewis Hay, Tom Johnson, Noel Polk, Jim West, and Margaret Yonce.

Special thanks for various kinds of textual assistance are due Dr. William S. Kable, of the University of South Carolina English Department, and Dr. Robert Bush.

Emendations and Textual Notes: As Good as a Comedy

Listed here are all changes made in the copy-text of *As Good as a Comedy*. The original 1852 reading appears to the left of the bracket, the emended Centennial edition reading to the right. Where no bracket appears the reading is the same in both texts and the refusal to emend is explained in parentheses. Where an explanation of the change is necessary it follows in parentheses.

5.17   Burger] Bürger (See Explanatory Note for this line.)

35.31   and the] the

37.19   demands] demand

37.20   Who's (The meaning is "whose"; but Simms may have intended to indicate word-play or eye dialect here.)

43.24   Fisher] Owens (This is the first mention of the character who is elsewhere called "Lazy Jake Owens," "Uncle Jake," and "Charley Owens." It seems more likely that Simms originally planned to call him Fisher, and later changed the name to Owens, than that Ned Ramsey, who is speaking here, would have mistaken the name.)

56.1   soul-hidden] ~∧~

64.22   field."] ~∧

70.34   "Flourish and Nabob"] "~" ~ "~"

82.23   *tête-a-tête*] *tête-à-tête*

83.29   "Graystreak,] ~"

96.32   sham-faced] shamefaced

97.4   scratch. The] ~, the

100.17 k——d (See Explanatory Note for this line.)

100.25 'good-looking too.' "] 'good-looking' too."

115.12 d—l] d——l

136.19 disappointed the] disappointed by the (Another possibility is "disappointed in the"; something is missing, and either word could have been squeezed out of a tight line, since "disappointed" is the last word of the line in the original text.)

150.title FETE] FÊTE

159.5   bcsom] bosom

161.12 wands] viands

163.22 Baraddee (See Explanatory Note for this line.)

178.5   "Lodge"] '~'

179.14 d——d] d——d

199.26 Wapoo (The Tennessean is referring to the battle of Wahoo Swamp, fought in November 1836. Though there is the possibility of a compositorial or authorial slip here, it seems more likely that the error, or mispronunciation, is deliberate on Simms's part, and a feature of the dialect characterization of the speaker. There may be an analogy, conscious or unconscious, with the Wapoo or Wappoo Creek near Charleston.)

201.29 him."] ~'

Explanatory Notes: Paddy McGann

213.Title-page   Shakespeare, *The Tempest*, III, ii.

215.epigraph   Shakespeare, *As You Like It*, II, i.

216.9   The first-person narrator, Stylus (named at 230.32), probably represents Simms himself, as author.

216.10   *Desilla:* Imaginary name, for a plantation in the Barnwell district. Simms apparently coined it from the Latin verb *desilire*, to leap down or dismount; hence, a place for dismounting.

216.11   Wharncliffe: Imaginary name, perhaps representing a combination of Simms himself, as country gentleman (see note for 241.29), and his close friend Charles R. Carroll. Wharncliffe refers to Frank Carroll (Dr. Francis F. Carroll) as "my kinsman . . . at Janina" (239.24-25); "kinsman" may be read as "son". See *Letters*, I, xcvii, and IV, 153.

217.1-2   Simms misquotes Cowper's "The Task": "How various his employments whom the world|Calls idle . . ." See *The Works of William Cowper, Esq.*, London, 1836, IX, 142.

218.30   well-shriven: Presumably *shriven* is a metaphor for *washed*, and the phrase means *well-washed*, or, less likely, *washed in a well*. (See also Textual Note.)

218.34   David F. Jamison (1810-64), lawyer and state legislator, was President of the Secession Convention of 1860. At Simms's suggestion he wrote a biography of Bertrand Du Guesclin (Charleston, 1864). In 1859 he had bought "Burwood," a neighboring plantation to Simms's "Woodlands."

219.8   Maxcy Gregg (1814-62), Brigadier General, C.S.A., was killed at Fredericksburg.

219.17   James Ryder Randall (1839-1908) was author of the poem "Maryland, My Maryland."

219.30-31   Horace, Ode XXIV. See *Horatius Restitutus*, ed. James Tate, London, 1837, p. 104. The lines are translated "What shame or measure should there be in grief for one so dear?" in the *Oxford Dictionary of Quotations*. (See also Textual Note.)

220.1 David Rumph Jones (1825-63), Major General, C.S.A.

220.2 Micah Jenkins (1835-64), Brigadier General, C.S.A.

220.12 Hollands: Gin made in the Netherlands; cf. 244.35.

220.15-16 Simms misquotes Cowper's "The Needless Alarm": "Beware of desperate steps. The darkest day,| Live till to-morrow, will have pass'd away." See *The Works*, X, 41.

220.26 Daniel Morgan (1736-1802), Revolutionary Brigadier General, won the battle of Cowpens, January 1781, for which he was praised and decorated by Congress.

220.34 Cold Harbor: Not the better-known battle of June 1864, but an earlier battle, sometimes called the battle of Gaines's Mill, fought June 1862.

222.epigraph The Pedagogue: Not identified.

222.13 bull: An individual raft, usually of timbers that had already been squared at a lumber mill. The 12″ × 12″ timbers were held together with pegs. Prize logs of cypress and long-leaf pine were cut in lengths up to eighty feet. The Edisto was an important artery for the lumber industry from the eighteenth century until World War I, when trucks began to supplant the rafts. See Alfred O. Halsey, "The Passing of a Great Forest and the History of the Mills . . . ," *Year Book 1937*, City of Charleston, S. C., pp. 198-210.

222.27 Although there were several John Brunsons in South Carolina at the time, Simms probably intends the one who was granted land in Barnwell district in 1824.

224.36 Abou Hassan: Simms appears to be using the name of the character in the *Arabian Nights* simply as a representative Arab name.

225.33 Valentine and Orson: Characters in an early French romance. The story first appeared in English about 1505 as the "History of the two valyaunte brethren Valentyne and Orson," by Henry Watson. Simms's source is probably a ballad about the brothers included in Thomas Percy's *"Reliques" of Ancient English Poetry* (1765).

227.3-4   Witch of Endor: I Samuel 28:7-14. Saul consults her.

227.13   Commodore Berry: Simms was a friend of Michael Berry, captain of the packet steamer *Charleston*. See *Letters*, V, 236.

227.28   Dunstan's metaphysics: St. Dunstan of Canterbury (909-988) was supposed to have been tempted by the devil in the form of a woman. He seized the apparition by the nose with red-hot smith's tongs.

227.30-31   Cagliostro . . . Faust: Count Alessandro Cagliostro (1743-95) was a self-styled alchemist or magician; in Simms's comparison Faust was a philosopher or metaphysician.

229.epigraph   Shakespeare, *A Midsummer Night's Dream*, IV, i. Simms's quotation is correct except for the addition of the word "but".

230.33   Ned Bucket: See 236.19. If Simms had a model for such a "series of backwoods satires" as he describes, it has not been found.

232.19   quizzing me: making fun of me.

232.28   Britton Elzy: No record has been found of a real person of this name, but William W. Ellzey (1822-87) and Thomas G. Ellzey (1825-99), brothers, are buried in the graveyard at Midway. See also 335.12-24.

235.epigraph   Shakespeare, *The Merry Wives of Windsor*, I, i. Simms's quotation is correct with two exceptions: "blessing" for "plessing" and "peradventure" for "peradventures".

236.10-11   Ferdinand . . . Miranda: See Shakespeare, *The Tempest*, III, i.

236.11-12   Simms misquotes Shakespeare, *Macbeth*, II, iii: "The labour we delight in, physicks pain."

237.11   A possible source for the Commedia dell'Arte are the Oscan *Atellanae Fabulae*, which were shows or farces introduced from the Italian town Atella and performed in the Italian dialect Oscan.

237.34   William of Deloraine: A medieval knight in Sir Walter Scott's "Lay of the Last Minstrel."

238.13-14 Daniel Defoe, *The Life and Strange Surprizing Adventures of Robinson Crusoe,* (1719). James Cook, *An Account of a Voyage round the World in the years 1768-71* (1773); *A Voyage towards the South Pole and round the World . . . in the years 1772-5* (1777); and *A Voyage to the Pacific Ocean . . . in the years 1776-80* (1784). Richard Johnson, *The Famous Historie of the Seven Champions of Christendom* (ca. 1597).

239.20-21 Sir William Howard Russell, as correspondent for the London *Times,* lost favor with the Union because of his description of the Union retreat after the First Battle of Bull Run. Simms's allusion is to one of Russell's letters (dated April 30 [1861]) which appeared in the London *Times* May 28, 1861; it was reprinted in the Charleston *Courier* June 18, 1861. Russell talked at length about the South Carolinians' admiration for the mother country and her monarchical system: "From all quarters has come to my ears the echoes of the same voice . . . . That voice says, 'If we could only get one of the Royal race of England to rule over us, we should be content.' "

241.29 only a mile distant: If Wharncliffe's residence is this close to those of Jamison and Carroll, it is additional evidence that Simms was drawing upon himself, and his own plantation, "Woodlands," in depicting Wharncliffe and "Desilla." (Cf. 216.11.)

245.32-35 These verses have not been identified. Perhaps Paddy's remark (245.37) that he has not heard them before is a hint that they are Simms's own.

248.9 Shakespeare, *Hamlet,* III, ii: "leave thy damnable faces, and begin."

250.12-36 The verses are obviously Simms's own. At 250.32, "Blackstone and Vattel" are two famous law commentaries: Sir William Blackstone (English) wrote *Commentaries on the Laws of England* (1813); Emmerich de Vattel (Swiss) wrote *Le Droit des Gens* (1758).

252.epigraph Shakespeare, *The Winter's Tale,* II, i.

253.35-36 all in my eye and Betty Martin: a colloquial English expression meaning "all humbug."

256.11 beginning, now, some six years ago: The chronology of Paddy's narrative is somewhat confused. The date he tells it to Wharncliffe and his friends is clearly established as November 1862 (215.8; references to Civil War battles on 219-221); his marriage appears to have taken place in March of 1861 (230.6, "last March was a year"); his trip to New York apparently occurred at least three years before his marriage (445.27), thus, about 1858, which would be consistent with the period of six years Paddy gives as the duration of his troubles with the devil, allowing him two years for the events that preceded his New York trip. The difficulty lies in the presence of Edgar Allan Poe at Miss Pynch's "Swarray" (427.30). Since Poe flourished in the New York salons after the publication of "The Raven" in 1845, and died in 1849, it seems likely that Simms first intended this part of Paddy's story to take place in the late 1840's, and failed to rectify his chronology when he gave the remainder of the story a later setting. This might well be an indication that Simms began the story a decade earlier than he finished it, or that the finished work included substantial elements of an earlier one. The ages of the literary figures at the gathering, and the dates of their works that are mentioned, appear to be an amalgam of a late 1840's and a late 1850's date for the "Swarray."

260.5-7 Abe Miller . . . W. P. Mills: Neither has been identified.

261.epigraph Shakespeare, *The Tempest*, III, ii.

261.18 Dicky: "In bad health, feeling very ill; inferior, sorry; insecure." See also 337.13. Eric Partridge, *A Dictionary of Slang and Unconventional English* (New York, 1951), p. 218.

264.5 wirra sthru!: The Irish exclamation "A Muire, is truaighe!" means "Oh Mary, what an affliction!" The *M* becomes *w* in exclamation.

266.16, 18 Shakespeare, *Othello*, II, iii.

268.epigraph Shakespeare, *Hamlet*, I, v.

268.12 Johann Kaspar Spurzheim (1776-1832), German phrenologist.

271.37-38 Midway is the village closest to Simms's plantation, "Woodlands." Carson and Whetstone are actual local names.

272.4-5 Kentucky Rifle Powder, three F.F.F.: A fine grade of gunpowder for small to medium caliber rifles.

277.epigraph Shakespeare, *As You Like It*, I, ii.

283.epigraph Shakespeare, *Macbeth*, III, iv.

288.26-27 Big Lake is an actual lake at "Woodlands."

288.31 A Charles Dewitt had property in the 1840's and 1850's near the fork of the North and South Edisto in Barnwell County, but there is no deed recording the transfer of land from Dewitt to Jamison or from Dewitt to intermediaries to Jamison.

290.4-5 Little Lake is an actual pond at "Woodlands."

290.33 Beckalee Place: The Beckley house is, in 1970, still partially intact near the Charleston Road at "Woodlands."

294.epigraph Ben Jonson, *Bartholomew Fair*, II, ii.

295.32-33 Both Moonbend and Turtle Cove are actual place names on the South Edisto near "Woodlands."

295.36 Horn Cove: Horn Branch, a tributary of the South Edisto, runs through "Woodlands."

297.22 Sand Field: Now known as Beech Tree Field, near Big Lake, at "Woodlands."

297.23 Holly Thick: An actual place name at "Woodlands."

299.18 Patterson's: Probably "Briarwood" Plantation, the home of the Patterson family to the east of "Woodlands."

301.2 Philip Pendleton Cooke (1816-50) published his *Froissart Ballads and Other Poems* in 1847.

301.7 John Esten Cooke (1830-86).

302.epigraph Simms cuts short the quotation from Froissart. The second sentence continues: "It is a fact, as the squire assured me, that the count de Foix was informed, the day after the battle of Aljubarota, of everything that had there happened, the same as I have related it, which surprised me exceedingly how this could possibly have been." Sir John Froissart's *Chronicles of England, France, Spain . . .*, trans. Thomas Johnes, London, 1855, II, 126.

303.28-30 Froissart's *Chronicles of England, France, Spain . . . ,* 2 vols., trans. Thomas Johnes. London: Henry G. Bohn, 1855. The passage Simms quotes is from Vol. II, Book III, Chapter 18, pp. 128-129.

307.26 Branchville is the junction point of the Charleston railroad, 5 miles from "Woodlands," one branch going to Columbia, the other to Augusta.

310.epigraph Shakespeare, *Hamlet*, I, i.

319.epigraph Shakespeare, *King Lear*, III, iv.

327.30 Balaam's ass: Numbers 22:22-35.

329.epigraph Shakespeare, *The Tempest*, V, i.

330.13-14 Job sees a shadow: There is frequent reference in Job to "visions of the night"; see 4:13, 20:8, 33:15. However, there is no reference to "shadows".

331.20 Forks: Paddy's farm evidently lay between the North Edisto and the South Edisto, somewhere near their junction.

331.29-30 a colt of Reliance's: Reliance was probably the registered stud foaled April 1835 on the farm of H. G. S. Key, Tudor Hall, Maryland. See *American Turf Register*, XIII (June 1842), 351.

331.34 me one: me alone; cf. 341.26, meself one; and 343.3, me one.

333.16 Captain John S. Jennings owned several miles of timber land on the opposite side of the South Edisto. After the burning of the house at "Woodlands" in 1862 he offered Simms free timber to rebuild it, expressing the pride of the community in Simms. See *Letters*, IV, 405-6.

333.18 Cannon's Bridge is still the name of the bridge across the South Edisto near "Woodlands."

333.32-33 railroad bridge: where the railroad from Charleston crossed the South Edisto above "Woodlands."

336.26-337.26 Paddy describes a route from Parker's Ferry on the Edisto to the entrance to the Ashley River near Charleston. The following place names have been found on 19th century maps and are correctly located by Simms: Parker's Ferry, Jacksonborough, Willtown Bluff, Slana's River, Slana's Bluff, White Point, Dawboo River (Dawhoo on some maps), New Cut, Stono River, Rantowles, Wappoo River, Ashley River. Church's Flats should come before New Cut rather than after it. Simms probably named the following for landmarks with which he was familiar but which did not lie along the route he describes: Peter's Cut, supposedly at the point where Slana's River branches from the Dawboo, was probably named for a landowner Peters, who held property on Big Edisto Island at a cut on another river; Reynold's mud-flat, supposedly across from the Big and Little Ingadoo, was probably named for Reynolds, who held property on Wadmalaw Island on Leadenwah Creek—probably marshy land similar to this. The Big and Little Ingadoo have not been located, but the Tugadoo River meets Wadmalaw River at the point where the Ingadoo would be in Simms's description; a river or creek adjacent to the Tugadoo would correspond to the Little Ingadoo. The following place names have not been located on any map although landmarks which they indicate did exist on the river journey at the places Simms describes them (i.e., there was an island where Black Island is indicated; there was a cut where Dead Man's Cut appears, etc.): Black Island Cut, Dead Man's Cut, Hop's and Long Creeks, the "Narrors," and Alligator (river or creek).

337.35-37 Proposals were made to link the Edisto with the Ashley River from the late eighteenth century on, but the plan was never carried out.

338.7-8 Paddy's remarks about the result of the blockading of the Stono River, which would cut Charleston off from the Edisto, are a little confusing, and the passage may be corrupt. If the Stono were blockaded, there would be no need for the enemy to run up the North Edisto in order to cut off the timber from Charleston. Nor would "running up North Edisto" affect the movement of rafts, like Captain Jennings', on the South Edisto.

339.20-21 Walker's Suck, Silliman's Ferry, and Graham's reaches are actual place names along the Edisto.

343.33-34 raccoon oysters: small, worthless oysters, fit to be eaten only by raccoons.

355.17-18   Sennacherib, with the Issyrians: Sennacherib was king of
Assyria (705-681 B.C.). The allusion here is probably to the biblical
account of the invasion of Judah by Sennacherib during the time of
Hezekiah. See II Kings 18-19.

355.18   Darius, with the Medes and Persians: There were three
kings of Persia named Darius. The allusion here is probably to
Darius I, the Great, who reigned from 521 to 486 B.C.

355.23   Dagons of Philistines: Dagon, represented as half man and
half fish, was the chief god of the ancient Philistines.

357.4   staddled: Paddy has earlier used the rare noun *staddle* for
a support of his woodpile (356.18); here he seems to be using it
as a verb, meaning held, or hemmed in. It is less likely that *staddled*
is a compositorial error for *straddled*; at this point Paddy does not
seem to have the log between his legs.

359.5-6   Queen of Sheba: The allusion is to I Kings 10:2: "And she
came to Jerusalem with a very great train, with camels that bare
spices, and very much gold, and precious stones . . . ." Paddy is
comparing the glory of the moon rising with the glory of Sheba's
coming to Jerusalem.

370.26   blister: Here, a blistering plaster.

370.33   the Adele, or Adela: the *Adela* was a British steamer cap-
tured off the Bahama Islands July 7, 1862 by the *U.S.S. Quaker
City* as a suspected blockade runner. The captain at that time was
James Walker. Captain Wilson has not been identified; however,
see Introduction, p. xxvi, for a discussion of his prototype in Simms's
own life.

379.10-11   Paddy misquotes Psalms 137:5, "If I forget thee, O
Jerusalem, let my right hand forget her cunning."

380.19   sawyers: trees with one end stuck in the river bottom, the
other projecting to the surface.

380.19   haricains: See 336.22-23.

380.28-30   The reference is apparently to the Nashville Convention
of 1850, which Robert Barnwell Rhett and others attempted to

persuade to indorse the principle of secession. Paddy also might be referring to the South Carolina ordinance of 1852 which declared the state's right to secede.

381.14 Providence burying ground: Probably the cemetery for Providence Church in Orangeburg County, about 30 miles from Bamberg.

381.27-382.6 Prominent among newspapers pursuing anti-Southern editorial policies was the *New-York Tribune*. Its editor, Horace Greeley, abhorred dueling, but he was severely caned by Arkansas Congressman Albert J. Rust in 1856. Although James Gordon Bennett's *New York Herald* was strongly national during the war, it had earlier been sympathetic toward the South. Bennett, however, is clearly referred to in the examples of "cowards" that Thompson gives. Frequently assaulted or horsewhipped, he usually chose to retaliate in the *Herald* with an account that would increase the circulation of his paper and make his enemy appear a bully. He is the one who "calls himself a *philosopher*"—a reference to Bennett's comparing himself with Zoroaster, Moses, Socrates, Seneca, and Luther. See Jeter Allen Isely, *Horace Greeley and the Republican Party, 1853-1861*, Princeton, 1947, pp. 147-48; and Don C. Seitz, *The James Gordon Bennetts . . .* , Indianapolis, 1928, pp. 56-57, 130-31. Simms despised James Watson Webb, editor of the *Enquirer*, and Henry J. Raymond, of the *New York Daily Times*, as well as Greeley; see *Letters*, IV, 266. Although the New York *Evening Post* was strongly abolitionist in the period before the war, it is doubtful that Simms would have maligned its editor, his friend William Cullen Bryant.

384.20 Lewis Gaylord Clark (1808-73) was editor of *The Knickerbocker Magazine*, 1834-61. Simms had contributed to it in the 1830's, when he was associated with the "Knickerbocker" group of writers, but he broke with Clark after a quarrel about payment for his contributions. In the 1840's Simms became associated with the "Young America" group, who were liberals in politics and nationalists in literature. The conservative Clark vilified them in print and particularly offended Simms with a comment that no one now read his "labored romances." See *Letters*, I, xcviii-xciv, and C. Hugh Holman's Introduction to Simms's *Views and Reviews in American Literature,* Cambridge, Mass., 1962, xxii-xxv.

385.2-4   Greeley and Bryant were both New Englanders, Webb and Raymond native New Yorkers. Bennett was a Scotsman.

385.18   Barnum's American Museum. P. T. Barnum directed it from 1842 to 1872. It became a national showplace for freaks and curiosities.

386.27   Grecians: The meaning is obscure, but this may be Paddy's misinterpretation of "greased ones": uncooked oysters were commonly referred to as being "in the grease."

389.21-22   snapper up of onconsidered trifles: Shakespeare, *The Winter's Tale,* IV, iii.

389.31   Tombs: a famous New York City prison.

390.6   Richard Henry Wilde (1789-1847).

390.10   Delmonico's: Restaurant catering to fashionable New Yorkers. It originally stood at the corner of 5th Avenue and 26th Street.

392.5   Fulton market: Built in 1821 and used until 1881, this market stood on the North side of Fulton between South and Front Streets.

395.21   Five P'ints: Originally the multiple intersection of Orange (now Baxter), Cross (now Park), and Anthony (now Worth) streets, by 1840 the name Five Points applied to the whole slum region of that area. See John A. Kouwenhoven, *The Columbia Historical Portrait of New York,* Garden City, 1953, p. 272.

405.17   Forrest: Simms was a friend of the American actor Edwin Forrest (1806-72).

407.25   stame chase: The metaphor suggests a race between two steam locomotives, with a probable play on "stern chase."

409.27-28   mobbed an English actor: In 1845 a rivalry developed between Edwin Forrest and the English Shakespearean actor William C. Macready. On May 10, 1849, when Macready was playing the Astor Place Opera House in New York, the audience and a mob outside the theatre took sides in the rivalry. When the mob stormed the theatre, the Militia, which had been called out in anticipation of the fracas, was forced to fire into the crowd, killing and injuring a number of people. Forrest was not present at the theatre and Macready escaped unharmed.

411.19-20 a man's a man for a' that: Burns, "For A' That and A' That." See *The Complete Works of Robert Burns* . . . , Boston, 1855, pp. 301-302.

412.27 Col. Dick Perry: not identified.

413.28 The caricature Anne Statia may be a composite satirical portrait of literary ladies of New York, the name echoing that of the learned Aspasia of ancient Greece. Simms may have had in mind Ann Sophia Stephens (1813-86) or Sarah Anna Blanche Robinson Lewis (1824-80), both of whom attended the literary soirees of Anne Lynch Botta. Mrs. Stephens wrote romances in the manner of Scott; Mrs. Lewis, the friend of Poe, wrote poetry in imitation of Byron.

414.36-37 John Howard Payne (1791-1852), the American dramatist and actor, is remembered today for the sentimental lyric "Home, Sweet Home," from his opera *Clari, or, The Maid of Milan.*

415.3-6 The quatrain is from Byron's "The Giaour":

> The cold in clime are cold in blood,
> Their love can scarce deserve the name;
> But mine was like the lava flood
> That boils in Ætna's breast of flame.

See *The Works of . . . Lord Byron,* London, 1815, II, 72.

417.16-17 Loves of the Oyster: "Extract from the Loves of the Shell-Fishes," a mock-heroic fragment by "Conch" was first published in the newspaper *New-York American,* XII, January 11, 1832. Simms may have read it in the *New-York Mirror,* IX, January 28, 1832, 239, where it was reprinted.

417.25-26 Shakespeare, *Twelfth Night,* II, iv. See under Textual Notes for Anne Statia's misquotation.

418.26 "transport and security entwine": From Campbell's "Gertrude of Wyoming," Part III. See *The Poetical Works of Thomas Campbell*, Boston, 1827, p. 76. Byron ridiculed the line in *Don Juan*, Canto I, lxxxviii-ix.

420.2 Anne Charlotte Lynch (1815-91) made her home in Waverly Place, near Washington Square, a center for the intellectual and literary life of New York. Her salon attracted such personalities as Bryant, Greeley, Margaret Fuller, and Poe. After her marriage to Professor Vincenzo Botta in 1855 she continued her salon at West 37th Street.

421.17 Fureyite: Fourierite.

421.19 Furey: François Marie Charles Fourier (1772-1837).

423.33-34 Jeems Adger: The *U.S.S. James Adger* was a Union steamer during the Civil War. Information about her pre-Civil War history has not been found, nor has her Captain Dickson (424.15) been identified.

425.18 Claryndin House: Clarendon House, a Broadway hotel of the 1840's.

426.25 Bowery Theatre: A famous New York theatre which was opened in 1826. It stood on Bowery between Bayard and Walker Streets.

427.26 Frances Sargent (Locke) Osgood (1811-50) wrote sentimental verse that was extravagantly praised by her friend Poe.

427.32 mosslem: mausoleum.

427.37 Caroline Stansbury Kirkland (1801-64) was best known for her first two books, *A New Home—Who'll Follow* (1839) and *Forest Life* (1842), about her life in the Michigan backwoods before she moved to New York City in 1843.

428.5 Margaret Fuller (1810-50) was author of *Woman in the Nineteenth Century* (1845), editor of *Dial*, and, later, literary critic for Greeley's *New-York Tribune*. She, her husband and child were drowned in a shipwreck off Fire Island.

428.10-11 Henry Theodore Tuckerman (1813-71) was an occasional critic and poet who is best known for his biography of John Pendleton Kennedy.

428.16   Maria McIntosh (1803-78) was best known for her volume of tales, *Aunt Kitty's Tales* (1847).

428.21   Rufus Wilmot Griswold (1815-57), Poe's literary executor, was apparently the victim of fraud when he married, reluctantly, Charlotte Myers of Charleston, S. C., in 1845. The marriage, never consummated, ended in divorce in 1852. In 1852 he remarried. In 1856 a group of his enemies attempted unsuccessfully to invalidate his divorce. See Joy Bayless, *Rufus Wilmot Griswold . . .*, Nashville, 1943, pp. 104-108, 222-223, 251.

429.1-2   Rev. Joel Tyler Headley (1813-97) produced a best-seller in *Napoleon and His Marshals* (1846). Asked by his publishers, Carey and Hart, to prepare a similar work on Washington and his generals, he carried the idea to Baker and Scribner and wrote the work for them. Meanwhile Griswold was commissioned by Carey and Hart to edit an authentic account of Washington's generals that would outsell Headley's fictional history. Simms was among the contributors. Both works appeared in 1847, precipitating an acrimonious literary quarrel. See Bayless, pp. 132-36.

429.31   "The Raven" appeared in the New York *Evening Mirror*, Jan. 29, 1845, and in the *American Review*, I (Feb. 1845), 143-45. There is still controversy over which actually came on the market first. See *Studies in Bibliography*, XVI (1963), 220-23. "The Conqueror Worm" first appeared in *Graham's Magazine*, XXII (Jan. 1843), 32. "The Haunted Palace" first appeared in the *American Museum of Literature and the Arts*, II (April 1839), 320.

430.11-12   Grace Greenwood was the pseudonym of Sara Jane (Clarke) Lippincott (1823-1904), popular journalist, essayist, and poet. She was best known for *Greenwood Leaves; a Collection of Sketches and Letters* (1850).

430.22,34   The "General" and his "boy" are satirical portraits of George Pope Morris (1802-64) and N. P. Willis (1806-67), editor and associate editor of the *New-York Mirror*. Simms had published frequently in this journal, but later contended that he had not been paid and refused to contribute. Enmity developed between him and both the editors.

432.22   Jemmy Greens: dandified greenhorns.

436.22 rattles: instruments then used by New York police to sound an alarm.

437.7 Jeremy Diddler: A swindler, from the character in James Kenney's farce *Raising the Wind* (1803).

439.25 Eutaw and Cowpens: Battles of the Revolutionary War, in South Carolina.

444.29 cypress *caps:* The meaning is obscure; however, Paddy may be referring to cypress "knees," the roots of cypress trees which grow perpendicularly out of the water.

444.30 *bays:* A piece of low, marshy ground producing large numbers of bay trees.

444.32 Nash Roach (c. 1792-1858) was Simms's father-in-law.

449.36 The poem has not been identified.

457.20 mumchance: silent.

458.5-6 Song VII, Isaac Watts, *Poetical Works*, Edinburgh, 1782, VII, 60.

468.25-26 The quotation has not been identified.

469.16 Kemble: Although John Philip Kemble (1757-1823) was well known in England for his performance of Macbeth, Simms probably has in mind Charles Kemble (1775-1854), who also played the role, touring the United States in 1832.

469.17-18 Shakespeare, *Macbeth*, II, ii.

469.26 Providence meeting-house: Providence Church or Chapel in Orangeburg County. See Explanatory Note for 381.14.

470.2 Jarsey: A Jersey wagon was a light wagon.

470.12-16 A widely known old rhyme, of which there are many versions.

471.24-25 A variant of an old nursery rhyme. See Iona and Peter Opie, *The Oxford Dictionary of Nursery Rhymes*, pp. 91-92. (See also Textual Note, 471.25.)

471.28 Parson Ballinger: the Reverend Lucius Bellinger, Jr., a friend of Simms.

485.2 Colonel Jim Meredith: Has not been identified.

485.30 Bomberg: Bamberg, a town several miles from Midway and "Woodlands."

485.38 *hafe cut:* half drunk.

488.4 Isaac S. Bamberg (1835-89) is buried in Restland Cemetery, Bamberg.

492.8 Edisto Swamp Scouters: Not an actual unit, though the "Edisto Rifles" was.

493.17 Father Abbot: A slightly satiric self-portrait by Simms, who created him as a vehicle for his own ideas in *Father Abbot, or, The Home Tourist; A Medley* (Charleston, 1849).

493.18 Lemurian Brotherhood: Apparently a jocular reference to Simms's Charleston coterie who, meeting at night, resembled the nocturnal lemurs. See also Textual Note.

493.23 Paul Hamilton Hayne (1830-86), poet, and friend of Simms, edited *Russell's Magazine* (1857-60).

493.23 24 John Dickson Bruns (1836 83), physician, and friend of Simms, also wrote verse.

496.25-26 what Wordsworth calls 'personal talk': Sonnet XXXVII. See *The Poetical Works of William Wordsworth*, London, 1837, III, 39.

500.18 Dr. Benjamin Sweat was another physician friend of Simms. He lived at "Briarwood," a few miles south of "Woodlands."

503.22 This line has not been identified.

509.17-18 Father Abbot misquotes Shakespeare, *Hamlet*, I, v: "There are more things in heaven and earth, Horatio,|Than are dreamt of in your philosophy."

509.20 Shakespeare, *Macbeth*, V, i.

Textual Introduction: Paddy McGann

Paddy McGann; or, The Demon of the Stump was first published in sixteen installments in the Richmond weekly *The Southern Illustrated News* from February 14 to May 30, 1863.[1] No manuscript or other printed form of the work exists, and the serial version is therefore copy-text for the Centennial edition of this novel.

However, the original text is in some ways a poor one, and a good deal of editorial correction and emendation has been necessary. It is highly unlikely that Simms himself had the opportunity of seeing proofs, and it is not surprising that the standard of composition, proofreading, and editorial supervision for this wartime Richmond newspaper was not high. For example, what seems to be a proofreader's query has survived in the printed newspaper text. The phrase *junk bottle* in the original is followed by *(Qu: chunk?)*; the query is legitimate, but not only did it go unanswered, the phrase was somehow incorporated into the text, presumably when a literal-minded compositor was making the proof corrections. (See Textual Note for 218.25.) There are frequent, obvious printer's errors, and a great many inconsistencies in spelling and punctuation are probably compositorial, or editorial, in origin, rather than authorial.

Nevertheless, many of the inconsistencies, particularly those in dialect passages, undoubtedly reflect the inconsistencies of Simms's manuscript, and a highly conservative editorial policy has been followed, with a minimum of regularization. Whether or not Simms consciously intended the variant spellings *leetle* and *leettle, scrimmage* and *skrimmage, mirac'lous* and *miracklously* to indicate variant pronunciations, even eye-dialect is an indication of the variety and vitality of the colloquial speech of Simms's backwoodsmen, and an aspect of the characterization of the speakers. Thus the given name *Sally,* which also appears, in dialect, as *Sallie* and *Salley,* is not regularized. In Paddy's narrative, three different spellings are used for the name of the local preacher who performs the marriage ceremony: *Bellinger, Ballinger,* and *Bollinger.* Though an actual person, the Reverend Lucius Bellinger, is referred to, and though the variants

[1] Feb. 14, pp. 4-5; Feb. 21, pp. 4-5; Feb. 28, pp. 4-5; March 7, pp. 4-5; March 14, pp. 4-5; March 21, pp. 4-5; March 28, pp. 6-7; April 4, pp. 6-7; April 11, pp. 6-7; April 18, pp. 4-6; April 25, pp. 5-7; May 2, pp. 5-7; May 9, pp. 5-7; May 16, pp. 5-7; May 23, p. 5-7; May 30, pp. 5-7.

[WRITTEN EXPRESSLY FOR THE SOUTHERN ILLUSTRATED NEWS.]

PADDY McGANN;

—OR,—

THE DEMON OF THE STUMP

BY W. GILMORE SIMMS,

AUTHOR OF "RICHARD HURDIS," "THE CASSIQUE OF KIAWAH," "BORDER BEAGLES," "THE YEMASSEE," &c.

"If thou be'est a man, shew thyself in thy likeness: If thou be'est a devil, take't as thou list."................."I defy thee."—SHAKSPEARE.

CHAPTER I.

" Now, my comates and brothers in exile,
Hath not old custom made this life more sweet
Than that of painted pomp? Are not these woods
More free from peril than the envious court?
Here feel we but the penalty of Adam,
The season's difference." .

[As You Like It.

It was November, and the delicious season that we call the Indian Summer; when, after two or three smart white frosts, and possibly a little ice, the cool spell passes off; the winds grow calm, and modestly beseem themselves, the temperature becomes sweet and genial—neither too cold nor too warm; when, after a heavy fog each morning, the sun suddenly bursts through the vaporous

which, by the way, does not, even in the Italian mind, signify merely the delight of doing nothing. At all events, if it implies the extremest measure of physical repose, it by no means implies the dormancy of the intellectual nature. On the contrary, with many, and the most superior minds, great mental activity is almost inseparable from extreme physical quiet; will, indeed, admit of no physical exertion, but seems to absorb, for its own uses, all the vital energies of the animal man.

It is Cowper who says, somewhere, "how various are the employments of those whom the world calls idle." Cowper was a busy man enough, and he too was a dreamer. But the difference between him and Wharncliffe was simply that he had had dreams, while Wharncliffe had good

land, largely contributing her stores of pine to the benighted cities of the North. It is great in its fish; and we are in the very neighborhood, which, in spring and summer, is so much frequented by amateurs of the Isaak Walton order, coming down from the precincts of Augusta and Columbia, to tickle their trout dexterously, and weave pretty sentiments out of their dying agonies. Here, with fashionable rods and lines, and painted flies, and artificial silver fish, they practice charms to wile the trout from his bed, and persuade perch, and bream, and rock, and pike, and cat, into their baskets. The bream and red-belly perch are great favorites, I notice, with the ladies. The trout and rock, not so delicate, but well flavoured and substantial, are commended by their portly dimensions to the masculine gender. You shall often capture a trout large enough to take a junk bottle (Qu : chunk?) into his jaws. The epicure specially rejoices in the blue cat of the Edisto, which is not only one of the largest, but the most delicate fish that swims in these regions. But beware how you subject him to vulgar treatment. Use none of your artificial and compounded sauces in costuming him for the table—nothing stronger than melted fresh butter, and fresh well-shriven parsley—no condiments ! Here, too, if sport only be your object, you may take, in the proper season, and after a peculiar manner, the monster sturgeon of a hundred pounds and upwards. He, too, commends himself to certain tastes, and more delicate, when on table, than many a politician when under it! But his dressing, like his person, has its own peculiarities !

Ah ! pleasant are the memories, most delightful views, that crowd the brain of the grateful visiters, when thou wast wont, in happy seasons, to beguile to thy green borders, and thy sweetly gushing streams. Sometimes there came the stately English-man, and the canny Scot, and the free-hand

could be the result of a compositorial misreading of Simms's manuscript *ə*, the spelling has not been regularized. On the other hand, where the proper (and historical) name *Jamison* appears in nondialectal passages, in the speech of educated persons who are well acquainted with General Jamison, a variant spelling like *Jamieson* is corrected as certainly representing an error which Simms did not intend.

Though as a rule punctuation has been left unregularized and unmodernized, order has been imposed upon the chaotic system of quotation marks in the original. Simms's surviving manuscripts reveal that he was frequently careless about closing quotations, and about distinguishing between quotations, and quotations within quotations. So presumably the irregularity of the original text of *Paddy McGann* in this respect is the fault of both author and compositor. Nevertheless, despite carelessness and inconsistency, Simms's manuscripts show that he intended to follow the customary system of omitting closing quotation marks at the end of a paragraph if the same speaker continues in the next paragraph, and of using single quotation marks for quotations within quotations. The Centennial text has been emended accordingly. However, the occasional use of quotation marks in indirect quotations, still acceptable in Simms's time, is not altered.

Simms often quotes other writers, particularly Shakespeare, and he often quotes them inaccurately. Clear and obvious printer's errors in these quotations have been corrected, though reluctantly; Simms may be quoting a faulty text (perhaps a cheap American reprint of an English classic). And for many of the Shakespearian quotations which are actually misquotations, to correct errors would conceal the significant fact that Simms was obviously quoting from memory.

Printer's copy for the Centennial edition of *Paddy McGann* was a typescript prepared from photocopies of the files of *The Southern Illustrated News* in the New-York Historical Society Library and the New York Public Library. Proofs were read against the file of the original newspaper in the South Caroliniana Library of the University of South Carolina, and against photocopies of the files in the Boston Athenaeum, the Huntington Library, the University of Virginia Library, and the Virginia State Library. In addition, where a reading, particularly of a punctuation point, was obscured by poor

inking or damage to the originals of these files, or by poor repro-
duction of the photocopy, reference was made to a photocopy of the
original of the file of the Charleston Library Society.

Proofs were read at least five times, in galley or page proof,
against an original or photocopy of the text. All members of the
Editorial Board read proof, as well as the following graduate stu-
dent research assistants of the University of South Carolina English
Department: Karen Boyle, Thorne Compton, George Ellison, Carl
Ficken, Eileen Gregory, Lewis Hay, Tom Johnson, Noel Polk, Jim
West, and Margaret Yonce. In addition, special thanks are due, for
their work upon the original typescript, to Dr. William S. Kable of
the University of South Carolina English Department, and Dr.
Bush; and to Dr. Bush for his work upon the proofs.

Emendations and Textual Notes: Paddy McGann

Listed here are all changes made in the copy-text of *Paddy Mc-
Gann*. The original 1863 reading appears to the left of the bracket,
the emended Centennial edition reading to the right. Where no
bracket appears the reading is the same in both texts and the refusal
to emend is explained in parentheses. Where an explanation of the
change is necessary it follows in parentheses.

215.epigraph   put] but
215.epigraph   [As] ∧~
215.epigraph   IT.]] ~∧
216.31   *dulce par niante*] *dolce far niente*
217.11   *racontour*] *raconteur*
218.3   mayily] mazily
218.25   junk bottle (Qu: chunk?)] junk bottle (Either "junk
bottle" or "chunk bottle" would be an acceptable reading, in the
context; the parenthetical phrase appears to be an editorial query,
probably added in proof and mistakenly added to the text. Cf.
Textual Note for 300.32.)
218.30   well-shriven (A smudge or spot between these two words
in all copies examined indicates the probability of a badly-inked
hyphen. See Explanatory Note.)
218.38   visiters] visitors
218.38   when] whom

219.30   perdor] pudor (See also Explanatory Note.)
220.15   "The] ∧~
220.16   away."] ~∧
220.25   fistcuff] fisticuff
220.35   the (second)] (the second)
222.12   'pilot's raft,'] "~"
224.36   Abon] Abou (See also Explanatory Note.)
224.37   Abon] Abou
 225.1   Djina] Djinn
229.epigraph   MIDSUMMER] A MIDSUMMER
 229.9   "Oh <quotation marks not overhanging>] ~ <quotation marks overhanging>
229.16   M] "~
229.20   "*wo*-men;] '~'
230.27   its] it's
 231.1   "I'm] ∧~
231.34   d—d] d——d
 234.4   Och] "~
234.12   man!] ~"
235.epigraph   [MERRY] THE MERRY
237.11   Oscar] Oscan (See also Explanatory Note.)
239.28   "The] ∧~
240.15   frends] friends
241.15   beaufat] beaufet (Although a number of variant spellings, including *beaufait,* occurred in the development of the word *buffet,* the copy-text reading is probably a compositorial misreading of *beaufet,* the most common American spelling.)
243.24   its] it's
244.26   its] it's
244.27   its] it's
245.32   "Love's] ∧~
246.27   "Clane] '~
246.28   hands."] ~∧'
 248.3   discoveries,] ~.
249.15   it] ~.
249.25   'That's] "~
249.27   stor.y] story
 250.8   dipthyrambic] dithyrambic

250.12   There] "~

250.36   throttle.] ~"

251.12   its] it's

252.epigraph   *"Her.*] _∧~

252.epigraph.3   *Mam,*] *Mam.*

252.epigraph   goblins."] ~_∧

252.epigraph   [WINTER'S] THE WINTER'S

253.2   Y u] You

253.5   Its] It's

254.14   But] "~

257.16   months, its] months, it's

257.16   and its] and it's

258.35   Sam] '~

259.35   besides."] ~_∧

260.2   wanted."] ~_∧

260.28   I d] I'd

262.36   tobacco."] ~_∧

263.19   its] it's

265.3   rifle!] ~'

265.4   h'd] he'd

265.12   Oh] "~

266.19   Besides] "~

267.13   it's] its

268.epigraph   —HAMLET] _∧~

270.11   'tis] ' '~

270.27   'narves.'] "~"

271.7   outside."] ~_∧

271.19   drink.] ~'

272.26   heart.'] ~_∧

273.37   it.'] ~"

274.10   most."] ~_∧

274.28   "Good] '~

276.8   d—d] d——d

276.24   works?] ~!

277.epigraph   working,] ~.

278.14   say,' then, (Although it is possible to make sense of the
passage as it stands, Simms may well have written: say, then,')

278.36   d—d] d——d
279.1   "I *think*] " '~
279.1   d—d] d——d
279.14   d—n] d——n
281.10   sh'd] she'd
283.epigraph   —MACBETH] ∧~
283.1   That] "~
283.12   try?"] ~'
284.27   "That's] " '~
284.29   religion.] ~'
285.36   Yes,"] ~'
287.25   think.] ~,
287.38   one."] ~' "
294.epigraph   What] "~
294.epigraph   this.] ~"
294.epigraph   —Ben] ∧~
298.37   strength] ~.
300.3   Midway"] ~."
300.24   "Hoo] '~
300.24   Hoo!"] ~'
300.32   bore!"¶ "Quere: Boar?"] bore!" (Another apparent editor's or proofreader's query; cf. Textual Note for 218.25.)
301.10   Johne's] Johnes'
302.epigraph   —SIR] ∧~
302.20   Bearn] Béarn
302.21   belife] belief
303.12   world?" "] ~.'
303.13   This] "~
303.28   Johne's] Johnes'
303.29   8 vo.] 8vo.
303.30   Bohen.] Bohn."
304.15   "Sir,"] '~'
304.23   Ay] '~
304.25   awile] awhile
304.32   You] '~
304.33   if] '~
304.37   sleep,] ~.

305.3   sow ———] ~———
305.24   'What] ∧~
305.28   Jamison?'"] ~"
305.29   mostly — Italians] ~—~
306.11   aud] and
307.1   a sleep] asleep
308.21   duck] dusk
310.epigraph   —HAMLET] ∧~
310.7   Clyme's] Clymes'
310.14   one's] ones
310.15   enough."] ~∧
312.5   wather!"] ~∧
314.29   children!] ~'
315.13   Where?] ~'
315.33   quick.'] ~∧
316.32   steps! ¶ You've] steps! < no ¶ > You've
318.14   "Hoo] '~
320.2   bring] brings
321.23   nothing!"] ~∧
321.33   "an] '~
321.34   him"] ~'
322.24   *first?*] ~"
323.3   your'e] you're
324.36   judgment] ~.
326.25   all] ~.
328.12   ef] of
328.35   good good] good
328.35   its] it's
328.38   me!] ~"
329.epigraph   —TEMPEST] THE TEMPEST
331.34   me one (See Explanatory Note.)
332.36   fight 1] ~!
333.19   nnd] and
333.22   "hands"] '~'
333.30   padlock,] ~.
336.1   to-night] to night
337.13   its] it's
337.34   Wharncliff] Wharncliffe

339.11	feet feet] feet
339.25	an, in] an' in
341.1	I'l] I'll
342.30	"Hoo] '~
342.30	Hoo!"] ~'
346.25	day—] ~"
346.35	fancy.'] ~"
352.1	I'member'd] I 'member'd
353.10	together] ~.
353.35	Hoo!] ~'
355.23	Philistiines] Philistines
355.27	knife!] ~'
357.4	staddled (See Explanatory Note.)
357.9	Wans't] Wasn't
357.15	drinking—] ~"
357.38	wept] wrept
358.15	"Hoo] '~
358.15	Hoo!"] ~'
358.27	"Oh] '~
358.27	joyful,"] ~'
358.36	' "You] " '~
361.2	*parénthese*] *parenthèse*
361.14	countervarsy.] ~',
361.24	nights.] ~,
362.1	"What's] " '~
362.7	fight?] ~'
362.20	spent (Simms may have written "spurt".)
362.26	"Hoo] '~
362.29	first] fist
363.7	' "And] " '~
363.8	What s] What's
363.9	misery."] ~'
363.10	So] "~
363.16	'It's] " '~
363.19	'It's] " '~
364.4	'I] "~
364.5-6	half sleeping] ~-~
364.27	senses] ~.

370.7   Jamieson] Jamison
371.5   ship,] ~.
371.17   <no indentation> "Then] <indentation> ~
372.5   A'ter] "~
373.12   And] "~
373.32   Capipn] Cappin
374.15   *greese*] *green* (To have green in one's eyes is the equivalent of being a greenhorn. Cf. 388.4.)
374.25   "ef] '~
374.32   skrimmage."] ~'
375.16   yit.'] ~' "
376.4   "Look] '~
376.6   people."] ~'
376.21   yo're] you're
377.2   'Restoorynut'] "~"
378.14   tarny (Presumably a dialect form, perhaps related to Paddy's "tarnal" for "eternal"; but possibly a compositorial misreading of "tarry.")
378.14   follows] fellows
379.10   it's] its
380.1   'Es] " '~
380.14   invintions.] ~'
380.15   " 'Well] "~
381.25   inimy."] ~'
381.30   p'int- | to] p'inting to
383.21   milliner (millionaire, we suppose,) (The use of parentheses for defining an unusual or dialect word was not unusual in Simms's time. However, see 427.12 for a use of square brackets in a similar case.)
386.4   derned —] ~ ——
386.10   'Ristorynut'] "~"
387.23   'It's] " '~
387.26   'Home] " '~
387.28   'Ef] " '~
387.29   hurry."] ~'
388.16   says he] says I
388.23   soon- | curried] ~ᴧ~
388.30   skunk."] ~'

388.36   him.'] ~ₐ
   388.   <Rule between last line of text and footnote>] <No
rule between last line of text and footnote>
389.24   oysters,] ~ₐ
389.24   (Shrewsbury)] ~,
  390.2   it.'] ~' "
390.22   pay.'] ~"
390.23   " 'Restaurant,'] "~"
390.23   'well] "~
390.24   Wharncliffe.'] ~"
390.25   " 'Take] "~
390.25   Paddy!'] ~"
  392.9   who who] who
392.19   d—d] d——d
392.36   'knock] "~
392.36   out,'] ~"
392.37   'who] "~
392.37   piper?'] ~"
393.24   d—d] d——d
394.30   d—d] d——d
396.28   he,' we'll] ~ₐ '~
397.12   d—n] d——n
397.12   you want to] you won't want to (The negative is essential;
it might also be emended: you don't.)
397.13   d—d] d——d
397.30   ' 'I'm] " '~
398.13   'Niggerknocker'] "~"
398.22   'saft,'] "~"
398.24   That] that
401.23   losses."] ~'
  402.8   subject."] ~'
402.35   quiet'] ~ₐ.
403.22   Brother ——] ~ ——
403.33   him,] ~.
404.26   have] ~.
406.28   fellow."] ~'
  407.5   " 'He] "~
407.28   about?"] ~'

408.12   'Niggerbotcher'] "~"
409.3   Liberty"] ~'
409.12   and and sturdy] and sturdy
409.29   Amesikin] Amerikin
410.23   divil.] ~"
411.5   When] "~
411.16   'a] "~
411.17   that!'] ~"
413.5   'Edisto Raftsman'] "~"
413.15   "Oh] " '~
413.20   'How] "~
413.21   solitude!'] ~"
413.27   clap!"] ~∧
414.14   Statia!] ~.
414.18   consolation."] ~'
414.36   'Home] "~
414.36   Home!'] ~"
415.3   " 'The] "~
415.6   flame!'] ~"
415.13   'Edisto Raftsman,'] "~"
415.32   was was] was
417.16   'Loves] "~
417.17   Oysters?'] ~"?
417.25   'To] "~
417.26   dam on cheek] damson cheek (Anne Statia is misquoting
Shakespeare, *Twelfth Night*, II, iv, "damask cheek".)
417.26   cheek!'] ~"
418.13   'Will] "~
418.13   miss?'] ~" '
418.26   'transport] "~
418.26   entwine!'] ~"
419.15   ma'am.' "] ~'∧
419.16   joke] yoke (Cf. 419.19.)
420.21   history!"] ~'
421.7   light."] ~'
421.35   brandy.'] ~' "
422.10   'swarray'] "~"
422.22   'clicks,'] "~"

422.23   'click,'] "~"
423.3   'click'] "~"
423.23   'swarray's'] "~"
423.23   'swarray'] "~"
423.28   " 'A'ter] "~
423.33   "Wait] " '~
424.23   time!"] ~'
425.22   dollars,"] ~'
425.33   open!"] ~'
427.8   Monday] "~
427.10   "Swarray"] '~'
427.12.   Die-out' [diet, I suppose]. (The words in square brackets are assumed to be those of Stylus, the narrator. Cf. 383.21.)
427.22   "Oh] " '~
427.30   'The Raven.'] "~"
427.31   'Raven'] "~"
427.33   'Nevermore!'] "~"
427.37   "And] " '~
428.3   kin.'] ~ₐ
429.3   'Napoleon] "~
429.3   Marshals,'] ~"
429.3   'Washington] "~
429.3   Generals.'] ~"
429.15   'Lord] " '~
429.31   'Raven,'] "~"
429.31   'Conquering Worm,'] "~"
429.31   'Haunted Palace.'] "~"
429.33   'The] "~
429.33   Wrack.'] ~"
430.33   'Home Journal,'] "~"
430.34   'mi boy,'] "~"
430.35   'mi boy.'] "~"
431.4-5   'Home Journal.'] "~"
431.13   'mi boy'] "~"
431.16   'Home Journal'] "~"
432.27   ship.] ~"
434.4   matey] Matey
434.5   place;"] ~'

434.27   " "All] " '~
435.5   lad] ~.
435.6   ' 'Lord] " '~
435.29   "Past] " '~
435.29   boys!"] ~'
436.34   I m] I'm
438.12   'I] "~
438.12   five——'] ~"
438.18   'we] "~
438.22   species.'] ~"
439.1   Citya nd] City and
439.2   P'nt] P'int
439.17   "My] " '~
442.36   says I.] ~"
444.36   afore.] ~"
446.12   Jamieson] Jamison
447.12   to to] to
447.22   it!] ~'
449.2   atime] a time
449.10   fine] fire
449.37   Polly] Salley (Cf. 452.epigraph, 455.12, etc.)
451.12   "Hear] ∧~
452.epigraph   Sally] Salley
456.14   Well,] ~'
456.18   wife 'll] wife'll
458.5   'Your] "~
458.6   eyes.'] ~"
460.32   'Birds] ∧~
460.36   heaven."] ~'
462.2   'snip,'] "~"
462.2   'snap.'] "~"
462.21   its] it's
462.22   a a-going] a-going
463.15   "This] '~
464.4   younke's] younker's
467.22   "Come] " '~
467.22   in,"] ~'
467.36   its] it's

468.21   'Because] "~
468.24   Abbe] Abbé
469.18   more] ~'
469.18   Macbeth] '~
470.12   " 'One] ʌʌ~
470.16   crows!'] ~ʌ
471.24   "Come] '~
471.25   Mr. Bond."] Mrs. Bond.' (In the old nursery rhyme, it is *Mrs.* Bond who sends John Ostler to the pond to kill ducks for the customers' supper. The analogy is appropriate if Paddy is seen as the victim of a woman, but not if he is the victim of a man. See Iona and Peter Opie, *Oxford Dictionary of Nursery Rhymes,* Oxford, 1951, pp. 91-92.)
471.32   I'] I'd
472.36   its] it's
476.3   em] '~
476.4   need't] need'nt
476.26   Its] It's
476.37   And] "~
477.14   " 'Stranger] " ' " ~
477.15   McGann.'] ~"
477.17   " 'Tell] " ' " ~
477.17   him,'] ~"
477.17   'that] "~
477.19   Its] It's
477.22   all.'] ~"
477.23   'never] "~
477.24   onderstand.'] ~"
482.6   Mr] ~.
482.15   its] it's
483.4   "Well] " '~
483.20   its] it's
483.32   "Yes,"] '~'
484.31   its] it's
485.8   wife."] ~'
486.29   Then] "~
488.37   its] it's
490.3   "So] " '~

490.9   its ence] it sence
490.12   creation!] ~"
490.38   you.] ~"
491.1   Jamieson] Jamison
491.24   its] it's
491.25   ts] it's
491.35   fressing] pressing
492.8   "Edisto] '~
492.8   Scouters,"] ~'
493.2   interuptions] interruptions
493.7   Padd ywas] Paddy was
493.12   Jamieson] Jamison
493.18   Lemarian] Lemurian (See Explanatory Note; no other
simple emendation appears to make sense of the word.)
493.24   Burns] Bruns (See Explanatory Note for this actual
name.)
493.25   the the] the
494.25   sophiscation] sophistication
495.6   I] "~
495.13   Of] "~
495.29   There] "~
495.35   "Ah!"] " '~'
495.35   "Wharncliffe] '~
495.37   is,"] ~'
496.1   "as] '~
496.2   myself."] ~'
496.3   Such] "~
496.19   In] "~
496.23   "Yes] " '~
496.23   *fool!*"] ~'
496.26   "personal talk."] '~'
496.29   " *He*] " '~
496.29   *last!*"] ~'
497.3   He] "~
497.3   the the] the
497.18   In] "~
497.27   Paddy] "~
497.29   months] ~'

497.35 Finding] "~
498.9 Returning] "~
498.18 The] "~
498.26 The] "~
498.33 Meanwhile] "~
498.36 The] "~
498.37 "daggers draw,"] 'daggers drawn,'
499.4 Meanwhile] "~
499.10 He] "~
499.13 His] "~
499.36 The] "~
500.10 This] "~
500.36 "Roll] '~
500.36 woman!"] ~'
501.4 When] "~
501.6 It] "~
501.19 Nevertheless] "~
501.35 He] "~
502.4 One] "~
502.10 Meanwhile] "~
502.20 Meanwhile] "~
502.26 At] "~
502.34 He] "~
502.36 It] "~
503.22 "One] ∧~
503.22 stood,"] ~∧
503.24 He] "~
503.29 Pogson] "~
503.32 "Stop,"] " '~'
503.32 "and] '~
503.35 father."] ~'
503.36 "Who | " '~
503.36 you?"] ~'
503.37 "Who] " '~
503.37 fact."] ~'
504.1 This] "~
504.6 "Mr.] " '~
504.9 longer."] ~'

504.10   The] "~
504.11   "I'll] " '~
504.11   house."] ~'
504.12   With] "~
504.20   Paddy] "~
504.22   it's] its
504.25   subject to] subject him to (A compositor may well have omitted this word, which would have come at the end of one line, or the beginning of the next, in the original text.)
504.28   "I] " '~
504.29   me!"] ~'
504.30   He] "~
504.32   "Never] " '~
504.32   agin,"] ~'
504.32   "unless] '~
504.33   can."] ~'
504.34   You] "~
505.3   I] "~
505.20   This] "~
505.24   Thus] "~
505.31   Fool!] ~"

APPENDIX

WORD DIVISION.

Table A

The following possible compounds, hyphenated at the end of a line in the Centennial edition of *As Good as a Comedy* and *Paddy McGann*, appear as one word in the copy-texts. All other compounds that are hyphenated at the end of a line in the Centennial edition (except those listed in Table C) are hyphenated within the line in the 1852 text and are omitted from this table.

6.37-7.1   school-|masters
10.4-5   great-grand-|mother
29.1-2   boy-|hood
30.38-31.1   school-|boys
31.18-9   step-|mother
36.7-8   horse-|manship
45.35-6   pack-|thread
52.4-5   home-|stead
85.25-6   White-|jacket
99.5-6   sweep-|stakes
141.5-6   over-|seer
218.13-4   neighbor-|hood
226.6-7   back-|woodsman
261.25-6   down-|hearted
333.32-3   rail-|road
333.37-334.1   pitch-|fork
338.8-9   rail-|road
359.9-10   moon-|light
374.23-4   blue-|bellied
380.1-2   news-|paper

382.10-1 news-|papers
385.7-8 over-|run
386.16-7 beef-|steak
398.22-3 back-|woods
418.15-6 backwoods-|man
425.30-1 ginger-|bread
431.19-20 Nigger-|knocker
472.16-7 bare-|legged
488.6-7 mean-|time

Table B

Listed here are compound words that fall within the line in the Centennial edition of *As Good as a Comedy* and *Paddy McGann* but whose intended form is ambiguous because they are hyphenated at the end of a line in the copy-texts. Where other examples of the same compound have been found within the line in the copy-texts, the form most frequently used has been adopted. Where no other examples of the same compound could be found within the line in the copy-texts, the Centennial edition has attempted to adopt the form of the compound which is most consistent with the copy-texts' handling of similar compounds and with Simms's handling of the same compound in other writings of approximately the same date.

5.7 stagecoach
6.36 schoolmaster (8.20)
18.31 shade-trees (67.4, 153.9)
19.3 well-bred (25.7, 139.17)
19.34 highway (24.3, 155.18)
25.7 well-looking (cf. 19.7, finer-looking)
25.25 good-fellowship (25.24)
29.1 ploughshare
35.36 carriage-poles
38.25 footrace
41.21 shirt-bosom
42.28 four-year
48.4 re-examine
48.5 new-comer (24.9, 25.1)
51.19 pocketbook (60.34)
52.11 homespun (20.32)

62.21   step-daughter   (54.37, 122.1, 125.15)
63.3   high-spirited   (63.6, 157.4)
63.20   to-day   (42.24)
67.4   card-players
72.7   stiff-capped
80.3   undervalued
81.17   step-mother   (66.26; but see 31.9, stepmother's)
83.14   horseflesh   (22.29, 102.24)
85.36   gypsy-jockey   (cf. 77.title, GYPSY JOCKEY)
89.23   wheelrocket
96.37   apple-brandy
99.27   apple-toddy   (96.35; cf. 160.13, brandy-toddy)
101.9   apple-toddy
103.14   brandy-cocktail
111.13   Sultana-like
123.35   step-mother   (See 81.17 above)
124.12   well-ordered
126.12   open-mouthed
127.3   millstone
134.6   repayment
135.13   step-mother   (See 81.17 above)
136.26   step-mother   (See 81.17 above)
150.4   birthday
153.25   shade-trees   (See 18.31 above)
156.23   girlhood
156.29   rope-skipping
158.24   mill-dam   (156.8)
162.8   pathways
162.25   dwelling-house
169.20   household
174.16   housekeeper   (132.37)
188.28   good-humor
189.28   marriage-fee
190.15   reappearance   (cf. 63.23, reappeared)
194.5   kind-hearted
209.25   overflowing   (cf. 18.26, overrun, 24.16, overslept, 210.25,
overflow)
210.25   back-room
210.35   sharp-sighted

217.12   intercourse
219.13   pike-fishing
220.7   dug-out   (222.14)
220.10   sunshine
220.39   State-rights
222.epigraph   schoolmaster
222.12   platform
223.22   under-song
224.19   tale-teller
224.35   household   (225.13)
227.5   self-esteem   (227.16, 19)
227.36   inkstand   (227.33)
229.20   *wo*-men
235.12   backwoods   (398.22, 23; but see also 435.24, back-woods)
235.15   to-day
236.21   backwoods (See 235.12 above)
241.15   side-board
244.32   loaf-sugar
253.21   toenail   (cf. finger nails, 457.38)
253.27   knee-high   (cf. 456.8, knee high and 473.27, knee high)
255.11   Jack-|of-all-trades
255.21   mid-winter
255.28   camp-hunt
258.24   witchcraft   (226.20)
260.36   witchcraft   (260.34)
261.24   night-waking
269.13   lightwood   (353.26)
270.25   now-a-|days
275.31   bad-mouth   (but see 258.32, 34, bad mouth)
287.7   brimstone   (315.17)
287.14   eyesight   (270.16; but see also 289.10, 16, eye sight)
288.18   meantime
291.12   brick-kiln
297.22   swamp-thick
304.26   bed-side
306.32   breastbone
313.19   peafields   (215.19)
320.7   eyesight   (See 287.14 above)
328.2   midnight

328.9   midnight
328.23   dug-out   (See 220.7 above)
329.7   meanwhile
332.34   odd-looking
338.14   railroad
338.22   good-bye
341.28   daylight
349.epigraph   Wood-Pile   (cf. 361.12, 362.9; but see also 352.22,
365.13, 367.23, wood pile)
350.29   lightwood   (See 269.13 above)
352.22   nonsense
352.37   moonshine
358.12   stand-up-to-the-|rack
358.20   lightwood   (See 269.13 above)
359.20   seesaw
361.12   wood-pile   (See 349.epigraph above)
363.2   sunshine
364.16   midnight
364.16   wood-pile   (See 349.epigraph above)
364.31   overboard   (359.37)
366.24   gray-bearded
371.24   north-easter   (cf. 372.16; but see also 371.3, northeast)
381.31   horse-whipt
387.5   backwoods   (See 235.12 above)
395.31   whiskey-punch   (cf. 401.7, whiskey punch)
396.5   shipwrackt   (380.9, 413.18, 442.28)
400.13   barefaced
407.10   knockdown
408.30   newspapers
409.34   newspapers
409.38   newspapers
412.19   westcote   (cf. 441.5, waistcoat)
413.18   shipwrack'd   (See 396.5 above)
418.10   tender-hearted
422.21   newspaper
424.17   shipwrack   (See 396.5 above)
427.32   graveyard   (cf. 254.2, churchyard)
428.10   alongside   (470.24)
433.5   to-night

436.26   daylight
438.27   nonsense
440.18   shot-bag
446.7   worthless
452.21   likewise
455.35   turn-uppy
460.25   tom-cat   (460.3)
461.19   tom-tiger
476.31   footsteps   (257.27)
484.11   to-morrow
486.23   owl-schreech
486.35   head-dress
487.4   head-dress
491.3   Honeymoon
491.14   settled-down
492.4   to-morrow
498.26   endless
499.35   outhouse
502.13   housekeeping
503.16   buckshot
503.19   dining-room
509.4   Brotherhood

Table C

Listed here are compounds, or possible compounds, which are hyphenated at the end of a line in the copy-texts and the Centennial edition text.

91.32-3   race-|course   (i.e., race-course)
132.37-133.1   house-|holder   (i.e., householder)
141.17-8   horse-|whip   (i.e., horsewhip; cf. 65.6)
180.14-5   handsomely-|turned   (i.e., handsomely-turned)
223.13-4   full-|grown   (i.e., full-grown)
274.14-5   marrow-|bones   (i.e., marrow-bones; cf. 349.18)
347.11-2   along-|side   (i.e., alongside)
372.16-7   north-|easter   (i.e., north-easter)
422.14-5   pepper-|vinegar   (i.e., pepper-vinegar)
424.27-8   onder-|writers   (i.e., onder-writers; cf. 423.36)